MARY HIGGINS CLARK

THREE BESTSELLING NOVELS

MARY HIGGINS CLARK

THREE BESTSELLING NOVELS

I'll Be Seeing You

~

Remember Me

~

Let Me Call You Sweetheart

WINGS BOOKS®
New York

CONTENTS

I'LL BE
SEEING YOU

For my newest grandchild
Jerome Warren Derenzo
"Scoochie"
With Love and Joy.

ACKNOWLEDGMENTS

The writing of this book required considerable research. It is with great gratitude I acknowledge those who have been so wonderfully helpful.

B. W. Webster, M.D., Associate Director, Reproductive Resource Center of Greater Kansas City; Robert Shaler, Ph.D., Director of Forensic Biology, New York City Medical Examiner's Office; Finian I. Lennon, Mruk & Partners, Management Consultants—Executive Search; Leigh Ann Winick, Producer Fox/5 TV News; Gina and Bob Scrobogna, Realty Executives, Scottsdale, Arizona; Jay S. Watnick, JD, ChFC, CLU, President of Namco Financial Associates, Inc.; George Taylor, Director—Special Investigation Unit, Reliance National Insurance Company; James F. Finn, Retired Partner, Howard Needles Tammen & Bergendoff, Consulting Engineers; Sergeant Ken Lowman (Ret.), Stamford, Conn., City Police.

Forever thanks to my longtime editor, Michael V. Korda, and his associate, senior editor Chuck Adams, for their terrific and vital guidance. Sine qua non.

As always, my agent Eugene H. Winick and my publicist Lisl Cade have been there every step of the way.

Special thanks to Judith Glassman for being my other eyes and my daughter Carol Higgins Clark for her ideas and for helping to put the final pieces of the puzzle together.

And to my dear family and friends, now that this is over, I'm happy to say I'll Be Seeing You!

His honour rooted in dishonour stood,
And faith unfaithful kept him falsely true.

—Alfred, Lord Tennyson

I'LL BE
SEEING YOU

1

*M*eghan Collins stood somewhat aside from the cluster of other journalists in Emergency at Manhattan's Roosevelt Hospital. Minutes before, a retired United States senator had been mugged on Central Park West and rushed here. The media were milling around, awaiting word of his condition.

Meghan lowered her heavy tote bag to the floor. The wireless mike, cellular telephone and notebooks were causing the strap to dig into her shoulder blade. She leaned against the wall and closed her eyes for a moment's rest. All the reporters were tired. They'd been in court since early afternoon, awaiting the verdict in a fraud trial. At nine o'clock, just as they were leaving, the call came to cover the mugging. It was now nearly eleven. The crisp October day had turned into an overcast night that was an unwelcome promise of an early winter.

It was a busy night in the hospital. Young parents carrying a bleeding toddler were waved past the registration desk through the door to the examination area. Bruised and shaken passengers of a car accident consoled each other as they awaited medical treatment.

Outside, the persistent wail of arriving and departing ambulances added to the familiar cacophony of New York traffic.

A hand touched Meghan's arm. "How's it going, Counselor?"

It was Jack Murphy from Channel 5. His wife had gone through NYU Law School with Meghan. Unlike Meghan, however, Liz was practicing law. Meghan Collins, Juris Doctor, had worked for a Park Avenue law firm for six months, quit and got a job at WPCD radio as a news reporter. She'd been there three years now and for the past month had been borrowed regularly by PCD Channel 3, the television affiliate.

"It's going okay, I guess," Meghan told him. Her beeper sounded.

"Have dinner with us soon," Jack said "It's been too long." He rejoined his cameraman as she reached to get her cellular phone out of the bag.

The call was from Ken Simon at the WPCD radio news desk. "Meg, the EMS scanner just picked up an ambulance heading for Roosevelt. Stabbing victim found on Fifty-sixth Street and Tenth. Watch for her."

The ominous ee-aww sound of an approaching ambulance coincided with the staccato tapping of hurrying feet. The trauma team was heading for the Emergency entrance. Meg broke the connection, dropped the phone in her bag and followed the empty stretcher as it was wheeled out to the semicircular driveway.

The ambulance screeched to a halt. Experienced hands rushed to assist in transferring the victim to the stretcher. An oxygen mask was clamped on her face. The sheet covering her slender body was bloodstained. Tangled chestnut hair accentuated the blue-tinged pallor of her neck.

Meg rushed to the driver's door. "Any witnesses?" she asked quickly.

"None came forward." The driver's face was lined and weary, his voice matter-of-fact. "There's an alley between two of those old tenements near Tenth. Looks like someone came up from behind, shoved her in it and stabbed her. Probably happened in a split second."

"How bad is she?"

"As bad as you can get."

"Identification?"

"None. She'd been robbed. Probably hit by some druggie who needed a fix."

The stretcher was being wheeled in. Meghan darted back into the emergency room behind it.

One of the reporters snapped, "The senator's doctor is about to give a statement."

The media surged across the room to crowd around the desk. Meghan did not know what instinct kept her near the stretcher. She watched as the doctor about to start an IV removed the oxygen mask and lifted the victim's eyelids.

"She's gone," he said.

Meghan looked over a nurse's shoulder and stared down into the unseeing blue eyes of the dead young woman. She gasped as she took in those eyes, the broad forehead, arched brows, high cheekbones, straight nose, generous lips.

It was as though she was looking into a mirror.

She was looking at her own face.

2

*M*eghan took a cab to her apartment in Battery Park City, at the very tip of Manhattan. It was an expensive fare, but it was late and she was very tired. By the time she arrived home, the numbing shock of seeing the dead woman was deepening rather than wearing off. The victim had been stabbed in the chest, possibly four to five hours before she was found. She'd been wearing jeans, a lined denim jacket, running shoes and socks. Robbery had probably been the motive. Her skin was tanned. Narrow bands of lighter skin on her wrist and several fingers suggested that rings and a watch were missing. Her pockets were empty and no hand-bag was found.

Meghan switched on the foyer light and looked across the room. From her windows she could see Ellis Island and the Statue of Liberty. She could watch the cruise ships being piloted to their berths on the Hudson River. She loved down-town New York, the narrowness of the streets, the sweeping majesty of the World Trade Center, the bustle of the financial district.

The apartment was a good-sized studio with a sleeping alcove and kitchen unit. Meghan had furnished it with her mother's castoffs, intending eventually to get a larger place and gradually redecorate. In the three years she'd worked for WPCD that had not happened.

She tossed her coat over a chair, went into the bathroom and changed into pajamas and a robe. The apartment was pleasantly warm, but she felt chilled to the point of illness. She realized she was avoiding looking into the vanity mirror. Finally she turned and studied herself as she reached for the cleansing cream.

Her face was chalk white, her eyes staring. Her hands trembled as she released her hair so that it spilled around her neck.

In frozen disbelief she tried to pick out differences between herself and the dead woman. She remembered that the vic-tim's face had been a little fuller, the shape of her eyes round rather than oval, her chin smaller. But the skin tone and the color of the hair and the open, unseeing eyes were so very like her own.

She knew where the victim was now. In the medical examiner's morgue, being photographed and fingerprinted. Dental charts would be made.

And then the autopsy.

Meghan realized she was trembling. She hurried into the kitchenette, opened the refrigerator and removed the carton of milk. Hot chocolate. Maybe that would help.

She settled on the couch and hugged her knees, the steaming cup in front of her. The phone rang. It was probably her mother, so she hoped her voice sounded steady when she answered it.

"Meg, hope you weren't asleep."

"No, just got in. How's it going, Mom?"

"All right, I guess. I heard from the insurance people today. They're coming over tomorrow afternoon again. I hope to God they don't ask any more questions about that loan Dad took out on his policies. They can't seem to fathom that I have no idea what he did with the money."

In late January, Meghan's father had been driving home to Connecticut from Newark Airport. It had been snowing and sleeting all day. At seven-twenty, Edwin Collins made a call from his car phone to a business associate, Victor Orsini, to set up a meeting the next morning. He told Orsini he was on the approach to the Tappan Zee Bridge.

In what may have been only a few seconds later, a fuel tanker spun out of control on the bridge and crashed into a tractor trailer, causing a series of explosions and a fireball that engulfed seven or eight automobiles. The tractor trailer smashed into the side of the bridge and tore open a gaping hole before plunging into the swirling, icy waters of the Hudson River. The fuel tanker followed, dragging with it the other disintegrating vehicles.

A badly injured eyewitness who'd managed to steer out of the direct path of the fuel tanker testified that a dark blue Cadillac sedan spun out in front of him and disappeared through the gaping steel. Edwin Collins had been driving a dark blue Cadillac.

It was the worst disaster in the history of the bridge. Eight lives were lost. Meg's sixty-year-old father never made it home that night. He was assumed to have died in the explosion. The New York Thruway authorities were still searching for scraps of wreckage and bodies, but now, nearly nine months later, no trace had as yet been found of either him or his car.

A memorial mass had been offered a week after the accident, but because no death certificate had been issued, Edwin and Catherine Collins' joint assets were frozen and the large insurance policies on his life had not been paid.

Bad enough for Mom to be heartbroken without the hassle these people are giving her, Meg thought. "I'll be up tomorrow afternoon, Mom. If they keep stalling, we may have to file suit."

She debated, then decided that the last thing her mother needed was to hear that a woman with a striking resemblance to Meghan had been stabbed to death. Instead she talked about the trial she'd covered that day.

FOR A LONG TIME, MEGHAN LAY IN BED, DOZING FITFULLY. Finally she fell into a deep sleep.

A high-pitched squeal pulled her awake. The fax began to whine. She looked at the clock: it was quarter-past four. What on earth? she thought.

She switched on the light, pulled herself up on one elbow and watched as paper slowly slid from the machine. She jumped out of bed, ran across the room and reached for the message.

It read: MISTAKE. ANNIE WAS A MISTAKE.

3

Tom Weicker, fifty-two-year-old news director of PCD Channel 3, had been borrowing Meghan Collins from the radio affiliate with increasing frequency. He was in the process of handpicking another reporter for the on-air news team and had been rotating the candidates, but now he had made his final decision: Meghan Collins.

He reasoned that she had good delivery, could ad lib at the drop of a hat and always gave a sense of immediacy and excitement to even a minor news item. Her legal training was a real plus at trials. She was damn good looking and had natural warmth. She liked people and could relate to them.

On Friday morning, Weicker sent for Meghan. When she knocked at the open door of his office, he waved her in. Meghan was wearing a fitted jacket in tones of pale blue and rust brown. A skirt in the same fine wool skimmed the top of her boots. Classy, Weicker thought, perfect for the job.

Meghan studied Weicker's expression, trying to read his thoughts. He had a thin, sharp-featured face and wore rimless glasses. That and his thinning hair made him look older than his age and more like a bank teller than a media powerhouse. It was an impression quickly dispelled, however, when he began to speak. Meghan liked Tom but knew that his nickname, "Lethal Weicker," had been earned. When he began borrowing her from the radio station he'd made it clear that it was a tough, lousy break that her father had lost his life in the bridge tragedy, but he needed her reassurance that it wouldn't affect her job performance.

It hadn't, and now Meghan heard herself being offered the job she wanted so badly.

The immediate, reflexive reaction that flooded through her was, I can't wait to tell Dad!

THIRTY FLOORS BELOW, IN THE GARAGE OF THE PCD BUILD-ing, Bernie Heffernan, the parking attendant, was in Tom Weicker's car, going through the glove compartment. By some genetic irony, Bernie's features had been formed to give him the countenance of a merry soul. His cheeks were plump, his chin and mouth small, his eyes wide and guileless, his hair thick and rumpled, his body sturdy, if somewhat rotund. At thirty-five the immediate impression he gave to observers was that he was a guy who, though wearing his best suit, would fix your flat tire.

He still lived with his mother in the shabby house in Jackson Heights, Queens, where he'd been born. The only times he'd been away from it were those dark, nightmarish periods when he was incarcerated. The day after his twelfth birthday he was sent to a juvenile detention center for the first of a dozen times. In his early twenties he'd spent three years in a psychiatric facility. Four years ago he was sentenced to ten months in Riker's Island. That was when the police caught him hiding in a college student's car. He'd been warned a dozen times to stay away from her. Funny, Bernie thought— he couldn't even remember what she looked like now. Not her and not any of them. And they had all been so important to him at the time.

Bernie never wanted to go to jail again. The other inmates frightened him. Twice they beat him up. He had sworn to Mama that he'd never hide in shrubs and look in windows again, or follow a woman and try to kiss her. He was getting very good at controlling his temper too. He'd hated the psychiatrist who kept warning Mama that one day that vicious temper would get Bernie into trouble no one could fix. Bernie knew that nobody had to worry about him anymore.

His father had taken off when he was a baby. His embittered mother no longer ventured outside, and at home Bernie had to endure her incessant reminders of all the inequities life had inflicted on her during her seventy-three years and how much he owed her.

Well, whatever he "owed" her, Bernie managed to spend most of his money on electronic equipment. He had a radio that scanned police calls, another radio powerful enough to receive programs from all over the world, a voice-altering device.

At night he dutifully watched television with his mother. After she went to bed at ten o'clock, however, Bernie snapped off the television, rushed down to the basement, turned on the radios and began to call talk show hosts. He made up names and backgrounds to give them. He'd call a right-wing host and rant liberal values, a liberal host and sing the praises of the extreme right. In his call-in persona, he loved arguments, confrontations, trading insults.

Unknown to his mother he also had a forty-inch television and a VCR in the basement and often watched movies he had brought home from porn shops.

The police scanner inspired other ideas. He began to go through telephone books and circle numbers that were listed in women's names. He would dial one of those numbers in the middle of the night and say he was calling from a cellular phone outside her home and was about to break in. He'd whisper that maybe he'd just pay a visit, or maybe he'd kill her. Then Bernie would sit and chuckle as he listened to the police scanners sending a squad car rushing to the address. It was almost as good as peeking in windows or following women, and he never had to worry about the headlights of a police car suddenly shining on him, or a cop on a loudspeaker yelling, "Freeze."

The car belonging to Tom Weicker was a gold mine of information for Bernie. Weicker had an electronic address book in the glove compartment. In it he kept the names, addresses and numbers of the key staff of the station. The big shots, Bernie thought, as he copied numbers onto his own electronic pad. He'd even reached Weicker's wife at home one night. She had begun to shriek when he told her he was at the back door and on his way in.

Afterwards, recalling her terror, he'd giggled for hours.

What was getting hard for him now was that for the first time since he was released from Riker's Island, he had that scary feeling of not being able to get someone out of his mind. This one was a reporter. She was so pretty that when he opened the car door for her it was a struggle not to touch her.

Her name was Meghan Collins.

4

*S*omehow Meghan was able to accept Weicker's offer calmly. It was a joke among the staff that if you were too gee-whiz-thanks about a promotion, Tom Weicker would ponder whether or not he'd made a good choice. He wanted ambitious, driven people who felt any recognition given them was overdue.

Trying to seem matter-of-fact, she showed him the faxed message. As he read it he raised his eyebrows. "What's this mean?" he asked. "What's the 'mistake'? Who is Annie?"

"I don't know. Tom, I was at Roosevelt Hospital when the stabbing victim was brought in last night. Has she been identified?"

"Not yet. What about her?"

"I suppose you ought to know something," Meghan said reluctantly. "She looks like me."

"She resembles you?"

"She could almost be my double."

Tom's eyes narrowed. "Are you suggesting that this fax is tied into that woman's death?"

"It's probably just coincidence, but I thought I should at least let you see it."

"I'm glad you did. Let me keep it. I'll find out who's handling the investigation on that case and let him take a look at it."

For Meghan, it was a distinct relief to pick up her assignments at the news desk.

IT WAS A RELATIVELY TAME DAY. A PRESS CONFERENCE AT the mayor's office at which he named his choice for the new police commissioner, a suspicious fire that had gutted a tenement in Washington Heights. Late in the afternoon, Meghan spoke to the medical examiner's office. An artist's sketch of the dead girl and her physical description had been issued by the Missing Persons Bureau. Her fingerprints were on the way to Washington to be checked against government and criminal files. She had died of a single deep stab wound in the chest. Internal bleeding had been slow but massive. Both legs and arms had been broken some years ago. If not claimed in thirty days, her body would be buried in potter's field in a numbered grave. Another Jane Doe.

At six o'clock that evening, Meghan was just leaving work. As she'd been doing since her father's disappearance, she was going to spend the weekend in Connecticut with her mother. On Sunday afternoon, she was assigned to cover an event at the Manning Clinic, an assisted reproduction facility located forty minutes from their home in Newtown. The clinic was having its annual reunion of children born as a result of in vitro fertilization carried out there.

The assignment editor collared her at the elevator. "Steve

will handle the camera on Sunday at Manning. I told him to meet you there at three."

"Okay."

During the week, Meghan used a company vehicle. This morning she'd driven her own car uptown. The elevator jolted to a stop at the garage level. She smiled as Bernie spotted her and immediately began trotting to the lower parking level. He brought up her white Mustang and held the door open for her. "Any news about your dad?" he asked solicitously.

"No, but thanks for asking."

He bent over, bringing his face close to hers. "My mother and I are praying."

What a nice guy! Meghan thought, as she steered the car up the ramp to the exit.

5

Catherine Collins' hair always looked as though she'd just run a hand through it. It was a short, curly mop, now tinted ash blond, that accentuated the pert prettiness of her heart-shaped face. She occasionally reminded Meghan that it was a good thing she'd inherited her own father's determined jaw. Otherwise, now that she was fifty-three, she'd look like a fading Kewpie doll, an impression enhanced by her diminutive size. Barely five feet tall, she referred to herself as the house midget.

Meghan's grandfather Patrick Kelly had come to the United States from Ireland at age nineteen, "with the clothes on my back and one set of underwear rolled under my arm," as the story went. After working days as a dishwasher in the kitchen of a Fifth Avenue hotel and nights with the cleaning crew of a funeral home, he'd concluded that, while there were a lot of things people could do without, nobody could give up eating or dying. Since it was more cheerful to watch people eat than lie in a casket with carnations scattered over them, Patrick Kelly decided to put all his energies into the food business.

Twenty-five years later, he built the inn of his dreams in Newtown, Connecticut, and named it Drumdoe after the village of his birth. It had ten guest rooms and a fine restaurant that drew people from a radius of fifty miles. Pat completed the dream by renovating a charming farmhouse on the adjoining property as a home. He then chose a bride, fathered Catherine and ran his inn until his death at eighty-eight.

His daughter and granddaughter were virtually raised in that inn. Catherine now ran it with the same dedication to excellence that Patrick had instilled in her, and her work there had helped her cope with her husband's death.

Yet, in the nine months since the bridge tragedy, she had found it impossible not to believe that someday the door would open and Ed would cheerfully call, "Where are my girls?" Sometimes she still found herself listening for the sound of her husband's voice.

Now, in addition to all the shock and grief, her finances had become an urgent problem. Two years earlier, Catherine had closed the inn for six months, mortgaged it and completed a massive renovation and redecoration project.

The timing could not have been worse. The reopening coincided with the downward trend of the economy. The payments on the new mortgage were not being met by present income, and quarterly taxes were coming due. Her personal account had only a few thousand dollars left in it.

For weeks after the accident, Catherine had steeled herself for the call that would inform her that her husband's body had been retrieved from the river. Now she prayed for that call to come and end the uncertainty.

There was such a total sense of incompletion. Catherine

would often think that people who ignored funeral rites didn't understand that they were necessary to the spirit. She wanted to be able to visit Ed's grave. Pat, her father, used to talk about "a decent Christian burial." She and Meg would joke about that. When Pat spotted the name of a friend from the past in the obituary column, she or Meg would tease, "Oh, by God, I hope he had a decent Christian burial."

They didn't joke about that anymore.

ON FRIDAY AFTERNOON, CATHERINE WAS IN THE HOUSE, GET-ting ready to go to the inn for the dinner hour. Talk about TGIF, she thought. Friday meant Meg would soon be home for the weekend.

The insurance people were due momentarily. If they'll even give me a partial payout until the Thruway divers find wreck-age of the car, Catherine thought as she fastened a pin on the lapel of her houndstooth jacket. I need the money. They're just trying to wiggle out of double indemnity, but I'm willing to waive that until they have the proof they keep talking about.

But when the two somber executives arrived it was not to begin the process of payment. "Mrs. Collins," the older of the two said, "I hope you will understand our position. We sympathize with you and understand the predicament you are in. The problem is that we cannot authorize payment on your husband's policies without a death certificate, and that is not going to be issued."

Catherine stared at him. "You mean it's not going to be issued until they have absolute proof of his death? But sup-pose his body was carried downriver clear into the Atlantic?"

Both men looked uneasy. The younger one answered her. "Mrs. Collins, the New York Thruway Authority, as owner and operator of the Tappan Zee Bridge, has conducted ex-haustive operations to retrieve both victims and wreckage from the river. Granted, the explosions meant that the vehi-cles were shattered. Nevertheless, heavy parts like transmissions and engines don't disintegrate. Besides the tractor trailer and fuel tanker, six vehicles went over the side, or seven if we were to include your husband's car. Parts from all the others have been retrieved. All the other bodies have been recovered as well. There isn't so much as a wheel or tire or door or engine part of a Cadillac in the riverbed below the accident site."

"Then you're saying . . ." Catherine was finding it hard to form the words.

"We're saying that the exhaustive report on the accident about to be released by the Thruway Authority categorically states that Edwin Collins could not have perished in the bridge tragedy that night. The experts feel that even though he may have been in the vicinity of the bridge, no one believes Edwin Collins was a victim. We believe he escaped being caught with the cars that were involved in the accident and took advantage of that propitious happening to make the disappearance he was planning. We think he reasoned he could take care of you and your daughter through the insurance and go on to whatever new life he had already planned to begin."

6

Mac, as Dr. Jeremy MacIntyre was known, lived with his seven-year-old son, Kyle, around the bend from the Collins family. The summers of his college years at Yale, Mac had worked as a waiter at the Drumdoe Inn. In those summers he'd formed a lasting attachment for the area and decided that someday he'd live there.

Growing up, Mac had observed that he was the guy in the crowd the girls didn't notice. Average height, average weight, average looks. It was a reasonably accurate description, but actually Mac did not do himself justice. After they took a second look, women *did* find a challenge in the quizzical expression in his hazel eyes, an endearing boyishness in the sandy hair that always seemed wind tousled, a comforting steadiness in the authority with which he would lead them on the dance floor or tuck a hand under their elbow on an icy evening.

Mac had always known he would be a doctor someday. By the time he began his studies at NYU medical school he had begun to believe that the future of medicine was in genetics. Now thirty-six, he worked at LifeCode, a genetic research laboratory in Westport, some fifty minutes southeast of Newtown.

It was the job he wanted, and it fit into his life as a divorced, custodial father. At twenty-seven Mac had married. The marriage lasted a year and a half and produced Kyle. Then one day Mac came home from the lab to find a babysitter and a note. It read: "Mac, this isn't for me. I'm a lousy wife and a lousy mother. We both know it can't work. I've got to have a crack at a career. Take good care of Kyle. Goodbye, Ginger."

Ginger had done pretty well for herself since then. She sang in cabarets in Vegas and on cruise ships. She'd cut a few records, and the last one had hit the charts. She sent Kyle expensive presents for his birthday and Christmas. The gifts were invariably too sophisticated or too babyish. She'd seen Kyle only three times in the seven years since she'd taken off.

Despite the fact that it had almost come as a relief, Mac still harbored residual bitterness over Ginger's desertion. Somehow, divorce had never been a part of his imagined future, and he still felt uncomfortable with it. He knew that his son missed having a mother, so he took special care and special pride in being a good, attentive father.

On Friday evenings, Mac and Kyle often had dinner at the Drumdoe Inn. They ate in the small, informal grill, where the special Friday menu included individual pizzas and fish and chips.

Catherine was always at the inn for the dinner hour. Growing up, Meg had been a fixture there too. When she was ten and Mac a nineteen-year-old busboy, she had wistfully told him that it was fun to eat at home. "Daddy and I do sometimes, when he's here."

Since her father's disappearance, Meg spent just about every weekend at home and joined her mother at the inn for dinner. But this Friday night there was no sign of either Catherine or Meg.

Mac acknowledged that he was disappointed, but Kyle, who always looked forward especially to seeing Meg, dismissed her absence. "So she's not here. Fine."

"Fine" was Kyle's new all-purpose word. He used it when he was enthusiastic, disgusted or being cool. Tonight, Mac wasn't quite sure what emotion he was hearing. But hey, he told himself, give the kid space. If something's really bothering him it'll come out sooner or later, and it certainly can't have anything to do with Meghan.

Kyle finished the last of the pizza in silence. He was mad at Meghan. She always acted like she really was interested in the stuff that he did, but Wednesday afternoon, when he was outside and had just taught his dog, Jake, to stand up on his hind legs and beg, Meghan had driven past and ignored him. She'd been going real slow, too, and he'd yelled to her to stop. He knew she'd seen him, because she'd looked right at him. But then she'd speeded up the car, driven off, and hadn't even taken time to see Jake's trick. Fine.

He wouldn't tell his dad about it. Dad would say that Meghan was just upset because Mr. Collins hadn't come home for a long time and might have been one of the people whose car went into the river off the bridge. He'd say that sometimes when people were thinking about something else, they could go right past people and not even see them. But Meg *had* seen Kyle Wednesday and hadn't even bothered to wave to him.

Fine, he thought. Just fine.

7

*W*hen Meghan arrived home she found her mother sitting in the darkened living room, her hands folded in her lap. "Mom, are you okay?" she asked anxiously. "It's nearly seven-thirty. Aren't you going to Drumdoe?" She switched on the light and took in Catherine's blotched, tear-stained face. She sank to her knees and grabbed her mother's hands. "Oh God, did they find him? Is that it?"

"No, Meggie, that's not it." Haltingly Catherine Collins related the visit from the insurers.

Not Dad, Meghan thought. He couldn't, wouldn't do this to Mother. Not to her. There had to be a mistake. "That's the craziest thing I ever heard," she said firmly.

"That's what I told them. But Meg, why would Dad have borrowed so much on the insurance? That haunts me. And even if he did invest it, I don't know where. Without a death certificate, my hands are tied. I can't keep up with expenses. Phillip has been sending Dad's monthly draw from the company, but that's not fair to him. Most of the money due him in commissions has been in for some time. I know I'm conservative by nature, but I certainly wasn't when I renovated the inn. I really overdid it. Now I may have to sell Drumdoe."

The inn. It was Friday night. Her mother should be there now, in her element, greeting guests, keeping a watchful eye on the waiters and busboys, the table settings, sampling the dishes in the kitchen. Every detail automatically checked and rechecked.

"Dad didn't do this to you," Meg said flatly. "I just know that."

Catherine Collins broke into harsh, dry sobs. "Maybe Dad used the bridge accident as a chance to get away from me. But why, Meg? I loved him so much."

Meghan put her arms around her mother. "Listen," she said firmly, "you were right the first time. Dad would never do this to you, and one way or the other, we're going to prove it."

The Collins and Carter Executive Search office was located in Danbury, Connecticut. Edwin Collins had started the firm when he was twenty-eight, after having worked five years for a Fortune 500 company based in New York. By then he'd realized that working within the corporate structure was not for him.

Following his marriage to Catherine Kelly, he'd relocated his office to Danbury. They wanted to live in Connecticut, and the location of Edwin's office was not important since he spent much of his time traveling throughout the country, visiting clients.

Some twelve years before his disappearance, Collins had brought Phillip Carter into the business.

Carter, a Wharton graduate with the added attraction of a law degree, had previously been a client of Edwin's, having been placed by him in jobs several times. The last one before they joined forces was with a multinational firm in Maryland.

When Collins was visiting that client, he and Carter would have lunch or a drink together. Over the years they had developed a business-oriented friendship. In the early eighties, after a difficult midlife divorce, Phillip Carter finally left his job in Maryland to become Collins' partner and associate.

They were opposites in many ways. Collins was tall, classically handsome, an impeccable dresser and quietly witty, while Carter was bluff and hearty, with attractively irregular features and a thick head of graying hair. His clothes were expensive, but never looked quite put together. His tie was often pulled loose from the knot. He was a man's man, whose stories over a drink brought forth bursts of laughter, a man with an eye for the ladies, too.

The partnership had worked. For a long time Phillip Carter lived in Manhattan and did reverse commuting to Danbury, when he was not traveling for the company. His name often appeared in the columns of the New York newspapers as having attended dinner parties and benefits with various women. Eventually he bought a small house in Brookfield, ten minutes from the office, and stayed there with increasing frequency.

Now fifty-three years old, Phillip Carter was a familiar figure in the Danbury area.

He regularly worked at his desk for several hours after everyone else had left for the day because, since a number of clients and candidates were located in the Midwest and on the West Coast, early evening in the East was a good time to contact them. Since the night of the bridge tragedy, Phillip rarely left the office before eight o'clock.

When Meghan called at five of eight this evening, he was reaching for his coat. "I was afraid it was coming to this," he said after she'd told him about the visit from the insurers. "Can you come in tomorrow around noon?"

After he hung up he sat for a long time at his desk. Then he picked up the phone and called his accountant. "I think we'd better audit the books right now," he said quietly.

9

*W*hen Meghan arrived at the Collins and Carter Executive Search offices at two o'clock on Saturday, she found three men working with calculators at the long table that usually held magazines and plants. She did not need Phillip Carter's explanation to confirm that they were auditors. At his suggestion, they went into her father's private office.

She had spent a sleepless night, her mind a battleground of questions, doubts and denial. Phillip closed the door and indicated one of the two chairs in front of the desk. He took the other one, a subtlety she appreciated. It would have hurt to see him behind her father's desk.

She knew Phillip would be honest with her. She asked, "Phillip, do you think it's remotely possible that my father is still alive and chose to disappear?"

The momentary pause before he spoke was answer enough. "You *do* think that?" she prodded.

"Meg, I've lived long enough to know that anything is possible. Frankly, the Thruway investigators and the insurers have been around here for quite a while asking some pretty direct questions. A couple of times I've wanted to toss them out bodily. Like everyone else, I expected Ed's car, or wreckage from it, would be recovered. It's possible that a lot of it would have been carried downstream by the tide or become lodged in the riverbed, but it doesn't help that not a trace of the car has been found. So to answer you, yes, it's possible. And no, I can't believe your father capable of a stunt like that."

It was what she expected to hear, but that didn't make it easier. Once when she was very little, Meghan had tried to take a burning piece of bread out of the toaster with a fork. She felt as though she was experiencing again the vivid pain of electrical current shooting through her body.

"And of course it doesn't help that Dad took the cash value out of his policies a few weeks before he disappeared."

"No, it doesn't. I want you to know that I'm doing the audit for your mother's sake. When this becomes public knowledge, and be sure it will, I want to be able to have a certified statement that our books are in perfect order. This sort of thing starts rumors flying, as you can understand."

Meghan looked down. She had dressed in jeans and a matching jacket. It occurred to her that this was the kind of outfit the dead woman was wearing when she was brought into Roosevelt Hospital. She pushed the thought away. "Was my father a gambler? Would that explain his need for a cash loan?"

Carter shook his head. "Your father wasn't a gambler, and I've seen enough of them, Meg." He grimaced. "Meg, I wish I could find an answer, but I can't. Nothing in Ed's business or personal life suggested to me that he would choose to disappear. On the other hand, the lack of physical evidence from the crash is necessarily suspicious, at least to outsiders."

Meghan looked at the desk, the executive swivel chair behind it. She could picture her father sitting there, leaning back, his eyes twinkling, his hands clasped, fingers pointing up in what her mother called "Ed's saint-and-martyr pose."

She could see herself running into this office as a child.

Her father always had candy for her, gooey chocolate bars, marshmallows, peanut brittle. Her mother had tried to keep that kind of candy from her. "Ed," she'd protest, "don't give her that junk. You'll ruin her teeth."

"Sweets to the sweet, Catherine."

Daddy's girl. Always. He was the fun parent. Mother was the one who made Meghan practice the piano and make her bed. Mother was the one who'd protested when she quit the law firm. "For heaven's sake, Meg," she had pleaded, "give it more than six months; don't waste your education."

Daddy had understood. "Leave her alone, love," he'd said firmly. "Meg has a good head on her shoulders."

Once when she was little Meghan had asked her father why he traveled so much.

"Ah, Meg," he'd sighed. "How I wish it wasn't necessary. Maybe I was born to be a wandering minstrel."

Because he was away so much, when he came home he always tried to make it up. He'd suggest that instead of going to the inn he'd whip up dinner for the two of them at home. "Meghan Anne," he'd tell her, "you're my date."

This office has his aura, Meg thought. The handsome cherrywood desk he'd found in a Salvation Army store and stripped and refinished himself. The table behind it with pictures of her and her mother. The lion's-head bookends holding leather-bound books.

For nine months she had been mourning him as dead. She wondered if at this moment she was mourning him more. If the insurers were right, he had become a stranger. Meghan looked into Phillip Carter's eyes. "They're not right," she said aloud. "I believe my father is dead. I believe that some wreckage of his car will still be found." She looked around. "But in fairness to you, we have no right to tie up this office. I'll come in next week and pack his personal effects."

"We'll take care of that, Meg."

"No. Please. I can sort things out better here. Mother's in rough enough shape without watching me do it at home."

Phillip Carter nodded. "You're right, Meg. I'm worried about Catherine too."

"That's why I don't dare tell her about what happened the other night." She saw the deepening concern on his face as she told him about the stabbing victim who resembled her and the fax that came in the middle of the night.

"Meg, that's bizarre," he said. "I hope your boss follows it up with the police. We can't let anything happen to you."

AS VICTOR ORSINI TURNED HIS KEY IN THE DOOR OF THE Collins and Carter offices, he was surprised to realize it was unlocked. Saturday afternoon usually meant he had the place to himself. He had returned from a series of meetings in Colorado and wanted to go over mail and messages.

Thirty-one years old with a permanent tan, muscular arms and shoulders and a lean disciplined body, he had the look of an outdoorsman. His jet black hair and strong features were indicative of his Italian heritage. His intensely blue eyes were a throwback to his British grandmother.

Orsini had been working for Collins and Carter for nearly seven years. He hadn't expected to stay so long, in fact he'd always planned to use this job as a stepping-stone to a bigger firm.

His eyebrows raised when he pushed open the door and saw the auditors. In a deliberately impersonal tone, the head man told Orsini that Phillip Carter and Meghan Collins were in Edwin Collins' private office. He then hesitantly acquainted Victor with the insurers' theory that Collins had chosen to disappear.

"That's crazy." Victor strode across the reception area and knocked on the closed door.

Carter opened it. "Oh, Victor, good to see you. We didn't expect you today."

Meghan turned to greet him. Orsini realized she was fighting back tears. He groped for something reassuring to say but could come up with nothing. He had been questioned by the investigators about the call Ed Collins made to him just before the accident. "Yes," he'd said at the time, "Edwin said he was getting on the bridge. Yes, I'm sure he didn't say he was getting off it. Do you think I can't hear? Yes, he wanted to see me the next morning. There wasn't anything unusual about that. Ed used his car phone all the time."

Victor suddenly wondered how long it would be before anyone questioned that it was his word alone that placed Ed Collins on the ramp to the Tappan Zee that night. It was not difficult for him to mirror the concern on Meghan's face when he shook the hand she extended to him.

10

At three o'clock on Sunday afternoon, Meg met Steve Boyle, the PCD cameraman, in the parking lot of the Manning Clinic.

The clinic was on a hillside two miles from Route 7 in rural Kent, a forty-minute drive north from her home. It had been built in 1890 as the residence of a shrewd businessman whose wife had had the good sense to restrain her ambitious husband from creating an ostentatious display on his meteoric rise to the status of merchant prince. She convinced him that, instead of the pseudopalazzo he had planned, an English manor house was better suited to the beauty of the countryside.

"Prepared for children's hour?" Meghan asked the cameraman as they trudged up the walk.

"The Giants are on and we're stuck with the Munchkins," Steve groused.

Inside the mansion, the spacious foyer functioned as a reception area. Oak-paneled walls held framed pictures of the children who owed their existence to the genius of modern science. Beyond, the great hall had the ambiance of a comfortable family room, with groupings of furniture that invited intimate conversations or could be angled for informal lectures.

Booklets with testimonials from grateful parents were scattered on tables. "We wanted a child so badly. Our lives were incomplete. And then we made an appointment at the Manning Clinic . . ." "I'd go to a friend's baby shower and try not to cry. Someone suggested I look into in vitro fertilization, and Jamie was born fifteen months later . . ." "My fortieth birthday was coming, and I knew it would soon be too late . . ."

Every year, on the third Sunday in October, the children who had been born as a result of IVF at the Manning Clinic were invited to return with their parents for the annual reunion. Meghan learned that this year three hundred invitations were sent and over two hundred small alumni accepted. It was a large, noisy and festive party.

In one of the smaller sitting rooms, Meghan interviewed Dr. George Manning, the silver-haired seventy-year-old director of the clinic, and asked him to explain in vitro fertilization.

"In the simplest possible terms," he explained, "IVF is a method by which a woman who has great difficulty conceiving is sometimes able to have the baby or babies she wants so desperately. After her menstrual cycle has been monitored, she begins treatment. Fertility drugs are administered so that her ovaries are stimulated to release an abundance of follicles, which are then retrieved.

"The woman's partner is asked to provide a semen sample to inseminate the eggs contained in the follicles in the laboratory. The next day an embryologist checks to see which, if any, eggs have been fertilized. If success was achieved, a physician will transfer one or more of the fertilized eggs, which are now referred to as embryos, to the woman's uterus. If requested, the rest of the embryos will be cryopreserved for later implantation.

"After fifteen days, blood is drawn for the first pregnancy test." The doctor pointed to the great hall. "And as you can see from the crowd we have here today, many of those tests prove positive."

"I certainly can," Meg agreed. "Doctor, what is the ratio of success to failure?"

"Still not as high as we'd prefer, but improving constantly," he said solemnly.

"Thank you, Doctor."

TRAILED BY STEVE, MEGHAN INTERVIEWED SEVERAL OF THE mothers, asking them to share their personal experiences with in vitro fertilization.

One of them, posing with her three handsome offspring, explained, "They fertilized fourteen eggs and implanted three. One of them resulted in a pregnancy, and here he is." She smiled down at her elder son. "Chris is seven now. The other embryos were cryopreserved, or, in simpler terms, frozen. I came back five years ago, and Todd is the result. Then I tried again last year, and Jill is three months old. Some of the embryos didn't survive thawing, but I still have two cryopreserved embryos in the lab. In case I ever find time on my hands for another kid," she said laughing as the four-year-old darted away.

"Have we got enough, Meghan?" Steve asked. "I'd like to catch the last quarter of the Giants game."

"Let me talk to one more staff member. I've been watching that woman. She seems to know everybody's name."

Meg went over to the woman and glanced at her name tag. "May I have a word with you, Dr. Petrovic?"

"Of course." Petrovic's voice was well modulated, with a

hint of an accent. She was of average height, with hazel eyes and refined features. She seemed courteous rather than friendly. Still, Meg noticed that she had a cluster of children around her.

"How long have you been at the clinic, Doctor?"

"It will be seven years in March. I'm the embryologist in charge of the laboratory."

"Would you care to comment on what you feel about these children?"

"I feel that each one of them is a miracle."

"Thank you, Doctor."

"We've got enough footage inside," Meg told Steve when they left Petrovic. "I do want a shot of the group picture, though. They'll be gathering for it in a minute."

The annual photo was taken on the front lawn outside the mansion. There was the usual confusion that attended lining up children from toddler age to nine-year-olds, with mothers holding infants standing in the last row and flanked by staff members.

The Indian summer day was bright, and as Steve focused the camera on the group, Meghan had the fleeting thought that every one of the children looked well dressed and happy. Why not? she thought. They were all desperately wanted.

A three-year-old ran from the front row to his pregnant mother, who was standing near Meghan. Blue eyed and golden haired, with a sweet, shy smile, he threw his arms around his mother's knees.

"Get a shot of that," Meghan told Steve. "He's adorable." Steve held the camera on the little boy as his mother cajoled him to rejoin the other children.

"I'm right here, Jonathan," she assured him as she placed him back in line. "You can see me. I promise I'm not going away." She returned to where she had been standing.

Meghan walked over to the woman. "Would you mind answering a few questions?" she asked, holding out the mike.

"I'd be glad to."

"Will you give us your name and tell us how old your little boy is?"

"I'm Dina Anderson, and Jonathan is almost three."

"Is your expected baby also the result of in vitro fertilization?"

"Yes, as a matter of fact, he's Jonathan's identical twin."

"Identical twin!" Meghan knew she sounded astonished.

"I know it sounds impossible," Dina Anderson said happily, "but that's the way it is. It's extremely rare, but an embryo can split in the laboratory just the way it would in the womb. When we were told that one of the fertilized eggs had divided, my husband and I decided that I would try to give birth to each twin separately. We felt that individually they might each have a better chance for survival in my womb, and actually it's practical. I've got a responsible job, and I'd hate to have left two infants with a nanny."

The photographer for the clinic had been snapping pictures. A moment later he yelled, "Okay kids, thanks." The children scattered, and Jonathan ran to his mother. Dina Anderson scooped up her son in her arms. "I can't imagine life without him," she said. "And in about ten days we'll have Ryan."

What a human interest segment that would make, Meghan thought. "Mrs. Anderson," she said persuasively, "if you're willing, I'd like to talk to my boss about doing a feature story on your twins."

11

On the way back to Newtown, Meghan used the car phone to call her mother. Her alarm at getting the answering machine turned to relief when she dialed the inn and was told

Mrs. Collins was in the dining room. "Tell her I'm on my way," she instructed the receptionist, "and that I'll meet her there."

For the next fifteen minutes Meghan drove as though on automatic pilot. She was excited about the possibility of the feature story she would pitch to Weicker. And she could get some guidance on it from Mac. He was a specialist in genetics. He'd be able to give her expert advice and reading material she could study to know more about the whole spectrum of assisted reproduction, including the statistics on success and failure rates. When the traffic slowed to a halt, she picked up her car phone and dialed his number.

Kyle answered. Meghan raised her eyebrow at the way his tone changed when he realized she was the caller. What's eating him? she wondered, as he pointedly ignored her greeting and passed the phone to his father.

"Hi, Meghan. What can I do for you?" As always the sound of Mac's voice gave Meghan a stab of familiar pain. She'd called him her best friend when she was ten, had a crush on him when she was twelve, and had fallen in love with him by the time she was sixteen. Three years later he married Ginger. She'd been at the wedding, and it was one of the hardest days of her life. Mac had been crazy about Ginger, and Meg suspected that even after seven years, if Ginger had walked in the door and dropped her suitcase, he'd *still* want her. Meg would never let herself admit that no matter how hard she tried, she'd never been able to stop loving Mac.

"I could use some professional help, Mac." As the car passed the blocked lane and picked up speed, she explained the visit to the clinic and the story she was putting together. "And I sort of need the information in a hurry so I can pitch the whole thing to my boss."

"I can give it to you right away. Kyle and I are just heading for the inn. I'll bring it along. Want to join us for dinner?"

"That works out fine. See you." She broke the connection.

It was nearly seven when she reached the outskirts of town. The temperature was dropping, and the afternoon breeze had turned to gusts of wind. The headlights caught the trees, still heavy with leaves that were now restlessly moving, sending shadows over the road. At this moment, they made her think of the dark, choppy water of the Hudson.

Concentrate on how you'll pitch the idea of doing a special on the Manning Clinic to Weicker, she told herself fiercely.

PHILLIP CARTER WAS IN DRUMDOE, AT A WINDOW TABLE SET for three. He waved Meghan over. "Catherine's in the kitchen giving the chef a hard time," he told her. "The people over there"—he nodded to a nearby table—"wanted the beef rare. Your mother said what they got could have passed for a hockey puck. In fact, it was medium rare."

Meghan sank into a chair and smiled. "The best thing that could happen to her would be if the chef quit. Then she'd have to get back in the kitchen. It would keep her mind off things." She reached across the table and touched Carter's hand. "Thanks for coming over."

"I hope you haven't eaten. I've managed to make Catherine promise to join me."

"That's great, but how about if I have coffee with you? Mac and Kyle should be here any minute, and I said I'd join them. The truth is, I need to pick Mac's brain."

At dinner, Kyle continued to be aloof to Meghan. Finally she raised her eyebrows in a questioning look at Mac, who shrugged and murmured, "Don't ask me." Mac cautioned her about the feature story she was planning. "You're right. There are a lot of failures, and it's a very expensive procedure."

Meg looked across the table at Mac and his son. They were so alike. She remembered the way her father had pressed her hand at Mac's wedding. He'd understood. He'd always understood her.

When they were ready to leave, she said, "I'll sit with Mother and Phillip for a few minutes." She put an arm around Kyle. "See you, buddy."

He pulled away.

"Hey, come on," Meghan said. "What's all this about?"

To her surprise she saw tears well in his eyes. "I thought you were my friend." He turned swiftly and ran to the door.

"I'll get it out of him," Mac promised as he rushed to catch up with his son.

AT SEVEN O'CLOCK, IN NEARBY BRIDGEWATER, DINA ANDERson was holding Jonathan on her lap and sipping the last of her coffee as she told her husband about the party at the Manning Clinic. "We may be famous," she said. "Meghan Collins, that reporter from Channel 3, wants to get the go-ahead from her boss to be in the hospital when the baby is born and get early pictures of Jonathan with his brand-new brother. If her boss agrees, she might want to do updates from time to time on how they interact."

Donald Anderson looked doubtful. "Honey, I'm not sure we need that kind of publicity."

"Oh, come on. It could be fun. And I agree with Meghan that if more people who want babies understood the different kinds of assisted birth, they'd realize IVF really is a viable option. This guy was certainly worth all the expense and effort."

"This guy's head is going in your coffee." Anderson got up, walked around the table and took his son from his wife's arms. "Bedtime for Bonzo," he announced, then added, "If you want to do it, it's okay with me. I guess it would be fun to have some professional tapes of the kids."

Dina watched affectionately as her blue-eyed, blond husband carried her equally fair child to the staircase. She had all Jonathan's baby pictures in readiness. It would be such fun to compare them with Ryan's pictures. She still had one cryopreserved embryo at the clinic. In two years we'll try for another baby, and maybe that one will look like me, she thought, glancing across the room to the mirror over the serving table. She studied her reflection, her olive skin, hazel eyes, coal black hair. "That wouldn't be too bad a deal either," she murmured to herself.

AT THE INN, LINGERING OVER A SECOND CUP OF COFFEE WITH her mother and Phillip, Meghan listened as he soberly discussed her father's disappearance.

"Edwin's borrowing so heavily on his insurance without telling you plays right into the insurers' hands. As they told you, they're taking it as a signal that for his own reasons he was accumulating cash. Just as they won't pay his personal insurance, I've been notified they won't settle the partnership insurance either, which would be paid to you as satisfaction for his senior partnership in Executive Search."

"Which means," Catherine Collins said quietly, "that because I cannot prove my husband is dead I stand to lose everything. Phillip, is Edwin owed any more money for past work?"

His answer was simple. "No."

"How is the headhunter business this year?"

"Not good."

"You've advanced us $45,000 while we've been waiting for Edwin's body to be found."

He suddenly looked stern. "Catherine, I'm glad to do it. I only wish I could increase it. When we have proof of Ed's death, you can repay me out of the business insurance."

She put a hand over his. "I can't let you do that, Phillip. Old Pat would spin in his grave if he thought I was living on borrowed money. The fact is, unless we can find some proof that Edwin did die in that accident, I will lose the place my father spent his life creating, and I'll have to sell my home." She looked at Meghan. "Thank God I have you, Meggie." That was when Meghan decided not to drive back to New York City as she had planned, but to stay the night.

· · ·

WHEN SHE AND HER MOTHER GOT BACK TO THE HOUSE, BY unspoken consent they did not talk any more about the man who had been husband and father. Instead they watched the ten o'clock news, then prepared for bed. Meghan knocked on the door of her mother's bedroom to say good night. She realized that she no longer thought of it as her parents' room. When she opened the door, she saw with a thrust of pain that her mother had moved her pillows to the center of the bed.

Meghan knew that was a clear message that if Edwin Collins was alive, there was no room for him anymore in this house.

12

*B*ernie Heffernan spent Sunday evening with his mother, watching television in the shabby sitting room of their bungalow-type home in Jackson Heights. He vastly preferred watching from the communications center he had created in the crudely finished basement room, but always stayed upstairs until his mother went to bed at ten. Since her fall ten years earlier, she never went near the rickety basement stairs.

Meghan's segment about the Manning Clinic was aired on the six o'clock news. Bernie stared at the screen, perspiration beading his brow. If he were downstairs now, he could be taping Meghan on his VCR.

"Bernard!" Mama's sharp voice broke into his reverie.

He plastered on a smile. "Sorry, Mama."

Her eyes were enlarged behind the rimless bifocals. "I asked you if they ever found that woman's father."

He'd mentioned Meghan's father to Mama once and always regretted it. He patted his mother's hand. "I told her that we're praying for her, Mama."

He didn't like the way Mama looked at him. "You're not thinking on that woman, are you, Bernard?"

"No, Mama. Of course not, Mama."

After his mother went to bed, Bernie went down to the basement. He felt tired and dispirited. There was only one way to get some relief.

He began his calls immediately. First the religious station in Atlanta. Using the voice-altering device, he shouted insults at the preacher until he was cut off. Then he dialed a talk show in Massachusetts and told the host he'd overheard a murder plot against him.

At eleven he began calling women whose names he had checked off in the phone book. One by one he warned them that he was about to break in. From the sound of their voices he could picture how they looked. Young and pretty. Old. Plain. Slim. Heavy. Mentally he'd create the face, filling in the details of their features with each additional word they said.

Except tonight. Tonight they all had the same face.

Tonight they all looked like Meghan Collins.

13

When Meghan went downstairs Monday morning at six-thirty she found her mother already in the kitchen. The aroma of coffee filled the room, juice had been poured and bread was in the toaster. Meghan's protest that her mother should not have gotten up so early died on her lips. From the deep shadows around Catherine Collins' eyes, it was clear that she had slept little if at all.

Like me, Meghan thought, as she reached for the coffeepot. "Mother, I've done a lot of thinking," she said. Carefully choosing her words, she continued, "I can't understand a single reason why Dad would choose to disappear. Let's say there was another woman. That certainly could happen, but if it did, Dad could have asked you for a divorce. You'd have been devastated, of course, and I'd have been angry for you, but in the end we're both realists, and Dad knew that. The insurance companies are hanging everything on the fact that they haven't found either his body or the car, and that he borrowed against his own policies. But they were *his* policies, and as you said, he may have wanted to make some kind of investment he knew you wouldn't approve of. It *is* possible."

"Anything's possible," Catherine Collins said quietly, "including the fact that I don't know what to do."

"I do. We're going to file suit demanding payment of those policies, including double indemnity for accidental death. We're not going to sit back and let those people tell us that Dad pulled this on you."

AT SEVEN O'CLOCK MAC AND KYLE SAT ACROSS FROM EACH other at their kitchen table. Kyle had gone to bed still refusing to discuss his coolness toward Meg, but this morning his mood had changed. "I was thinking," he began.

Mac smiled. "That's a good start."

"I mean it. Remember last night Meg was talking about the case she was covering in court all day Wednesday?"

"Yes."

"Then she couldn't have been up here Wednesday afternoon."

"No, she wasn't."

"Then I didn't see her drive by the house."

Mac looked into his son's serious eyes. "No, you wouldn't have seen her Wednesday afternoon. I'm sure of that."

"I guess it was just somebody who looked a lot like her." Kyle's relieved smile revealed two missing teeth. He glanced down at Jake, who was stretched out under the table. "Now, by the time Meg gets a chance to see Jake when she comes home next weekend, he'll be *perfect* at begging."

At the sound of his name, Jake jumped up and lifted his front paws.

"I'd say he's perfect at begging now," Mac said dryly.

MEGHAN DROVE DIRECTLY TO THE WEST FIFTY-SIXTH STREET garage entrance of the PCD building. Bernie had the driver's door open at the exact moment she shifted into Park. "Hi, Miss Collins." His beaming smile and warm voice brought a responsive smile to her lips. "My mother and I saw you at that clinic, I mean we saw the news last night with you on. Must have been fun to be with all those kids." His hand came out to assist her from the car.

"They were awfully cute, Bernie," Meghan agreed.

"My mother said it seems kind of weird—you know what I mean—having babies the way those people do. I'm not much for all these crazy scientific fads."

Breakthroughs, not fads, Meghan thought. "I know what you mean," she said. "It does seem a little like something out of *Brave New World.*"

Bernie stared blankly at her.

"See you." She headed for the elevator, her leather folder tucked under her arm.

Bernie watched her go, then got in her car and drove it down to the lower level of the garage. Deliberately he put it in a dark corner at the far wall. During lunch break all the guys chose a car to relax in, where they'd eat and read the paper or doze. The only management rule was to make sure you didn't smear ketchup on the upholstery. Ever since some dope burned the leather armrest of a Mercedes, no one was allowed to smoke, even in cars where the ashtray was filled with butts. The point was, nobody saw anything funny about always taking a break in the same car or the same couple of cars. Bernie felt happy sitting in Meghan's Mustang. It had a hint of the perfume she always wore.

MEGHAN'S DESK WAS IN THE BULL PEN ON THE 30TH FLOOR. Swiftly she read the assignment sheet. At eleven o'clock she was to be at the arraignment of an indicted inside stock trader.

Her phone rang. It was Tom Weicker. "Meg, can you come in right away?"

There were two men in Weicker's private office. Meghan recognized one of them, Jamal Nader, a soft-spoken black detective whom she'd run into a number of times in court. They greeted each other warmly. Weicker introduced the other man as Lt. Story.

"Lt. Story is in charge of the homicide you covered the other night. I gave him the fax you received."

Nader shook his head. "That dead girl really is a look-alike for you, Meghan."

"Has she been identified?" Meghan asked.

"No." Nader hesitated. "But she seems to have known you."

"Known me?" Meghan stared at him. "How do you figure that?"

"When they brought her into the morgue Thursday night they went through her clothing and found nothing. They sent everything to the district attorney's office to be stored as evidence. One of our guys went over it again. The lining of the jacket pocket had a deep fold. He found a sheet of paper torn from a Drumdoe Inn notepad. It had your name and direct phone number at WPCD written on it."

"My name!"

Lt. Story reached into his pocket. The piece of paper was

encased in plastic. He held it up. "Your first name and the number."

Meghan and the two detectives were standing at Tom Weicker's desk. Meghan gripped the desktop as she stared at the bold letters, the slanted printing of the numbers. She felt her lips go dry.

"Miss Collins, do you recognize that handwriting?" Story asked sharply.

She nodded. "Yes."

"Who . . . ?"

She turned her head, not wanting to see that familiar writing anymore. "My father wrote that," she whispered.

14

*O*n Monday morning, Phillip Carter reached the office at eight o'clock. As usual he was the first to arrive. The staff was small, consisting of Jackie, his fifty-year-old secretary, the mother of teenagers; Milly, the grandmotherly part-time bookkeeper; and Victor Orsini.

Carter had his own computer adjacent to his desk. In it he kept files that only he could access, files that listed his personal data. His friends joked about his love for going to land auctions, but they would have been astonished at the amount of rural property he had quietly amassed over the years. Unfortunately for him, much of the land he had acquired cheaply had been lost in his divorce settlement. The property he bought at sky-high prices he acquired after the divorce.

As he inserted the key in the computer he reflected that

when Jackie and Milly learned that Edwin Collins' presumed death was being challenged, they would not lack for noon-hour gossip.

His essential sense of privacy recoiled at the notion that he would ever be the subject of one of the avid discussions Jackie and Milly shared as they lunched on salads that seemed to him to consist mostly of alfalfa sprouts.

The subject of Ed Collins' office worried him. It had seemed the decent thing to leave it as it was until the official pronouncement of his death, but now it was just as well Meghan had said she wanted to pack up her father's personal effects. One way or the other, Edwin Collins would never use it again.

Carter frowned. Victor Orsini. He just couldn't like the man. Orsini had always been closer to Ed, but he did a damn good job, and his expertise in the field of medical technology was absolutely necessary today, and particularly valuable now that Ed was gone. He had handled most of that area of the business.

Carter knew there was no way to avoid giving Orsini Ed's office when Meghan had finished clearing it out. Victor's present office was cramped and had only one small window.

Yes, for the present, he needed the man, like him or not.

Nevertheless, Phillip's intuition warned him that there was an elusive factor about Victor Orsini's makeup that should never be ignored.

LT. STORY ALLOWED A COPY OF THE PLASTIC-ENCLOSED scrap of paper to be made for Meghan. "How long ago were you assigned that phone number at the radio station?" he asked her.

"In mid-January."

"When was the last time you saw your father?"

"On January 14th. He was leaving for California on a business trip."

"What kind of business?"

Meghan's tongue felt thick, her fingers were chilled as she held the photocopy with her name looking incongruously bold against the white background. She told him about Collins and Carter Executive Search. It was obvious that Detective Jamal Nader had already told Story that her father was missing.

"Did your father have this number in his possession when he left?"

"He must have. I never spoke to him or saw him again after the fourteenth. He was due home on the twenty-eighth."

"And he died in the Tappan Zee Bridge accident that night."

"He called his associate Victor Orsini as he was starting onto the bridge. The accident happened less than a minute after their phone conversation. Someone reported seeing a dark Cadillac spin into the fuel tanker and go over the side." It was useless to conceal what this man could learn by one phone call. "I must tell you that the insurance companies have now refused to pay his policies on the basis that at least parts of all the other vehicles have been found, but there's been no trace of my father's car. The Thruway divers claim that if the car went into the river at that point, they should have located it." Meghan's chin went up. "My mother is filing suit to have the insurance paid."

She could see the skepticism in the eyes of all three men. To her own ears—and with this paper in her hand—she sounded like one of those unfortunate witnesses she had seen in court trials, people who stick doggedly to their testimony even in the face of irrefutable proof that they are either mistaken or lying.

Story cleared his throat. "Miss Collins, the young woman who was murdered Thursday night bears a striking resemblance to you and was carrying a slip of paper with your name and phone number written on it in your father's handwriting. Have you any explanation?"

Meghan stiffened her back. "I have no idea why that young

woman was carrying that piece of paper. I have no idea how she got it. She did look a lot like me. For all I know my father might have met her and commented on the similarity and said, 'If you're ever in New York, I'd like you to meet my daughter.' People do resemble each other. We all know that. My father was in the kind of business where he met many people; knowing him, that would be the kind of comment he'd make. There is one thing I am sure of, if my father were alive, he would not have deliberately disappeared and left my mother financially paralyzed."

She turned to Tom. "I'm assigned to cover the Baxter arraignment. I'd better get moving."

"You okay?" Tom asked. There was no hint of pity in his manner.

"I'm absolutely fine," Meghan said quietly. She did not look at Story or Nader.

It was Nader who spoke. "Meghan, we're in touch with the FBI. If there's been any report of a missing woman who fits the description of Thursday night's stabbing victim, we'll have it soon. Maybe a lot of answers are tied up together."

15

$\mathcal{H}$elene Petrovic loved her job as embryologist in charge of the laboratory of the Manning Clinic. Widowed at twenty-seven, she had emigrated to the United States from Rumania, gratefully accepted the largess of a family friend, worked for her as a cosmetician and begun to go to school at night.

Now forty-eight, she was a slender, handsome woman whose eyes never smiled. During the week, Helene lived in New Milford, Connecticut, five miles from the clinic, in the furnished condo she rented. Weekends were spent in Lawrenceville, New Jersey, in the pleasant colonial-style house she owned. The study off her bedroom there was filled with pictures of the children she had helped bring into life.

Helene thought of herself as the chief pediatrician of a nursery for newborns on the maternity ward of a fine hospital. The difference was that the embryos in her care were more vulnerable than the frailest preemie. She took her responsibility with fierce seriousness.

Helene would look at the tiny vials in the laboratory, and, knowing the parents and sometimes the siblings, in her mind's eye she saw the children who might someday be born. She loved them all, but there was one child she loved the best, the beautiful towhead whose sweet smile reminded her of the husband she had lost as a young woman.

THE ARRAIGNMENT OF THE STOCKBROKER BAXTER ON INSIDE trader charges took place in the courthouse on Centre Street. Flanked by his two attorneys, the impeccably dressed defendant pleaded not guilty, his firm voice suggesting the authority of the boardroom. Steve was Meg's cameraman again. "What a con artist. I'd almost rather be back in Connecticut with the Munchkins."

"I wrote up a memo and left it for Tom—about doing a feature on that clinic. This afternoon I'm going to pitch it to him," Meghan said.

Steve winked. "If I ever have kids, I hope I have them the old-fashioned way, if you know what I mean."

She smiled briefly. "I know what you mean."

AT FOUR O'CLOCK, MEGHAN WAS AGAIN IN TOM'S OFFICE. "Meghan, let me get this straight. You mean this woman is about to give birth to the identical twin of her three-year-old?"

"That's exactly what I mean. That kind of divided birth has been done in England, but it's news here. Plus the mother in this case is quite interesting. Dina Anderson is a bank vice president, very attractive and well spoken, and obviously a terrific mother. And the three-year-old is a doll.

"Another point is that so many studies have shown that identical twins, even when separated at birth, grow up with identical tastes. It can be eerie. They may marry people with the same name, call their children by the same names, decorate their houses in the same colors, wear the same hairstyle, choose the same clothes. It would be interesting to know how the relationship would change if one twin is significantly older than the other.

"Think about it," she concluded. "It's only fifteen years since the miracle of the first test tube baby, and now there are thousands of them. There are more new breakthroughs in assisted reproduction methods every day. I think ongoing segments on the new methods—and updates on the Anderson twins—could be terrific."

She spoke eagerly, warming to her argument. Tom Weicker was not an easy sell.

"How sure is Mrs. Anderson that she's having the identical twin?"

"Absolutely positive. The cryopreserved embryos are in individual tubes, marked with the mother's name, Social Security number and date of her birth. And each tube is given its own number. After Jonathan's embryo was transferred, the Andersons had two embryos, his identical twin and one other. The tube with his identical twin was specially labeled."

Tom got up from his desk and stretched. He'd taken off his coat, loosened his tie and opened his collar button. The effect was to soften his usual flinty exterior.

He walked over to the window, stared down at the snarled traffic on West Fifty-sixth Street, then turned abruptly. "I liked what you did with the Manning reunion yesterday. We've gotten good response. Go ahead with it."

He was letting her do it! Meghan nodded, reminding herself that enthusiasm was out of order.

Tom went back to his desk. "Meghan, take a look at this. It's an artist's sketch of the woman who was stabbed Thursday night." He handed it to her.

Even though she had seen the victim, Meghan's mouth went dry when she looked at the sketch. She read the statistics, "Caucasian, dark brown hair, blue-green eyes, 5'6", slender build, 120 pounds, 24–28 years old." Add an inch to the height and they'd describe her.

"If that 'mistake' fax was on the level and meant you were the intended victim, it's pretty clear why this girl is dead," Weicker commented. "She was right in this neighborhood, and the resemblance to you is uncanny."

"I simply don't understand it. Nor do I understand how she got that slip of paper with my father's writing."

"I spoke to Lt. Story again. We both agreed that until the killer is found it would be better to pull you off the news beat, just in case there is some kind of nut gunning for you."

"But, Tom—" she protested. He cut her off.

"Meghan, concentrate on that feature. It could make a darned good human interest story. If it works, we'll do future segments on those kids. But as of now, you are off the news beat. Keep me posted," he snapped as he sat down and pulled out a desk drawer, clearly dismissing her.

16

By Monday afternoon, the Manning Clinic had settled down from the excitement of the weekend reunion. All traces of the festive party were gone, and the reception area was restored to its usual quiet elegance.

A couple in their late thirties was leafing through magazines as they waited for their first appointment. The receptionist, Marge Walters, looked at them sympathetically. She had had no problem having three children in the first three years of her marriage. Across the room an obviously nervous woman in her twenties was holding her husband's hand. Marge knew the young woman had an appointment to have embryos implanted in her womb. Twelve of her eggs had become fertilized in the lab. Three would be implanted in the hope that one might result in a pregnancy. Sometimes more than one embryo developed, leading to a multiple birth.

"That would be a blessing, not a problem," the young woman had assured Marge when she signed in. The other nine embryos would be cryopreserved. If a pregnancy did not result this time, the young woman would come back and be implanted with some of those embryos.

Dr. Manning had called an unexpected lunchtime staff meeting. Unconsciously, Marge riffled her fingers through short blond hair. Dr. Manning had told them that PCD Channel 3 was going to do a television special on the clinic and tie it in with the impending birth of Jonathan Anderson's identical twin. He asked that all cooperation be given to Meghan Collins, respecting of course the privacy of the clients. Only those clients who agreed in writing would be interviewed.

Marge hoped that she'd get to appear in the special. Her boys would get such a kick out of it.

To the right of her desk were the offices for senior staff. The door leading to those offices opened and one of the new secretaries came out, her step brisk. She paused at Marge's desk long enough to whisper, "Something's up. Dr. Petrovic just came out of Manning's office. She's very upset, and when I went in, he looked as though he was about to have a heart attack."

"What do you think is going on?" Marge asked.

"I don't know, but she's cleaning out her desk. I wonder if she quit—or was fired?"

"I can't imagine her choosing to leave this place," Marge said in disbelief. "That lab is her whole life."

ON MONDAY EVENING, WHEN MEGHAN PICKED UP HER CAR, Bernie had said, "See you tomorrow, Meghan."

She had told him that she wouldn't be around the office for a while, that she would be on special assignment in Connecticut. Saying that to Bernie had been easy, but as she drove home, she wrestled with the problem of how to explain to her mother that she'd been switched from the news team after just getting the job.

She'd simply have to say that the station wanted the feature to be completed quickly because of the impending birth of the Anderson baby. Mom's upset enough without having to worry that I might have been an intended murder victim, Meghan thought, and she'd be a wreck if she knew about the slip of paper with Dad's writing.

She exited Interstate 84 onto Route 7. Some trees still had leaves, although the vivid colors of mid-October had faded. Fall had always been her favorite season, she reflected. But not this year.

A part of her brain, the legal part, the portion that separated emotion from evidence, insisted that she begin to consider all the reasons why that paper with her name and phone number could have been in the dead woman's pocket. It's not disloyal to examine all the possibilities, she reminded herself fiercely. A good defense lawyer must always see the case through the prosecutor's eyes as well.

Her mother had gone through all the papers that were in the wall safe at home. But she knew her mother had not examined the contents of the desk in her father's study. It was time to do that.

She hoped she had taken care of everything at the newsroom. Before she left, Meg made a list of her ongoing assignments for Bill Evans, her counterpart from the Chicago affiliate, who would sub for her on the news team while the murder investigation was going on.

Her appointment with Dr. Manning was set for tomorrow at eleven o'clock. She'd asked him if she could go through an initial information and counseling session as though she were a new client. During a sleepless night, something else had occurred to her. It would be a nice touch to get some tape on Jonathan Anderson helping his mother prepare for the baby. She wondered if the Andersons had any home videos of Jonathan as a newborn.

When she reached home, the house was empty. That had to mean her mother was at the inn. Good, Meghan thought. It's the best place for her. She lugged in the fax machine they'd lent her at the office. She'd hook it up to the second line in her father's study. At least I won't be awakened by crazy, middle-of-the-night messages, she thought as she closed and locked the door and began switching on lights against the rapidly approaching darkness.

Meghan sighed unconsciously as she walked around the house. She'd always loved this place. The rooms weren't large. Her mother's favorite complaint was that old farmhouses always looked bigger on the outside than they actually were. "This place is an optical illusion," she would lament. But in Meghan's eyes there was great charm in the intimacy of the rooms. She liked the feel of the slightly uneven floor with its wide boards, the look of the fireplaces and the French doors and the built-in corner cupboards of the dining room. In her eyes they were the perfect setting for the antique maple furniture with its lovely warm patina, the deep comfortable upholstery, the colorful hand-hooked rugs.

Dad was away so much, she thought as she opened the door of his study, a room that she and her mother had avoided since the night of the bridge accident. But you always knew he was coming back, and he was so much fun.

She snapped on the desk lamp and sat in the swivel chair. This room was the smallest on the first floor. The fireplace was flanked by bookshelves. Her father's favorite chair, maroon leather with a matching ottoman, had a standing lamp on one side and a piecrust table on the other.

The table as well as the mantel held clusters of family pictures: her mother and father's wedding portrait; Meghan as a baby; the three of them as she grew up; old Pat, bursting with pride in front of the Drumdoe Inn. The record of a happy family, Meghan thought, looking from one to another of a group of framed snapshots.

She picked up the picture of her father's mother, Aurelia. Taken in the early thirties when she was twenty-four, it showed clearly that she had been a beautiful woman. Thick wavy hair, large expressive eyes, oval face, slender neck, sable skins over her suit. Her expression was the dreamy posed look that photographers of that day preferred. "I had the prettiest mother in Pennsylvania," her father would say, then add, "and now I have the prettiest daughter in Connecticut. You look like her." His mother had died when he was a baby.

Meghan did not remember ever having seen a picture of Richard Collins. "We never got along," her father had told her tersely. "The less I saw of him, the better."

The phone rang. It was Virginia Murphy, her mother's right-hand at the inn. "Catherine wanted me to see if you were home and if you wanted to come over for dinner."

"How is she, Virginia?" Meghan asked.

"She's always good when she's here, and we have a lot of reservations tonight. Mr. Carter is coming at seven. He wants your mother to join him."

Hmm, Meghan thought. She'd always suspected that Phillip Carter was developing a warm spot in his heart for Catherine Collins. "Will you tell Mom that I have an interview in Kent tomorrow and need to do a lot of research for it? I'll fix something here."

When she hung up, she resolutely got out her briefcase and pulled from it all the newspaper and magazine human interest stories on in vitro fertilization a researcher at the station had assembled for her. She frowned when she found several cases where a clinic was sued because tests showed the woman's husband was not the biological father of the child. "That is a pretty serious mistake to make," she said aloud, and decided that it was an angle that should be touched on in one segment of the feature.

At eight o'clock she made a sandwich and a pot of tea and carried them back to the study. She ate while she tried to absorb the technical material Mac had given her. It was, she decided, a crash course in assisted reproductive procedures.

The click of the lock a little after ten meant that her mother was home. She called, "Hi, I'm in here."

Catherine Collins hurried into the room. "Meggie, you're all right?"

"Of course. Why?"

"Just now when I was coming up the driveway I got the queerest feeling about you, that something was wrong—almost like a premonition."

Meghan forced a chuckle, got up swiftly and hugged her mother. "There *was* something wrong," she said. "I've been trying to absorb the mysteries of DNA, and believe me, it's tough. I now know why Sister Elizabeth told me I had no head for science."

She was relieved to see the tension ease from her mother's face.

HELENE PETROVIC SWALLOWED NERVOUSLY AS SHE PACKED the last of her suitcases at midnight. She left out only her toiletries and the clothes she would wear in the morning. She was frantic to be finished with it all. She had become so jumpy lately. The strain had become too much, she decided. It was time to put an end to it.

She lifted the suitcase from the bed and placed it next to the others. From the foyer, the faint click of a turning lock reached her ears. She jammed her hand against her mouth to muffle a scream. He wasn't supposed to come tonight. She turned around to face him.

"Helene?" His voice was polite. "Weren't you planning to say goodbye?"

"I . . . I was going to write you."

"That won't be necessary now."

With his right hand, he reached into his pocket. She saw the glint of metal. Then he picked up one of the bed pillows and held it in front of him. Helene did not have time to try to escape. Searing pain exploded through her head. The future that she had planned so carefully disappeared with her into the blackness.

AT FOUR A.M. THE RINGING OF THE PHONE TORE MEGHAN from sleep. She fumbled for the receiver.

A barely discernible, hoarse voice whispered, "Meg."

"Who is this?" She heard a click and knew her mother was picking up the extension.

"It's Daddy, Meg. I'm in trouble. I did something terrible."

A strangled moan made Meg fling down the receiver and rush into her mother's room. Catherine Collins was slumped on the pillow, her face ashen, her eyes closed. Meg grasped her arms. "Mom, it's some sick, crazy fool," she said urgently. "Mom!"

Her mother was unconscious.

17

At seven-thirty Tuesday morning, Mac watched his lively son leap onto the school bus. Then he got in his car for the drive to Westport. There was a nippy bite in the air, and his glasses were fogging over. He took them off, gave them a quick rub and automatically wished that he were one of the happy contact lens wearers whose smiling faces reproached him from poster-sized ads whenever he went to have his glasses adjusted or replaced.

As he drove around the bend in the road he was astonished to see Meg's white Mustang about to turn into her driveway. He tapped the horn and she braked.

He pulled up beside her. In unison they lowered their windows. His cheerful, "What are you up to?" died on his lips as he got a good look at Meghan. Her face was strained and pale, her hair disheveled, a striped pajama top visible between the lapels of her raincoat. "Meg, what's wrong?" he demanded.

"My mother's in the hospital," she said tonelessly.

A car was coming up behind her. "Go ahead," he said. "I'll follow you."

In the driveway, he hurried to open the car door for Meg. She seemed dazed. How bad is Catherine? he thought, worried. On the porch, he took Meg's house key from her hand. "Here, let me do that."

In the foyer, he put his hands on her shoulders. "Tell me."

"They thought at first she'd had a heart attack. Fortunately they were wrong, but there is a chance that she's building up to one. She's on medication to head it off. She'll be in the hospital for at least a week. They asked—get this—had she been under any stress?" An uncertain laugh became a stifled sob. She swallowed and pulled back. "I'm okay, Mac. The tests showed no heart damage as of now. She's exhausted, heartsick, worried. Rest and some sedatives are what she needs."

"I agree. Wouldn't hurt you either. Come on. You could use a cup of coffee."

She followed him into the kitchen. "I'll make it."

"Sit down. Don't you want to take your coat off?"

"I'm still cold." She attempted a smile. "How can you go out on a day like this without a coat?"

Mac glanced down at his gray tweed jacket. "My topcoat has a loose button. I can't find my sewing kit."

When the coffee was ready, he poured them each a cup and sat opposite her at the table. "I suppose with Catherine in the hospital you'll come here to sleep for a while."

"I was going to anyhow." Quietly she told him all that had been happening: about the victim who resembled her, the note that had been found in the victim's pocket, the middle-of-the-night fax. "And so," she explained, "the station wants me off the firing line for the time being, and my boss gave me the Manning Clinic assignment. And then early this morning the phone rang and . . ." She told him about the call and her mother's collapse.

Mac hoped the shock he was feeling did not show in his face. Granted, Kyle had been with them Sunday night at dinner. She might not have wanted to say anything in front of him. Even so, Meg had not even hinted that less than three days earlier she had seen a murdered woman who might have died in her place. Likewise, she had not chosen to confide in Mac about the decision of the insurers.

From the time she was ten years old and he was a college sophomore working summers at the inn, he'd been the willing confidante of her secrets, everything from how much she missed her father when he was away, to how much she hated practicing the piano.

The year and a half of Mac's marriage was the only time he hadn't seen the Collinses regularly. He'd been living here since the divorce, nearly seven years now, and believed that he and Meg were back on their big brother-little sister basis. Guess again, he thought.

Meghan was silent now, absorbed in her own thoughts, clearly neither looking for nor expecting help or advice from him. He remembered Kyle's remark: *I thought you were my friend.* The woman Kyle had seen driving past the house on Wednesday, the one he'd thought was Meghan. Was it possible that she was the woman who died a day later?

Mac decided instantly not to discuss this with Meghan until he had questioned Kyle tonight and had a chance to think. But he did have to ask her something else. "Meg, forgive me, but is there any chance however remote that it was your father calling this morning?"

"No. No. I'd know his voice. So would my mother. The one we heard was surreal, not as bad as a computer voice, but not right."

"He said he was in trouble."

"Yes."

"And the note in the stabbing victim's pocket was in his writing."

"Yes."

"Did your father ever mention anyone named Annie?"

Meghan stared at Mac.

Annie! She could hear her father teasing as he called, *Meg . . . Meggie . . . Meghan Anne . . . Annie . . .*

She thought in horror, *Annie* was always his pet name for me.

18

On Tuesday morning, from the front windows of her home in Scottsdale, Arizona, Frances Grolier could see the first glimmer of light begin to define the McDowell Mountains, light that she knew would become strong and brilliant, constantly changing the hues and tones and colors reflected on those masses of rock.

She turned and walked across the long room to the back windows. The house bordered on the vast Pima Indian reservation and offered a view of the primordial desert, stark and open, edged by Camelback Mountain; desert and mountain now mysteriously lighted in the shadowy pink glow that preceded the sunrise.

At fifty-six, Frances had somehow managed to retain a fey quality that suited her thin face, thick mass of graying brown hair and wide, compelling eyes. She never bothered to soften the deep lines around her eyes and mouth with makeup. Tall and reedy, she was most comfortable in slacks and a loose smock. She shunned personal publicity, but her work as a sculptor was known in art circles, particularly for her consummate skill in molding faces. The sensitivity with which she captured below-the-surface expressions was the hallmark of her talent.

Long ago she had made a decision and stuck by it without regret. Her lifestyle suited her well. But now . . .

She shouldn't have expected Annie to understand. She should have kept her word and told her nothing. Annie had listened to the painful explanation, her eyes wide and shocked. Then she'd walked across the room and deliberately knocked over the stand holding the bronze bust.

At Frances' horrified cry, Annie had rushed from the house, jumped in her car and driven away. That evening Frances tried to phone her daughter at her apartment in San Diego. The answering machine was on. She'd phoned every day for the last week and always got the machine. It would be just like Annie to disappear indefinitely. Last year, after she'd broken her engagement to Greg, she'd flown to Australia and backpacked for six months.

With fingers that seemed to be unable to obey the signals from her brain, Frances resumed her careful repair of the bust she had sculpted of Annie's father.

FROM THE MOMENT SHE ENTERED HIS OFFICE AT TWO o'clock on Tuesday afternoon, Meghan could sense the difference in Dr. George Manning's attitude. On Sunday, when she'd covered the reunion, he had been expansive, cooperative, proud to display the children and the clinic. On the phone yesterday, when she'd made the appointment, he'd been quietly enthusiastic. Today the doctor looked every day of his seventy years. The healthy pink complexion she had noted earlier had been replaced by a gray pallor. The hand that he extended to her had a slight tremor.

This morning, before he left for Westport, Mac had insisted that she phone the hospital and check on her mother. She was told that Mrs. Collins was sleeping and that her blood pressure had improved satisfactorily and was now in the high-normal range.

Mac. What had she seen in his eyes as he said goodbye? He'd brushed her cheek with his usual light kiss, but his eyes held another message. Pity? She didn't want it.

She'd lain down for a couple of hours, not sleeping but at least dozing, sloughing off some of the heavy-eyed numbness. Then she'd showered, a long, hot shower that took some of the achiness from her shoulders. She'd dressed in a dark green suit with a fitted jacket and calf-length skirt. She wanted to look her best. She had noticed that the adults at the Manning Clinic reunion were well dressed, then reasoned that people who could afford to spend somewhere between ten and twenty thousand dollars in the attempt to have a baby certainly had discretionary income.

At the Park Avenue firm where she'd set out to practice law, it was a rule that no casual dress was permitted. As a radio and now television reporter, Meghan had observed that people being interviewed seemed to be naturally more expansive if they felt a sense of identity with the interviewer.

She wanted Dr. Manning to subconsciously think of her and talk to her as he would to a prospective client. Now, standing in front of him, studying him, she realized that he was looking at her the way a convicted felon looked at the sentencing judge. Fear was the emotion emanating from him. But why should Dr. Manning be afraid of her?

"I'm looking forward to doing this special more than I can tell you," she said as she took the seat across the desk from him. "I—"

He interrupted. "Miss Collins, I'm afraid that we can't cooperate on any television feature. The staff and I had a meeting, and the feeling was that many of our clients would be most uncomfortable if they saw television cameras around here."

"But you were happy to have us on Sunday."

"The people who were here on Sunday have children. The women who are newcomers, or those who have not succeeded in achieving a successful pregnancy, are often anxious and depressed. Assisted reproduction is a very private matter." His voice was firm, but his eyes betrayed his nervousness. About what, she wondered?

"When we spoke on the phone," she said, "we agreed that no one would be interviewed or caught on-camera who wasn't perfectly willing to discuss being a client here."

"Miss Collins, the answer is no, and now I'm afraid I'm due at a meeting." He rose.

Meghan had no choice but to stand up with him. "What happened, Doctor?" she asked quietly. "You must know I'm aware that there's got to be a lot more to this sudden change than belated concern for your clients."

He did not reply. Meghan left the office and walked down the corridor to the reception area. She smiled warmly at the receptionist and glanced at the nameplate on the desk. "Mrs. Walters, I have a friend who'd be very interested in any literature I can give her about the clinic."

Marge Walters looked puzzled. "I guess Dr. Manning forgot to give you all the stuff he had his secretary put together for you. Let me call her. She'll bring it out."

"If you would," Meghan said. "The doctor *was* willing to cooperate with the story I've been planning."

"Of course. The staff loves the idea. It's good publicity for the clinic. Let me call Jane."

Meghan crossed her fingers, hoping Dr. Manning had not told his secretary of his decision to refuse to be involved in the planned special. Then, as she watched, Walters' expression changed from a smile to a puzzled frown. When she replaced the receiver, her open and friendly manner was gone. "Miss Collins, I guess you know that I shouldn't have asked Dr. Manning's secretary for the file."

"I'm only asking for whatever information a new client might request," Meghan said.

"You'd better take that up with Dr. Manning." She hesitated. "I don't mean to be rude, Miss Collins, but I work here. I take orders."

It was clear that there would be no help from her. Meghan turned to go, then paused. "Can you tell me this? Was there very much concern on the part of the staff about doing the feature? I mean, was it everybody or just a few who objected at the meeting?"

She could see the struggle in the other woman. Marge Walters was bursting with curiosity. The curiosity won. "Miss Collins," she whispered, "yesterday at noon we had a staff meeting and everyone applauded the news that you were doing a special. We were joking about who'd get to be on-camera. I can't imagine what changed Dr. Manning's mind."

19

Mac found his work in the LifeCode Research Laboratory, where he was a specialist in genetic therapy, to be rewarding, satisfying and all-absorbing.

After he left Meghan, he drove to the lab and got right to work. As the day progressed, however, he admitted to himself that he was having trouble concentrating. A dull sense of apprehension seemed to be paralyzing his brain and permeating his entire body so that his fingers, which could as second nature handle the most delicate equipment, felt heavy and clumsy. He had lunch at his desk and, as he ate, tried to analyze the tangible fear that was overwhelming him.

He called the hospital and was told that Mrs. Collins had been removed from the intensive care unit to the cardiac section. She was sleeping, and no calls were being put through.

All of which is good news, Mac thought. The cardiac section was probably only a precaution. He felt sure Catherine would be all right and the enforced rest would do her good.

It was his worry about Meghan that caused this blinding unease. Who was threatening her? Even if the incredible were true and Ed Collins was still alive, surely the danger was not coming from him.

No, his concern all came back to the victim who looked like Meghan. By the time he'd tossed out the untasted half of his sandwich and downed the last of his cold coffee, Mac knew that he would not rest until he had gone to the morgue in New York to see that woman's body.

STOPPING AT THE HOSPITAL ON HIS WAY HOME THAT EVE-ning, Mac saw Catherine, who was clearly sedated. Her speech was markedly slower than her usual spirited delivery. "Isn't this nonsense, Mac?" she asked.

He pulled up a chair. "Even stalwart daughters of Erin are allowed time out every now and then, Catherine."

Her smile was acknowledgment. "I guess I've been traveling on nerve for a while. You know everything, I suppose."

"Yes."

"Meggie just left. She's going over to the inn. Mac, that new chef I hired! I swear he must have trained at a takeout joint. I'll have to get rid of him." Her face clouded. "That is, if I can figure a way to hang on to Drumdoe."

"I think you'd better put aside that kind of worry for at least a little while."

She sighed. "I know. It's just that I can *do* something about a bad chef. I can't *do* anything about insurers who won't pay and nuts who call in the middle of the night. Meg said that kind of sick call is just a sign of the times, but it's so rotten, so upsetting. She's shrugging it off, but you can understand why I'm worried."

"Trust Meg." Mac felt like a hypocrite as he tried to sound reassuring.

A few minutes later he stood up to go. He kissed Catherine's forehead. Her smile had a touch of resiliency. "I have a great idea. When I fire the chef, I'll send him over to this place. Compared to what they served me for dinner, he comes through like Escoffier."

MARIE DILEO, THE DAILY HOUSEKEEPER, WAS SETTING THE table when Mac got home, and Kyle was sprawled on the floor doing his homework. Mac pulled Kyle up on the couch beside him. "Hey, fellow, tell me something. The other day, how much of a look did you get at the woman you thought was Meg?"

"A pretty good look," Kyle replied. "Meg came over this afternoon."

"She did?"

"Yes. She wanted to see why I was mad at her."

"And you told her?"

"Uh-huh."

"What'd she say?"

"Oh, just that Wednesday afternoon she was in court and that sometimes when people are on television other people like to see where they live. That stuff. Just like you, she asked how good a look I got at that lady. And I told her that the lady was driving very, very slow. That's why when I saw her, I ran down the driveway and I called to her. And she stopped the car and looked at me and rolled down the window and then she just took off."

"You didn't tell me all that."

"I said that she saw me and then drove away fast."

"You didn't say she stopped and rolled down the window, pal."

"Uh-huh. I *thought* she was Meg. But her hair was longer. I told Meg that too. You know, it was around her shoulders. Like that picture of Mommy."

Ginger had sent Kyle one of her recent publicity pictures, a head shot with her blond hair swirling around her shoulders, her lips parted, revealing perfect teeth, her eyes wide and sensuous. In the corner she'd written, "To my darling little Kyle, Love and kisses, Mommy."

A publicity picture, Mac had thought in disgust. If he'd been home when it arrived, Kyle would never have seen it.

AFTER STOPPING TO SEE KYLE, VISITING HER MOTHER AND checking on the inn, Meghan arrived home at seven-thirty. Virginia had insisted on sending dinner home with her, a chicken potpie, salad and the warm salty rolls Meghan loved. "You're as bad as your mother," Virginia had fussed. "You'll forget to eat."

I probably would have, Meghan thought as she changed quickly into old pajamas and a robe. It was an outfit that dated back to college days and was still her favorite for an early, quiet evening of reading or watching television.

In the kitchen, she sipped a glass of wine and nibbled on the salt roll as the microwave oven zapped the temperature of the potpie to steaming hot.

When it was ready, she carried it on a tray into the study and settled down in her father's swivel chair. Tomorrow she would begin digging into the history of the Manning Clinic. Researchers at the television station could quickly come up with all the background available on it. And on Dr. Manning, she thought. I'd like to know if there are any skeletons in *his* closet, she told herself.

Tonight she had a different project in mind, however. She absolutely had to find any shred of evidence that might link her father to the dead woman who resembled her, the woman whose name might be Annie.

A suspicion had insinuated itself into her mind, a suspicion so incredible that she could not bring herself to consider it yet. She only knew that it was absolutely essential to go through all her father's personal papers immediately.

Not surprisingly the desk drawers were neat. Edwin Collins had been innately tidy. Writing paper, envelopes and stamps were precisely placed in the slotted side drawer. His day-at-a-glance calendar was filled out for January and early February. After that, only standing dates were entered. Her mother's birthday. Her birthday. The spring golf club outing. A cruise her parents had planned to take to celebrate their thirtieth wedding anniversary in June.

Why would anyone who was planning to disappear mark his calendar for important dates months in advance? she wondered. That didn't make sense.

The days he had been away in January or had planned to be away in February simply carried the name of a city. She knew the details of those trips would have been listed in the business appointment book he carried with him.

The deep bottom drawer on the right was locked. Meghan searched in vain for a key, then hesitated. Tomorrow she might be able to get a locksmith, but she did not want to wait. She went into the kitchen, found the toolbox and brought back a steel file. As she hoped, the lock was old and easily forced open.

In this drawer stacks of envelopes were held together by rubber bands. Meghan picked up the top packet and glanced through it. All except the first envelope were written in the same hand.

That one contained only a newspaper clipping from the *Philadelphia Bulletin*. Below the picture of a handsome woman, the obituary notice read:

Aurelia Crowley Collins, 75, a lifelong resident of Philadelphia, died in St. Paul's Hospital on 9 December of heart failure.

Aurelia Crowley Collins! Meghan gasped as she studied the picture. The wide-set eyes, the wavy hair that framed the oval face. It was the same woman, now aged, whose portrait was prominently placed on the table a few feet away. *Her grandmother.*

The date on the clipping was two years old. Her grandmother had been alive until two years ago! Meghan leafed through the other envelopes in the packet she was holding. They all came from Philadelphia. The last one was postmarked two and a half years ago.

She read one, then another, and another. Unbelieving, she went through the other stacks of envelopes. At random, she kept reading. The earliest note went back thirty years. All contained the same plea.

Dear Edwin,

   I had hoped that perhaps this Christmas I might have word from you. I pray that you and your family are well. How I would love to see my granddaughter. Perhaps someday you will allow that to happen.
                    With love,
                    Mother

Dear Edwin,

   We are always supposed to look ahead. But as one grows older, it is much easier to look back and bitterly regret the mistakes of the past. Isn't it possible for us to talk, even on the telephone? It would give me so much happiness.
                    Love,
                    Mother

After a while Meg could not bear to read any more, but it was clear from their worn appearance that her father must have pored over them many times.

Dad, you were so kind, she thought. Why did you tell everyone your mother was dead? What did she do to you that was so unforgivable? Why did you keep these letters if you were never going to make peace with her?

She picked up the envelope that had contained the obituary

notice. There was no name, but the address printed on the flap was a street in Chestnut Hill. She knew that Chestnut Hill was one of Philadelphia's most exclusive residential areas.

Who was the sender? More important, what kind of man had her father really been?

20

*I*n Helene Petrovic's charming colonial home in Lawrenceville, New Jersey, her niece, Stephanie, was cross and worried. The baby was due in a few weeks, and her back hurt. She was always tired. As a surprise, she had gone to the trouble of preparing a hot lunch for Helene, who had said she planned to get home by noon.

At one-thirty, Stephanie had tried to phone her aunt, but there was no answer at the Connecticut apartment. Now, at six o'clock, Helene had still not arrived. Was anything wrong? Perhaps some last-minute errands came up and Helene had lived alone so long she was not used to keeping someone else informed of her movements.

Stephanie had been shocked when on the phone yesterday Helene told her that she had quit her job, effective immediately. "I need a rest and I'm worried about you being alone so much," Helene had told her.

The fact was that Stephanie loved being alone. She had never known the luxury of being able to lie in bed until she decided to make coffee and get the paper that had been delivered in the predawn hours. On really lazy days, still resting in bed, she would eventually watch the morning television programs.

She was twenty but looked older. Growing up, it had been her dream to be like her father's younger sister, Helene, who had left for the United States twenty years ago, after her husband died.

Now that same Helene was her anchor, her future, in a world that no longer existed as she knew it. The bloody, brief revolution in Rumania had cost her parents their lives and destroyed their home. Stephanie had moved in with neighbors whose tiny house had no room for another occupant.

Over the years, Helene had occasionally sent a little money and a gift package at Christmas. In desperation, Stephanie had written to her imploring help.

A few weeks later she was on the plane to the United States.

Helene was so kind. It was just that Stephanie fiercely wanted to live in Manhattan, get a job in a beauty salon and go to cosmetician school at night. Already her English was excellent, though she'd arrived here last year knowing only a few English words.

Her time had almost come. She and Helene had looked at studio apartments in New York. They found one in Greenwich Village that would be available in January, and Helene had promised they would go shopping to decorate it.

This house was on the market. Helene had always said she was not going to give up her job and the place in Connecticut until it sold. What had made her change her mind so abruptly now, Stephanie wondered?

She brushed back the light brown hair from her broad forehead. She was hungry again and might as well eat. She could always warm up dinner for Helene when she arrived.

At eight o'clock, as she was smiling at a rerun of *The Golden Girls,* the front door bell pealed.

Her sigh was both relieved and vexed. Helene probably had an armful of packages and didn't want to search for her key. She gave a last look at the set. The program was about to end. After being so late, couldn't Helene have waited one more minute? she wondered as she hoisted herself up from the couch.

Her welcoming smile faded and vanished at the sight of a tall policeman with a boyish face. In disbelief she heard that Helene Petrovic had been shot to death in Connecticut.

Before grief and shock encompassed her, Stephanie's one clear thought was to frantically ask herself, *what will become of me?* Only last week Helene had talked about her intention of changing her will, which left everything she had to the Manning Clinic Research Foundation. Now it was too late.

21

*B*y eight o'clock on Tuesday evening, traffic in the garage had slowed down to a trickle. Bernie, who frequently worked overtime, had put in a twelve hour day and it was time to go home.

He didn't mind the overtime. The pay was good and so were the tips. All these years the extra money had paid for his electronic equipment.

This evening when he went to the office to check out he was worried. He hadn't realized the big boss was on the premises when at lunchtime that day he'd sat in Tom Weicker's car and flipped through the glove compartment again for possible items of interest. Then he'd looked up to see the boss staring through the car window. The boss had just walked away, not saying a word. That was even worse. If he'd snarled at him it would have cleared the air.

Bernie punched the time clock. The evening manager was sitting in the office and called him over. His face wasn't friendly. "Bernie, clean out your locker." He had an envelope in his hand. "This covers salary, vacation and sick days and two weeks severance."

"But . . . " The protest died on Bernie's lips as the manager raised a hand.

"Listen, Bernie, you know as well as I do that we've had complaints of money and personal items disappearing from cars that were parked in this garage."

"I never took a thing."

"You had no damn business going through Weicker's glove compartment, Bernie. You're through."

When he got home, still angry and upset, Bernie found that his mother had a frozen macaroni and cheese dinner ready to be put in the microwave. "It's been a terrible day," she complained as she took the wrapper off the package. "The kids from down the block were yelling in front of the house. I told them to shut up and they called me an old bat. You know what I did?" She did not wait for an answer. "I called the cops and complained. Then one of them came over, and he was rude to me."

Bernie grasped her arm. "You brought the cops in here, Mama? Did they go downstairs?"

"Why would they go downstairs?"

"Mama, I don't want the cops in here, ever."

"Bernie, I haven't been downstairs in years. You're keeping it clean down there, aren't you? I don't want dust filtering up. My sinuses are terrible."

"It's clean, Mama."

"I hope so. You're not a neat person. Like your father." She slammed the door of the microwave. "You hurt my arm. You grabbed it hard. Don't do that again."

"I won't, Mama. I'm sorry, Mama."

THE NEXT MORNING, BERNIE LEFT FOR WORK AT THE USUAL time. He didn't want his mother to know he got fired. Today, however, he headed for a car wash a few blocks from the house. He paid to have the full treatment on his eight-year-old Chevy. Vacuum, clean out trunk, polish the dashboard, wash, wax. When the car came out, it was still shabby but respectable, the basic dark green color recognizable.

He never cleaned his car except for the few times a year his mother announced she was planning to go to church on the following Sunday. Of course it would be different if he were taking Meghan for a ride. He'd really have it shining for her.

Bernie knew what he was going to do. He had thought about it all night. Maybe there was a reason he'd lost the job at the garage. Maybe it was all part of a greater plan. For weeks it hadn't been enough to see Meghan only in the few minutes when she dropped off or picked up her Mustang or a Channel 3 car.

He wanted to be around her, to take pictures of her that he could play during the night on his VCR.

Today he'd buy a video camera on Forty-seventh Street.

But he had to make money. No one was a better driver, so he could earn it by using his car as a gypsy cab. That would give him a lot of freedom too. Freedom to drive to Connecticut where Meghan Collins lived when she wasn't in New York.

He had to be careful not to be noticed.

"It's called 'obsession,' Bernie," the shrink at Riker's Island had explained when Bernie begged to know what was wrong with him. "I think we've helped you, but if that feeling comes over you again, I want you to talk to me. It will mean that you might need some medication."

Bernie knew he didn't need any help. He just needed to be around Meghan Collins.

22

*T*he body of Helene Petrovic lay all Tuesday in the bedroom where she had died. Never friendly with her neighbors, she'd already said goodbye to the few with whom she exchanged greetings, and her car was hidden from sight in the garage of her rented condo.

It was only when the owner of the condo stopped by late that afternoon that she found the dead woman at the foot of the bed.

The death of a quiet embryologist in New Milford, Connecticut, was briefly mentioned on New York television news programs. It wasn't much of a story. There was no evidence of a break-in, no apparent sexual attack. The victim's purse with two hundred dollars in it was in the room, so robbery was ruled out.

A neighbor across the street volunteered that Helene Petrovic had one visitor she'd observed, a man who always came late at night. She'd never really gotten a good look at him but knew he was tall. She figured he was a boyfriend, because he always pulled his car into the other side of Petrovic's garage. She knew he had to have left during the night, because she'd never seen him in the morning. How often had she seen him? Maybe a half-dozen times. The car? A late model dark sedan.

AFTER THE DISCOVERY OF HER GRANDMOTHER'S OBITUARY notice, Meghan had phoned the hospital and was told that her mother was sleeping and that her condition was satisfactory. Tired to the bone, she'd rummaged through the medicine cabinet for a sleeping pill, then gone to bed and slept straight through until her alarm woke her at 6:30 A.M.

An immediate call to the hospital reassured her that her mother had had a restful night and her vital signs were normal.

Meghan read the *Times* over coffee, and in the Connecticut section was shocked to read of the death of Dr. Helene Petrovic. There was a picture of the woman. In it, the expression in her eyes was both sad and enigmatic. I talked with her at Manning, Meghan thought. She was in charge of the lab with the cryopreserved embryos. Who had murdered that quiet, intelligent woman? Meghan wondered. Another thought struck her. According to the paper, Dr. Petrovic had quit her job and had planned on moving from Connecticut the next morning. Did her decision have anything to do with Dr. Manning's refusal to cooperate on the television special?

It was too early to call Tom Weicker, but it probably wasn't too late to catch Mac before he left for work. Meghan knew there was something else she had to face, and now was as good a time as any.

Mac's hello was hurried.

"Mac, I'm sorry. I know this is a bad time to call but I have to talk to you," Meghan said.

"Hi, Meg. Sure. Just hang on a minute."

He must have put his hand over the phone. She heard his muffled but exasperated call, "Kyle, you left your homework on the dining room table."

When he got back on he explained, "We go through this every morning. I tell him to put his homework in his schoolbag at night. He doesn't. In the morning he's yelling that he lost it."

"Why don't *you* put it in his schoolbag at night?"

"That doesn't build character." His voice changed. "Meg, how's your mother?"

"Good. I really think she's okay. She's a strong lady."

"Like you."

"I'm not that strong."

"Too strong for my taste, not telling me about that stab-bing victim. But that's a conversation we'll have another time."

"Mac, could you stop by for three minutes on your way out?"

"Sure. As soon as His Nibs gets on the bus."

MEGHAN KNEW THAT SHE HAD NO MORE THAN TWENTY MIN-utes to shower and dress before Mac arrived. She was brush-ing her hair when the bell rang. "Have a quick cup of coffee," she said. "What I'm about to ask isn't easy."

Was it only twenty-four hours ago they had sat across from each other at this table? she wondered. It seemed so much longer. But yesterday she'd been in near-shock. Today, knowing her mother was almost certainly all right, she was able to face and accept whatever stark truth came to light.

"Mac," she began, "you're a DNA specialist."

"Yes."

"The woman who was stabbed Thursday night, the one who resembles me so much?"

"Yes."

"If her DNA was compared to mine, could kinship be established?"

Mac raised his eyebrows and studied the cup in his hand. "Meg, this is the way it works. With DNA testing we can positively know if any two people had the same mother. It's complicated, and I can show you in the lab how we do it. Within the ninety-ninth percentile we can establish if two people had the same father. It's not as absolute as the mother-child scenario, but we can get a very strong indication of whether or not we're dealing with half siblings."

"Can that test be done on me and the dead woman?"

"Yes."

"You don't seem surprised that I'm asking about it, Mac."

He put down the coffee cup and looked at her squarely. "Meg, I already had decided to go to the morgue and see that woman's body this afternoon. They have a DNA lab in the medical examiner's office. I was planning to make sure they were preserving a sample of her blood before she's removed to potter's field."

Meg bit her lip. "Then you're thinking in the same direction I am." She blinked her eyes to blot out the vivid memory of the dead woman's face. "I have to see Phillip this morning and stop in at the hospital," she continued. "I'll meet you at the medical examiner's. What time is good for you?"

They agreed to meet around two o'clock. As Mac drove away he reflected that there was no good time to look down at the dead face of a woman who resembled Meghan Collins.

23

*P*hillip Carter heard the news report detailing Dr. Helene Petrovic's death on his way to the office. He made a mental note to have Victor Orsini follow up immediately on the vacancy her death had left at Manning Clinic. She had, after all, been hired at Manning through Collins and Carter. Those jobs paid well, and there would be another good fee if Collins and Carter was commissioned to find a replacement.

He arrived at the office at a quarter of nine and spotted Meghan's car parked in one of the stalls near the entrance of the building. She had obviously been waiting for him, because she got out of her car as he parked.

"Meg, what a nice surprise." He put an arm around her.

"But for goodness sake, you have a key. Why didn't you go inside?"

Meg smiled briefly. "I've just been here a minute." Besides, she thought, I'd feel like an intruder walking in.

"Catherine's all right, isn't she?" he asked.

"Doing really well."

"Thank God for that," he said heartily.

The small reception room was pleasant with its brightly slipcovered couch and chair, circular coffee table and paneled walls. Meghan once again had a reaction of intense sadness as she hurried through it. This time they went into Phillip's office. He seemed to sense that she did not want to go into her father's office again.

He helped her off with her coat. "Coffee?"

"No thanks. I've had three cups already."

He settled behind his desk. "And I'm trying to cut down, so I'll wait. Meg, you look pretty troubled."

"I am." Meghan moistened her lips. "Phillip, I'm beginning to think I didn't know my father at all."

"In what way?"

She told him about the letters and the obituary notice she had found in the locked drawer, then watched as Phillip's expression changed from concern to disbelief.

"Meg, I don't know what to tell you," he said when she finished. "I've known your father for years. Ever since I can remember, I've understood that his mother died when he was a kid, his father remarried and he had a lousy childhood, living with the father and stepmother. When my father was dying, your dad said something I never forgot. He said, 'I envy you being able to mourn a parent.' "

"Then you never knew either?"

"No, of course not."

"The point is, why did he have to lie about it?" Meg asked, her voice rising. She clasped her hands together and bit her lip. "I mean, why not tell my mother the truth? What did he have to gain by deceiving her?"

"Think about it, Meg. He met your mother, told her his

family background as he'd told it to everyone else. When they started getting interested in each other it would have been pretty difficult to admit he'd lied to her. And can you imagine your grandfather's reaction if he'd learned that your father was ignoring his own mother for whatever reason?"

"Yes, I can see that. But Pop's been dead for so many years. Why couldn't he . . . ?" Her voice trailed off.

"Meg, when you start living a lie, it gets harder with every passing day to straighten it out."

Meghan heard the sound of voices in the outside office. She stood up. "Can we keep this between us?"

"Of course."

He got up with her. "What are you going to do?"

"As soon as I'm sure Mother is okay I'm going to the address in Chestnut Hill that was on the envelope with the obituary notice. Maybe I'll get some answers there."

"How's the feature story on the Manning Clinic going?"

"It's not. They're stonewalling me. I've got to find a different in vitro facility to use. Wait a minute. You or Dad placed someone at Manning, didn't you?"

"Your dad handled it. As a matter of fact, it's that poor woman who was shot yesterday."

"Dr. Petrovic? I met her last week."

The intercom buzzed. Phillip Carter picked up the phone. "Who? All right, I'll take it."

"A reporter from the *New York Post,*" he explained to Meghan. "God knows what they want of me."

Meghan watched as Phillip Carter's face darkened. "That's absolutely impossible." His voice was husky with outrage. "I . . . I will not comment until I have personally spoken with Dr. Iovino at New York Hospital."

He replaced the receiver and turned to Meghan. "Meg, that reporter has been checking on Helene Petrovic. They never heard of her at New York Hospital. Her credentials were fraudulent, and we're responsible for her getting the job in the laboratory at Manning."

"But didn't you check her references before you submitted her to the clinic?"

Even as she asked the question, Meghan knew the answer, she could see it in Phillip's face. Her father had handled Helene Petrovic's file. It would have been up to him to validate the information on her curriculum vitae.

24

*D*espite the best efforts of the entire staff of the Manning Clinic there was no hiding the tension that permeated the atmosphere. Several new clients watched uneasily as a van with a CBS television logo on the sides pulled into the parking area and a reporter and cameraman hurried up the walkway.

Marge Walters was at her receptionist best, firm with the reporter. "Dr. Manning declines to be interviewed until he has investigated the allegations," she said. She was unable to stop the cameraman, who began to videotape the room and its occupants.

Several clients stood up. Marge rushed over to them. "This is all a misunderstanding," she pleaded, suddenly realizing she was being recorded.

One woman, her hands shielding her face, exploded in anger. "This is an outrage. It's tough enough to have to resort to this kind of procedure to have a baby without being on the eleven o'clock news." She ran from the room.

Another said, "Mrs. Walters, I'm leaving too. You'd better cancel my appointment."

"I understand." Marge forced a sympathetic smile. "When would you like to reschedule?"

"I'll have to check my appointment book. I'll call."

Marge watched the retreating women. No you won't, she thought. Alarmed, she noticed Mrs. Kaplan, a client on her second visit to the clinic, approach the reporter.

"What's this all about?" she demanded.

"What it's all about is that the person in charge of the Manning Clinic lab for the last six years apparently was not a doctor. In fact her only training seems to have been as a cosmetologist."

"My God. My sister had in vitro fertilization here two years ago. Is there any chance she didn't receive her own embryo?" Mrs. Kaplan clenched her hands together.

God help us, Marge thought. That's the end of this place. She'd been shocked and saddened when she heard on the morning news of Dr. Helene Petrovic's death. It was only when she arrived at work an hour ago that she'd heard the rumor of something being wrong with Petrovic's credentials. But hearing the reporter's stark statement and watching Mrs. Kaplan's response made her realize the enormity of the possible consequences.

Helene Petrovic had been in charge of the cryopreserved embryos. Dozens upon dozens of test tubes, no bigger than half an index finger, each one containing a potentially viable human being. Mislabel even one of them and the wrong embryo might be implanted in a woman's womb, making her a host mother, but not the biological mother of a child.

Marge watched the Kaplan woman rush from the room followed by the reporter. She looked out the window. More news vans were pulling in. More reporters were attempting to question the women who had just left the reception area.

She saw the reporter from PCD Channel 3 getting out of a car. Meghan Collins. That was her name. She was the one who'd been planning to do the television special that Dr. Manning called off so abruptly . . .

MEGHAN WAS NOT SURE IF SHE REALLY SHOULD BE HERE, especially since her father's name was certain to come up in the course of the investigation into Helene Petrovic's credentials. As she left Phillip Carter's office she'd been beeped by the news desk and told that Steve, her cameraman, would meet her at the Manning Clinic. "Weicker okayed it," she was assured.

She'd tried to reach Weicker earlier, but he was not yet in. She felt she had to speak to him about the possible conflict of interest. It was easier for the moment, however, to simply accept the assignment. The odds were that the lawyers for the clinic would not permit any interviews with Dr. Manning anyway.

She did not attempt to join the rest of the media in flinging questions to the departing clients. Instead she spotted Steve and motioned for him to follow her inside. She opened the door quietly. As she had hoped, Marge Walters was at her desk, speaking urgently into the phone. "We've got to cancel all of today's appointments," she was insisting. "You'd better tell them in there that they've got to make some kind of statement. Otherwise the only thing the public is going to see is women bolting out of here."

As the door closed behind Steve, Walters looked up. "I can't talk anymore," she said hurriedly and clicked down the receiver.

Meghan did not speak until she was settled in the chair across from Walters' desk. The situation required tact and careful handling. She had learned not to fire questions at a defensive interviewee. "This is a pretty rough morning for you, Mrs. Walters," she said soothingly.

She watched as the receptionist brushed a hand over her forehead. "You bet it is."

The woman's tone was guarded, but Meghan sensed in her the same conflict she had noticed yesterday. She realized the need for discretion, but she was dying to talk to someone about all that had been going on. Marge Walters was a born gossip.

"I met Dr. Petrovic at the reunion," Meghan said. "She seemed like a lovely person."

"She was," Walters agreed. "It's hard to believe she wasn't qualified for the job she was doing. But her early medical training was probably in Rumania. With all the changes in government over there, I'll bet anything they find out she had all the degrees she needed. I don't understand about New York Hospital saying she didn't train there. I bet that's a mistake too. But finding that out may come too late. This bad publicity will ruin this place."

"It could," Meghan agreed. "Do you think that her quitting had something to do with Dr. Manning's decision to cancel our session yesterday?"

Walters looked at the camera Steve was holding.

Quickly Meghan added, "If you can tell me anything that will balance all this negative news I'd like to include it."

Marge Walters made up her mind. She trusted Meghan Collins. "Then let me tell you that Helene Petrovic was one of the most wonderful, hardest working people I've ever met. No one was happier than she when an embryo was brought to term in its mother's womb. She loved every single embryo in that lab and used to insist on having the emergency generator tested regularly to be sure that in case of power failure the temperature would stay constant."

Walters' eyes misted. "I remember Dr. Manning telling us at a staff meeting last year how he'd rushed to the clinic during that terrible snowstorm in December, when all the electricity went down, to make sure the emergency generator was working. Guess who arrived a minute behind him? Helene Petrovic. And she hated driving in snow or ice. It was a special fear of hers, yet she drove here in that storm. She was that dedicated."

"You're telling me exactly what I felt when I interviewed her," Meghan commented. "She seemed to be a very caring person. I could see it in the way she was interacting with the children during the picture session on Sunday."

"I missed that. I had to go to a family wedding that day. Can you turn off the camera now?"

"Of course." Meghan nodded to Steve.

Walters shook her head. "I wanted to be here. But my cousin Dodie finally married her boyfriend. They've only been living together for eight years. You should have heard my aunt. You'd think a nineteen-year-old out of convent school was the bride. I swear to God the night before the wedding I bet she told Dodie how babies come to be born."

Walters grimaced as the incongruity of her remark in this clinic occurred to her. "How most of them come to be born, I mean."

"Is there any chance I can see Dr. Manning?" Meghan knew if there was a chance it was through this woman.

Walters shook her head. "Just between us, an assistant state attorney and some investigators are with him now."

That wasn't surprising. Certainly they were looking into Helene Petrovic's abrupt departure from the clinic and asking questions about her personal life. "Did Helene have any particularly close friends here?"

"No. Not really. She was very nice but a little formal—you know what I mean. I thought maybe it was because she was from Rumania. Although when you think about it, the Gabor women came from there, and they've had more than their share of close friends, especially Zsa Zsa."

"I'm quite sure the Gabors are Hungarian, not Rumanian. So Helene Petrovic didn't have any particular friends or an intimate relationship you're aware of?"

"The nearest to it was Dr. Williams. He used to be Dr. Manning's assistant, and I wondered if there wasn't a little something going on between him and Helene. I saw them at dinner one night when my husband and I went to a little out-of-the-way place. They didn't look happy when I stopped by their table to say hello. But that was just one time six years ago, right after she started working here. I have to say I kept my eye on them after that and they never acted at all special to each other."

"Is Dr. Williams still here?"

"No. He was offered a job to open and run a new facility and he took it. It's the Franklin Center in Philadelphia. It has a wonderful reputation. Between us, Dr. Williams was a top-drawer manager. He put together the whole medical team here, and believe me, he did a terrific job."

"Then he was the one who hired Petrovic?"

"Technically, but they always hire the top staff through one of those headhunter outfits that recruits and screens them for us. Even so, Dr. Williams worked here for about six months after Helene came on staff, and believe me, he'd have noticed if she seemed incompetent."

"I'd like to talk with him, Mrs. Walters."

"Please call me Marge. I wish you *would* talk to him. He'd tell you how wonderful Helene was in that lab."

Meghan heard the front door opening. Walters looked up. "More cameras! Meghan, I'd better not say any more."

Meghan stood up. "You've been a great help."

Driving home, Meghan reflected that she would not give Dr. Williams the chance to put her off over the phone. She'd go to the Franklin Center in Philadelphia and try to see him. With luck she could persuade him to tape an interview for the in vitro feature.

What would he have to say about Helene Petrovic? Would he defend her, like Marge Walters? Or would he be outraged that Petrovic had managed to deceive him, as she had deceived all her other colleagues?

And, Meghan wondered, what would she learn at her other stop in the Philadelphia area? The house in Chestnut Hill, from which someone had notified her father of his mother's death.

25

$\mathcal{V}$ictor Orsini and Phillip Carter never socialized for lunch. Orsini knew that Carter considered him to be Edwin Collins' protégé. When the job at Collins and Carter had come up nearly seven years ago it had been between Orsini and another candidate. Orsini had been Ed Collins' choice. From the beginning his relationship with Carter was cordial, but never warm.

Today, however, after they had both ordered the baked sole and house salad, Orsini was in full sympathy with Carter's obvious distress. There had been reporters in the office and a dozen phone calls from the media asking how it was possible that Collins and Carter had not detected the lies in Helene Petrovic's curriculum vitae.

"I told them the simple truth," Phillip Carter said as he drummed his fingers nervously on the tablecloth. "Ed always researched prospective candidates meticulously, and it was his case. It only adds fuel to the fire that Ed is missing and the police are openly saying they don't believe he died in the bridge accident."

"Does Jackie remember anything about the Petrovic case?" Orsini asked.

"She'd just started working for us then. Her initials are on the letter, but she has no memory of it. Why should she? It was a usual glowing recommendation attached to the curriculum vitae. After he received it Dr. Manning had a meeting with Petrovic and hired her."

Orsini said, "Of all the fields in which to have been caught verifying fraudulent references, medical research is about the worst."

"Yes, it is," Phillip agreed. "If any mistakes were made by Helene Petrovic and the Manning Clinic is sued, there's a damn good chance the clinic will sue us."

"And win."

Carter nodded glumly. "And win." He paused. "Victor, you worked more directly with Ed than you did with me. When he called you from the car phone that night, he talked about wanting to meet with you in the morning. Was that all he said?"

"Yes, that's all. Why?"

"Damn it, Victor," Phillip Carter snapped, "let's stop playing games! If Ed did manage to get over the bridge safely, do you have any inkling from that conversation whether he might have been in the state of mind to use the accident as his opportunity to disappear?"

"Look, Phillip, he said he wanted to make sure I was in the office in the morning," Orsini replied, his voice taking on an edge. "It was a lousy connection. That's all I can tell you."

"I'm sorry. I keep looking for anything that might start to make sense." Carter sighed. "Victor, I've been meaning to speak to you. Meghan is clearing out Ed's personal things from his office on Saturday. I want you to take that office as of Monday. We haven't had a great year but we can certainly refurbish it within reason."

"Don't worry about that right now."

They had little else to say to each other.

Orsini noticed that Phillip Carter did not hint that after the matter of Ed Collins' legal situation was somehow straightened out, he would offer Orsini a partnership. He knew that offer would never be made. For his part it was only a matter of weeks before the position he'd almost gotten on the Coast last year became available again. The guy they'd hired for the job didn't work out. This time Orsini was being offered a bigger salary, a vice presidency and stock options.

He wished that he could leave today. Pack up and fly out there right now. But under the circumstances that was impossible. There was something he wanted to find, something he wanted to check out at the office, and now that he could move into Ed's old office, the search might be easier.

26

*B*ernie stopped at a diner on Route 7 just outside Danbury. He settled on a stool at the counter and ordered the deluxe hamburger, French fries and coffee. Increasingly content as he munched and swallowed, he reviewed with satisfaction the busy hours he'd spent since he left home this morning.

After the car was cleaned up, he'd purchased a chauffeur's hat and dark jacket at a secondhand store in lower Manhattan. He'd reasoned that outfit would give him a leg up on all the other gypsy cabs in New York. Then he'd headed for La Guardia Airport and stood near the baggage area, with the other chauffeurs waiting to make pickups.

He lucked out right away. Some guy about thirty or so came down the escalator and searched the name cards drivers were holding. There was no one waiting for him. Bernie could read the guy's mind. He'd probably hired a driver from one of the dirt-cheap services and was kicking himself. Most of the drivers from those places were guys who had just arrived in New York and spent their first six months on the job getting lost.

Bernie had approached the man, offered to take him into the city, warned that he didn't have a fancy limo but a nice clean car and bragged he was the best driver anyone could hire. He quoted a price of twenty bucks to drive the fellow to West Forty-eighth Street. He got him there in thirty-five minutes and received a ten-dollar tip. "You are a hell of a driver," the man said as he paid.

Bernie remembered the compliment with pleasure as he reached for a French fry and smiled to himself. If he kept making money this way, adding it to his severance and vacation pay, he could last a long time before Mama knew he wasn't at the old job. She never called him there. She didn't like talking on the phone. She said it gave her one of her headaches.

And here he was, free as a bird, not accountable to anyone and out to see where Meghan Collins lived. He had bought a street map of the Newtown area and studied it. The Collins house was on Bayberry Road, and he knew how to get there.

At exactly two o'clock he was driving slowly past the white-shingled house with the black shutters. His eyes narrowed as he drank in every detail. The large porch. Nice. Kind of elegant. He thought of the people next door to his house in Jackson Heights who had poured concrete over most of their minuscule backyard and now grandly referred to the lumpy surface as their patio.

Bernie studied the grounds. There was a huge rhododendron at the left corner of the macadam driveway, a weeping willow off center in the middle of the lawn. Evergreens made a vivid hedge separating the Collins place from the next property.

Well satisfied, Bernie leaned his foot on the accelerator. In case he was being watched, he certainly wouldn't be dope enough to do a U-turn here. He drove around the bend, then jammed on his brakes. He'd almost hit a stupid dog.

A kid came flying across the lawn. Through the window, Bernie could hear him frantically calling the dog. "Jake! Jake!"

The dog ran to the kid, and Bernie was able to start up the car again. The street was quiet enough that through the closed window, he could hear the kid yell, "Thanks, mister. Thanks a lot."

. . .

MAC ARRIVED AT THE MEDICAL EXAMINER'S OFFICE ON EAST Thirty-first Street at one-thirty. Meghan was not due until two o'clock, but he had phoned and made an appointment with Dr. Kenneth Lyons, the director of the lab. He was escorted to the fifth floor, where in Dr. Lyons' small office, he explained his suspicions.

Lyons was a lean man in his late forties with a ready smile and keen, intelligent eyes. "That woman has been a puzzle. She certainly didn't have the look of someone who would simply disappear and not be missed. We were planning to take a DNA sample from her before the body is taken to potter's field anyway. It will be very simple to take a sample from Miss Collins as well and see if there's the possibility of kinship."

"That's what Meghan wants to do."

The doctor's secretary was seated at a desk near the window. The phone rang and she picked it up. "Miss Collins is downstairs."

It wasn't just the normal apprehension of viewing a dead body in the morgue that Mac saw in Meghan's face as he stepped from the elevator. Something else had added to the pain in her eyes, the drawn, tired lines around her mouth. It seemed to him that there was a sadness in her that was removed from the grief she had lived with since her father's disappearance.

But she smiled when she saw him, a quick, relieved smile. She's so pretty, he thought. Her chestnut hair was tousled around her head, a testament to the sharp afternoon wind. She was wearing a black-and-white tweed suit and black boots. The zippered jacket reached her hips, the narrow skirt was calf length. A black turtleneck sweater accentuated the paleness of her face.

Mac introduced her to Dr. Lyons. "You'll be able to study the victim more closely downstairs than in the viewing room," Lyons said.

The morgue was antiseptically clean. Rows of lockers lined the walls. The murmur of voices could be heard from behind the closed door of a room with an eight-foot window on the corridor. The curtains were drawn over the window. Mac was sure an autopsy was being performed.

An attendant led them down the corridor almost to the end. Dr. Lyons nodded to him and he reached for the handle of a drawer.

Noiselessly, the drawer slid out. Mac stared down at the nude, refrigerated body of the young woman. There was a single deep stab wound in her chest. Slender arms lay at her sides; her fingers were open. He took in the narrow waist, slim hips, long legs, high-arched feet. Finally he studied the face.

The chestnut hair was matted on her shoulders, but he could imagine it with the same wind-tossed life as Meghan's hair. The mouth, generous and with the promise of warmth, the thick eyelashes that arched over the closed eyes, the dark brows that accentuated the high forehead.

Mac felt as though a violent punch had caught him in the stomach. He felt dazed, nauseated, light-headed. This could be Meg, he thought, *this was meant to happen to Meg.*

27

Catherine Collins touched the button at her hand, and the hospital bed tilted noiselessly up until she stopped it at a semireclining position. For the last hour, since the lunch tray was taken out, she had tried to sleep, but it was useless. She was irritated at herself for her desire to escape into sleep. It's time to face up to life, my girl, she told herself sternly.

She wished she had a calculator and the account books of the inn. She needed to figure out for herself how long she could hold on before she was forced to sell Drumdoe. The mortgage, she thought—that damn mortgage! Pop would never have put so much money in the place. Do without and make do, that had been his slogan when he was a greenhorn. How often had she heard that?

But once he got his inn and his house he'd been the most generous husband and father. Provided you weren't ridiculously extravagant, of course.

And I was ridiculous giving that decorator so much leeway, Catherine thought. But that's water under the bridge.

The analogy made her shiver. It brought to mind the horrible photographs of wrecked cars being hauled to the surface from under the Tappan Zee Bridge. She and Meghan had studied the photos with magnifying glasses, dreading to find what they were expecting to see: some part of a dark blue Cadillac.

Catherine threw back the covers, got out of bed and reached for her robe. She walked across the room to the tiny bathroom and splashed water on her face, then looked in the mirror and grimaced. Put on a little war paint, dear, she told herself.

Ten minutes later she was back in bed and feeling somewhat better. Her short blond hair was brushed; blusher on her cheeks and lipstick had camouflaged the gaunt pallor she had seen in the mirror; a blue silk bed jacket made her feel presentable to possible visitors. She knew Meghan was in New York for the afternoon, but there was always the chance someone else might drop by.

Someone did. Phillip Carter tapped on the partially open door. "Catherine, may I come in?"

"You bet."

He bent down and kissed her cheek. "You look much better."

"I feel much better. In fact I'm trying to get out of here, but they want me to stay a couple of days more."

"Good idea." He pulled the one comfortable chair close to the bed and sat down.

He was wearing a casual tan jacket, dark brown slacks and a brown-and-beige print tie, Catherine noticed. His strong male presence made her ache for her husband.

Edwin had been strikingly handsome. She had met him thirty-one years ago, at a party after a Harvard-Yale football game. She was dating one of the Yale players. She had noticed Ed on the dance floor. The dark hair, the deep blue eyes, the tall thin body.

The next dance, Edwin had cut in on her, and the next day he was ringing the bell at the farmhouse, a dozen roses in his hand. "I'm courting you, Catherine," he'd announced.

Now Catherine tried to blink back sudden tears.

"Catherine?" Phillip's hand was holding hers.

"I'm fine," she said, withdrawing her hand.

"I don't think you'll feel that way in a few minutes. I wish I could have spoken to Meg before I came."

"She had to go into the city. What is it, Phillip?"

"Catherine, you may have read about the woman who was murdered in New Milford."

"That doctor. Yes. How awful."

"Then you haven't heard that she wasn't a doctor, that her credentials were falsified and that she was placed at the Manning Clinic by our company?"

Catherine bolted up. "What?"

A nurse hurried in. "Mrs. Collins, there are two investigators from the New Milford police in the lobby who need to speak with you. The doctor is on his way. He wants to be here but said I should warn you they'll be up in a few minutes."

Catherine waited until she heard retreating footsteps in the corridor before she asked, "Phillip, you know why those people are here."

"Yes, I do. They were in the office an hour ago."

"Why? Forget about waiting for the doctor. I have no intention of collapsing again. Please, I do need to know what I'm facing."

"Catherine, the woman who was murdered last night in New Milford was Ed's client. Ed had to have known her credentials were falsified." Phillip Carter turned away as though to avoid seeing the pain he knew he was going to inflict. "You know that the police don't think Ed was drowned in the bridge accident. A neighbor who lives across the street from Helene Petrovic's apartment said Petrovic was visited regularly late at night by a tall man who drove a dark sedan." He paused, his expression grim. "She saw him there two weeks ago. Catherine, when Meg called the ambulance the other night a squad car came as well. When you came to, you told the policeman you'd had a call from your husband."

Catherine tried to swallow but could not. Her mouth and lips were parched. She had the incongruous thought that this is what it must be like to experience severe thirst. "I was out of it. I meant to say Meg had a call from someone saying he was her father."

There was a tap on the door. The doctor spoke as he came in. "Catherine, I'm terribly sorry about this. The assistant state attorney insists that the investigators of a murder in New Milford ask you a few questions, and I could not in conscience say you weren't well enough to see them."

"I'm well enough to see them," Catherine said quietly. She looked at Phillip. "Will you stay?"

"I certainly will." He got up as the investigators followed a nurse into the room.

Catherine's first impression was surprise that one of them was a woman, a young woman around Meghan's age. The other was a man she judged to be in his late thirties. It was he who spoke first, apologizing for the intrusion, promising to take only a few moments of her time, introducing himself and his partner. "This is Special Investigator Arlene Weiss. I'm Bob Marron." He got straight to the point. "Mrs. Collins, you were brought here in shock because your daughter received a phone call in the middle of the night from someone who claimed to be your husband?"

"It wasn't my husband. I'd know his voice anywhere, under any circumstances."

"Mrs. Collins, I'm sorry to ask you this, but do you still believe your husband died last January?"

"I absolutely believe he is dead," she said firmly.

"Beautiful roses for you, Mrs. Collins," a voice chirped as the door was pushed open. It was one of the volunteers in pink jackets who delivered flowers to the rooms, brought around the book cart and helped feed the elderly patients.

"Not now," Catherine's doctor snapped.

"No, it's all right. Just put them on the nightstand." Catherine realized she welcomed the intrusion. She needed a moment to get hold of herself. Again stalling for time, she reached for the card the volunteer was detaching from the ribbon on the vase.

She glanced at it, then froze, her eyes filled with horror. As everyone stared at her, she held up the card with trembling fingers, fighting to retain her composure. "I didn't know dead people could send flowers," she whispered.

She read it aloud. " 'My dearest. Have faith in me. I promise this will all work out.' " Catherine bit her lip. "It's signed, 'Your loving husband, Edwin.' "

Part Two

28

On Wednesday afternoon, investigators from Connecticut drove to Lawrenceville, New Jersey, to question Stephanie Petrovic about her murdered aunt.

Trying to ignore the restless stirring in her womb, Stephanie clasped her hands together to keep them from trembling. Having grown up in Rumania under the Ceauşescu regime, she had been trained to fear the police, and even though the men who were sitting in her aunt's living room seemed very kind and were not wearing uniforms, she knew enough not to trust them. People who trusted the police often ended up in prison, or worse.

Her aunt's lawyer, Charles Potters, was there as well, a man who reminded her of an official of the village where she had been born. He too was being kind, but she sensed that his kindness was of the impersonal variety. He would do his duty and he had already informed her that his duty was to carry out the terms of Helene's will, which left her entire estate to the Manning Clinic.

"She intended to change it," Stephanie had told him. "She planned to take care of me, to help me while I went to cosmetology school, to get me an apartment. She promised she would leave money to me. She said I was like a daughter to her."

"I understand. But since she did not change her will, the only thing I can say is that until this house is sold you may live in it. As trustee, I can probably arrange to hire you as a caretaker until a sale is completed. After that, I'm afraid, legally you're on your own."

On her own! Stephanie knew that unless she could get a green card and a job there was no way she could stay in this country.

One of the policemen asked if there were any man who had been her aunt's particular friend.

"No. Not really," she answered. "Sometimes in the evening we go to parties given by other Rumanians. Sometimes Helene would go to concerts. Often on Saturday or Sunday, she would go out for three or four hours. She never told me where." But Stephanie knew of no man at all in her aunt's life. She told again how surprised she had been when Helene abruptly quit her job. "She was planning to give up work as soon as she sold her house. She wanted to move to France for a while." Stephanie knew she was stumbling over the English words. She was so afraid.

"According to Dr. Manning, he had no inkling that she was contemplating leaving the clinic," the investigator named Hugo said in Rumanian.

Stephanie flashed a look of gratitude at him and switched to her native language as well. "She told me that Dr. Manning would be very upset and she dreaded breaking the news to him."

"Did she have another job in mind? It would have meant her credentials being checked again."

"She said she wanted to take some time off to rest."

Hugo turned to the lawyer. "What was Helene Petrovic's financial situation?"

Charles Potters answered, "I can assure you it was quite good. Doctor, or rather Ms. Petrovic lived very carefully and made good investments. This house was paid off, and she had eight hundred thousand dollars in stocks, bonds and cash."

So much money, Stephanie thought, and now she would not have a penny of it. She rubbed her hand across her forehead. Her back hurt. Her feet were swollen. She was so tired. Mr. Potters was helping her arrange the funeral mass. It would be held at St. Dominic's on Friday.

She looked around. This room was so pretty, with its blue brocaded upholstery, polished tables, fringed lamps and pale blue carpet. This whole house was so pretty. She'd liked being in a place like this. Helene had promised that she could take some things from here for her apartment in New York. What would she do now? What was the policeman asking?

"When do you expect your baby, Stephanie?"

Tears gushed down her cheeks as she answered. "In two weeks." She burst out, "He told me it was my problem and he's moved to California. He won't help me. I don't know where to find him. I don't know what to do."

29

The shock that Meghan had felt at once again seeing the dead woman who resembled her had dulled by the time a vial of blood was drawn from her arm.

She did not know quite what reaction she expected from Mac when he viewed the body. The only one she had detected was a tightening of his lips. The only comment he made was that he found the resemblance so startling he felt the DNA comparison was absolutely necessary. Dr. Lyons voiced the same opinion.

Neither she nor Mac had eaten lunch. They left the medical examiner's office in separate cars and drove to one of Meg's favorite spots, Neary's on Fifty-seventh Street. Seated side by side on a banquette in the cozy restaurant, over a club sandwich and coffee, Meghan told Mac about Helene Petrovic's falsified credentials and her father's possible involvement.

Jimmy Neary came over to inquire about Meghan's mother. When he learned Catherine was in the hospital, he brought his portable phone to the table for Meghan to call her.

Phillip answered.

"Hi, Phillip," Meghan said. "Just thought I'd phone and see how Mom is doing. Would you put her on, please?"

"Meg, she's had a pretty nasty shock."

"What kind of shock?" Meghan demanded.

"Somebody sent her a dozen roses. You'll understand when I read the card to you."

Mac had been looking across the room at the framed pictures of the Irish countryside. At Meghan's gasp, he turned to her, then watched as her eyes widened in shock. Something's happened to Catherine, he thought. "Meg, what is it?" He took the phone from her shaking fingers. "Hello . . ."

"Mac, I'm glad you're there."

It was Phillip Carter's voice, even now, sounding confident and in charge.

Mac put his arm around Meghan as Carter tersely related the events of the past hour. "I'm staying with Catherine for a while," he concluded. "She was pretty upset at first, but she's calmer now. She says she wants to speak to Meg."

"Meg, it's your mother," Mac said, holding the receiver out to her. For a moment he wasn't sure Meghan had heard him, but then she reached for the phone. He could see the effort she was making to sound matter-of-fact.

"Mom, you're sure you're okay? . . . What do I think? I think it's some kind of cruel joke too. You're right, Dad would never do anything like that. . . . I know . . . I know how tough it is. . . . Come on, you certainly do have the strength to handle this. You're old Pat's daughter, aren't you?

"I have an appointment with Mr. Weicker at the station in an hour. Then I'll come directly to the hospital. . . . Love you too. Let me talk to Phillip for a minute.

"Phillip, stay with her, won't you? She shouldn't be alone now. . . . Thanks."

When Meg replaced the receiver, she cried, "It's a miracle my mother didn't have a full-blown heart attack, what with investigators asking about Dad and those roses being delivered." Her mouth quivered and she bit her lip.

Oh, Meg, Mac thought. He ached to put his arms around her, to hold her to him, to kiss the pain from her eyes and lips. Instead he tried to reassure her about the primary fear that he knew was paralyzing her.

"Catherine isn't going to have a heart attack," he said firmly. "At least put that worry out of your mind. I mean it, Meg. Now, did I get it right from Phillip that the police are trying to tie your dad to that Petrovic woman's death?"

"Apparently. They kept coming back to the neighbor who said a tall man with a dark late-model sedan visited Petrovic regularly. Dad was tall. He drove a dark sedan."

"So do thousands of other tall men, Meg. That's ridiculous."

"I know it is. Mom knows it too. But the police categorically don't believe Dad was in the bridge accident, which means to them that he's probably still alive. They want to know why he vouched for Petrovic's falsified credentials. They asked Mom if she thought he might have had some kind of personal relationship with Petrovic."

"Do you believe that he's alive, Meg?"

"No, I don't. But if he put Helene Petrovic in that job knowing she was a fraud, something was wrong. Unless she somehow fooled him too."

"Meg, I've known your father since I was a college freshman. If there's one point on which I can reassure you, it's that Edwin Collins is or was a very gentle man. What you told Catherine is absolutely true. That middle-of-the-night phone call and sending those flowers your mother received just aren't things your father would have done. They're the kind of games cruel people play."

"Or demented people." Meghan straightened up as though just aware of Mac's arm around her. Quietly, Mac removed it.

He said, "Meg, flowers have to be paid for, with cash, with a credit card, with a charge account. How was the payment for the roses handled?"

"I gather the investigators are hot onto that scenario."

Jimmy Neary offered an Irish coffee.

Meghan shook her head. "I sure could use one, Jimmy, but we'd better take a rain check. I have to get to the office."

Mac was going back to work. Before they got into their cars, he put his hands on her shoulders. "Meg, one thing. Promise me you'll let me help."

"Oh, Mac," she sighed, "I think you've had your share of the Collins family's problems for a while. How long did Dr. Lyons say it would take to get the results of the DNA comparison?"

"Four to six weeks," Mac said. "I'll call you tonight, Meg."

HALF AN HOUR LATER, MEGHAN WAS SITTING IN TOM Weicker's office. "That was a hell of a good interview with the receptionist at the Manning Clinic," he told her. "No one else has anything like it. But in view of your father's connection to Petrovic, I don't want you to go near that place again."

It was what she expected to hear. She looked squarely at him. "The Franklin Center in Philadelphia has a terrific reputation. I'd like to substitute that in vitro facility for Manning in the feature." She waited, dreading to hear that he was pulling her off that too.

She was relieved when he said, "I want the feature completed as soon as possible. Everybody's buzzing about in vitro fertilization because of Petrovic. The timing is great. When can you go to Philadelphia?"

"Tomorrow."

She felt dishonest not telling Tom that Dr. Henry Williams, who headed the Franklin Center, had worked with Helene Petrovic at Manning. But, she reasoned, if she had any chance of getting in to talk to Williams it would be as a PCD reporter, not as the daughter of the man who had submitted Petrovic's bogus résumé and glowingly recommended her.

BERNIE DROVE TO MANHATTAN FROM CONNECTICUT. SEEING Meghan's house brought back memories of all the other times he'd followed a girl home, then hidden in her car or garage or even in the shrubbery around her house, just so he could watch her. It was like being in a different world where it was just the two of them alive, even though the girl didn't know he was there.

He knew he had to be near Meghan, but he'd have to be careful. Newtown was a ritzy little community, and cops in places like that were always on the lookout for strange cars driving around a neighborhood.

Suppose I'd hit that dog, Bernie thought as he drove through the Bronx toward the Willis Avenue bridge. The kid who owned it probably would have started yelling his head off. People would have rushed out to see what happened. One of them might have started asking questions, like what's a guy in a gypsy cab doing in this neighborhood, on a dead end street? If somebody'd called the cops, they might have checked my record, Bernie thought. He knew what that would mean.

There was only one thing for him to do. When he got to midtown Manhattan, he drove to the discount shop on Forty-seventh Street where he acquired most of his electronic gadgets. For a long time he'd had his eye on a real state-of-

the-art video camera there. Today he bought that and a police scanner radio for the car.

He then went to an art supply store and bought sheets of
pink paper. This year pink was the color of the press passes
the police issued to the media. He had one at home. A reporter had dropped it in the garage. On his computer, he
could copy it and make up a press pass that looked official,
and he'd also make himself a press parking permit to stick in
his windshield.

There were bunches of local cable stations around that no
one paid any attention to. He'd say he was from one of them.
He'd be Bernie Heffernan, news reporter.

Just like Meghan.

The only problem was, he was going through his vacation
and severance pay too fast. He had to keep money coming
in. Fortunately he managed to pick up a fare to Kennedy
Airport and one back into the city before it was time to go
home.

AT DINNER HIS MOTHER WAS SNEEZING. "ARE YOU GETTING
a cold, Mama?" he asked solicitously.

"I don't get colds. I just have allergies," she snapped. "I
think there's dust in this house."

"Mama, you know there's no dust here. You're a good
housekeeper."

"Bernard, are you keeping the basement clean? I'm trusting you. I don't dare attempt those stairs after what happened."

"Mama, it's fine."

They watched the six o'clock news together and saw
Meghan Collins interviewing the receptionist at the Manning
Clinic.

Bernie leaned forward, drinking in Meghan's profile as she
asked questions. His hands and forehead grew damp.

Then the remote selector was yanked from his hand. As
the television clicked off, he felt a stinging slap on his face.

"You're starting again, Bernard," his mother screamed. "You're watching that girl. I can tell. I can just tell! Don't you ever learn?"

WHEN MEGHAN GOT TO THE HOSPITAL, SHE FOUND HER mother fully dressed. "Virginia brought me some clothes. I've got to get out of here," Catherine Collins said firmly. "I can't just lie in this bed and think. It's too unsettling. At least at the inn I'll be busy."

"What did the doctor say?"

"At first he objected, of course, but now he agrees, or at least he's willing to sign me out." Her voice faltered. "Meggie, don't try to change my mind. It really is better if I'm home."

Meghan hugged her fiercely. "Are you packed yet?"

"Down to the toothbrush. Meg, one more thing. Those investigators want to talk to you. When we get home, you have to call and set up an appointment with them."

THE PHONE WAS RINGING WHEN MEGHAN PUSHED OPEN THE front door of the house. She ran to get it. It was Dina Anderson. "Meghan. If you're still interested in being around when the baby is born, start making plans. The doctor is going to put me into Danbury Medical Center on Monday morning and induce labor."

"I'll be there. Is it all right if I come up Sunday afternoon with a cameraman and take some pictures of you and Jonathan getting ready for the baby?"

"That will be fine."

CATHERINE COLLINS WENT FROM ROOM TO ROOM, TURNING on the lights. "It's so good to be home," she murmured.

"Do you want to lie down?"

"That's the last thing in the world I want to do. I'm going

to soak in a tub and get properly dressed and then we're going to have dinner at the inn."

"Are you sure?" Meghan watched as her mother's chin went up and her mouth settled in a firm line.

"I'm very sure. Things are going to get a lot worse before they get better, Meg. You'll see that when you talk to those investigators. But no one is going to think that we're hiding out."

"I think Pop's exact words were, 'Don't let the bastards get you.' I'd better call those people from the state attorney's office."

JOHN DWYER WAS THE ASSISTANT STATE ATTORNEY ASSIGNED to the Danbury courthouse. His jurisdiction included the town of New Milford.

At forty, Dwyer had been in the state attorney's office for fifteen years. During those years, he'd sent some upstanding citizens, pillars of the community, to prison for crimes ranging from fraud to murder. He'd also prosecuted three people who'd faked their deaths in an attempt to collect insurance.

Edwin Collins' supposed death in the Tappan Zee Bridge tragedy had generated much sympathetic coverage in the local media. The family was well known in the area, and the Drumdoe Inn was an institution.

The fact that Collins' car almost certainly had not gone over the side of the bridge and his role in the verification of Helene Petrovic's bogus credentials had changed a shocking suburban murder to a statewide scandal. Dwyer knew that the State Department of Health was sending medical investigators to the Manning Clinic to determine how much damage Petrovic might have done in the lab there.

Late Wednesday afternoon, Dwyer had a meeting in his office with the investigators from the New Milford police, Arlene Weiss and Bob Marron. They had managed to get Petrovic's file from the State Department in Washington.

Weiss reviewed the specifics of it for him. "Petrovic came

to the United States twenty years ago, when she was twenty-seven. Her sponsor ran a beauty salon on Broadway. Her visa application lists her education as high school graduate with some training at a cosmetology school in Bucharest."

"No medical training?" Dwyer asked.

"None that she listed," Weiss confirmed.

Bob Marron looked at his notes. "She went to work at her friend's salon, stayed there eleven years and in the last couple took secretarial courses at night."

Dwyer nodded.

"Then she was offered a job as a secretary at the Dowling Assisted Reproduction Center in Trenton, New Jersey. That's when she bought the Lawrenceville house.

"Three years later, Collins placed her at the Manning Clinic as an embryologist."

"What about Edwin Collins? Does his background check out?" Dwyer asked.

"Yes. He's a Harvard Business graduate. Never been in trouble. Senior partner in the firm. Got a gun permit about ten years ago after he was held up at a red light in Bridgeport."

The intercom buzzed. "Miss Collins returning Mr. Marron's call."

"That's Collins' daughter?" Dwyer asked.

"Yes."

"Get her in here tomorrow."

Marron took the phone and spoke to Meghan, then looked at the assistant state attorney. "Eight o'clock tomorrow morning all right? She's driving to Philadelphia on assignment and needs to come in early."

Dwyer nodded.

After Marron confirmed the appointment with Meghan and replaced the receiver, Dwyer leaned back in his swivel chair. "Let's see what we have. Edwin Collins disappeared and is presumed dead. But now his wife receives flowers from him, which you tell me were charged to his credit card."

"The order was phoned in to the florist. The credit card

has never been canceled. On the other hand, until this afternoon, it hasn't been used since January," Weiss said.

"Wasn't it tagged after his disappearance to see if there was activity on the account?"

"Until the other day, Collins was presumed to have drowned. There was no reason to put an alert on his cards."

Arlene Weiss was looking over her notes. "I want to ask Meghan Collins about something her mother said. That phone call that landed Mrs. Collins in the hospital, the one that she swears didn't sound like her husband . . ."

"What about it?"

"She thought she heard the caller say something like, 'I'm in terrible trouble.' What did that mean?"

"We'll ask the daughter what she thinks when we talk to her tomorrow," Dwyer said. "I know what I think. Is Edwin Collins still listed as missing-presumed-dead?"

Marron and Weiss nodded together. Assistant State Attorney Dwyer got up. "We probably should change that. Here's the way I see it. One, we've established Collins' connection to Petrovic. Two, he almost certainly did not die in the bridge accident. Three, he took all the cash value from his insurance policies a few weeks before he disappeared. Four, no trace of his car has been found, but a tall man in a dark sedan regularly visited the Petrovic woman. Five, the phone call, the use of the credit card, the flowers. I say it's enough. Put out an APB on Edwin Collins. Make it, 'Wanted for questioning in the murder of Helene Petrovic.'"

30

*J*ust before five o'clock, Victor Orsini received the call he was afraid might come. Larry Downes, president of Downes and Rosen, phoned to tell him that it would be better all around if he held off giving notice at Collins and Carter.

"For how long, Larry?" Victor asked quietly.

"I don't know," Downes said evasively. "This fuss about the Petrovic woman will all die down eventually, but you have too much negative feedback attached to you for you to come here now. And if it turns out that Petrovic mixed up any of those embryos at the clinic, there'll be hell to pay, and you know it. You guys placed her there, and you'll be held responsible."

Victor protested. "I'd just started when Helene Petrovic's application was submitted to the Manning Clinic. Larry, you let me down last winter."

"I'm sorry, Victor. But the fact is, you were there six weeks before Petrovic began working at Manning. That means you were there when the investigation into her credentials should have been taking place. Collins and Carter is a small operation. Who's going to believe you weren't aware of what was going on?"

Orsini swallowed. When he spoke to the reporters he'd said that he'd never heard of Petrovic, that he'd barely been hired when she was okayed for Manning. They hadn't picked up that he'd obviously been in the office when her application was processed. He tried one more argument. "Larry, I've helped you people a lot this year."

"Have you, Victor?"

"You placed candidates with three of our best accounts."

"Perhaps our candidates for the jobs were stronger."

"Who told you those corporations were looking to fill positions?"

"I'm sorry, Victor."

Orsini stared at the receiver as the line went dead. Don't call us. We'll call you, he thought. He knew the job with Downes and Rosen probably would never be given to him now.

Milly poked her head into his office. "I'm on my way. Hasn't it been a terrible day, Mr. Orsini? All those reporters coming in and all those calls." Her eyes were snapping with excitement.

Victor could just see her at her dinner table tonight, repeating with relish every detail of the day. "Is Mr. Carter back?"

"No. He phoned that he was going to stay with Mrs. Collins at the hospital and then go directly home. You know, I think he's getting sweet on her."

Orsini did not answer.

"Well, good night, Mr. Orsini."

"Good night, Milly."

WHILE HER MOTHER WAS DRESSING, MEGHAN SLIPPED INTO the study and took the letters and obituary notice from the drawer in her father's desk. She hid them in her briefcase and prayed her mother would not notice the faint scratches on the desk where the file had slipped when she was breaking into the drawer. Meghan would have to tell her about the letters and the death notice eventually, but not yet. Maybe after she'd been to Philadelphia she might have some sort of explanation.

She went upstairs to her own bathroom to wash her face and hands and freshen her makeup. After hesitating a moment, she decided to call Mac. He had said he'd call her, and she didn't want him to think anything was wrong. More wrong than it already is, she corrected herself.

Kyle answered. "Meg!" It was the Kyle she knew, delighted to hear her voice.

"Hi, pal. How's it going?"

"Great. But today was really bad."

"Why?"

"Jake nearly got killed. I was throwing a ball to him. He's getting real good at catching it, but I threw too hard and it went in the street and he ran out and some guy almost hit him. I mean you should have seen the guy stop his car. Like just *stop*. That car *shook*."

"I'm glad Jake's okay, Kyle. Next time toss the ball to him in the backyard. You've got more room."

"That's what Dad said. He's grabbing the phone, Meg. See you."

Mac came on. "I was not grabbing it. I reached for it. Hi, Meg. You've gotten all the news from this end. How's it going?"

She told him that her mother was home. "I'm driving to Philadelphia tomorrow for the feature I'm trying to put together."

"Will you also check out that address in Chestnut Hill?"

"Yes. Mother doesn't know about that or those letters."

"She won't hear it from me. When will you get back?"

"Probably not before eight o'clock. It's nearly a four-hour drive to Philadelphia."

"Meg." Mac's voice became hesitant. "I know that you don't want me interfering, but I wish you'd let me help. I sense sometimes that you're avoiding me."

"Don't be silly. We've always been good buddies."

"I'm not sure we are anymore. Maybe I've missed something. What happened?"

What happened, Meghan thought, is that I can't think of that letter I wrote you nine years ago, begging you not to marry Ginger, without writhing in humiliation. What happened is that I'll never be anything more than your little buddy and I've managed to separate myself from you. I can't risk going through Jeremy MacIntyre withdrawal again.

"Nothing happened, Mac," she said lightly. "You're still

my buddy. I can't help it if I don't talk about piano lessons anymore. I gave them up years ago."

THAT NIGHT WHEN SHE WENT TO HER MOTHER'S ROOM TO turn down the bed she switched the ringer on the phone to the off position. If there were any more nocturnal calls, they would be heard only by her.

31

*D*r. Henry Williams, the sixty-five-year-old head of the Franklin Assisted Reproduction Center in the renovated old town section of Philadelphia, was a man who looked vaguely like everyone's favorite uncle. He had a head of thick graying hair, a gentle face that reassured even the most nervous patient. Very tall, he had a slight stoop that suggested he was in the habit of bending down to listen.

Meghan had phoned him after her meeting with Tom Weicker, and he had readily agreed to an appointment. Now Meghan sat in front of his desk in the cheerful office with its framed pictures of babies and young children covering the walls.

"Are these all children born through in vitro fertilization?" Meghan asked.

"Born through assisted reproduction," Williams corrected. "Not all are in vitro births."

"I understand, or at least I believe I do. In vitro is when

the eggs are removed from the ovaries and fertilized with semen in the laboratory."

"Correct. You realize that the woman has been given fertility drugs so that her ovaries will release a number of eggs at the same time?"

"Yes. I understand that."

"There are other procedures we practice, all variations of in vitro fertilization. I suggest I give you some literature that explains them. Basically it amounts to a lot of heavy-duty terms that all boil down to assisting a woman to have the successful pregnancy she craves."

"Would you be willing to be interviewed on-camera, to let us do some footage on the facilities and speak to some of your clients?"

"Yes. Frankly we're proud of our operation, and favorable publicity is welcome. I would have one stipulation. I'll contact several of our clients and ask if they'd be willing to speak to you. I don't want you approaching them. Some people do not choose to let their families know that they have used assisted birth procedures."

"Why would they object? I should think they'd just be happy to have the baby."

"They are. But one woman whose mother-in-law learned about the assisted birth openly said that, because of her son's very low sperm count, she doubted if it was her son's child. Our client actually had DNA testing done on her, the husband and the baby to prove it was the biological offspring of both parents."

"Some people do use donor embryos, of course."

"Yes, those who simply cannot conceive on their own. It's actually a form of adoption."

"I guess it is. Doctor, I know this is a terrible rush, but could I come back late this afternoon with a cameraman? A woman in Connecticut is giving birth very soon to the identical twin of her son who was born three years ago through in vitro fertilization. We'll be doing follow-up stories on the progress of the children."

Williams' expression changed, becoming troubled. "Sometimes I wonder if we don't go too far. The psychological aspects of identical twins being born at separate times concerns me greatly. Incidentally, when the embryo splits in two and one is cryopreserved, we call it the clone, not the identical twin. But to answer your question, yes, I'd be available later today."

"I can't tell you how grateful I am. We'll do some establishing shots outside and in the reception area. I'll lead in with when the Franklin Center started. That's about six years ago, I understand."

"Six years ago this past September."

"Then I'll stick to specific questions about in vitro fertilization and the freezing, I mean cryopreservation, of the clone, as in Mrs. Anderson's case."

Meghan got up to go. "I've got some fast arrangements to make. Would four o'clock be all right for you?"

"It should be fine."

Meghan hesitated. She had been afraid to ask Dr. Williams about Helene Petrovic before she established some rapport with him, but she could not wait any longer. "Dr. Williams, I don't know if the papers here have carried the story, but Helene Petrovic, a woman who worked in the Manning Clinic, was found murdered, and it's come out that her credentials were falsified. You knew her and actually worked with her, didn't you?"

"Yes, I did." Henry Williams shook his head. "I was Dr. Manning's assistant, and I knew everything that went on in that clinic and who was doing the job. Helene Petrovic certainly fooled me. She kept that lab the way labs should be kept. It's terrible that she falsified credentials, but she absolutely seemed to know what she was doing."

Meghan decided to take a chance that this kindly man would understand why she needed to ask probing questions. "Doctor, my father's firm and specifically my father have been accused of verifying Helene Petrovic's lies. Forgive me, but I must try to find out more about her. The receptionist at

Manning Clinic saw you and Helene Petrovic at dinner. How well did you get to know her?"

Henry Williams looked amused. "You mean Marge Walters. Did she also tell you that as a courtesy I always took a new staff member at Manning to dinner? An informal welcome . . ."

"No, she didn't. Did you know Helene Petrovic before she went to Manning?"

"No."

"Have you had any contact with her since you left?"

"None at all."

The intercom buzzed. He picked up the receiver and listened. "Hold it for a moment, please," he said, turning to Meghan.

She took her cue. "Doctor, I won't take any more of your time. Thank you so much." Meghan picked up her shoulder bag and left.

When the door closed behind her, Dr. Henry Williams again put the receiver to his ear. "Put the call through now, please."

He murmured a greeting, listened, then said nervously, "Yes, of course I'm alone. She just left. She'll be back at four with a cameraman. Don't tell me to be careful. What kind of fool do you take me for?"

He replaced the receiver, suddenly infinitely weary. After a moment, he picked it up again and dialed. "Everything under control over there?" he asked.

HER SCOTTISH ANCESTORS CALLED IT SECOND SIGHT. THE gift had turned up in a woman in different generations of Clan Campbell. This time it was Fiona Campbell Black who was granted it. A psychic who was regularly called upon by police departments throughout the country to help solve crimes and by families frantic to find missing loved ones, Fiona treated her extraordinary abilities with profound respect.

Married twenty years, she lived in Litchfield, Connecticut, a lovely old town that was settled in the early seventeenth century.

On Thursday afternoon Fiona's husband, Andrew Black, a lawyer with offices in town, came home for lunch. He found her sitting in the breakfast room, the morning paper spread in front of her, her eyes reflective, her head tilted as though she were expecting to hear a voice or sound she did not want to miss.

Andrew Black knew what that meant. He took off his coat, tossed it on a chair and said, "I'll fix us something."

Ten minutes later when he came back with a plate of sandwiches and a pot of tea, Fiona raised her eyebrows. "It happened when I saw this." She held up the local newspaper with Edwin Collins' picture on the front page. "They want this man for questioning in the Petrovic woman's death."

Black poured the tea. "I read that."

"Andrew, I don't want to get involved, but I think I have to. I'm getting a message about him."

"How clear is it?"

"It isn't. I have to handle something that belongs to him. Should I call the New Milford police or go directly to his family?"

"I think it's better to go through the police."

"I suppose so." Slowly, Fiona ran her fingertips over the grainy reproduction of Edwin Collins' face. "So much evil," she murmured, "so much death and evil surrounding him."

32

*B*ernie's first fare on Thursday morning was from Kennedy Airport. He parked the Chevy and wandered over to where the suburban buses picked up and deposited passengers. Bernie glanced at the schedule. A bus for Westport was due in, and a group of people were waiting for it. One couple in their thirties had two small kids and a lot of luggage. Bernie decided that they'd be good prospects.

"Connecticut?" he asked them, his smile genial.

"We're not taking a cab," the woman snapped impatiently as she grabbed the two-year-old's hand. "Billy, stay with me," she scolded. "You can't run around here."

"Forty bucks plus tolls," Bernie said. "I've got a pickup around Westport, so any fare I get is found money."

The husband was trying to hang onto a squirming three-year-old. "You've got a deal." He did not bother to look to his wife for approval.

Bernie had run his car through the car wash and vacuumed the interior again. He saw the disdain that initially flashed on the woman's face turn to approval at the Chevy's clean interior. He drove carefully, never above the speed limit, no quick changes from lane to lane. The man sat in front with him. The woman was in the back, the kids strapped in beside her. Bernie made a mental note to buy some car seats and keep them in the trunk.

The man directed Bernie to Exit 17 off the Connecticut Turnpike. "It's just a mile and a half from here." When they reached the pleasant brick home on Tuxedo Road, Bernie was rewarded with a ten dollar tip.

He drove back to the Connecticut Turnpike, south to Exit 15 and once again got on Route 7. It was as though he couldn't stop the car from going to where Meghan lived. Be careful, he tried to tell himself. Even with the camera and the press pass it might look suspicious for him to be on her street.

He decided to have a cup of coffee and think about it. He pulled in at the next diner. There was a newspaper vending machine in the vestibule between the outer and inner doors. Through the glass, Bernie saw the headline, all about the Manning Clinic. That was where Meghan had done the interview yesterday, the one he and Mama had watched. He fished in his pocket for change and bought a paper.

Over coffee he read the article. The Manning Clinic was about forty minutes away from Meghan's town. There'd probably be media hanging around there because they were checking out the laboratory where that woman had worked.

Maybe Meghan would be there too. She'd been there yesterday.

Forty minutes later Bernie was on the narrow, winding road that led from the quaint center of Kent to the Manning Clinic. After he left the diner he'd sat in the car and studied the map of this area so carefully that it was easy to figure out the most direct way to get there.

Just as he'd hoped, there were a number of media vans in the parking lot of the clinic. He parked at a distance from them and stuck his parking permit in the windshield. Then he studied the press pass he'd created. It would have taken an expert to spot that it wasn't genuine. It listed him as Bernard Heffernan, Channel 86, Elmira, New York. It was a local community station, he reminded himself. If anyone asked why that community would be interested in this story, he'd say they were thinking of building a facility like the Manning Clinic there.

Satisfied that he had his story straight, Bernie got out of the car and pulled on his windbreaker. Most reporters and cameramen didn't dress up. He decided to wear dark glasses, then got his new video camera from the trunk. State of the art, he told himself proudly. It had cost a bundle. He'd put it on his credit card. He'd rubbed some dust on it from the basement so it didn't look too new, and he'd painted the Channel 86 call letters on the side.

THERE WERE A DOZEN OR SO REPORTERS AND CAMERAMEN IN the clinic's lobby. They were interviewing a man who Bernie could see was stonewalling them. He was saying, "I repeat, the Manning Clinic is proud of its success in assisting women to have the children they so ardently desire. It is our belief that, despite the information on her visa application, Helene Petrovic may have trained as an embryologist in Rumania. None of the professionals who worked with her detected the slightest word or action on her part that suggested she did not thoroughly know her job."

"But if she made mistakes?" one reporter asked. "Suppose she mixed up those frozen embryos and women have given birth to other people's children?"

"We will perform DNA analysis for any parents who wish the clinical test for themselves and their child. The results take four to six weeks to achieve, but they are irrefutable. If parents wish to have that testing done at a different facility, we will pay the expense. Neither Dr. Manning nor any of the senior staff expect a problem in that area."

Bernie looked around. Meghan wasn't here. Should he ask people if they'd seen her? No, that would be a mistake. Just be part of the crowd, he cautioned himself.

But as he'd hoped, no one was paying any attention to him. He pointed his camera at the guy answering questions and turned it on.

When the interview was over, Bernie left with the group, taking care not to get too close to any of the others. He had spotted a PCD cameraman but did not recognize the burly man who was holding the mike. At the foot of the porch steps, a woman stopped her car and got out. She was pregnant and obviously upset. A reporter asked, "Ma'am, are you a client here?"

Stephanie Petrovic tried to shield her face from the cameras as she cried. "No. No. I just came to beg them to share my aunt's money with me. She left everything to the clinic. I am thinking that perhaps somebody from here killed her because they were afraid that after she quit she would change her will. If I could prove that, wouldn't her money be mine?"

FOR LONG MINUTES, MEGHAN SAT IN HER CAR IN FRONT OF the handsome limestone house in Chestnut Hill, twenty miles from downtown Philadelphia. The graceful lines of the three-story residence were accentuated by the mullioned windows, antique oak door and the slate roof that gleamed in shades of deep green in the early afternoon sun.

The walkway that threaded through the broad expanse of lawn was bordered by rows of azaleas that Meghan was sure would bloom with vivid beauty in the spring. A dozen slender white birches were scattered like sentinels throughout the property.

The name on the mailbox was C. J. Graham. Had she ever heard that name from her father? Meghan didn't think so.

She got out of the car and went slowly up the walk. She hesitated a moment, then rang the bell and heard the faint peal of chimes sound inside the house. A moment later the door was opened by a maid in uniform.

"Yes?" Her inquiry was polite but guarded.

Meghan realized she did not know who she should ask to see. "I would like a word with whoever lives in this house who might have been a friend of Aurelia Collins."

"Who is it, Jessie?" a man's voice called.

Behind the maid, Meghan saw a tall man with snow white hair, approaching the door.

"Invite the young woman in, Jessie," he directed. "It's cold out there."

Meghan stepped inside. As the door closed, the man's eyes narrowed. He waved her closer. "Come in, please. Under the light." A smile broke over his face. "It's Annie, isn't it? My dear, I'm glad to see you again."

33

Catherine Collins had an early breakfast with Meghan before Meg left to meet with the investigators at the Danbury courthouse and then to drive to Philadelphia. Catherine carried a second cup of coffee upstairs and turned on the television in her room. On the local news she heard that her husband's official listing with the law was no longer missing-presumed-dead, but had been changed to wanted-for-questioning in the Petrovic death.

When Meg called to say she was finished with the investigators and about to leave for Philadelphia, Catherine asked, "Meg, what did they ask you?"

"The same kind of questions they asked you. You know they're convinced Dad is alive. So far they have him guilty of fraud and murder. God knows what else they'll come up with. You're the one who warned me yesterday that it was going to get worse before it got better. You sure were right."

Something in Meg's voice chilled Catherine. "Meg, there's something you're not telling me."

"Mom, I have to go. We'll talk tonight, I promise."

"I don't want anything held back."

"I swear to God I won't hold anything back."

THE DOCTOR HAD CAUTIONED CATHERINE TO STAY AT HOME and rest for at least a few days. Rest and give myself a real heart attack worrying, she thought as she dressed. She was going to the inn.

She'd been away only a few days, but she could see a

difference. Virginia was good but missed small details. The flower arrangement on the registration desk was drooping. "When did this come?" Catherine asked.

"Just this morning."

"Call the florist and ask him to replace it." The roses she had received in the hospital were dewy fresh, Catherine remembered.

The tables in the dining room were set for lunch. Catherine walked from one to the other, examining them, a busboy behind her. "We're short a napkin here, and on the table by the window. A knife is missing there and that saltcellar looks grimy."

"Yes, ma'am."

She went into the kitchen. The old chef had retired in July after twenty years. His replacement, Clive D'Arcette, had come with impressive experience, despite being only twenty-six years old. After four months, Catherine was coming to the conclusion that he was a good second banana, but couldn't yet do the job on his own.

He was preparing the luncheon specials when Catherine entered the kitchen. She frowned as she noticed the grease spatters on the stove. Clearly they came from the dinner preparation the night before. The garbage bin had not been emptied. She tasted the hollandaise sauce. "Why is it salty?" she asked.

"I wouldn't call it salty, Mrs. Collins," D'Arcette said, his tone just missing politeness.

"But I would, and I suspect anyone who orders it would."

"Mrs. Collins, you hired me to be the chef here. Unless I can be the chef and prepare food my way, this situation won't work."

"You've made it very easy for me," Catherine said. "You're fired."

She was tying an apron around her waist when Virginia Murphy hurried in. "Catherine, where's Clive going? He just stormed past me."

"Back to cooking school, I hope."

"You're supposed to be resting."

Catherine turned to her. "Virginia, my salvation is going to be at this stove for as long as I can hang onto this place. Now what specials did Escoffier line up for today?"

They served forty-three lunches as well as sandwiches in the bar. It was a good seating. As the new orders slowed down, Catherine was able to go into the dining room. In her long white apron, she went from table to table, stopping for a moment at each. She could see the questioning eyes behind the warm smiles of greeting.

I don't blame people for being curious, with all they're hearing, she thought. I would be too. But these are my friends. This is my inn, and no matter what truth comes out, Meg and I have our place in this town.

CATHERINE SPENT THE LATE AFTERNOON IN THE OFFICE going over the books. If the bank will let me refinance and I hock or sell my jewelry, she decided, I might be able to hang on for six months longer at least. By then maybe we'll know something about the insurance. She closed her eyes. If only she hadn't been fool enough to put the house in both her and Edwin's names after Pop died . . .

Why did I do it? she wondered. I know why. I didn't want Edwin to think of himself as living in my house. Even when Pop was alive, Edwin had always insisted on paying for the utilities and repairs. "I have to feel as though I belong here," he'd said. Oh, Edwin! What had he called himself? Oh yes, "a wandering minstrel." She'd always thought of that as a joke. Had he meant it as a joke? Now she wasn't so certain.

She tried to remember verses of the old Gilbert and Sullivan song he used to sing. Only the opening line and one other came back to her. The first line was, "A wandering minstrel, I, a thing of shreds and patches." The other line: "And to your humors changing, I tune my subtle song."

Plaintive words when you analyzed them. Why had Edwin felt they applied to him?

Resolutely, Catherine went back to studying the accounts. The phone rang as she closed the last book. It was Bob Marron, one of the investigators who had come to see her in the hospital. "Mrs. Collins, when you weren't home I took a chance on calling you at the inn. Something has come up. We felt we needed to pass on this information to you, though we certainly don't necessarily recommend that you act on it."

"I don't know what you're talking about," Catherine said flatly.

She listened as Marron told her that Fiona Black, a psychic who had worked with them on cases of missing persons, had called. "She says she is getting very strong vibrations about your husband and would like to be able to handle something of his," Marron concluded.

"You're trying to send me some quack?"

"I know how you feel, but do you remember the Talmadge child who was missing three years ago?"

"Yes."

"It was Mrs. Black who told us to concentrate the search in the construction area near the town hall. She saved that kid's life."

"I see." Catherine moistened her lips with her tongue. Anything is better than not knowing, she told herself. She tightened her grasp on the receiver. "What does Mrs. Black want of Edwin's? Clothing? A ring?"

"She's here now. She'd like to come to your house and select something if that's possible. I'd bring her over in half an hour."

Catherine wondered if she should wait for Meg before she met this woman. Then she heard herself say, "Half an hour will be fine. I'm on my way home now."

MEGHAN FELT FROZEN IN TIME AS SHE STOOD IN THE FOYER with the courtly man who obviously believed they had met before. Through lips almost too numb to utter the words, she managed to say, "My name isn't Annie. It's Meghan. Meghan Collins."

Graham looked closely at her. "You're Edwin's daughter, aren't you?"

"Yes, I am."

"Come with me, please." He took her arm and guided her through the door to the study, on the right of the foyer. "I spend most of my time in here," he told her as he led her to the couch and settled himself in a high-backed wing chair. "Since my wife passed away, this house seems awfully big to me."

Meghan realized that Graham had seen her shock and distress and was trying to defuse it. But she was beyond phrasing her questions diplomatically. She opened her purse and took out the envelope with the obituary notice. "Did you send this to my father?" she asked.

"Yes, I did. He didn't acknowledge it, but then I never expected that he would. I was so sorry when I read about the accident last January."

"How do you know my father?" Meghan asked.

"I'm sorry," he apologized. "I don't think I've introduced myself. I'm Cyrus Graham. Your father's stepbrother."

His stepbrother! I never knew this man existed, Meghan thought.

"You called me 'Annie' just now," she said. "Why?"

He answered her with a question. "Do you have a sister, Meghan?"

"No."

"And you don't remember meeting me with your father and mother about ten years ago in Arizona?"

"I've never been there."

"Then I'm totally confused," Graham told her.

"Exactly when and where in Arizona did you think we met?" Meghan asked urgently.

"Let's see. It was in April, close to eleven years ago. I was in Scottsdale. My wife had spent a week in the Elizabeth Arden Spa, and I was picking her up the next morning. The evening before, I stayed at the Safari Hotel in Scottsdale. I was just leaving the dining room when I spotted Edwin. He was sitting with a woman who might have been in her early forties and a young girl who looked very much like you." Graham looked at Meghan. "Actually, both you and she resemble Edwin's mother."

"My grandmother."

"Yes." Now he looked concerned. "Meghan, I'm afraid this is distressing you."

"It's very important that I know everything I can about the people who were with my father that night."

"Very well. You realize it was a brief meeting, but since it was the first time I'd seen Edwin in years it made an impression on me."

"When had you seen him before that?"

"Not since he graduated from prep school. But even though thirty years had passed, I recognized him instantly. I went over to the table and got a mighty chilly reception. He introduced me to his wife and daughter as someone he'd known growing up in Philadelphia. I took the hint and left immediately. I knew through Aurelia that he and his family lived in Connecticut and simply assumed that they were vacationing in Arizona."

"Did he introduce the woman he was with as his wife?"

"I think so. I can't be sure about that. He may have said something like 'Frances and Annie, this is Cyrus Graham.' "

"You're positive the girl's name was *Annie?*"

"Yes, I am. And I know the woman's name was Frances."

"How old was Annie then?"

"About sixteen, I should think."

Meghan thought, that would make her about twenty-six now. She shivered. And she's lying in the morgue in my place.

She realized Graham was studying her.

"I think we could use a cup of tea," he said. "Have you had lunch?"

"Please don't bother."

"I'd like you to join me. I'll ask Jessie to put something together for us."

When he left the room, Meghan clasped her hands on her knees. Her legs felt weak and wobbly, as though if she stood up they would not support her. *Annie,* she thought. A vivid memory sprang into her mind of discussing names with her father. "How did you pick Meghan Anne for me?"

"My two favorite names in the world are Meghan and Annie. And that's how you became Meghan Anne."

You got to use your two favorite names, after all, Dad, Meghan thought bitterly. When Cyrus Graham returned, followed by the maid carrying a luncheon tray, Meghan accepted a cup of tea and a finger sandwich.

"I can't tell you how shocked I am," she said, and was glad she was able to at least sound calm. "Now tell me about *him.* Suddenly my father has become a total stranger to me."

It was not a pretty story. Richard Collins, her grandfather, had married seventeen-year-old Aurelia Crowley when she became pregnant. "He felt it was the honorable thing," Graham said. "He was much older and divorced her almost immediately, but he did support her and the baby with reasonable generosity. A year later, when I was fourteen, Richard and my mother married. My own father was dead. This was the Graham family home. Richard Collins moved in, and it was a good marriage. He and my mother were both rather rigid, joyless people, and as the old saying goes, God made them and matched them."

"And my father was raised by his mother?"

"Until he was three years old, at which point Aurelia fell madly in love with someone from California who did not want to be saddled with a child. One morning she arrived here and deposited Edwin with his suitcases and toys. My mother was furious. Richard was even more furious, and little Edwin was devastated. He worshiped his mother."

"She abandoned him to a family where he wasn't wanted?" Meghan asked incredulously.

"Yes. Mother and Richard took him in out of duty, but certainly not out of desire. I'm afraid he was a difficult little boy. I can remember him standing every day with his nose pressed to the window, so positive was he that his mother would come back."

"And did she?"

"Yes. A year later. The great love affair went sour, and she came back and collected Edwin. He was overjoyed and so were my parents."

"And then . . ."

"When he was eight, Aurelia met someone else and the scenario was repeated."

"Dear God!" Meghan said.

"This time Edwin was really impossible. He apparently thought that if he behaved very badly they'd find a way to send him back to his mother. It was an interesting morning around here when he put the garden hose in the gas tank of Mother's new sedan."

"Did they send him home?"

"Aurelia had left Philadelphia again. He was sent to boarding school and then to camp during the summer. I was away at college and then in law school and only saw him occasionally. I did visit him at school once and was astonished to see that he was very popular with his schoolmates. Even then he was telling people that his mother was dead."

"Did he ever see her again?"

"She came back to Philadelphia when he was sixteen. This time she stayed. She had finally matured and taken a job in a law office. I understand she tried to see Edwin, but it was too late. He wanted nothing to do with her. The pain was too deep. From time to time over the years she contacted me to ask if I ever heard from Edwin. A friend had sent me a clipping reporting his marriage to your mother. It gave the name and address of his firm. I gave the clipping to Aurelia. From what she told me, she wrote to him around his birthday and at Christmas every year but never heard back. In one of our conversations I told her about the meeting in Scottsdale. Perhaps I had no business sending the obituary notice to him."

"He was a wonderful father to me and a wonderful husband to my mother," Meghan said. She tried to blink back the tears that she felt welling in her eyes. "He traveled a great deal in his job. I can't believe he could have had another life, another woman he may have called his wife, perhaps another daughter he must have loved too. But I'm beginning to think it must be true. How else do you explain Annie and Frances? How can anybody expect my mother and me to forgive that deception?"

It was a question she was asking of herself, not of Cyrus Graham, but he answered it. "Meghan, turn around." He pointed to the prim row of windows behind the couch. "That center window is the one where a little boy stood watch every afternoon, looking for his mother. That kind of abandonment does something to the soul and the psyche."

34

*A*t four o'clock, Mac phoned Catherine at home to see how she was feeling. When he did not get an answer he tried her at the inn. Just as the operator was about to put him through to Catherine's office, the intercom on his desk began to buzz. "No, that's all right," he said hurriedly. "I'll try her later."

The next hour was busy, and he did not get to phone again. He was just at the outskirts of Newtown when he dialed her at the house from the car phone. "I thought if you were home I'd stop by for few minutes, Catherine," he said.

"I'd be glad for the moral support, Mac." Catherine quickly told him about the psychic and that she and the investigator were on their way.

"I'll be there in five minutes." Mac replaced the receiver

and frowned. He didn't believe in psychics. God knows what Meg is hearing about Edwin in Chestnut Hill today, he thought. Catherine's just about at the end of her rope, and they don't need some charlatan creating any more trouble for them.

He pulled into the Collins driveway as a man and a woman were getting out of a car in front of the house. The investigator and the psychic, Mac thought.

He caught up with them on the porch. Bob Marron introduced first himself and then Mrs. Fiona Black, saying only that she was someone who hoped to assist in locating Edwin Collins.

Mac was prepared to see a real display of hocus-pocus and calculated fakery. Instead he found himself in grudging admiration of the contained and poised woman who greeted Catherine with compassion. "You've had a very bad time," she said. "I don't know if I can help you, but I know I have to try."

Catherine's face was drawn, but Mac saw the flicker of hope that came into it. "I believe in my heart that my husband is dead," she told Fiona Black. "I know the police don't believe that. It would be so much easier if there were some way of being certain, some way of proving it, of finding out once and for all."

"Perhaps there is." Fiona Black pressed Catherine's hands in hers. She walked slowly into the living room, her manner observant. Catherine stood next to Mac and Investigator Marron, watching her.

She turned to Catherine. "Mrs. Collins, do you still have your husband's clothes and personal items here?"

"Yes. Come upstairs," she said, leading the way.

Mac felt his heart beating faster as they followed her. There was something about Fiona Black. She was not a fraud.

Catherine brought them to the master bedroom. On the dresser there was a twin frame. One picture was of Meghan. The other of Catherine and Edwin in formal dress. Last New Year's Eve at the inn, Mac thought. It had been a festive night.

Fiona Black studied the picture, then said, "Where is his clothing?"

Catherine opened the door to a walk-in closet. Mac remembered that years ago she and Edwin had broken through the wall to the small adjoining bedroom and made two walk-in closets for themselves. This one was Edwin's. Rows of jackets and slacks and suits. Floor-to-ceiling shelves with sport shirts and sweaters. A shoe rack.

Catherine was looking at the contents of the closet. "Edwin had wonderful taste in clothes. I always had to pick out my father's ties," she said. It was as though she was reminiscing to herself.

Fiona Black walked into the closet, her fingers lightly touching the lapel of one coat, the shoulder of another. "Do you have favorite cuff links or a ring of his?"

Catherine opened a dresser drawer. "This was the wedding ring I gave him. He mislaid it one day. We thought it was lost. He was so upset I replaced it, then found this one where it had slipped behind the dresser. It had gotten a bit tight, so he kept wearing the new one."

Fiona Black took the thin band of gold. "May I take this for a few days? I promise not to lose it."

Catherine hesitated, then said, "If you think it will be useful to you."

THE CAMERAMAN FROM THE PCD PHILADELPHIA AFFILIATE met Meghan at quarter of four outside the Franklin Center. "Sorry this is such a rush job," she apologized.

The lanky cameraman, who introduced himself as Len, shrugged. "We're used to it."

Meghan was glad that it was necessary to concentrate on this interview. The hour she had spent with Cyrus Graham, her father's stepbrother, was so painful that she had to put thoughts of it aside until, bit by bit, she could accept it. She had promised her mother she would hold nothing back from her. It would be difficult, but she would keep that promise. Tonight they would talk it out.

She said, "Len, at the opening, I'd like to get a wide shot of the block. These cobbled streets aren't the way people think about Philadelphia."

"You should have seen this area before the renovation," Len said as he began to roll tape.

Inside the Center they were greeted by the receptionist. Three women sat in the waiting room. All looked well groomed and were carefully made up. Meghan was sure these were the clients whom Dr. Williams had contacted to be interviewed.

She was right. The receptionist introduced her to them. One was pregnant. On-camera she explained that this would be her third child to be born by in vitro fertilization. The other two each had one child and were planning to attempt another pregnancy with their cryopreserved embryos.

"I have eight frozen embryos," one of them said happily as she smiled into the lens. "They'll transfer three of them, hoping one will take. If not, I'll wait a few months, then I'll have others thawed and try again."

"If you succeed immediately in achieving a pregnancy, will you be back next year?" Meghan asked.

"Oh no. My husband and I only want two children."

"But you'll still have cryopreserved embryos stored in the lab here, won't you?"

The woman agreed. "Yes, I will," she said. "We'll pay to have them stored. Who knows? I'm only twenty-eight. I might change my mind. In a few years I may be back, and it's nice to know I have other embryos already available to me."

"Provided any of them survive the thawing process?" Meghan asked.

"Of course."

Next they went into Dr. Williams' office. Meg took a seat opposite him for the interview. "Doctor, again thank you for having us," she said. "What I wish you would do at the outset is explain in vitro fertilization as simply as you did to me earlier. Then, if you'll allow us to have some footage of the lab, and show us how cryopreserved embryos are kept, we won't take up any more of your time."

Dr. Williams was an excellent interview. Admirably succinct, he quickly explained the reasons why women might have trouble conceiving and the procedure of in vitro fertilization. "The patient is given fertility drugs to stimulate the production of eggs; the eggs are retrieved from her ovaries; in the lab they are fertilized, and the desired result is that we achieve viable embryos. Early embryos are transferred to the mother's womb, usually two or three at a time, in hopes that at least one will result in a successful pregnancy. The others are cryopreserved, or in layman's language, frozen, for eventual later use."

"Doctor, in a few days, as soon as it is born, we are going to see a baby whose identical twin was born three years ago," Meghan said. "Will you explain to our viewers how it is possible for identical twins to be born three years apart?"

"It is possible, but very rare, that the embryo divides into two identical parts in the Petri dish just as it could in the womb. In this case, apparently the mother chose to have one embryo transferred immediately, the other cryopreserved for transfer later. Fortunately, despite great odds, both procedures were successful."

Before they left Dr. Williams' office, Len panned the camera across the wall with the pictures of children born through assisted reproduction at the Center. Next they shot footage of the lab, paying particular attention to the long-term storage containers where cryopreserved embryos, submerged in liquid nitrogen, were kept.

It was nearly five-thirty when Meghan said, "Okay, it's a wrap. Thanks everyone. Doctor, I'm so grateful."

"I am too," he assured her. "I can guarantee you that this kind of publicity will generate many inquiries from childless couples."

Outside, Len put his camera in the van and walked with Meghan to her car. "Kind of gets you, doesn't it?" he asked. "I mean, I have three kids and I'd hate to think they started life in a freezer like those embryos."

"On the other hand, those embryos represent lives that

wouldn't have come into existence at all without this process," Meghan said.

As she began the long drive back to Connecticut she realized that the smooth, pleasant interview with Dr. Williams had been a respite.

Now her thoughts were back to the moment Cyrus Graham had greeted her as Annie. Every word he said in their time together replayed in her mind.

THAT SAME EVENING, AT 8:15, FIONA BLACK PHONED BOB Marron. "Edwin Collins is dead," she said quietly. "He has been dead for many months. His body is submerged in water."

35

*I*t was nine-thirty when Meghan arrived home on Thursday night, relieved to find that Mac was waiting with her mother. Seeing the question in his eyes, she nodded. It was a gesture not lost on her mother.

"Meg, what is it?"

Meg could catch the lingering aroma of onion soup. "Any of that left?" She waved her hand in the direction of the kitchen.

"You didn't have any dinner? Mac, pour her a glass of wine while I heat something up."

"Just soup, Mom, please."

When Catherine left, Mac came over to her. "How bad was it," he asked, his voice low.

She turned away, not wanting him to see the weary tears that threatened to spill over. "Pretty bad."

"Meg, if you want to talk to your mother alone, I'll get out of here. I just thought she needed company, and Mrs. Dileo was willing to stay with Kyle."

"That was nice of you, Mac, but you shouldn't have left Kyle. He looks forward to you coming home so much. Little kids shouldn't be disappointed. Don't ever let him down."

She felt that she was babbling. Mac's hands were holding her face, turning it to him.

"Meggie, what's the matter?"

Meg pressed her knuckles to her lips. She must not break down. "It's just . . ."

She could not go on. She felt Mac's arms around her. Oh God, to just let go, to be held by him. The letter. Nine years ago he had come to her with the letter she had written, the letter that begged him not to marry Ginger . . .

"I think you'd rather I didn't save this," he'd said then. He'd put his arm around her then as well, she remembered. "Meg, someday you'll fall in love. What you feel for me is something else. Everyone feels that way when a best friend gets married. There's always the fear that everything will be different. It won't be that way between us. We'll always be buddies."

The memory was as sharp as a dash of cold water. Meg straightened up and stepped back. "I'm all right, I'm just tired and hungry." She heard her mother's footsteps and waited until she was back in the room. "I have some pretty disturbing news for you, Mom."

"I think I should leave you two to talk it out," Mac said.

It was Catherine who stopped him. "Mac, you're family. I wish you'd stay."

They sat at the kitchen table. It seemed to Meghan that she could feel her father's presence. He was the one who would fix the late-evening supper if the restaurant had been crowded and her mother too busy to eat. He was a perfect mimic, taking on the mannerisms of one of the captains dealing with a cranky guest. "This table is not satisfactory? The banquette? Of course. A draft? But there is no window open. The inn is sealed shut. Perhaps it is the air flowing between your ears, madame."

Sipping a glass of wine, the steaming soup so appetizing, but untouched until she could tell them about the meeting in Chestnut Hill, Meghan talked about her father. She deliberately told about his childhood first, about Cyrus Graham's belief that the reason he turned his back on his mother was that he could not endure the chance of her abandoning him again.

Meghan watched her mother's face and found the reaction she had hoped for, pity for the little boy who had not been wanted, for the man who could not risk being hurt a third time.

But then it was necessary to tell her about the meeting in Scottsdale between Cyrus Graham and Edwin Collins.

"He introduced another woman as his wife?" There was no expression in her mother's voice.

"Mom, I don't know. Graham knew that Dad was married and had a daughter. He assumed that Dad was with his wife and daughter. Dad said something to him like, 'Frances and Annie, this is Cyrus Graham.' Mom, did Dad have any other relatives you know about? Is it a possibility that we have cousins in Arizona?"

"For God's sake, Meg, if I didn't know that your grandmother was alive all those years, how would I know about cousins?" Catherine Collins bit her lip. "I'm sorry." Her expression changed. "You say your father's stepbrother thought you were Annie. You looked that much like her?"

"Yes." Meg looked imploringly at Mac.

He understood what she was asking. "Meg," he said, "I don't think there's any point in not telling your mother why we went to New York yesterday."

"No, there isn't. Mom, there's something else you have to

know . . ." She looked steadily at her mother as she told her what she had hoped to conceal.

When she finished, her mother sat staring past her as though trying to understand what she had been hearing.

Finally, in a steady voice that was almost a monotone, she said, "A girl was stabbed who looked like you, Meg? She was carrying a piece of paper from Drumdoe Inn with your name and work number in Dad's handwriting? Within hours after she died, you got a fax that said, 'Mistake. Annie was a mistake'?"

Catherine's eyes became bleak and frightened.

"You went to have your DNA checked against hers because you thought you might be related to that girl."

"I did it because I'm trying to find answers."

"I'm glad I saw that Fiona woman tonight," Catherine burst out. "Meg, I don't suppose you'll approve, but Bob Marron of the New Milford police phoned this afternoon . . ."

Meg listened as her mother spoke of Fiona Black's visit. It's bizarre, she thought, but no more bizarre than anything else that's happened these last months.

At ten-thirty, Mac got up to leave. "If I may give advice, I'd suggest that both of you go to bed," he said.

MRS. DILEO, MAC'S HOUSEKEEPER, WAS WATCHING TELEVI-sion when he arrived home. "Kyle was so disappointed when you didn't get home before he fell asleep," she said. "Well, I'll be on my way."

Mac waited until her car pulled out, then turned off the outside lights and locked the door. He went in to look at Kyle. His small son was hunched in the fetal position, the pillow bunched under his head.

Mac tucked the covers around him, bent down and kissed the top of his head. Kyle seemed to be just fine, a pretty normal kid, but now Mac asked himself if he was ignoring any signals that Kyle might be sending out. Most other seven-

year-olds grew up with mothers. Mac wasn't sure if the overwhelming surge of tenderness he felt now was for his son, or
for the little boy Edwin Collins had been fifty years ago in
Philadelphia. Or for Catherine and Meghan, who surely were
the victims of the unhappy childhood of their husband and
father.

MEGHAN AND CATHERINE SAW STEPHANIE PETROVIC'S IMPAS-
sioned interview at the Manning Clinic on the eleven o'clock
news. Meg listened as the anchorman reported that Stephanie
Petrovic had lived with her aunt in their New Jersey home.
"The body is being shipped to Rumania; the memorial mass
will be held at noon in St. Dominic's Rumanian Church in
Trenton," he finished.

"I'm going to that mass," Meghan told her mother. "I
want to talk to that girl."

AT EIGHT O'CLOCK FRIDAY MORNING, BOB MARRON RE-
ceived a call at home. An illegally parked car, a dark blue
Cadillac sedan, had been ticketed in Battery Park City, Manhattan, outside Meghan Collins' apartment house. The car
was registered to Edwin Collins, and appeared to be the car
he was driving the evening he disappeared.

As Marron dialed State Attorney John Dwyer he said to
his wife, "The psychic sure dropped the ball on this one."

Fifteen minutes later, Marron was telling Meghan about
the discovery of her father's car. He asked if she and Mrs.
Collins could come to John Dwyer's office. He would like to
see them together as soon as possible.

36

*E*arly Friday morning, Bernie watched again the replay of the interview he had taped at the Manning Clinic. He didn't hold the camera steady enough, he decided. The picture wobbled. He'd be more careful next time.

"Bernard!" His mother was yelling for him at the top of the stairs. Reluctantly he turned off the equipment.

"I'll be right there, Mama."

"Your breakfast is getting cold." His mother was wrapped in her flannel robe. It had been washed so often that the neck and the sleeves and the seat were threadbare. Bernie had told her that she washed it too much, but Mama said she was a clean person, that in her house you could eat off the floors.

This morning Mama was in a bad mood. "I was sneezing a lot last night," she told him as she dished out oatmeal from the pot on the stove. "I think I smelled dust coming from the basement just now. You do mop the floor down there, don't you?"

"Yes, I do, Mama."

"I wish you'd fix those cellar stairs so I can get down there and see for myself."

Bernie knew that his mother would never take a chance on those stairs. One of the steps was broken, and the bannister was wobbly.

"Mama, those stairs are dangerous. Remember what happened to your hip—and now, what with your arthritis, your knees are really bad."

"Don't think I'm taking a chance like that again," she

snapped. "But see that you keep it mopped. I don't know why you spend so much time down there anyhow."

"Yes, you do, Mama. I don't need much sleep, and if I have the television on in the living room, it keeps you awake." Mama had no idea about all the electronic equipment he had and she never would.

"I didn't sleep much last night. My allergies were at me."

"I'm sorry, Mama." Bernie finished the lukewarm oatmeal. "I'll be late." He grabbed his jacket.

She followed him to the door. When he was going down the walk, she called after him, "I'm glad to see you're keeping the car decent for a change."

AFTER THE PHONE CALL FROM BOB MARRON, MEGHAN HURriedly showered, dressed and went down to the kitchen. Her mother was already there, preparing breakfast.

Catherine's attempt at a cheery "Good morning, Meg" froze on her lips as she saw Meg's face. "What is it?" she asked. "I did hear the phone ring when I was in the shower, didn't I?"

Meg took both her mother's hands in hers. "Mom, look at me. I'm going to be absolutely honest with you. I thought for months that Daddy was lost on the bridge that night. With all that's happened this past week I need to make myself think as a lawyer and reporter. Look at all the possibilities, weigh each one carefully. I tried to make myself consider whether he might be alive and in serious trouble. But I know . . . I am sure . . . that what has gone on these last few days was something Dad would never do to us. That call, the flowers . . . and now . . ." She stopped.

"And now, what, Meg?"

"Dad's car was found in the city, illegally parked outside my apartment building."

"Mother of God!" Catherine's face went ashen.

"Mom, someone else put it there. I don't know why, but there's a reason behind all of this. The assistant state attorney wants to see us. He and his investigators are going to try to persuade us that Dad is alive. They didn't know him. We did. Whatever else may have been wrong in his life, he wouldn't send those flowers or leave his car where he'd be sure it would be found. He'd know how frantic we'd be. When we have this meeting, we're going to stick to our guns and defend him."

Neither one of them cared about food. They brought steaming cups of coffee out to the car. As Meghan backed out of the garage, trying to sound matter-of-fact, she said, "It may be illegal to drive one-handed, but coffee does help."

"That's because we're both so cold, inside and out. Look, Meg. The first dusting of snow is on the lawn. It's going to be a long winter. I've always loved winter. Your father hated it. That was one of the reasons he didn't mind traveling so much. Arizona is warm all year, isn't it?"

When they passed the Drumdoe Inn, Meghan said, "Mom, look over there. When we get back I'm going to drop you at the inn. You're going to work, and I'm going to start looking for answers. Promise me you won't say anything about what Cyrus Graham told me yesterday. Remember, he only assumed the woman and girl Dad was with ten years ago were you and me. Dad never introduced them except by their names, Frances and Annie. But until we can do some checking on our own, let's not give the state attorney any more reason to destroy Dad's reputation."

MEGHAN AND CATHERINE WERE ESCORTED IMMEDIATELY TO John Dwyer's office. He was waiting there with investigators Bob Marron and Arlene Weiss. Meghan took the chair next to her mother, her hand protectively covering hers.

It was quickly apparent what was wanted. All three, the attorney and the officers, were convinced that Edwin Collins was alive and about to directly contact his wife and daughter. "The phone call, the flowers, now his car," Dwyer pointed out. "Mrs. Collins, you knew your husband had a gun permit?"

"Yes, I did. He got it about ten years ago"

"Where did he keep the gun?"

"Locked up in his office or at home."

"When did you last see it?"

"I don't remember having seen it in years."

Meghan broke in, "Why are you asking about my father's gun? Was it found in the car?"

"Yes, it was," John Dwyer said quietly.

"That wouldn't be unusual," Catherine said quickly. "He wanted it for the car. He had a terrible experience in Bridgeport ten years ago when he was stopped at a traffic light."

Dwyer turned to Meghan. "You were away all day in Philadelphia, Miss Collins. It's possible your father is aware of your movements and knew you had left Connecticut. He might have assumed that you could be found in your apartment. What I must emphatically request is that if Mr. Collins does contact either one of you, you must insist that he come here and talk with us. It will be much better for him in the long run."

"My husband won't be contacting us," Catherine said firmly. "Mr. Dwyer, didn't some people try to abandon their cars that night on the bridge?"

"Yes. I believe so."

"Wasn't a woman who left her car hit by one of the other vehicles, and didn't she barely escape being dragged over the side of the bridge?"

"Yes."

"Then consider this. My husband might have abandoned his car and gotten caught in that carnage. Someone else might have driven it away."

Meghan saw exasperation mingled with pity in the assistant state attorney's face.

Catherine Collins saw it too. She got up to go. "How long does it usually take Mrs. Black to reach a premise about a missing person?" she asked.

Dwyer exchanged glances with his investigators. "She already has," he said reluctantly. "She believes your husband has been dead a long time, that he is lying in water."

Catherine closed her eyes and swayed. Involuntarily, Meghan grasped her mother's arms, afraid she was about to faint.

Catherine's entire body was trembling. But when she opened her eyes, her voice was firm as she said, "I never thought I would find comfort in a message like that, but in this place, and listening to you, I *do* find comfort in it."

THE CONSENSUS OF THE MEDIA ABOUT STEPHANIE PETROVIC'S impassioned interview was that she was a disappointed potential heir. Her accusation of a possible plot by the Manning Clinic to kill her aunt was dismissed as frivolous. The clinic was owned by a private group of investors and run by Dr. Manning, whose credentials were impeccable. He still refused to speak to the press, but it was clear that in no way did he stand to personally gain by Helene Petrovic's bequest to embryo research at the clinic. After her outburst Stephanie had been taken to the office of a Manning Clinic senior staff member who would not comment on the conversation.

Helene's lawyer, Charles Potters, was appalled when he read about the episode. On Friday morning before the memorial mass, he came to the house and with ill-concealed outrage imparted his feelings to Stephanie. "No matter what her background turns out to be, your aunt was devoted to her work at the clinic. For you to create a scene like that would have been horrifying to her."

When he saw the misery in the young woman's face, he relented. "I know you've been through a great deal," he told her. "After the mass you'll have a chance to rest. I thought some of Helene's friends from St. Dominic's were planning to stay with you."

"I sent them home," Stephanie said. "I hardly know them, and I'm better off by myself."

After the lawyer left, she propped pillows on the couch and lay down. Her unwieldy body made it difficult to get comfortable. Her back hurt all the time now. She felt so alone. But she didn't want those old women around, eyeing her, talking about her.

She was grateful that Helene had left specific instructions that upon her death there was to be no wake, that her body was to be sent to Rumania and buried in her husband's grave.

She dozed off and was awakened by the peal of the telephone. Who now, she wondered wearily. It was a pleasant woman's voice. "Miss Petrovic?"

"Yes."

"I'm Meghan Collins from PCD Channel 3. I wasn't at the Manning Clinic when you were there yesterday, but I saw your statement on the eleven o'clock news."

"I don't want to talk about that. My aunt's lawyer is very upset with me."

"I wish you would talk with me. I might be able to help you."

"How can you help me? How can anyone help me?"

"There are ways. I'm calling from my car phone. I'm on my way to the mass. May I take you out to lunch afterwards?"

She sounds so friendly, Stephanie thought, and I need a friend. "I don't want to be on television again."

"I'm not asking you to be on television. I'm asking you to talk to me."

Stephanie hesitated. When the service is over, she thought, I don't want to be with Mr. Potters and I don't want to be with those old women from the Rumanian Society. They're all gossiping about me. "I'll go to lunch with you," she said.

MEGHAN DROPPED HER MOTHER AT THE INN, THEN DROVE to Trenton as fast as she dared.

On the way she made a second phone call to Tom Weicker's office to tell him that her father's car had been located.

"Does anyone else know about the car being found?" he asked quickly.

"Not yet. They're trying to keep it quiet. But we both know it's going to leak out." She tried to sound offhand. "At least Channel 3 can have the inside track."

"It's turning into a big story, Meg."

"I know it is."

"We'll run it immediately."

"That's why I'm giving it to you."

"Meg, I'm sorry."

"Don't be. There's a rational answer to all this."

"When is Mrs. Anderson's baby due?"

"They're putting her in the hospital on Monday. She's willing to have me go to her home Sunday afternoon and tape her and Jonathan getting the room ready for the baby. She has infant pictures of Jonathan that we can use. When the baby is born, we'll compare the newborn shots."

"Stay with it, at least for the present."

"Thanks, Tom," she said, "and thanks for the support."

PHILLIP CARTER SPENT MUCH OF FRIDAY AFTERNOON BEING questioned about Edwin Collins. With less and less patience, Carter answered questions that grew more and more pointed. "No, we have never had another instance in which there was a question of fraudulent credentials. Our reputation has been impeccable."

Arlene Weiss asked about the car. "When it was found in New York it had twenty-seven thousand miles on the odometer, Mr. Carter. According to the service record booklet, it had been serviced the preceding October, just a little over a year ago. At that time it had twenty-one thousand miles on it. How many miles did Mr. Collins put on the car in an average month?"

"I would say that depended entirely on his schedule. We have company cars and turn them in every three years. It's up to us to have them serviced. I'm fairly meticulous. Edwin tended to be a bit lax."

"Let me put it this way," Bob Marron said, "Mr. Collins

vanished in January. Between October last year and January, was it likely that he put six thousand miles on the car?"

"I don't know. I can give you his appointments for those months and try to figure out through expense accounts to which of those he would have driven."

"We need to try to estimate how much the car has been used since January," Marron said. "We'd also like to see the car phone bill for January."

"I assume you want to check on the time he made the call to Victor Orsini. The insurance company has already looked into that. The call was made less than a minute before the accident on the Tappan Zee Bridge."

They asked about Collins and Carter's financial status. "Our books are in order. They have been thoroughly audited. The last few years, like many businesses, we experienced the cutbacks of the recession. The kind of companies we deal with were letting people go, not hiring them. However, I know of no reason why Edwin would have had to borrow several hundred thousand dollars on his life insurance."

"Your firm would have received a commission from the Manning Clinic for placing Petrovic?"

"Of course."

"Did Collins pocket that commission?"

"No, the auditors found it."

"No one questioned Helene Petrovic's name on the $6,000 payment when it came in?"

"The copy of the Manning client statement in our files had been doctored. It reads 'Second installment due for placing Dr. Henry Williams.' There was no second installment due."

"Then clearly Collins didn't place her so he could swindle the firm out of $6,000."

"I would say that's obvious."

When they finally left, Phillip Carter tried without success to concentrate on the work on his desk. He could hear the phone in the outer office ringing. Jackie buzzed him on the intercom. A reporter from a supermarket tabloid was on the phone. Phillip curtly refused the call, realizing that the only calls that day had come from the media. Collins and Carter had not heard from a single client.

37

*M*eghan slipped into St. Dominic's church at twelve-thirty, at the midpoint of the sparsely attended mass for Helene Petrovic. In keeping with the wishes of the deceased, it was a simple ceremony without flowers or music.

There was a scattering of neighbors from Lawrenceville in attendance as well as a few older women from the Rumanian Society. Stephanie was seated with her lawyer, and as they left the church, Meghan introduced herself. The young woman seemed glad to see her.

"Let me say goodbye to these people," she said, "and then I'll join you."

Meghan watched as the polite murmurs of sympathy were expressed. She saw no great manifestation of grief from anyone. She walked over to two women who had just come out of church. "Did you know Helene Petrovic well?" she asked.

"As well as anyone," one of them replied pleasantly. "Some of us go to concerts together. Helene joined us occasionally. She was a member of the Rumanian Society and was notified of any of our activities. Sometimes she would show up."

"But not too often."

"No."

"Did she have any very close friends?"

The other woman shook her head. "Helene kept to herself."

"How about men? I met Mrs. Petrovic. She was a very attractive woman."

They both shook their heads. "If she had any special men friends, she never breathed a word about it."

Meghan noted that Stephanie was saying goodbye to the last of the people from church. As she walked over to join her, she heard the lawyer caution, "I wish you would not speak to that reporter. I'd be glad to drive you home or take you to lunch."

"I'll be fine."

Meghan took the young woman's arm as they walked down the rest of the steps. "These are pretty steep."

"And I'm so clumsy now. I keep getting in my own way."

"This is your territory," Meghan said when they were in the car. "Where would you like to eat?"

"Would you mind if we went back to the house? People have left so much food there, and I'm feeling so tired."

"Of course."

When they reached the Petrovic home, Meghan insisted that Stephanie rest while she prepared lunch. "Kick your shoes off and put your feet up on the couch," she said firmly. "We have a family inn, and I was raised in the kitchen there. I'm used to preparing meals."

As she heated soup and laid out a plate of cold chicken and salad, Meghan studied the surroundings. The kitchen had a French country house decor. The tiled walls and terracotta floor were clearly custom made. The appliances were top of the line. The round oak table and chairs were antiques. Obviously a lot of care—and money—had gone into the place.

They ate in the dining room. Here too the upholstered armchairs around the trestle table were obviously expensive. The table shone with the patina of fine old furniture. Where did the money come from? Meghan wondered. Helene had worked as a cosmetician until she got a job as a secretary in the clinic in Trenton, and from there she went to Manning.

Meghan did not have to ask questions. Stephanie was more than willing to discuss her problems. "They are going to sell this house. All the money from the sale and eight hundred thousand dollars is going to the clinic. But it's so unfair. My aunt promised to change her will. I'm her only relative. That's why she sent for me."

"What about the baby's father?" Meghan asked. "He can be made to help you."

"He's moved away."

"He can be traced. In this country there are laws to protect children. What is his name?"

Stephanie hesitated. "I don't want to have anything to do with him."

"You have a right to be taken care of."

"I'm going to give up the baby for adoption. It's the only way."

"It may not be the only way. What is his name and where did you meet him?"

"I . . . I met him at one of the Rumanian affairs in New York. His name is Jan. Helene had a headache that night and left early. He offered to drive me home." She looked down. "I don't like to talk about being so foolish."

"Did you go out with him often?"

"A few times."

"You told him about the baby?"

"He called to say he was going to California. That was when I told him. He said it was my problem."

"When was that?"

"Last March."

"What kind of work does he do?"

"He's a . . . mechanic. Please, Miss Collins, I don't want anything to do with him. Don't lots of people want babies?"

"Yes, they do. But that was what I meant when I said I could help you. If we find Jan, he'll have to support the baby and help you at least until you can get a job."

"Please leave him alone. I'm afraid of him. He was so angry."

"Angry because you told him he was the father of your baby?"

"Don't keep asking me about him!" Stephanie pushed her chair away from the table. "You said you'd help. Then find me people who will take the baby and give me some money."

Meghan said contritely, "I'm sorry, Stephanie. The last thing I came here to do was to upset you. Let's have a cup of tea. I'll clean up later."

In the living room she propped an extra pillow behind Stephanie's back and pulled an ottoman over for her feet.

Stephanie smiled apologetically. "You're very kind. I was rude. It is just that so much has happened so fast."

"Stephanie, what you're going to need is to have someone sponsor you for a green card until you can get a job. Surely your aunt had one good friend who might help you out."

"You mean if one of her friends sponsored me, I might be able to stay."

"Yes. Isn't there someone, maybe someone who owes your aunt a favor?"

Stephanie's expression brightened. "Oh, yes, there may indeed be someone. Thank you, Meghan."

"Who is the friend?" Meghan asked swiftly.

"I may be wrong," Stephanie said, suddenly nervous. "I must think about it."

She would not say anything more.

IT WAS TWO O'CLOCK. BERNIE HAD GOTTEN A COUPLE OF trips out of La Guardia Airport in the morning, then took a fare from Kennedy Airport to Bronxville.

He had had no intention of going to Connecticut that afternoon. But when he left the Cross County he found himself turning north. He had to go back to Newtown.

There was no car in the driveway of Meghan's house. He cruised along the curving road to the cul-de-sac, then turned around. The kid and his dog were nowhere in sight. That was good. He didn't want to be noticed.

He drove past Meghan's house again. He couldn't hang around here.

He drove past the Drumdoe Inn. Wait a minute, he thought. This is the place her mother owns. He'd read that in the paper yesterday. In an instant he'd made a U-turn and driven into the parking lot. There's got to be a bar, he thought. Maybe I can have a beer and even order a sandwich.

Suppose Meghan was there. He'd tell her the same story he told the others, that he was working for a local cable station in Elmira. There was no reason she shouldn't believe him.

The inn's lobby was medium size and had paneled walls and blue-and-red checked carpeting. There was no one behind the desk. To the right, he could see a few people in the dining room and busboys clearing tables. Well, lunch hour was pretty well over, he thought. The bar was to the left. He could see that it was empty, except for the bartender. He went to the bar, sat on one of the stools, ordered a beer and asked for the menu.

After he decided on a hamburger he started talking to the bartender. "This is a nice place."

"Sure is," the bartender agreed.

The guy had a name tag that read "Joe"; he looked to be about fifty. The local newspaper was on the back bar. Bernie pointed to it.

"I read yesterday's paper. Looks like the family that owns this place has a lot of problems."

"They sure do," Joe agreed. "Damn shame. Mrs. Collins is the nicest woman you'd ever want to know and her daughter, Meg, is a doll."

Two men came in and sat at the end of the bar. Joe filled their orders, then stayed talking with them. Bernie looked around as he finished his hamburger and beer. The back windows looked out over the parking lot. Beyond that was a wooded area that extended behind the Collins house.

Bernie had an interesting thought. If he drove here at night he could park in the lot with the cars from the dinner crowd and slip into the woods. Maybe from there he could take pictures of Meghan in her house. He had a zoom lens. It should be easy.

Before he left he asked Joe if they had valet parking.

"Just on Friday and Saturday nights," Joe told him.

Bernie nodded. He decided that he'd be back Sunday night.

MEGHAN LEFT STEPHANIE PETROVIC AT TWO O'CLOCK. AT THE door she said, "I'll keep in touch with you and I want to know when you're going to the hospital. It's tough to have your first baby without anyone close to you around."

"I'm getting scared about it," Stephanie admitted. "My mother had a hard time when I was born. I just want it over with."

The image of the troubled young face stayed with Meghan. Why was Stephanie so adamant about not trying to get child support from the father? Of course if she was determined to give the baby up for adoption, it was probably a moot point.

There was another stop Meghan wanted to make before she started home. Trenton was not far from Lawrenceville, and Helene Petrovic had worked there as a secretary in the Dowling Center, an assisted reproduction facility. Maybe somebody there would remember the woman, although she'd left the place for the Manning Clinic six years ago. Meghan was determined to find out more about her.

THE DOWLING ASSISTED REPRODUCTION CENTER WAS IN A small building connected to Valley Memorial Hospital. The reception room held only a desk and one chair. Clearly this place was not on the scale of the Manning Clinic.

Meghan did not show her PCD identification. She was not here as a reporter. When she told the receptionist she wanted to speak to someone about Helene Petrovic, the woman's face changed. "We have nothing more to say on the matter. Mrs. Petrovic worked here as a secretary for three years. She never was involved in any medical procedures."

"I believe that," Meghan said. "But my father is being held responsible for placing her at the Manning Clinic. I need to speak to someone who knew her well. I need to know if my father's firm ever requested a reference for her."

The woman looked hesitant.

"Please," Meghan said quietly.

"I'll see if the director is available."

THE DIRECTOR WAS A HANDSOME GRAY-HAIRED WOMAN OF about fifty. When Meghan was escorted into her office, she introduced herself as Dr. Keating. "I'm a Ph.D., not a physician," she said briskly. "I'm concerned with the business end of the center."

She had Helene Petrovic's file in her drawer. "The state attorney's office in Connecticut requested a copy of this two days ago," she commented.

"Do you mind if I take notes?" Meghan asked.

"Not at all."

The file contained information that had been reported in the papers. On her application form to Dowling, Helene Petrovic had been truthful. She had applied for a secretarial position, giving her work background as a cosmetician and citing her recently acquired certificate from the Woods Secretarial School in New York.

"Her references checked out," Dr. Keating said. "She made a nice appearance and had a pleasant manner. I hired her and was very satisfied with her the three years she was here."

"When she left, did she tell you she was going to the Manning Clinic?"

"No. She said that she planned to take a job as a cosmetician in New York again. She said a friend was opening a salon. That's why we didn't find it surprising that we were never contacted for a reference."

"Then you had no dealings with Collins and Carter Executive Search?"

"None at all."

"Dr. Keating, Mrs. Petrovic managed to pull the wool over the eyes of the medical staff in the Manning Clinic. Where do you think she got the knowledge to handle cryopreserved embryos?"

Keating frowned. "As I told the Connecticut investigators, Helene was fascinated with medicine and particularly the kind that is done here, the process of assisted reproduction. She used to read the medical books when work was slow and often would visit the laboratory and observe what was going on there. I might add that she would never have been allowed to step into the laboratory alone. As a matter of fact, we never allow fewer than two qualified staff people to be present. It's a sort of fail-safe system. I think it should be a law in every facility of this kind."

"Then you think she picked up her medical knowledge through observation and reading?"

"It's hard to believe that someone who had no opportunity to do hands-on work under supervision would be able to fool experts, but it's the only explanation I have."

"Dr. Keating, all I hear is that Helene Petrovic was very nice, well respected but a loner. Was that true here?"

"I would say so. To the best of my knowledge she never socialized with the other secretaries or anyone on this staff."

"No male friends?"

"I don't know for sure, but I always suspected that she was seeing someone from the hospital. Several times when she was away from her desk one of the other girls picked up her phone. They began to tease her about who was her Dr. Kildare. Apparently the message was to call an extension in the hospital."

"You wouldn't know which extension?"

"It was over six years ago."

"Of course." Meghan got up. "Dr. Keating, you've been so kind. May I give you my phone number just in case you remember anything that you think might be of assistance?"

Keating reached out her hand. "I know the circumstances, Miss Collins. I wish I could help."

When she was getting into her car, Meghan studied the impressive structure that was Valley Memorial Hospital. Ten stories high, half the length of a city block, hundreds of windows from which lights were beginning to gleam in the late afternoon.

Was it possible that behind one of those windows there was a doctor who had helped Helene Petrovic to perfect her dangerous deception?

MEGHAN WAS EXITING ONTO ROUTE 7 WHEN THE FIVE o'clock news came on. She listened to the WPCD radio station bulletin: "Assistant State Attorney John Dwyer has confirmed that the car Edwin Collins was driving the night of the Tappan Zee Bridge disaster last January has been located outside the Manhattan apartment of his daughter. Ballistic tests show that Collins' gun, found in the car, was the murder weapon that killed Helene Petrovic, the laboratory worker whose fraudulent credentials he allegedly presented to the Manning Clinic. A warrant has just been issued for Edwin Collins' arrest on suspicion of homicide."

38

*D*r. George Manning left the clinic at five o'clock on Friday afternoon. Three new patients had canceled their appointments, so far only a half dozen or so worried parents had called to inquire about DNA tests to assure themselves that their children were their biological offspring. Dr. Manning knew that it would take only one verified case of a mixup to cause alarm in every woman who had borne a child through treatment at the clinic. For good and sufficient reasons he dreaded the next few days.

Wearily he drove the eight miles to his home in South Kent. It was such a shame, such a damn shame, he thought. Ten years of hard work and a national reputation ruined, virtually overnight. Less than a week ago he had been celebrating the annual reunion and looking forward to retirement. On his seventieth birthday last January he had announced that he would stay at his post just one more year.

The most galling memory was that Edwin Collins had called when he read an account of the birthday celebration and retirement plans and asked if Collins and Carter could once again serve the Manning Clinic!

ON FRIDAY EVENING, WHEN DINA ANDERSON PUT HER THREE-year-old son to bed, she hugged him fiercely. "Jonathan, I think your twin isn't going to wait till Monday to be born," she told him.

"How's it going, honey?" her husband asked when she went downstairs.

"Five minutes apart."

"I'd better alert the doctor."

"So much for Jonathan and me being on-camera, getting the room ready for Ryan." She winced. "You'd better tell my mother to get right over, and let the doctor know I'm on my way to the hospital."

HALF AN HOUR LATER, IN DANBURY MEDICAL CENTER, DINA Anderson was being examined. "Would you believe the contractions stopped?" she asked in disgust.

"We're going to keep you," the obstetrician told her. "If nothing happens during the night, we'll start an IV to induce labor in the morning. You might as well go home, Don."

Dina pulled her husband's face down for a kiss. "Don't look so worried, Daddy. Oh, and will you phone Meghan Collins and alert her that Ryan will probably be around by tomorrow. She wants to be there to tape him as soon as he's in the nursery. Be sure to bring the pictures of Jonathan as a newborn. She's going to show them with the baby so everyone can see that they're exactly alike. And let Dr. Manning know. He was so sweet. He called today to ask how I was doing."

THE NEXT MORNING, MEGHAN AND HER CAMERAMAN, STEVE, were in the lobby of the hospital, awaiting word of the delivery of Ryan. Donald Anderson had given them Jonathan's newborn infant pictures. When the baby was in the nursery, they would be allowed to videotape him. Jonathan would be brought to the hospital by Dina's mother, and they'd be able to take a brief shot of the family together.

With a reporter's eye, Meghan observed the activity in the lobby. A young mother, her infant in her arms, was being wheeled to the door by a nurse. Her husband followed, struggling with suitcases and flower arrangements. From one of the bouquets floated a pink balloon inscribed, "It's a Girl."

An exhausted-looking couple came out of the elevator holding the hands of a four-year-old with a cast on his arm and a bandage on his head. An expectant mother crossed the lobby and entered the door marked ADMITTANCE.

Seeing these families, Meghan was reminded of Kyle. What kind of mother would walk out on a six-month-old baby?

The cameraman was studying Jonathan's pictures. "I'll get the same angle," he said. "Kind of weird when you think you know exactly what the kid's gonna look like."

"Look," Meghan said. "That's Dr. Manning coming in. I wonder if he's here because of the Andersons."

· · ·

UPSTAIRS IN THE DELIVERY ROOM, A LOUD WAIL BROUGHT A smile to the faces of the doctors, the nurses and the Andersons. Pale and exhausted, Dina looked up at her husband and saw the shock on his face. Frantically she pulled herself up on one elbow. "Is he okay?" she cried. "Let me see him."

"He's fine, Dina," the doctor said, holding up the squalling infant with the shock of bright red hair.

"That's not Jonathan's twin!" Dina screamed. "Whose baby have I been carrying?"

39

"It always rains on Saturday," Kyle grumbled as he flipped from channel to channel on the television set. He was sitting cross-legged on the carpet, Jake beside him.

Mac was deep in the morning paper. "Not always," he said absently. He glanced at his watch. It was almost noon. "Turn to Channel 3. I want to catch the news."

"Okay." Kyle clicked the remote. "Look, there's Meg!"

Mac dropped the paper. "Turn up the volume."

"You're always telling me to turn it down."

"Kyle!"

"Okay. Okay."

Meg was standing in the lobby of a hospital. "There is a frightening new development in the Manning Clinic case. Following the murder of Helene Petrovic, and the discovery of her fraudulent credentials, there has been concern that the late Ms. Petrovic may have made serious mistakes in handling the cryopreserved embryos. An hour ago a baby, expected to be the clone of his three-year-old brother, was born here in Danbury Medical Center."

Mac and Kyle watched as the camera angle widened.

"With me is Dr. Allan Neitzer, the obstetrician who just delivered Dina Anderson of a son. Doctor, will you tell us about the baby?"

"The baby is a healthy, beautiful eight-pound boy."

"But it is not the identical twin of the Andersons' three-year-old son?"

"No, it is not."

"Is it Dina Anderson's biological child?"

"Only DNA tests can establish that."

"How long will they take?"

"Four to six weeks."

"How are the Andersons reacting?"

"Very upset. Very worried."

"Dr. Manning was here. He went upstairs before we could speak to him. Has he seen the Andersons?"

"I can't comment on that."

"Thank you, Doctor." Meghan turned to face the camera directly. "We'll be here with this unfolding story. Back to you in the newsroom, Mike."

"Turn it off, Kyle."

Kyle pressed the remote button, and the screen went blank. "What did that mean?"

It means big problems, Mac thought. How many more mistakes had Helene Petrovic made at Manning? Whatever they were, no doubt Edwin Collins would be held equally responsible for them. "It's pretty complicated, Kyle."

"Is anything wrong for Meg? "

Mac looked into his son's face. The sandy hair so like his own that never stayed in place was falling on his forehead. The brown eyes that he'd inherited from Ginger had lost their usual merry twinkle. Except for the color of the eyes, Kyle was a MacIntyre through and through. What would it be like, Mac wondered, to look in your son's face and realize he might not belong to you.

He put an arm around Kyle. "Things have been rough for Meg lately. That's why she looks worried."

"Next to you and Jake, she's my best friend," Kyle said soberly.

At the mention of his name, Jake thumped his tail.

Mac smiled wryly. "I'm sure Meg will be flattered to hear it." Not for the first time in these last few days, he wondered if his blind stupidity in not realizing his feelings for Meg had forever relegated him in her eyes to the status of friend and buddy.

MEGHAN AND THE CAMERAMAN SAT IN THE LOBBY OF DAN-bury Medical Center. Steve seemed to know that she did not want to talk. Neither Donald Anderson nor Dr. Manning had come downstairs.

"Look, Meg," Steve said suddenly, "isn't that the other Anderson kid?"

"Yes, it is. That must be the grandmother with him."

They both jumped up, followed them across the lobby and caught them at the elevator. Meg turned on the mike. Steve began to roll tape.

"I wonder if you would speak to us for a moment," Meghan asked the woman. "Aren't you Dina Anderson's mother and Jonathan's grandmother?"

"Yes, I am." The well-bred voice was distressed. Silver hair framed a troubled face.

By her expression, Meghan knew the woman was aware of the problem.

"Have you spoken to your daughter or son-in-law since the baby was born?"

"My son-in-law phoned me. Please. We want to get up-stairs. My daughter needs me." She stepped into the elevator, the little boy's hand grasped tightly in her own.

Meghan did not try to detain her.

Jonathan was wearing a blue jacket that matched the blue of his eyes. His cheeks were rosy accents to his fair complexion. His hood was down, and raindrops had beaded the white-gold hair that was shaped in Buster Brown style. He smiled and waved. "Bye-bye," he called as the elevator doors began to close.

"That's some good-looking kid," Steve observed.

"He's beautiful," Meghan agreed.

They returned to their seats. "Do you think Manning will give a statement?" Steve asked.

"If I were Dr. Manning, I'd be talking to my lawyers." And Collins and Carter Executive Search will need their lawyers too, she thought.

Meghan's beeper sounded. She pulled out her cellular phone, called the news desk and was told that Tom Weicker wanted to talk to her. "If Tom's in on Saturday, something's up," she murmured.

Something was up. Weicker got right to the point. "Meg, Dennis Cimini is on his way to relieve you. He took a helicopter, so he should be there soon."

She was not surprised. The special about identical twins being born three years apart had become a much bigger story. It was now tied into the Manning Clinic scandal and the murder of Helene Petrovic.

"All right, Tom." She sensed there was more.

"Meg, you told the Connecticut authorities about the dead woman who resembles you and the fact that she had a note in her pocket in your father's handwriting."

"I felt I had to tell them. I was sure the New York detectives would contact them at some point about it."

"There's been a leak somewhere. They also learned that you went to the morgue for a DNA test. We've got to carry the story right away. The other stations have it."

"I understand, Tom."

"Meg, as of now you're on leave. Paid leave of course."

"All right."

"I'm sorry, Meg."

"I know you are. Thanks." She broke the connection. Dennis Cimini was coming through the revolving door to the lobby. "I guess that does it. See you around, Steve," she said. She hoped her bitter disappointment wasn't obvious to him.

40

*T*here was an auction coming up on property near the Rhode Island border. Phillip Carter had planned to take a look at it.

He needed a day away from the office and the myriad problems of the past week. The media had been omnipresent. The investigators had been in and out. A talk show host had actually asked him to be on a program about missing persons.

Victor Orsini had not been off the mark when he said that every word uttered or printed about Helene Petrovic's fraudulent credentials was a nail in the coffin of Collins and Carter.

On Saturday just before noon, Carter was at his front door when the phone rang. He debated about answering, then picked up the receiver. It was Orsini.

"Phillip, I had the television on. The fat's in the fire. Helene Petrovic's first known mistake at the Manning Clinic was just born."

"What's that supposed to mean?"

Orsini explained. As Phillip listened, his blood chilled.

"This is just the beginning," Orsini said. "How much insurance does the company have to cover this?"

"There isn't enough insurance in the world to cover it," Carter said quietly as he hung up.

You believe you have everything under control, he thought, but you never do. Panic was not a familiar emotion, but suddenly events were closing in on him.

In the next moment he was thinking of Catherine and Meghan. There was no further consideration of a leisurely drive to the country. He would call Meg and Catherine later. Maybe he could join them for dinner this evening. He wanted to know what they were doing, what they were thinking.

WHEN MEG GOT HOME AT ONE-THIRTY, CATHERINE HAD lunch ready. She'd seen the news brief broadcast from the hospital.

"It was probably my last one for Channel 3," Meg said quietly.

For a little while, both too overwhelmed to speak, the two women ate in silence. Then Meg said, "Mom, as bad as it is for us, can you imagine how the women feel who underwent in vitro fertilization at the Manning Clinic? With the Anderson mix-up there isn't one of them who isn't going to wonder if she received her own embryo. What will happen when errors can be traced and a biological and host mother both claim the same child?"

"I can imagine what it would be like." Catherine Collins reached across the table and grasped Meg's hand. "Meggie, I've lived for nearly nine months on such an emotional seesaw that I'm punch drunk."

"Mom, I know how it's been for you."

"Hear me out. I have no idea how all this will end, but I do know one thing. *I can't lose you.* If somebody killed that poor girl thinking it was you, I can only pity her with all my heart and thank God on my knees that you're the one who's alive."

They both jumped as the door bell rang.

"I'll get it," Meg said.

It was an insured package for Catherine. She ripped it open. Inside was a note and a small box. She read the note aloud: "Dear Mrs. Collins, I am returning your husband's wedding ring. I have rarely felt such certainty as I did when I told investigator Bob Marron that Edwin Collins died many months ago.

"My thoughts and prayers are with you, Fiona Campbell Black."

Meghan realized that she was glad to see tears wash away some of the pain that was etched on her mother's face.

Catherine took the slender gold ring from the box and closed her hand over it.

41

*L*ate Saturday in Danbury Medical Center, a sedated Dina Anderson was dozing in bed, Jonathan asleep beside her. Her husband and mother were sitting silently by the bedside. The obstetrician, Dr. Neitzer, came to the door and beckoned to Don.

He stepped outside. "Any word?"

The doctor nodded. "Good, I hope. On checking your blood type, your wife's, Jonathan's and the baby's, we find that the baby certainly could be your biological child. You are A positive, your wife is O negative, the baby is O positive."

"Jonathan is A positive."

"Which is the other blood type consistent with the child of A positive and O negative parents."

"I don't know what to think," Don said. "Dina's mother swears the baby looks like her own brother when he was born. There's red hair on that side of the family."

"The DNA test will establish absolutely whether or not the baby is biologically yours, but that will take four weeks minimum."

"And what do we do in the meantime?" Don asked, angrily. "Bond to it, love it and maybe find out we have to give it to someone else from the Manning Clinic? Or do we let it lie in a nursery until we know whether or not it's ours?"

"It isn't good for any baby in the early weeks of life to be left in a nursery," Doctor Neitzer replied. "Even our very sick babies are handled as much as possible by the mothers and fathers. And Dr. Manning says—"

"Nothing Dr. Manning says interests me," Don interrupted. "All I've ever heard since the embryo split nearly four years ago was how the embryo of Jonathan's twin was in a specially marked tube."

"Don, where are you?" a weak voice called.

Anderson and Dr. Neitzer went back into the room. Dina and Jonathan were both awake. She said, "Jonathan wants to see his new brother."

"Honey, I don't know . . ."

Dina's mother stood up and looked hopefully at her daughter.

"I do. I agree with Jonathan. I carried that baby for nine months. For the first three I was spotting and terrified I'd lose it. The first moment I felt life I was so happy I cried. I love coffee and couldn't have one sip of it because that kid doesn't like coffee. He's been kicking me so hard I haven't had a decent sleep in three months. Whether or not he's my biological child, by God I've earned him and I want him."

"Honey, Dr. Neitzer says the blood tests show it may be our child."

"That's good. Now, will you please have someone bring my baby to me."

. . .

AT TWO-THIRTY DR. MANNING, ACCOMPANIED BY HIS LAWYER
and a hospital official, entered the hospital's auditorium.

The hospital official made a firm announcement. "Dr.
Manning will read a prepared statement. He will not take
questions. After that I request that all of you leave the premises. The Andersons will not make any statements, nor will
they permit any pictures."

Dr. Manning's silver hair was rumpled, and his kindly face
was strained as he put on his glasses and in a hoarse voice
began to read:

"I can only apologize for the distress the Anderson family
is experiencing. I firmly believe Mrs. Anderson gave birth to
her own biological child today. She had two cryopreserved
embryos in the laboratory at our clinic. One was her son
Jonathan's identical twin; the other his sibling.

"Last Monday, Helene Petrovic admitted to me that she
had had an accident in the laboratory at the time she was
handling the Petri dishes containing those two embryos. She
slipped and fell. Her hand hit and overturned one of the lab
dishes before the embryos were transferred to the test tubes.
She believed the remaining dish contained the identical twin
and put it in the specially marked tube. The other embryo
was lost."

Dr. Manning took off his glasses and looked up.

"If Helene Petrovic was telling the truth, and I have no
reason to doubt it, I repeat, Dina Anderson today gave birth
to her biological son."

Questions were shouted at him. "Why didn't Petrovic tell
you at that time?"

"Why didn't you warn the Andersons immediately?"

"How many more mistakes do you think she made?"

Dr. Manning ignored them all and walked unsteadily from
the room.

. . .

VICTOR ORSINI CALLED PHILLIP CARTER AFTER THE SATUR-
day evening news broadcast. "You'd better think of getting
lawyers in to represent the firm," he told Carter.

Carter was just ready to leave for dinner at the Drumdoe
Inn. "I agree. This is too big for Leiber to handle, but he can
probably recommend someone."

Leiber was the lawyer the company kept on retainer.

"Phillip, if you don't have plans for the evening, how about
dinner? There's an old saying, misery loves company."

"Then I've got the right plans. I'm meeting Catherine and
Meg Collins."

"Give them my best. See you Monday."

Orsini hung up and walked over to the window. Candlewood Lake was tranquil tonight. The lights from the houses
that bordered it were brighter than usual. Dinner parties,
Orsini thought. He was sure his name would come up at all
of them. Everyone around here knew he worked for Collins
and Carter.

His call to Phillip Carter had elicited the information he
wanted: Carter was safely tied up for the evening. Victor
could go to the office now. He'd be absolutely alone and
could spend a couple of hours going through the personal
files in Edwin Collins' office. Something had begun to nag at
him, and it was vital that he give those files a final check
before Meghan moved them out.

MEGHAN, MAC AND PHILLIP MET FOR DINNER AT THE
Drumdoe Inn at seven-thirty. Catherine was in the kitchen
where she'd been since four o'clock.

"Your mother has guts," Mac said.

"You bet she does," Meg agreed. "Did you catch the
evening news? I watched PCD, and the lead story was the
combination of the Anderson baby mix-up, the Petrovic
murder, my resemblance to the woman in the morgue and
the warrant for Dad's arrest. I gather all the stations led
with it."

"I know," Mac said quietly.

Phillip raised his hand in a gesture of helplessness. "Meg, I'd do anything to help you and your mother, anything to try to find some explanation for Edwin sending Petrovic to Manning."

"There is an explanation," Meg said. "I believe that and so does Mother, which is what gave her the courage to come down here and put on an apron."

"She's not planning to handle the kitchen herself indefinitely?" Phillip protested.

"No. Tony, the head chef who retired last summer, phoned today and offered to come back and help out for a while. I told him that was wonderful but warned him not to take over. The busier Mother is, the better for her. But he's in there now. She'll be able to join us soon."

Meghan felt Mac's eyes on her and looked down to avoid the compassion she saw in them. She had known that tonight everyone in the dining room would be studying her and her mother to see how they were holding up. She had deliberately chosen to wear red: a calf-length skirt and cowl-neck cashmere sweater with gold jewelry.

She'd made herself up carefully with blusher and lipstick and eyeshadow. I guess I don't look like an unemployed reporter, she decided, glimpsing herself in the mirror as she left the house.

The disconcerting part was that she was sure that Mac could see behind her façade. He'd guess that in addition to everything else, she was worried sick about her job.

Mac had ordered wine. When it was poured, he raised his glass to her. "I have a message from Kyle. When he knew we were having dinner together he said to tell you he's coming to scare you tomorrow night."

Meg smiled. "Of course; tomorrow's Halloween. What's Kyle wearing?"

"Very original. He's a ghost, a really scary ghost, or so he claims. I'm taking him and some other kids trick-or-treating tomorrow afternoon, but he wants to save you for tomorrow night. So if there's a thump on the window after dark, be prepared."

"I'll make sure I'm home. Look, here's Mother."

Catherine kept a smile on her lips as she walked across the dining room. She was constantly stopped by people jumping up from their tables to embrace her. When she joined them, she said, "I'm so glad we came here. It's a heck of a lot better than sitting at home thinking."

"You look *wonderful,*" Phillip said. "You're a real trouper."

The admiration in his eyes was not lost on Meg. She glanced at Mac. He had seen it too.

Be careful, Phillip. Don't crowd Mother, Meghan thought.

She studied her mother's rings. The diamonds and emeralds she was wearing shone brilliantly under the small table lamp. Earlier that evening her mother had told her that on Monday she intended to hock or sell her jewelry. A big tax payment was due on the inn the following week. Catherine had said, "My only regret about giving up the jewelry is that I so wanted it for you."

I don't care about myself, Meg thought now, but . . .

"Meg? Are you ready to order?"

"Oh, sorry." Meghan smiled apologetically and glanced down at the menu in her hand.

"Try the Beef Wellington," Catherine said. "It's terrific. I should know. I made it."

During dinner, Meg was grateful that Mac and Phillip steered the conversation onto safe subjects, everything from the proposed paving of local roads to Kyle's championship soccer team.

Over cappuccino, Phillip asked Meg what her plans were. "I'm so sorry about the job," he said.

Meg shrugged. "I'm certainly not happy about it, but maybe it will turn out all right. You see, I keep thinking that nobody really knows anything about Helene Petrovic. She's the key to all this. I'm determined to turn up something about her that may give us some answers."

"I wish you would," Phillip said. "God knows *I'd* like some answers."

"Something else," Meg added, "I never got to clear out Dad's office. Would you mind if I go in tomorrow?"

"Go in whenever you want, Meg. Can I help you?"

"No thanks. I'll be fine."

"Meg, call me when you're finished," Mac said. "I'll come over and carry things to the car."

"Tomorrow's your day to trick or treat with Kyle," Meg reminded him. "I can handle it." She smiled at the two men. "Many thanks, guys, for being with us tonight. It's good to have friends at a time like this."

IN SCOTTSDALE, ARIZONA, AT NINE O'CLOCK ON SATURDAY night, Frances Grolier sighed as she put down her pearwood-handled knife. She had a commission to do a fifteen-inch bronze of a young Navaho boy and girl as a presentation to the guest of honor at a fund-raising dinner. The deadline was fast approaching and Frances was totally unsatisfied with the clay model she had been working on.

She had not managed to capture the questioning expression she had seen in the sensitive faces of the children. The pictures she had taken of them had caught it, but her hands were simply unable to execute her clear vision of what the sculpture should be.

The trouble was that she simply could not concentrate on her work.

Annie. She had not heard from her daughter for nearly two weeks now. All the messages she'd left on her answering machine had been ignored. In the last few days she'd called Annie's closest friends. No one had seen her.

She could be anywhere, Frances thought. She could have accepted an assignment to do a travel article on some remote, godforsaken place. As a free-lance travel writer, Annie came and went on no set schedule.

I raised her to be independent, Frances told herself. I raised her to be free, to take chances, to take from life what she wanted.

Did I teach her that to justify my own life? she wondered.

It was a thought that had come to her repeatedly in the last few days.

There was no use trying to work any more tonight. She went to the fireplace and added logs from the basket. The day had been warm and bright, but now the desert night was sharply cool.

The house was so quiet. There might never again be the heart-pounding anticipation of knowing that he was coming soon. As a little girl, Annie often asked why Daddy traveled so much.

"He has a very important job with the government," Frances would tell her.

As Annie grew up she became more curious. "What kind of job is it, Dad?"

"Oh, a sort of watchdog, honey."

"Are you in the CIA?"

"If I were, I'd never tell you."

"You are, aren't you?"

"Annie, I work for the government and get a lot of frequent-flyer miles in the process."

Remembering, Frances went into the kitchen, put ice in a glass and poured a generous amount of Scotch over it. Not the best way to solve problems, she told herself.

She put the drink down, went into the bath off the bedroom and showered, scrubbing away the bits of dried clay that were clinging to the crevices in her palms. Putting on gray silk pajamas and a robe, she retrieved the Scotch and settled on the couch in front of the fireplace. Then she picked up the Associated Press item she had torn from page ten of the morning newspaper, a summary of the report issued by the New York State Thruway Authority on the Tappan Zee Bridge disaster.

In part it read: "The number of victims who perished in the accident has been reduced from eight to seven. Exhaustive search has revealed no trace of the body of Edwin R. Collins, nor wreckage from his car."

Now Frances was haunted by the question, is it possible that Edwin is still alive?

He'd been so upset about business the morning he left.

He'd had a growing fear that his double life would be exposed and that both his daughters would despise him.

He'd had chest pains recently, which were diagnosed as being caused by anxiety.

He'd given her a bearer bond for two hundred thousand dollars in December. "In case anything happens to me," he had said. Had he been planning to find a way to drop out of both his lives when he said that?

And where was Annie? Frances agonized, with a growing sense of foreboding.

Edwin had an answering machine in his private office. Over the years, if Frances ever had to reach him, the arrangement was that she would call between midnight and 5 A.M. Eastern time. He always beeped in for messages by six o'clock and then erased them.

Of course that number was disconnected. Or was it?

It was a few minutes past ten in Arizona, past midnight on the East Coast.

She picked up the receiver and dialed. After two rings, Ed's recorded announcement began. "You have reached 203-555-2867. At the beep please leave a brief message."

Frances was so startled at hearing his voice that she almost forgot why she was calling. Could this possibly mean that he is alive? she wondered. And if Ed is alive somewhere, does he ever check this machine?

She had nothing to lose. Hurriedly Frances left the message they'd agreed upon. "Mr. Collins, please call Palomino Leather Goods. If you're still interested in that briefcase, we have it in stock."

. . .

VICTOR ORSINI WAS IN EDWIN COLLINS' OFFICE, STILL GOING through the files, when the private phone rang. He jumped. Who in hell would call an office at this hour?

The answering machine clicked on. Sitting in Collins' chair, Orsini listened to the modulated voice as it left the brief message.

When the call was completed, Orsini sat staring at the machine for long minutes. No business calls about a briefcase are made at this hour, he thought. That's some kind of code. Someone expects Ed Collins to get that message. It was one more confirmation that some mysterious person believed Ed was alive and out there somewhere.

A few minutes later, Victor left. He had not found the object of his search.

42

On Sunday morning, Catherine Collins attended the ten o'clock mass at St. Paul's, but she found it difficult to keep her mind on the sermon. She had been christened in this church, married in it, buried her parents from it. She had always found comfort here. For so long she had prayed at mass that Edwin's body would be found, prayed for resignation to his loss, for the strength to go on without him.

What was she asking of God now? Only that He keep Meg safe. She glanced at Meg, sitting beside her, completely still, seemingly attentive to the homily, but Catherine suspected that her daughter's thoughts were far away as well.

A fragment from the *Dies Irae* came unbidden into Catherine's mind. "Day of wrath and day of mourning. Lo, the world in ashes burning."

I'm angry and I'm hurt and my world is in ashes, Catherine thought. She blinked back sudden tears and felt Meg's hand close over hers.

When they left church they stopped for coffee and sticky buns at the local bakery, which had a half-dozen tables in the rear of the shop. "Feel better?" Meg asked.

"Yes," Catherine said briskly. "These sticky buns will do it every time. I'm going with you to Dad's office."

"I thought we'd agreed I should clear it out. That's why we're in two cars."

"It's no easier for you than it is for me. It will go faster if we're together, and some of that stuff will be heavy to carry."

Her mother's voice held the note of finality that Meghan knew ended further debate.

MEGHAN'S CAR WAS FILLED WITH BOXES FOR PACKING. SHE and her mother lugged them to the building. When they opened the door into the Collins and Carter office suite, they were surprised to find that it was warm and the lights were on.

"Ten to one Phillip came in early to get the place ready," Catherine observed. She looked around the reception room. "It's surprising how seldom I came here," she said. "Your dad traveled so much, and even when he wasn't on the road he was usually out on appointments. And of course I was always tied to the inn."

"I probably was here more than you," Meg agreed. "I used to come here after school sometimes and catch a ride home with him."

She pushed open the door to her father's private office. "It's just as he left it," she told her mother. "Phillip has been awfully generous to keep it undisturbed this long. I know Victor really should have been using it."

For a long moment they both studied the room: his desk,

the long table behind it with their pictures, the wall unit with bookcases and file cabinets in the same cherrywood finish as the desk. The effect was uncluttered and tasteful.

"Edwin bought and refinished that desk," Catherine said. "I'm sure Phillip wouldn't mind if we had it picked up."

"I'm sure he wouldn't."

They began by collecting the pictures and stacking them in a box. Meghan knew they both sensed that the faster the office took on an impersonal look, the easier it would be. Then she suggested, "Mom, why don't you start with the books. I'll go through the desk and files."

It was only when she was seated at the desk that she saw the blinking light on the answering machine, which sat on a low table next to the swivel chair.

"Look at this."

Her mother came over to the desk. "Is anyone still leaving messages on Dad's machine?" she asked incredulously, then leaned down to look at the call display. "There's just one. Let's hear it."

Bewildered, they listened to the message and then the computer voice of the machine saying, "Sunday, October thirty-first, 12:09 A.M. End of final message."

"That message came in only hours ago!" Catherine exclaimed. "Who leaves a business message in the middle of the night? And when would Dad have ordered a brief-case?"

"It could be a mistake," Meghan said. "Whoever called didn't leave a return number or a name."

"Wouldn't most salespeople leave a phone number if they wanted to confirm an order, especially if the order was placed months ago? Meg, that message doesn't make sense. And that woman doesn't sound like an order clerk to me."

Meg slipped the tape out of the machine and put it in her shoulder bag. "It doesn't make sense," she agreed. "We're only wasting time trying to figure it out here. Let's get on with this packing and listen to it again at home."

She looked quickly through the desk drawers and found

the usual assortment of stationery, notepads, paper clips, pens and highlighters. She remembered that when he went over a candidate's curriculum vitae, her father had marked the most favorable aspects of the résumé in yellow, the least favorable in pink. Quickly she transferred the contents of the desk to boxes.

Next she tackled the files. The first one seemed to have copies of her father's expense account reports. Apparently the bookkeeper kept the original and returned a photocopy with Paid stamped across the top.

"I'm going to take these files home," she said. "They're Dad's personal copies of originals already in the company records."

"Is there any point in taking them?"

"Yes, there just might be some reference to Palomino Leather Goods."

They were finishing the last box when they heard the outside door open. "It's me," Phillip called.

He came in, wearing a shirt open at the neck, sleeveless sweater, corduroy jacket and slacks. "Hope it was comfortable when you got here," he said. "I stopped by this morning for a minute. This place gets mighty chilly over a weekend if the thermostat is down."

He surveyed the boxes. "I knew you'd need a hand. Catherine, will you please put down that box of books."

"Dad called her 'Mighty Mouse,' " Meg said. "This is nice of you, Phillip."

He saw the top of an expense file sticking out of one of the boxes. "Are you sure you want all that stuff? It's nuts and bolts, and you and I went all through it, Meg, looking for any insurance policies that might not have been in the safe."

"We might as well take it," Meg said. "You'd only have to dispose of it anyhow."

"Phillip, the answering machine was blinking when we came in here." Meghan took out the tape, snapped it into the machine and played it.

She saw the look of astonishment on his face. "Obviously you don't get it either."

"No. I don't."

It was fortunate that both she and her mother had brought their cars. The trunks and backseats were crammed by the time the last box had been carried down.

They refused Phillip's offer to follow them and help unload. "I'll have a couple of the busboys from the inn take care of it," Catherine said.

As Meghan drove home she knew that every hour she was not tracking down information on Helene Petrovic she would be going through every line of every page of her father's records.

If there was someone else in Dad's life, she thought, and if that woman in the morgue is the Annie that Cyrus Graham met ten years ago, there might be some link in his files that I can trace back to them.

Some instinct told her that Palomino Leather Goods might prove to be that link.

IN KYLE'S EYES, THE TRICK-OR-TREATING HAD BEEN ABSO-lutely great. On Sunday evening he spread his collection of assorted candies, cookies, apples and pennies on the den floor while Mac prepared dinner.

"Don't eat any of that junk now," Mac warned.

"I know, Dad. You told me twice."

"Then maybe it'll start sinking in." Mac tested the hamburgers on the grill.

"Why do we always have hamburgers on Sunday when we're home?" Kyle asked. "They're better at McDonald's."

"Many thanks." Mac flipped them onto toasted buns. "We have hamburgers on Sunday because I cook hamburgers better than anything else. I take you out most Fridays. I make pasta when we're home on Saturdays, and Mrs. Dileo cooks good food the rest of the week. Now eat up if you want to put your costume on again and scare Meg."

Kyle took a couple of bites of his hamburger. "Do you like Meg, Dad?"

"Yes, I do. Very much. Why?"

"I wish she'd come here more. She's fun."

I wish she'd come here more too, Mac thought, but it doesn't look as though that's going to happen. Last night when he'd offered to help her with the packing up of her father's office she'd cut him off so fast his head had been spinning.

Stay away. Don't get too close. We're just friends. She might as well put up a sign.

She'd certainly grown up a lot from the nineteen-year-old kid who had a crush on him and wrote a letter telling him she loved him and please don't marry Ginger.

He wished he had the letter now. He also wished she'd feel that way again. He certainly regretted he hadn't taken her advice about Ginger.

Then Mac looked at his son. No I don't, he thought. I couldn't and wouldn't undo having this kid.

"Dad, what's the matter?" Kyle asked. "You look worried."

"That's what you said about Meg when you saw her on television yesterday."

"Well, she did and so do you."

"I'm just worried that I might have to learn how to cook something else. Finish up and get your costume on."

IT WAS SEVEN-THIRTY WHEN THEY LEFT THE HOUSE. KYLE deemed it satisfactorily dark outside for ghosts. "I bet there really are ghosts out," he said. "On Halloween all the dead people get out of their graves and walk around."

"Who told you that?"

"Danny."

"Tell Danny that's a tall tale everyone tells on Halloween."

They walked around the curve in the road and reached the Collins property. "Now, Dad, you wait here near the hedge where Meg can't see you. I'll go around in back and bang on the window and howl. Okay?"

"Okay. Don't scare her too much."

Swinging his skull-shaped lantern, Kyle raced around the back of the Collins house. The dining room shades were up, and he could see Meg sitting at the table with a bunch of papers in front of her. He had a good idea. He'd go right to the edge of the woods and run from there to the house, yelling "Whoo, whoo," and then he'd bang on the window. That should really scare Meg.

He stepped between two trees, spread his arms and began to wave them about. As his right hand went back, he felt flesh, smooth flesh, then an ear. He heard breathing. Whirling his head around, he saw the form of a man, crouching behind him, the light reflecting off a camera lens. A hand grabbed his neck. Kyle wiggled loose and began to scream. Then he was shoved forward with a violent push. As he fell, he dropped his lantern and began clawing the ground, his hand closing over something. Still screaming, he scrambled to his feet and ran toward the house.

That's some realistic yell, Mac thought, when he first heard Kyle's scream. Then, as the terrified shriek continued, he began to run toward the woods. Something had happened to Kyle. With a burst of speed he raced across the lawn and behind the house.

From inside the dining room, Meg heard the screaming and ran to the back door. She yanked it open and grabbed Kyle as he stumbled through the door and fell into her arms, sobbing in terror.

That was the way Mac found them, their arms around each other, Meg rocking his son back and forth, soothing him. "Kyle, it's okay. It's okay," she kept repeating.

It took minutes before he could tell them what had happened. "Kyle, it's all those stories about the dead walking that makes you think you're seeing things," Mac said. "There was nothing there."

Calmer now, drinking the hot cocoa Meg had made for

him, Kyle was adamant. "There was so a man there, and he had a camera. I know. I fell when he pushed me, but I picked up something. Then I dropped it when I saw Meg. Go see what it is, Dad."

"I'll get a flashlight, Mac," Meg said.

Mac went outside and began moving the beam back and forth over the ground. He did not have to go far. Only a few feet from the back porch he found a gray plastic box, the kind used to carry videotapes.

He picked it up and walked back to the woods, still shining the light before him. He knew it was useless. No intruder stands around waiting to be discovered. The ground was too hard to see footprints, but he found Kyle's lantern directly in line with the dining room windows. From where he was standing he could see Meg and Kyle clearly.

Someone with a camera had been here watching Meg, maybe taping her. Why?

Mac thought of the dead girl in the morgue, then hurried back across the lawn to the house.

THAT STUPID KID! BERNIE THOUGHT AS HE RAN THROUGH the woods to his car. He'd parked it near the end of the Drumdoe Inn parking lot but not so far away that it stood out. There were about forty cars scattered through the lot now, so his Chevy certainly wouldn't have been particularly noticed. He hurriedly tossed his camera in the trunk and drove through town toward Route 7. He was careful to go not more than five miles above the speed limit. But he knew that driving too slow was a red flag to the cops too.

Had that kid gotten a good look at him? He didn't think so. It was dark, and the kid was scared. A few seconds more and he could have moved backwards and the kid wouldn't have known he was there.

Bernie was furious. He'd been enjoying watching Meghan through the camera, and he'd had such a clear view of her. He was sure he had great tapes.

On the other hand he'd never seen anyone so frightened as that kid had been. He felt tingly and alive and almost energized just thinking about it. To have such power. To be able to record someone's expressions and movements and secret little gestures, like the way Meghan kept tucking her hair behind her ear when she was concentrating. To scare someone so much that he screamed and cried and ran like that little kid just now.

To watch Meghan, her hands, her hair . . .

43

*S*tephanie Petrovic had a fitful night, finally falling into a heavy sleep. When she awakened at ten-thirty on Sunday morning, she opened her eyes lazily and smiled. At last things were working out.

She had been warned never to breathe his name, to forget she'd ever met him, but that was before Helene was murdered and before Helene lost the chance to change her will.

On the telephone he was so kind to her. He promised he would take care of her. He would make arrangements to have the baby adopted by people who would pay one hundred thousand dollars for it.

"So much?" she had asked, delighted.

He reassured her that there would be no problem.

He would also arrange to get her a green card. "It will be fake, but no one will ever be able to tell the difference," he had said. "However, I suggest that you move someplace where no one knows you. I wouldn't want anyone to recognize you. Even in a big place like New York City people bump into each other, and in your case they'd start asking questions. You might try California."

Stephanie knew she would love California. Maybe she could get a job in a spa there, she thought. With one hundred thousand dollars she'd be able to get the training she'd need. Or maybe she could just get a job right away. She was like Helene. Being a beautician came to her naturally. She loved that kind of work.

He was sending a car for her at seven o'clock tonight. "I don't want the neighbors to see you moving out," he'd told her.

Stephanie wanted to luxuriate in bed, but she was hungry. Only ten days more and the baby will be born and then I can go on a diet, she promised herself.

She showered, then dressed in the maternity clothes she had come to hate. Then she began to pack. Helene had tapestry luggage in the closet. Why shouldn't I have it? Stephanie thought. Who deserves it more?

Because of the pregnancy, she had so few clothes, but once she was back to her normal size she'd fit in Helene's things again. Helene had been a conservative dresser, but all her clothes were expensive and in good taste. Stephanie went through the closet and dresser drawers, rejecting only what she absolutely did not like.

Helene had a small safe on the floor of her closet. Stephanie knew where she kept the combination, so she opened it. It didn't contain much jewelry, but there were a few very good pieces, which she slipped into a cosmetic bag.

It was a shame she couldn't move the furniture out there. On the other hand, she knew from pictures she'd seen that in California they didn't use old-fashioned upholstered furniture and dark woods like mahogany.

She did go through the house and chose some Dresden figurines to take with her. Then she remembered the table silver. The big chest was too heavy to carry, so she put the silver in plastic bags and fastened rubber bands around them to keep it from rattling in the suitcase.

The lawyer, Mr. Potters, called at five o'clock to see how she was feeling. "Perhaps you'd like to join my wife and me for dinner, Stephanie."

"Oh, thank you," she said, "but someone from the Rumanian Society is going to drop in."

"Fine. We just didn't want you to be lonesome. Remember, be sure to call me if you need anything."

"You're so kind, Mr. Potters."

"Well, I only wish I could do more for you. Unfortunately, where the will is concerned, my hands are tied."

I don't need your help, Stephanie thought as she hung up the phone.

Now it was time to write the letter. She composed three versions before she was satisfied. She knew that some of her spelling was bad, and she had to look up some words, but at last it seemed to be all right. It was to Mr. Potters:

Dear Mr. Potters,

I am happy to say that Jan, the father of my baby, is the one who came to see me. We are going to get maried and he will take care of us. He must get back to his job right awaye so I am leaving with him. He now works in Dallas.

I love Jan very much and I know you will be pleassed for me.

Thank you.

Stephanie Petrovic

The car came for her promptly at seven. The driver carried her bags out. Stephanie left the note and house key on the dining room table, turned off the lights, closed the door behind her and hurried through the darkness, down the flagstone walk to the waiting vehicle.

ON MONDAY MORNING, MEGHAN TRIED TO PHONE STEPHANIE Petrovic. There was no answer. She settled down at the dining room table, where she had begun to go through her father's business files.

She immediately noticed something. He'd been registered and billed for five days at the Four Seasons Hotel in Beverly Hills, from 23 January to 28 January, the day he flew to Newark and disappeared. After the first two days there were no extra charges on that bill. Even if he ate most of his meals out, Meghan thought, people send for breakfast or make a phone call or open the room bar and have a drink—something.

On the other hand, if he'd been on the concierge floor, it would be very like her father just to go to the courtesy buffet and help himself to juice, coffee and a roll. He was a light-breakfast eater.

The first two days, however, did have extra charges on the bill, like the valet, a bottle of wine, an evening snack, phone calls. She made a note of the dates of the three days when there were no extra expenses.

There might be a pattern, she thought.

At noon she tried Stephanie again, and again the phone was not answered. At two o'clock she began to be alarmed and phoned the lawyer, Charles Potters. He assured her that Stephanie was fine. He'd spoken to her the evening before and she'd said someone from the Rumanian Society was dropping by.

"I'm glad," Meghan said. "She's a very frightened girl."

"Yes, she is," Potters agreed. "Something that isn't generally known is that when someone leaves an entire estate to a charity or a medical facility such as the Manning Clinic, if a close relative is needy and inclined to try to break the will, the charity or facility may quietly offer a settlement. However, after Stephanie went on television literally accusing the clinic of being responsible for her aunt's murder, any such settlement was out of the question. It would seem like hush money."

"I understand," Meghan said. "I'll keep trying Stephanie, but will you ask her to call me if you hear from her? I still think someone should go after the man who got her pregnant. If she gives away her baby, she may someday regret it."

Meghan's mother had gone to the inn for the breakfast and lunch service, and she returned to the house just as Meg was finishing the conversation with Potters. "Let me get busy with you," she said, taking a seat next to her at the dining room table.

"Actually you can take over," Meghan told her. "I really have to drive to my apartment and get clothes and pick up my mail. It's the first of November, and all the little window envelopes will be in."

The evening before, when her mother had returned from the inn, she had told her about the man with the camera who had frightened Kyle. "I asked someone at the station to check it out for me; I haven't heard yet, but I'm sure one of those sleazy programs is putting together a story on us and Dad and the Andersons," she said. "Sending someone to spy on us is the way they work." She had not allowed Mac to call the police.

She showed her mother what she was doing with the files. "Mom, watch the hotel receipts for times when there were no extra expenses for three or four days in a row. I'd like to see if it only happened when Dad was in California." She did not say that Los Angeles was half an hour by plane from Scottsdale.

"And as for Palomino Leather Goods," Catherine said, "I don't know why, but that name has been churning around in my mind. I feel as though I've heard it before, but a long time ago."

Meghan still had not decided if she would stop at PCD on her way to the apartment. She was wearing comfortable old slacks and a favorite sweater. It'll do, she thought. That was one of the aspects she had loved about the job, the behind-the-scenes informality.

She brushed her hair quickly and realized that it was growing too long. She liked it to be collar length. Now it was touching her shoulders. The dead girl's hair had been on her shoulders. Her hands suddenly cold, Meghan reached back, twisted her hair into a French knot and pinned it up.

When she was leaving, her mother said, "Meg, why don't you go out to dinner with some of your friends? It will do you good to get away from all this."

"I'm not much in the mood for social dinners," Meg said, "but I'll call and let you know. You'll be at the inn?"

"Yes."

"Well, when you're here after dark be sure to keep the draperies drawn." She raised her hand, palm upright and outward, fingers spread. "As Kyle would say, 'Give me a high five.'"

Her mother raised her hand and touched her daughter's palm in response. "You've got it."

They looked at each other for a long minute, then Catherine said briskly, "Drive carefully."

It was the standard warning ever since Meg had gotten her driving permit at age sixteen.

Her answer was always in the same vein. Today she said, "Actually I thought I'd tailgate a tractor trailer." Then she wanted to bite her tongue. The accident on the Tappan Zee Bridge had been caused by a fuel truck tailgating a tractor trailer.

She knew her mother was thinking the same thing when she said, "Dear God, Meg, it's like walking through a mine field, isn't it? Even the kind of joking remark that has been part of the fabric of our lives has been tainted and twisted. Will it ever end?"

THAT SAME MONDAY MORNING, DR. GEORGE MANNING WAS again questioned in Assistant State Attorney John Dwyer's office. The questions had become sharper with an edge of sarcasm in them. The two investigators sat quietly as their boss handled the interrogation.

"Doctor," Dwyer asked, "can you explain why you didn't tell us immediately that Helene Petrovic was afraid that she had mixed up the Anderson embryos?"

"Because she wasn't sure." George Manning's shoulders

slumped. His complexion, usually a healthy pink, was ashen. Even the admirable head of silver hair seemed a faded, graying white. Since the Anderson baby's birth he had aged visibly.

"Dr. Manning, you've said repeatedly that founding and running the assisted reproduction clinic has been the great achievement of your lifetime. Were you aware that Helene Petrovic was planning to leave her rather considerable estate to research at your clinic?"

"We had talked about it. You see, the level of success in our field is still not anything like what we would wish. It's very expensive for a woman to have in vitro fertilization, anywhere from ten to twenty thousand dollars. If a pregnancy is not achieved, the process starts all over. While some clinics claim a one out of five success ratio, the honest figure is closer to one out of ten."

"Doctor, you are very anxious to see the ratio of successful pregnancies at your clinic improved?"

"Yes, of course."

"Wasn't it quite a blow to you last Monday when Helene Petrovic not only quit but admitted she might have made a very serious mistake?"

"It was devastating."

"Yet, even when she was found murdered, you withheld the very important reason for quitting that she had given you." Dwyer leaned across his desk. "What else did Ms. Petrovic tell you at that meeting last Monday, Doctor?"

Manning folded his hands together. "She said that she was planning to sell her house in Lawrenceville and move away, that she might go to France to live."

"And what did you think of that plan?"

"I was stunned," he whispered. "I was sure she was running away."

"Running away from what, Doctor?"

George Manning knew it was all over. He could not protect the clinic any longer. "I had the feeling that she was afraid that if the Anderson baby was not Jonathan's twin, it would start an investigation that might reveal many mistakes in the lab."

"The will, Doctor. Did you also think that Helene Petrovic would change her will?"

"She told me she was sorry, but it was necessary. She planned to take a long time off from work and now she had family to consider."

John Dwyer had found the answer he had guessed was there. "Dr. Manning, when was the last time you spoke to Edwin Collins?"

"He called me the day before he disappeared." Dr. George Manning did not like what he saw in Dwyer's eyes. "It was the first contact I had had with him either by phone or letter since he placed Helene Petrovic in my clinic," he said, looking away, unable to cope with the disbelief and mistrust he was reading in the demeanor of the assistant state attorney.

44

*M*eghan decided to skip going to the office and reached her apartment building at four o'clock. Her mailbox was overflowing. She fished out all the envelopes and ads and throwaways, then took the elevator up to her fourteenth-floor apartment.

She immediately opened the windows to blow away the smell of stale heat, then stood for a moment looking out over the water to the Statue of Liberty. Today the lady seemed remote and formidable in the shadows cast by the late afternoon sun.

Often when she looked at it she thought of her grandfather, Pat Kelly, who had come to this country as a teenager with nothing and worked so hard to make his fortune.

What would her grandfather think if he knew that his daughter Catherine might lose everything he had worked for because her husband had cheated on her for years?

Scottsdale, Arizona. Meg looked over the waters of New York Harbor and realized what had been bothering her. Arizona was in the Southwest. Palomino had the sound of the Southwest.

She went over to the phone, dialed the operator and asked for the area code for Scottsdale, Arizona.

Next she dialed Arizona information.

When she reached that operator, she asked, "Do you have a listing for an Edwin Collins or an E. R. Collins?"

There was none.

Meg asked another question. "Do you have a listing for Palomino Leather Goods?"

There was a pause, then the operator said, "Please hold for the number."

Part
Three

45

On Monday evening when Mac got home from work, Kyle was his usual cheerful self. He informed his father that he had told all the kids at school about the guy in the woods.

"They all said how scared they'd be," he explained with satisfaction. "I told them how I really ran fast and got away from him. Did you tell your friends about it?"

"No, I didn't."

"It's okay if you want to," Kyle said magnanimously.

As Kyle turned away, Mac held his arm. "Kyle, wait a minute."

"What's the matter?"

"Let me take a look at something."

Kyle was wearing an open-necked flannel shirt. Mac pushed it back, revealing yellowish and purple bruises at the base of his son's neck. "Did you get these last night?"

"I told you that guy grabbed me."

"You said he pushed you."

"First he grabbed me, but I got away."

Mac swore under his breath. He had not thought to examine Kyle the night before. He'd been wearing the ghost costume, and under that, a white turtleneck shirt. Mac had thought that Kyle had only been pushed by the intruder with the camera. Instead he had been grabbed around the neck. Strong fingers had caused those bruises.

Mac kept an arm around his son as he dialed the police. Last night he had reluctantly gone along with Meghan when she pleaded with him not to call them.

"Mac, it's bad enough now without giving the media a fresh angle on all this," she had said. "Mark my words, somebody will write that Dad is hanging around the house. The assistant state attorney is sure he's going to contact us."

I've let Meg keep me out of this long enough, Mac thought grimly. She's not going to any longer. That wasn't just some cameraman hanging around out there.

The phone was answered on the first ring. "State Trooper Thorne speaking."

FIFTEEN MINUTES LATER A SQUAD CAR WAS AT THE HOUSE. IT was clear the two policemen were not pleased that they had not been called earlier. "Dr. MacIntyre, last night was Halloween. We're always worried that some nut might be hanging around, hoping to pick up a kid. That guy might have gone somewhere else in town."

"I agree I should have called," Mac said, "but I don't think that man was looking for children. He was directly in line with the dining room windows of the Collins' home, and Meghan Collins was in full view."

He saw the looks the cops exchanged. "I think the state attorney's office should know about this," one of them said.

ALL THE WAY HOME FROM HER APARTMENT, THE BITTER truth had been sinking in. Meghan knew she now had virtual confirmation that her father had a second family in Arizona.

When she'd phoned the Palomino Leather Goods Shop she'd spoken to the owner. The woman was astonished when asked about the message on the answering machine. "That call didn't come from here," she said flatly.

She did confirm that she had a customer named Mrs. E. R. Collins who had a daughter in her twenties. After that she refused to give further information over the phone.

It was seven-thirty when Meg reached Newtown. She turned into the driveway and was surprised to see Mac's red Chrysler and an unfamiliar sedan parked in front of the house. Now what? she thought, alarmed. She pulled up behind them, parked and hurried up the porch steps, realizing that any unexpected occurrence was enough to start her heart pounding with dread.

SPECIAL INVESTIGATOR ARLENE WEISS WAS IN THE LIVING room with Catherine, Mac and Kyle. There was no apology in Mac's voice when he told Meg why he'd called the local police and then the assistant state attorney's office about the intruder. In fact, Meg was sure from the clipped way he spoke to her that he was angry. Kyle had been manhandled and terrified; he might have been strangled by some lunatic, and I wouldn't let Mac notify the police, she thought. She didn't blame him for being furious.

Kyle was sitting between Catherine and Mac on the couch. He slid down and came across the room to her. "Meg, don't look so sad. I'm okay." He put his hands on her cheeks. "Really, I'm okay."

She looked into his serious eyes, then hugged him fiercely. "You bet you are, pal."

Weiss did not stay long. "Miss Collins, believe it or not, we want to help you," she said as Meghan accompanied her to the door. "When you don't report, or allow other people to report, incidents like last night's, you are hindering this investigation. We could have had a police vehicle here in a few minutes if you'd called. According to Kyle, that man was carrying a large camera that would have slowed him down. Please, is there anything else we should know?"

"Nothing," Meg said.

"Mrs. Collins tells me that you were at your apartment. Did you find any more faxed messages?"

"No." She bit her lip, thinking of her call to Palomino Leather Goods.

Weiss stared at her. "I see. Well, if you remember anything that you think will interest us, you know where to reach us."

When Weiss left, Mac said to Kyle, "Go into the den. You can watch television for fifteen minutes. Then we have to go."

"That's okay, Dad. There's nothing good on. I'll stay here."

"It wasn't a suggestion."

Kyle jumped up. "Fine. You don't have to get sore about it."

"Right, Dad," Meghan agreed. "You don't have to get sore about it."

Kyle gave her a high five as he passed her chair.

Mac waited until he heard the click of the den door. "What did you find out while you were at your apartment, Meghan?"

Meg looked at her mother. "The location of the Palomino Leather Goods Shop and that they have a customer named Mrs. E. R. Collins."

Ignoring her mother's gasp, she told them about her call to Scottsdale.

"I'm flying out there tomorrow," she said. "We have to know if their Mrs. Collins is the woman Cyrus Graham saw with Dad. We can't be sure until I meet her."

Catherine Collins hoped the hurt she saw in her daughter's face was not mirrored in her own expression when she said quietly, "Meggie, if you look so much like that dead young woman, and the woman in Scottsdale is that girl's mother, it could be terrible for her to see you."

"Nothing is going to make it easy for whoever turns out to be the mother of that girl."

She was grateful that they did not try to dissuade her.

Instead Mac said, "Meg, don't tell anyone, and I mean *any-one,* where you're going. How long do you expect to stay?"

"Overnight at the most."

"Then for all anyone will know, you're at your apartment. Leave it at that."

When he collected Kyle, he said, "Catherine, if Kyle and I come to the inn tomorrow night, do you think you'd have time to join us for dinner?"

Catherine managed a smile. "I'd love to. What should I have on the menu, Kyle?"

"Chicken McNuggets?" he asked hopefully.

"Are you trying to run me out of business? Come on inside. I brought home some cookies. Take a couple with you." She led him into the kitchen.

"Catherine is very tactful," Mac said. "I think she knew I wanted a minute with you. Meg, I don't like you going out there alone, but I think I understand. Now I want the truth. Is there anything you're holding back?"

"No."

"Meg, I won't let you shut me out anymore. Get used to that idea. How can I help?"

"Call Stephanie Petrovic in the morning, and if she's not there, call her lawyer. I have a funny feeling about Stephanie. I've tried to reach her three or four times, and she's been out all day. I even called her from the car half an hour ago. Her baby is due in ten days and she feels lousy. The other day she was exhausted after her aunt's funeral and couldn't wait to lie down. I can't imagine her being gone so long. Let me give you the numbers."

When Mac and Kyle left a few minutes later, Mac's kiss was not the usual friendly peck on the cheek. Instead, as his son had done earlier, he held Meg's face in his hands.

"Take care of yourself," he ordered, as his lips closed firmly over hers.

46

*M*onday had been a bad day for Bernie. He got up at dawn, settled in the cracked Naugahyde recliner in the basement, and began to watch over and over the video he'd taken of Meghan from his hiding place in the woods. He'd wanted to see it when he got home last night, but his mother had demanded he keep her company.

"I'm alone too much, Bernard," she'd complained. "You never used to go out so much on weekends. You haven't got a girl have you?"

"Of course not, Mama," he'd said.

"You know all the trouble you've gotten into because of girls."

"None of that was my fault, Mama."

"I didn't say it was your fault. I said that girls are poison for you. Stay away from them."

"Yes, Mama."

When Mama got in one of those moods, the best thing Bernie could do was to listen to her. He was still afraid of her. He still shivered thinking of the times when he was growing up and she'd suddenly appear with the strap in her hands. "I saw you looking at that smut on television, Bernard. I can read those filthy thoughts in your head."

Mama would never understand that what he felt for Meghan was pure and beautiful. It was just that he wanted to be around Meghan, wanted to see her, wanted to feel like he could always get her to look up and smile at him. Like last night. If he had tapped at the window and she'd recognized him, she wouldn't have been scared. She'd have run to the door to let him in. She'd have said, "Bernie, what are you doing here?" Maybe she'd have made a cup of tea for him.

Bernie leaned forward. He was getting to the good part again, where Meghan looked so intent on what she was doing as she sat at the head of the dining room table with all those papers in front of her. With the zoom lens he'd managed to get close-ups of her face. There was something about the way she was beginning to moisten her lips that thrilled him. Her blouse was open at the neck. He wasn't sure if he could see the beat of her pulse there or if he only imagined that.

"Bernard! Bernard!"

His mother was at the head of the stairs, shouting down to him. How long had she been calling?

"Yes, Mama. I'm coming."

"It took you long enough," she snapped when he reached the kitchen. "You'll be late for work. What were you doing?"

"Straightening up a little. I know you want me to leave it neat."

Fifteen minutes later he was in the car. He drove down the block, unsure of where to go. He knew he should try to pick up some fares at the airport. With all the equipment he was buying, he needed to make some money. He had to force himself to turn the wheel and head in the direction of La Guardia.

He spent the day driving back and forth to the airport. It went well enough until late afternoon when some guy kept complaining to him about the traffic. "For Pete's sake, get in the left lane. Can't you see this one is blocked?"

Bernie had begun thinking about Meghan again, about whether it would be safe to drive past her house once it got dark.

A minute later the passenger snapped, "Listen, I knew I should have taken a cab. Where'd you learn to drive? Keep up with the traffic, for God's sake."

Bernie was at the last exit on the Grand Central Parkway before the Triborough Bridge. He took a sharp right onto the street parallel to the parkway and pulled the car to the curb.

"What the hell do you think you're doing?" the passenger demanded.

The guy's big suitcase was next to Bernie in the front seat. He leaned over, opened the door and pushed it out. "Get lost," he ordered. "Get yourself a taxi."

He spun his head to look into the passenger's face. Their eyes locked.

The passenger's expression changed to one of panic. "All right, take it easy. Sorry if I got you upset."

He jumped out of the car and yanked his suitcase away just as Bernie floored the accelerator. Bernie cut through side streets. He'd better go home. Otherwise he'd go back and smash that big mouth.

He began to take deliberate deep breaths. That's what the prison psychiatrist told him to do when he felt himself getting mad. "You've got to handle that anger, Bernie," he'd warned him. "Unless you want to spend the rest of your life in here."

Bernie knew he could never go back to prison again. He'd do anything to keep that from happening.

ON TUESDAY MORNING, MEGHAN'S ALARM WENT OFF AT 4 A.M. She had a reservation on America West Flight 9, leaving from Kennedy Airport at 7:25. She had no trouble getting up. Her sleep had been uneasy. She showered, running the water as hot as she could stand it, glad to feel some of the taut muscles in her neck and back loosen.

As she pulled on underwear and stockings she listened to the weather report on the radio. It was below freezing in New York. Arizona, of course, was another matter. Cool in the evenings at this time of year, but she understood it could be fairly warm during the day.

A tan, lightweight wool jacket and slacks with a print blouse seemed to be a good choice. Over it she'd wear her Burberry without the lining. She quickly packed the few things she'd need for an overnight stay.

The smell of coffee greeted her as she started down the

stairs. Her mother was in the kitchen. "You shouldn't have gotten up," Meg protested.

"I wasn't sleeping." Catherine Collins toyed with the belt of her terry-cloth robe. "I didn't offer to go with you, Meg, but now I'm having second thoughts. Maybe I shouldn't let you do this alone. It's just that if there is another Mrs. Edwin Collins in Scottsdale, I don't know what I could say to her. Was she as ignorant as I about what was going on? Or did she knowingly live a lie?"

"I hope by the end of the day I'll have some answers," Meg said, "and I absolutely know that it's better I do this alone." She took a few sips of grapefruit juice and swallowed a little coffee. "I've got to get going. It's a long ride to Kennedy Airport. I don't want to get caught in rush-hour traffic."

Her mother walked her to the door. Meg hugged her briefly. "I get into Phoenix at eleven o'clock, mountain time. I'll call you late this afternoon."

She could feel her mother's eyes on her as she walked to the car.

THE FLIGHT WAS UNEVENTFUL. SHE HAD A WINDOW SEAT AND for long periods of time gazed down at the puffy cushion of white clouds. She thought of her fifth birthday when her mother and father took her to DisneyWorld. It was her first flight. She'd sat at the window, her father beside her, her mother across the aisle.

Over the years her father had teased her about the question she'd asked that day. "Daddy, if we got out of the plane, could we walk on the clouds?"

He'd told her that he was sorry to say the clouds wouldn't hold her up. "But I'll always hold you up, Meggie Anne," he'd promised.

And he had. She thought of the awful day when she'd tripped just before the finish line of a race and had cost her high school track team the state championship. Her father had been waiting when she'd slunk out of the gym, not wanting to hear the consoling words of her teammates or see the disappointment on their faces.

He had offered understanding, not consolation. "There are some events in our lives, Meghan," he'd told her, "that no matter how old we get, the memory still hurts. I'm afraid you've just chalked up one of those events."

A wave of tenderness swept over Meghan and then was gone as she remembered the times when her father's claim of pressing business had kept him away. Sometimes even on holidays like Thanksgiving and Christmas. Was he celebrating them in Scottsdale? With his other family? Holidays were always so busy at the inn. When he wasn't home, she and her mother would have dinner there with friends, but her mother would be up and down greeting guests and checking the kitchen.

She remembered being fourteen and taking jazz dance lessons. When her father came home from one of his trips, she'd shown him the newest steps she'd mastered.

"Meggie," he'd sighed, "jazz is good music and a fine dance form, but the waltz is the dance of the angels." He'd taught her the Viennese waltz.

It was a relief when the pilot announced that they were beginning the descent into Sky Harbor International Airport, where the outside temperature was seventy degrees.

Meghan took her things from the overhead compartment and waited restlessly for the cabin door to open. She wanted to get through this day as quickly as possible.

The car rental agency was in the Barry Goldwater terminal. Meghan stopped to look up the address of the Palomino Leather Goods Shop and when she signed for a car asked the clerk for directions.

"That's in the Bogota section of Scottsdale," the clerk said. "It's a wonderful shopping area that will make you think you're in a medieval town."

On a map she outlined the route for Meghan. "You'll be there in twenty-five minutes," she said.

As she drove, Meghan absorbed the beauty of the moun-

tains in the distance and the cloudless, intensely blue sky.
When she had cleared the commercial sections, palms and
orange trees and saguaro cactus began to dot the landscape.

She passed the adobe-style Safari Hotel. With its bright
oleanders and tall palms, it looked serene and inviting. This
was where Cyrus Graham said he had seen his stepbrother,
her father, nearly eleven years ago.

The Palomino Leather Goods Shop was a mile farther
down on Scottsdale Road. Here the buildings had castlelike
towers and crenellated parapet walls. Cobblestone streets
contributed to an old-world effect. The boutiques that lined
the streets were small, and all of them looked expensive.
Meghan turned left into the parking area past Palomino
Leather Goods and got out of the car. She found it disconcerting to realize that her knees were trembling.

The pungent scent of fine leather greeted her when she
entered the shop. Purses ranging in size from clutches to tote
bags were tastefully grouped on shelves and tables. A display
case held wallets, key rings and jewelry. Briefcases and luggage were visible in the larger area a few steps down and to
the rear of the entry level.

There was only one other person in the shop, a young
woman with striking Indian features and thick, dark hair that
cascaded down her back. She looked up from her position
behind the cash register and smiled. "May I help you?" There
was no hint of recognition in her voice or manner.

Meghan thought quickly. "I hope so. I'm only in town for
a few hours and I wanted to look up some relatives. I don't
have their address and they're not listed in the phone book. I
know they shop here and I hoped I might be able to get the
address or phone number from you."

The clerk hesitated. "I'm new. Maybe you could come
back in about an hour. The owner will be in then."

"Please," Meghan said. "I have so little time."

"What's the name? I can see if they have an account."

"E. R. Collins."

"Oh," the clerk said, "you must have called yesterday."

"That's right."

"I was here. After she spoke to you, the owner, Mrs. Stoges, told me about Mr. Collins' death. Was he a relative?"

Meghan's mouth went dry. "Yes. That's why I'm anxious to stop in on the family."

The clerk turned on the computer. "Here's the address and phone number. I'm afraid I have to phone Mrs. Collins and ask permission to give it to you."

There was nothing to do but nod. Meghan watched the buttons on the phone being rapidly pressed.

A moment later the clerk said into the receiver, "Mrs. Collins? This is the Palomino Leather Goods Shop. There's a young lady here who would like to see you, a relative. Is it all right if I give her your address?"

She listened then looked at Meghan. "May I ask your name?"

"Meghan. Meghan Collins."

The clerk repeated it, listened, then said goodbye and hung up. She smiled at Meg. "Mrs. Collins would like you to come right over. She lives only ten minutes from here."

47

*F*rances stood, looking out the window at the back of the house. A low stucco wall crowned by a wrought-iron rail enclosed the pool and patio. The property ended at the border of the vast expanse of desert that was the Pima Indian Reservation. In the distance, Camelback Mountain glistened under the midday sun. An incongruously beautiful day for all secrets to be laid open, she thought.

Annie had gone to Connecticut after all, had looked up Meghan and sent her here. Why should Annie have honored her father's wishes, Frances asked herself fiercely. What loyalty does she owe to him or to me?

In the two-and-a-half days since she'd left the message on Edwin's answering machine, she'd waited in an agony of hope and dread. The call she'd just received from Palomino was not the one she'd hoped to get. But at least Meghan Collins might be able to tell her when she had seen Annie, perhaps where Frances could reach her.

The chimes rang through the house, soft, melodious, but chilling. Frances turned and walked to the front door.

WHEN MEGHAN STOPPED IN FRONT OF 1006 DOUBLETREE Ranch Road she found a one-story, cream-colored stucco house with a red tile roof, on the edge of the desert. Vivid red hibiscus and cactus framed the front of the dwelling, complementing the stark beauty of the mountain range in the distance.

On her way to the door she passed the window and caught a glimpse of the woman inside. She couldn't see her face but could tell that the woman was tall and very thin, with hair loosely pinned in a chignon. She seemed to be wearing some sort of smock.

Meghan rang the bell, then the door opened.

The woman gave a startled gasp. Her face went ashen. "Dear God," she whispered. "I knew you looked like Annie, but I had no idea. . . ." Her hand flew up to her mouth, pressing against her lips in a visible effort to silence the flow of words.

This is Annie's mother and she doesn't know that Annie is dead. Horrified, Meghan thought, It's going to be worse for her that I'm here. What would it be like for Mom if Annie had been the one to go to Connecticut and tell her I was dead?

"Come in, Meghan." The woman stood aside, still clutching the handle of the door, as though supporting herself on it. "I'm Frances Grolier."

Meghan did not know what kind of person she had expected to find, but not this woman with her fresh-scrubbed looks, graying hair, sturdy hands and thin, lined face. The eyes she was looking into were shocked and distressed.

"Didn't the clerk at Palomino call you Mrs. Collins when she phoned?" Meghan asked.

"The tradespeople know me as Mrs. Collins."

She was wearing a gold wedding band. Meghan looked at it pointedly.

"Yes," Frances Grolier said. "For appearance sake, your father gave that to me."

Meghan thought of the way her mother had convulsively gripped the wedding band the psychic had returned to her. She looked away from Frances Grolier, suddenly filled with an overwhelming sense of loss. Impressions of the room filtered through the misery of this moment.

The house was divided into living and studio areas extending from the front to the back.

The front section was the living room. A couch in front of the fireplace. Earth-tone tiles on the floor.

The maroon leather chair and matching ottoman to the side of the fireplace, exact replicas of the ones in her father's study, Megan realized with a start. Bookshelves within easy reach of the chair. Dad certainly liked to feel at home wherever he was, Meghan thought bitterly.

Framed photographs prominently displayed on the mantel drew her like a magnet. They were family groups of her father with this woman and a young girl who might easily be her sister, and who was—or rather had been—her half sister.

One picture especially riveted her. It was a Christmas scene. Her father holding a five- or six-year-old on his lap, surrounded by presents. A young Frances Grolier kneeling behind him, arms around his neck. All wearing pajamas and robes. A joyous family.

Was that one of the Christmas Days I spent praying for a miracle, that suddenly Daddy would come through the door? Meghan wondered.

Sickening pain encompassed her. She turned away and saw against the far wall the bust on a pedestal. With feet that now seemed too leaden to move she made her way to it.

A rare talent had shaped this bronze image of her father. Love and understanding had caught the hint of melancholy behind the twinkle in the eyes, the sensitive mouth, the long, expressive fingers folded under the chin, the fine head of hair with the lock that always strayed forward onto his forehead.

She could see that cracks along the neck and forehead had been skillfully repaired.

"Meghan?"

She turned, dreading what she must now tell this woman.

Frances Grolier crossed the room to her. Her voice pleading, she said, "I'm prepared for anything you feel about me, but *please* . . . I must know about Annie. Do you know where she is? And what about your father? Has he been in touch with you?"

KEEPING HIS PROMISE TO MEGHAN, MAC TRIED UNSUCCESS-fully to phone Stephanie Petrovic at nine o'clock on Tuesday morning. Hourly phone calls continued to bring no response.

At twelve-fifteen he called Charles Potters, the lawyer for the estate of Helene Petrovic. When Potters got on the phone, Mac identified himself and stated his reason for phoning and was immediately told that Potters too was concerned.

"I tried Stephanie last night," Potters explained. "I could tell that Miss Collins was disturbed by her absence. I'm going over to the house now. I have a key."

He promised to call back.

An hour and a half later, his voice trembling with indignation, Potters told Mac about Stephanie's note. "That deceitful girl," he cried. "She helped herself to whatever she could carry! The silver. Some lovely Dresden. Practically all of Helene's wardrobe. Her jewelry. Those pieces were insured for over fifty thousand dollars. I'm notifying the police. This is a case of common theft."

"You say she left with the father of her baby?" Mac asked. "From what Meghan told me, I find that very hard to believe. She had the sense that Stephanie was frightened at the suggestion that she go after him for child support."

"Which may have been an act," Potters said. "Stephanie Petrovic is a very cold young woman. I can assure you that the main source of her grief over her aunt's death was the fact that Helene had not changed her will as Stephanie claimed she planned to do."

"Mr. Potters, do you believe Helene Petrovic planned to change her will?"

"I have no way of knowing that. I do know that in the weeks before her death, Helene had put her house on the market and converted her securities to bearer bonds. Fortunately those were not in her safe."

When Mac put down the phone, he leaned back in his chair.

How long could any amateur, no matter how gifted, pull the wool over the eyes of trained experts in the field of reproductive endocrinology and in vitro fertilization? he mused. Yet Helene Petrovic had managed it for years. I couldn't have done it, Mac thought, remembering his intense medical training.

According to Meghan, while Petrovic was working at the Dowling Assisted Reproduction Center she spent a lot of time hanging around the laboratory. She might also have been seeing a doctor from Valley Memorial, the hospital with which the center was affiliated.

Mac made up his mind. He would take tomorrow off. There were some things best handled in person. Tomorrow he was going to drive to Valley Memorial in Trenton and see the director of the facility. He needed to try to get some records.

Mac had met and liked Dr. George Manning but was shocked and concerned that Manning had not immediately warned the Andersons about the potential embryo mix-up. There was no question he'd been hoping for a cover-up.

Now Mac wondered if there was any possibility that Helene Petrovic's abrupt decision to quit the clinic, change her will, sell her house and move to France might have more sinister reasons than her fear of an error in the laboratory. Particularly, he reasoned, since it might still be proven that the Andersons' baby was their biological child, if not the identical twin they'd expected.

Mac wanted to learn if there was any possibility that Dr. George Manning had been connected to Valley Memorial at any point in the several years that Helene Petrovic worked in the adjacent facility.

Manning would not be the first man to throw aside his professional life for a woman, nor would he be the last. Technically, Petrovic had been hired through Collins and Carter Executive Search. Yet only yesterday Manning had admitted that he had spoken to Edwin Collins the day before Collins disappeared. Had they been in collusion over those credentials? Or had someone else on the Manning staff helped her out? The Manning Clinic was only about ten years old. Their annual reports would list the names of the senior staff. He'd get his secretary to copy them for him.

Mac pulled out a pad, and in his neat penmanship, which his colleagues joked was so uncharacteristic of the medical profession, wrote:

1. Edwin Collins believed dead in bridge accident, 28 January; no proof.
2. Woman who resembles Meg (Annie?) fatally stabbed, 21 October.
3. "Annie" may have been seen by Kyle the day before her death.
4. Helene Petrovic fatally shot hours after she quit her job at Manning, 25 October.

(Edwin Collins placed Helene Petrovic at Manning Clinic, vouching for the accuracy of her false credentials.)

5. Stephanie Petrovic claimed conspiracy by Manning Clinic to prevent her aunt from changing her will.

6. Stephanie Petrovic vanished sometime between late afternoon of 31 October and 2 November, leaving a note claiming she was rejoining the father of her child, a man she apparently feared.

None of it made sense. But there was one thing he was convinced was true. Everything that had happened was connected in a logical way. Like genes, he thought. The minute you understand the structure everything falls into place.

He put aside the pad. He had work to do if he was planning to take tomorrow off for the trip to Dowling. It was four o'clock. That meant it was two o'clock in Arizona. He wondered how Meg was doing, how the day, which must be incredibly difficult for her, was progressing.

MEG STARED AT FRANCES GROLIER. "WHAT DO YOU MEAN have I heard from my father?"

"Meghan, the last time he was here, I could see that the world was closing in on him. He was so frightened, so depressed. He said he wished he could just disappear.

"Meghan, you must tell me. *Have you seen Annie?*"

Only a few hours ago, Meg had remembered her father's warning that some events cause unforgettable pain. Compassion engulfed her as she saw the dawning horror in the eyes of Annie's mother.

Frances grasped her arms. "Meghan, is Annie sick?"

Meghan could not speak. She answered the note of hope in the frantic question with a barely perceptible shake of her head.

"Is she . . . is Annie dead?"

"I'm so sorry."

"No. That can't be." Frances Grolier's eyes searched Meghan's face, pleading. "When I opened the door . . . even though I knew you were coming . . . for that split second, I thought it was Annie. I knew how alike you were. Ed showed me pictures." Grolier's knees buckled.

Meghan grasped her arms, helped her to sit down on the couch. "Isn't there someone I can call, somebody you'd like to have with you now?"

"No one," Grolier whispered. "No one." Her pallor turning a sickly gray, she stared into the fireplace as though suddenly unaware of Meghan's presence.

Meghan watched helplessly as Frances Grolier's pupils became dilated, her expression vacant. She's going into shock, Meghan thought.

Then, in a voice devoid of emotion, Grolier asked, "What happened to my daughter?"

"She was stabbed. I happened to be in the emergency room when she was brought in."

"Who . . . ?"

Grolier did not complete the question.

"Annie may have been a mugging victim," Meghan said quietly. "She had no identification except a slip of paper with my name and phone number on it."

"The Drumdoe Inn notepaper?"

"Yes."

"Where is my daughter now?"

"The . . . the medical examiner's building in Manhattan."

"You mean the morgue."

"Yes."

"How did you find me, Meghan?"

"Through the message you left the other night to call the Palomino Leather Goods Shop."

A ghastly smile tugged at Frances Grolier's lips. "I left that message hoping to reach your father. Annie's father. He always put you first, you know. So afraid that you and your mother would find out about us. Always so afraid."

Meghan could see that shock was being replaced by anger

and grief. "I am so sorry." It was all she could think to say. From where she was sitting, she could see the Christmas picture. I'm so sorry for all of us, she thought.

"Meghan, I have to talk to you, but not now. I need to be alone. Where are you staying?"

"I'll try to get a room at the Safari Hotel."

"I'll call you there later. Please go."

As Meghan closed the door, she heard the steady sobbing, low rhythmic sounds that tore at her heart.

She drove to the hotel, praying that it would not be full, that no one would see her and think she was Annie. But the check-in was fast, and ten minutes later she closed the door of the room and sank down on the bed, her emotions a combination of enormous pity, shared pain and icy fear.

Frances Grolier clearly believed it possible that her lover, Edwin Collins, was alive.

48

On Tuesday morning, Victor Orsini moved into Edwin Collins' private office. The day before, the cleaning service had washed the walls and windows and cleaned the carpet. Now the room was antiseptically clean. Orsini had no interest in even thinking about redecorating it. Not with the way things were going.

He knew that on Sunday Meghan and her mother had cleared the office of Collins' personal effects. He assumed they had heard the message on the answering machine and taken the tape. He could only imagine what they thought of it.

He had hoped they wouldn't bother with Collins' business records, but they'd taken all of them. Sentiment? He doubted it. Meghan was smart. She was looking for something. Was it the same thing he was so anxious to find? Was it somewhere in those papers? Would she find it?

Orsini paused in the unpacking of his books. He'd spread the morning paper on the desk, the desk that belonged to Edwin Collins and soon would be moved to the Drumdoe Inn. A front-page update on the Manning Clinic scandal announced that state medical investigators had been in the clinic on Monday and already rumors were rampant that Helene Petrovic may have made many serious mistakes. Empty vials had been found among the ones containing cryo-preserved embryos, suggesting that Petrovic's lack of medical skill may have resulted in embryos being improperly labeled or even destroyed.

An independent source who refused to be identified pointed out that, at the very least, clients who were paying handsomely for maintenance of their embryos were being overcharged. In the worst possible scenario, women who might not be able to again produce eggs for possible fertilization might have lost their chance for biological motherhood.

Featured next to the story was a reproduction of Edwin Collins' letter strongly recommending "Dr." Helene Petrovic to Dr. George Manning.

The letter had been written 21 March, nearly seven years ago, and was stamped received on 22 March.

Orsini frowned, hearing again the accusing, angry voice of Collins, calling him from the car phone that last night. He stared at the newspaper and Edwin's bold signature on the letter of recommendation. Perspiration broke out on his forehead. Somewhere in this office or in the files Meghan Collins had taken home is the incriminating evidence that will bring down this house of cards, he thought. But will anyone find it?

*   *   *

FOR HOURS, BERNIE WAS UNABLE TO CALM THE RAGE THE sneering passenger had triggered in him. As soon as his mother went to bed Monday night, he'd rushed downstairs to play his videotapes of Meghan. The news tapes had her voice, but the one he'd taken from the woods behind her house was his favorite. It made him wildly restless to be near her again.

He played the tapes through the night, only going to bed as a hint of dawn flickered through the slit in the cardboard he had placed over the narrow basement window. Mama would notice if his bed had not been slept in.

He got into bed fully dressed and pulled up the covers just in time. The creaking of the mattress in the next room warned that his mother was waking up. A few minutes later the door of his room opened. He knew she was looking in at him. He kept his eyes shut. She wouldn't expect him to wake up for another fifteen minutes.

After the door closed again, he hunched up in bed, planning his day.

Meghan had to be in Connecticut. But where? At her house? At the inn? Maybe she gave her mother a hand in running the inn. What about the New York apartment? Maybe she was there.

He got up promptly at seven, took off his sweater and shirt, put on his pajama top in case Mama saw him and went out to the bathroom. There he splashed water on his face and hands, shaved, brushed his teeth and combed his hair. He smiled at his reflection in the mirror on the medicine cabinet. Everyone had always told him he had a warm smile. Trouble was the silver was peeling behind the glass, and the mirror gave back a distorted image like the ones in amusement parks. He didn't look warm and friendly now.

Then, as Mama had taught him to do, he reached down for the can of cleanser, shook a liberal amount of the gritty powder into the sink, rubbed it in vigorously with a sponge, rinsed it away and dried the sink with the rag Mama always left folded over the side of the tub.

Back in the bedroom he made his bed, folded his pajama top, put on a clean shirt and carried the soiled one to the hamper.

Today Mama had bran flakes in his cereal bowl. "You look tired, Bernard," she said sharply. "Are you getting enough rest?"

"Yes, Mama."

"What time did you go to bed?"

"I guess about eleven o'clock."

"I woke up to go to the bathroom at eleven-thirty. You weren't in bed then."

"Maybe it was a little later, Mama."

"I thought I heard your voice. Were you talking to some-one?"

"No, Mama. Who would I be talking to?"

"I thought I heard a woman's voice."

"Mama, it was the television." He gulped the cereal and tea. "I have to be at work early."

She watched him from the door. "Be home on time for dinner. I don't want to be fussing in the kitchen all night."

He wanted to tell her that he expected to work overtime but didn't dare. Maybe he'd call her later.

Three blocks away he stopped at a public telephone. It was cold, but the shiver he felt as he dialed Meghan's apartment had more to do with anticipation than chill. The phone rang four times. When the answering machine clicked on, he hung up.

He then dialed the house in Connecticut. A woman answered. It must be Meghan's mother, Bernie thought. He deepened his voice, quickened its pace. He wanted to sound like Tom Weicker.

"Good morning, Mrs. Collins. Is Meghan there?"

"Who is this?"

"Tom Weicker of PCD."

"Oh, Mr. Weicker, Meg will be sorry she missed your call. She's out of town today."

Bernie frowned. He wanted to know where she was. "Can I reach her?"

"I'm afraid not. But I'll be hearing from her late this afternoon. May I have her phone you?"

Bernie thought swiftly. It would sound wrong if he didn't say yes. But he wanted to know when she'd be back. "Yes, have her call. Do you expect her to be home this evening?"

"If not tonight, surely tomorrow."

"Thank you." Bernie hung up, angry that he couldn't reach Meghan, but glad he hadn't wasted a trip to Connecticut. He got back in the car and headed for Kennedy Airport. He might just as well get some fares today, but they'd better not tell him how to drive.

THIS TIME THE SPECIAL INVESTIGATORS OF HELENE PE-trovic's death did not go to Phillip Carter. Instead, late Tuesday morning they phoned and asked if it would be convenient for him to stop in for an informal chat at the assistant state attorney's office in the Danbury courthouse.

"When would you like me to come?" Carter asked.

"As soon as possible," Investigator Arlene Weiss told him.

Phillip glanced at his calendar. There was nothing on it that he couldn't change. "I can make it around one," he suggested.

"That will be fine."

After he replaced the receiver he tried to concentrate on the morning mail. There were a number of references in on candidates whom they were considering offering to two of their major clients. As least so far those clients hadn't pulled back.

Could Collins and Carter Executive Search weather the storm? He hoped so. One thing he would do in the very near future would be to change the name to Phillip Carter Associates.

In the next room he could hear the sounds of Orsini moving into Ed Collins' office. Don't get too settled, Phillip thought. It was too soon to get rid of Orsini. He needed him for now, but Phillip had several replacements in mind.

He wondered if the police had been questioning Catherine and Meghan again.

He dialed Catherine at home. When she answered, he said, cheerfully, "It's me. Just checking to see how it's going."

"That's nice of you, Phillip." Her voice was subdued.

"Anything wrong, Catherine?" he asked quickly. "The police haven't been bothering you, have they?"

"No, not really. I'm going through Edwin's files, the copies of his expense accounts, that sort of thing. You know what Meg pointed out?" She did not wait for an answer. "There are times when even though Edwin was billed for four or five days in a hotel, after the first day or two there were absolutely no additional charges on his bill. Not even for a drink or a bottle of wine at the end of the day. Did you ever notice that?"

"No. I wouldn't be the one to look at Edwin's expense accounts, Catherine."

"All the files I have seem to go back seven years. Is there a reason for that?"

"That would be right. That's as long as you're supposed to retain records for possible audit. Of course the IRS will go back much further if they suspect deliberate fraud."

"What I'm seeing is that whenever Edwin was in California that pattern of noncharges showed up in the hotel bills. He seemed to go to California a great deal."

"California was where it was at, Catherine. We used to make a lot of placements there. It's just changed in the last few years."

"Then you never wondered about his frequent trips to California?"

"Catherine, Edwin was my senior partner. We both always went where we thought we'd find business."

"I'm sorry, Phillip. I don't mean to suggest that you should have seen something that I as Edwin's wife of thirty years never even suspected."

"Another woman?"

"Possibly."

"It's such a rotten time for you," Phillip said vehemently. "How's Meg doing? Is she with you?"

"Meg's fine. She's away today. It would be the one day her boss phoned her."

"Are you free for dinner tonight?"

"No, I'm sorry. I'm meeting Mac and Kyle at the inn." Catherine hesitated. "Do you want to join us?"

"I don't think so, thanks. How about tomorrow night?"

"It depends on when Meg gets back. May I call you?"

"Of course. Take care of yourself. Remember, I'm here for you."

TWO HOURS LATER PHILLIP WAS BEING INTERROGATED IN Assistant State Attorney John Dwyer's office. Special investigators Bob Marron and Arlene Weiss were present with Dwyer, who was asking the questions. Some of them were the same ones Catherine had raised.

"Didn't you at any time suspect your partner might be leading a double life?"

"No."

"Do you think so now?"

"With that dead girl in the morgue in New York who looks like Meghan? With Meghan herself requesting DNA tests? Of course I think so."

"From the pattern of Edwin Collins' travels, can you suggest where he might have been involved in an intimate relationship?"

"No, I can't."

The assistant state attorney looked exasperated. "Mr. Carter, I get the feeling that everyone who was close to Edwin Collins is trying in one way or another to protect him. Let me put it this way. We believe he is alive. If he had another situation, particularly a long-term one, he may be there now. Just off the top of your head, where do you think that could be?"

"I simply don't know," Phillip repeated.

"All right, Mr. Carter," Dwyer said brusquely. "Will you give us permission to go through all the Collins and Carter files if we deem it necessary, or will it be necessary to subpoena them?"

"I wish you *would* go through the files!" Phillip snapped. "Do anything you can to bring this dreadful business to a conclusion and let decent people get on with their lives."

On his way back to the office, Phillip Carter realized he had no desire for a solitary evening. From his car phone he again dialed Catherine's number. When she answered, he said, "Catherine, I've changed my mind. If you and Mac and Kyle can put up with me, I'd very much like to have dinner with you tonight."

AT THREE O'CLOCK, FROM HER HOTEL ROOM, MEGHAN phoned home. It would be five o'clock in Connecticut, and she wanted to be able to talk to her mother before the dinner hour at the inn.

It was a painful conversation. Unable to find words to soften the impact, she told about the grueling meeting with Frances Grolier. "It was pretty awful," she concluded. "She's devastated, of course. Annie was her only child."

"How old was Annie, Meg?" her mother asked quietly.

"I don't know. A little younger than I am, I think."

"I see. That means they were together for many years."

"Yes, it does," Meghan agreed, thinking of the photographs she had just seen. "Mom, there's something else. Frances seems to think that Dad is still alive."

"She *can't* think he's still alive!"

"She does. I don't know more than that. I'm going to stay in this hotel until I hear from her. She said she wants to talk to me."

"What more could she have to say to you, Meg?"

"She still doesn't know very much about Annie's death." Meghan realized she was too emotionally drained to talk any more. "Mom, I'm going to get off the phone now. If you get a chance to tell Mac about this without Kyle hearing, go ahead."

Meghan had been sitting on the edge of the bed. When she said goodbye to her mother, she leaned back against the pillows and closed her eyes.

She was awakened by the ringing of the telephone. She sat up, aware that the room was dark and chilly. The lighted face of the clock radio showed that it was five past eight. She leaned over and picked up the phone. To her own ears, her voice sounded strained and husky when she murmured, "Hello."

"Meghan, this is Frances Grolier. Will you come and see me tomorrow morning as early as possible?"

"Yes." It seemed insulting to ask her how she was. How could any woman in her situation be? Instead, Meghan asked, "Would nine o'clock be all right?"

"Yes, and thank you."

ALTHOUGH GRIEF WAS ETCHED DEEPLY IN HER FACE, FRANCes Grolier seemed composed the next morning when she opened the door for Meghan. "I've made coffee," she said.

They sat on the couch, holding the cups, their bodies angled stiffly toward each other. Grolier did not waste words. "Tell me how Annie died," she commanded. "Tell me everything. I need to know."

Meghan began, "I was on assignment in Roosevelt-St. Luke's Hospital in New York . . ." As in the conversation with her mother, she did not attempt to be gentle. She told about the fax message she had gotten, *Mistake. Annie was a mistake.*

Grolier leaned forward, her eyes blazing. "What do you think that means?"

"I don't know." She continued, omitting nothing, beginning with the note found in Annie's pocket, including Helene Petrovic's false credentials and death and finishing with the warrant issued for her father's arrest. "His car was found. You may or may not know that Dad had a gun permit. His gun was in the car and was the weapon that killed Helene Petrovic. I do not and cannot believe that he could take anyone's life."

"Nor do I."

"Last night you told me you thought my father might be alive."

"I think it's possible." Frances Grolier said, "Meghan, after today I hope we never meet again. It would be too difficult for me and, I suppose, for you as well. But you and your mother are owed an explanation.

"I met your father twenty-seven years ago in the Palomino Leather Shop. He was buying a purse for your mother and debating between two of them. He asked me to help make the choice, then invited me to lunch. That's how it began."

"He'd only been married three years at that time," Meghan said quietly. "I know my father and mother were happy together. I don't understand why he needed a relationship with you." She felt she sounded accusing and pitiless, but she couldn't help it.

"I knew he was married," Grolier said. "He showed me your picture, your mother's picture. On the surface, Edwin had it all: charm, looks, wit, intelligence. Inwardly he was, or is, a desperately insecure man. Meghan, try to understand and forgive him. In so many ways your father was still that hurt child who feared he might be abandoned again. He needed to know he had another place to go, a place where someone would take him in."

Her eyes welled with tears. "It suited us both. I was in love with him but didn't want the responsibility of marriage. I wanted only to be free to become the best sculptor that I was capable of being. For me the relationship worked, open-ended and without demands."

"Wasn't a child a demand, a responsibility?" Meghan asked.

"Annie wasn't part of the plan. When I was expecting her, we bought this place and told people that we were married. After that, your father was desperately torn, always trying to be a good father to both of you, always feeling he was failing both of you."

"Didn't he worry about being discovered?" Meghan asked. "About someone bumping into him here the way his step-brother did?"

"He was haunted by that fear. As she grew up, Annie asked more and more questions about his job. She wasn't buying the story that he had a top-secret government job. She was becoming known as a travel writer. You were being seen on television. When Edwin had terrible chest pains last November he wouldn't let himself be admitted to the hospital for observation. He wanted to get back to Connecticut. He said, 'If I die, you can tell Annie I was on some kind of government assignment.' The next time he came he gave me a bearer bond for two hundred thousand dollars."

The insurance loan, Meghan thought.

"He said that if anything happened to him, you and your mother were well taken care of, but I was not."

Meghan did not contradict Frances Grolier. She knew it had not occurred to Grolier that because his body had not been found a death certificate had not been issued for her father. And she knew with certainty that her mother would lose everything rather than take the money back that her father had given this woman.

"When was the last time you saw my father?" she asked.

"He left here on January twenty-seventh. He was going to San Diego to see Annie, then take a flight home on the morning of the twenty-eighth."

"Why do you believe he's still alive?" Meghan had to ask before she left. More than anything, she wanted to get away from this woman whom she realized she both deeply pitied and bitterly resented.

"Because when he left he was terribly upset. He'd learned something about his assistant that horrified him."

"Victor Orsini?"

"That's the name."

"What did he learn?"

"I don't know. But business had not been good for several years. Then there was a write-up in the local paper about a seventieth birthday party that had been given for Dr. George Manning by his daughter, who lives about thirty miles from here. The article quoted Dr. Manning as saying that he planned to work one more year, then retire. Your father said that the Manning Clinic was a client, and he called Dr. Manning. He wanted to suggest that he be commissioned to start the search for Manning's replacement. That conversation upset him terribly."

"Why?" Meghan asked urgently. "Why?"

"I don't know."

"Try to remember. Please. It's very important."

Grolier shook her head. "When Edwin was leaving, his last words were, 'It's becoming too much for me . . .' All the papers carried the story of the bridge accident. I believed he was dead and told people he had been killed in a light-plane accident abroad. Annie wasn't satisfied with that explanation.

"When he visited her at her apartment that last day, Edwin gave Annie money to buy some clothes. Six one-hundred-dollar bills. He obviously didn't realize that the slip of Drumdoe Inn notepaper with your name and number fell out of his wallet. She found it after he left and kept it."

Frances Grolier's lip quivered. Her voice broke as she said, "Two weeks ago, Annie came here for what you'd call a showdown. She had phoned your number. You'd answered 'Meghan Collins,' and she hung up. She wanted to see her father's death certificate. She called me a liar and demanded to know where he was. I finally told her the truth and begged her not to contact you or your mother. She knocked over that bust I'd sculpted of Ed and stormed out of here. I never saw her again."

Grolier stood up, placed her hand on the mantel and leaned her forehead against it. "I spoke to my lawyer last night. He's going to accompany me to New York tomorrow afternoon to identify Annie's body and arrange to have it brought back here. I'm sorry for the embarrassment this will cause you and your mother."

Meghan had only one more question she needed to ask. "Why did you leave that message for Dad the other night?"

"Because I thought if he were still alive, if that line were still connected, he might check it out of habit. It was my way of contacting him in case of emergency. He used to beep in to that answering machine early every morning." She faced Meghan again.

"Let no one tell you that Edwin Collins is capable of killing anyone, because he isn't." She paused. "But he *is* capable of beginning a new life that does not include you and your mother. Or Annie and me."

Frances Grolier turned away again. There was nothing left to say. Meghan took a last look at the bronze bust of her father and left, closing the door quietly behind her.

49

On Wednesday morning, as soon as Kyle was on the school bus, Mac left for Valley Memorial Hospital in Trenton, New Jersey.

At dinner the night before, when Kyle had left the table for a moment, Catherine had quickly told Mac and Phillip about Meghan's call. "I don't know very much except that this woman has had a long-term relationship with Edwin; she thinks he's still alive, and the dead girl who looks like Meg was her daughter."

"You seem to be taking it very well," Phillip had commented, "or are you still in denial?"

"I don't know what I feel anymore," Catherine had answered, "and I'm worried about Meg. You know how she felt about her father. I never heard anyone sound so hurt as she did when she called earlier." Then Kyle was back and they changed the subject.

Driving south on Route 684 through Westchester, Mac tried to tear his thoughts away from Meghan. She had been crazy about Edwin Collins, a real Daddy's girl. He knew that these past months since she'd thought her father was dead had been hell for her. How many times Mac had wanted to ask her to talk it out with him, not to hold everything inside. Maybe he should have insisted on breaking through her reserve. God, how much time he had wasted nursing his wounded pride over Ginger's dumping him.

At last we're getting honest, he told himself. Everybody knew you were making a mistake tying up with Ginger. You could feel the reaction when the engagement was announced. Meg had the guts to say it straight out, and she was only nineteen. In her letter she'd written that she loved him and that he ought to have the sense to know she was the only girl for him. "Wait for me, Mac," was the way she'd ended it.

He hadn't thought about that letter for a long time. Now he found that he was thinking about it a lot.

It was inevitable that as soon as Annie's body was claimed, it would be public knowledge that Edwin had led a double life. Would Catherine decide she didn't want to live in the same area where everyone had known Ed, that she would rather start fresh somewhere else? It could happen, especially if she lost the inn. That would mean Meg wouldn't be around either. The thought made Mac's blood run cold.

You can't change the past, Mac thought, but you can do something about the future. Finding Edwin Collins if he's still alive, or learning what happened to him if he's not, would release Meg and Catherine from the misery of uncertainty. Finding the doctor Helene Petrovic might have dated when she was a secretary at the Dowling Center in Trenton could be the first step to solving her murder.

Mac normally enjoyed driving. It was a good time for thinking. Today, however, his thoughts were in a jumble, filled with unsettled issues. The trip across Westchester to the Tappan Zee Bridge seemed longer than usual. The Tappan Zee Bridge—where it all began almost ten months ago, he thought.

It was another hour-and-a-half drive from there to Trenton. Mac arrived at Valley Memorial Hospital at ten-thirty and asked for the director. "I called yesterday and was told he could see me."

FREDERICK SCHULLER WAS A COMPACT MAN OF ABOUT forty-five whose thoughtful demeanor was belied by his quick, warm smile. "I've heard of you, Dr. MacIntyre. Your work in human gene therapy is becoming pretty exciting, I gather."

"It is exciting," Mac agreed. "We're on the cutting edge of finding the way to prevent an awful lot of diseases. The hardest job is to have the patience for trial and error when there are so many people waiting for answers."

"I agree. I don't have that kind of patience, which is why I'd never have been a good researcher. Which means that since you're giving up a day to drive down here, you must have a very good reason. My secretary said that it's urgent."

Mac nodded. He was glad to get to the point. "I'm here because of the Manning Clinic scandal."

Schuller frowned. "That really is a terrible situation. I can't believe that any woman who worked in our Dowling facility as a secretary was able to get away with passing herself off as an embryologist. Somebody dropped the ball on that one."

"Or somebody trained a very capable student, although trained her not well enough, obviously. They're finding a lot of problems in that lab, and we're talking about major problems like possibly mislabeling test tubes containing cryopreserved embryos or even deliberately destroying them."

"If any field is calling for national legislation, assisted reproduction is first on the list. The potential for mistakes is enormous. Fertilize an egg with the wrong semen, and if the embryo is successfully transferred, an infant is born whose genetic structure is fifty percent different from what the parents had the right to expect. The child may have genetically inherited medical problems that can't be foreseen. It—" He stopped abruptly. "Sorry, I know I'm preaching to the converted. How can I help?"

"Meghan Collins is the daughter of Edwin Collins, the man who is accused of placing Helene Petrovic at the Manning Clinic with false credentials. Meg's a reporter for PCD Channel 3 in New York. Last week she spoke to the head of the Dowling Center about Helene Petrovic. Apparently, some of Petrovic's coworkers thought she might be seeing a doctor from this hospital, but no one knows who he is. I'm trying to help Meg find him."

"Didn't Petrovic leave Dowling more than six years ago?"

"Nearly seven years ago."

"Do you realize how large our medical staff is here, Doctor?"

"Yes, I do," Mac said. "And I know you have consultants who are not on staff but are called in regularly. It's a shot in the dark, but at this stage, when the investigators are convinced Edwin Collins is Petrovic's murderer, you can imagine how desperately his daughter wants to know if there was someone in her life with a reason to kill her."

"Yes, I can." Schuller began to make notes on a pad. "Have you any idea how long Petrovic might have been seeing this doctor?"

"From what I understand, a year or two before she went up to Connecticut. But that's only a guess."

"It's a start. Let's go back into the records for the three

years she worked at Dowling. You think this person may have been the one who helped her to acquire enough skill to pass herself off as thoroughly trained?"

"Again, a guess."

"All right. I'll see that a list is compiled. We won't leave out people who worked in the fetal research or DNA labs either. Not all the technicians are MDs, but they know their business." He stood up. "What are you going to do with this list? It will be a long one."

"Meg is going to dig into Helene Petrovic's personal life. She's going to collect names of Petrovic's friends and acquaintances from the Rumanian Society. We'll compare names from the personal list with the one you send us."

Mac reached into his pocket. "This is a copy of a roster I compiled of everyone on the medical staff at the Manning Clinic while Helene was there. For what it's worth, I'd like to leave it with you. I'd be glad if you would run these names through your computer first."

He got up to go. "It's a big fishnet, but we do appreciate your help."

"It may take a few days, but I'll get the information you want," Schuller said. "Shall I send it to you?"

"I think directly to Meghan. I'll leave her address and phone number."

Schuller walked him to the door of his office. Mac took the elevator down to the lobby. As he stepped into the corridor, he passed a boy about Kyle's age in a wheelchair. Cerebral palsy, Mac thought. One of the diseases they were starting to get a handle on through gene therapy. The boy gave him a big smile. "Hi. Are you a doctor?"

"The kind who doesn't treat patients."

"My kind."

"Bobby!" his mother protested.

"I have a son your age who'd get along fine with you." Mac tousled the boy's hair.

The clock over the receptionist's desk showed that it was quarter past eleven. Mac decided that if he picked up a sandwich and Coke in the coffee shop off the lobby he could eat it later in the car and drive right through. That way he'd be back in the lab by two o'clock at the latest and get in an afternoon of work.

He reflected that when you passed a kid in a wheelchair, you didn't want to lose any more time than necessary if your job was trying to unlock the secrets of genetic healing.

AT LEAST HE'D MADE A COUPLE HUNDRED BUCKS DRIVING yesterday. That was the only consolation Bernie could find when he awakened Wednesday morning. He'd gone to bed at midnight and slept right through because he was really tired, but now he felt good. This was sure to be a better day; he might even see Meg.

His mother, unfortunately, was in a terrible mood. "Ber-NARD, I was awake half the night with a sinus headache. I was sneezing a lot. I want you to fix those steps and tighten the railing so I can get down to that basement again. I'm sure you're not keeping it clean. I'm sure there's dust filtering up from there."

"Mama, I'm not good at fixing things. That whole staircase is weak. I can feel another step getting loose. You wanna really hurt yourself?"

"I can't afford to hurt myself. Who'd keep this place nice? Who'd cook meals for you? Who'd make sure you don't get in trouble?"

"I need you, Mama."

"People need to eat in the morning. I always fix you a nice breakfast."

"I know you do, Mama."

Today the cereal was lukewarm oatmeal that reminded him of prison food. Nonetheless, Bernie dutifully scraped every spoonful from the bowl and drained his glass of apple juice.

He felt relaxed as he backed out of the driveway and waved goodbye to Mama. He was glad that he'd lied and told her another basement step was loose. One night, ten years ago, she'd said that she was going to inspect the basement the next day to see if he was keeping it nice.

He'd known he couldn't let that happen. He'd just bought his first police scanner radio. Mama would have realized it was expensive. She thought he just had an old television set down there and watched it after she went to bed so she wouldn't be disturbed.

Mama never opened his credit card bill. She said he had to learn to take care of it himself. She handed him the phone bill unopened too, because, she said, "I never call anybody." She had no idea how much he spent on equipment.

That night when he could hear her deep snores and knew she was in a sound sleep, he'd loosened the top steps. She'd had some fall. Her hip really had been smashed. He'd had to wait on her hand and foot for months, but it had been worth it. Mama go downstairs again? Not after that.

Bernie reluctantly decided to work at least for the morning. Meghan's mother had said she would be back today. That could mean *anytime* today. He couldn't phone and say he was Tom Weicker again. Meghan might have already called the station and found out that Tom hadn't tried to get her.

It was not a good day for fares. He stood near the baggage claim area with the other gypsy drivers and those fancy-limousine chauffeurs who were holding cards with the names of the people they were meeting.

He approached arriving passengers as they came down the escalator. "Clean car, cheaper than a cab, great driver." His lips felt stuck in a permanent smile.

The trouble was, the Port Authority had put so many signs around, warning travelers against taking a chance on getting into cars not licensed by the Taxi and Limousine Commission. A number of people started to say yes to him, then changed their minds.

One old woman let him carry her suitcases to the curb, then said she'd wait for him, that he should go for his car. He tried to take the bags with him, but she yelled at him to put them down.

People turned their heads to look at him.

If he had her alone! Trying to get him in trouble when all he wanted to do was be nice. But of course he didn't want to attract attention, so he said, "Sure, ma'am. I'll get the car real quick."

When he drove back five minutes later, she was gone.

That was enough to set him off. He wasn't going to drive any jerks today. Ignoring a couple who called out to him to ask his rate to Manhattan, he pulled away, got on the Grand Central Parkway and, paying the toll on the Triborough Bridge, chose the Bronx exit, the one that led to New England.

By noon he was having lunch, a hamburger and beer, at the bar of the Drumdoe Inn, where Joe the bartender welcomed him back as a regular patron.

50

Catherine went to the inn on Wednesday morning and worked in her office until eleven-thirty. There were twenty reservations for lunch. Even allowing for drop-ins, she knew that Tony could handle the kitchen perfectly well. She would go home and continue to go through Edwin's files.

When she passed the reception area, she glanced into the bar. There were ten or twelve people already seated there, a couple of them with menus. Not bad for a weekday. No question business in general was picking up. The dinner hour especially was almost back to where it had been before the recession.

But that still didn't mean that she could hang onto this place.

She got in her car, reflecting that it was crazy that she didn't make herself walk the short distance between the house and the inn. I'm always in a hurry, she thought, but unfortunately that might not be necessary much longer.

The jewelry she'd hocked on Monday hadn't brought in anything like what she'd expected. A jeweler had offered to take everything on consignment but warned that the market was down. "These are lovely pieces," he'd said, "and the market will be improving. Unless you absolutely need the money now, I urge you not to sell."

She hadn't sold. By pawning them all at Provident Loan, at least she got enough to pay the quarterly tax on the inn. But in three months it would be due again. There was a message from an aggressive commercial real estate agent on her desk. "Would you be interested in selling the inn? We may have a buyer."

A distress sale is what that vulture wants, Catherine told herself as she drove along the macadam to the parking lot exit. And I may have to accept it. For a moment she stopped and looked back at the inn. Her father had fashioned it after a fieldstone manor in Drumdoe, which as a boy he had thought so grand that only the gentry would dare set foot in it.

"I'd welcome the errand that would send me to the place," he'd told Catherine. "And from the kitchen I'd peek in to see the more of it. One day, the family was out and the cook took pity on me. 'Would you like to see the rest?' she asked, taking me by the hand. Catherine, that good woman showed me the entire house. And now we have one just like it."

Catherine felt a lump form in her throat as she studied the graceful Georgian-style mansion with its lovely casement windows and sturdy carved oak door. It always seemed to her that Pop was lurking inside, a benevolent ghost still strutting around, still taking his rest in front of the fire in the sitting room.

He'd really haunt me if I sold it, she thought as she pressed down on the accelerator.

THE PHONE WAS RINGING WHEN SHE UNLOCKED THE DOOR to the house. She rushed to pick it up. It was Meghan.

"Mom, I have to hurry. The plane is starting to board. I saw Annie's mother again this morning. She and her lawyer are flying into New York tonight to identify Annie's body. I'll tell you about it when I get home. That should be around ten o'clock."

"I'll be here. Oh, Meg, I'm sorry. Your boss, Tom Weicker, wanted you to call him. I didn't think to tell you when we talked yesterday."

"It would have been too late to get him at the office anyhow. Why don't you call him now and explain that I'll get back to him tomorrow. I'm sure he isn't offering me an assignment. I'd better rush. Love you."

That job is so important to Meg, Catherine berated herself. How could I have forgotten to tell her about Mr. Weicker's call? She flipped through her memo book, looking for the number of Channel 3.

Funny he didn't give me his direct line, she reflected as she waited for the operator to put her through to Weicker's secretary. Then she reasoned that of course Meg would know it.

"I'm sure he'll want to speak to you, Mrs. Collins," the secretary said when she gave her name.

Catherine had met Weicker about a year ago when Meg had showed her around the station. She'd liked him, although as she'd observed afterwards, "I wouldn't want to have to face Tom Weicker if I'd caused some kind of major foul-up."

"How are you, Mrs. Collins, and how is Meg?" Weicker said as he picked up.

"We're all right, thanks." She explained why she was calling.

"I didn't speak to you yesterday," he said.

My God, Catherine thought, I'm not going crazy as well as everything else, am I? "Mr. Weicker, somebody called and used your name. Did you authorize anyone to phone?"

"No. Specifically, what did this person say to you?"

Catherine's hands went clammy. "He wanted to know where Meg was and when she'd be home." Still holding the receiver, she sank down onto a chair. "Mr. Weicker, somebody was photographing Meg from behind our house the other night."

"Do the police know about that?"

"Yes."

"Then let them know about this call too. And please keep me posted if you get any more of them. Tell Meg we miss her."

He meant it. She knew he did, and he sounded genuinely concerned. Catherine realized that Meg would have given Weicker the exclusive story of what she had learned in Scottsdale about the dead girl who resembled her.

There's no hiding it from the media, Catherine thought. Meg said that Frances Grolier is coming to New York tomorrow to claim her daughter's body.

"Mrs. Collins, are you all right?"

Catherine made up her mind. "Yes, and there's something you should know before anyone else. Meg went to Scottsdale, Arizona, yesterday because . . ."

She told him what she knew, then answered his questions. The final one was the hardest.

"As a newsman, I have to ask you this, Mrs. Collins. How do you feel about your husband now?"

"I don't know how I feel about my husband," Catherine answered. "I do know I'm very, very sorry for Frances Grolier. Her daughter is dead. My daughter is alive and will be with me tonight."

When she was finally able to replace the receiver, Catherine went into the dining room and sat at the table where the files were still spread out as she had left them. With her fingertips, she rubbed her temples. Her head was beginning to ache, a dull, steady pain.

The door chimes pealed softly. Pray God it isn't the state attorney's people or reporters, she thought as she wearily got up.

Through the living room window she could see that a tall man was standing on the porch. Who? She caught a glimpse of his face. Surprised, she hurried to open the door.

"Hello, Mrs. Collins," Victor Orsini said. "I apologize. I should have called but I was nearby and thought I'd take a chance and stop in. I'm hoping that some papers I need might have been put in Edwin's files. Would you mind if I go through them?"

MEGHAN TOOK AMERICA WEST FLIGHT 292 LEAVING PHOENIX at 1:25 and due to arrive in New York at 8:05 P.M. She was grateful she'd been given a window seat. The middle one was not occupied, but the fortyish woman on the aisle seemed to be a talker.

To avoid her, Meg reclined the seat and closed her eyes. In her mind she replayed every detail of her meeting with Frances Grolier. As she reviewed it, her emotions seemed to be on a roller-coaster ride, going from one extreme to another.

Anger at her father. Anger at Frances.

Jealousy that there had been another daughter whom her father loved.

Curiosity about Annie. She was a travel writer. She must have been intelligent. She looked like me. She was my half-sister, Meghan thought. She was still breathing when they put her in the ambulance. I was with her when she died and I'd never known that she existed.

Pity for everyone: for Frances Grolier and Annie, for her mother and herself. And for Dad, Meghan thought. Maybe someday I'll see him the way Frances does. A hurt little boy who couldn't be secure unless he was sure there was a place for him to go, a place where he was wanted.

Still, her father had known two homes where he was loved, she thought. Did he need both of them to make up for the two he'd known as a child, places where he was neither wanted nor loved?

The plane's bar service began. Meghan ordered a glass of red wine and sipped it slowly, glad for the warmth that began to seep through her system. She glanced to one side. Happily, the woman on the aisle was engrossed in a book.

Lunch was served. Meghan wasn't hungry but did have the salad and roll and coffee. Her head began to clear. She took a pad from her shoulder bag and over a second cup of coffee began to jot down notes.

That scrap of paper with her name and phone number had triggered Annie's confrontation with Frances, her demand to know the truth. Frances said that Annie called me and hung up when I answered, Meghan thought. *If only she'd spoken to me then.* She might never have come to New York. She might still be alive.

Kyle had obviously seen Annie when she'd been driving around Newtown. Had anyone else seen her there?

I wonder if Frances told her where Dad worked, Meghan thought, and jotted down the question.

Dr. Manning. According to Frances, Dad was upset after speaking to him the day before Dad disappeared. According to the papers, Dr. Manning said the conversation was cordial. Then what got Dad upset?

Victor Orsini. Was he the key to all this? Frances said that Dad was horrified by something he'd learned about him.

Orsini. Meghan underlined his name three times. He had come to work around the time Helene Petrovic was presented as a candidate to the Manning Clinic. Was there a connection?

The last notation Meghan made consisted of three words. *Is Dad alive?*

The plane landed at eight o'clock, exactly on time. As Meghan unsnapped her seat belt, the woman on the aisle closed her book and turned to her. "I've just figured it out," she said happily. "I'm a travel agent and I understand that when you don't want to talk, you shouldn't be bothered. But I knew I'd met you somewhere. It was at an ASTA meeting in San Francisco last year. You're Annie Collins, the travel writer, aren't you?"

BERNIE WAS AT THE BAR WHEN CATHERINE LOOKED IN AS SHE was leaving the hotel. He watched her reflection in the mirror but immediately averted his eyes and picked up the menu when she looked in his direction.

He didn't want her to notice him. It was never a good idea for people to pay special attention to you. They might start asking questions. Just from that glance in the mirror, he could tell that Meghan's mother looked like a smart lady. You couldn't put too much over on her.

Where was Meghan? Bernie ordered another beer, then wondered if the bartender, Joe, wasn't starting to look at him with the kind of expression the cops had when they'd stop him and ask what he was up to.

All you had to do was say, "I'm just hanging around," and they were all over you with questions. "Why?" "Who do you know around here?" "Do you come here much?"

Those were the questions he didn't want people around here to even start thinking.

The big thing was to have people used to seeing him. When you're used to seeing someone all the time, you never really see him. He and the prison psychiatrist had talked about that.

Something inside him was warning that it would be dangerous to go into the woods behind Meghan's house again. With the way that kid had been screaming, someone had probably called the cops. They might be keeping a watch on the place now.

But if he never ran into Meghan on a job because she was on leave from Channel 3, and he couldn't get near her house, how would he get to see her?

While he sipped his second beer, the answer came to him, so easy, so simple.

This wasn't just a restaurant, it was an *inn.* People stayed here. There was a sign outside that announced VACANCY. From the windows on the south side you should have a clear view of Meghan's house. If he rented a room he could come and go and no one would think anything of it. They'd *expect* his car to be there all night. He could say that his mother was in a hospital but would be getting out in a few days and needed a quiet place where she could take it easy and not have to cook.

"Are these rooms expensive?" he asked the bartender. "I need to find a place for my mother, so she can get her strength back, if you know what I mean. She's not sick anymore, but kind of weak and can't be fussing for herself."

"The guest rooms are great," Tony told him. "They were renovated only two years ago. They're not expensive right now. It's between seasons. In about three weeks, around Thanksgiving, they go up and stay up through the skiing season. Then they get discounted again until April or May."

"My mother likes a lot of sun."

"I know half the rooms are empty. Talk to Virginia Murphy. She's Mrs. Collins' assistant and handles everything."

The room Bernie chose was more than satisfactory. On the south side of the inn, it directly faced the Collins house. Even with all the electronic equipment he'd bought lately he wasn't near the limit on his credit card. He could stay here a long time.

Murphy accepted it with a pleasant smile. "What time will your mother check in, Mr. Heffernan?" she asked.

"She won't be here for a few days," Bernie explained. "I want to be able to use the room till she's out of the hospital. It's too long a trek to drive back and forth from Long Island every day."

"It certainly is and the traffic can be bad too. Do you have luggage?"

"I'll come back with it later."

Bernie went home. After dinner with Mama he told her the boss wanted him to drive a customer's car to Chicago. "I'll be gone three or four days, Mama. It's an expensive new car, and they don't want me to speed. They'll send me back on the bus."

"How much are they paying you?"

Bernie picked a figure out of the air. "Two hundred dollars a day, Mama."

She snorted. "I get sick when I think of the way I worked to support you and got paid next to nothing and you get two hundred dollars a day to drive a fancy car."

"He wants me to start tonight." Bernie went into the bedroom and threw some clothes in the black nylon suitcase that Mama had bought at a garage sale years ago. It didn't look bad. Mama had cleaned it up.

He made sure to bring plenty of tape cassettes for his video camera, all his lenses and his cellular telephone.

He told Mama goodbye, but didn't kiss her. They never kissed. Mama didn't believe in kissing. As usual, she stood at the door to watch him drive away.

Her last words to him were, "Don't get in any trouble, Bernard."

MEGHAN REACHED HOME SHORTLY BEFORE TEN-THIRTY. HER mother had cheese and crackers and grapes on the coffee table in the living room and wine chilling in the decanter. "I thought you might need a little sustenance."

"I need something. I'll be right down. I'm going to get comfortable."

She carried her bag upstairs, changed into pajamas, a robe and slippers, washed her face, brushed her hair and anchored it back with a band.

"That feels better," she said when she returned to the living room. "Do you mind if we don't talk about everything tonight? You know the essentials. Dad and Annie's mother have had a relationship for twenty-seven years. The last time she saw him was when he left to come home to us and never arrived. She and her lawyer are taking the 11:25 red-eye tonight from Phoenix. They'll get to New York around six tomorrow morning."

"Why didn't she wait until tomorrow? Why would anyone want to fly all night?"

"I suspect she wants to be in and out of New York as fast as possible. I warned her that the police would certainly want to see her and there'd probably be extensive media coverage."

"Meg, I hope I did the right thing." Catherine hesitated. "I told Tom Weicker about your trip to Scottsdale. PCD carried the story about Annie on the six o'clock news and I'm sure they'll repeat it at eleven. I think they were as kind to you and me as possible, but it isn't a pretty story. I might add I turned the ringer off on the phone and turned on the answering machine. A couple of reporters have come to the door, but I could see their vans outside and didn't answer. They showed up at the inn, and Virginia said I was out of town."

"I'm glad you gave the story to Tom," Meg said. "I enjoyed working for him. I want him to have the exclusive." She tried to smile at her mother. "You're gutsy."

"We might as well be. And, Meg, he *didn't* call you yesterday. I realize now that whoever did call was trying to find out where you were. I called the police. They're going to keep an eye on the house and check the woods regularly." Catherine's control snapped. "Meg, I'm frightened for you."

Meg thought, who on earth would have known to use Tom Weicker's name?

She said, "Mom, I don't know what's going on. But for now, the alarm is set, isn't it?"

"Yes."

"Then we might as well watch the news. It's time."

IT'S ONE THING TO BE GUTSY, MEG THOUGHT, IT'S ANOTHER to know that a few hundred thousand people are watching a story that makes mincemeat of your private life.

She watched and listened as, with appropriately serious

demeanor, Joel Edison, the PCD eleven o'clock anchor, opened the program. "As reported exclusively on our six o'clock newscast, Edwin Collins, missing since January 28th and a suspect in the Manning Clinic murder case, is the father of the young victim, stabbed to death in mid-Manhattan twelve days ago. Mr. Collins . . .

"Also the father of Meghan Collins of this news team . . . warrant for arrest . . . had two families . . . known in Arizona as husband of the prominent sculptor, Frances Grolier . . ."

"They've obviously been doing their own investigation," Catherine said. "I didn't tell them that."

Finally a commercial came.

Meg pushed the Off button on the remote, and the television went dark. "One thing Annie's mother told me is that the last time he was in Arizona, Dad was horrified by something he'd learned about Victor Orsini."

"Victor Orsini!"

The shock in her mother's voice startled Meg. "Yes. Why? Has something come up about him?"

"He was here today. He asked to go through Edwin's files. He claimed that papers he needed were in them."

"Did he take anything? Did you leave him alone with them?"

"No. Or maybe just for a minute. He was here about an hour. When he left he seemed disappointed. He asked if I was sure that these were all the files we'd brought home. Meg, he begged me for the present not to say anything to Phillip about being here. I promised, but I didn't know what to make of it."

"What I make of it is that there's something in those files that he doesn't want us to find." Meg stood up. "I suggest we both get some sleep. I can assure you that tomorrow the media will be all over the place again, but you and I are spending the day going through those files."

She paused, then added, "I only wish to God we knew what we're looking for."

*   *   *

BERNIE WAS AT THE WINDOW OF HIS ROOM IN THE DRUMDOE Inn when Meg arrived home. He had his camera with the telescopic lens ready and began taping when she turned on the light in her bedroom. He sighed with pleasure as she took off her jacket and unbuttoned her blouse.

Then she came over and tilted the blinds but didn't completely close them, and he was able to get glimpses of her moving back and forth as she undressed. He waited impatiently when she went downstairs. He couldn't see whatever part of the house she was in.

What he did see made him realize how clever he'd been. A squad car drove slowly past the Collins house every twenty minutes or so. Besides that he saw the beams of flashlights in the woods. The cops had been told about him. They were looking for him.

What would they think if they knew he was right here watching them, laughing at them? But he had to be careful. He wanted a chance to be with Meghan, but he realized now it couldn't be around her house. He'd have to wait until she drove away alone in her car. When he saw her going toward the garage, all he had to do was get downstairs quickly, get into his own car and be ready to pull out behind her when she passed the inn.

He needed to be alone with her, talk to her like a real friend. He wanted to watch the way her lips went up in a curve when she smiled, the way her body moved like just now when she took off her jacket and opened her blouse.

Meghan would understand that he'd never hurt her. He just wanted to be her friend.

Bernie didn't get much sleep that night. It was too interesting to watch the cops driving back and forth.

Back and forth.

Back and forth.

51

*P*hillip was the first one to call on Thursday morning. "I heard the newscast last night and it's all over the papers this morning. May I come by for a few minutes?"

"Of course," Catherine told him. "If you can pick your way through the press. They're camped outside the house."

"I'll go around to the back."

It was nine o'clock. Meg and Catherine were having breakfast. "I wonder if anything new has developed?" Catherine said. "Phillip sounds upset."

"Remember you promised you wouldn't say anything about Victor Orsini being here yesterday," Meg cautioned. "Anyhow I'd like to do my own checking on him."

When Phillip arrived it was clear that he was very concerned.

"The dam has burst, if that's the proper metaphor," he told them. "The first lawsuit was filed yesterday. A couple who have been paying for storage of ten cryopreserved embryos at the Manning Clinic have been notified there are only seven in the lab. Clearly, Petrovic was making a lot of mistakes along the line and falsifying records to cover them. Collins and Carter have been named as codefendants with the clinic."

"I don't know what to say anymore except that I'm so sorry," Catherine told him.

"I shouldn't have told you. It isn't even the reason I'm here. Did you see Frances Grolier being interviewed when she arrived at Kennedy this morning?"

"Yes, we did." It was Meg who answered.

"Then what do you think of her statement that she believes Edwin is alive and may have started a totally new life?"

"We don't believe that for a minute," Meghan said.

"I have to warn you that John Dwyer is so sure Ed is hiding somewhere that he's going to grill you on that. Meg, when I saw Dwyer Tuesday, he practically accused me of obstructing justice. He asked a hypothetical question: Assuming Ed had a relationship somewhere, where did I think it would be? Clearly you knew where to look for it."

"Phillip," Meghan asked, "you're not suggesting that my father is alive and I know where he is, are you?"

There was no evidence of Carter's usually cheerful and assured manner. "Meg," he said, "I certainly don't believe you know where to reach Edwin. But that Grolier woman knew him so well." He stopped, aware of the impact of his words. "Forgive me."

Meghan knew Phillip Carter was right, that the assistant state attorney would be sure to ask how she knew to go to Scottsdale.

When he left, Catherine said, "This is dragging Phillip down too."

An hour later, Meghan tried calling Stephanie Petrovic. There was still no answer. She called Mac at his office to see if he had managed to reach her.

When Mac told her about the note Stephanie had left, Meghan said flatly, "Mac, that note is a fraud. Stephanie never went with that man willingly. I saw her reaction when I suggested going after him for child support. She's mortally afraid of him. I think Helene Petrovic's lawyer had better report her as a missing person."

Another mysterious disappearance, Meghan thought. It was too late to drive to southern New Jersey today. She would go tomorrow, starting out before daylight. That way she might evade the press.

She wanted to see Charles Potters and ask him to take her through the Petrovic house. She wanted to see the priest who had conducted the service for Helene. He obviously knew the Rumanian women who had attended it.

The terrible possibility was that Stephanie, a young woman about to give birth, might have known something about her aunt that was dangerous to Helene Petrovic's killer.

52

Special investigators Bob Marron and Arlene Weiss requested and received permission from the Manhattan district attorney to question Frances Grolier late Thursday morning.

Martin Fox, her attorney, a silver-haired retired judge in his late sixties, was by her side in a suite in the Doral Hotel, a dozen blocks from the medical examiner's office. Fox was quick to reject questions he felt inappropriate.

Frances had been to the morgue and identified Annie's body. It would be flown to Phoenix and met by a funeral director from Scottsdale. Grief was carved on her face as implacably as it would be in one of her sculptures, but she was composed.

She answered for Marron and Weiss the same questions she had answered for the New York homicide detectives. She knew of no one who might have accompanied Annie to New York. Annie had no enemies. She would not discuss Edwin Collins except to say that, yes, she did think there was a possibility he chose to disappear.

"Did he ever express any desire to be in a rural setting?" Arlene Weiss asked.

The question seemed to penetrate Grolier's lethargy. "Why do you want to know that?"

"Because even though his car had been recently washed

when it was found in front of Meghan Collins' apartment building, there were traces of mud and bits of straw embedded in the tread on the tires. Ms. Grolier, do you think that's the kind of place he might choose to hide?"

"It's possible. Sometimes he interviewed staff members at rural colleges. When he talked about those trips, he always said that life seemed so much less complicated in the country."

WEISS AND MARRON WENT FROM NEW YORK DIRECTLY TO Newtown to talk to Catherine and Meghan again. They asked them the same question.

"The last place in the world I could see my husband is on a farm," Catherine told them.

Meghan agreed. "There's something that keeps bothering me. Doesn't it seem odd that if my father were driving his car, he'd not only leave it where it was sure to be noticed and ticketed but would also leave a murder weapon in it?"

"We haven't closed the door to any possibilities," Marron told her.

"But you're concentrating on *him*. Maybe if you take him out of the picture completely, a different pattern will start to emerge."

"Let's talk about why you made that sudden trip to Arizona, Miss Collins. We had to hear about it on television. Tell us yourself. When did you learn that your father had a residence there?"

When they left an hour later, they took the tape containing the Palomino message with them.

"Do you believe anyone in that office is looking beyond Dad for answers?" Meghan asked her mother.

"No, and they don't intend to," Catherine said bitterly.

They went back into the dining room where they'd been studying the files. Analysis of the California hotel charges pinpointed year by year the times Edwin Collins had probably stayed in Scottsdale.

"But that isn't the kind of information that Victor Orsini would care about," Meg said. "There's got to be something else."

ON THURSDAY AT THE COLLINS AND CARTER OFFICE, JACKIE, the secretary, and Milly, the bookkeeper, conferred in whispers about the tension between Phillip Carter and Victor Orsini. They agreed that it was caused by all the terrible publicity about Mr. Collins and the law suits being filed.

Things had never been right since Mr. Collins died. "Or at least since we thought he died," Jackie said. "It's hard to believe that with a nice, pretty wife like Mrs. Collins, he'd have someone on the side all these years.

"I'm so worried," she went on. "Every penny of my salary is saved for college for the boys. This job is so convenient. I'd hate to lose it."

Milly was sixty-three and wanted to work for two more years until she could collect a bigger social security check. "If they go under, who's going to hire me?" It was a rhetorical question that she frequently asked these days.

"One of them is coming in here at night," Jackie whispered. "You know you can tell when someone's been going through the files."

"Why would anyone do that? They can have us dig for anything they want," Milly protested. "That's what we're paid for."

"The only thing I can figure is that one of them is trying to find the file copy of the letter to the Manning Clinic recommending Helene Petrovic," Jackie said. "I've looked and looked and I can't put my hands on it."

"You'd only been here a few weeks when you typed it. You were just getting used to the filing system," Milly reminded her. "Anyhow, what difference does it make? The police have the original and that's what counts."

"Maybe it makes a lot of difference," Jackie said. "The truth is, I don't remember typing that letter, but then it was seven years ago and I don't remember half the letters that go out of here. And my initials *are* on it."

"So?"

Jackie pulled out her desk drawer, removed her purse and plucked from it a folded newspaper clipping. "Ever since I saw the letter to the Manning Clinic about Petrovic reprinted in the paper, something's been bothering me. Look at this."

She handed the clipping to Milly. "See the way the first line of each paragraph is indented? That's the way I type letters for Mr. Carter and Mr. Orsini. Mr. Collins always had his letters typed in block form, no indentation at all."

"That's right," Milly agreed, "but that certainly looks like Mr. Collins' signature."

"The experts say it's his signature, but I say it's awfully funny a letter he signed went out typed like that."

AT THREE O'CLOCK, TOM WEICKER PHONED. "MEG, I JUST wanted you to know that we're going to run the story you did on the Franklin Clinic in Philadelphia, the one we were going to use with the identical twin special. We'll schedule it on both news broadcasts tonight. It's a good, succinct piece on in vitro fertilization and ties in with what's happened at the Manning Clinic."

"I'm glad you're running it, Tom."

"I wanted to be sure you saw it," he said, his voice surprisingly kind.

"Thanks for letting me know," Meg replied.

MAC PHONED AT FIVE-THIRTY. "HOW ABOUT YOU AND CATHerine coming over here for dinner for a change? I'm sure you won't want to go to the inn tonight."

"No, we don't," Meg agreed. "And we could use the company. Is six-thirty all right? I want to watch the Channel 3 news. A feature I did is being run."

"Come over now and watch it here. Kyle can show off that he's learned to tape."

"All right."

IT WAS A GOOD STORY. A NICE MOMENT WAS THE SEGMENT taped in Dr. Williams' office, when he pointed to the walls filled with pictures of young children. "Can you imagine how much happiness these kids are bringing into people's lives?"

Meg had instructed the cameraman to pan slowly over the photographs as Dr. Williams continued to speak. "These children were born only because of the methods of assisted reproduction available here."

"Plug for the center," Meg commented. "But it wasn't too heavy."

"It was a good feature, Meg," Mac said.

"Yes, I think so. Suppose we skip the rest of the news. We all know what it's going to be."

BERNIE STAYED IN THE ROOM ALL DAY. HE TOLD THE MAID that he wasn't feeling well. He told her that he guessed all the nights he'd spent at the hospital when his mother was so sick were catching up with him.

Virginia Murphy called a few minutes later. "We usually only have continental breakfast room service, but we'll be glad to send up a tray whenever you're ready."

They sent up lunch, then later Bernie ordered dinner. He had the pillows propped up so it looked like he'd been in bed resting. The minute the waiter left, Bernie was back at the window, sitting at an angle so nobody who happened to look up would notice him.

He watched as Meghan and her mother left the house a little before six. It was dark, but the porch light was on. He debated following them, then decided that as long as the mother was along, he would be wasting his time. He was glad he hadn't bothered when the car went right instead of left. He figured they must be going to the house where that kid lived. That was the only one in the cul-de-sac.

The squad cars came regularly through the day, but not every twenty minutes anymore. During the evening, he noticed flashlights in the woods only once. The cops were easing up. That was good.

Meghan and her mother got back home around ten. An hour later, Meghan undressed and got into bed. She sat up for about twenty minutes, writing something in a notebook.

Long after she turned off the light, Bernie stayed at the window thinking about her, imagining being in the room with her.

53

*D*onald Anderson had taken two weeks off from work to help with the new baby. Neither he nor Dina wanted outside assistance. "You relax," he told his wife. "Jonathan and I are in charge."

The doctor had signed the release the night before. He wholeheartedly agreed that it was better if they could avoid the media. "Ten to one some of the photographers will be in the lobby between nine and eleven," he'd predicted. That was the time new mothers and babies usually were discharged.

The phone had been ringing all week with requests for interviews. Don screened them with the answering machine and did not return any of them. On Thursday their lawyer phoned. There was definite proof of malfeasance at the Manning Clinic. He warned them that they'd be urged to join the class action suit that was being proposed.

"Absolutely not," Anderson said. "You can tell that to anyone who calls you."

Dina was propped up on the couch, reading to Jonathan. Stories about Big Bird were his new favorites. She glanced up at her husband. "Why not just turn off that phone?" she suggested. "Bad enough I wouldn't even look at Nicky for hours after he was born. All he'd need to know when he grows up is that I sued someone because he's here instead of another baby."

They'd named him Nicholas after Dina's grandfather, the one her mother swore he resembled. From the nearby bassinet, they heard a stirring, a faint cry, then a wholehearted wail as their infant woke up.

"He heard us talking about him," Jonathan said.

"Maybe he did, love," Dina agreed as she kissed the top of Jonathan's silky blond head.

"He's just plain hungry again," Don announced. He bent down, picked up the squirming bundle and handed it to Dina.

"Are you sure he's not my twin?" Jonathan asked.

"Yes, I'm sure," Dina said. "But he's your brother, and that's every bit as good."

She put the baby to her breast. "You have my olive skin," she said as she gently stroked his cheek to start him nursing. My little paisano."

She smiled at her husband. "You know something, Don. It's really only fair that one of our kids looks like me."

MEGHAN'S EARLY START ON FRIDAY MORNING MEANT THAT she was able to be in the rectory of St. Dominic's church on the outskirts of Trenton at ten-thirty.

She had called the young pastor immediately after dinner the night before and set up the appointment.

The rectory was a narrow, three-story frame house typical of the Victorian era, with a wraparound porch and gingerbread trim. The sitting room was shabby but comfortable with heavy, overstuffed chairs, a carved library table, old-fashioned standing lamps and a faded Oriental carpet. The fireplace glowed with burning logs and breaking embers, dispelling the chill of the minuscule foyer.

Fr. Radzin had opened the door for her, apologized that he was on the phone, ushered her into this room and vanished up the stairs. As Meghan waited, she mused that this was the kind of room where troubled people could unburden themselves without fear of condemnation or reproach.

She wasn't sure exactly what she would ask the priest. She did know from the brief eulogy he'd delivered at the memorial mass that he'd known and liked Helene Petrovic.

She heard his footsteps on the stairs. Then he was in the room, apologizing again for keeping her waiting. He chose a chair opposite hers and asked, "How can I help you, Meghan?"

Not "What can I do for you?" but "How can I help you?" A subtle difference that was oddly consoling. "I have to find out who Helene Petrovic really was. You're aware of the situation at the Manning Clinic?"

"Yes, of course. I've been following the story. I also saw in this morning's paper a picture of you and that poor girl who was stabbed. The resemblance is quite remarkable."

"I haven't seen the paper, but I know what you mean. Actually, that's what started all this." Meghan leaned forward, locking her fingers, pressing her palms together. "The assistant state attorney investigating Helene Petrovic's murder believes that my father is responsible for Helene being hired at Manning and for her death too. I don't. Too many things don't make sense. Why would he want to see the clinic hire someone who wasn't qualified for the job? What did he have to gain by placing Helene in the lab in the first place?"

"There's always a reason, Meghan, sometimes several, for every action any human being makes."

"That's what I mean. I can't find one, never mind several. It just makes no sense. Why would my father have even become involved with Helene if he knew she was a fraud? I know he was conscientious about his job. He took pride in matching the right people to his clients. We used to talk about it often.

"It's reprehensible to put an unqualified person in a sensitive medical situation. The more they investigate the lab at the Manning Clinic, the more errors they're finding. I can't understand why my father would deliberately cause all that. And what about Helene? Didn't she have any conscience in the matter? Didn't she worry about preembryos being damaged or destroyed because of her sloppiness, carelessness or ignorance? At least some stored embryos were intended to be transferred in the hope that they'd be born."

"Transferred and born," Fr. Radzin repeated. "An interesting ethical question. Helene was not a regular churchgoer, but when she did come to mass, it was always the last one on Sunday and she would stay for coffee hour. I had the feeling there was something on her mind that she couldn't bring herself to talk about. But I must tell you that if I were applying adjectives to her, the last three that would come to mind are 'sloppy, careless and ignorant.' "

"What about her friends? Who was she close to?"

"No one I know of. Some of her acquaintances have been in touch with me this week. They've commented on how little they really knew Helene."

"I'm afraid something may have happened to her niece, Stephanie. Did you ever meet the young man who is her baby's father?"

"No. And neither did anyone else from what I understand."

"What did you think of Stephanie?"

"She's nothing like Helene. Of course she's very young and in this country less than a year. Now she's alone. It may just be that the baby's father showed up again and she decided to take a chance on him."

He wrinkled his forehead. Mac does that, Meghan thought. Fr. Radzin looked to be in his late thirties, a little

older than Mac. Why was she comparing them? It was because there was something so wholesome and good about
them, she decided.

She stood up. "I've taken enough of your time, Fr. Radzin."

"Stay another minute or two, Meghan. Sit down, please.
You've raised the question of your father's motivation in
placing Helene at the clinic. If you can't get information
about Helene, my advice is to keep searching until you find
the reason for *his* participation in the situation. Do you think
he was romantically involved with her?"

"I very much doubt it." She shrugged. "He seems to have
been sufficiently troubled trying to balance his time between
my mother and Annie's mother."

"Money?"

"That doesn't make sense either. The Manning Clinic paid
the usual fee to Collins and Carter for the placement of Helene and Dr. Williams. My experience in studying law and
human nature has taught me that love or money are the
reasons most crimes are committed. Yet I can't make either
fit here." She stood up. "Now I really must go. I'm meeting
Helene's lawyer at her Lawrenceville house."

CHARLES POTTERS WAS WAITING WHEN MEGHAN ARRIVED.
She had met him briefly at Helene's memorial service. Now
as she had a chance to focus on him, she realized that he
looked like the kind of family lawyer portrayed in old movies.

His dark blue suit was ultraconservative, his shirt crisp
white, his narrow blue tie subdued, his skin tone pink, his
sparse gray hair neatly combed. Rimless glasses enhanced
surprisingly vivid hazel eyes.

Whatever items from the house Stephanie had taken with
her, the appearance of this room, the first they entered, was
unchanged. It looked exactly as Meghan had seen it less than
a week ago. Powers of observation, she thought. Concen-

trate. Then she noticed that the lovely Dresden figures she'd admired were missing from the mantel.

"Your friend Dr. MacIntyre dissuaded me from immediately reporting Stephanie's theft of Helene's property, Miss Collins, but I'm afraid I cannot wait any longer. As trustee I'm responsible for all of Helene's possessions."

"I understand that. I simply wish that some effort could be made to find Stephanie and persuade her to return them. If a warrant is sworn out for her arrest, she might be deported.

"Mr. Potters," she continued, "my concern is much more serious than worrying about the things Stephanie took with her. Do you have the note she left?"

"Yes. Here it is."

Meghan read it through.

"Did you ever meet this Jan?"

"No."

"What did Helene think about her niece's pregnancy?"

"Helene was a kind woman, reserved but kind. Her only comments to me about the pregnancy were quite sympathetic."

"How long have you handled her affairs?"

"For about three years."

"You believed she was a medical doctor?"

"I had no reason not to believe her."

"Didn't she build up a rather considerable estate? She had a very good salary at Manning of course. She was paid there as an embryologist. But she certainly couldn't have made very much money as a medical secretary for the three years before that."

"I understood she'd been a cosmetologist. Cosmetology can be lucrative, and Helene was a shrewd investor. Miss Collins, I don't have much time. I believe you said you would like to walk through the house with me? I want to be sure it's properly secured before I leave."

"Yes, I would."

Meghan went upstairs with him. Here too nothing seemed

to be out of order. Stephanie's packing had clearly not been rushed.

The master bedroom was luxurious. Helene Petrovic had not denied herself creature comforts. The coordinated wall hanging, spread and draperies looked very expensive.

French doors opened into a small sitting room. One wall was covered with pictures of children. "These are duplicates of the ones at the Manning Clinic," she said.

"Helene showed them to me," Potters told her. "She was very proud of the successful births achieved through the clinic."

Meg studied the pictures. "I saw some of these kids at the reunion less than two weeks ago." She picked out Jonathan. "This is the Anderson child whose family you've been reading about. That's the case that started the state investigation of the lab at Manning." She paused, studying the photograph on the top corner. It was of two children, a boy and girl, in matching sweaters with their arms around each other. What was it about them that she should be noticing?

"I really have to lock up now, Miss Collins."

There was an edge in the attorney's voice. She couldn't delay him any longer. Meg took another long look at the picture of the children in matching sweaters, committing it to memory.

BERNIE'S MOTHER WAS NOT FEELING WELL. IT WAS HER ALlergies. She'd been sneezing a lot, and her eyes were itchy. She thought she felt a draft in the house too. She wondered if Bernard had forgotten and left a window open downstairs.

She knew she shouldn't have let Bernard drive that car to Chicago, even for two hundred dollars a day. Sometimes when he was off by himself too long, he got fanciful. He started to daydream and to want things that could get him in trouble.

Then his temper started. That's when she needed to be there; she could control an outburst when she saw it coming.

She kept him on the straight and narrow. Kept him nice and clean, well fed, saw that he got to his job and then stayed in with her watching television at night.

He'd been doing well for such a long time now. But he'd been acting kind of funny lately.

He was supposed to call. Why didn't he? When he got to Chicago he wouldn't start following a girl and try to touch her, would he? Not that he'd mean to harm her, but there'd been too many times when Bernard got nervous if a girl screamed. A couple of girls he'd hurt real bad.

They said that if it happened again, they wouldn't let him come home. They'd keep him locked up. He knew it too.

THE ONLY THING I HAVE REALLY ESTABLISHED IN ALL THESE hours is the number of times my husband was cheating on me, Catherine thought as she pushed the files away late Friday afternoon. She no longer had any desire to go through them. What good would knowing all this serve her now? It hurts so much, she thought.

She stood up. Outside it was a blustery November afternoon. In three weeks it would be Thanksgiving. That was always a busy time at the inn.

Virginia had phoned. The real estate company was being persistent. Was the inn for sale? They must be serious, she reported. They'd even named the price at which they'd start negotiating. They had another place in mind if Drumdoe wasn't available, or so they said. But it might be true.

Catherine wondered how long she and Meg could twist in the wind like this.

Meg. Would she close in on herself because of her father's betrayal as she had when Mac married Ginger? Catherine had never let on that she knew how heartbroken Meg had been over Mac. Edwin was always the one their daughter had turned to for comfort. Natural enough. Daddy's girl. It ran in the family. I was Daddy's girl too, Catherine thought.

Catherine could see the way Mac looked at Meg these days. She hoped it wasn't too late. Edwin had never forgiven his mother for rejecting him. Meg had built up a wall around herself where Mac was concerned. And great as she was with Kyle in her own way, she chose not to see how hopefully he was always reaching out to her.

Catherine caught a glimpse of a figure in the woods. She froze, then relaxed. It was a policeman. At least they were keeping an eye on the place.

She heard the click of a key in the lock.

Catherine breathed a prayer of gratitude. The daughter who made everything else bearable was safe.

Now maybe for the moment she could stop being haunted by the pictures that had run side by side in the newspapers today, the official publicity head shot of Meg from Channel 3 and the professional head shot Annie had used for her travel articles.

At Catherine's insistence, Virginia had sent over all the papers delivered to the inn, including the tabloids. The *Daily News,* besides using the pictures, had printed a photocopy of the fax Meg had received the night Annie was stabbed.

The headline of their article read: DID THE WRONG SISTER DIE?

"Hi, Mom. I'm home."

For reassurance, Catherine took one more glance at the policeman at the edge of the woods, then turned to greet her daughter.

VIRGINIA MURPHY WAS THE SEMIOFFICIAL SECOND IN COMMAND of the Drumdoe Inn. Technically hostess at the restaurant, and reservation clerk as needed, she was in fact Catherine's eyes and ears when Catherine was not around or when she was busy in the kitchen. Ten years younger than Catherine, six inches taller and handsomely rounded, she was a good friend as well as a faithful employee.

Knowing the financial situation at the inn, Virginia worked diligently to cut corners where it wouldn't show. She passionately wanted Catherine to be able to keep the inn. She knew that when all this terrible publicity died down, Catherine's best chance to get on with her life began here.

It galled Virginia that she'd aided and abetted Catherine when that crazy interior designer came in with her violently expensive swatches and tile samples and plumbing-supply books. And that after the expense of the much-needed renovation!

The place looked lovely, Virginia admitted, and it certainly had needed a face-lift, but the irony would be to go through the inconvenience and financial drain of renovating and redecorating only to have someone else come in and buy Drumdoe at a fire-sale price.

The last thing Virginia wanted to do was to cause Catherine any more concern, but now she was getting worried about the man who had checked into room 3A. He'd been in bed since he arrived, claiming he was exhausted from running back and forth from Long Island to New Haven, where his mother was in the hospital.

It wasn't a big deal to send a tray up to his room. They could certainly handle that. The problem was that he might be seriously sick. How would it look if something happened to him while he was here?

Virginia thought, I'm not going to bother Catherine yet. I'm going to let it go at least for another day. If he's still in bed tomorrow night, I'll go up and have a talk with him myself. I'll insist that he allow a doctor to see him.

FREDERICK SCHULLER FROM VALLEY MEMORIAL HOSPITAL IN Trenton called Mac late Friday afternoon. "I've sent the roster of medical staff to Miss Collins by overnight mail. She'll have a lot of reading to do unless she knows what name she's looking for."

"That was very quick," Mac said sincerely. "I'm grateful."

"Let's see if it's helpful. There is one thing that might interest you. I was looking over the Manning Clinic list and saw Dr. Henry Williams' name on it. I'm acquainted with him. He's head of Franklin Clinic in Philadelphia now."

"Yes, I know," Mac said.

"This may not be relevant. Williams was never on staff here, but I remembered that his wife was in our long-term care facility for two of the three years Helene Petrovic worked at Dowling. I used to run into him here occasionally."

"Do you think there's any chance he's the doctor Petrovic may have been seeing when she was at Dowling?" Mac asked quickly.

There was a hesitation, then Schuller said, "This borders on gossip, but I did make a few inquiries in the long-term unit. The head nurse has been there twenty years. She remembers Dr. Williams and his wife very well."

Mac waited. Let this be the connection we're looking for, he prayed.

It was clear that Frederick Schuller was reluctant to continue. After another brief pause he said, "Mrs. Williams had a brain tumor. She had been born and raised in Rumania. As her condition worsened, she lost her ability to communicate in English. Dr. Williams spoke only a few words of Rumanian, and a woman friend came regularly to Mrs. Williams' room to translate for him."

"Was it Helene Petrovic?" Mac asked.

"The nurse never was introduced to her. She described her as a dark-haired, brown-eyed woman in her early to mid-forties, quite attractive." Schuller added, "As you can see, this is very tenuous."

No it isn't, Mac thought. He tried to sound calm when he thanked Frederick Schuller, but when he hung up the phone, he said a silent prayer of gratitude.

This was the first break! Meg had told him that Dr. Williams denied having known Petrovic before she joined the staff of the Manning Clinic. Williams was the expert who could have taught Petrovic the skills she needed to pass herself off as an embryologist.

54

"Kyle, shouldn't you be starting your homework?" Marie Dileo, the sixty-year-old housekeeper gently prodded.

Kyle was watching the tape he'd made of Meg's interview at the Franklin Clinic. He looked up. "In a minute, Mrs. Dileo, honest."

"You know what your Dad says about too much television."

"This is an educational tape. That's different."

Dileo shook her head. "You have an answer for everything." She studied him affectionately. Kyle was such a nice child, smart as a whip, funny and little-boy appealing.

The segment with Meg was ending, and he turned off the set. "Meg is really a good reporter, isn't she?"

"Yes, she is."

Trailed by Jake, Kyle followed Marie into the kitchen. She could tell something was wrong. "Didn't you come home from Danny's a little early?" she asked.

"Uh-huh." He spun the fruit bowl.

"Don't do that. You'll knock it over. Anything happen at Danny's?"

"His mother got a little mad at us."

"Oh?" Marie looked up from the meat loaf she was preparing. "I'm sure there was a reason."

"They put in a new laundry chute in his house. We thought we'd try it out."

"Kyle, you two wouldn't fit in a laundry chute."

"No, but Penny fits."

"You put Penny in the chute!"

"It was Danny's idea. He put her in and I caught her at the bottom and we put a big quilt and pillows down in case I missed, but I didn't, not once. Penny didn't want to stop, but Danny's mother's real mad. We can't play together all week."

"Kyle, if I were you, I'd have my homework done when your father gets home. He is not going to be happy about this."

"I know." With a deep sigh Kyle went for his backpack and dumped his books on the kitchen table. Jake curled up on the floor at his feet.

That desk he got for his birthday was a waste of money, Marie thought. She'd been about to set the table. Well, that could wait. It was only ten past five. The routine was that she prepared dinner and then left when Mac got home around six. He didn't like to eat the minute he walked in, so he always served the meal himself, after Marie had left.

The phone rang. Kyle jumped up. "I'll get it." He answered, listened, then handed the receiver to Marie. "It's for you, Mrs. Dileo."

It was her husband saying that her father had been taken to the hospital from the nursing home.

"Is something the matter?" Kyle asked when she replaced the receiver.

"Yes. My Dad's been sick for a long time. He's very old. I have to get right to the hospital. I'll drop you at Danny's and leave a note for your father."

"Not Danny's," Kyle said, alarmed. "His mother wouldn't like that. Leave me at Meg's. I'll call her." He pressed the automatic dial button on the phone. Meg's number was directly under those of the police and fire departments. A moment later he announced, beaming, "She said come right over."

Mrs. Dileo scribbled a note to Mac. "Take your homework, Kyle."

"Okay." He ran into the living room and grabbed the tape he'd made of Meg's interview. "Maybe she'll want to watch it with me."

THERE WAS A BRISKNESS ABOUT MEG THAT CATHERINE DID not understand. In the two hours since she'd come back from Trenton, Meg had been through Edwin's files, extracted some papers and made several phone calls from the study. Then she sat at Edwin's desk, writing furiously. It reminded Catherine of when Meg was in law school. Whenever she came home for a weekend, she spent most of it at that desk, totally preoccupied with her case studies.

At five o'clock, Catherine looked in on her. "I thought I'd fix chicken and mushrooms for dinner. How does that grab you?"

"Fine. Sit down for a minute, Mom."

Catherine chose the small armchair near the desk. Her eyes slid past Edwin's maroon leather chair and ottoman. Meg had told her that they were duplicated in Arizona. Once an endearing reminder of her husband, they were now a mockery.

Meg put her elbows on the desk, clasped her hands and rested her chin on them. "I had a nice talk with Fr. Radzin this morning. He offered the memorial mass for Helene Petrovic. I told him I couldn't find any reason why Dad would have placed Petrovic at the Manning Clinic. He said words to the effect that there was always a reason for someone's actions, and if I couldn't find it, maybe I should reexamine the whole premise."

"What do you mean?"

"Mom, I mean that several traumatic things happened to us at once. I saw Annie's body when she was brought to the hospital. We learned that Dad almost certainly had not died in the bridge accident and we began to suspect that he had been leading a double life. On the heels of that, Dad was blamed for Helene Petrovic's false credentials and now for her murder."

Meg leaned forward. "Mom, if it hadn't been for the shock of the double life and Petrovic's death, when the insurers refused to pay, we would have taken a much longer look at the reason we thought Dad was on that bridge when the accident happened. Think about it."

"What do you mean?" Catherine was bewildered. "Victor Orsini was talking to Dad just as he was driving onto the ramp. Someone on the bridge saw his car go over the edge."

"That someone on the bridge obviously was mistaken. And Mom, we only have Victor Orsini's word that Dad was calling him from that spot. Suppose, just suppose, Dad had already crossed the bridge when he called Victor. He might have seen the accident happening behind him. Frances Grolier remembered that Dad had been angry about something Victor had done, and that when Dad called Dr. Manning from Scottsdale, he had seemed really distraught. I was in New York. You were away overnight. It would be just like Dad to tell Victor he wanted to see him immediately, instead of next morning, as Victor said. Dad may have been insecure in his personal life, but I don't think he ever had any doubts professionally."

"You're saying that Victor's a liar?" Catherine looked astounded.

"It would be a safe lie, wouldn't it? The time of the call from Dad's car phone was exactly right and could be verified. Mom, Victor had been at the office a month or so when the recommendation for Petrovic went to Manning. He could have sent it. He was working directly under Dad."

"Phillip never has liked him," Catherine murmured. "But, Meg, there's no way to prove this. And you come up with the same question: Why? Why would Victor, any more than Dad, put Petrovic in that lab? What would he have to gain?"

"I don't know yet. But don't you see that as long as the police think Dad is alive, they're not going to seriously examine any alternative answers in Helene Petrovic's murder?"

The phone rang. "Ten to one it's Phillip for you," Meg said as she picked it up. It was Kyle.

"We've got company for dinner," she told Catherine when she replaced the receiver. "Hope you can stretch the chicken and mushrooms."

"Mac and Kyle?"

"Yes."

"Good." Catherine got up. "Meg, I wish I could be as enthusiastic as you about all these possibilities. You have a theory and it's a good defense argument for your father. But maybe it's just that."

Meg held up a sheet of paper. "This is the January bill for Dad's car phone. Look at how much that last call cost. He and Victor were on for eight minutes. It doesn't take eight minutes to set up a meeting, does it?"

"Meg, Dad's signature was on the letter to the Manning Clinic. That's been verified by experts."

AFTER DINNER, MAC SUGGESTED THAT KYLE HELP CATHERINE with clearing the table. Alone with Meghan in the living room he told her about Dr. Williams' connection to Dowling and possibly to Helene.

"Dr. Williams!" Meghan stared at him. "Mac, he absolutely denied knowing Petrovic before Manning Clinic. The receptionist at Manning saw them having dinner together. When I asked Dr. Williams about it, he claimed that he always took a new staff member out for dinner as a friendly gesture."

"Meg, I think we're onto something, but we still can't be *sure* it was Helene Petrovic who accompanied Williams when he visited his wife," Mac cautioned.

"Mac, it fits. Williams and Helene must have been involved with each other. We know she had a tremendous interest in lab work. He's the perfect one to have helped her falsify her curriculum vitae and to have guided her when she arrived at Manning."

"But Williams left Manning Clinic six months after Petrovic started to work there. Why would he do that if he was involved with her?"

"Her home is in New Jersey, not far from Philadelphia. Her niece said that she was often away for hours on Saturday and Sunday. Much of that time may have been spent with him."

"Then where does your father's letter of recommendation come in? He placed Williams at Manning, but why would he have helped Petrovic get her job there?"

"I have a theory about that, and it involves Victor Orsini. It's starting to fit, all of it."

She smiled up at him, the closest he'd seen to a genuine smile on her lips for a long time.

They were standing in front of the fireplace. Mac put his arms around her. Meghan immediately stiffened and shifted to move out of his embrace, but he would have none of it. He turned her to face him.

"Get it straight, Meghan," Mac said. "You were right nine years ago. I only wish I had seen it then." He paused. "You're the only one for me. I know it now, and you do too. We can't keep wasting time."

He kissed her fiercely, then released her, stepping back. "I won't let you keep pushing me away. Once your life settles down again, we're going to have a long talk about *us.*"

KYLE BEGGED TO SHOW THE TAPE OF MEG'S INTERVIEW. "IT'S only three minutes, Dad. I want to show Meg how I can tape programs now."

"I think you're stalling," Mac told him. "Incidentally, Danny's mother caught me at home when I was reading Mrs. Dileo's note. You're grounded. Show Meg the tape, but then don't even *think* television for a week."

"What'd you do?" Meg asked in a whisper when Kyle sat beside her.

"I'll tell you in a minute. See, here you are."

The tape ran. "You did a good job with that," Meg assured him.

THAT NIGHT MEGHAN LAY IN BED FOR A LONG TIME, UNABLE to sleep. Her mind was in turmoil, going over all the new developments, the connection of Dr. Williams to Petrovic, her suspicions about Victor Orsini. Mac. I told the police if they'd stop concentrating on Dad they'd find the real answers, she thought. But Mac? She wouldn't let herself think about him now.

All this, yet there was something else, she realized, something that was eluding her, something terribly, terribly important. What was it? It had something to do with the tape of her interview at the Franklin Center. I'll ask Kyle to bring it over tomorrow, she thought. I have to see it again.

FRIDAY WAS A LONG DAY FOR BERNIE. HE HAD SLEPT UNTIL seven-thirty, real late for him. He suspected right away that he had missed Meghan, that she'd left very early. Her blinds were up, and he could see her bed was made.

He knew he should call Mama. She'd told him to call, but he was afraid. If she had any idea he wasn't in Chicago, she'd be angry. She'd make him come home.

He sat by the window all day, watching Meghan's house, waiting for Meghan to return. He pulled the phone as far as the cord would stretch so he didn't lose sight of the house when he phoned for breakfast and lunch.

He'd unlock the door, then when the waiter knocked, Bernie would leap into bed and call, "Come in." It drove him crazy that he might miss Meghan again while the waiter was fussing with the tray.

When the maid knocked and tried to open the door with her master key she was stopped by the chain. He knew she couldn't see in.

"May I just change the towels?" she asked.

He figured he'd better let her do that at least. Didn't want her to get suspicious.

Yet as she passed him, he noticed that she looked at him funny, the way people do when they're sizing you up. Bernie tried hard to smile at her, tried to sound sincere when he thanked her.

It was late afternoon when Meghan's white Mustang turned into her driveway. Bernie pressed his nose against the window, straining to catch a glimpse of her walking up the path to the house. Seeing her made him happy again.

Around five-thirty, he saw the kid dropped off at Meghan's house. If it wasn't for the kid, Bernie could be hiding in the woods. He could be closer to Meg. He'd be taping her so that he could keep her. Could watch her and be with her whenever he wanted. Except for that stupid kid. He hated that kid.

He didn't think to order dinner. He wasn't hungry. Finally at ten-thirty his wait was over. Meghan turned on the light in her bedroom and undressed.

She was so beautiful!

AT FOUR O'CLOCK FRIDAY AFTERNOON, PHILLIP ASKED Jackie, "Where's Orsini?"

"He had an appointment outside the office, Mr. Carter. He said he'd be back around four-thirty."

Jackie stood in Phillip Carter's office, trying to decide what to do. When Mr. Carter was upset he was a little scary. Mr. Collins never used to get upset.

But Mr. Carter was the boss now, and last night her husband, Bob, told her that she owed it to him to tell him that Victor Orsini was going through all the files at night.

"But maybe it's Mr. Carter doing it," she had suggested.

"If it is Carter, he'll appreciate your concern. Don't forget, if there's any trouble between them, Orsini is the one who'll leave, not Carter."

Bob was right. Now Jackie said firmly, "Mr. Carter, it may

be none of my business, but I'm pretty sure Mr. Orsini is coming in here at night and going through all the files."

Phillip Carter was very quiet for a long minute, then his face hardened and he said, "Thank you, Jackie. Have Mr. Orsini see me when he comes in."

I wouldn't want to be in Mr. Orsini's boots, she thought.

Twenty minutes later she and Milly dropped all pretense of not listening as through the closed door of Phillip Carter's office, they could hear his raised voice castigating Victor Orsini.

"For a long time I have suspected you of working hand-in-glove with Downes and Rosen," he told him. "This place is in trouble now, and you're preparing to land on your feet by going with them. But you seem to forget that you have a contract that specifically prohibits you from soliciting our accounts. Now get out and don't bother to pack. You've probably taken plenty of our files already. We'll send your personal items on to you."

"So that's what he was doing," Jackie whispered. "That is really bad." Neither she nor Milly looked up at Orsini when he passed their desks on his way out.

If they had, they would have seen that his face was white with fury.

ON SATURDAY MORNING, CATHERINE WENT TO THE INN FOR the breakfast hour. She checked her mail and phone calls, then had a long talk with Virginia. Deciding not to stay for the lunch serving, she returned to the house at eleven o'clock. She found that Meg had been taking the files to her father's study and analyzing them, one by one.

"The dining room is such a mess that I can't concentrate," Meg explained. "Victor was looking for something important, and we're not seeing the forest for the trees."

Catherine studied her daughter. Meg was wearing a plaid silk shirt and chinos. Her chestnut hair was almost shoulder length now, and brushed back. That's what it is, Catherine thought. Her hair is just that little bit longer. The picture of Annie Collins in yesterday's newspapers came to mind.

"Meg, I've thought it through. I'm going to accept that offer on Drumdoe."

"You're *what?*"

"Virginia agrees with me. The overhead is simply too high. I don't want the inn to end up on the auction block."

"Mom, Dad founded Collins and Carter, and even under these circumstances, there must be some way you can take some money out of it."

"Meg, if there were a death certificate, there would be partnership insurance. With lawsuits pending there won't be a business before long."

"What does Phillip say? By the way, he's been around a lot lately," Meg said, "more than in all the years he worked with Dad."

"He's trying to be kind, and I appreciate that."

"Is it more than kindness?"

"I hope not. He'd be making a mistake. I have too much to deal with before I even think in that direction with anyone." She added quietly, "But you don't."

"What's that supposed to mean?"

"It means that Kyle isn't the greatest busboy. He was keeping an eye on you two and reported with great satisfaction that Mac was kissing you."

"I am not interested—"

"Stop it, Meg," Catherine commanded. She stepped around the desk, yanked open the bottom drawer, pulled out a half-dozen letters and threw them on the desk. "Don't be like your father, an emotional cripple because he couldn't forgive rejection."

"He had every reason not to forgive his mother!"

"As a child, yes. As an adult with a family who deeply loved him, no. Maybe he wouldn't have needed Scottsdale if he'd gone to Philadelphia and made peace with her."

Meg raised her eyebrows. "You can play rough, can't you?"

"You bet I can. Meg, you love Mac. You always have. Kyle needs you. Now for God's sake, put yourself on the line and quit being afraid that Mac would be imbecile enough to want Ginger if she ever showed up in his life again."

"Dad always called you Mighty Mouse." Meg felt tears burning behind her eyes.

"Yes, he did. When I go back to the inn, I'm going to call the real estate people. One thing I can promise. I'll raise their ante till they beg for mercy."

AT ONE-THIRTY, JUST BEFORE SHE RETURNED TO THE INN, Catherine poked her head into the study. "Meg, remember I said Palomino Leather Goods sounded familiar? I think Annie's mother may have left the same message on our home phone for Dad. It would have been mid-March seven years ago. The reason I can pinpoint it is that I was so furious when Dad missed your twenty-first birthday party that when he finally got home with a leather purse for you, I told him I'd like to hit him over the head with it."

ON SATURDAY, BERNIE'S MOTHER COULD NOT STOP SNEEZ-ing. Her sinuses were beginning to ache, her throat was scratchy. She had to do something about it.

Bernard had let dust pile up in the basement, she just knew it. No question about it, that had to be it. Now the dust was filtering through the house.

She became angrier and more agitated by the minute. Finally, at two o'clock, she couldn't stand it anymore. She had to get down there and clean.

First she heaved the broom and shovel and mop into the basement. Then she filled a plastic bag with rags and cleanser and threw it down the stairs. It landed on the mop.

Finally Mama tied on her apron. She felt the bannister. It wasn't that loose. It would hold her. She'd go slowly, a step at a time, and test each stair before she put her weight on it.

She still didn't know how she'd managed to fall so hard ten years ago. One minute she'd been starting down the stairs, the next she was in an ambulance.

Step by step, with infinite care, she descended. Well, I did it, she thought as she stepped on the basement floor. The toe of her shoe caught in the bag of rags and she fell heavily to the side, her left foot bending beneath her.

The sound of Mama's ankle bone breaking resounded through the clammy basement.

55

*A*fter her mother went back to the inn, Meghan phoned Phillip at home. When he answered, she said, "I'm glad to get you. I thought you might be in New York or at one of your auctions today."

"It's been a rough week. I had to fire Victor yesterday afternoon."

"Why?" Meg asked, distressed at this sudden twist of events. She needed Victor available while she was trying to tie him to the Petrovic recommendation. Suppose he left town? So far she didn't have any proof, couldn't go to the police with her suspicions about him. That would take time.

"He's a slippery one, Meg. Been stealing our clients. Frankly, from one or two remarks your dad made just before he disappeared, I think he suspected that Victor was up to something."

"So do I," Meg said. "That's why I'm calling. I think he might have sent out the Petrovic letter when Dad was away.

Phillip, we don't have any of Dad's Daily Reminders with his business appointments. Are they in the office?"

"They should have been with the files you took home."

"I would think so, but they're not. Phillip, I'm trying to reach Annie's mother. Like a fool I didn't get her private number when I was out there. The Palomino Leather Goods Shop contacted her and then gave me directions to her house. I have an idea that Dad may not have been in the office when that letter about Petrovic went to Manning. It's dated March 21st, isn't it?"

"I believe so."

"Then I'm onto something. Annie's mother can verify it. I did reach the lawyer who came out here with her. He wouldn't give me the number but said he'd contact her for me."

She paused, then said, "Phillip, there's something else. I think Dr. Williams and Helene Petrovic were involved, certainly while they worked together and maybe even before then. And if so, it's possible he's the man Petrovic's neighbor saw visiting her apartment.

"Meg, that's incredible. Do you have any proof?"

"Not yet, but I don't think it will be hard to get."

"Just be careful," Phillip Carter warned her. "Williams is very well respected in medical circles. Don't even mention his name until you can back up what you say."

FRANCES GROLIER PHONED AT QUARTER TO THREE. "YOU wanted to talk to me, Meghan."

"Yes. You told me the other day that you only used the Palomino code a couple of other times in all those years. Did you ever phone our house with that message?"

Grolier did not ask why Meg wanted to know. "Yes, I did. It was nearly seven years ago, on March 10th. Annie had been in a head-on collision and wasn't expected to live. I'd tried the machine in the office, but as it turned out, it had been accidentally unplugged. I knew Edwin was in Connecticut and I *had* to reach him. He flew out that night and was here two weeks until Annie was out of danger."

Meg thought of March 18th seven years ago, her twenty-first birthday. A black-tie dinner dance at Drumdoe. Her father's phone call that afternoon. He had a virus and was too sick to get on the plane. Two hundred guests. Mac with Ginger, showing pictures of Kyle.

She'd spent the night trying to smile, trying not to show how bitterly disappointed she was that her father was not with her on this special night.

"Meghan?" Frances Grolier's controlled voice at the other end of the phone was questioning.

"I'm sorry. Sorry about everything. What you've just told me is terribly important. It's tied to so much of what's happened."

Meghan returned the receiver to its cradle, but held onto it for several minutes. Then she dialed Phillip. "Confirmation." Quickly she explained what Frances Grolier had just told her.

"Meg, you're a whiz," Phillip told her.

"Phillip, there's the bell. It must be Kyle. Mac is dropping him off. I asked him to bring something over for me."

"Go ahead. And Meg, don't talk about this until we get a complete picture to present to Dwyer's office."

"I won't. Our assistant state attorney and his people don't trust me anyhow. I'll talk to you."

KYLE CAME IN SMILING BROADLY.

Meghan bent down to kiss him.

"Never do that in front of my friends," he warned.

"Why not?"

"Jimmy's mother waits at the road and kisses him when he gets off the bus. Isn't that disgusting?"

"Why did you let me kiss you?"

"It's okay in private. Nobody saw us. You were kissing Dad last night."

"He kissed me."

"Did you like it?"

Meg considered. "Let's just say that it wasn't disgusting. Want some cookies and milk?"

"Yes, please. I brought the tape for you to watch. Why do you want to see it again?"

"I'm not sure."

"Okay. Dad said he'll be about an hour. He had to pick up some stuff at the store."

Meghan brought the plate of cookies and the glasses of milk into the den. Kyle sat on the floor at her feet; using the remote control, he once again started the tape of the Franklin Center interview. Meg's heart started to pound. She asked herself, What is it I saw in this tape?

In the last scene in Dr. Williams' office, when the camera panned over the pictures of the children born through in vitro fertilization, she found what she was looking for. She grabbed the remote from Kyle and snapped the Pause button.

"Meg, it's almost over," Kyle protested.

Meg stared at the picture of the little boy and girl with identical sweaters. She had seen the same picture on the wall of Helene Petrovic's sitting room in Lawrenceville. "It *is* over, Kyle. I know the reason."

The phone rang. "I'll be right back," she told him.

"I'll rewind. I know how."

It was Phillip Carter. "Meg, are you alone?" he asked quickly.

"Phillip! I just found confirmation that Helene Petrovic knew Dr. Williams. I think I know what she was doing at the Manning Clinic."

It was as though he hadn't heard her. "Are you alone?" he repeated.

"Kyle is in the den."

"Can you drop him off at his house?" His voice was low, agitated.

"Mac's out. I can leave him at the inn. Mother's there. Phillip, what is it?"

Now Carter sounded unbelieving, near hysteria. "I just heard from Edwin! He wants to see both of us. He's trying to decide if he should turn himself in. Meg, he's desperate. Don't let anyone know about this until we have a chance to see him."

"Dad? Phoned you?" Meg gasped. Stunned, she grasped the corner of the desk for support. In a voice so shocked it was barely a whisper, she demanded, "Where is he? I've got to go to him."

56

*W*hen Bernie's mother regained consciousness, she tried to shout for help, but she knew none of the neighbors could hear her. She'd never make it up the stairs. She'd have to drag herself into Bernard's TV area where there was a phone. It was all his fault for not keeping the place clean. Her ankle hurt so much. The pains were shooting up her leg. She opened her mouth and took big gulps of air. It was agony to drag herself along the dirty, rough concrete floor.

Finally she made her way into the alcove her son had fashioned for himself. Even with all the pain she was in, Mama's eyes widened in amazed fury. That big television! Those radios! Those machines! What was Bernard doing, throwing away money on all these things?

The phone was on the old kitchen table that he'd carried in when one of their neighbors put it at the curb. She couldn't reach it, so she pulled it down by the cord. It clattered on the floor.

Hoping she hadn't broken it, Bernie's mother dialed 911. At the welcome sound of a dispatcher's voice, she said, "Send an ambulance."

She was able to give her name and address and tell what had happened before she fainted again.

"KYLE," MEG SAID HURRIEDLY, "I'M GOING TO HAVE TO leave you at the inn. I'll put a note on the door for your dad. Just tell my mother that something came up, that I had to leave right away. You stay with her. No going outside, okay?"

"Why are you so worried, Meg?"

"I'm not. It's a big story. I have to cover it."

"Oh, that's great."

At the inn, Meg watched until Kyle had reached the front door. He waved and she waved back, forcing a smile. Then she put her foot on the accelerator.

She was meeting Phillip at a crossroads in West Redding, about twenty miles from Newtown. "You can follow me from there," he had hurriedly told her. "It's not far after that, but it would be impossible for you to find it alone."

Meg did not know what to think. Her mind was a jumble of confused thoughts and confused emotions. Her mouth was so dry. Her throat simply would not swallow. *Dad was alive and he was desperate!* Why? Surely not because he was He-lene Petrovic's murderer. Please, dear God, anything but that.

When Meg found the intersection of the narrow country roads, Phillip's black Cadillac was waiting. It was easy to spot him. There was no other car in sight.

He did not take the time to speak to her but held up his hand and motioned for her to follow him. Half a mile later he turned sharply onto a narrow hard-packed dirt road. Fifty yards after that the road twisted through a wooded area and Meghan's car vanished from the view of anyone driving past.

· · · ·

VICTOR ORSINI HAD NOT BEEN SURPRISED BY THE SHOW-
down with Phillip Carter Friday afternoon. It had never been
a question of *if* it would happen. The question for months
had been *when.*

At least he had found what he needed before he lost access
to the office. When he left Carter, he had driven directly to
his house at Candlewood Lake, fixed himself a martini and
sat where he could look over the water and consider what he
ought to do.

The evidence he had was not enough alone and without
corroboration, would not stand up in court. And in addition,
how much could he tell them and still not reveal things that
could hurt him?

He'd been with Collins and Carter nearly seven years, yet
suddenly all that mattered was that first month. It was the
linchpin connecting everything that had happened recently.

Victor had spent Friday evening weighing the pros and
cons of going to the assistant state attorney and laying out
what he thought had happened.

The next morning he jogged along the lake for an hour, a
long healthy run that cleared his head and strengthened his
resolve.

Finally, at two-thirty Saturday afternoon, he dialed the
number Special Investigator Marron had given him. He half-
expected that Marron might not be in his office on Saturday,
but he answered on the first ring.

Victor identified himself. In the calm, reasoned voice that
inspired confidence in clients and job candidates, he asked,
"Would it be convenient if I stopped by in half an hour? I
think I know who murdered Helene Petrovic . . ."

FROM THE FRONT DOOR OF THE DRUMDOE INN, KYLE
looked back and watched Meghan drive away. She was on a
story. Cool. He wished he was going with her. He used to

think he'd be a doctor like Dad when he grew up but had decided being a reporter was more fun.

A moment later a car zoomed out of the parking lot, a green Chevy. That's the guy who didn't run over Jake, Kyle thought. He was sorry he didn't get a chance to talk to him and thank him. He watched as the Chevy turned down the road in the direction Meg had gone.

Kyle went into the lobby and spotted Meg's mother and Mrs. Murphy at the desk. They both looked serious. He went over to them. "Hi."

"Kyle, what are you doing here?" That's a heck of a way to greet a kid, Catherine thought. She ruffled his hair. "I mean, did you and Meg come over for some ice cream or something?"

"Meg dropped me off. She said to stay with you. She's working on a story."

"Oh, did she get a call from her boss?"

"Somebody called her and she said she had to leave right away."

"Wouldn't that be great if she's being reinstated?" Catherine said to Virginia. "It would be such a morale booster for her."

"It sure would," Murphy agreed. "Now what do you think we should do about that guy in 3A? Frankly, Catherine, I think there's something a little wrong with him."

"Just what we need."

"How many people would stay in a room for nearly three days and then go charging out so fast he almost knocked people down? You just missed him, but I can tell you there appeared to be nothing sick about Mr. Heffernan. He tore down the stairs and ran through the lobby, carrying a video camera."

"Let's take a look at the room," Catherine said. "Come with us, Kyle."

The air in 3A was stale. "Has this room been cleaned since he checked in?" Catherine asked.

"No," Murphy said. "Betty said he would let her in just to

change the towels, that he just about threw her out when she tried to clean up."

"He must have been out of bed sometime. Look at the way that chair is pulled up to the window," Catherine commented. "Wait a minute!" She crossed the room, sat in the chair and looked out. "Dear God," she breathed.

"What is it?" Virginia asked.

"From here you can look directly into Meg's bedroom windows." Catherine rushed to the phone, glanced at the emergency numbers listed on the receiver and dialed.

"State police. Officer Thorne speaking."

"This is Catherine Collins at the Drumdoe Inn in Newtown," she snapped. "I think a man staying at the inn has been spying on our house. He's been locked in his room for days, and just now he drove away in a mad hurry." Her hand flew to her mouth. "Kyle, when Meg dropped you off did you see if a car followed her?"

Kyle sensed that something was very wrong, but surely it couldn't be because of the nice guy who was such a good driver. "Don't worry. The guy in the green Chevy is okay. He saved Jake's life when he drove past our house last week."

In near despair, Catherine cried, "Officer, he's following my daughter now. She's driving a white Mustang. He's in a green Chevy. *Find her! You've got to find her!*"

57

The squad car pulled into the driveway of the shabby one-story frame house in Jackson Heights, and two policemen jumped out. The shrill ee-aww of an approaching EMS ambulance sounded over the screech of a braking elevated train at the station less than a block away.

The cops ran around the house to the back door, forced it open and pounded down the stairs to the basement. A loose step gave way under the weight of the rookie, but he grabbed the railing and managed to keep from falling. The sergeant stumbled over the mop at the foot of the stairs.

"No wonder she got hurt," he muttered. "This place is booby-trapped."

Low moans from a crudely enclosed area drew them to Bernie's alcove. The police officers found the elderly woman sprawled on the floor, the telephone beside her. She was lying near an unsteady table with an enameled-steel top heaped with phone books. A worn Naugahyde recliner was directly in front of a forty-inch television set. A shortwave radio, police scanner, typewriter and fax machine crowded the top of an old dresser.

The younger cop dropped down on one knee beside the injured woman. "Police Officer David Guzman, Mrs. Heffernan," he said soothingly. "They're bringing a stretcher to take you to the hospital."

Bernie's mother tried to speak. "My son doesn't mean any harm." She could barely get the words out. She closed her eyes, unable to continue.

"Dave, look at this!"

Guzman jumped up. "What is it, Sarge?"

The Queens telephone directory was spread open. On those pages nine or ten names were circled. The sergeant pointed to them. "They look familiar? In the last few weeks all of these people reported threatening phone calls."

They could hear the EMS team. Guzman ran to the foot of the stairs. "Watch out or you'll break your necks coming down here," he warned.

In less than five minutes, Bernie's semiconscious mother had been secured to a stretcher and carried to the ambulance.

The police officers did not leave. "We've got enough probable cause to take a look around," the sergeant commented.

He picked up papers next to the fax machine and began to thumb through them.

Officer Guzman pulled open the knobless drawer of the table and spotted a handsome wallet. "Looks as though Bernie might do a little mugging on the side," he commented.

As Guzman stared at Annie Collins' picture on her driver's license, the sergeant found the original of the fax message. He read it aloud. " 'Mistake. Annie was a mistake.' "

Guzman grabbed the phone from the floor. "Sarge," he said, "you'd better let the chief know we found ourselves a murderer."

EVEN FOR BERNIE IT WAS HARD TO KEEP FAR ENOUGH BEHIND Meghan's car to avoid being seen. From the distance he watched her begin to follow the dark sedan. He almost lost both cars after the intersection, when they suddenly seemed to vanish. He knew they must have turned off somewhere, so he backed up. The dirt road through the woods was the only place they could have gone. He turned onto it cautiously.

Now he was coming to a clearing. Meghan's white car and the dark sedan were shaking up and down as they covered the uneven, rutted ground. Bernie waited until they were past the clearing and into another wooded area, then drove the Chevy through the clearing.

The second clump of woods wasn't nearly as deep as the first. Bernie had to jam on his brakes to avoid being seen when the narrow track abruptly turned into open fields again. Now the road led directly to a distant house and barn. The cars were heading there.

Bernie grabbed his camera. With his zoom lens it was possible to track them, until they drove behind the barn.

He sat quietly, considering what he should do. There was a cluster of evergreens near the house. Maybe he could hide the Chevy there. He had to try.

· · ·

IT WAS PAST FOUR, AND THE FADING SUNLIGHT WAS OB-
scured by thickening clouds. Meg drove behind Phillip along
the winding, bumpy road. They came out of the wooded
area, crossed a field, went through another stretch of woods.
The road straightened out. In the distance she saw buildings,
a farmhouse and barn.

Is Dad here in this godforsaken place? Meg wondered. She
prayed that when she came face to face with him, she would
find the right words to say.

I love you, Daddy, the child in her wanted to cry.

Dad, what happened to you? Dad, why? the hurt adult
wanted to scream.

Dad, I've missed you. How can I help you? Was that the
best way to start?

She followed Phillip's car around the dilapidated buildings.
He parked, got out of his sedan, walked over and opened the
door of Meg's car.

Meg looked up at him. "Where's Dad?" she asked. She
moistened lips that now felt cracked and dry.

"He's nearby." Phillip's eyes locked with hers.

It was the abrupt way he answered that caught her attention. He's as nervous about this as I am, she thought as she
got out of the car.

58

*V*ictor Orsini had agreed to be at John Dwyer's office
in the Danbury courthouse at three o'clock. Special investigators Weiss and Marron were there when he arrived. An hour

later, from their impassive faces, he still did not know if they were putting any stock in what he was telling them.

"Let's go through this again," Dwyer said.

"I've gone through it a dozen times," Victor snapped.

"I want to hear it again," Dwyer said.

"All right, all right. Edwin Collins called me on his car phone the night of January 28th. We spoke for about eight minutes until he disconnected because he was on the ramp of the Tappan Zee Bridge and the driving was very slippery."

"When do you tell us everything you talked about?" Weiss demanded. "What took eight minutes to say?"

This part of the story was what Victor had hoped to gloss over, but he knew unless he told the complete truth he would not be believed. Reluctantly, he admitted, "Ed had learned a day or two before that I'd been tipping off one of our competitors to positions our major clients would be looking to fill. He was outraged and ordered me to be in his office the next morning."

"And that was your last contact with him?"

"On January 29th I was waiting in his office at eight o'clock. I knew Ed was going to fire me, but I didn't want him to think I'd cheated the firm out of money. He'd told me that if he found proof that I'd been pocketing commissions, he'd prosecute. At the time I thought he meant kickbacks. Now I think he was referring to Helene Petrovic. I don't think he knew anything about her, then must have found out and thought I was trying to pull a fast one."

"We know the commission for placing her at the Manning Clinic went into the office account," Marron said.

"He wouldn't have known that. I've checked and found that it was deliberately buried in the fee received for placing Dr. Williams there. Obviously Edwin was never supposed to find out anything about Petrovic."

"Then who recommended Petrovic to Manning?" Dwyer asked.

"Phillip Carter. It had to be. When the letter endorsing her credentials was sent to Manning on March 21st almost seven years ago, I'd only been at Collins and Carter a short time. I'd never even heard that woman's name until she was murdered less than two weeks ago. And I'd bet my life Ed didn't either. He was away from the office the end of March that year, including March 21st."

He paused. "As I've told you, when I saw the newspaper with the reprint of the letter supposedly signed by him, I knew it was a phony."

Orsini pointed to the sheet of paper he had given to Dwyer. "With his old secretary, who was a gem, Ed had gotten in the habit of leaving a stack of signed letterheads she could use if he wanted to dictate over the phone. He trusted her completely. Then she'd retired, and Ed wasn't that impressed with her replacement, Jackie. I can remember him ripping up those signed letterheads and telling me that from then on he wanted to see everything that went out over his signature. On the blank letterheads he always signed in the same place, where his longtime secretary had left a light pencil mark: thirty-five lines down and beginning on the fiftieth character. You've got one in your hands now.

"I've been going through Ed's files, hoping that there might be other signed letterheads that he'd missed. I found the one you're holding in Phillip Carter's desk. A locksmith made a key for me. I imagine Carter was saving this in case he needed to produce something else signed by Edwin Collins.

"You can believe me or not," Orsini continued, "but thinking back to that morning of January 29th, when I waited in Ed's office, I had the distinct feeling he'd been there recently. The *H* through *O* drawer in the filing cabinet was open. I'd swear he had been looking at the Manning file for any record of Helene Petrovic.

"While I was waiting for him, Catherine Collins phoned, worried that Ed wasn't home. She'd been at a reunion in Hartford the night before and found the house empty when she returned. She tried the office, to see if we'd heard from him. I told her about speaking to him the night before when he was on the ramp of the Tappan Zee Bridge. At that time I didn't know anything about the accident. She was the one who suggested that Ed might have been one of the victims.

"I realized it was possible, of course," Victor said. "Ed's last words to me were about how slippery the ramp was, and we know the accident took place less than a minute later. After talking to Catherine, I tried to call Phillip. His phone was busy, and since he lives only ten minutes from the office, I drove to his house. I had some idea we might want to drive down to the bridge and see if they were pulling victims out of the water.

"When I arrived, Phillip was in the garage, just getting in his car. His jeep was there as well. I remember he made a point of telling me he'd brought it down from the country to have it serviced. I knew he had a jeep that he used to get around his farm property. He'd drive the sedan up and then switch.

"At the time I thought nothing of it. But in this last week I reasoned that if Ed wasn't involved in that accident, went to the office and found something that sent him to Carter's home, whatever happened to him took place there. Carter could have driven Ed away in his own car and hidden it somewhere. Ed always said Phillip had a lot of rural property."

Orsini looked at the inscrutable faces of his interrogators. I've done what I had to do, he thought. If they don't believe me, at least I tried.

Dwyer said in a noncommittal tone, "This may be helpful. Thank you, Mr. Orsini. You'll hear from us."

When Orsini left, the assistant state attorney said to Weiss and Marron, "It fits. And it explains the findings of the forensic lab." They had just received word that analysis of Edwin Collins' car revealed traces of blood in the trunk.

59

*I*t was nearly four o'clock when Mac completed his last errand and started home. The butcher, the baker, the candlestick maker, he thought. He'd gone to the barber, picked up the dry cleaning and stopped at the supermarket. Mrs. Dileo might not be back from taking care of her father to do the usual shopping on Monday.

Mac felt good. Kyle had been thrilled to be visiting with Meg. There'd certainly be no problem for Kyle if Mac succeeded in rekindling the feelings Meg had once had for him. Meggie, you don't have a chance, Mac vowed. You're not getting away from me again.

It was a cold, overcast day, but Mac had no thought of weather as he turned onto Bayberry Road. He thought of the hope in Meg's face when they'd talked about Petrovic's connection to Dr. Williams and the possibility that Victor Orsini had forged Edwin's name to Petrovic's letter of recommendation. She'd realized then that her father might be proven innocent of any connection to the Petrovic case and the Manning Clinic scandal.

Nothing can change the fact that Ed had a double life all those years, Mac thought. But if his name is cleared of murder and fraud, it will be a hell of a lot easier for Meg and Catherine.

The first warning that something was wrong came as Mac neared the inn. There were police cars in the driveway, and the parking lot was blocked. A police helicopter was landing. He could see another one with the logo of a New Haven television station already on the ground.

He pulled his car onto the lawn and ran toward the inn.

The door of the inn was flung open, and Kyle rushed out. "Dad, Meg's boss didn't call her to cover a story," he sobbed. "The man who didn't run over Jake is the guy who's been watching Meg. He's following her in his car."

Meg! For a split second Mac's vision blurred. He was in the morgue looking down at the dead face of Annie Collins, Meg's half sister.

Kyle grabbed his father's arm. "The cops are here. They're sending helicopters to look for Meg's car and the guy's green car. Mrs. Collins is crying." Kyle's voice broke. "Dad, don't let anything happen to Meg."

TAILING MEGHAN AS SHE FOLLOWED THE CADILLAC DEEPER into the countryside, Bernie felt slow, burning anger. He'd wanted to be alone with her with no one else around. Then she'd met up with that other car. Suppose the guy Meg was with tried to give him trouble? Bernie patted his pocket. It was there. He never could remember if he had it with him. He wasn't supposed to carry it, and he'd even tried to leave it in the basement. But when he met somebody he liked and started to think about her all the time, he got nervous and a lot of things started to be different.

Bernie left the car behind the clump of evergreens, took his camera and carefully approached the cluster of ramshackle buildings. Now that he was up close he could see that the farmhouse was smaller than it seemed from a distance. What he'd thought was an enclosed porch was actually a storage shed. Next to that was the barn. There was just enough space for him to slide in sideways between the house and the storage shed.

The passageway was dark and musty, but he knew it was a good hiding place. From behind the buildings he could hear their voices clearly. He knew that, like the window in the inn, this was a good place for him to watch and not be seen.

Reaching the end of the passageway, he peeked out just enough to see what was going on.

Meghan was with a man Bernie had never seen before, and they were standing near what appeared to be an old well, about twenty feet away. They were facing each other, talking. The sedan was parked between them and where Bernie was hiding, so he crouched down and crept forward, hidden from sight by the car. Then he stopped, lifted his camera and began to videotape them.

60

"*P*hillip, before Dad gets here, I think I know the reason for Helene Petrovic being at Manning."

"What is it, Meg?"

She ignored the oddly detached tone in Phillip's voice. "When I was in Helene Petrovic's house yesterday, I saw pictures of young children in her study. Some of them are the same pictures I'd seen on the walls of Dr. Williams' office at the Franklin Center in Philadelphia.

"Phillip, those kids weren't born through the Manning Clinic, and I'm sure I understand Helene's connection to them. She wasn't losing embryos at Manning through carelessness. I believe she was stealing those embryos and giving them to Dr. Williams for use in his donor program at Franklin."

Why was Phillip looking at her like that? she wondered suddenly. Didn't he believe her? "Think about it, Phillip," she urged. "Helene worked under Dr. Williams for six months at Manning. For three years before that, when she was a secretary at Dowling, she used to haunt the laboratory. Now we can connect her to Williams at that time as well."

Now Phillip seemed at ease. "Meg, it fits. And you think that Victor, not your father, sent the letter recommending Petrovic to Manning?"

"Absolutely. Dad was in Scottsdale. Annie had been in an accident and was close to death. We can prove Dad wasn't in the office when that letter was sent."

"I'm sure you can."

THE CALL FROM PHILLIP CARTER TO DR. HENRY WILLIAMS had come in at 3:15 Saturday afternoon. Carter had demanded that Williams be summoned from examining a client. The conversation had been brief but chilling.

"Meghan Collins has tied you to Petrovic," Carter told him, "although she thinks Orsini sent the letter of recommendation. And I know that Orsini's been up to something, and may even suspect what happened. We could still be all right, but no matter what, keep your mouth shut. Refuse to answer questions."

Somehow Henry Williams managed to get through the rest of his appointments. The last one was completed at four-thirty. That was when the Franklin Assisted Reproduction Center closed on Saturdays.

His secretary looked in on him. "Dr. Williams, is there anything else I can do for you?"

Nobody can do anything for me, he thought. He managed a smile. "No, nothing, thank you, Eva."

"Doctor, are you all right? You don't look well."

"I'm fine. Just a bit weary."

By 4:45 everyone on the staff had left and he was alone. Williams reached for the picture of his deceased wife, leaned back in his chair and studied it. "Marie," he said softly, "I didn't know what I was getting into. I honestly thought that I was accomplishing some good. Helene believed that too."

He replaced the picture, folded his hands under his chin and stared ahead. He did not notice that the shadows outside were deepening.

Carter had gone mad. He had to be stopped.

Williams thought of his son and daughter. Henry Jr. was an obstetrician in Seattle. Barbara was an endocrinologist in San Francisco. What would this scandal do to them, especially if there was a long trial?

The truth was going to come out. It was inevitable. He knew that now.

He thought of Meghan Collins, the questions she had asked him. Had she suspected that he was lying to her?

And her father. Appalling enough to know without having to ask that Carter had murdered Helene to silence her. Had he anything to do with Edwin Collins' disappearance as well? And should Edwin Collins be blamed for what others had done?

Should Helene be blamed for mistakes she hadn't made?

Dr. Henry Williams took a pad from his desk and began to write. He had to explain, to make it very clear, to try to undo the harm he had done.

When he was finished, he put the pages he had written in an envelope. Meghan Collins was the one who deserved to present this to the authorities. He had done her and her family a grave disservice.

Meghan had left her card. Williams found it, addressed the envelope to her at Channel 3 and carefully stamped it.

He stopped for a long minute to study the pictures of the children who had been born because their mothers had come to his clinic. For an instant the bleakness in his heart was relieved at the sight of their young faces.

Dr. Henry Williams turned out the light as he left his office for the last time.

He carried the envelope to his car, stopped at a nearby mailbox and dropped it in. Meghan Collins would receive it by Tuesday.

By then it wouldn't matter to him anymore.

. . .

THE SUN WAS GETTING LOWER. A WIND WAS FLATTENING THE short blades of yellowed grass. Meghan shivered. She'd grabbed her Burberry when she'd rushed out of the house, forgetting she'd removed the lining for her trip to Scottsdale.

Phillip Carter was wearing jeans and a boxy winter jacket. His hands were in its roomy pockets. He was leaning against the open fieldstone well.

"Do you think Victor killed Helene Petrovic because she decided to quit?" he asked.

"Victor or Dr. Williams. Williams might have panicked. Petrovic knew so much. She could have sent both of them to prison for years if she ever talked. Her parish priest told me he felt she had something on her mind that troubled her terribly."

Meg began to tremble. Was it just nerves and the cold? "I'm going to sit in the car till Dad gets here, Phillip. How far does he have to come?"

"Not far, Meg. In fact he's amazingly nearby." Phillip took his hands out of his pockets. The right hand held a gun. He gestured toward the well. "Your psychic was right, Meg. Your dad's under water. And he's been dead a long time."

DON'T LET ANYTHING HAPPEN TO MEG! IT WAS THE PRAYERful plea Mac whispered as he and Kyle entered the inn. Inside, the reception area was teeming with police and media. Employees and guests watched from doorways. In the adjacent sitting room, Catherine was perched at the edge of the small sofa, Virginia Murphy beside her. Catherine's face was ashen.

When Mac approached her, she reached up and clasped his hands. "Mac, Victor Orsini's talked to the police. Phillip was behind all this. Can you believe it? I trusted him so completely. We think he's the one who called Meg, pretending to be Edwin. And there's a man who's following her, a dangerous man with a history of obsessive attachments to unsuspecting women. He's probably the one who scared Kyle on Halloween. The New York police phoned John Dwyer about him. And now Meghan is gone, and we don't know why she left or where she is. I'm so afraid I don't know what to do. I can't lose her, Mac. I couldn't stand that."

Arlene Weiss rushed into the sitting room. Mac recognized her. "Mrs. Collins, a traffic helicopter crew thinks they spotted the green car on an old farm near West Redding. We told them to stay out of the area. We'll be there in less than ten minutes."

Mac gave Catherine what he hoped was a reassuring embrace. "I'll find Meg," he promised. "She'll be all right."

Then he ran outside. The reporter and cameraman from New Haven were rushing toward their helicopter. Mac followed them, scrambling behind them into the chopper. "Hey, you can't get on here," the burly reporter shouted over the roar of the engine revving up for takeoff.

"Yes, I can," Mac said. "I'm a doctor. I may be needed."

"Shut the door," the reporter yelled to the pilot. "Get this thing in the air."

MEGHAN STARED IN CONFUSION. "PHILLIP, I . . . I DON'T UNderstand," she stammered. "My father's body is in that well?" Meg stepped forward, placing her hands on the rough, rounded surface. Her fingertips curled over the edge, feeling the clammy dampness of the stone. She was no longer aware of Phillip or the gun he was pointing at her or the barren fields behind him or the cold, biting wind.

She stared down into the yawning hole with numbing horror, imagining her father's body lying at the bottom.

"You won't be able to see him, Meg. There isn't much water down there, hasn't been for years, but enough to cover him. He was dead when I pushed him in, if that's any consolation. I shot him the night of the bridge accident."

Meg whirled on him. "How could you have done that to

him? He was your friend, your partner. How could you have done that to Helene and Annie?"

"You give me too much credit. I had nothing to do with Annie's death."

"You meant to kill me. You sent me the fax saying Annie's death was a mistake." Meg's eyes darted around. Was there any way she could get to her car? No, he'd shoot her before she'd taken a step.

"Meghan, *you* told me about the fax. It was like a gift. I needed people to believe that Ed was still alive, and you delivered the way I could do it."

"What did you do to my father?"

"Ed called me from the office the night of the accident. He was in shock. Talked about how close he'd come to being caught in the bridge explosion. Told me he knew Orsini was cheating on us. Told me that Manning had talked about us placing an embryologist named Petrovic Ed had never heard of. He'd gone directly to the office and had been through the Manning file and couldn't find any reference to her. Blamed it on Orsini.

"Meghan, try to understand. It would have been all over. I told him to come to my house, that we'd figure it out, confront Orsini together in the morning. By the time he walked in my door he was ready to accuse me. He'd pieced it all together. Your father was very smart. He left me no choice. I knew what I had to do."

I'm so cold, Meghan thought, so cold.

"Everything was fine for a while," Phillip continued. "Then Petrovic quit, telling Manning she'd made a mistake that was going to cause a lot of trouble. I couldn't take a chance that she'd give everything away, could I? The day you came to the office and talked about the girl who'd been stabbed, how much she looked like you, that was when you told me about the fax. I knew your father had something going out West somewhere. It wasn't hard to figure he might have had a daughter there. This seemed the perfect time to bring him back to life."

"You may not have sent the fax, but you made the phone call that sent Mother to the hospital. You ordered those roses and sat next to her when they were delivered. How could you have done that to her?"

Only yesterday, Meghan thought, Fr. Radzin told me to look for the reason.

"Meghan, I lost a lot of money in my divorce. I spent top dollar for property I'm trying to hold on to. I had a miserable childhood. I was one of ten kids living in a three-bedroom house. I'm not going back to being poor again. Williams and I found a way to make money with nobody hurt. And Petrovic cashed in, too."

"Stealing embryos for the Franklin Center donor program?"

"You're not as smart as I thought, Meghan. There's so much more to it than that. Donor embryos are small time."

He raised the pistol. She could see the muzzle aimed at her heart. She watched his finger tighten on the trigger, heard him say, "I kept Edwin's car in the barn till last week. I'll keep yours in its place. And you can join him."

In a reflex action, Meghan threw herself to the side.

His first bullet went over her head. His second hit her shoulder.

Before he could fire again, a figure came hurtling from nowhere. A heavy figure with a rigid outstretched arm. The fingers that grasped the knife and the shimmering blade itself were one, an avenging sword that sought out Phillip and found his throat.

Meghan felt blinding pain in her left shoulder. Blackness enveloped her.

61

*W*hen Meghan regained consciousness she was lying on the ground, her head in someone's lap. She forced her eyes open, looked up and saw Bernie Heffernan's cherubic smile, then felt his moist kisses on her face and lips and neck.

From somewhere in the distance she heard a whirring sound. A plane? A helicopter. Then it faded and was gone.

"I'm glad I saved you, Meghan. It's all right to use a knife to save someone, isn't it?" Bernie asked. "I never want to hurt anybody. I didn't want to hurt Annie that night. It was a mistake." He repeated it softly, like a child. "Annie was a mistake."

MAC LISTENED TO THE RADIO EXCHANGE BETWEEN THE PO-lice helicopter and the squad cars that were rushing to the area. They were coordinating strategy.

Meg is with two killers, he realized suddenly—that nut who was in the woods Sunday night and Phillip Carter.

Phillip Carter, who betrayed and murdered his partner, then posed as protector to Catherine and Meghan, privy to every step of Meg's search for truth.

Meghan. Meghan.

They were in a rural area. The helicopters were beginning to descend. Vainly Mac searched the ground below. It was going to be dark in fifteen minutes. How could they pick out a car when it was dark?

"We're at the outskirts of West Redding," the pilot said, pointing ahead. "We're a couple of minutes from where they spotted the green Chevy."

· · ·

HE'S CRAZY, MEG THOUGHT. THIS WAS BERNIE, THE CHEER-ful parking attendant who often told her about his mother. How did he get here? Why was he following her? And he said he had killed Annie. Dear God, he killed Annie!

She tried to sit up.

"Don't you want me to hold you, Meg? I'd never hurt you."

"Of course you wouldn't." She knew she had to soothe him, keep him calm. "It's just that the ground is so cold."

"I'm sorry. I should have known that. I'll help you." He kept his arm around her, hugging her as they awkwardly struggled together to their feet.

The pressure of his arm around her shoulder intensified the pain from the bullet wound. She mustn't antagonize him. "Bernie, would you try not to . . ." She was going to pass out again. "Bernie," she pleaded, "my shoulder hurts so much."

She could see the knife he had used to kill Phillip lying on the ground. Was this the knife that had taken Annie's life?

Phillip's gun was still clutched in his hand.

"Oh, I'm sorry. If you want I'll carry you." His lips were on her hair. "But, stand here for just a minute. I want to take your picture. See my camera?"

His camera. Of course. He must have been the cameraman in the woods who had almost strangled Kyle. She leaned against the well as he videotaped her and watched as he walked around Phillip's body, taping him.

Then Bernie laid the camera down and came over to her. "Meghan, I'm a hero," he bragged. His eyes were like shiny blue buttons.

"Yes, you are."

"I saved your life."

"Yes you did."

"But I'm not allowed to carry a weapon. A knife is a weapon. They'll put me away again, in the prison hospital. I hate it there."

"I'll talk to them."

"No, Meghan. That's why I had to kill Annie. She started to scream. All I did when I saw her that night was to walk up behind her and say, 'This is a dangerous block. I'll take care of you.' "

"You said that?"

"I thought it was you, Meghan. You'd have been glad to have me take care of you, wouldn't you?"

"Yes, of course I would."

"I didn't have time to explain. There was a police car coming. I didn't mean to hurt her. I didn't even know I was carrying the knife that night. Sometimes I don't remember I have it."

"I'm glad you were carrying it now." The car, Meg thought. My keys are in it. It's my only chance. "But Bernie, I don't think you should leave your knife here for the police to find." She pointed to it.

He looked back over his shoulder. "Oh, thank you, Meghan."

"And don't forget your camera."

If she wasn't fast enough, he'd know that she was trying to get away. And he'd have the knife in his hand. But when he turned and started to walk the half-dozen steps to Phillip's body, Meghan whirled, stumbling in her weakness and haste, yanked open her car door and slid behind the wheel.

"Meghan, what are you doing?" Bernie shrieked.

His hands grabbed the handle of the car door as she clicked the lock. He hung onto the handle as she threw the car into gear and plunged her foot down on the gas pedal.

The car leaped forward. Bernie kept his grip on the handle for ten feet, shouting at her, then let go and fell. She careened around the buildings. He was emerging from the passageway between the house and shed when she headed down the dirt road through the open fields.

She had not reached the wooded area when in the rearview mirror she saw his car lurch forward in pursuit.

. . .

THEY WERE PASSING OVER A WOODED AREA. THE POLICE helicopter was in front of them. The photographer and cameraman were straining their eyes.

"Look!" the pilot shouted. "There's the farmhouse."

Mac never knew what made him look back. "Turn around," he shouted. "Turn around."

Meg's white Mustang shot out of the woods, a green car inches behind it, repeatedly smashing into it. As Mac watched, the Chevy pulled alongside the Mustang and began sideswiping it, trying to run it off the road.

"Go down," Mac shouted to the pilot. "That's Meghan in the white car. Can't you see he's trying to kill her."

MEGHAN'S CAR WAS FASTER, BUT BERNIE WAS A BETTER driver. She had managed to stay ahead of him for a short time, but now could not escape him. He was slamming into the driver's side door. Meghan's body whipped back and forth as the air bag ballooned from the center of the wheel. For an instant she could not see, but she kept her foot on the accelerator, and the car zigzagged wildly through the field as Bernie kept attacking it.

The driver's side door smashed into her shoulder as the Mustang teetered and flipped over on its side. An instant later flames burst through the hood of the engine.

BERNIE WANTED TO WATCH MEGHAN'S CAR BURN, BUT THE police were coming. He could hear the scream of approaching sirens. Overhead he heard the din of a helicopter coming closer. He had to get away.

Someday you'll hurt someone, Bernie. That's what worries us. That's what the psychiatrist had told him. But if he got home to Mama, she'd take care of him. He'd get another job parking cars where he could be home every night with her. From now on he'd only make phone calls to women. Nobody would find out about that.

Meghan's face was fading from his mind. He'd forget her the way he forgot all the others he had liked. I never really hurt anyone before and I didn't mean to hurt Annie, he reminded himself as he drove through the hastening darkness. Maybe they'll believe me if they find me.

He drove through the second patch of woods and reached the intersection where they'd turned off onto the dirt road. Headlights snapped on. A loudspeaker said, "Police, Bernie. You know what to do. Get out of the car with your hands in the air."

Bernie began to cry. "Mama, Mama," he sobbed as he opened the door and lifted his arms.

THE CAR WAS ON ITS SIDE. THE DRIVER'S DOOR WAS PRESSING against her. Meghan felt for the button to release the seat belt but could not find it. She was disoriented.

She smelled smoke. It began pouring through the vent. Oh God, Meghan thought. I'm trapped. The car was resting on the passenger door.

Waves of heat began to attack her. Smoke filled her lungs. She tried to scream but no sound came.

MAC LED THE FRANTIC RACE FROM THE HELICOPTER TO Meg's car. Flames from the engine shot up higher just as they reached it. He could see Meg inside, struggling to free herself, her body illuminated by the flames that were spreading across the hood. "We've got to get her out through the passenger door," he shouted.

As one, he, the pilot, the reporter and cameraman put their hands on the superheated roof of the Mustang. As one they pushed, rocked, pushed again.

"Now," Mac shouted. With a groan they threw their weight against the car, held while tortured palms blistered.

And then the car began to move, slowly, resistantly, then finally in rapid surrender it slammed onto its tires, once more upright.

The heat was becoming unbearable. As in a dream, Meghan saw Mac's face and somehow managed to reach over and release the door lock before she passed out.

62

*T*he helicopter landed at the Danbury Medical Center. Dazed and blinded with pain, Meghan was aware of being taken from Mac's arms, lifted onto a stretcher.

Another stretcher. Annie being rushed into Emergency. No, she thought, no. "Mac."

"I'm here, Meggie."

Blinding lights. An operating room. A mask over her face. *The mask being removed from Annie's face in Roosevelt Hospital.* "Mac."

A hand over hers. "I'm here, Meggie."

SHE AWOKE IN THE RECOVERY ROOM, AWARE OF A THICK bandage on her shoulder, a nurse looking down at her. "You're fine."

Later they wheeled her to a room. Her mother. Mac. Kyle. Waiting for her.

Her mother's face, miraculously peaceful when their eyes met. Seeming to read her thoughts. "Meg, they recovered Dad's body."

Mac's arm around her mother. His bandaged hands. Mac, her tower of strength. Mac, her love.

Kyle's tearstained face next to hers. "It's all right if you want to kiss me in front of people, Meg."

. . .

ON SUNDAY NIGHT, THE BODY OF DR. HENRY WILLIAMS WAS
found in his car on the outskirts of Pittsburgh, Pennsylvania,
in the quiet neighborhood where he and his wife had grown
up and met as teenagers. He had taken a lethal dose of sleeping pills. Letters to his son and daughter contained messages
of love and pleas for forgiveness.

MEGHAN WAS ABLE TO LEAVE THE HOSPITAL ON MONDAY
morning. Her arm was in a sling, her shoulder a vague,
constant ache. Otherwise she was recovering rapidly.

When she arrived home, she went upstairs to her room to
change to a comfortable robe. As she started to undress, she
hesitated, then went to the windows and closed the blinds
firmly. I hope I get over doing that, she thought. She knew it
would be a long time before she would be able to banish the
image of Bernie shadowing her.

Catherine was getting off the phone. "I've just cancelled
the sale of the inn," she said. "The death certificate has been
issued, and that means all the joint assets Dad and I held are
unfrozen. The insurance adjustors are processing payment of
all Dad's personal policies as well as the one from the business. It's a lot of money, Meg. Remember, the personal policies have a double indemnity clause."

Meg kissed her mother. "I'm so glad about the inn. You'd
be lost without Drumdoe." Over coffee and juice she scanned
the morning papers. In the hospital, she'd seen the early
morning television news reports about the Williams suicide.
"They're combing the Franklin Center records to try to find
out who received the embryos Petrovic stole from Manning."

"Meg, what a terrible thing it must be for people who had
cryopreserved embryos there to wonder if their biological
child was born to a stranger," Catherine Collins said. "Is
there enough money in the world for anyone to do something
like that?"

"Apparently there is. Phillip Carter told me he needed money. But Mom, when I asked him if that was what Petrovic was doing, stealing embryos for the donor program, he told me I wasn't as smart as he'd thought. There was more to it. I only hope they find out what in the records at the center."

Meghan sipped the coffee. "What could he have meant by that? And what happened to Stephanie Petrovic? Did Phillip kill that poor girl? Mom, her baby was due around this time."

THAT NIGHT WHEN MAC CAME, SHE SAID, "DAD WILL BE BURied day after tomorrow. Frances Grolier should be notified about that and told the circumstances of Dad's death, but I dread calling her."

Mac's arms around her. All the years she'd waited for them.

"Why not let me take care of it, Meggie?" Mac asked.

And then they'd talked. "Mac, we don't know everything yet. Dr. Williams was the last hope for understanding what Phillip meant."

ON TUESDAY MORNING, AT NINE O'CLOCK, TOM WEICKER phoned. This time he did not ask the teasing-but-serious question he'd asked yesterday: "Ready to come back to work, Meg?"

Nor did he ask how she was feeling. Even before he said, "Meg, we've got a breaking story," she sensed the difference in his tone.

"What is it, Tom?"

"There's an envelope marked 'Personal and Confidential' for you from Dr. Williams."

"Dr. Williams! Open it. Read it to me."

"You're sure?"

"Tom, open it."

There was a pause. She visualized him slitting the envelope, pulling out the contents.

"Tom?"

"Meg, this is Williams' confession."

"Read it to me."

"No. You have the fax machine you took home from the office?"

"Yes."

"Give me the number again. I'll fax it to you. We'll read it together."

Meghan gave the number to him and rushed downstairs. She got to the study in time to hear the high-pitched squeal of the fax. The first page of the statement from Dr. Henry Williams slowly began to emerge on the thin, slick paper.

It was five pages long. Meghan read and reread it. Finally the reporter in her began to pick out specific paragraphs and isolated sentences.

The phone rang. She knew it was Tom Weicker. "What do you think, Meghan?"

"It's all there. He needed money because of the bills from his wife's long illness. Petrovic was a naturally gifted person who should have been a doctor. She hated seeing cryopreserved embryos destroyed. She saw them as children who could fill the lives of childless couples. Williams saw them as children people would pay a fortune to adopt. He sounded out Carter, who was more than willing to place Petrovic at Manning, using my father's signature."

"They had everything covered," Weicker said, "a secluded house where they brought illegal aliens willing to be host mothers in exchange for ten thousand dollars and a bogus green card. Not a high price when you think Williams and Carter were selling the babies for a minimum of one hundred thousand dollars each.

"In the past six years," Weicker went on, "they've placed more than two hundred babies and were planning to open other facilities."

"And then Helene quit," Meghan said, "claiming she'd made a mistake that was going to become public.

"The first thing Dr. Manning did after Petrovic quit was to call Dr. Williams and tell him about it. Manning trusted Williams and needed to talk to someone. He was horrified at the prospect of the clinic losing its reputation. He told Williams how upset Petrovic was and that she thought she'd lost the Anderson baby's identical twin when she slipped in the lab.

"Williams called Carter, who immediately panicked. Carter had a key to Helene's apartment in Connecticut. They weren't romantically involved. Sometimes he'd need to transport embryos she'd brought from the clinic immediately after they were fertilized and before they were cryopreserved. He'd rushed them to Pennsylvania to be transferred to a host womb."

"Carter panicked and killed her," Weicker agreed. "Meg, Dr. Williams gave you the address of the place where he and Carter kept those pregnant girls. We're obliged to give that information to the authorities, but we want to be there when they arrive. Are you up to it?"

"You bet I am. Tom, can you send a helicopter for me? Make it one of the big ones. You're missing something important in the Williams statement. He was the person Stephanie Petrovic contacted when she needed help. He was the one who had transferred an embryo into her womb. She's due to give birth now. If there's one redeeming feature about Henry Williams, it's that he didn't tell Phillip Carter that he'd hidden Stephanie Petrovic. If he had, her life wouldn't have been worth a plugged nickel."

TOM PROMISED TO HAVE A HELICOPTER AT THE DRUMDOE Inn within the hour. Meghan made two phone calls. One to Mac. "Can you get away, Mac? I want you with me for this." The second call was to a new mother. "Can you and your husband meet me in an hour?"

. . .

THE RESIDENCE DR. WILLIAMS DESCRIBED IN HIS CONFESSION was forty miles from Philadelphia. Tom Weicker and the crew from Channel 3 were waiting when the helicopter carrying Meghan, Mac and the Andersons touched down in a nearby field.

A half-dozen official cars were parked nearby.

"I struck a deal that we'll go in with the authorities," Tom told them.

"Why are we here, Meghan?" Dina Anderson asked as they got into a waiting Channel 3 car.

"If I was sure, I would tell you," Meghan said. Every instinct told her she was right. In his confession, Williams had written, "I had no idea when Helene brought Stephanie to me and asked me to transfer an embryo into her womb that if a pregnancy resulted, Helene intended to raise the baby as her own."

THE YOUNG WOMEN IN THE OLD HOUSE WERE IN VARIOUS stages of pregnancy. Meghan saw the heartsick fear on their faces when they were confronted by the authorities. "You will not send me home, please?" a teenager begged. "I did just what I promised. When the baby is born, you will pay me, please?"

"Host mothers," Mac whispered to Meghan. "Did Williams indicate if they kept any records of whose babies these girls are carrying?"

"His confession said they're all the babies of women who have embryos cryopreserved at Manning," Meghan said. "Helene Petrovic came here regularly to be sure these girls were well cared for. She wanted all the cryopreserved embryos to have a chance to be born."

Stephanie Petrovic was not there. A weeping practical nurse said, "She's at the local hospital. That's where all our girls give birth. She's in labor."

. . .

"WHY ARE WE HERE?" DINA ANDERSON ASKED AGAIN AN
hour later, when Meghan returned to the hospital lobby.

Meghan had been allowed to be with Stephanie in the last
moments of her labor.

"We're going to see Stephanie's baby in a few minutes,"
she said. "She had it for Helene. That was their bargain."

Mac pulled Meghan aside. "Is it what I think?"

She did not answer. Twenty minutes later the obstetrician
who had delivered Stephanie's baby stepped off the elevator
and beckoned to them. "You can come up now," he said.

Dina Anderson reached for her husband's hand. Too overwhelmed to speak, she wondered, Is it possible?

Tom Weicker and the cameraman accompanied them and
began taping as a smiling nurse brought the blanket-wrapped
infant to the window of the nursery and held it up.

"It's Ryan!" Dina Anderson shrieked. "It's Ryan!"

THE NEXT DAY, AT A PRIVATE FUNERAL MASS AT ST. PAUL'S,
the mortal remains of Edwin Richard Collins were consigned
to the earth. Mac was at the grave with Catherine and Meg.

I've shed so many tears for you, Dad, Meg thought. I don't
think I have any left in me. And then she whispered so silently
that no one could hear, "I love you, Daddy."

Catherine thought of the day when her door bell had rung
and there stood Edwin Collins, handsome, with the quick
smile she'd so loved, a dozen roses in his hands. *I'm courting
you, Catherine.*

After a while I'll remember only the good times, she promised herself.

Hand in hand the three walked to the waiting car.

REMEMBER ME

Acknowledgments

Twenty years ago I came across a book called *The Narrow Land* by Elizabeth Reynard. The myths and legends and folk chronicles I found in there are the reason this book exists. My gratitude for background material also belongs to these writers of the past: Henry C. Kittredge for his *Cape Codders: People and Their History* and *Mooncussers of Cape Cod;* Doris Doane for *A Book of Cape Cod Houses* with drawings by Howard L. Rich; Frederick Freeman for *The History of Cape Cod;* and William C. Smith for his *History of Chatham.*

Profound and heartfelt thanks to Michael V. Korda, my longtime editor, and his associate, senior editor Chuck Adams. As always, guys, sine qua non.

Garlands to Frank and Eve Metz for consistently terrific jacket design and interior design. Sainthood to Gypsy da Silva for her magnificent copy supervision.

Blessings on Eugene H. Winick, my agent, and Lisl Cade, my publicist, valued companions of this journey called writing a book.

Kudos to Ina Winick for the professional guidance to understanding post-traumatic stress disorder. Special thanks to the Eldredge Library, Sam Pinkus, Dr. Marina Stajic, the Coast Guard Group at Woods Hole, the Chatham Police Department, the

Barnstable County District Attorney's office, Ron Aires of Aires Jewelers. If I didn't get any of the technicalities straight, it certainly wasn't your fault.

A tip of the hat to my daughter Carol Higgins Clark for her insight and suggestions.

And now, dear family and friends. If you Remember Me, give me a call. I'm available for dinner.

In joyful memory of
Maureen Higgins Dowling, "Mo,"
Sister-in-law and friend
With love

*B*Y 9 P.M. *the storm had broken with full force, and a stiff wind was sending powerful waves crashing against the eastern shore of Cape Cod. We're going to get more than a touch of the nor'easter, Menley thought as she reached over the sink to close the window. It might actually be fun, she thought, in an effort to reassure herself. The Cape airports were closed, so Adam had rented a car to drive from Boston. He should be home soon. There was plenty of food on hand. She had stocked up on candles, just in case the electricity went out, although if she was right about what she was beginning to suspect, the thought of being in this house with only candlelight was frightening.*

She switched on the radio, twisted the dial and found the Chatham station that played forties music. She raised an eyebrow in surprise as the Benny Goodman orchestra went into the opening notes of "Remember."

A particularly appropriate song when you're living in a place called Remember House, she thought. Pushing aside the inclination to flip the dial again, she picked up a serrated knife and began to slice tomatoes for a salad. When he phoned, Adam told her he hadn't had time to eat. "But you forgot to remember," the vocalist warbled.

The unique sound that the wind made when it rushed past the house was starting again. Perched high on the embankment over the churning water, the house became a kind of bellows in a wind storm, and the whooshing sound it emitted had the effect of a distant voice calling out "Remember, Remember . . ." The legend was that over the decades that peculiarity had given the house its name.

Menley shivered as she reached for the celery. Adam will be here soon, she promised herself. He'd have a glass of wine while she made some pasta.

There was a sudden noise. What was that? Had a door blown open? Or a window? Something was wrong.

She snapped off the radio. The baby! Was she crying? Was that a cry or a muffled, gagging sound? Menley hurried to the counter, grabbed the monitor and held it to her ear. Another choking gasp and then nothing. The baby was choking!

She rushed from the kitchen into the foyer, toward the staircase. The delicate fan-shaped window over the front door sent gray and purple shadows along the wide-plank floor.

Her feet barely touched the stairs as she raced to the second floor and down the hall. An instant later she was at the door of the nursery. There was no sound coming from the crib. "Hannah, Hannah," she cried.

Hannah was lying on her stomach, her arms outstretched, her body motionless. Frantically, Menley leaned down, turning the baby as she picked her up. Then her eyes widened in horror.

The china head of an antique doll rested against her hand. A painted face stared back at her.

Menley tried to scream, but no sound came from her lips. And then from behind her a voice whispered, "I'm sorry, Menley. It's all over."

*A*FTERWARDS, steadfastly through the question-
ing, Scott Covey tried to make everyone understand just how it had
happened.

He and Vivian had been napping on a quilt spread on the boat's
deck, the hazy sun and gentle lapping of the water lulling them into
sleepy contentment.

He had opened one eye and yawned. "I'm hot," he said. "Want
to check out the ocean floor?"

Vivian had brushed her lips against his chin. "I don't think I'm
in the mood." Her soft voice was lazy, a contented murmur.

"I am." He sprang up decisively and looked over the side. "It's
perfect down there. Water's clear as a bell."

It was nearly four o'clock. They were about a mile off Monomoy
Island. The haze of humidity lay like shimmering chiffon, but a
faint breeze had begun to stir.

"I'll get my gear," Scott told her. He crossed the deck and
reached down into the small cabin they used as a storage area.

Vivian had gotten up, shaking off her drowsiness. "Get my stuff
too."

He had turned. "Are you sure, honey? I'm just going in for a few minutes. Why don't you just nap?"

"No way." She'd rushed to him and put her arms around his neck. "When we go to Hawaii next month I want to be able to explore those coral reefs with you. Might as well get some practice."

Later he tearfully pleaded that he hadn't noticed all the other boats had disappeared while they napped. No, he hadn't turned on the radio to check the weather.

They had been down twenty minutes when the squall hit. The water became violent. They struggled to reach the anchored boat. Just as they surfaced, a five-foot wave hit them. Vivian disappeared. He had searched and searched, diving into the water again and again, until his own air was running out.

They knew the rest. The emergency call was received by the Coast Guard as the full force of the fast-moving squall was at its peak. "My wife is missing!" Scott Covey had shouted. "My wife is missing!"

July 28th

2

*E*LAINE ATKINS sat across the table from Adam Nichols. They were at Chillingsworth, the restaurant in Brewster where Elaine took all her important real estate clients. Now, at the peak of the Cape Cod season, every table was filled.

"I don't think you have to eavesdrop to know what they're talking about," she said quietly. Her hand moved slightly in a gesture that encompassed the room. "A young woman, Vivian Carpenter, disappeared scuba diving a couple of weeks ago. She bought her house in Chatham from me, and we became very friendly. While you were on the phone I was told that her body was washed ashore an hour ago."

"I was on a fishing boat once when someone hooked a body that had been in the water for a couple of weeks," Adam said quietly. "It wasn't a pretty sight. How did it happen?"

"Vivian was a good swimmer but not an experienced diver. Scott was teaching her. They hadn't listened to the warning on the radio about the storm. The poor guy is devastated. They'd only been married three months."

Adam raised an eyebrow. "Sounds as though it was pretty careless, to go diving just before a storm."

"Pretty tragic," Elaine said firmly. "Viv and Scott were very happy. She's the one who knew these waters. Like you, growing up she spent every summer on the Cape. It's such a damn shame. Till she met Scott, Viv was kind of a lost soul. She's one of the Carpenters from Boston. Youngest in a family of achievers. Dropped out of college. Pretty much on the outs with the family. Worked at a variety of jobs. Then three years ago, when she turned twenty-one, she came into the trust her grandmother left her. That's when she bought the house. She worshipped Scott, wanted to do everything with him."

"Including scuba diving in bad weather? What does this guy do?"

"Scott? He was assistant business manager for the Cape Playhouse last year. That's when he met Viv. I guess she visited him over the winter. Then he came back for good in May, and the next thing anyone knew they were married."

"What's his last name?"

"Covey. Scott Covey. He's from the Midwest somewhere."

"A stranger who marries a rich girl and the rich girl dies three months later. If I were the cops I'd want to read her will fast."

"Oh, stop," Elaine protested. "You're supposed to be a defense attorney, not a prosecutor. I saw a lot of those two. I was showing them houses. They were looking for something bigger. They were planning to start a family and wanted more room. Trust me. It was a horrible accident."

"Probably." Adam shrugged. "Maybe I'm getting to be too much of a skeptic."

They were sipping wine. Elaine sighed. "Let's change the subject," she said. "This is supposed to be a festive occasion. *You* look great, Adam. More than that—you look happy, content, pleased with life. Everything really is okay, isn't it? With Menley, I mean. I'm so eager to meet her."

"Menley's a trooper. She'll be fine. Incidentally, when she gets up here, don't mention that I told you about those anxiety attacks. She doesn't like to talk about them."

"I can understand that." Elaine studied him. Adam's dark brown hair was beginning to show flecks of gray. Like her, he'd be thirty-nine on his next birthday. Long and lean, he'd always had a quicksilver quality. She'd known him from the time they were both sixteen, when his family hired a summer housekeeper from the employment service her mother managed.

Nothing ever changes, Elaine thought. She'd noticed the glances other women had given him when he joined her at the table.

The waiter brought over menus. Adam studied his. "Steak tartare, well done," he suggested with a laugh.

She made a face at him. "Don't be mean. I was a kid when I pulled that."

"I'll never let you forget it. 'Laine, I'm awfully glad you made me come up to see Remember House. When the other place fell through I didn't think we'd hit on a desirable rental for August."

She shrugged. "These things happen. I'm just glad it worked out. I can't believe that rental I found for you in Eastham turned out to have all those plumbing problems. But this one is a real gem. As I told you, it wasn't occupied for thirty-five years. The Paleys saw the place, realized it had possibilities and picked it up for a song a couple of years ago. They'd finished the worst of the renovating when Tom had the heart attack. He'd put in twelve hours on a hot day when it happened. Jan Paley finally decided it was too much house for one person, and that's why it's on the market. There aren't that many authentic captain's houses available, so it won't last long, you know. I'm hoping you two will decide to buy it."

"We'll see. I'd like to have a place up here again. If we're going to continue to live in the city, it makes sense. Those old sailors knew how to build a home."

"This one even has a story attached to it. It seems that Captain Andrew Freeman built it for his bride in 1703 and ended up deserting her when he found she'd been engaged in hanky-panky with some guy from town while he was at sea."

Adam grinned. "My grandmother told me the early settlers were Puritans. Anyhow I won't be doing any renovating. This is vacation for us, although it's inevitable that I'll be going back and forth to the city for a few days at a time. I've got to do some work on the retrial of the Potter case. Maybe you read about it. The wife got a bum rap. I wish I'd defended her in the first place."

"I'd like to see you in action in court someday."

"Come to New York. Tell John to bring you down. When are you getting married?"

"We haven't quite set the date, but sometime in the fall. Predictably, John's daughter is less than thrilled about the engagement. She's had John to herself for a long time. Amy starts college in September, so we figure around Thanksgiving would be about right."

"You look happy, 'Laine. And you also look great. Very attractive and very successful. You're skinnier than I've ever seen you. Also your hair's blonder, which I like."

"Compliments from you? Don't ruin our relationship." Elaine laughed. "But I thank you. I am very happy indeed. John's the Mr. Right I've been waiting for. And I thank the gods that you look like yourself again. Believe me, Adam, last year when you came up after you and Menley separated, I was worried about you."

"It was a pretty rough period."

Elaine studied the menu. "This one is on Atkins Real Estate. No arguments, please. Remember House is for sale, and if you decide after renting it that it would be a great buy I get the commission."

After they'd ordered, Adam said, "The phone was busy when I tried Menley before. I'll give a quick call now."

He returned a minute later, looking troubled. "Still busy."

"Don't you have Call Waiting?"

"Menley hates it. She says it's so rude to keep telling people 'wait a minute' and going off the line."

"She has a point, but it still is mighty handy." Elaine hesitated. "All of a sudden you seem worried. Is she really okay now?"

"She seems to be fine," Adam said slowly. "But when those anxiety attacks come, they're hell. She's practically a basket case when she relives the accident. I'll try her again in a minute, but in the meantime, did I show you a picture of the baby?"

"Have you got a picture with you?"

"Is the Pope Catholic?" He reached in his pocket. "Here's the most recent. Her name is Hannah. She was three months old last week. Isn't she a knockout?"

Elaine studied the picture carefully. "She's absolutely beautiful," she said sincerely.

"She looks like Menley, so she's going to stay gorgeous," Adam said decisively. He returned the snapshot to his wallet and pushed back his chair. "If the line's still busy I'm going to ask the operator to interrupt."

Elaine watched him wend his way through the room. He's nervous about her being alone with the baby, she thought.

"Elaine."

She looked up. It was Carolyn March, a fiftyish New York advertising executive to whom she'd sold a house. March did not wait to be greeted. "Have you heard how much Vivian Carpenter's trust fund was? *Five million dollars!* The Carpenters never talk money, but one of the cousins' wives let that slip. And Viv told people that she'd left everything to her husband. Don't you think that much money should dry Scott Covey's tears?"

3

*T*HAT MUST BE ADAM. He said he'd call around now. Menley juggled the baby on her shoulder as she reached for the phone. "Come on, Hannah," she murmured. "You've finished half the second bottle. At this rate you'll be the only three-month-old in Weight Watchers."

She held the receiver between her ear and shoulder as she patted the baby's back. Instead of Adam, it was Jane Pierce, editor-in-chief of *Travel Times* magazine. As usual, Jane did not waste words. "Menley, you *are* going to the Cape in August, aren't you?"

"Keep your fingers crossed about that," Menley said. "We heard last night that the house we were supposed to rent has major plumbing problems. I never thought chamber pots were cute, so Adam drove up this morning to see what else we could get."

"It's pretty late to get anything, isn't it?" Jane asked.

"We have one ace in the hole. An old friend of Adam's owns a real estate agency. Elaine found the first place for us and swears she has a terrific replacement. Let's hope Adam agrees."

"In that case, if you do go up . . ."

"Jane, if we do go up I'm going to research another book for the David series. I've heard so much about the Cape from Adam that I may want to set the next one there." David was the ten-year-old continuing character in a series of novels that had made Menley a well-known children's book author.

"I know this is begging a favor, Menley, but it's that special way you weave in historical background that I need for this piece," the editor pleaded.

When Menley hung up the phone fifteen minutes later, she had been talked into doing an article about Cape Cod for *Travel Times*.

"Oh well, Hannah," she said as she gave one final pat to the baby's back, "Jane did give me my first break ten years ago. Right? It's the least I can do."

But Hannah was contentedly asleep on her shoulder. Menley strolled over to the window. The twenty-eighth-floor apartment on East End Avenue afforded a stunning view of the East River and the bridges that spanned it.

Moving back to Manhattan from Rye after they lost Bobby had saved her sanity. But it would be good to get away for August. After the first terrible anxiety attack, her obstetrician had encouraged her to see a psychiatrist. "You're having what is called delayed post-traumatic stress disorder, which is not uncommon after a frightful experience, but there is treatment available, and I'd recommend it."

She'd been seeing the psychiatrist, Dr. Kaufman, weekly, and Kaufman wholeheartedly endorsed the idea of a vacation. "The episodes are understandable and in the long run beneficial," she said. "For nearly two years after Bobby's death, you were in denial. Now that you have Hannah, you're finally dealing with it. Take this vacation. Get away. Enjoy yourself. Just take your medication. And, of course, call me at any time if you need me. Otherwise, I'll see you in September."

We will enjoy ourselves, Menley thought. She carried the sleeping baby into the nursery, laid her down and quickly changed and covered her. "Now be a love and take a nice long nap," she whispered, looking down into the crib.

Her shoulders and neck felt tight, and she stretched out her arms and rotated her head. The brown hair that Adam described as being the color of maple syrup bounced around the collar of her sweat suit. For as long as she could remember, Menley had wished to grow taller. But at thirty-one she'd reconciled herself to a permanent height of five feet four. At least I can be strong, she'd consoled herself, and her sturdy, slender body was testimony to her daily trips to the exercise room on the second floor of the building.

Before she turned out the light she studied the baby. Miracle, miracle, she thought. She'd been raised with an older brother who had turned her into a tomboy. As a result she'd always scorned dolls and preferred tossing a football to playing house. She was always comfortable with boys and in her teens became the favorite confidante and willing baby-sitter of her two nephews.

But nothing had prepared her for the torrents of love she'd felt when Bobby was born and that were evoked now by this perfectly formed, roundfaced, sometimes cranky infant girl.

The phone rang as she reached the living room. I bet it's Adam and he was trying to get me while I was talking to Jane, she thought as she rushed to answer.

It was Adam. "Hi, love," she said joyously. "Have you found us a house?"

He ignored the question. "Hi, sweetheart. How do you feel? How's the baby?"

Menley paused for a moment. She knew she really couldn't blame him for worrying, still she couldn't resist taking a little jab. "I'm fine, but I really haven't checked on Hannah since you left this morning," she told him. "Wait a minute and I'll give a look."

"Menley!"

"I'm sorry," she said, "but Adam, it's the way you ask; it's as though you're expecting bad news."

"*Mea culpa,*" he said contritely. "I just love you both so much. I want everything to be right. I'm with Elaine. We've got a terrific place. A nearly three-hundred-year-old captain's house on Morris

Island in Chatham. The location is magnificent, a bluff overlooking the ocean. You'll be crazy about it. It even has a name, Remember House. I'll tell you all about it when I get home. I'll start back after dinner."

"That's a five-hour drive," Menley protested, "and you've already done it once today. Why don't you stay over and get an early start in the morning?"

"I don't care how late it is. I want to be with you and Hannah tonight. I love you."

"I love you too," Menley said fervently.

After they said good-bye, she replaced the receiver and whispered to herself, "I only hope the real reason for rushing home isn't that you're afraid to trust me alone with the baby."

July 31st

4

*H*ENRY SPRAGUE held his wife's hand as they walked along the beach. The late afternoon sun was slipping in and out of clouds, and he was glad he had fastened the warm scarf around Phoebe's head. He mused that the approaching evening brought a different look to the landscape. Without the bathers, the vistas of sand and cooling ocean waters seemed to return to a primal harmony with nature.

He watched as seagulls hopped about at the edge of the waves. Clam shells in subtle tones of gray and pink and white were clustered on the damp sand. An occasional piece of flotsam caught his eye. Years ago he had spotted a life preserver from the *Andrea Doria* that had washed ashore here.

It was the time of day he and Phoebe had always enjoyed most. It was on this beach four years ago that Henry had first noticed the signs of forgetfulness in her. Now, with a heavy heart, he acknowledged that he wouldn't be able to keep her at home much longer. The drug tacrine had been prescribed, and sometimes she seemed to be making genuine improvement, but several times recently she had slipped out of the house while his back was turned. Just the other day at dusk he'd found her on this beach, waist-deep in the ocean. Even as he ran toward her, a wave had knocked her over. Totally disoriented, she'd been within seconds of drowning.

We've had forty-six good years, he told himself. I can visit her at the home every day. It will be for the best. He knew all this was true, still it was so difficult. She was trudging along at his side, quiet, lost in a world of her own. Dr. Phoebe Cummings Sprague, full professor of history at Harvard, who no longer remembered how to tie a scarf or whether she'd just had breakfast.

He realized where they were and looked up. Beyond the dune, on the high ground, the house was silhouetted against the horizon. It had always reminded him of an eagle, perched as it was on the embankment, aloof and watchful. "Phoebe," he said.

She turned and stared at him, frowning. The frown had become automatic. It had begun when she still was trying desperately not to give the appearance of being forgetful.

He pointed to the house above them. "I told you that Adam Nichols is renting there for August, with his wife, Menley, and their new baby. I'll ask them to visit us soon. You always liked Adam."

Adam Nichols. For an instant the murky fog that had invaded Phoebe's mind, forcing her to grope for understanding, parted. That house, she thought. It's original name was Nickquenum.

Nickquenum, the solemn Indian word that meant "I am going home." I was walking around, Phoebe told herself. I was in that house. Someone I know—who was it?—doing something strange ... Adam's wife must *not* live there ... the fog rushed back into her brain and enveloped it. She looked at her husband. "Adam Nichols," she murmured slowly. "Who is that?"

August 1st

5

Scott Covey had not gone to bed until midnight. Even so he was still awake when the first hints of dawn began to cast shadows through the bedroom. After that he fell into an uneasy doze and woke up with a sensation of tightness in his forehead, the beginning of a headache.

Grimacing, he threw back the covers. The night had turned sharply cooler, but he knew the drop in temperature was temporary. By noon it would be a fine Cape day, sunny with the midsummer heat tempered by salt-filled ocean breezes. But it was still cool now, and if Vivian were here he'd have closed the windows before she got out of bed.

Today Vivian was being buried.

As he got up, Scott glanced down at the bed and thought of how often in the three months they'd been married he'd brought coffee to her when she woke up. Then they would snuggle in bed and drink it together.

He could see her still, her scrunched up knees supporting the saucer, her back against a pile of pillows, remember her joking about the brass headboard.

"Mother redecorated my room when I was sixteen," she'd told him in that breathy voice she had. "I wanted one of these so much, but Mother said I didn't have any flair for interior decoration and brass beds were getting too common. The first thing I did when I got my hands on my own money was to buy the most ornate one I could find." Then she'd laughed. "I have to admit that an uphol-stered headboard is a lot more comfortable to lean against."

He'd taken the cup and saucer from her hand that morning and placed it on the floor. "Lean against me," he'd suggested.

Funny that particular memory hitting him now. Scott went into the kitchen, made coffee and toast, and sat at the counter. The front of the house faced the street, the back overlooked Oyster Pond. From the side window through the foliage he could see the corner of the Spragues' place.

Vivian had told him that Mrs. Sprague would be put in a nursing home soon. "Henry doesn't like me to visit her anymore, but we'll have to invite him over to dinner when he's alone," she had said.

"It's fun to have company when we do it together," she'd added. Then she had wrapped her arms around his neck and hugged him fiercely. "You *do* really love me, don't you, Scott?"

How many times had he reassured her, held her, stroked her hair, comforted her until, once again cheerful, she'd switched to listing reasons why she loved him. "I always hoped my husband would be over six feet tall, and you are. I always hoped he'd be blond and handsome so that everyone would envy me. Well, you are, and they do. But most important of all, I wanted him to be crazy about me."

"And I am." Over and over again he had told her that.

Scott stared out the window, thinking over the last two weeks, reminding himself that some of the Carpenter family cousins, and many of Viv's friends, had rushed to console him from the minute she was reported missing. But a significant number of people had not. Her parents had been especially aloof. He knew that in the eyes of many he was nothing more than a fortune hunter, an opportunist. Some of the news accounts in the Boston and Cape papers had printed interviews with people who were openly skeptical of the circumstances of the accident.

The Carpenter family had been prominent in Massachusetts for generations. Along the way they had produced senators and governors. Anything that happened to them was news.

He got up and crossed to the stove for more coffee. Suddenly the thought of the hours ahead, of the memorial service and the burial, of the inevitable presence of the media was overwhelming. Everyone would be watching him.

"Damn you all, we were in love!" he said fiercely, slamming the percolator down on the stove.

He took a quick gulp of coffee. It was boiling hot. His mouth burning, he rushed to the sink and spat it out.

6

*T*HEY STOPPED in Buzzards Bay long enough to pick up coffee, rolls and a copy of the *Boston Globe*. As they drove over the Sagamore Bridge in the packed station wagon, Menley sighed, "Do you think there's coffee in heaven?"

"There'd better be. Otherwise you won't stay awake long enough to enjoy your eternal reward." Adam glanced over at her, a smile in his eyes.

They'd gotten an early start, on the road by seven. Now at eleven-thirty they were crossing Cape Cod Canal. After howling for the first fifteen minutes, an unusually cooperative Hannah had slept the rest of the trip.

The late morning sun gave a silvery sheen to the metal structure of the bridge. In the canal below, a cargo ship was slowly steaming through the gently lapping water. Then they were on Route 6.

"It was at this point every summer that my dad used to shout, 'We're back on the Cape!' " Adam said. "It was always his real home."

"Do you think your mother regrets selling?"

"No. The Cape wasn't the same for her after Dad died. She's happier in North Carolina near her sisters. But I'm like Dad. This place is in my blood; our family has summered here for three centuries."

Menley shifted slightly so that she could watch her husband. She was happy to finally be here with him. They had planned to come up the summer Bobby was born, but the doctor hadn't wanted her to be so far away in late pregnancy. The next year they'd just bought the house in Rye and were settling in, so it didn't make sense to come to the Cape.

The next summer they'd lost Bobby. And after that, Menley thought, all I knew was the awful numbness, the feeling of being detached from every other human being, the inability to respond to Adam.

Last year, Adam had come up here alone. She had asked him for a trial separation. Resigned, he had agreed. "We certainly can't go on like this, Men," he had admitted, "going through the motions of being married."

He had been gone for three weeks when she realized she was pregnant. In all that time he hadn't called her. For days she had agonized about telling him, wondering what his reaction would be.

Finally she had phoned. His impersonal greeting had made her heart sink, but when she said, "Adam, maybe this isn't the news you want to hear but I'm pregnant and I'm very happy about it," his whoop of joy had thrilled her.

"I'm on my way home," he had said without a pause.

Now she felt Adam's hand in hers. "I wonder if we're thinking the same thing," he said. "I was up here when I heard her nibs was on the way."

For a moment they were silent; then Menley blinked back tears and began to laugh. "And remember how after she was born Phyllis carried on about naming her Menley Hannah." She mimicked the strident tone of her sister-in-law. "I think it's very nice to keep the family tradition of naming the first daughter Menley, but please don't call her Hannah. That's so old-fashioned. Why not name her Menley Kimberly and then she can be Kim? Wouldn't that be cute?"

Her voice resumed its normal pitch. "Honestly!"

"Don't ever get mad at me, honey," Adam chuckled. "I hope Phyllis doesn't wear out your mother." Menley's mother was traveling in Ireland with her son and daughter-in-law.

"Phyl is determined to research both sides of the family tree. It's a safe bet that if she finds horse thieves among her ancestors we'll never hear about it."

From the backseat they heard a stirring. Menley looked over her shoulder. "Well, it looks like her ladyship is going to be joining us soon, and I bet she'll be one hungry character." Leaning over, she popped the pacifier into Hannah's mouth. "Say a prayer that holds her until we get to the house."

She put the empty coffee container in a bag and reached for the newspaper. "Adam, look. There's a picture of the couple you told me about. She's the one who drowned when they were scuba diving. The funeral is today. The poor guy. What a tragic accident."

Tragic accident. How many times had she heard those words. They triggered such terrible memories. They flooded over her. *Driv-*

*ing on that unfamiliar country road, Bobby in the backseat. A
glorious sunny day. Feeling so great. Singing to Bobby at the top of
her lungs. Bobby joining in. The unguarded railroad crossing. And
then feeling the vibrations. Looking out the window. The conduc-
tor's frantic face. The roar and the screech of metal as the braking
train bore down on them. Bobby screaming, "Mommy, Mommy."
Flooring the accelerator. The crash as the train hit the back door
next to Bobby. The train dragging the car. Bobby sobbing,
"Mommy, Mommy." Then his eyes closing. Knowing he was dead.
Rocking him in her arms. Screaming and screaming, "Bobby, I
want Bobby. Bobbbbyyyyyyyyy."*

Once again Menley felt the perspiration drenching her body. She
began to shiver. She pressed her hands on her legs to control the
trembling spasms of her limbs.

Adam glanced at her. "Oh my God." They were approaching a
rest stop. He pulled into it, braked the car and turned to wrap his
arms around her. "It's okay, sweetheart. It's okay."

In the backseat, Hannah began to wail.

Bobby wailing, "Mommy, Mommy."

Hannah wailing . . .

"Make her stop!" Menley screamed. *"Make her stop!"*

7

*I*T WAS QUARTER of twelve, Elaine realized, glancing at the dashboard clock. Adam and Menley should be arriving
any minute, and she wanted to check the house before they got

there to make sure everything was in order. One of the services she offered her clients was that a rental property would be thoroughly cleaned before and after a tenancy. She pressed her foot more firmly on the accelerator. She was running late because of attending the funeral service for Vivian Carpenter Covey.

Impulsively, she stopped at the supermarket.

I'll pick up some of the smoked salmon that Adam loves, she thought. It would go nicely with the bottle of chilled champagne she always left for high-ticket clients. Then she could just scribble a welcoming note and be out of the house before they arrived.

The overcast morning had evolved into a splendid day, sunny, in the mid-seventies, sparkling clear. Elaine reached up, opened the sunroof and thought about what she had told the television reporter. As the funeral cortege was preparing to leave the church, she had noticed him stopping people at random to ask for comments. Deliberately, she'd gone over to him. "May I say something?"

She'd looked into the camera squarely. "I'm Elaine Atkins. I sold Vivian Carpenter her home in Chatham three years ago, and the day before her death I was showing larger places to her and her husband. They were very happy and planning to start a family. What has happened is a tragedy, not a mystery. I think the people who are spreading ugly rumors about Mr. Covey should just check to see how many people there were in boats that day who hadn't heard the Coast Guard warning and were nearly swamped when the squall hit."

The memory brought a satisfied smile. She was sure Scott Covey had been watching from inside the limo.

She drove past the lighthouse to the Quitnesset section of Morris Island, down past the Monomoy National Wildlife Refuge; she turned onto Awarks Trail, then veered onto the private road that led to Remember House. When she rounded the bend, and the place came into view, she tried to imagine Menley's reaction upon seeing it for the first time.

Larger and more graceful than much of the architecture of the early eighteenth century, it stood as a tribute to the love Captain Andrew Freeman had initially felt for his young bride. With its starkly beautiful lines, and perched as it was on the bluff, it made a majestic silhouette against the background of sky and sea. Morning glories and holly berries vied with wild roses to splash color throughout the property. Locust trees and oaks, heavy with age, offered oases of shade from the brilliant sunshine.

The paved driveway led from the side of the house to the parking area behind the kitchen. Elaine frowned as Carrie Bell's van came into view. Carrie was an excellent cleaning woman, but she was always late. She should have been out of there by now.

Elaine found Carrie in the kitchen, her purse under her arm. Her thin, strong-featured face was pale. When she spoke, her voice, always a shade too loud, was rushed and subdued. "Oh, Miss Atkins. I know I'm a little behind, but I had to drop Tommy off at my mother's. Everything's shipshape, but let me tell you I'm glad to be getting out of here."

"What's wrong?" Elaine asked quickly.

"I got the fright of my life," Carrie said, her voice still tremulous. "I was in the dining room when I was sure I heard footsteps upstairs. I thought you might have come in so I called out to you. When nobody answered, I went up to take a look. Miss Atkins, you know that antique cradle that's in the bedroom with the single bed and crib?"

"Of course I know it."

Carrie's face went a shade paler. She clutched Elaine's arm. "Miss Atkins, the windows were closed. There was absolutely no breeze. But the spread on the bed was a little wrinkled, the way it would be if someone was sitting on it. And the cradle was moving. *Someone I couldn't see was sitting on the side of that bed, rocking the cradle!*"

"Now, Carrie, you've just heard those silly stories people made up about this house when it was abandoned," Elaine told her.

"Those old floors are uneven. If that cradle was moving, it's because you're so heavy footed and probably stepped on a loose board."

From behind she could hear the sound of a car coming up the driveway. Adam and his family were here. "The whole idea is ridiculous," she said sternly. "Don't you dare say a word about that to the Nicholses," she warned, turning to watch as Adam and Menley got out of the station wagon. She knew her warning was pointless, however—Carrie Bell would share that story with everyone she met.

8

*N*ATHANIEL COOGAN had been on the Chatham police force for eighteen years. A Brooklyn native, Nat had been attending John Jay College in Manhattan, working toward a degree in criminal science, when he met his wife, a lifelong resident of Hyannis. Deb had no interest in living in New York, so after graduation he had willingly applied for a job in police work on the Cape. Now a detective and the forty-year-old father of two teenage sons, he was one of those rare birds, an easygoing, happy man, content with his family and job, his only major concern being the unwanted fifteen or so pounds his wife's excellent cooking had added to his already ample frame.

Earlier that day, however, another concern had surfaced. Actually it had been bothering him for some time. Nat knew that his boss, Chief of Police Frank Shea, firmly believed that Vivian Carpenter Covey's death had been an accident. "We had two other near-drownings that day," Frank pointed out. "It was Vivian Carpenter's boat. She knew those waters better than her husband did. If anyone should have thought to turn on the radio, she was the one." Still it bothered Nat, and like a dog worrying a bone, he was unwilling to let go until his suspicions were justified or put to rest.

That morning, Nat had gotten into the office early and studied the autopsy pictures the ME had sent from Boston. Even though he had long ago taught himself to be clinically objective about the photographs of victims, the sight of the slender body—or what was left of it—swollen with water, mangled by fish bites, hit him like a dentist's drill on an exposed nerve. Murder victim or accident victim? Which was it?

At nine o'clock he went into Frank's office and asked to be assigned to the case. "I really want to stay on it. It's important."

"One of your hunches?" Shea asked.

"Yep."

"I think you're wrong, but it won't hurt to be thorough. Go ahead."

At ten Nat was at the memorial service. No eulogy for the poor kid, he thought. What did the stony faces of Vivian Carpenter's parents and sisters hide? Grief that it was noblesse oblige to conceal from prying eyes? Anger at a senseless tragedy? Guilt? The media had written plenty about Vivian Carpenter's forlorn history. It was nothing like that of her older sisters, one of them a surgeon, one a diplomat, both suitably married, whereas Vivian, thrown out of boarding school for smoking pot, later became a college dropout. Although she didn't need the money, when she moved to the Cape she took a job, then gave it up, something she would do a half-dozen times.

Scott Covey sat alone in the first pew, weeping through the service. He looks the way I'd feel if something happened to Deb, Nat Coogan thought. Almost convinced that he was barking up the wrong tree, he left the church at the end of the service, then hung around outside to pick up the remarks people were making.

They made good listening. "Poor Vivian. I'm so sorry for her, but she kind of wore you out, didn't she?"

The middle-aged woman who had been addressed sighed. "I know. She could never just relax."

Nat remembered that Covey had said that he had unsuccessfully urged his wife to keep napping while he went scuba diving.

A television reporter was rounding up people to tape. Nat watched as an attractive blond woman went to the reporter on her own. He recognized her, Elaine Atkins, the real estate agent. He sidled over to hear her comments.

When she was finished, Nat jotted down a note. Elaine Atkins said that the Coveys had been looking for a new house and were planning to start a family. She seemed to know them reasonably well. He decided he would have to talk to Miss Atkins himself.

When he got back to the office, he took out the autopsy pictures again, trying to figure out what it was that bothered him about them.

9

MENLEY WIGGLED from under Adam's arm and moved quietly to her side of the bed. He half murmured her name but did not awaken. She got up, slipped on her robe and looked down at him, a smile tugging at her lips.

The dynamic criminal lawyer who could sway juries with his rhetoric looked utterly defenseless in sleep. He was lying on his side, his head pillowed on one arm. His hair was tousled, the patches of gray more apparent, the faint beginning of a tonsure clearly visible.

The room was chilly, so Menley leaned down and drew the blanket over his shoulders, brushing her lips against his forehead. On her twenty-fifth birthday she'd decided that she'd probably never find anyone she wanted to marry. Two weeks later, she'd met Adam on an ocean liner, the *Sagafjord.* The ship was making a round-the-world tour, and because she had written extensively about the Far East, Menley had been invited to lecture on the leg between Bali and Singapore.

On the second day out, Adam had stopped by her deck chair to chat. He'd been taking depositions in Australia and impulsively signed up for the same leg of the voyage. "Great stops along the way, and I can use a week's vacation," he'd explained. By the end of that day, she had realized that Adam was the reason she'd broken her engagement three years earlier.

It had been different for him. He'd fallen in love with her gradually, over the course of the next year. Menley sometimes wondered whether she would ever have heard from him again if they hadn't lived three blocks apart in Manhattan.

It helped that they had some important things in common. Both were active New Yorkers and each was passionate about Manhattan, although they had been raised in distinctly different worlds. Adam's family had a Park Avenue duplex, and he'd gone to Collegiate. She had been brought up in Stuyvesant Town, on Fourteenth Street, where her mother still lived, and she had attended the local parochial schools. But by coincidence they both had graduated from Georgetown University, although eight years apart. They both loved the ocean, and Adam had spent his summers on Cape Cod, while she had gone swimming on day trips to Jones Beach.

When they started dating it was obvious to Menley that at thirty-two Adam was very content with his bachelor life. And why not? He was a successful defense attorney. He had a handsome apartment; a string of girlfriends. Sometimes weeks would go by between his calls.

When he had proposed, Menley suspected that it had something to do with his approaching thirty-third birthday. She didn't care. When they were married something her grandmother had told her years before echoed in her ears: "In marriage, one often is more in love than the other. It's better if the woman is the one who doesn't love as deeply."

Why is it better? Menley had wondered, and asked herself again as she looked at him sleeping so peacefully. What's *wrong* with being the one who loves the most?

It was seven o'clock. The strong sunlight was forcing its way into the room around the edges of the drawn shades. The spacious room was simply furnished with a four-poster, a two-on-three dresser, an armoire, a night table and a straight-backed chair. All the pieces were obviously authentic. Elaine had told her that just before Mr. Paley died, he and his wife had been going to auctions to collect early-eighteenth-century furniture.

Menley loved the fact that each of the bedrooms had a fireplace, although they were unlikely to need them in August. The room next to theirs was small, but it seemed perfect for the baby. Menley wrapped the robe around her more tightly as she stepped into the hall.

When she opened the door to Hannah's room, a brisk breeze greeted her. I should have covered her with a quilt, Menley thought, dismayed at her omission. They'd looked in on the baby at eleven when they went to bed, debated about the quilt, then decided it wasn't necessary. Obviously it had gotten much cooler than expected during the night.

Menley hurried over to the crib. Hannah was sleeping soundly; the quilt was tucked securely around her. Surely I couldn't have forgotten coming in during the night, Menley thought. Who covered her?

Then she felt foolish. Adam must have gotten up and looked in on the baby, although it was something that rarely happened, since he was a heavy sleeper. Or I might have come in myself, she realized. The doctors had prescribed a bedtime sedative that made her terribly groggy.

She wanted to kiss Hannah but knew if she did she risked instant awakening. "See you later, babe," she whispered. "I need a peaceful cup of coffee first."

At the bottom of the staircase she paused, suddenly aware of the rapid beating of her heart, of a sensation of overwhelming sadness. The thought leaped into her head: *I'm going to lose Hannah too.* No! No! That's ridiculous, she told herself fiercely. Why even *think* like that?

She went into the kitchen and put the coffee on to perk. Ten minutes later, a steaming cup in her hand, she stood in the front parlor, looking out at the Atlantic Ocean as the sun rose higher in the sky.

The house faced Monomoy Strip, the narrow sandbar between ocean and bay that Menley had been told was the scene of countless shipwrecks. A few years ago the ocean had broken through the sandbar; Adam had pointed out where houses had tumbled into the sea. But Remember House, he assured her, was set far enough back so that it would always be safe.

Menley watched as the ocean charged against the sandbar, spraying fountains of salt-filled mist into the air. Sunbeams danced on the whitecaps. The horizon was already dotted with fishing boats. She opened the window and listened to the hawking of the gulls, the thin, noisy chirping of the sparrows.

Smiling, she turned from the window. After three days she felt comfortably settled here. She walked from room to room, planning what she would do if she were decorating them. The master bedroom contained the only authentic furniture. Most of the furnishings in the other rooms were the kind people put in homes that they are planning to rent—inexpensive couches, Formica tables, lamps that looked like they might have been purchased at a garage sale.

But the deacon's bench, now painted a garish green, could be sanded down and refinished. She ran her hand over it, imagining the velvety walnut grain.

The Paleys had done massive structural repairs to the building. There was a new roof, new plumbing, new wiring, a new heating system. A lot of cosmetic work remained to be done—faded wallpaper in a jarring modern design was an eyesore in the dining room; dropped acoustical ceilings destroyed the noble height of the parlors and library—but none of those things mattered. The house itself was the important thing. It would be a joy to complete the restoration. There was a double parlor, for example —if she owned the house, she'd use one of them as a den. Later on Hannah and her friends would enjoy having a gathering place.

She ran her fingers over the minister's cabinet that was built into the wall next to the fireplace. She'd heard the stories of the early settlers and how a little glass of spirits was offered to the minister when he came to call. The poor man probably needed it, she thought. In those days there was rarely a fire laid in parlors. The ordained must have been blue with cold.

Early Cape families lived in the keeping room, as the kitchen was called, the room where the great fireplace gave warmth, where the air was inviting with the aroma of cooking, where children did their schoolwork by candlelight on the refectory table, where the family passed the long winter evenings together. She wondered about the generations of families who had replaced the original ill-fated owners here.

She heard footsteps on the stairs and went into the foyer. Adam was coming down, Hannah in his arms. "Who says I don't hear her when she cries?" He sounded very pleased with himself. "She's changed and hungry."

Menley reached for the baby. "Give her to me. Isn't it wonderful to have her to ourselves with only a part-time baby-sitter? If Elaine's future stepdaughter is half as good a sitter as she's supposed to be, we'll have a terrific summer."

"What time is she coming?"

"Around ten, I think."

At exactly ten o'clock, a small, blue car pulled into the driveway. Menley watched Amy as she came up the walk, noting her slim figure, her long ash blond hair clipped into a ponytail. It struck Menley that there was something aggressive about the girl's posture, the way her hands were jammed into the pockets of her cut-offs, the belligerent thrust of her shoulders.

"I don't know," Menley murmured as she went to open the door.

Adam looked up from the office work he had spread out on the table. "You don't know what?"

"Ssh," Menley cautioned.

Once in the house, however, the girl gave a different impression. She introduced herself, then went right over to the baby, who was in the small daytime crib they'd set up for her in the kitchen. "Hi, Hannah." She moved her hand gently until Hannah grabbed at her finger. "Good girl. You've got some grip. Are you going to be my buddy?"

Menley and Adam exchanged glances. The affection seemed genuine. After a few minutes of talking with Amy, Menley felt that, if anything, Elaine had understated the girl's expertise. She'd been baby-sitting since she was thirteen and most recently had stayed with a family with year-old twins. She was planning to be a nursery school teacher.

They agreed that she would come in for several afternoons a week, to help out while Menley was doing research for her writing projects, and occasionally would stay for the evening if they wanted to go out for dinner.

As the girl was leaving, Menley said, "I'm so glad Elaine suggested you, Amy. Now do you have any questions for me?"

"Yes . . . I . . . no, never mind."

"What is it?"

"Nothing, honest, nothing."

When she was well out of earshot, Adam said quietly, "That kid is afraid of something."

10

HENRY SPRAGUE sat on the couch in the sunroom, the photo album on his lap. Phoebe was beside him, seemingly attentive. He was pointing out pictures to her. "This is the day we took the kids to see the Plymouth Rock for the first time. At the rock you told them the story of the pilgrims landing. They were only six and eight then, but they were fascinated. You always made history sound like an adventure story."

He glanced at her. There was no hint of recognition in her eyes, but she nodded, anxious to please him. It had been a rough night. He'd awakened at two to find Phoebe's side of the bed empty. Heartsick, he'd rushed to see if she'd gotten out of the house again. Even though he'd put special locks on the doors, she had somehow managed to leave through the kitchen window last week. He'd reached her just as she was about to start the car.

Last night she'd been in the kitchen with the kettle on and one of the gas jets open.

Yesterday he had heard from the nursing home. There would be an opening on September first. "Please reserve it for my wife," he had told them miserably.

"What nice children," Phoebe said. "What are their names?"

"Richard and Joan."

"Are they all grown up?"

"Yes. Richard is forty-three. He lives in Seattle with his wife and boys. Joan is forty-one, and she lives in Maine with her husband and daughter. You have three grandchildren, dear."

"I don't want to see any more pictures. I'm hungry."

One of the effects of the disease was that her brain sent false signals to her senses. "You had breakfast just a few minutes ago, Phoebe."

"No, I didn't." Her voice became stubborn.

"All right. Let's go in and fix something for you." As they got up, he put his arm around her. He'd always been proud of her tall, elegant body, the way she held her head, the poised warmth that emanated from her. *I wish we could have just one more day the way it used to be,* he thought.

As Phoebe hungrily ate a roll and gulped milk, he told her that they were having company. "A man named Nat Coogan. It's business."

There was no use trying to explain to Phoebe that Coogan was a detective who was coming to talk to him about Vivian Carpenter Covey.

As Nat drove past Vivian Carpenter's house, he studied it carefully. It was vintage Cape, the kind of house that had been added to and expanded over the years so that now it rambled agreeably along the property. Surrounded by blue and purple hydrangeas, impatiens spilling from the window boxes, it was a postcard-perfect residence, although he knew that in all likelihood the rooms were fairly small. Still, it was obviously well kept and on valuable property. According to the real estate agent, Elaine Atkins, Vivian and Scott Covey had been looking for a larger home for the family they planned to start.

How much would this place go for, Nat wondered? Situated on Oyster Pond, maybe an acre of property? Half a million? Since

Vivian's will left everything to her husband, this would be another asset Scott Covey had inherited.

The Sprague residence was the next house. Another very attractive place. This one was an authentic saltbox, probably built in the late eighteenth century. Nat had never met the Spragues but used to enjoy the articles Professor Phoebe Sprague wrote for the *Cape Cod Times.* They all had to do with legends from the early Cape. He hadn't seen any new ones in recent years, however.

When Henry Sprague answered the bell, invited him in and introduced him to his wife, Nat understood immediately why Phoebe Sprague was no longer contributing articles. Alzheimer's, he thought, and with compassion became aware of the tired creases etched around Henry Sprague's mouth, of the quiet pain in his eyes.

He refused the offer for coffee. "I won't be long. Just a few questions, sir. How well did you know Vivian Carpenter Covey?"

Henry Sprague wanted to be kind. Painfully honest, he also did not want to dissemble. "As you probably know, Vivian bought that house three years ago. We introduced ourselves to her. You can see my wife is not well. Her problem was just beginning to become obvious at that time. Unfortunately, Vivian began to drop in on us constantly. She was taking a course in cooking and kept bringing over samples of food she had prepared. It got to the point where my wife was becoming very nervous. Vivian meant to be kind, but I finally had to ask her to stop visiting unless we specifically had plans to get together."

He paused and added, "Emotionally, Vivian was an extremely needy young woman."

Nat nodded. It fit in with what he had heard from others. "How well do you know Scott Covey?"

"I've met him, of course. He and poor Vivian were married very quietly, I gather, but she did have a reception at home that we attended. That was in early May. Her family was there and so were a smattering of friends and other neighbors."

"What did you think of Scott Covey?"

Henry Sprague avoided a direct answer. "Vivian was radiantly happy. I was pleased for her. Scott seemed very devoted."

"Have you seen much of them since then?"

"Only from a distance. They seemed to go out on the boat quite a bit. Sometimes when we were all barbecuing in the back we'd exchange pleasantries."

"I see." Nat sensed that Henry Sprague was holding something back. "Mr. Sprague, you've said that Covey seemed very devoted to his wife. Did you get the feeling he was honestly in love with her?"

Sprague did not have a problem answering that question. "He certainly acted as though he was."

But there was more, and again Henry Sprague hesitated. He felt he might be guilty of simple gossip if he told the detective something that had happened in late June. He'd dropped Phoebe off at the hairdresser, and Vivian had been there as well, having her hair done. To kill time, he'd gone across the street to the Cheshire Pub, to have a beer and watch the Red Sox and Yankees game.

Scott Covey had been sitting on a stool in the bar. Their eyes met, and Henry went over to greet him. He didn't know why, but he had the impression that Covey was nervous. A moment later a flashy brunette in her late twenties came in. Covey had jumped up. "For heaven's sake, Tina, what are *you* doing here?" he'd said. "I thought you had a run-through Tuesday afternoons."

She had looked at him dumbfounded but recovered quickly. "Scott, how *nice* to bump into you. No rehearsal today. I was supposed to meet some of the other kids from the show either here or at the Impudent Oyster. I'm late, so if they're not here I'll rush over there."

When she left, Scott told Henry that Tina was in the chorus of the musical currently at the Cape Playhouse. "Vivian and I went to opening night and started talking to her at the cast party in the Playhouse Restaurant," he had explained carefully.

Henry had ended up having a sandwich and beer with Scott while they watched the game. At two-thirty Covey left. "Viv should be finished now," he had said.

But when Henry picked up Phoebe a half hour later, Covey was still in the reception area of the salon, waiting for his wife. When she finally came out, tremulously proud of the blond highlights in her hair, he had overheard Covey reassure her that he hadn't minded waiting at all, that he and Henry had watched the game together over lunch. At the time Henry had wondered if Scott's omission of the meeting with Tina had been deliberate.

Maybe not, Henry thought now. Maybe he forgot because it simply wasn't important to him. Maybe it had all been Henry's imagination that Covey had seemed nervous that day. Don't be a meddlesome gossip, he told himself as he sat with the detective. There's no point in bringing this up.

What aren't you telling me? Nat wondered as he gave Henry Sprague his card.

11

MENLEY DROVE Adam to the Barnstable Airport. "You're very grumpy," she teased as she stopped at the drop-off area.

A smile quickly cleared the frown from his face. "I admit it. I don't want to have to go back and forth to New York. I don't want to leave you and Hannah. I don't want to leave the Cape." He paused, "Let's see, what else?"

"Poor baby," Menley said mockingly, taking his face between her hands. "We'll miss you." She hesitated, then added, "It's really been a great couple of days, hasn't it?"

"Spectacular."

She straightened his tie. "I think I like you better in cutoffs and sandals."

"I like myself better. Men, are you sure you don't want to have Amy stay overnight with you?"

"Positive. Adam, please . . ."

"Okay, sweetheart. I'll call you tonight." He leaned into the backseat and touched Hannah's foot. "Stay out of trouble, Toots," he told her.

Hannah's sunny if toothless grin followed him as with a final wave he disappeared into the terminal.

After lunch, Adam had received an urgent call from his office. There was an emergency hearing scheduled to revoke the Potter woman's bail. The prosecution claimed that she had made threats against her mother-in-law. Adam had expected to have at least ten days at the Cape before having to go back to New York overnight, but this seemed like a genuine emergency, and he decided it was necessary to handle it personally.

Menley steered the car out of the airport, turned onto the rotary and followed the sign to Route 28. She came to the railroad crossing and felt icy perspiration form on her forehead. She stopped, then glanced fearfully both ways. A freight train was far down the tracks. It was not moving. The warning lights weren't flashing. The gates were up. Even so for a moment she sat paralyzed, unable to move.

The impatient beep of car horns behind her forced her to take action. She jammed her foot on the accelerator. The car leapt across the tracks. Then she had to hit the brake to avoid slamming into the car ahead. Oh God, she thought, help me, please. Hannah bounced in the car seat and began to cry.

Menley pulled the car into the parking lot of a restaurant and drove to the most distant spot. There she stopped, got in the back and took Hannah from the car seat.

She cradled the baby against her and they cried together.

12

GRAHAM CARPENTER could not sleep. He tried to lie quietly in the king-sized bed that had long ago replaced the double bed he and Anne had shared in the early days of their marriage. As they were approaching their twentieth anniversary they had both admitted that they wanted more room and made the change. More room to stretch out, more free time, more travel. With their second daughter in college it was all possible.

The night this bed had arrived, they had toasted each other with champagne. Vivian was conceived shortly after that. Sometimes he wondered if from the very beginning she had known that she was unwanted. Was her lifelong hostility to them and insecurity with others triggered in the womb?

A fanciful notion. Vivian had been a demanding, malcontent child who became a problem teenager and a difficult adult. An underachiever at school, self-pitying, her motto had been, "I do my best."

To which his angry response was, "No, damn it, you *don't* do your best. You don't know the meaning of the word."

At the boarding school where the older girls had excelled, Vivian was suspended twice, then finally dismissed. For a while she had flirted with drugs, fortunately something she hadn't continued. And then there was the apparent constant need to annoy Anne. She'd ask her to go shopping for clothes, then refuse to follow any of Anne's suggestions.

She didn't finish college, didn't ever stay longer than six months on any job. Years ago he had begged his mother not to let her have access to her trust fund until she was thirty. But she'd come into it all at twenty-one, bought that house and afterwards rarely contacted them. It was an absolute shock when in May she had phoned to invite them to her house to a reception. She had gotten married.

What could he say about Scott Covey? Good looking, well mannered, bright enough, certainly devoted to Vivian. She had literally glowed with happiness. The only sour note had come when one of her friends joked about a prenuptial agreement. She had flared, "No, we *don't* have one. In fact, we're making wills in favor of each other."

Graham had wondered what Scott Covey had to leave anyone. Vivian insinuated he had a private income. Maybe.

About one thing, for once, Vivian had been telling the unvarnished truth. She had changed her will the same day she was married, and now Scott would inherit all the money from her trust fund, along with her house in Chatham. And they had been married twelve week. *Twelve weeks.*

"Graham." Anne's voice was soft.

He reached for her hand. "I'm awake."

"Graham, I know Vivy's body was in very bad shape. What about her right hand?"

"I don't know, dear. Why?"

"Because, nobody has said anything about her emerald ring. Maybe her hand was gone. But if it wasn't, Scott may have the ring, and I'd like to have it back. It's always been in our family, and I can't imagine some other woman wearing it."

"I'll find out, dear."

"Graham, why couldn't I ever reach Vivian? What did I do wrong?"

He grasped her hand more tightly. There was no answer he could give her.

That day he and Anne played golf. It was physical and emotional therapy for both of them. They got home around five, showered, and he fixed them cocktails. Then he said. "Anne, while you were dressing I tried to reach Scott. There's a message on the machine. He's on the boat and will be back around six. Let's swing by and ask him about the ring. Then we'll go out to dinner." He paused. "I mean you and I will go out for dinner."

"If he has the ring, he doesn't have to part with it. It was Vivian's to leave to him."

"If he has the ring we'll offer to buy it at fair market value. If that doesn't work, we'll pay him whatever he asks for it."

Graham Carpenter's mouth set in a grim line. Scott's reaction to this request would allay or verify the suspicion and doubt that was choking his soul.

13

*I*T WAS FIVE-THIRTY when Menley and Hannah finally got back to Chatham. When they left the parking lot, she had forced herself to drive over the railroad crossing again. Then she had circled the rotary and driven over it a third time. No more panicky driving for me, she vowed. Not when it means I'm jeopardizing Hannah.

The sun was still high over the ocean, and to Menley it seemed as though the house had a contented air about it as it basked in the warm rays that enveloped it. Inside, the sun streaming through the stained glass of the fan-shaped window over the door cast a rainbow of colors onto the bare oak floor.

Holding Hannah tightly, Menley walked to the front window and looked out over the ocean. She wondered if, when this house was first built, the young bride had ever watched to see the mast of her husband's ship as he returned from a voyage. Or had she been too busy dallying with her lover?

Hannah stirred restlessly. "Okay, chow time," Menley said, wishing once again that she had been able to nurse Hannah. When the post-traumatic stress symptoms began, the doctor had ordered tranquilizers and discontinued the nursing. "You need tranquilizers, but she doesn't," he had explained.

Oh well, you're certainly thriving anyway, Menley thought as she poured formula into the bottle and warmed it in a saucepan.

At seven o'clock she tucked Hannah into the crib, this time snug in a sleeping bag. A glance about the room confirmed that the quilt was folded on the bed where it belonged. Menley stared at it uneasily. She had casually asked Adam if he had covered the baby during the night. No, he had replied, obviously wondering why she asked.

She had thought quickly and said, "Then she isn't as much a kicker up here as she was at home. Probably the sea air keeps her sleeping quietly."

He hadn't realized there had been a far different reason for the question.

She hesitated outside the baby's room. It was silly to leave the hall light on. It was much too bright. But for some reason Menley felt uneasy about the prospect of coming upstairs later with only a tiny night-light to guide her footsteps.

She had her evening mapped out. There were fresh tomatoes in the refrigerator. She'd fix a quick pomodoro sauce, pour it over linguine and make a watercress salad. There was a half loaf of Italian bread in the freezer.

That will be perfect, Menley thought. And while I eat, I'll make some notes for the book.

The few days in Chatham had already given her ideas on what she would do with the story line. With Adam away, she would spend the long, calm evening fleshing them out.

14

*H*E HAD SPENT the whole day on *Viv's Toy*. The twenty-two-foot inboard/outboard motorboat was in excellent shape. Vivian had been talking about replacing it with a sailboat. "Now that I've got a captain for it, should we get one big enough to do serious sailing?"

So many plans! So many dreams! Scott hadn't been scuba diving since that last day with Vivian. Today he fished for a while, checked his lobster pots and was rewarded with four two-pounders, then put on his scuba gear and went down for a while.

He docked the boat at the marina and reached home at five-thirty, then immediately went next door to the Sprague house with two of the lobsters. Henry Sprague answered the door.

"Mr. Sprague, I know at our reception your wife seemed to enjoy the lobster. I caught some today and hoped you might like to have a couple of them."

"That's very kind," Henry said sincerely. "Won't you come in?"

"No, that's fine. Just enjoy them. How is Mrs. Sprague?"

"About the same. Would you like to say hello? Wait, here she is."

He turned as his wife came down the hall. "Phoebe, dear, Scott has brought lobster for you. Isn't that nice of him?"

Phoebe Sprague looked at Scott Covey, her eyes widening. "Why was she crying so hard?" she asked. "Is she all right now?"

"Nobody was crying, dear," Henry Sprague said soothingly. He put an arm across her shoulders.

Phoebe Sprague pulled away from him. "Listen to me," she shrieked. "I keep telling you there's a woman living in my house and you won't believe me. Here, you." She grabbed Scott's arm and pointed to the mirror over the foyer table. The three of them were reflected in it. "See that woman." She reached over and touched her own image. "She's living in my house and he won't believe me."

Somewhat troubled by Phoebe Sprague's ramblings, Scott went home, deep in thought. He had planned to steam one of the remaining lobsters for himself, but he found he had no taste for food. He made a drink and checked the answering machine. There were two messages: Elaine Atkins had phoned. Did he want to leave the house on the market? She had a prospective buyer. The other was from Vivian's father. He and his wife had an urgent matter to discuss. They would stop by around six-thirty. It would take only a few minutes.

What's *that* about? Scott wondered. He checked his watch; it was ten after six already. He set down the drink and hurried in for a quick shower. He dressed in a dark blue knit shirt, chinos and Docksiders. He was just combing his hair when the bell rang.

It was the first time Anne Carpenter had been in her daughter's home since the body was found. Not knowing what she was looking for, she searched the living room with her eyes. In the three years Vivian had owned the house, Anne had only been in it a few times, and it looked about the same as she remembered. Vivian had replaced the bedroom furniture but left this room pretty much as she had found it. On her first visit Anne had suggested that her daughter get rid of the loveseat and some of the cheap prints, but Vivian had flared up at her, despite the fact that she *had* asked for suggestions.

Scott insisted they have a drink. "I just made one. Please join me. I haven't wanted people around, but it's awfully good to see you."

Reluctantly, Anne admitted to herself that his demeanor seemed genuinely sad. He was so strikingly good looking with his blond hair and tanned skin and hazel eyes, it was easy to see how Vivian had fallen in love with him. But what did he see in her except her money? Anne asked herself, then recoiled at her own question. What a horrible thought for a mother, she scolded herself.

"What are your plans, Scott?" Graham Carpenter asked.

"I don't have any. I still have the feeling that this is all a bad dream. I don't think I've come to grips with reality yet. You know Viv and I had been looking for a bigger house. The upstairs bedrooms are really small, and when we had a baby we'd have wanted a place where live-in help wouldn't be under our feet all the time. We even had names picked out. Graham for a boy, Anne for a girl. She told me that she always felt she was a big disappointment to the two of you and she wanted to make it up to you. She felt it was her fault, not yours."

Anne felt a lump in her throat. She watched the convulsive tightening of her husband's mouth. "We always seemed to be at cross-purposes," she said quietly. "Sometimes it happens like that, and as a parent you hope it will change. I'm glad if Vivy truly wanted it to change. We certainly did."

The phone rang. Scott jumped up. "Whoever it is, I'll call back." He hurried into the kitchen.

A moment later Anne watched with curiosity as her husband picked up his drink and walked down the hall to the bathroom. He returned just as Scott came back.

"I just wanted to put a dash more water in the scotch," Graham explained.

"You should have gotten some ice water from the kitchen. There was nothing private about the phone conversation. That was the real estate agent wanting to know if it was all right to bring a prospective buyer around tomorrow," Scott said. "I told her to take the house off the market."

"Scott, there is something we need to ask." Graham Carpenter clearly was trying to keep his emotions under control. "The emerald ring Vivian always wore. It's been in her mother's family for generations. Do you have it?"

"No, I don't."

"You identified the body. She never took it off her finger. She wasn't wearing it when she was found?"

Scott looked away. "Mr. Carpenter, I'm grateful you and Mrs. Carpenter didn't see the body. It had been so badly attacked by marine life that there was very little left to identify. But if I had that ring I would have given it to you immediately. I knew it was a family treasure. Is there anything else of Vivian's that you want? Would her clothes fit her sisters?"

Anne winced. "No . . . no."

The Carpenters got up together. "We'll call you for dinner soon, Scott," Anne said.

"Please do. I only wish we'd gotten to know each other better."

"Unless you can't part with them, perhaps you'll assemble some pictures of Vivian for us," Graham Carpenter said.

"Of course."

When they reached the car and started to drive away, Anne turned to her husband. "Graham, you never put water in your scotch. What were you doing?"

"I wanted to get a look at the bedroom. Anne, didn't you notice that there wasn't a single picture of Vivian in the living room? Well, I have news. There isn't a picture of her in the bedroom either. I'll bet you there isn't a trace of our daughter anywhere in that house. I don't like Covey and I don't trust him. He's a phony. He knows more than he's telling, and I'm going to get to the bottom of it."

15

*T*HEY HAD SET UP a computer, printer and fax machine on the desk in the library. The computer and printer took up most of the surface, but it would suffice, especially since Menley didn't intend to devote all that much time to working. Adam had his portable typewriter, which Menley was always trying to get him to discard but which could be set up anywhere.

Adam had so far successfully resisted Menley's efforts to get him to learn how to use a computer. But then Menley had been equally stubborn about learning to play golf.

"You're well coordinated. You'd be good at it," Adam insisted.

The memory made Menley smile as she worked at the long refectory table in the kitchen. No, not the kitchen, the keeping room, she reminded herself. Let's get the jargon right, especially if I'm going to set a book here. Alone in the house with just the baby, it seemed cozier to work in this wonderfully shabby room, with its huge fireplace and side oven, and the smell of the garlic bread lingering in the air. And she was only going to make notes tonight. She always did them in a loose-leaf notebook. "Here we go again," she murmured aloud as she wrote *David's Adventures in the Narrow Land.* It's so crazy how all this had worked out, she thought.

After college she had managed to get the job at *Travel Times.* She knew that she wanted to be a writer but what kind of a writer she wasn't sure. Her mother had always hoped she would concentrate on art, but she knew that wasn't right for her.

Her break at the magazine came when the editor in chief asked her to cover the opening of a new hotel in Hong Kong. The article had been accepted almost without editing. Then hesitantly she had shown the watercolor paintings she'd made of the hotel and its surrounding area. The magazine had illustrated the article with the paintings, and at twenty-two Menley became a senior travel editor.

The idea for doing a series of children's books using a "yesterday and today" theme, in which David, a contemporary child, goes back into the past and follows the life of a child from another century, evolved gradually. But now she had completed four of them, doing both the text and artwork. One was set in New York, one in London, one in Paris and one in San Francisco. They had become popular immediately.

Listening to all Adam's stories about the Cape had made her interested in setting the next book here. It would be about a boy in Pilgrim times growing up on the Cape, the Narrow Land as the Indians had called it.

Like all the other ideas that had eventually ended up as a book, once hatched, it would not go away. The other day they had gone to the library in Chatham and she had borrowed books on the early history of the Cape. Then she'd found some dusty old books in a cabinet in the library at Remember House. So tonight she sat down to read; soon she was happily lost in her research.

At eight o'clock the phone rang. "Mrs. Nichols?"

She did not recognize the voice. "Yes," she said cautiously.

"Mrs. Nichols, I'm Scott Covey. Elaine Atkins gave me your number. Is Mr. Nichols there?"

Scott Covey! Menley recognized the name. "I'm afraid my husband isn't here," she said. "He'll be back tomorrow. You can reach him by late afternoon."

"Thank you. I'm sorry to have bothered you."

"No bother. And I'm so sorry about your wife."

"It's been pretty awful. I'm only praying that your husband can help me. It's bad enough to have lost Viv, but now the police are acting as though they think it wasn't an accident."

Adam called a few minutes later, sounding weary. "Kurt Potter's family is determined to see that Susan goes back to prison. They know she killed him in self-defense, but to admit it also means admitting that they'd ignored the warning signs."

Menley could tell he was exhausted. After only three days of vacation he was already back in the office. She did not have the heart to bring up Scott Covey's request now. When he got back tomorrow, she'd ask him to meet with Covey. Of all people, she understood what it was like to have the police question a tragic accident.

She assured Adam that she and Hannah were fine, that they both missed him and that she was keeping busy doing research for the new book.

The talk with Scott Covey and then with Adam had broken her concentration, however, and at nine o'clock she turned out the lights and went upstairs.

She checked the peacefully sleeping Hannah, then sniffed the air. There was a musty smell in the room. Where was it coming from? she wondered. She opened the window a few inches more. A strong, salty sea breeze quickly swept through the room. That's better, she thought.

Sleep did not come easily. The railroad crossing today had brought back vivid memories of the terrible accident. This time she thought about the signal light that day. She was sure she had glanced at it—it was something she did automatically—but the sun was so strong that she hadn't realized it was flashing. The first indication of what was happening was the vibrations caused by the train rushing toward them. Then she heard the frantic, shrill scream of its whistle.

Her throat went dry, her lips felt bloodless. But at least this time she did not begin to perspire or tremble. At last she fell into an uneasy sleep.

At two o'clock she sat bolt upright. The baby was screaming, and the sound of an oncoming train was echoing through the house.

August 5th

16

*A*DAM NICHOLS could not overcome the sense that something was wrong. He slept fitfully, and each time he awoke it was with the knowledge that he'd just had a vague, troublesome dream and could not remember what it was.

At six o'clock, as dawn broke over the East River, he threw back the sheet and got up. He made coffee and brought it out on the terrace, wishing that it were seven-thirty and he could call Menley. He would wait till then, since the baby was usually sleeping past seven now.

A smile flickered on his lips as he thought of Menley and Hannah. His family. The miracle of Hannah's birth three months ago. The grief of losing Bobby finally beginning to ease for both of them. A year ago at this time he'd been at the Cape alone and wouldn't have bet a nickel that their marriage would survive. He'd spoken to a counselor about it and had been told that the death of a child frequently caused the end of the marriage. The counselor had said there was so much pain the parents sometimes couldn't exist under the same roof.

Adam had begun to think that maybe it would be better for both of them to start over separately. Then Menley had phoned and Adam knew he desperately wanted their marriage to work.

Menley's pregnancy had been uneventful. He had been with her in the labor room. She'd been in a lot of pain but doing great. Then from down the hall they could hear a woman screaming. The change in Menley had been dramatic. Her face went ashen. Those enormous blue eyes grew even larger, then she had covered them with her hands. "No . . . no . . . help me, please," she had cried, as she trembled and sobbed. The tension in her body dramatically increased the strength of the contractions, the difficulty of the birth.

And when Hannah was finally born, and the doctor had laid her in Menley's arms in the delivery room, incredibly she had pushed her away. "I want Bobby," she had sobbed. "I want Bobby."

Adam had taken the baby and held her against his neck, whispering, "It's all right, Hannah. We love you, Hannah," as though he was afraid she could understand Menley's words.

Later Menley had told him, "At the moment they gave her to me, I was reliving holding Bobby after the accident. It was the first time I really knew what I'd felt at that moment."

That was the beginning of what the doctors called the post-traumatic stress disorder. The first month had been very difficult. Hannah had started out as a colicky infant who screamed for hours. They'd had a live-in nurse, but one afternoon when the nurse was on an errand, the baby had started shrieking. Adam came home to find Menley sitting on the floor by the crib, pale and trembling, her fingers in her ears. But miraculously a formula change turned Hannah into a sunny baby, and Menley's anxiety attacks for the most part passed.

I still shouldn't have left her alone so soon, Adam thought. I should have insisted that at least the baby-sitter stay over.

At seven o'clock he couldn't wait any longer. He phoned the Cape.

The sound of Menley's voice brought a rush of relief. "Her nibs get you up early, honey?"

"Just a bit. We like the morning."

There was something in Menley's voice. Adam bit back the question that came too easily to his lips. *You okay?* Menley resented his hovering over her.

"I'll be up on the four o'clock flight. Want to get Amy to mind Hannah and we'll go out to dinner?"

Hesitation. What was wrong? But then Menley said, "That sounds great. Adam . . ."

"What is it, honey?"

"Nothing. Just that we miss you."

When he hung up, Adam called the airline. "Is there any earlier flight I can get on?" he asked. He would be out of court by noon. There was a one-thirty flight he might be able to make.

Something was wrong, and the worst part of it was that Menley wasn't going to tell him what it was.

17

*E*LAINE ATKINS' real estate office was on Main Street in Chatham. Location, location, location, she thought as a passerby stopped to look at the pictures that she had taken of available homes. Since she'd moved to Main Street, the drop-in traffic had improved dramatically, and more and more she'd been able to convert these expressions of preliminary interest into an excellent percentage of sales.

This summer she'd tried a new gimmick. She'd had aerial photographs taken of houses with particularly good locations. One of them was Remember House. When she'd arrived at work this morning at ten, Marge Salem, her assistant, told her there had already been two inquiries about it.

"That aerial photo really does the trick. Do you think it was wise to rent it to the Nicholses without asking for the right to show it?" Marge asked.

"It was necessary," Elaine said briskly. "Adam Nichols isn't the type who's going to want people trooping through a house he's renting, and he did pay top dollar for it. But we're not losing a sale. My hunch is that the Nicholses will decide to buy that place."

"I would have thought that he'd look in Harwich Port. That's where his family came from and always summered."

"Yes, but Adam always liked Chatham. And he knows a good buy when he sees it. He also likes to own, not rent. I think he regrets not buying the family home when his mother sold it. If his wife is happy here, we've got a customer. Watch and see." She smiled at Marge. "And if by chance he doesn't, well, Scott Covey loves that place. When things settle down for him he'll be in the market again. He won't want to keep Vivian's house."

Marge's pleasant face became serious. The fifty-year-old housewife had started working for Elaine at the beginning of the summer and found that she thoroughly enjoyed the real estate business. She also loved gossip and, as Elaine joked, could pick it out of the air. "There are a lot of rumors floating around about Scott Covey."

Elaine made a quick gesture with her hand, always a sign of impatience. "Why don't they leave that poor guy alone? If Vivian hadn't come into that trust fund, everyone would be keening with him. That's the trouble with people in these parts. On principle, they don't like to see family money go to an outsider."

Marge nodded. "God knows that's true."

They were interrupted by the tingling of the bell over the front door, signaling the arrival of a potential client. After that they were busy all morning. At one o'clock, Elaine got up, went into the bathroom and came out wearing fresh lipstick and with her hair recombed.

Marge studied her. Elaine was wearing a white linen dress and sandals, making an attractive contrast to her deeply tanned arms and legs. Her dark blond hair streaked with highlights was pulled back by a band. "If I hadn't mentioned it before, you look terrific," Marge said. "Obviously being engaged suits you."

Elaine wiggled her ring finger, and the large solitaire on it glittered. "I agree. I'm meeting John for lunch at the Impudent Oyster. Hold the fort."

When she returned an hour later, Marge said, "There've been a bunch of calls. The top one is the most interesting."

It was from Detective Nat Coogan. It was imperative that he speak with Miss Atkins at her earliest convenience.

18

*B*Y MID-MORNING, Menley had begun to convince herself that the terror that had awakened her had been simply a vivid dream. With Hannah held tightly in her arms she walked outside to the edge of the embankment. The sky was vividly blue and reflected in the water that broke gently against the shoreline. It was low tide, and the long expanse of sandy beach was tranquil.

Even without the ocean it's a wonderful piece of property, she thought as she studied the grounds. In the many years the house had been abandoned, the locust and oak trees had grown unchecked. Now heavily laden with leaves, they were in natural harmony with the velvety fullness of the pines.

The lush midsummer look, Menley thought. Then she noticed an occasional leaf already tinged with rust. Autumn would be beautiful here as well, she reflected.

Her father had died when her brother Jack was eleven and she was only three. Education was more important than a house, her mother had decided, and had used whatever she could save from her salary as a nurse supervisor at Bellevue Hospital to send them both to Georgetown. She still lived in that same four-room apartment where Menley and Jack had grown up.

Menley had always wanted to live in a house. As a little girl she drew pictures of the one she would have someday. And it was pretty much like this place, she thought. She'd had so many plans for the house she and Adam had bought in Rye. But after Bobby was gone it held too many memories. "Living in Manhattan is right for us," she said aloud to Hannah. "Daddy can be home from work in ten minutes. Grandma enjoys baby-sitting and I'm a city slicker. But Daddy's family has always been on the Cape. They were among the first settlers. It might be kind of wonderful to have this house for the summer and holidays and long weekends. What do you think?"

The baby turned her head and together they looked at the house behind them. "There's still a load of work to do," Menley said. "But it would be fun to really restore it to the way it used to be. I guess it was just the two of us being here alone that made the dream seem so real when I was waking up. Don't you agree?"

Hannah wriggled impatiently, and her lip drooped. "Okay, you're getting tired," Menley said. "God, you're a crabby kid." She started back toward the house, then paused and studied it again. "It has a wonderful sheltering look, doesn't it?" she murmured.

She felt suddenly lighthearted, hopeful. Adam would be home

this afternoon and their vacation could get back on track. Except . . .

Except if Alan decides to represent Scott Covey, she thought. Adam never does anything halfheartedly. It would take a lot of his time. Even so I hope he does represent him. She remembered the horror when, two weeks after Bobby's funeral, Adam had received a phone call. The assistant district attorney was considering prosecuting Menley for reckless manslaughter.

"He said that you've had a couple of speeding tickets. He thinks he can prove that you ignored the warning signal at the crossing because you were racing to beat the train." Then Adam's face had become grim. "Don't worry, honey. He won't get to first base." The D.A. had backed off when Adam produced a formidable list of other fatal accidents at that crossing.

Elaine had told them that one of the reasons Scott Covey was being judged harshly was because some people said he should have known about the squall.

Menley thought, I don't care if it does cut into our vacation. Covey needs help just as I did.

19

THE CARPENTER SUMMER HOME in Osterville was not visible from the road. As Detective Nat Coogan drove through the gates and along the wide driveway, he observed the manicured lawn and flower beds. I'm suitably impressed, he thought. Big, big bucks, but old money. Nothing flamboyant.

He stopped in front of the house. It was an old Victorian mansion with a wide porch and gingerbread latticework. The unpainted shakes had weathered to a mellow gray, but the shutters and window frames gleamed snowy white in the afternoon sun.

When he had phoned this morning asking for an interview, he had been somewhat surprised at how readily Vivian Carpenter's father had agreed to see him.

"Do you want to come today, Detective Coogan? We were planning to play golf this afternoon but there's plenty of time for that."

It was not the reaction Nat had expected. The Carpenters did not have the reputation of being accessible people. He had anticipated a frosty response, a demand to know why he wanted to see them.

Interesting, he thought.

A maid led him to the sunporch at the back of the house where Graham and Anne Carpenter were seated on brightly cushioned wicker chairs, sipping iced tea. At the funeral service, Nat had gotten the impression that these were cold people. The only tears he had seen shed for Vivian Carpenter Covey had been her husband's. Looking at the couple in front of him, he was embarrassed to realize how wrong he'd been. Both her parents' patrician faces were visibly strained, their expressions filled with sadness.

They greeted him quietly, offered iced tea or whatever beverage he preferred. On his refusal, Graham Carpenter came directly to the point. "You're not here to offer condolences, Mr. Coogan."

Nat had chosen a straight-backed chair. He leaned forward, his hands linked, a habit his colleagues would have recognized as his unconscious posture when he felt he was onto something. "I do offer condolences, but you're right, Mr. Carpenter. That is not the reason I'm here. I'm going to be very blunt. I'm not satisfied that your daughter's death was an accident, and until I am satisfied I'm going to be seeing a lot of people and asking a lot of questions."

It was as though he had jolted them with a live wire. The lethargy disappeared from their expressions. Graham Carpenter looked at his wife, "Anne, I told you . . ."

She nodded. "I didn't want to believe . . ."

"What didn't you want to believe, Mrs. Carpenter?" Nat asked quickly.

They described for him their reasons for being suspicious of their son-in-law, but Coogan found them disappointing. "I understand your feelings about not finding a picture of your daughter anywhere in her home," he told them, "but it's been my experience that after this kind of tragedy, people react differently. Some will bring out every picture they can find of the person they've lost, while others will immediately store or even destroy pictures and mementos, give away the clothes, sell the car of the deceased, even change homes. It's almost as though they believe removing any reminder will make it easier to get over the pain."

He tried a new tack. "You met Scott Covey after your daughter married him. Since he was a stranger, you must have been concerned. By any chance did you investigate his background?"

Graham Carpenter nodded. "Yes, I did. Not a very in-depth investigation, but everything he told us was true. He was born and raised in Columbus, Ohio. His father and stepmother retired to California. He attended but did not graduate from the University of Kansas. He tried acting but didn't get far and worked as a business manager for a couple of small theatrical companies. That's how Vivian met him last year." He smiled mirthlessly. "Vivian insinuated that he had a private income. I think that was a fabrication for our benefit."

"I see." Nat stood up. "I'll be honest. So far everything I've been told checks out. Your daughter was crazy about Covey, and he certainly acted as though he was in love with her. They were planning to go to Hawaii, and she'd told a number of people that she was determined to be a good scuba diver by the time they got there. She wanted to do everything with him. He's an excellent swimmer but had never handled a boat before he met her. The squall wasn't supposed to come in until midnight. Frankly, *she's* the one who was experienced and should have known to turn on the radio in order to monitor the weather."

"Does that mean you're giving up the investigation?" Carpenter asked.

"No. But it *does* mean that except for the obvious factors that Vivian was a wealthy young woman and they had been married only a brief time, there's really nothing to go on."

"I see. Well, I thank you for sharing this with us. I'll walk you out."

They had reached the door of the sunporch when Anne Carpenter called after them. "Mr. Coogan."

Both Nat and Graham Carpenter turned.

"Just one thing. I know my daughter's body was in terrible condition because of the length of time it was in the water and the marine life attacking it . . ."

"I'm afraid that's true," Nat agreed.

"Anne, dear, why torture yourself," her husband protested.

"No, hear me out. Mr. Coogan, were the fingers of my daughter's right hand intact, or missing?"

Nat hesitated. "One hand was badly mutilated. The other was not. I believe it was the right hand that was in bad shape, but I'd want to check the autopsy pictures. Why do you ask?"

"Because my daughter always wore a very valuable emerald on the ring finger of her right hand. From the day my mother gave it to her, Vivian never took it off. We asked Scott about it because it was a family piece and we wanted it back if it had been found. But he told us in so many words that her hand was mutilated and the ring missing."

"I'll call you within the hour," Nat said.

Back in his office, Nat studied the autopsy pictures for long minutes before he called the Carpenters.

All ten fingertips were missing. On the left hand the wedding band was on the ring finger. But it was the ring finger of the right hand that was a mess. Between the knuckle and hand it had been eaten to the bone. What had attracted the scavengers to it? Nat wondered.

There was no sign of the emerald ring.

When he called the Carpenters, Nat was careful not to jump to conclusions. He told Graham Carpenter that his daughter's right hand had suffered massive trauma and the ring was missing.

"Do you know if it was a loose or tight fit?" he asked.

"It had become tight," Carpenter said. Then he paused before asking, "What are you saying?"

"I'm not saying anything, Mr. Carpenter. It is simply one more circumstance to consider. I'll stay in touch."

As he hung up, Nat thought about what he had just learned. Could this be the smoking gun? he wondered. I'd bet the ranch that Covey ripped the ring off and then swam away from that poor kid. If the finger was bruised, there was blood near the surface, and that drew the scavengers.

August 6th

20

"*ELAINE OWES ME ONE*," Adam muttered as he looked through the window of the keeping room and watched a car turn in from the driveway. They'd taken a picnic basket to the beach while Hildy, the cleaning woman Elaine had sent, went through the house. At two o'clock they went up for the appointment Adam had made with Scott Covey.

Adam showered and changed to shorts and a tee shirt. Menley was still in her bathing suit and cover-up when they heard Covey's car drive up.

"I'm glad he's here," she told Adam. "While you're busy, I'll grab a nap with Hannah. I want to be sharp when I meet all your old buddies."

Elaine was having a buffet supper in their honor at her home and had invited some of the people Adam had grown up with during summers at the Cape.

He caught her around the waist. "When they tell you how fortunate you are, be sure to agree."

"Puh . . . leeze."

The doorbell rang. Menley glanced at the stove. There was no way she could grab Hannah's bottle and be out of the kitchen before Scott Covey came in. She was curious about meeting the man with whom she felt so much empathy, but she also wanted to stay out of the way in case Adam for any reason decided not to represent him. Curiosity won out, however; she decided to wait.

Adam strode to the door. His greeting for Scott Covey was cordial but reserved.

Menley stared at the visitor. No wonder Vivian Carpenter fell for him, she thought immediately.

Scott Covey was stunningly good looking, with even but strong features, a deep tan and dark blond hair that waved and curled even though he wore it short. He was lean as well, but broad shoulders added a hint of strength. When Adam introduced him to Menley, however, it was his eyes she found most compelling. They were a rich, deep hazel, but it wasn't just the color that fascinated her. Rather, she saw in them the same anguish she'd seen in her own eyes when she looked in the mirror after Bobby had died.

He's innocent, she decided. I'd stake my life on it. She was holding Hannah in her right arm. With a smile she shifted the baby and held out her hand. "I'm glad to meet you . . ." she said, then hesitated. He was about her age, she reasoned, and he was a good friend of one of Adam's best friends. So what should she call him? Mr. Covey sounded stilted. ". . . Scott," she finished. She reached for the baby's bottle. "And now Hannah and I will let you two have a chance to talk."

Again she hesitated. It was impossible to ignore the reason he was there. "I know I told you on the phone the other night, but I'm very sorry about your wife."

"Thank you." His voice was low, deep and musical. The kind of voice you could trust, she thought.

Hannah had no intention of going to sleep. When Menley put her down, she howled, pushed away the bottle and kicked off the blankets. "I may list you with an adoption agency," Menley threatened with a smile. She looked at the antique cradle. "I wonder."

The small single bed in the room had two pillows on it. She put one in the cradle, laid a still-fussing Hannah on top of it and covered her with the light quilt. Then she sat on the edge of the bed and began to rock the cradle. Hannah's fussing tapered off. In a few minutes her eyes began to close.

Menley's eyes were heavy too. I should get out of this bathing suit before I nap, she thought. But it's bone dry now, so what's the difference? She lay down and pulled up the folded afghan at the foot of the bed. Hannah whimpered. "Okay, okay," she murmured, reaching out her hand and rocking the cradle gently.

She didn't know how long it was before the sound of light footsteps awakened her. Opening her eyes, she realized she must have dreamed them, since no one was there. But there was a chill in the room. The window was open, and the breeze must have gotten sharper. She blinked and looked over the edge of the bed. Hannah was blissfully asleep.

Boy, the service you get, kid, she thought. Even in my sleep I wait on you!

The cradle was moving from side to side.

21

"*THIS IS A WONDERFUL HOUSE,*" Scott Covey said as he followed Adam into the library. "My wife and I were looking at it just a few days before she died. She intended to make an offer on it, but like a true New Englander she had no intention of looking eager to have it."

"Elaine told me about that." Adam indicated one of the battered club chairs by the windows and settled in the other one. "I don't have to point out that the furnishings are garage-sale rejects."

Covey smiled briefly. "Viv was filled with ideas about going to antique shops and really giving the rooms the look they had in the early seventeen hundreds. Last summer she'd worked for a short time for an interior designer. She was like a kid in a candy store at the prospect of doing this big house herself."

Adam waited.

"I'd better get down to business," Covey said. "First, thank you for seeing me. I know it's your vacation and I know you wouldn't have done it if Elaine hadn't asked you."

"That's true. Elaine is an old friend, and she obviously believes you need help."

Covey lifted his hands in a gesture of futility. "Mr. Nichols—"

"Adam."

"Adam, I understand why there's so much talk. I'm a stranger. Vivian was wealthy. But on the Bible, I swear I had no idea she had so much money. Viv was desperately insecure and could be secretive. She loved me, but she was just beginning to understand how much I loved her. Her self-image was terrible. She was so afraid people only bothered with her because of her family background and her money."

"Why was her self-image that bad?"

Covey's expression became bitter. "Her whole damn family. They always put her down. In the first place, her parents didn't want to have her, and when she was born, they tried to make her a carbon copy of her sisters. Her grandmother was the one exception. She understood Viv, but unfortunately she was an invalid who spent most of her time in Florida. Viv told me her grandmother had left her a million-dollar trust and that three years ago, at twenty-one, she came into it. She told me she had paid six hundred thousand for the house, was living on the rest and wouldn't come into another dime until she was thirty-five. By anybody's standards she was well off, but I understood that the balance of the trust reverted to her grandmother's estate if anything happened to her. Yes, because of her death I received the house, but I never thought her estate went beyond a couple hundred thousand dollars more. I had absolutely no idea she'd already received five million dollars."

Adam linked his fingers and looked up at the ceiling, thinking aloud. "Even if she was only worth the amount of money she told you, people could justifiably say that for a marriage of three months, you did mighty well."

He looked back at Covey and shot the next question. "Was anyone else aware that your wife had not shared her true financial status with you?"

"I don't know."

"No close friend who was a confidante?"

"No. Vivian didn't have what I would call close friends."

"Did her father and mother approve of the marriage?"

"They never knew about it until it was over. That was Vivian's decision. She wanted a quiet wedding at city hall, a honeymoon in Canada and then a home reception when we got back. I know her parents were shocked and I don't blame them. It's possible she did tell them that I didn't know the extent of the inheritance. In a way, as much as she defied them, Vivian desperately wanted their approval."

Adam nodded. "On the phone you said that a detective has been asking you about a family ring."

Scott Covey looked directly at Adam. "Yes, it was an emerald, a family heirloom, I believe. I absolutely remember that Viv was wearing the ring on the boat. The only thing that makes sense is she must have changed it to her left hand that morning. When I was going through her things I found her engagement ring in the drawer at home. Her wedding ring was a narrow gold band. She always wore the engagement and wedding rings together."

He bit his lip. "The emerald ring had been getting tight to the point it was cutting off circulation. That last morning Viv was tugging at it and twisting it. When I was leaving for the store I told her if she was determined to get it off to soap or grease her finger first. She bruised very easily. When I got back we took off for the boat and I didn't think to ask about it and she never mentioned it. But Viv was superstitious about that ring. She never went anywhere without it. I think when I identified her body and didn't see the ring I assumed it was because her right hand was mutilated."

His face suddenly became contorted. He pushed his knuckles against his mouth to stifle the dry sobs that shook his shoulders. "You just can't understand. No one can. One minute we're down there, swimming next to each other, watching a school of striped bass go by, the water so clear and calm. Her eyes were so happy, like a little kid in an amusement park. And then, in a second, it all changed." He buried his face in his hands.

Adam studied Scott Covey intently. "Go on," he said.

"The water went gray, got so rough. I could see Viv was panicking. I grabbed her hand and put it on my belt. She knew I meant that she should hang on to me. I started to swim for the boat, but it was so far away. The anchor must have been dragging, because the current was fierce. We weren't making progress, so Viv let go of my belt and started to swim next to me again. I could tell that she thought we'd make better time if we both swam. Then, just as we were surfacing, a huge wave came and she was gone. She was gone."

He dropped his hands from his face and blurted, "Christ, how can anyone think I'd deliberately allow my wife to die? I'm haunted thinking I should have been able to save her. It was my fault for not being able to find her, but before God, I tried."

Adam straightened up. He remembered the night of Bobby's death, with Menley sedated, barely conscious, sobbing over and over, "It was my fault, my fault . . ." He reached over and squeezed Scott Covey's shoulder. "I'll represent you, Scott," he said, "and try to relax. You'll get through this. Everything will be all right."

22

*A*MY ARRIVED at seven o'clock to baby-sit Hannah. She greeted Menley, then immediately knelt in front of the baby swing Adam had set up in the keeping room.

"Hi, Hannah," Amy said softly. "Did you go swimming today?"

Hannah looked at her visitor complacently.

"You should have seen her splashing in a puddle in the sand," Menley said. "She yelled when I took her out of it. You'll find that Hannah lets you know when she isn't happy."

Amy smiled briefly. "That's what my mother used to say about me."

Menley knew that Elaine was engaged to Amy's father, but she didn't know whether he was divorced or a widower. It seemed to her that Amy was inviting the question. "Tell me about your mother," she suggested. "I can see she raised a nice daughter."

"She died when I was twelve." The girl's voice was flat, emotionless.

"That's rough." It was on the tip of Menley's tongue to suggest that it was so nice that Elaine would be Amy's new mother, but she suspected that wasn't the way Amy saw it. She remembered how her brother Jack had objected to their mother dating. One man, a doctor, liked her a lot. Whenever he phoned, Jack would call out, "Stanley Beamish for you, Ma." Stanley Beamish was a nerdy character in a mercifully brief TV series that had aired when they were kids.

Her mother would hiss, "His name is Roger!" but her lips would be twitching with a smile when she reached for the phone. Then Jack would flap his arms in imitation of Stanley Beamish, who had the ability to fly.

Roger hadn't lasted long as a potential stepfather. He was a nice guy, Menley thought now, and who knows? Mother might have been much happier if she'd toughed it out, instead of telling Roger that it wouldn't work. Maybe I'll have a chance to talk to Amy a bit this month, she thought. It might make it easier for her.

"It's time to put the crown princess away for the night," she said. "I've made a list of the emergency telephone numbers: police, fire, ambulance. And Elaine's number."

"That one I know." Amy straightened up. "Is it okay if I hold Hannah?"

"Sure. I think it's a good idea."

With the baby in her arms, Amy seemed more confident. "You look awfully pretty, Mrs. Nichols," she said.

"Thank you." Menley felt inordinately pleased by the compliment. She realized she'd been a bit nervous about meeting Adam's friends. She didn't have the knockout looks of the models he used to date, and she knew that over the years he had brought some of them to the Cape. Far more important than that, however, she was sure she must be the object of speculation. Everyone knew her history. Adam's wife who had driven the car over the railroad track and lost his son. Adam's wife who wasn't with him last year in the month he spent at the Cape.

Oh, they'll be eyeing me all right, she thought. After several false starts, she'd chosen to wear a peacock blue raw silk jumpsuit with a blue-and-white corded belt and white sandals.

"Why don't we try to get Hannah settled before I go?" She led the way to the stairs. "The television is in this parlor. But I'd like you to leave the baby monitor on high volume and look in on Hannah every half hour or so. She's great for kicking off the blankets, and the cleaning woman put both sleepers in the wash. The dryer isn't hooked up yet."

"Carrie Bell. She was here?" Amy's voice sounded incredulous.

"Well, no, this woman's name is Hildy. She'll be coming in once a week. Why?"

They were at the top of the stairs. Menley stopped and turned to look at Amy.

Amy blushed. "Oh, nothing. I'm sorry. I knew Elaine was going to suggest someone else to you."

Menley took Hannah from Amy. "Her dad will want to say good night." She went into the master bedroom. Adam was just putting on his navy linen sports jacket. "One of your younger admirers to pay homage," she told him.

He kissed Hannah. "No late dates, Toots, and don't give Amy a hard time." The tenderness in his face belied his flippant tone. Menley felt her heart twist. Adam had been crazy about Bobby. If anything happened to Hannah . . .

Why do you keep thinking that? she asked herself fiercely. She forced her own voice to sound bantering. "Your daughter thinks you look terrific. She wants to know if you're getting gussied up for all your old girlfriends?"

"Nope." Adam leered at her. "I've just got one girl. No," he corrected, "two girls." He addressed the baby. "Hannah, tell your mommy that she looks very sexy and I wouldn't throw her out of bed for anybody."

Laughing, Menley brought the baby back to the nursery. Amy was standing by the side of the crib, her head tilted as though she was listening for something. "Do you get a funny feeling in this room, Mrs. Nichols?" she asked.

"What do you mean?"

"I'm sorry. I don't know what I mean." Amy looked embarrassed. "Please don't mind me. I'm just being silly. Have a great time. I promise you Hannah will be fine and I'll be on the phone in a shot if there's any kind of problem. Besides, Elaine's house is less than two miles away."

Menley paused for a moment. Was there something odd about the baby's room? Hadn't she felt it herself? Then shaking her head at her own silliness, Menley settled Hannah in the crib and popped the pacifier in her mouth before she could launch a protest.

23

ELAINE LIVED NEAR the Chatham Bars Inn in a small Cape that had started its existence in 1780 as a half house. Over the years it had been enlarged and renovated so that now it blended handsomely with its more impressive neighbors.

At seven o'clock she made a quick final inspection. The house gleamed. The guest towels were in the powder room, the wine was chilled, the table attractively set. She had made the lobster salad herself, a long, tiresome job; the rest of the buffet was prepared by the caterer. She was expecting twenty people in all and had hired one man to serve, another to tend the bar.

John had offered to handle the bar, but she'd declined. "You're my host, aren't you?"

"If that's what you want."

Whatever Elaine wants, Elaine gets, she thought, knowing just what he would say before he said it.

"Whatever Elaine wants, Elaine gets," John said with a rumble of laughter. He was a big, solid man with a deliberate manner. At fifty-three his thinning hair was completely gray. His full face was open and pleasant. "Come here, sweetie."

"John, don't muss my hair."

"I like it mussed, but I won't. I just want to give you a little hostess gift."

Elaine took the small package. "John, how sweet. What is it?"

"A bottle of olives, what else? Open it."

It was an olive bottle but inside there appeared to be only a wad of blue tissue.

"Now what's this about?" Elaine asked as she unscrewed the top of the jar and reached into it. She began to pull out the tissue.

"Go easy," he cautioned. "Those olives are expensive."

She held the tissue in her hand and opened it. Inside were crescent-shaped onyx earrings edged with diamonds. "John!"

"You said you were wearing a black and silver skirt, so I thought you ought to have earrings to match."

She put her arms around his neck. "You are too nice to be true. I'm not used to being pampered."

"It's going to be my pleasure to pamper you. You've worked hard enough, long enough, and you deserve it."

She held his face between her hands and drew his lips to hers. "Thank you."

The bell rang. Someone was standing at the screen door. "Will you two stop necking and let your company in?"

The first guests had arrived.

. . .

It's a very nice party, Menley told herself as she came back from the buffet table and reclaimed her seat on the couch. Six of the couples were lifelong summer Capeys, and some of them were into reminiscing. "Adam, remember the time we took your dad's boat to Nantucket. He was seriously unhappy."

"I forgot to mention our plans to him," Adam said with a grin.

"It was my mother who went on the warpath," Elaine said. "She went on and on about my being the only girl with five young men. 'What will people think?' "

"The rest of us were furious we weren't invited," the quiet brunette from Eastham drawled. "We all had a crush on Adam."

"You didn't have a crush on me?" her husband protested.

"That started the next year."

"The time we dug the pit for the clam bake . . . I nearly broke my neck collecting seaweed . . . That stupid kid who ran down the beach and almost fell into the pit . . . The year we . . ."

Menley smiled and tried to listen, but her mind was elsewhere.

Elaine's fiancé, John Nelson, was sitting on the chair next to the couch. He turned to Menley. "What were you doing as a teenager when these people were cavorting at the Cape?"

Menley turned to him with relief. "I was doing the same thing Amy is doing right now, baby-sitting. I went down to the Jersey shore three years straight with a family with five kids."

"Not much of a vacation."

"It was okay. They were nice kids. Incidentally, I do want to tell you that Amy is a lovely girl. She's terrific with my baby."

"Thank you. I don't mind telling you it's a problem that she resents Elaine."

"Don't you think that going to college and meeting new friends will change that?"

"I hope so. She used to worry that I'd be lonesome when she went to college. Now she seems to be afraid that after Elaine and I are married, she won't have a home anymore. Ridiculous, but my fault because I made her feel like the lady of the house, and now she doesn't want to be bumped." He shrugged. "Oh well. She'll get over it. Now I just hope, young lady, that you learn to enjoy the Cape the way I did. We came here from Pennsylvania on a vacation twenty years ago, and my wife liked it so much we pulled up stakes. Fortunately I was able to sell my insurance business and buy into one in Chatham. Whenever you're ready to purchase a house, I'll take good care of you. Lots of people don't really understand insurance. It's a fascinating business."

Ten minutes later Menley excused herself to get another cup of coffee. Insurance is not *that* fascinating, she thought, then felt guilty for thinking it. John Nelson was a very nice man, even if he was a little dull.

Adam joined her as she refilled her cup. "Having fun, honey? You were in such a deep discussion with John that I couldn't catch your eye. How do you like my friends?"

"They're great." She tried to sound enthusiastic. The fact was she'd much rather be home alone with Adam. This first week of their vacation was almost over, and he'd spent two days of it in New York. Then this afternoon they had come up from the beach for his appointment with Scott Covey, and tonight they were with all these people who were strangers to her.

Adam was looking past her. "I haven't had a chance to talk to Elaine privately," he said. "I want to tell her about the meeting with Covey."

Menley reminded herself that she'd been delighted when Adam told her he'd decided to take Scott's case.

The bell rang and without waiting for a response a woman in her sixties opened the screen door and came in. Elaine jumped up. "Jan, I'm so glad you made it."

Adam said, "Elaine told me she was inviting Jan Paley, the woman who owns Remember House."

"Oh, that's interesting. I'd love to get a chance to talk to her."

Menley studied Mrs. Paley as she embraced Elaine. Attractive, she thought. Jan Paley wore no makeup. Her gray-white hair had a natural wave. Her skin was finely wrinkled, with the look of someone who was indifferent about exposure to the sun. Her smile was warm and generous.

Elaine brought her to meet Menley and Adam. "Your new tenants, Jan," she said.

Menley caught the look of sympathy that came into the other woman's eyes. Clearly Elaine had told her about Bobby. "The house is wonderful, Mrs. Paley," she said sincerely.

"I'm so glad you like it." Paley refused Elaine's offer to prepare a plate for her. "No thanks. I left a dinner party at the club. Coffee will be fine."

It was a good time to let Adam talk to Elaine about Scott Covey. People had begun to drift around the room. "Mrs. Paley, why don't we?" Menley nodded toward the empty loveseat.

"Perfect."

As they settled, Menley could hear the beginning of another story about a long-ago summer adventure.

"I went with my husband to his fiftieth high school reunion a couple of years ago," Jan Paley said. "The first evening I thought I'd go out of my mind hearing about the good old days. But after they got it out of their systems, I had a lovely time."

"I'm sure it's like that."

"I must apologize," Paley said. "Most of the furniture in the house is really dreadful. We hadn't completed the renovation and simply used what was there when we bought it until we were ready to decorate."

"The master bedroom pieces are beautiful."

"Yes. I'd seen them at an auction and couldn't pass them up. The cradle, however, I found under a load of junk in the basement. It's authentic early seventeenth century, I believe. It may even have been part of the original furnishings. The house has quite a history you know."

"The version I heard is that a ship captain built it for his bride and then left her when he learned she was involved with someone else."

"There's more to it than that. Supposedly the wife, Mehitabel, swore she was innocent and on her deathbed vowed to stay in the house until her baby was returned to her. But of course half the old houses on the Cape have developed legends. Some perfectly sensible people swear they live in haunted houses."

"Haunted!"

"Yes. In fact one of my good friends bought an old place that had really been ruined by do-it-yourselfers. After the house was completely restored and authentically decorated, early one morning, when she and her husband were asleep, she awakened when she heard footsteps coming up the stairs. Then her bedroom door opened and she swears she could see the impression of footsteps on the carpet."

"I think I'd have died of fright."

"No, Sarah said she experienced the most benevolent feeling, the kind you have as a child when you wake up and your mother is tucking the blankets around you. Then she felt a pat on her shoulder, and in her head she could hear a voice saying, 'I'm so pleased with the care you have taken of my house.' She was sure it was the lady for whom it had been built letting her know how happy she was to have it restored."

"Did she ever see a ghost?"

"No. Sarah is a widow now and quite elderly. She says she sometimes senses a benevolent presence and feels they're two old girls enjoying their home together."

"Do you believe that?"

"I don't disbelieve it," Jan Paley said slowly.

Menley sipped coffee and then found the courage to ask a question. "Did you experience any sense of something odd about the baby's room in Remember House, the small front room next to the master bedroom?"

"No, but we never used it. Frankly for a while after my husband died last year I really thought I'd keep Remember House. But then I sometimes felt such overwhelming sadness that I knew it would be better to let it go. I should never have let Tom do so much of the heavy restoration himself, even though he thoroughly enjoyed every minute of it."

Do we all feel guilty when we lose someone we love? Menley wondered. She glanced across the room. Adam was standing in a group with three other men. She smiled ruefully as she watched Margaret, the thin brunette from Eastham, join them and smile brilliantly up at Adam. A little leftover crush? she thought. I can't say I blame you.

Jan Paley said, "I bought your four David books for my grandson. They're simply wonderful. Are you working on one now?"

"I've decided to set the next one on the Cape in the late sixteen hundreds. I'm just starting to do some research."

"The pity is that the one to have talked to a few years ago would have been Phoebe Sprague. She was a great historian and was preparing notes for a book on Remember House. Perhaps Henry would let you see some of her material."

The party broke up at ten-thirty. On the way home Menley told Adam about Jan Paley's suggestion. "Do you think it would be too pushy to ask Mr. Sprague about his wife's notes or at least ask where she found the best source material?"

"I've known the Spragues all my life," Adam said. "I intended to call them anyway. Who knows? Henry might enjoy sharing Phoebe's research with you."

Amy was watching television in the parlor when they arrived. "Hannah never woke up," she said. "I checked her every half hour."

As Menley walked the girl to the door, Amy said shyly, "I feel so dumb about what I said earlier, that there was something

funny about Hannah's room. I guess it's because of that story
Carrie Bell was telling people, about the cradle rocking by itself and
the spread mussed the way it would be if someone was sitting on
the bed.''

Menley felt her throat go dry. "I didn't know about that, but it's
ridiculous," she said.

"I guess so. Good night, Mrs. Nichols."

Menley went directly to the baby's room. Adam was already
there. Hannah was blissfully asleep in her favorite position, her
arms over her head. "We can't call her 'her crabbiness' anymore,"
Adam murmured.

"How many names do we have for this poor kid?" Menley asked
as she slipped into bed a few minutes later.

"I can't count that high. Good night, honey." Adam held her
tightly. "I hope you had a good time."

"I did." Later she murmured, "I'm not sleepy. Will it bother you
if I read for a while?"

"You know I can sleep through a festival of lights." He
scrunched his pillow. "Listen, when Hannah wakes up, shake me
alive. I'll take care of her. You've been getting up with her all
week."

"Great." Menley reached for her reading glasses and began to
read one of the books about early Cape history that she had found
in the library. It was heavy, and the watersoaked cover was curling.
Inside, the pages were flaking and dusty. Even so it made fascinating reading.

She was intrigued to learn that boys went to sea when they were
only ten years old and that some of them became captains of their
own ships when they were still in their early twenties. She decided
that in the new David book it would be interesting to have a
seventeenth-century boy who had made seafaring his career.

She came to a chapter that gave brief biographies of some of the
most prominent seafarers. One name caught her eye. Captain Andrew Freeman, born in 1663 in Brewster, went to sea as a child and

became master of his own ship, the *Godspeed,* at twenty-three. Pilot and skipper, he had the reputation of being absolutely fearless, and even pirates learned to give a wide berth to the *Godspeed.* He drowned in 1707, when against all reason he set sail knowing a nor'easter was coming. The masts broke, and the ship foundered and sank with its entire crew. The wreckage was strewn for miles along the Monomoy sandbar.

I've got to find out more about him, Menley thought. When she finally laid the book on the night table and turned out the light at two o'clock she felt the exhilaration that always came when a story line was firmly rooted in her mind.

Hannah started fussing at quarter of seven. As she had promised, Menley shook Adam awake and settled back with her eyes closed. In a few minutes he returned, the baby leaning against his shoulder, still half asleep. "Menley, why did you switch Hannah to the cradle last night?"

Menley sat up with a start and stared at him.

Confused and slightly alarmed, she thought, I don't remember going in to her. But if I say that, Adam will think I'm crazy. Instead she yawned and murmured, "When Hannah woke up, she wouldn't settle down, so I rocked her for a while."

"That's what I thought," Adam agreed.

Hannah lifted her head from his shoulder and turned. The shades were down, and the light that peeked around their edges was muted. Hannah yawned elaborately and fluttered her eyelids, then smiled and stretched.

In the shadowy room, the contours of her face were so like Bobby's, Menley thought. That was the way Bobby had awakened, too, yawning and smiling and stretching.

Menley looked up at Adam. She did not want him to see that she was on the verge of panicking. She rubbed her eyes. "I read so late. I'm still sleepy."

"Sleep as long as you want. Here, give the morning star a kiss and I'll take her downstairs. I'll take good care of her."

He handed her the baby. "I know you will," Menley said. She held Hannah so that the little face was only inches from her own. "Hi, angel," she whispered as she thought, Your daddy can take good care of you and I promise you this: if the day ever comes when I think I can't, I'll be history.

August 7th

24

*H*ENRY AND PHOEBE SPRAGUE sat at a table outside the Wayside Inn. For the first time this season Henry had brought Phoebe out for Sunday brunch, and a pleased smile was playing on her lips. She had always been a people watcher, and the main street of Chatham was lively today. Tourists and residents were window-shopping, drifting in and out of the specialty shops or heading for one of the many restaurants.

Henry glanced down at the menu the hostess had given him. We'll order eggs Benedict, he thought. Phoebe always enjoys them here.

"Good morning. Are you ready to order, sir?"

Henry looked up and then stared at the boldly pretty waitress. It was Tina, the young woman whom he'd seen in the pub across the street from the hairdresser in early July, the one whom Scott Covey had explained was an actress appearing at the Cape Playhouse.

There was no hint of recognition on her face, but then she'd barely glanced at him before she rushed out of the pub that day. "Yes, we can order," he said.

Throughout breakfast, Henry Sprague kept up a running commentary on the passersby. "Look, Phoebe, there are Jim Snow's grandchildren. Remember how we used to go to the theater with the Snows?"

"Stop asking me if I remember," Phoebe snapped. "Of course I do." She went back to sipping coffee. A moment later she hunched forward and looked around, her eyes darting from table to table. "So many people," she murmured. "I don't want to be here."

Henry sighed. He'd hoped that the outburst had been a good sign. For some people, tacrine was a remarkably helpful drug, temporarily stopping, even reversing, deterioration in Alzheimer's patients. Since it had been prescribed for Phoebe, he thought he had seen occasional flashes of clarity. Or was he grasping at straws?

Their waitress came with the bill. When Henry laid the money down, he glanced up at her. The young woman's expression was worried and subdued, the exuberant smile singularly absent. She's recognized me, Henry thought, and wonders if I've put her together with Scott Covey.

He enjoyed the realization and was not about to tip his hand. With an impersonal smile he got up and pulled back Phoebe's chair. "Ready, dear?"

Phoebe got up and looked at the waitress. "How are you, Tina?" she asked.

25

*N*AT COOGAN and his wife, Debbie, owned a twenty-foot outboard. They'd bought it secondhand when the boys were little, but because of the care Nat had lavished on it, it was still in excellent condition. Since the boys were spending the afternoon with friends in Fenway Park at the Red Sox game, Nat had suggested to Debbie that they go for a picnic on the boat.

She raised an eyebrow. "You don't like picnics."

"I don't like sitting in fields with ants crawling all over everything."

"I thought you were going to check the lobster pots and then come back and watch the game." She shrugged. "There's something else going on here that I'm not getting, but okay. I'll make some sandwiches."

Nat looked at his wife affectionately. Can't put anything over on Deb, he thought. "No, you just relax for a few minutes. I'll take care of everything."

He went to the delicatessen where he bought salmon, pâté, crackers and grapes. Might as well do everything they did, he thought.

"Pretty fancy," Deb observed as she put the food in a hamper. "Were they out of liverwurst?"

"No. This is what I wanted." From the refrigerator he plucked the chilled bottle of wine.

Debbie read the label. "Are you guilt-complexed for some reason? That's expensive stuff."

"I know it is. Come on. The weather's going to change later."

They dropped anchor exactly one and a half miles from Monomoy Island. Nat did not tell his wife that this was the spot where Vivian Covey had spent her last hours. It might unsettle her.

"This actually is fun," Debbie admitted. "But what have you suddenly got against the deck chairs?"

"Just thought a change of pace would be interesting." He spread an old beach blanket on the deck and laid out the food. He had brought cushions for them to sit on. Finally he poured wine into their glasses.

"Hey, take it easy," Debbie protested. "I don't want to get a buzz on."

"Why not?" Nat asked. "We can nap when we're finished."

The sun was warm. The boat rocked gently. They sipped the wine, nibbled on the cheese and pâté, picked at the grapes. An hour later, Debbie looked drowsily at the empty bottle. "I can't believe we drank all that," she said.

Nat wrapped up the leftover food and put it in the picnic hamper. "Want to stretch out?" he asked as he arranged the cushions side by side on the blanket. He knew she was not a daytime drinker.

"Great idea." Debbie settled down and immediately closed her eyes.

Nat stretched out beside her and began to review some of what he had learned the past few days. Friday after he'd studied the autopsy pictures he'd dropped in on Scott Covey. Covey's explanation that his wife had probably switched the emerald ring to her other hand seemed to him a little glib and perhaps rehearsed.

He glanced at the empty wine bottle warming in the sun. The autopsy report showed that Vivian Carpenter had consumed several glasses of wine shortly before her death. But when he queried her parents about her drinking habits, they'd both told him that she was not a daytime drinker. A single glass of wine made her sleepy, especially in the sun, the same reaction Deb was having.

Would anyone who was sleepy from drinking wine, and who was just learning to scuba dive, have insisted on joining her husband when he said he was going to take a brief underwater swim?

Nat didn't think so.

At three o'clock he sensed a subtle change in the motion of the boat. Heavy rain showers had been predicted for about three-thirty.

Nat stood up. This spot was on line with the entrance to the harbor, and as he watched, from all directions small craft were heading in.

Covey claimed he and Vivian had been down about twenty minutes when the squall hit. That meant that when he got up from the nap that afternoon, he *must* have noticed small craft going in toward shore. There must have been some sense of the current getting stronger.

At that point anyone with half a brain would have turned on the radio and checked the weather report, Nat reasoned.

Deb stirred and sat up. "What are you doing?"

"Thinking." He looked down at her as she stretched. "Want to go for a quick swim, honey?"

Debbie lay back and closed her eyes.

"Forget it," she murmured. "I'm too sleepy."

26

*S*COTT COVEY spent Sunday in the house. Relieved that Adam Nichols had agreed to represent him, he still was uneasy about one of the specific warnings Adam had given him. "When a rich wife dies in an accident shortly after her marriage to a man no one knows well, and that man is the only one present at her death, there's bound to be talk. You've cooperated with the police, and that was all to the good. Now stop cooperating. Refuse to answer any more questions."

That admonition was fine with Scott.

Nichols' second piece of advice was easy to follow too. "Don't change your lifestyle. Don't start throwing money around."

He had no intention of being that much of a fool.

Finally Adam had said, "And very important—don't be seen with another woman while the police are openly suspicious."

Tina. Should he explain to Adam that before he met Viv, he'd been involved with her? That the relationship had started last year when he was working at the playhouse? Would Adam understand that he'd had nothing to do with her after he met Viv?

He could explain that Tina hadn't realized he'd come back to the Cape. Then of all the damn luck she quit her job in Sandwich and started working at the Wayside Inn. After she saw him and Viv having dinner there she started calling him. The one time he'd agreed to meet her in person, Henry Sprague, of all people, had to be sitting beside him in the pub! Sprague was nobody's fool. Should he explain to Adam that Tina only stopped by the house one time after Viv was missing, to offer sympathy?

At four o'clock the phone rang. Grimly, Scott went to answer it. It had better not be that detective, he thought.

It was Elaine Atkins, inviting him to a barbecue at her fiancé's place. "Some of John's friends will be here," she said. "Important people, the kind you should be seen with. I saw Adam last night, by the way. He told me he's going to represent you."

"I can't thank you enough for that, Elaine. And of course I'll be happy to join you."

As he drove down the street an hour later, he noticed Nat Coogan's eight-year-old Chevy parked in front of the Sprague house.

27

NAT COOGAN had dropped in on the Spragues without phoning in advance. It was not something he did without calculation, however. He knew there was something Henry Sprague had not told him about Scott Covey, and he hoped that the element of surprise might encourage Sprague to answer the question he planned to ask him.

Sprague's cool greeting gave Nat the message he expected. A phone call ahead of time would have been appreciated. They were expecting guests.

"It will just take a minute."

"In that case, please come in."

Henry Sprague hastily led the way through the house to the deck. Once there, Nat realized the reason he was hurrying. Sprague had left his wife alone outside, and in the minute he was gone she had started to walk across the lawn to the Carpenter/Covey house.

Sprague quickly caught up with her and guided her back to the deck. "Sit down, dear. Adam and his wife are going to visit us." He did not invite Nat to be seated.

Nat decided to lay all his cards on the table. "Mr. Sprague, I believe that Scott Covey deliberately abandoned his wife when they were scuba diving, and I'm going to do everything in my power to prove it. The other day I had the very strong sense that there was something you were debating about telling me. I know you're the kind of man who minds his own business, but this *is* your business. Picture how terrified Vivian was when she knew she was going to drown. Imagine how *you'd* feel if someone deliberately led your wife into danger and then abandoned her."

For some time, Henry Sprague had been valiantly trying to give up smoking. Now he found himself reaching into the breast pocket of his sports shirt for the pipe he had left in his desk drawer. He promised himself that he would get it when he let this detective out. "Yes, you're right, there was one thing. Three weeks before Vivian's death I happened to be in the Cheshire Pub at the same time Scott Covey was there," he said reluctantly. "A young woman named Tina came in. I'm sure they were planning to meet. He made a pretense of being surprised to see her, and she took the cue and ran off. She was not someone I knew. But then I saw her again this morning. She's a waitress at the Wayside Inn."

"Thank you," Nat said quietly.

"There's one thing more. My wife knew her by name. I don't know when they could have met except . . ."

He looked over at Vivian Carpenter Covey's home. "Several times lately when I've turned my back, Phoebe has walked over to the Carpenter place. The house isn't air-conditioned, and the windows are usually open. She may have seen Tina there. It's the only explanation I can come up with."

28

"*I* THINK it was a good idea to get Amy to mind Hannah for a couple of hours," Adam said as they drove past the lighthouse and through the center of Chatham. "From what I understand, Phoebe can't handle much distraction. I gather also that she probably won't be able to discuss her notes, but I'm really glad that Henry was receptive to the idea of sharing them with you."

"I am too." Menley tried to sound enthusiastic, but it was a struggle. It should have been a perfect day, she thought. They'd spent a couple of hours on the beach, then read the Sunday papers while Hannah napped. Around three-thirty, when the thunderstorm broke, they stood at the window and watched the rain lash at the ocean and the angry surge of the waves. An easy, comfortable day, time spent together, sharing things, the kind of day they used to know.

Except that now always in Menley's mind was the specter of a breakdown. What was happening to her? she wondered. She had not told Adam about the panic attack at the railroad crossing, even though he would have understood. But to tell him that the night he was in New York she had awakened to the sound of a train, thundering as though it were roaring through the house! What would any rational human being think about a story like that? Likewise, could she tell him that she had no memory of being in the baby's room last night? No, never!

It would have seemed like whining to let him know that at Elaine's party she felt isolated by the camaraderie she witnessed but could not share. I have plenty of friends, Menley reassured herself. It's just that here I'm an outsider. If we *do* decide to buy Remember House I'll get to know everyone really well. And I'll bring my own friends up to visit.

"You're very quiet suddenly," Adam said.

"Just daydreaming."

The Sunday afternoon traffic was heavy and they inched their way down Main Street. At the rotary they turned left and drove a mile to the Sprague home on Oyster Pond.

As Adam braked in front of the house, a blue Chevy pulled away. Henry Sprague was standing in the doorway. His greeting to them was cordial, but it was clear that he was preoccupied.

"I hope Phoebe's okay," Adam murmured to Menley as they followed him to the deck.

Henry had told his wife they were coming. Mrs. Sprague pretended to recognize Adam and smiled absently at Menley.

Alzheimer's, Menley thought. How awful to lose touch with reality. At Bellevue, her mother had sometimes had patients with Alzheimer's on the floor she supervised. Menley tried to remember some of the stories her mother had told her about helping them to retrieve memory.

"You've researched a great deal about the early history of the Cape," she said. "I'm going to write a children's story about the Cape in the sixteen hundreds."

Mrs. Sprague nodded but did not answer.

Henry Sprague was describing Nat Coogan's visit to Adam. "I felt like a damn gossip," he said, "but there's something about that Covey fellow that doesn't ring true. If there's any chance he let that poor girl drown . . ."

"Elaine doesn't think so, Henry. She sent Scott Covey to me last week. I agreed to represent him."

"You! I thought you were on vacation, Adam."

"I'm supposed to be, but it's obvious that Covey is right to be concerned. The police are on a fishing expedition. He needs representation."

"Then I'm talking out of turn."

"No. If it comes to an indictment, the defense has the right to know which witnesses will be called. I'll want to talk to this Tina myself."

"Then I feel better." Henry Sprague gave a relieved sigh and turned to Menley. "This morning I collected what I could find of Phoebe's files on the early Cape days. I always told her that her research notes were an awful hodgepodge for someone who turned out polished articles and essays." He chuckled. "Her answer was to tell me that she worked in orderly chaos. I'll get them for you."

He went into the house and returned in a few minutes with an armful of thickly packed expandable manila files.

"I'll take good care of them and get them back to you before we go home," Menley promised. She looked at the material longingly. "It will be a treat to dig into this."

"Henry, we're giving some serious thought to buying Remember House," Adam said. "Have you been in it since it was renovated?"

Phoebe Sprague's expression changed suddenly, became fearful. "I don't want to go to Remember House," she said. "They made me go in the ocean. That's what they're going to do to Adam's wife."

"Dear, you're confused. You haven't been in Remember House," Henry said patiently.

She looked uncertain. "I thought I was."

"No, you were on the beach near it. This is Adam's wife you're with now."

"Is it?"

"Yes, dear."

He lowered his voice. "A few weeks ago Phoebe wandered out about eight o'clock at night. Everyone was searching for her. We always enjoyed walking on your beach, and I decided to drive over there. I found her in the ocean not far from your house. Another few minutes and it would have been too late."

"I couldn't see their faces but I know them," Phoebe Sprague said sadly. "They wanted to hurt me."

August 8th

29

O N *MONDAY MORNING,* Adam called the Wayside Inn, established that a waitress named Tina was scheduled to work there that day, then called Scott Covey and made an appointment to meet him at the inn.

Menley had arranged for Amy to come and mind Hannah while she delved into Phoebe Sprague's files, something it was obvious she was looking forward to. "You won't miss me," Adam laughed. "You've got a look in your eye like a pirate chasing a ship full of gold."

"Being in this house helps so much to capture the sense of the early days," Menley said eagerly. "Did you know that the door of the main parlor is so large because it was made wide enough to get a casket through it?"

"That's cheerful," Adam said. "My grandmother used to tell me stories about the old house she lived in. I've forgotten most of them." He paused, wistful for a moment. "Well, I'm off to begin the defense of my new client." Menley was feeding Hannah cereal. Adam kissed the top of Menley's head and gave a friendly pat to Hannah's foot. "You're too messy to kiss, Toots," he told her.

He hesitated, trying to decide whether or not to mention that he planned to walk past Elaine's real estate agency and drop in on her if she was there. He decided not to say anything about it. He did not want Menley to know the reason for that visit.

. . .

Adam arrived at the Wayside Inn fifteen minutes before Covey was due. It was easy to spot Tina from Henry Sprague's description. As he walked in, she was clearing a small table near the window. He asked the hostess to seat him there.

Very attractive in a showy way, he thought as he took the menu from her. Tina had shiny dark hair, lively brown eyes, a pink-and-white complexion and perfect teeth that were displayed in a radiant smile. An unnecessarily tight uniform displayed every line of her rounded figure. Late twenties, he decided, and she's been around.

Her cheery "Good morning, sir," was followed by a frankly admiring stare. A phrase from the song "Paper Doll," which his mother used to sing, popped into his mind: "flirty, flirty eyes . . ." Tina *definitely* had flirty, flirty eyes, he decided.

"Just coffee for now," he said. "I'm waiting for someone."

Scott Covey came in exactly at nine. From across the room, Adam watched his expression change when he realized Tina would be their waitress. But when he sat down and she came over with the menu, he accepted it without acknowledging her, and she likewise gave no outward sign of recognition, saying merely, "Good morning, sir."

They both ordered juice, coffee and a Danish. "I don't have much appetite these days," Covey said quietly.

"You'll have even less if you play games with me," Adam warned.

Covey looked startled. "What's that supposed to mean?"

Tina was clearing a nearby table. Adam nodded toward her. "It means that the police know that you met that lovely young lady in the Cheshire Pub before your wife died, and that she may have been in your house."

"Henry Sprague." Covey looked disgusted.

"Henry Sprague knew you hadn't just bumped into her at the

pub. But if you hadn't given him a cock-and-bull story about her being in the cast of the play at the Cape Playhouse, he wouldn't have said anything to the detective. And how does Mrs. Sprague know Tina?"

"She doesn't."

"Phoebe knew enough to call her by name. How often has Tina been at your house?"

"Once. She dropped by when Viv was missing. That Sprague woman doesn't know what she's doing. It's pretty spooky to see her staring in the window or opening the door and walking in. Since she got so bad, she gets confused about the houses. She must have been hanging around when Tina came that one time. Don't forget, Adam, a lot of people dropped by in those weeks."

"What was your relationship with Tina before your wife died?"

"Absolutely none from the minute I met Viv. Before that, yes. Last year when I was working in the office at the playhouse I was dating her."

Adam raised an eyebrow. "Dating?"

"I was involved with her." Scott Covey looked anguished. "Adam, I was single. She was single. Look at her. Tina's a party girl. We both knew it was going nowhere, that when the season was over I'd be leaving. She used to work at the Daniel Webster Inn in Sandwich. It's just hard luck that she got a job here and Viv and I ran into her. She called me that one time, to ask me to meet her for a drink. She came to the house to tell me how sorry she was about Viv. That's all."

Tina was heading toward them with the coffeepot. "Another cup, sir?" she asked Scott.

"Tina, this is my attorney, Adam Nichols," Scott said. "He's going to represent me. You know the rumors."

She looked uncertain and said nothing.

"It's all right, Tina," Scott told her. "Mr. Nichols knows we're old friends, that we used to date and that you stopped by the house to offer condolences."

"Why did you want to meet Scott in the Cheshire Pub that day when Henry Sprague was there?" Adam asked.

She looked directly at him. "When Scott left the Cape at the end of the season last year, I never heard from him again. Then when he came in here with his wife, I was furious. I thought he'd been seeing her while we were going together. But that wasn't true. He met her at the end of the summer. I just needed to hear that."

"I would suggest you make sure that you tell the police that story," Adam said, "because you're going to be questioned by the police. I will have another coffee and the check, please."

When she left the table, Adam leaned across to Scott. "Listen as you've never listened before. I have agreed to represent you but I must tell you there are a lot of negative factors piling up. At your expense, I'm going to put an investigator on this."

"An investigator! Why?"

"His job will be to do exactly the same fieldwork the Chatham police are engaged in. If there's a grand jury hearing, we can't afford surprises. We need to see the autopsy pictures, the diving gear your wife was wearing, know the currents that day, find other boaters to testify about nearly being swamped because the storm came up so fast."

He paused as Tina laid down the check and left again; then he resumed. "We need more witnesses like Elaine who can testify to how great your marriage was. And finally my investigator is going to investigate you just as the cops are doing right now. If you've got any blemishes in your background, I need to know them and be able to explain them away."

He glanced at the bill and pulled out his wallet.

"Here, let me." Scott reached for it.

Adam smiled. "Don't worry. It's on the expense account."

As they walked down the outside steps of the inn, the blue Chevy Adam had seen leaving the Spragues' pulled up and parked. "Tina has a visitor," Adam said dryly as Detective Coogan got out of the car and walked into the restaurant.

30

*A*MY ARRIVED at nine-thirty. After greeting Menley, instead of going immediately to Hannah she lingered by the refectory table, which was now piled with the books and files Menley was planning to sort through.

"Mrs. Nichols, my dad and Elaine had some people over for a barbecue last night, and Scott Covey was there. He's *gorgeous!*"

So that's the reason for the bright eyes this morning, Menley thought. "He certainly is," she agreed.

"I'm glad Mr. Nichols is going to represent him. He's so nice, and the police are giving him a hard time."

"That's what we understand."

"It's weird to think that he and his wife were looking at this house only a day or two before she died."

"Yes, it is."

"He talked to me for a while. His mother died and he has a stepmother. He told me that at first he wouldn't let himself like her and then afterwards he was sorry he had wasted so much time being mean to her. They're really close."

"I'm glad he told you that, Amy. Does it make you feel a little better about your dad getting married?"

She sighed. "I guess so. Listening to him made me believe it will be okay."

Menley got up from the table and put her hands on the young girl's shoulders. "It will be better than okay. You'll see."

"I guess so," Amy said. "It's just . . . no, it'll be all right. I just want my dad to be happy."

Hannah was in the playpen, examining a rattle. Now she shook it vigorously.

Menley and Amy looked down at her and laughed. "Hannah does not like to be ignored," Menley said. "Why don't you put her in the carriage and sit outside for a while?"

When they left, she opened the Sprague files, stacked the contents on the refectory table and began to try to put the papers and books and clippings in some kind of order. It was a treasure chest of historical research. There were copies of letters that dated back to the sixteen hundreds. There were bills and genealogies and old maps and page upon page of memos Phoebe Sprague had made, noting their sources.

Menley found files marked with dozens of categories, among them SHIPWRECKS; PIRATES; MOONCUSSERS; MEETING ROOMS; HOUSES; SEA CAPTAINS. As Henry Sprague had warned, the papers within the files were far from orderly. They were simply there, some folded, some torn scraps, some with highlighted paragraphs.

Menley decided to glance into each file to get a sense of its contents and try to establish an overall picture. She was also on the alert for any mention of Captain Andrew Freeman, in hopes of learning more about Remember House.

An hour later she came across the first one. In the file marked HOUSES there was a reference to a house being built by Tobias Knight for Captain Andrew Freeman. "A dwelling house of goodly size, so as to house the chatles he has transported." The year was 1703. That must refer to this house, Menley thought.

Further back in that file she found a copy of a letter Captain Freeman had written to Tobias Knight, directing the construction of the house. One sentence stood out: "Mehitabel, my wife, be of gentle size and strength. Let the boards be tightly joined so no unseemly draft penetrate to chill her."

Mehitabel. That was the unfaithful wife. "Of gentle size and strength," Menley thought. ". . . so that no unseemly draft penetrate to chill her." Why would any woman deceive a man who cared for her like that? She pushed back the chair, got up, walked to the front parlor and looked out. Amy had placed the carriage almost at the end of the bluff and was sitting by it, reading.

How long had Mehitabel lived in this house? Menley wondered. Was she ever in love with Captain Freeman? When he was due to return home from a voyage, did she ever go up to the widow's walk to watch for him?

She had asked Adam about the small railed platform that crowned the roofs of many old Cape houses. He'd told her they were called widow's walks because in the early days, when a sea captain was expected home, his wife would keep a vigil there, straining her eyes for the first sight of his ship's masts appearing over the horizon. So many vessels did not return that in time the platforms became known as widow's walks.

She mused that the one on this house must command a sweeping view of the ocean. She could imagine a slender young woman standing on it. It would be one of the sketches she would make to illustrate the book.

Then she smiled as she looked out at the carriage where Hannah was sleeping in the sunshine. She felt suddenly calm and at peace. I'll be fine, she thought. I worry too much. Work always puts me back on balance.

She returned to the kitchen and began to go through more files and compile her own lists—names typical of the times; descriptions of clothing; references to weather.

It was quarter past twelve when she glanced at the clock. I'd better think about lunch, she decided and went out to fetch Amy and Hannah.

Hannah was still fast asleep. "This air is like a sedative, Amy," Menley said, smiling. "When I think of the way this kid wouldn't close an eye for the first six weeks of her life!"

"She was unconscious the minute the carriage started rolling," Amy said. "I should charge you half price."

"Not a bit of it. You being here meant I've had a wonderful

couple of hours. The files I've been studying have terrific background material."

Amy looked at her curiously. "Oh, I thought I caught a glimpse
of you standing up there." She pointed to the widow's walk.

"Amy, except for a few minutes looking out the downstairs window, I haven't budged until just now." Shading her eyes, Menley
looked up at the widow's walk. "There's a strip of metal on the left
chimney. The way the sun is hitting it, it looks as though something
is moving."

Amy looked unconvinced, but she shook her head and said,
"Well, the sun was in my eyes when I looked up, and I had to
squint. I guess I just thought I saw you."

Later, while Amy was feeding Hannah, Menley slipped upstairs.
A folding staircase in a second-floor closet led to the widow's walk.
She opened the closet door and felt a blast of cold air. Where's that
draft coming from? she wondered.

She pulled the ladder down, climbed the rungs, unlocked and
pushed up the trapdoor, then stepped out. Cautiously, she tapped
the flooring. It was secure. She walked a few steps and put her hand
on the railing. It was almost as high as her waist. That too was
secure.

What did Amy see when she thought I was up here? she asked
herself. The walk was about ten feet square and nestled between
the two massive chimneys. She crossed it and looked out at the spot
more than one hundred feet away where Amy had been sitting.
Then she turned to examine the space behind her.

Was the metal strip on the corner of the left chimney what had
caught Amy's eye? The sunbeams were dancing off the metal, creating moving shadows.

I still don't know how she could make a mistake like that, Menley thought as she went back down the ladder. God, it's clammy in
here. She shivered at the deepening chill within the narrow closet.

At the bottom of the steps she became immobilized as a sudden
thought leapt into her mind. Was it possible that Amy was right?

When I was picturing Mehitabel watching for her captain from the widow's walk, was the image so vivid because I came up here myself? Menley wondered.

Could I really be losing touch like that? The possibility filled her with despair.

31

ADAM LEFT HIS CAR at the Wayside Inn and walked the two blocks to Elaine's real estate office. Through the window he could see her sitting at her desk. He was in luck. She was alone.

The window was filled with pictures of available properties. As he turned toward the door the aerial photo of Remember House caught his eye and he studied it. Good picture, he thought. It had captured the panorama of the view from the house; the ocean, sandbar, beach, cliff, a fishing boat, all depicted with remarkable clarity. He read the card attached to the picture: REMEMBER HOUSE. FOR SALE. No way, he thought.

When the door opened, Elaine glanced up, then pushed back her chair and hurried into the reception area. "Adam, what a nice surprise." She kissed him lightly.

He followed her back into her office and settled in a comfortable chair. "Hey, what are you trying to do, sell my house from under me?"

She raised an eyebrow. "I wasn't aware you were buying it."

"Let's call it a definite maybe. I just haven't told you yet. Menley loves it, but I don't want to rush her into making a commitment. We have an option till September, don't we?"

"Yes, and I was sure you'd want it."

"Then why the picture in the window?"

She laughed. "It brings in business. People inquire and I say it's optioned and steer them onto someplace else."

"You always were a smart cookie."

"I had to be. Poor Mother never could hold a job. She always picked a fight with someone and got fired."

Adam's eyes softened. "You didn't have it easy, growing up, 'Laine. I hate to be paying too many compliments, but I have to tell you that you look great all the time these days."

Elaine made a face at him. "You're just getting mellow."

"No, not really," Adam said quietly. "Maybe just a little less dense. I don't know if I ever thanked you for being so terrific when I came up here last year."

"Between losing Bobby and separating from Menley you were in pretty bad shape. I was glad to be around for you."

"I'm going to ask for more help now."

"Is anything wrong?" she asked quickly.

"No, not really. It's just that I'll have to go back and forth to New York more than I expected. I'm not happy about leaving Menley alone so much. I think she's having more episodes of that post-traumatic stress than she's letting on. I think she feels she has to tough it out by herself, and maybe she does."

"Would it help if Amy stayed over?"

"Menley doesn't want that. My thought was that some nights when I'm away, Amy could stay with Hannah, and you, or you and John, might invite Menley out for dinner. When I'm home it's good for us to spend most of the time together. We're still . . . Well, never mind."

"Adam, what is it?"

"Nothing."

Elaine knew enough not to urge Adam to finish whatever he had been about to say. Instead she said, "Let me know when you're going to New York again."

"Tomorrow afternoon."

"I'll call late today, invite both of you to dinner tomorrow, then insist that Menley come alone."

"And I'll insist from my end." Adam smiled. "That's a relief. Incidentally I had breakfast with Scott Covey."

"And?" Elaine's eyes opened wide.

"Nothing I can talk about now. Attorney-client privilege."

"I always end up on the outside," she said, then sighed. "Oh, that reminds me. Big news. Circle your calendar for the Saturday after Thanksgiving. John and I are getting married."

"Terrific. When did you set the date?"

"Last night. We had a barbecue, and Scott Covey was there. He talked with Amy about his stepmother, and later Amy told her father that she was happy for us. John called me at midnight. Scott really made the difference."

"Well you keep telling me Covey's a nice guy." Adam got up. "Walk me to the door."

In the reception area he put his arm over Elaine's shoulders. "So will John get mad if I come running to you with a problem after you're hitched?"

"Of course not."

At the door he hugged her and kissed her cheek. "You used to do better than that," she laughed. In a sudden move, she turned his face and pressed her lips firmly on his.

Adam stepped back and shook his head. "That's called long-term memory, 'Laine."

32

*T*HE BREAKFAST SERVICE was virtually over. Only a few stray diners lingered over coffee. The manager had told Tina to sit at one of the tables at the far end of the room and talk to the detective. She brought coffee for both of them. Then she lit a cigarette.

"I'm trying to stop," she told Nat after the first puff. "And I only lapse once in a while."

"Like when you're nervous?" Nat suggested.

Tina's eyes narrowed. "I'm not nervous," she snapped. "Why should I be?"

"You tell me," Nat suggested. "One reason I could give is like maybe if you were running around with a newly married man whose rich wife died suddenly. And if that death turned out to be a homicide, a lot of people might wonder how much you knew about the bereaved husband's plans. Hypothetical case, of course."

"Listen, Mr. Coogan," Tina said, "I dated Scott last year. He always said that at the end of the summer he'd be on his way. I'm sure you've heard of summer romances."

"And I've heard of some that didn't end when summer was over," Nat said.

"This one did. It was only when I saw him with his wife, right in this room, and asked around and found out he'd been seeing her last August that I got mad. I had a guy who was crazy about me, even wanted to get married, and I dumped him for Scott."

"And that's why a month ago you met Scott in that pub?"

"Like I just told Mr. Nichols—"

"Mr. Nichols?"

"He's Scott's lawyer. He was here with Scott this morning. I explained to him that it was me who called Scott, not the other way around. He didn't want to see me, but I insisted. Then when I got to the pub, some man was talking to Scott and I could tell Scott didn't want it to look like I was meeting him, so I didn't hang around."

"But you *did* see him another time?"

"I called him. He asked me to say what I had to say over the phone. So I told him off."

"Told him off?"

"I told him I wished he'd never come around, that if he'd just left me alone I'd have married Fred and I'd be in great shape now. Fred was crazy about me, and he had money."

"But you said you knew all along that Scott intended to take off after the season at the playhouse was over."

Tina took a long drag on the cigarette and sighed. "Listen, Mr. Coogan, when a guy like Scott rushes you and tells you he's crazy about you, you think to yourself that maybe you're the one who can hang onto him. Lots of girls have landed guys who swore they'd never get married."

"I suppose that's true. So your beef with Scott was that he was probably pulling the same line on Vivian at the same time."

"But he wasn't. She met him the last week he was here. She wrote to him. She visited him when he got a job at the theater in Boca Raton. She chased him. At least that made me feel a little better."

"Scott told you that?"

"Yeah."

"And then you paid a consolation call after his wife disappeared. Maybe you hoped he'd turn to you in his hour of need."

"Well, he didn't." Tina pushed back the chair. "And it wouldn't have done him a bit of good if he had. I'm seeing Fred again, so you see, there's no reason for you to be bothering me. It's been nice meeting you, Mr. Coogan. My coffee break's over."

• • •

On his way out, Nat stopped at the business office of the Wayside Inn and asked to see the application Tina had filled out when she applied for the waitressing job. From it he learned that she was from New Bedford, had been on the Cape for five years, and her last job was at the Daniel Webster Inn in Sandwich.

In the references she'd supplied, he found the name he was looking for. Fred Hendin, a carpenter in Barnstable. Barnstable was the next town over from Sandwich. He'd bet anything that Fred Hendin was the big spender Tina had dropped last year and then taken up with again. He hadn't wanted to ask Tina too much about him. He didn't want her to warn him that he'd be questioned.

It would be interesting to talk to Tina's patient suitor and to her fellow employees at the Daniel Webster Inn.

A brazen young lady, Nat thought as he handed back Tina's job application. And pretty smug. She thinks she's handled me pretty well. We'll see.

33

ANNE AND GRAHAM CARPENTER had enjoyed house guests for the weekend; their daughters Emily and Barbara had visited with their families. They all went sailing, then the adults golfed while the three teenage grandchildren were at the beach with friends. Saturday night they had dinner at the club. That there was none of the discord and contention that Vivian had brought to such family gatherings served in a perverse way to make Anne all the more aware of her absence.

None of us loved her the way she needed to be loved, she said to herself. That thought and the question of the emerald ring lurked constantly in the back of her mind. The ring was the one object that Vivian had sincerely treasured. Had it been ripped from her finger by the only person who had made her feel loved? The question plagued Anne Carpenter all weekend.

On Monday morning over breakfast, she brought up the subject of the ring. "Graham, I think Emily had a good idea about the emerald."

"What's that, dear?"

"She pointed out that it's still on our insurance policy. She feels we should report it as missing. In a situation like this, wouldn't we be covered?"

"We might be. But we'd be giving the money to Scott as Vivian's heir."

"I know. But that ring was valued at $250,000. Don't you think that if we hinted to the insurance company that we question Scott's version of how it got lost, they might put an investigator on him?"

"Detective Coogan is conducting an investigation. You know that, Anne."

"Would it hurt if the insurance company got involved?"

"I suppose not."

Ann nodded as the housekeeper came to the table with the coffeepot. "I will have a little more, Mrs. Dillon, thank you."

She sipped in silence for a few minutes, then said, "Emily reminded me that Vivy had complained about the ring being tight when she took it off to clean it. Remember? She broke that finger when she was little and the knuckle was enlarged. But the ring fit fine once it was in place, so Scott's story about her moving it to her other hand doesn't make sense."

Her eyes glistened with tears as she said, "I remember the stories my grandmother told me about emeralds. One story was that it's very bad luck to lose an emerald. The other is that emeralds have the reputation of finding their way back home."

34

*J*AN PALEY had spent a quiet Sunday. For her it was the most difficult day of the week. There were too many memories of pleasant Sundays when she and her husband, Tom, read the papers, shared the crossword puzzle, walked on the beach.

She lived on Lower Road in Brewster, in the same house they'd bought thirty years ago. They'd planned to sell it when the renovations to Remember House were completed. Now she was extremely grateful that they hadn't already moved when she lost Tom.

Jan was always relieved when Monday came and her weekday activities resumed. Recently she had become a volunteer at the Brewster Ladies Library, working there on Monday afternoons. It was a pleasant and useful pastime, and she enjoyed the company of the other women.

Today as she drove to the library she thought about Menley Nichols. She had taken an instant liking to the young woman, which was gratifying since she admired her books enormously. She was also glad that the next book in the David series was going to be set on the Cape. On Saturday night, when she and Menley had talked about Remember House, Menley had indicated that she might use Captain Andrew Freeman as the model for the story of a young boy growing up and going to sea.

Jan wondered if Menley had acted on her suggestion to ask Henry Sprague about Phoebe's research files, but as she drove down the tree-lined highway, another thought occurred to her. At the beginning of the eighteenth century it was common practice for a sea captain to take his wife and even his children with him on a long voyage. Some of those wives had kept journals that were now in the collection of the Brewster Ladies Library. She hadn't gotten around to reading them yet, but it would be interesting to browse through them now and see if by any chance Captain Freeman's wife had been one of the contributors.

It was a beautiful day, and predictably the only car in the parking lot belonged to Alana Martin, the other Monday volunteer. I'll have plenty of time to read this afternoon, Jan thought.

"Those gals got around," she murmured to Alana an hour later as she sat at one of the long tables with a dozen handwritten journals stacked around her. "One of them wrote that she 'was two years on board.' Went to China and India, had a baby born during an Atlantic storm and came home 'refreshed and tranquil of spirit despite some hardships along the way.' This is the jet age, but I've never been to China."

The journals made fascinating reading, but she could find no reference to Captain Andrew Freeman's wife. Finally she gave up. "I guess Captain Freeman's wife didn't take pen in hand, or if she did, we don't have her memoirs here."

Alana was checking the shelves for out-of-order books. She paused and took off her glasses, a habit she had when she was trying to remember something. "Captain Freeman," she mused. "I remember finding some stuff on him years ago for Phoebe Sprague. It seems to me we even have a sketch of him somewhere. He grew up in Brewster."

"I didn't know that," Jan said. "I thought he was from Chatham."

Alana put her glasses back on. "Let me take a look."

A few minutes later, Jan was reading through the annals of

Brewster and jotting notes. She culled from the book the fact that Andrew's mother was Elizabeth Nickerson, daughter of William Nickerson of Yarmouth, who in 1653 married Samuel Freeman, a farmer. As a wedding gift, she received from her father a grant of forty acres of upland and ten acres in Monomoit, as Chatham was then known.

I wonder if the Chatham property was where Remember House was eventually built, Jan thought.

Samuel and Elizabeth Freeman had three sons, Caleb, Samuel and Andrew. Only Andrew lived past babyhood, and at age ten he went to sea in the *Mary Lou,* a sloop under the command of Captain Nathaniel Baker.

In 1702 Andrew, age thirty-eight, now the captain of his own ship, the *Godspeed,* married Mehitabel Winslow, age sixteen, daughter of the Reverend Jonathan Winslow of Boston.

I can't wait to tell Menley Nichols I found all this, Jan exulted. Of course she may have Phoebe's files and already have come across it.

"Want to take a peek at Captain Andrew Freeman?"

Jan looked up. Alana was at her elbow, smiling triumphantly. "I knew I'd seen a sketch of him. It must have been drawn by someone on his ship. Isn't he impressive?"

The pen-and-ink drawing depicted Captain Andrew Freeman at the helm of the *Godspeed.* A large man, broad and tall, with a short dark beard, strong features, a firm mouth, eyes that were narrowed as though he was looking into the sun. There was an air of confidence and command about him.

"He had the reputation of being fearless, and he looks the part, doesn't he?" Alana commented. "I tell you, I wouldn't want to be the wife who cheated on him and got caught."

"Do you think it's all right if I make a copy of this?" Jan asked. "I'll be careful."

"Sure."

When she went home later that afternoon, Jan called Menley and told her that she had some interesting material for her. "One find is really special," she promised. "I'll drop everything off for you tomorrow. Will you be home around four o'clock?"

"That would be fine," Menley agreed. "I've been doing some sketching today for the illustrations, and of course Mrs. Sprague's files are glorious. Thank you for suggesting them." She hesitated, then asked, "Do you think there's any chance there might be a picture of Mehitabel anywhere?"

"I don't know," Jan said. "But I'll certainly keep looking."

When she hung up, Jan was lost in thought. Menley Nichols sounded genuinely glad to hear from her, but there was something in her voice that made Jan uneasy. What was it? And then the unanswered question once again ran through her mind.

Tom had suffered the heart attack at Remember House. He'd come in from working outside, clutching his chest. She'd made him lie down, then ran to phone the doctor. When she came back, he'd grabbed her hand and pointed to the fireplace. "Jan, I just saw . . ."

What had Tom seen? He didn't live long enough to finish the sentence.

35

MENLEY HAD SENT AMY home at two o'clock, after Hannah had been tucked in for an afternoon nap. Several times she had caught the teenager studying her and was slightly unnerved by the scrutiny. It was the same expression she so often saw on Adam's face, and it made her uncomfortable. She was relieved when she heard Amy's car start down the driveway.

Adam wouldn't be home for another hour or so, she knew. After his meeting with Scott Covey he had a golf date with three of the friends who'd been at Elaine's party. Well, maybe they'll get all the "do-you-remember's" out of their systems, she thought, then felt a little guilty. Adam loves golf and has so little opportunity to play, and it's good that he has friends here.

It's just that I'm so confused, she mused. Hearing the train, not remembering putting Hannah in the cradle, not absolutely sure I wasn't on the widow's walk when Amy thought she saw me. But I'll go mad if Adam insists on having someone here all the time. She hated thinking of that first month after Hannah was born, when she'd been having the frequent anxiety attacks and they'd had a live-in nurse. She could still hear the well-intentioned soothing, but incredibly irritating, voice constantly urging her away from the baby. "Now Mrs. Nichols, why don't you have a nice rest? I'll take care of Hannah."

She couldn't allow that to happen again. She went to the sink and splashed cold water on her face. I've got to get over these flashbacks and lapses, she thought to herself.

Menley settled down at the refectory table and went back to Phoebe Sprague's files. The one marked SHIPWRECKS made fascinating reading. Sloops and packets and schooners and whaling vessels—during the seventeenth and eighteenth centuries so many of them foundered in vicious ocean storms in this area, even right below this house. In those days the Monomoy strip was known as the White Graveyard of the Atlantic.

There was a reference to the *Godspeed,* which in fierce battle had overcome the "pasel of roughes on a pirate ship," and whose captain, Andrew Freeman, personally hauled down the "bloodie flagg" the pirates had run up to the masthead.

The tough side of the captain, Menley thought. He must have

been quite a guy. A mental image of him was forming in her mind. Lean face. Skin creased and roughened by the sun and wind. A close-cropped beard. Strong, irregular features dominated by piercing eyes. She reached for her sketchpad and with quick, sure strokes transferred the mental image to paper.

It was three-fifteen when she looked up again. Adam would be along soon, and Hannah was due to wake up. She had just time enough to glance through one more file. She chose the one marked MEETING ROOMS. On the Cape in the early days, the meeting rooms were the churches.

Phoebe Sprague had copied old records she had obviously found interesting. The pages included stories of fiery ministers who stood in the pulpit expounding the "Appetising of God" and the "Prompt Confusion of the Devil"; timid young ministers who gratefully accepted the salary of fifty pounds per annum and "a house and land and a good supply of firewood cut and brought to the door." Fining a member of the congregation for small violations of the Sabbath had obviously been a common occurrence. There was a long list of minor infractions, like whistling, or allowing a pig to run loose on the Lord's Day.

Then, as she was just about to close the file, Menley came across the name Mehitabel Freeman.

On December 10, 1704, at meeting, several goodwives stood up to testify that in the past month while Captain Andrew Freeman was at sea, they had observed Tobias Knight visiting Mehitabel Freeman "at unseemly hours."

According to the account, Mehitabel, three months pregnant at the time, had jumped up to deny the charge hotly, but Tobias Knight, "humble and contrite, did confess his adultery and welcome the chance to cleanse his soul."

The judgment of the deacons was to commend Tobias Knight for his pious renunciation of his sin and "to refuse to put him to open punishment but sentence him to pay for the said offence the sum of five pounds to the poor of the burough." Mehitabel was given the opportunity to renounce her unchastity. Her furious refusal and scathing denunciation of both Tobias Knight and her accusers sealed her fate.

It was decreed that at the first town meeting six weeks after her delivery, "the adulteress Mehitabel Freeman would be presented to receive forty stripes save one."

My God, Menley thought. How awful. She couldn't have been more than eighteen at the time and, to quote her husband, "of gentle size and strength."

There was a notation in Phoebe Sprague's handwriting: "The *Godspeed* returned from a voyage to England on March 1st and sailed again on March 15th. Was the captain present for the baby's birth? Birth registered as being on June 30th, as child of Andrew and Mehitabel, so no question seems to have been raised that he was the father. He returned mid-August, around which time her sentence would have been carried out. Sailed again immediately, taking baby, and was away nearly two years. Next record of *Godspeed* returning is August 1707."

And all that time she didn't know where her baby was or if it was even alive, Menley thought.

"Hey, you're really into that material."

Menley looked up, startled. "Adam!"

"That's my name."

Clearly relaxed, he was smiling. The visor of his cap shaded his face, but his blue sports shirt was open at the neck and revealed a touch of fresh sunburn, which was also apparent on his arms and legs. He leaned over Menley and put his arms around her. "When you're this deep into research there's no point in asking if you missed me."

Trying to pull herself back into the present, Menley leaned her head against his arm. "I counted every minute you were gone."

"Now that's serious. How's her nibs?"

"Fast asleep."

Menley looked up and saw him glance at the baby monitor. He's making sure it's on, she thought. A cry, passionate and heartbreaking raced through her head. "Oh, love, why can you not trust me?"

36

*W*HEN FRED HENDIN pulled his car into the driveway of his modest Cape Cod home in Barnstable, he quickly learned that the man in the car parked across the street was waiting for him.

Nat Coogan, shield in hand, caught him at the door. "Mr. Hendin?"

Fred glanced at the shield. "I gave at the office." His half smile belied the suggestion of sarcasm.

"I'm not selling tickets for the policemen's ball," Nat said pleasantly, quickly assessing the man in front of him. Late thirties, he thought. Norwegian or Swedish background. The man was barely medium height, with strong arms and neck, faded blondish hair in need of trimming. He was wearing denim overalls and a perspiration-soaked tee shirt.

Hendin inserted his key in the lock. "Come in." He moved and spoke deliberately, as though he thought through everything before speaking or acting.

The room they entered reminded Nat of the first house he'd bought when he and Deb were married. It was made up of essentially small rooms, but there was a compact hominess to the floor plan that always appealed to him.

Fred Hendin's living room might have been furnished from a catalogue. Imitation leather couch and matching recliner, walnut veneer end tables, matching coffee table, artificial flower arrangement, threadbare beige carpet, prim beige curtains that didn't quite reach the windowsills.

The obviously expensive entertainment center housed in a fine cherrywood breakfront seemed out of place. It consisted of a forty-inch television set, VCR and stereo system with CD player. There were shelves of videotapes. Nat unabashedly inspected them, then whistled. "You've got a great collection of classic films," he commented. Then he examined the cassettes and CDs. "You must like forties and fifties music. My wife and I are nuts for it too."

"Jukebox music," Hendin said. "I've been collecting for years."

On the top shelves there were a half-dozen wooden sculptures of sailing vessels. "If I'm being too intrusive just say so," Nat said as he reached up and carefully removed an exquisitely carved schooner. "You did this?"

"Uh-huh. I carve while I'm listening to the music. A good hobby. And relaxing. What do you do when you listen to it?"

Nat replaced the carving and turned to face Hendin. "Sometimes I'll be fixing something around the house or tinkering with the car. If the kids are away and we're in the mood, my wife and I dance."

"You've got me there. I have two left feet. I'm getting myself a beer. Want one? Or a soda?"

"No thanks."

Nat watched Hendin's back as he disappeared through the door frame. Interesting guy, he thought. He looked again at the top shelves of the breakfront, appreciating the finely carved sculptures. He's a real craftsman, he thought. Somehow he could not picture this man and Tina together as a couple.

When Hendin returned he was carrying cans of beer and soda. "It's there if you change your mind," he said as he placed the soda in front of Nat. "All right, what do you want?"

"This is routine. You may have heard or read about Vivian Carpenter Covey's death?"

Hendin's eyes narrowed. "And last year Scott Covey was running around with my girlfriend and you want to know if he's still involved with her."

Nat shrugged. "You don't waste time, Mr. Hendin."

"Fred."

"Okay, Fred."

"Tina and I are going to get married. We started dating early last summer, and then Covey came along. Talk about old smoothie. I warned Tina that she was wasting her time, but listen, you've seen the guy. He fed her a line like you wouldn't believe. Unfortunately, she did."

"How did you feel about it?"

"Sore. And in a funny way, sorry for Tina. She's not as tough as she looks or sounds."

Yes she is, Nat thought.

"It was just as I figured," Hendin said. "Covey did a disappearing act at the end of the summer."

"And Tina came running back to you."

Hendin smiled. "That's what I kind of liked. She's got spunk. I went to see her where she was waitressing and said I knew Covey was gone and I thought he was a louse. She told me not to waste my pity."

"Meaning she was still in touch with him?" Nat asked quickly.

"No way. Meaning she wasn't going to be grateful to me. We only dated once in a while over the winter. She saw a lot of other guys. Then in the spring she finally came around to figuring I'm not so bad."

"Did she tell you she contacted Scott Covey when he moved back here?"

Hendin's forehead became a mass of furrows. "Not right away. She told me a couple of weeks ago. You got to realize Tina isn't the kind to let things go. She was damn sore and had to get it out of her system." He gestured. "See this room, this house? It was my mother's. I moved in a couple of years ago after she died." He took a long swallow of beer.

"When Tina and I started talking about getting married, she told me there was no way she was going to live with all this junk. She's right. I just didn't bother to change anything except for making the breakfront and setting up my films and tapes in it. Tina wants a bigger house. We're looking around for a 'handyman's special.' But what I mean is, Tina says it straight."

Nat consulted his notes. "Tina lives in a rented condo in Yarmouth."

"Uh-huh. Just over the town line, a couple of miles from here. Makes it convenient for the two of us."

"Why did she give up her job at the Daniel Webster Inn and go to work in Chatham? That's a good forty-minute drive from here in summer traffic."

"She liked the Wayside Inn. The hours are better. The tips are good. Listen, Coogan. Stay off Tina's case."

Hendin put his beer down and stood up. There was no mistaking that he was not about to discuss Tina any further.

Nat sank deeper into the chair and became aware of the sharp edges of broken plastic around the worn spot behind his head. "Then of course you totally condoned Tina's visit to Scott Covey when his wife was still missing."

Bull's eye, Nat thought as he watched Hendin's face cloud. A faint flush darkened the skin tone of his face, accentuating the prominent cheekbones. "I think we've talked enough," he said flatly.

37

*I*T HAD BEEN a remarkably pleasant day. As happened occasionally, for some inexplicable reason, Phoebe had experienced brief moments of lucidity.

At one point she'd asked about the children and Henry had quickly placed a conference call. Listening in on an extension, he'd heard the joy in Richard and Joan's voices as they spoke to their mother. For a few minutes there'd been a real exchange.

Then she asked, "And how are . . ."

Henry understood the pause. Phoebe was groping for the names of the grandchildren. Swiftly he provided them.

"I know." Now Phoebe's voice was irritable. "At least you didn't start by saying 'Remember . . .' " Her sigh was an angry reproach.

"Dad," Joan sounded near tears.

"Everything's fine," he warned her.

A click told him that Phoebe had hung up. The wonderful moments of reprieve apparently were over. Henry stayed on the phone long enough to tell his children that the nursing home had an opening on September first.

"Take it for her," Richard said firmly. "We'll come down and stay through Labor Day."

"So will we," Joan echoed.

"You're good kids," Henry said, trying to push back the huskiness that was enveloping his throat.

"I want to be with someone who thinks of me as a kid," his daughter told him, a catch in her voice.

"See you in a couple of weeks, Dad," Richard promised. "Hang in there."

Henry had been on the bedroom extension, Phoebe in her old office. Now Henry hurried to the foyer, the worry that Phoebe in a split second might wander away always with him. But she had not strayed; he found her sitting at the desk where she had spent so many productive hours.

The bottom drawer, which had held so many files, was open and empty. Phoebe was staring at it. The hair she used to wear in a smooth chignon was slipping from the pins that Henry had used to try to secure it in a bun.

She turned when she heard him come in. "My notes." She pointed to the empty drawer. "Where are they?"

Even now he would not refuse her truth. "I lent them to Adam's wife. She wants to consult them for a book she's writing. She'll credit you, Phoebe."

"Adam's wife." The look of irritation that had crossed her face evolved into a questioning frown.

"She was here yesterday. She and Adam live in Remember House. She's going to write a book about the time when the house was built and use the story of Captain Freeman."

Phoebe Sprague's eyes took on a dreamy quality. "Someone should clear Mehitabel's name," she said. "That's what I wanted to do. Someone should investigate Tobias Knight."

She slammed shut the drawer. "I'm hungry. I'm always hungry."

Then as Henry walked toward her, she looked directly at him. "I love you, Henry. Help me, please."

38

*W*HEN HANNAH WOKE UP Menley and Adam went for a late afternoon swim. The Remember House property granted private beach rights, which meant that, while anyone could walk on their beach, no one could settle on it.

The midday warmth was edged now with a hint of early autumn. The breeze was cool, and there were no more strollers passing by.

Adam sat beside Hannah, comfortably propped up in her stroller while Menley swam. "Your mama certainly loves the water, kiddo," he said as he watched Menley dive into the increasingly turbulent waves. Alarmed, he stood up as he saw her venturing farther out.

Finally he walked to the water's edge and waved to her, beckoning her to come in.

Had she not seen him, or pretended not to see him? he wondered as she swam farther out. A strong wave gathered, crested and broke. She rode it in and emerged from the surf, sputtering and smiling, her salt-filled hair hanging around her face.

"Terrific!" she exulted.

"And dangerous. Menley, this is the Atlantic Ocean."

"No kidding. I thought it was a wading pool."

Together they walked across the beach to where Hannah still sat, complacently observing a seagull hopping along the shore.

"Men, I'm not joking. When I'm not here, I don't want you swimming out so far."

She stopped. "And be sure to leave the monitor on when your daughter is asleep. Right? And don't you think it would be nice to have Amy stay overnight? To mind *me*, not Hannah, *me*? Right? And isn't your little weapon the implied threat that we need full-time live-in help because maybe this post-traumatic stress thing is a problem? After all, I was the one who drove the car in front of the train when your son was killed."

Adam grasped her arms. "Menley, stop it. Damn it. You keep blaming me for not forgiving you for Bobby's death, but there's no question of blame here. The only problem is that you can't forgive yourself."

They went back to the house, stiffly aware that each had hurt the other deeply and that they should talk this one through. The phone was ringing as they opened the door, however, and Adam ran for it. Any talk would have to come later. Menley tossed a towel over her damp swimsuit, picked up Hannah and listened.

"Elaine! How are you?"

Menley watched as a look of concern came over his face. What was Elaine saying to him? she wondered. And a moment later, What did he mean when he said, "Thanks for telling me"?

Then his tone changed, becoming cheerful again. "Tomorrow

night? I'm sorry but I'm on my way to New York. But listen, maybe Menley . . ."

No, Menley thought.

Adam covered the receiver with one hand. "Men, Elaine and John are having dinner tomorrow night at the Captain's Table in Hyannis. They want you to join them."

"Many thanks, but I want to just stay in and work. Another time." Menley nuzzled Hannah. "You're a terrific kid," she murmured.

"Men, Elaine really wants you to come. I hate to think of you alone in this place. Why don't you go? You can get Amy to sit for a few hours."

The implied threat, Menley thought. Go and show how sociable you are, or Adam will want someone to be with you at all times. She forced herself to smile. "That sounds wonderful."

Adam was back on the phone. " 'Laine, Menley would love to come. Seven should be fine." He covered the receiver with his hand again and said, "Men, they think it would be a good idea if Amy stays over. They don't want her driving home late."

Menley looked at Adam. She knew that even Hannah had felt the tension in her body. The baby stopped smiling and began to whimper. "Tell *'Laine,"* Menley said, emphasizing the name and Adam's personal abbreviation of it, "that I am perfectly capable of being alone in this or any other house, and if Amy can't drive home at ten o'clock on a summer evening, then she is too immature to be minding my child."

The thaw began at dinner. While Menley fed and bathed Hannah, Adam made a quick trip to the market and returned with fresh lobsters, watercress, green beans and a crisp loaf of Italian bread.

They prepared dinner together, sipped a cold chardonnay while the lobsters steamed and at the end of the meal brought their cups of espresso with them while they strolled to the end of the property and watched powerful waves pound the shoreline.

The taste of the salt-filled wind on her lips calmed Menley. If Adam were the one going through these bouts of anxiety and depression, I'd be worried too, she reminded herself.

Later, when they were going to bed, they checked Hannah for the last time that night. She had moved around in the crib so that she was lying from side to side. Adam straightened her, covered her and for a moment rested his hand on her back.

Something else Menley had gleaned from the files flashed through her mind. In the old Cape days the special love between a father and his baby daughter had been acknowledged and even named. The daughter was her father's *tortience*.

Later, their arms around each other, drifting off to sleep, Adam asked the question he could no longer suppress. "Men," he whispered, "why didn't you want Amy to know you'd been on the widow's walk?"

39

WHEN NAT COOGAN got to work on Tuesday morning, he found a note on his desk. "See me." It was signed by his boss, Frank Shea, the chief of police.

What's up? he wondered as he headed for his boss's office. He found Frank on the phone with the district attorney. Shea's fingers were drumming on the desk. His usual amiable expression was missing.

Nat settled in a chair, listening to the half of the conversation he could hear and guessing the rest.

The heat was on. Graham Carpenter's insurance company had gotten in on the act. They were more than happy to subscribe to Carpenter's theory that his daughter had experienced foul play, that her emerald ring had been forced from her finger by Scott Covey and was now in his possession.

Nat raised his eyebrows as he realized that the next part of the discussion had to do with the study of ocean currents. He gathered that Coast Guard experts were willing to testify that if Vivian Carpenter Covey had been scuba diving where her husband claimed they were when they got separated, her body would not have washed ashore in Stage Harbor but instead would have been carried out toward Martha's Vineyard.

When Shea got off the phone, he said, "Nat, I'm glad you listened to that bird-dog hunch of yours. The DA was very pleased to hear that we already have an active investigation going. It's good that we've got a head start, because when the media get wind of this, it'll turn into a circus. Remember what they did with the von Bulow case."

"Yes, of course. And we face some of the same problems the prosecution did in that case. Innocent or guilty, von Bulow got off because he had a good lawyer. I'm convinced Covey is guilty as sin, but proving it is another matter. He has a damn good lawyer too. It's a lousy break for us that Adam Nichols took on Covey's case."

"We may have a chance to find out how good Nichols is soon enough.

"We're about to find more hard evidence. On the basis of the missing emerald ring and everything else we know, the DA is getting a search warrant for Covey's home and boat. I want you there when his people go in."

Nat got up. "I can hardly wait."

. . .

In the privacy of his own office, Nat gave vent to some of the irritation he felt. Now that it was obvious that the media would pick up the scent on the case and start howling for news, the district attorney was going to have the state police take over the investigation. It's not just that I want to break this case myself, Nat thought. It's that I think it's a stupid grandstand play, rushing it to a grand jury before we have something absolutely solid to go on.

He took off his jacket, rolled up his sleeves and loosened his tie. Now he was comfortable. Deb was always after him not to loosen his tie when they went out to dinner. She'd say, "Nat, you look so nice, but when you pull your tie down and open the top button of your shirt you spoil it. I swear you must have been hanged in a previous incarnation. They say that's the reason some people can't wear anything tight around the neck."

Nat sat at his desk a few moments longer, thinking about Deb, about how lucky he was to have her, thinking about the bond between them, the love and the trust.

He picked up the coffee mug, went out to the machine in the hall, absentmindedly poured a cup and carried it back to the office.

Trust. A good word. How much had Vivian Carpenter trusted her husband? If you could believe Scott Covey, she didn't trust him enough to tell him the full extent of her inheritance.

Seated at his desk again, Nat leaned back and sipped the coffee while he stared at the ceiling. If Vivian had been as insecure as everyone seemed to indicate, wouldn't she have been watching for signs that everything was not right with Covey?

Phone calls. Did Tina ever call Covey at home, and if so, was Vivian aware of it? Vivian's phone bill. For sure she was the one who paid the expenses. Would Covey have ever been dope enough to call Tina from his home? He would have to check that out.

Something else. Vivian's lawyer, the one who prepared the new will after the marriage. It would be worth ambling over to see him.

The phone rang. It was Deb. "I was listening to the news," she said. "There was a big story about an investigation into Vivian Carpenter's death. Did you expect that?"

"I just heard about it." Briefly Nat filled his wife in on his meeting with Jack Shea and what he was planning to do now. He had long ago learned that Deb was an excellent sounding board for him.

"The phone bills are a good idea," Deb said. "I'll bet anything that he wouldn't be dumb enough to call a girlfriend's apartment from home, but you say this Tina is a waitress at the Wayside Inn. Calls from his house to the Inn wouldn't be listed, but you could ask whether Tina got many personal calls there and if anyone knows who made them."

"Very smart," Nat said admiringly. "I've certainly educated you to think like a cop."

"Spare me. But another thing. Go to Vivian's beauty parlor. They're hotbeds of gossip. Or better yet, maybe I should start going there. I might hear something. You told me she went to Tresses, didn't you?"

"Yes."

"I'll make an appointment for this afternoon."

"Are you sure this is strictly business?" Nat asked.

"No, it isn't. I've been dying to get my hair frosted. They do a good job but they're expensive. Now I don't have to feel guilty. Bye, dear."

40

*A*FTER ADAM'S QUESTION about Menley's not wanting Amy to know she'd been on the widow's walk, they had not talked any more but lay unhappily side by side, not touching, each aware that the other was awake. Just before dawn Menley had gotten up to check the baby. She found Hannah sleeping contentedly, the blankets cozy around her.

In the faint glow of the night-light, Menley stood over the crib, drinking in the exquisite little features, the tiny nose, the soft mouth, the lashes that cast shadows on the round cheeks, the wisps of golden hair that had begun to curl around the baby's face.

I can't swear that I *wasn't* on the widow's walk when Amy thought she saw me, but I do know that I would never neglect or forget or hurt Hannah, she thought. I have to understand Adam's concern, she warned herself, but he must realize that I will *not* have a baby-sitter reporting about me to his old buddy Elaine.

That resolve firmly made, it was easier to settle back into bed, and when Adam's arm crept around her, she did not pull away.

At eight o'clock Adam went out for fresh bagels and the newspapers. As they ate and sipped coffee, Menley was aware that they were both trying to put aside the last vestiges of tension. She knew that when he left for New York this afternoon, neither one of them wanted to have the remnants of a quarrel still hanging between them.

He offered her her pick of the newspapers.

She smiled. "You know you want to start with *The New York Times.*"

"Well, maybe."

"That's fine." She opened the first section of the *Cape Cod Times* and a moment later said, "Oh boy, look at this." She slid the paper across the table.

Adam scanned the story she was pointing to, then jumped up. "Damn it! They're really gunning for Scott. Right now there must be a hell of a lot of pressure on the DA to call for a grand jury."

"Poor Scott. Do you think there's a chance they'd actually indict him?"

"I think the Carpenter family is howling for blood, and they've got plenty of pull. I've got to talk to him."

Hannah had had enough of the playpen. Menley picked her up, held her on her lap and gave her the end of a bagel to gnaw on. "Feels good, doesn't it?" she asked. "I think you've got a couple of teeth on the way."

Adam was holding the phone. "Covey's not home and he didn't leave his machine on. He should know enough to keep in touch with me. He has to have seen the paper."

"Unless he went fishing early," Menley suggested.

"Well, if he did, I hope there's nothing in his house that the police will find interesting. You can bet your boots that before the day is over some judge will be signing a search warrant." He slammed down the receiver. "Damn!"

Then he shook his head and walked over to her. "Listen, bad enough I have to go to New York. There's nothing I can do until Covey calls me, so let's not waste our time. You girls game for the beach?"

"Sure. We'll get dressed."

Menley was wearing a flowered cotton robe. Adam smiled down at her. "You look about eighteen," he commented. He smoothed her hair, then rested his hand on her cheek. "You're an awfully pretty lady, Menley McCarthy Nichols."

Menley's heart melted. One of the good moments, she thought— the kind I used to take for granted. I love him so much.

But then Adam asked, "What time did you say Amy is coming?"

She had planned to tell him this morning that this would be Amy's last day, but she didn't want to start a quarrel. Not now. "I asked her to be here around two," she said, trying to sound casual. "I'll work on the book this afternoon after I come back from the airport. Oh, I forgot to tell you. Jan Paley found some interesting facts about Captain Andrew Freeman. She's dropping in around four."

"That's great," he said, stroking her head. She knew Adam's

enthusiastic reaction was an indication of his desire to have her surrounded by people.

Just don't suggest that I ask Jan to stay the night, she thought bitterly, clutching the baby as she pushed his hand away and got up.

41

SCOTT COVEY did not realize how deeply the meeting with Adam the previous day had upset him until he took the boat out early Tuesday morning. The word was that the blues were running off Sandy Point. When the sun rose at 6:00 A.M. he was anchored in the location where they'd supposedly been spotted.

As he sat patiently holding the rod, Scott forced himself to think of the warnings Adam Nichols had given him. And Adam had said he was going to have his own investigator on him to find any "blemishes" he might have in his background.

It occurred to him that he had not spoken to his father and stepmother in five years. It's not my fault, he thought. They moved to San Mateo; her family is all around, and when I go out there's no room for me to stay overnight. But there might be questions about why his family had not come to either the wedding reception or the funeral service. He decided to call his father and ask for his support.

It was another beautiful August day in a string of sunny, low-humidity days. The horizon was dotted with boats ranging in size from dinghys to yachts.

Vivian had wanted a sailboat. "I just bought this one so I could get used to handling a boat on my own," she'd explained. "That's why I called it *Viv's Toy.*"

Now, riding in the boat with that name painted on the side, he felt weighted down. When he'd been walking down the dock this morning, Scott had seen several men standing next to the boat, looking at it and talking quietly. Speculating about the accident, no doubt.

As soon as this was settled, he'd change the name. No. Better than that. He'd sell the boat.

A strong tug on his line brought him sharply back to the present. He had a big one to land.

Twenty minutes later a thirty-two-pound striped bass was thrashing wildly on the deck.

Perspiration streaming from his forehead, Scott observed its dying struggle. Then revulsion seized him. He cut the line, managed to get a grip on the flailing fish and threw it back into the ocean. He had no stomach for fishing today, he decided, and headed for home.

On impulse Scott went to Clancy's in Dennisport for lunch. It was a cheerful, gregarious place, and he felt the need to be in the company of a lot of other people. He sat at the bar and ordered a beer and a hamburger. Several times he noticed the glances other people directed at him.

When the stools next to him were vacated, two attractive young women grabbed them. They quickly opened up a conversation by explaining that this was their first visit to the Cape and asked him if he could tell them the fun places to go.

Scott swallowed the last of his hamburger. "You're in one of the best," he said pleasantly and signaled for his bill. That's all I need, he thought. With my luck Sprague will come waltzing in and see me talking to these girls.

At least tonight he'd be able to relax. Elaine Atkins and her boyfriend had invited him to dinner at the Captain's Table in Hyannis. They were bringing Menley Nichols too, and she'd been genuinely kind to him.

On the way home he decided to stop for a paper. He tossed it on the seat beside him and did not open it until he was in the house. That was when he saw the front page headline: CARPENTER FAMILY DEMANDS ANSWERS.

"Oh, Christ," he murmured and rushed to the phone. His call was to Adam Nichols, but there was no answer.

An hour later the front doorbell pealed. He went to the door and opened it. A half-dozen grim-faced men were standing there. Scott only recognized one of them, the detective from Chatham who'd questioned him earlier.

In a daze he saw a piece of paper waved before him, then heard the frightening words, "We have a search warrant for these premises."

42

MENLEY GOT BACK from dropping Adam at the airport at quarter of two. The phone was ringing as she opened the door, and still clutching Hannah in one arm, she rushed to answer it.

It was her mother calling from Ireland. After the first joyous exchange, she found herself trying to reassure her mother that all was well. "What do you mean you have a feeling that something's wrong, Mom? That's crazy. The baby's great . . . We're having a wonderful time . . . The house we've rented is fascinating . . . We're even thinking of buying it . . . Weather's wonderful . . . Tell me about Ireland. How's the itinerary I made out for you?"

She had been to Ireland a half-dozen times on writing assignments and had helped plan her mother's trip. It was a relief to hear that the arrangements were highly satisfactory. "And how are Phyllis and Jack enjoying it?"

"They're having a great time," her mother said. Then she lowered her voice, adding, "Needless to say Phyl is hell-bent on looking up her family tree. We spent two days in Boyle while she was going through old county records. But score one for her. She did locate her great-grandfather's farm in Ballymote."

"I never doubted she would," Menley said, laughing, then tried to persuade Hannah to coo and gurgle for Grandma.

Before the conversation ended, Menley again assured her mother that she was feeling fine, that she'd hardly had a trace of PTSD.

"And wouldn't it be nice if that were true?" she asked Hannah ruefully when she hung up the phone.

Amy arrived a few minutes later. Menley greeted her coolly and knew Amy was perceptive enough to pick up the change in her attitude.

While Amy put Hannah in her carriage and took her outside, Menley settled down to the Sprague files. A note Phoebe Sprague had written about the meeting house built in 1700 intrigued her. After the building statistics—"20 ft by 32 and 13 feet in the walls," the names of the men who were appointed to "get the timber and frame the house," "to bring boards and planks" and "to buy more finishing"—Mrs. Sprague had written, "Nickquenum (Remember House) was much larger than the meeting house, which probably caused a great deal of discontent in the town. People were undoubtedly ready to believe the worst of Mehitabel Freeman."

Then in what was clearly a later memo she had penciled in, "Tobias Knight," followed by a question mark.

The builder. What was the question about him? Menley wondered.

Shortly before three an agitated Scott Covey phoned, looking for Adam. The police had arrived with a search warrant. He wanted to know if there was anything he could do to stop them.

"Adam tried to reach you this morning," Menley said, and gave him Adam's New York office number. "I do know this," she told him, "once a judge issues a warrant, no lawyer can get it canceled, but it can be challenged later in court." Then she added softly, "I'm so sorry, Scott."

Jan Paley arrived promptly at four. Menley had the feeling of being on firm ground when she greeted the handsome older woman. "It's so kind of you to do research for me."

"Not at all. When Tom and I became interested in this house, we used to talk to Phoebe Sprague about it. She was fascinated by the story of poor Mehitabel. I'm glad Henry lent you Phoebe's papers." She glanced at the table. "I can see you are caught up in them," she said, smiling as she surveyed the stacks of files.

Menley checked on Amy and the baby, put on a kettle for tea, then placed cups and sugar and milk at the end of the table.

"Believe it or not, I have a computer and printer and all the trimmings set up in the library, but there's something so inviting about this kitchen, or keeping room I guess I should call it, that I'm happiest working here."

Jan Paley nodded in understanding. She ran her hand over a protruding brick on the face of the massive fireplace. "I can see you're very into the spirit of the house. In the early days the keeping room was the only room they really lived in. The winters were so bitterly cold. The family slept in the bedrooms under piles of quilts and then rushed down here. And think about it. When you have a party at home, no matter how much room you have, the guests will usually manage to work their way into the kitchen. Same principle. Warmth and food and life."

She gestured toward the pantry door opposite the fireplace.

"That used to be the borning room," she said. "It's where the woman gave birth or where the sick person was brought to be nursed back to health or to die. Obviously it made sense. The fire kept that room warm as well."

For a moment her eyes brightened, and she blinked back tears. "I hope you do decide to buy this place," she said. "It could make a wonderful home, and you have the feel for it."

"I believe I do," Menley agreed. It was on the tip of her tongue to tell this intelligent, sympathetic woman about the unexplainable business of the figure on the widow's walk, of Hannah being moved during the night to the cradle and the sound of the train rushing through the house, but she could not. She did not want anyone else to look at her as though speculating on her emotional stability.

Instead she busied herself at the stove, where the kettle was now whistling, poured boiling water into the teapot to warm it and reached for the tea cannister.

"You know how to make a cup of tea," Jan Paley observed.

"I hope so. My grandmother had a heart attack if anyone used teabags. She said that the Irish and the English always knew how to make a proper cup."

"A lot of the early sea captains carried tea as part of their cargo," Jan Paley commented. As they sipped the tea and nibbled on cookies, she reached for her oversized shoulder bag. "I told you I'd found some interesting material on Captain Freeman." She brought out a manila envelope and handed it to Menley. "Something that occurred to me: Captain Freeman's mother was a Nickerson. From the beginning the various branches of the family began to spell the name differently—Nickerson, Nicholson, Nichols. Was your husband a descendant of the first William Nickerson?"

"I have no idea. I do know his ancestor came over in the early sixteen hundreds," Menley said. "Adam never was terribly interested in tracing the line."

"Well, if you do decide to buy this house, he might become

interested. Captain Freeman could turn out to be a thirty-fifth cousin, generations removed."

Jan watched as Menley began to read quickly through the material from the Brewster Library. "The coup I promised is on the last page."

"Great." Menley reached for a file on the table. "This is some of the data I've culled so far. I'd like you to take a look at it."

As she turned to the last page of the Brewster material, Menley heard Jan Paley's disappointed protest: "Oh, look, you already have the captain's picture, and I thought I was going to give you a treat by digging it up for you."

Menley felt her lips go dry.

Jan was looking at the sketch Menley had made when she envisioned how she would portray the mature Captain Andrew Freeman in the new David book.

She was staring down at the copy Jan had made of the sketch of Captain Andrew Freeman at the wheel of his schooner.

The faces were identical.

43

*S*COTT COVEY carried a beer out onto the deck while the team of policemen and detectives searched his home. His face set in grim lines, he sat with his back to the Sprague house. The last thing he needed was to see Henry Sprague watching what he had helped set in motion. *If Tina's name hadn't come into this, the cops wouldn't be here now,* was the thought that he could not shake off.

Then he tried to reassure himself. He had nothing to worry about. What did they expect to find? No matter how much they searched, there was nothing in the house to incriminate him.

Adam Nichols had told him to stay put until everything about Viv's death and will was settled, but Scott knew he was beginning to hate this house and to hate the Cape as well. He knew that for him it would always be like living in a goldfish bowl.

He'd worked last winter in the office of a struggling playhouse in Boca Raton, Florida. He had liked it there, so that was where he would buy a home when this was all over. Maybe he would even buy into that playhouse, too, instead of starting a new one here, the way he and Viv had planned.

Think ahead, he urged himself. They have nothing on me and nothing to go on except suspicion and jealousy and dirty minds. There is nothing that will stand up in a court of law.

"This place is clean," an investigator from the district attorney's office told Nat Coogan.

"It's too clean," Nat snapped as he continued to go through the desk. What little personal mail they had found was addressed to Vivian, letters from friends congratulating her on her marriage; postcards from cousins traveling in Europe.

There was a small, neat pile of bills, all marked paid. No mortgage; no credit card installments; no car loan: sure keeps things simple, Nat mused. Also helps one to stay mobile, with nothing to tie him down.

The phone bill was not very high. He knew Tina's phone number but there had not been a single call to it in the three months of the marriage.

He also had Vivian's lawyer's phone number. There were no calls to him in the last three months.

The bank records were somewhat interesting. Vivian kept a single checking account in the local bank, and it was in her name only. If Covey had his own money, he didn't keep it locally. If he had been dependent on her for cash, she had been doling it out to him. Of course, a good lawyer could argue that the lack of records in the house validated Covey's story that his wife had not admitted to him the extent of her holdings.

The Carpenters had told Nat about the house being stripped of pictures of Vivian. Nat found them in the guest room. Covey had also prepared a box to return to the family. He had not included any pictures in which he appeared with Vivian. Nat grudgingly acknowledged that that did show sensitivity.

On the other hand, the pictures of Covey and Vivian together were piled on the floor of a storage closet. Not exactly the place you keep sentimental objects, he thought.

Vivian's clothes were packed neatly in her expensive luggage. Who was going to be the recipient? he wondered. Not Tina. She was too heavy for them. Nat's bet was that the clothes and suitcases were headed for a secondhand shop.

He hadn't really expected that they would come across the emerald ring. Even if Covey had it, he wouldn't be stupid enough to keep it where it could be found. Vivian apparently wasn't really into jewelry. They had found her engagement ring, some chains and bracelets and earrings, all in a small jewelry box in the master bedroom. Nothing, including the engagement ring, had any significant value.

Nat decided to make his own inspection of the garage. Attached to the house, it was a good-sized structure, capable of holding two cars. Shelves in the back were neatly stacked with diving and fishing gear, an ice chest, some tools—the usual paraphernalia. The diving gear Vivian had been wearing when her body washed in was still being evaluated.

Covey and Vivian had only one car, a late-model BMW. Nat knew that it had belonged to Vivian. The more he'd seen this afternoon, the more he'd thought of his mother's disgust when her older sister married years ago. "Jane's worked all these years for everything she has," his mother had fumed. "What did she see in that

miserable leech? He went into the marriage with one set of underwear."

It looked to Nat as though Covey had brought about the same
amount of worldly goods to his union with Vivian.

Then his eyes brightened. The BMW was on the left side of the
garage. The floor on the right side was stained with oil.

Nat got down on his knees. There was no sign of oil drippings
from the BMW, and he knew there were no oil stains in the driveway.

Who had parked here, not once but a number of times, he wondered, and why would a visitor's car be driven into the garage? One
reason, of course, would be to ensure that no one would know it
was there.

Nat knew that his next stop would be to see if Tina's car leaked
oil.

44

*D*EB COOGAN was having a marvelous time.
Usually she washed her own short, curly hair, toweled it dry and
went every six weeks or so to the small hairdresser's at the other
end of town to have it shaped. This was her first visit to Tresses,
the premier beauty salon in Chatham.

She was relaxed, thoroughly enjoying the luxurious pink-and-
green interior of the chic salon, the prolonged shampoo that included a neck massage, the frosting that brought gold highlights to
her medium-brown hair, the hot-oil manicure and the first-time

pedicure. Deciding that it was her civic duty to try to get into conversation with as many operators as possible, she'd elected to have all these services.

Any fear she had that the salon's employees might be reluctant to talk disappeared quickly. Everyone in the place was buzzing with the news that Scott Covey might be a suspect in his wife's death.

Deb found it easy to get Beth, who shampooed her hair, to talk about the late Vivian Carpenter Covey, but all she learned was that Beth nearly fainted when she read that Vivian was worth so much money. "Never a tip to me and just a chintzy one to the hairdresser. And take my word for it. One drop of water got near her ear and she'd howl about her sensitive eardrums. I ask you, how sensitive could they be? She was always bragging about learning to scuba dive."

The hairdresser was a bit more charitable. "Oh, we all had a turn having Vivian as a client. She was always worried that she didn't look just right. And it was always the operator's fault, of course, if she thought she didn't. It's really a shame. She was a pretty woman but shifted between being on her Carpenter family high horse and getting upset about everything. She'd drive a saint crazy."

The manicurist was also gossipy but, unfortunately, not especially helpful: "She was crazy about that husband of hers. Isn't *he* gorgeous? One day he was crossing the street to pick her up, and one of our new girls saw him through the window. She said, 'Excuse me, I'm going to run out and throw myself in front of that hunk.' She was joking, of course, but wouldn't you know she was just finishing Vivian's nails? Talk about going through the roof. Vivian yelled at her. 'Why does every tramp in the world want to make a play for my husband?' "

Want to make a play, Deb thought. That suggests he did not take them up on it. "When did that happen?" she asked.

"Oh, about two or three weeks before she drowned."

It was when she was having her pedicure that Debbie knew her afternoon had not been an extravagant waste. The pedicures were given in a separate, screened-off area with two raised chairs side by side over footbaths.

"Try to keep your toes still, Mrs. Coogan," said Marie, the pedicurist. "I don't want to cut you."

"I can't help it," Debbie confessed. "I have very ticklish toes."

Marie laughed. "So does one of my other clients. She almost never has pedicures, but when she was getting married we all told her she absolutely had to have pretty feet."

Recognizing an opening, Debbie brought up Vivian's name. "When you think that Vivian Carpenter only lived three months after she was married . . ." She sighed and let her voice trail off.

"I know. It was awful, wasn't it. Sandra, the client I was telling you about, the one who never wants to have pedicures?"

"Yes."

"Well, the day she had one for her wedding, she was sitting right in this chair and Vivian was next to her. They started talking. Sandra's the kind who tells you all her business."

"What was she talking about that day?"

"She was telling Vivian that she was on her way to her lawyer's office to meet her fiancé to sign a very tight prenuptial agreement."

Debbie sat up straighter. "What did Vivian say?"

"Well, she said something like, 'I think if you can't go into a marriage loving and trusting each other, you shouldn't go into it.'"

Marie applied lotion to Debbie's feet and began to massage them. "Sandra wasn't the kind to take that lying down. She told Vivian that she'd been married once before, and they broke up after three years. Sandra has a couple of boutiques. Her ex claimed he helped her a lot because—get this—at night she talked about her expansion plans to him. He got a big settlement. Sandra said when she married him he didn't know what the word 'boutique' meant and he still didn't know what it meant when they separated. She told Vivian that when one spouse has money and the other doesn't, if the marriage breaks up, the one with money pays through the nose."

"What did Vivian say?" Debbie asked.

"Vivian looked kind of upset. She said that that was very interesting and a good point. She said, 'Maybe I'd better call my lawyer.' "

"Was she joking?"

"I don't know. With her you never could tell." Marie pointed to the trays of polish. "Same color as your fingers, strawberry sorbet?"

"Please."

Marie shook the bottle, unscrewed the cap and with careful strokes began to paint Debbie's toenails. "Such a shame," she sighed. "Underneath, Vivian was really a nice person, just so insecure. That day she was talking to Sandra was the last time I ever saw her. She died three days later."

45

THE CAPTAIN'S TABLE restaurant, housed in the Hyannis Yacht Club, overlooked the harbor.

As a longtime member of the club and frequent customer of the restaurant, John had secured a desirable table in the dining room's glassed-in addition. He insisted that Menley sit facing the window so that she could enjoy the view of Nantucket Sound, the graceful sailboats, the sleek yachts and the ponderous island steamships that brought tourists back and forth from Martha's Vineyard and Nantucket.

When Menley had left Remember House at quarter of seven, Hannah was already tucked in for the night. Now as she sipped champagne, a thought haunted her. Was there a likeness of Captain Andrew Freeman in the Sprague files, one that she had glimpsed and that had made a subconscious impression on her as she was going through that vast mound of papers? That was what she let Jan Paley believe. And then she wondered, how often in the last few days had she used the words "unconscious" and "subconscious"? She reminded herself that even the infrequent tranquilizers she was taking could make her feel fuzzy.

She shook her head to push away the distracting thoughts. Now that she was at the restaurant, she was glad she had come. Maybe that was why Adam was anxious for her to have people around. She used to be a truly outgoing person, but after Bobby's death, it had become a real effort to try to seem cheerful and interested in anyone or anything.

During her pregnancy with Hannah, she'd been writing the last David book and was glad to be totally involved with finishing it. She had found that when she wasn't busy, she would start to worry that something might go wrong, that maybe she would miscarry or the baby would be stillborn.

And since Hannah's birth, she'd been battling the harrowing episodes of PTSD—flashbacks, anxiety attacks, depression.

A pretty dreary litany of problems for a man like Adam who has a superstressful job to live with, she thought. Earlier she had been so resentful of Adam's transparent efforts to make her go out, to have Amy stay overnight. Now she desperately wished he were beside her at this table.

Menley knew she was at last looking like her old self. Her waistline was completely back to normal, and tonight she had chosen to wear a pale gray silk suit with a bolero jacket and wide-cut slacks. Charcoal gray cuffs accentuated the charcoal gray camisole. Her hair, bleaching from the sun, was tied back in a simple knot at the nape of her neck. The silver-and-diamond choker and matching earrings Adam had given her when they were engaged complemented the outfit. She realized that it felt good to dress up again.

It had been a not-unpleasant surprise to find that Scott Covey was John and Elaine's other guest. Menley was aware of the appreciation in his eyes when the maître d' brought her to the table. A part of his charm, she acknowledged to herself, was that Scott seemed to be oblivious to his astonishing good looks. His manner was, if anything, a trifle shy, and he had the gift of paying close attention to whoever was speaking.

He referred briefly to the search warrant. "Your advice was right, Menley. When I reached Adam, he told me he couldn't do anything about it, but he did tell me to stay in closer touch and leave the answering machine on all the time."

"Adam's a very decisive guy," Elaine smiled.

"I'm damn glad he's in my corner," Covey said, but then added, "let's not spoil the evening by talking about it. One consolation about having nothing to hide: It's a terrible invasion when the police are ransacking your home to try to prove you're a criminal, but there's a big difference between being outraged and being worried."

Heatedly, Elaine snapped, "Don't get me started. The Carpenters should have shown half the concern for Vivian when she was alive as they think they're showing now that she's dead. I tell you, when that poor kid bought her house three years ago, she seemed so alone. I brought over a bottle of champagne later, and it was pathetic how grateful she was. She was just sitting there by herself."

"Elaine," John warned.

When she saw the tears welling in Scott's eyes, Elaine bit her lip. "Oh God, Scott, I'm so sorry. You're right. Let's change the subject."

"I will," John beamed. "We're having our wedding reception here, and you two are the first to be officially notified that the exact time is four o'clock on Saturday, November twenty-sixth. We even decided on the menu: turkey stew." His laugh was a *heh-heh-heh* sound. "Don't forget, that's two days after Thanksgiving." He squeezed Elaine's hand.

Elaine looked like a bride, Menley thought. Her white cowl-neck dress was set off by a pearl-and-gold necklace. Her soft-brushed blond hair flattered her thin, somewhat angular face. The large pear-shaped diamond on her left hand was a clear and present sign of John's generosity.

And the downside, Menley decided over dessert, is that John *does* love to talk about insurance and should *not* tell jokes. She was used to Adam's quick, sharp wit, and it was excruciating to hear John begin, yet again, "That reminds me of a story about . . ."

At one point, during a tedious recital, Scott Covey raised an eyebrow to her, and she felt her lips twitch. Coconspirator, she thought.

But John was a solid, good man, and a lot of women probably envied Elaine.

Still when they rose from the table, Menley was more than ready, even anxious, to get home. John suggested that he and Elaine follow her to the door to make sure she arrived safely.

"Oh, no, please, I'm fine." She tried not to sound irritated. I'm developing too much of a knee-jerk reaction to any hint of protection, she thought.

Hannah was peacefully asleep when Menley arrived home. "She's been great," Amy said. "Do you want me to come by tomorrow around the same time, Mrs. Nichols?"

"No, that won't be necessary," Menley said evenly. "I'll be in touch." She regretted the hurt she saw in Amy's crestfallen face but realized that she was looking forward to being alone with Hannah until Adam got back from New York tomorrow.

It was harder to go to sleep tonight. It wasn't that she was nervous. It was just that in her mind she kept going through the pile of pictures and sketches in Phoebe Sprague's files. She'd thought she'd barely glanced at them. They were mostly sketches of early settlers, some of them unnamed, and landmark buildings; property maps; sailing ships—an unsorted mishmash, really.

Was it possible that she'd come across one that didn't have a name attached to it and subconsciously copied it when she was trying to envision Captain Andrew Freeman? His looks weren't that unusual. A lot of the early-eighteenth-century seamen had short, dark beards.

And then by coincidence, I'd actually drawn his face? she mocked herself. *Subconsciously, unconsciously*—those words again, she thought. Dear God what is happening to me?

Three times before 2:00 A.M. she got up to check on Hannah and found her in a sound sleep. In just a little over a week up here, she looks bigger, Menley mused as she lightly touched the small outstretched hand.

Finally she felt her own eyes growing heavy and knew she soon would be drifting off. She settled back in bed and touched Adam's pillow, missing him acutely. Had he phoned tonight? Probably not. Amy would have told her. But why hadn't he tried around ten-thirty? He knew she'd be home by then.

Or I could have called him, Menley thought. I should have let him know I'd enjoyed the evening. He might have been afraid to call me for fear I'd be complaining about going out.

Oh, God, I just want to be myself, I just want to be normal.

At four o'clock the sound of a train roaring toward her thundered through the house.

She was at the railroad crossing, trying to get through it in time. The train was coming.

She bolted up, shoved her fingers in her ears, trying to drown out the sound, and stumbled wildly to the nursery. She had to save Bobby.

Hannah was screaming, her arms flailing, her legs kicking the blankets away.

The train was going to kill her too, Menley thought, her mind racing to grasp some sense of reality in all the confusion.

But then it was over. The train was going away, the clickedy-click of the wheels vanishing into the night.

Hannah was screaming.

"Stop it," Menley shouted at the baby. "Stop it! Stop it!"

Hannah screeched louder.

Menley sank down on the bed opposite the crib, trembling, hugging herself, afraid to trust herself to pick up Hannah.

And then from downstairs, she heard him calling her, his voice excited and joyous, summoning her to him, "Mommy, Mommy."

Arms outstretched, sobbing his name, she rushed to find Bobby.

August 10th

46

*T*HE DISTRICT ATTORNEY called a meeting for Wednesday afternoon at his office in the Barnstable courthouse. Scheduled to be present were the three officers from his staff who had participated in the search of the Covey house, the medical examiner who had conducted the autopsy, two expert witnesses from the Coast Guard group in Woods Hole—one to testify about the currents the day Vivian Carpenter drowned, the second to discuss the condition of the diving gear she was wearing—and Nat Coogan.

"That means I get an early start today," Nat told Debbie on Wednesday morning. "I want to take a look at Tina's car and see if it drips oil, and I want to talk to Vivian's lawyer to see if she contacted him."

Deb was placing a new batch of waffles on her husband's plate. Their two sons had already finished breakfast and taken off for their summer jobs.

"I shouldn't feed these to you," she sighed. "You're supposed to lose twenty pounds."

"I need the energy today, doll."

"Sure you do." Debbie shook her head.

From the breakfast table Nat looked admiringly at the glints of light in her hair. "You do look great," he said. "I'll take you out to dinner tonight to show you off. By the way, you never did tell me how much it cost to get all that done."

"Eat your waffles," Debbie said as she passed him the syrup. "You don't want to know."

Nat's first stop was the Wayside Inn. He poked his head in the dining room. As he had hoped, Tina was working. Then he went to the office, where he found only the secretary.

"Just a question," he said, "about Tina."

The secretary shrugged. "I guess it's all right. They let you look at her file the other day."

"Who would know if she received many personal calls here?" Nat asked.

"She wouldn't have received them. Unless it's a real emergency, we take a message and the waitress calls back on her break."

I guess it's a blind alley, he thought. "Would you happen to know what kind of car Tina drives?"

She pointed out the window to the parking lot in the back of the building. "That green Toyota is Tina's."

The car was at least ten years old. Rust spots on the fenders were deteriorating into breaks in the steel. Grunting as he squatted down, Nat peered at the undercarriage. Glistening drops of oil were clearly visible. There were stains on the macadam.

Just as I thought, he exulted. He labored to his feet and looked inside through the driver's window. Tina's car was sloppy. Tape cassettes were scattered on the front passenger seat. Empty soda cans were clumped on the floor. He looked through the back window. Newspapers and magazines were strewn on the seat. And then, half covered by paper bags, he saw two empty pint-sized oil cans on the floor.

He hurried into the office again. "One last question—by any chance does Tina take a turn at the reservations desk?"

"Well, yes, she does," the secretary replied. "She's assigned there from eleven to eleven-thirty, during Karen's break."

"So she could have received personal calls there?"

"I suppose so."

"Thank you very much." Nat's step was buoyant as he headed for his next stop, a chat with Vivian's lawyer.

Leonard Wells, Esquire, had a comfortable suite of offices a block from Main Street in Hyannis. A reserved-looking man in his fifties, with frameless glasses that magnified thoughtful brown eyes, he was crisply dressed in a beige lightweight suit. Nat had the immediate impression that Wells was the kind of man who never opened his collar and loosened his tie in public.

"You are aware, Detective Coogan, that I've already been visited by the district attorney's staff, the Carpenter family's attorney and the representative of the insurance company that carried the policy on the emerald ring. I fail to understand how much more I can contribute to the investigation."

"Perhaps you can't, sir," Nat said pleasantly. "But there's always the chance that something has been overlooked. I do, of course, know the terms of the will."

"Every cent Vivian had, as well as her home, boat, car and jewelry, were inherited by her new husband." Frosty disapproval dripped from Wells' voice.

"Who was the beneficiary of her prior will?"

"There was no prior will. Vivian came to me three years ago, at the time she inherited the principal of her trust, five million dollars."

"Why did she come to you? I mean, surely her family has lawyers."

"I'd done some work for one of her friends, who apparently was quite satisfied with me. And Vivian said at the time that she did not want to be represented by her family's legal advisors. She asked my advice about which bank I would suggest she go to in order to open a safety deposit box. She wanted the name of a conservative broker with whom she could review her considerable stock portfolio. She asked my advice about her potential heirs."

"She wanted to make out a will?"

"No, she specifically did *not* want to make one out. She wanted to know who would inherit in case of her death. I told her it would be her family."

"She was satisfied with that?" Nat asked.

"She told me she didn't want to leave it as a gift to them because they didn't deserve it, but since there was no one in the world she gave a damn about, they might just as well have it de facto. Of course, all that changed when she met Covey."

"Did you urge her to have a prenuptial agreement?"

"It was too late. She was already married. I did urge her to sign a more complex will. I pointed out that the way the will stood, her husband would inherit everything, and that she should write in provisions for unborn children. She said she'd face that issue when she became pregnant. I also urged her to consider the fact that if the marriage did fail, there were steps she should be aware of that would protect her assets."

Nat looked around the room. Paneled walls with a fine patina; law books stacked neatly on floor-to-ceiling shelves behind the mahogany desk. Handsomely framed English hunting scenes; an Oriental area rug. The overall effect was harmonious good taste, an appropriate background for Leonard Wells. Nat decided he liked this man.

"Mr. Wells, did Vivian consult with you often?"

"No. I do understand that she took my advice to keep only a relatively modest checking account in the local bank. She was satisfied with the securities expert I recommended and had quarterly meetings with him in Boston. She left the key to her safety deposit box in my office. When she occasionally came in to get it, we'd exchange pleasantries."

"Why did she leave her safety deposit box key here?" Nat asked.

"Vivian tended to be careless. Last year she lost the key twice and had to pay a heavy replacement fee. Since the bank is right next door, she decided to make us custodians. While she was alive she was the only one with access. Since her death, of course, the contents have been taken out and listed, as I'm sure you know."

"Did Vivian call you three days before she died?"

"Yes. The call came while I was on vacation."

"Do you know why she was contacting you?"

"No, I don't. She wasn't looking for her key and would not speak to my associate. She left word for me to phone as soon as I returned. Unfortunately, by then she'd been missing two days."

"What was her manner when she spoke to your secretary? Did she seem upset?"

"Vivian was always upset if people she wanted to see weren't readily available to her."

Not much help there, Nat thought. Then he asked, "Did you ever meet Scott Covey, Mr. Wells?"

"Only once. At the reading of the will."

"What did you think of him?"

"My opinion, of course, is just that. Prior to meeting him, I'd already decided in my own mind that he was a gold digger who had charmed a vulnerable, highly emotional young woman. I still feel that it is a disgrace that an entire Carpenter fortune will be enjoyed by a stranger. There are plenty of distant Carpenter cousins who could use a windfall. I confess that afterward I felt differently. I was most favorably impressed by Scott Covey. He seemed genuinely heartsick about his wife's death. And unless he's a magnificent actor, he was stunned to realize the extent of her fortune."

47

*H*ENRY SPRAGUE had a bad taste in his mouth. Tuesday afternoon he'd observed the police cars when they pulled up to Scott Covey's driveway. Feeling like a Peeping Tom, he had watched from the side window as what he assumed to be a search warrant was handed to Covey. Later, when he and Phoebe were sitting on the deck, he had been uncomfortably aware of Covey sitting on his deck, his posture reflecting dejection and despair.

If it weren't for seeing that Tina woman in the Cheshire Pub, I wouldn't have one single reason to suspect Scott Covey, Henry had reminded himself during the sleepless night.

He remembered back to the first time he had met Phoebe. She had been a doctoral candidate at Yale. He had an M.B.A. from Amos Tuck and was in the family import-export business. From the minute he laid eyes on her, the other girls he had dated became unimportant. One of them, her name was Kay, had really been hurt and had kept calling him.

Suppose I had agreed to see Kay after I was married, just to talk it out, and someone misinterpreted the meeting? Henry thought. Could that be the case here?

On Wednesday morning, he knew what he had to do. Betty, their longtime cleaning woman, was there, and he knew he could trust her to keep an eye on Phoebe.

Sensing that he might be told to stay home, he did not phone Scott. Instead at ten o'clock he walked across the lawn and rang the back doorbell. Through the screen he could see Scott, seated at the kitchen table, drinking coffee and reading the newspaper.

Henry reminded himself that Covey had no reason to look pleased when he realized who his visitor was.

He came to the door but did not open it. "What do you want, Mr. Sprague?"

Henry did not mince words. "I feel I owe you an apology."

Covey was wearing a sports shirt, khaki shorts and leather thongs. His dark blond hair was damp, as though he'd just showered. His frown disappeared. "Why don't you come in?"

Without asking, he got another mug from the cabinet and poured coffee. "Vivian told me that you're a coffee-holic."

It was good, even excellent, coffee, Henry was pleased to note. He took the seat opposite Covey at the small table and sipped quietly for a few moments. Then, choosing his words carefully, he tried to convey to Scott his regret that he had told the detective about meeting Tina that afternoon in the pub.

He liked the fact that Covey did not demur. "Look, Mr. Sprague, I understand that you did what you felt you had to do. I also understand where the police are coming from and the attitude of Viv's family and friends. I do have to point out, Viv didn't have many friends who really cared about her. I'm just glad if you can begin to realize it's tough as hell to be missing my wife so much and at the same time have people treat me like a murderer."

"Yes, I think I'm beginning to understand."

"You know what's really scary?" Scott asked. "It's the way the Carpenters are stirring everyone up; there's a damn good chance I'll be indicted for murder."

Henry stood up. "I've got to get back. If there's anything I can do to help you, count on me. I should not have allowed myself to be talked into gossiping. I can promise you this: If I'm asked to testify, I'll say loud and clear that from the day you and Vivian were married, I witnessed the transformation of a very unhappy young woman."

"That's all I ask of you, sir," Scott Covey said. "If everyone would tell the simple truth, I'd be all right."

"Henry."

Both men turned as Phoebe opened the screen door and walked in. She looked around, her eyes clouded. "Did I tell you about Tobias Knight?" she asked vaguely.

"Phoebe . . . Phoebe . . ." Jan Paley was a few steps behind her. "Oh, Henry, I'm so sorry. I dropped by for a minute and I told Betty to go ahead with her work, that I'd sit with Phoebe. I turned my back and . . ."

"I understand," Henry said. "Come along, dear." He shook Scott's hand reassuringly, then put his arm around his wife and patiently led her home.

48

MENLEY'S FRANTIC search of the downstairs rooms had not revealed where Bobby's voice was coming from. Finally Hannah's wails had penetrated her consciousness, and she had made her way back to the nursery. By then Hannah's sobs had become gulping hiccups.

"Oh, sweet baby," Menley had murmured, shocked into awareness that Hannah had been crying for a long time. She had picked up her daughter, wrapped the covers around her and dropped onto the bed opposite the crib.

Crawling under the quilt, she had slid her shoulder strap down and put the baby's lips to her breast. She had not been able to nurse, but her breast pulsated as the tiny lips sucked at her nipple. Finally the hiccups had subsided, and Hannah had slept contentedly in her arms.

She wanted to keep the baby with her, but exhaustion was a cloud that pushed Menley into a stuporlike state. As she had done a few days ago, she placed a pillow in the cradle, laid Hannah on it, tucked the blankets around her, and fell into a dead sleep herself, her hand on the cradle, one tiny finger encircling her thumb.

The ringing of the phone woke her at eight o'clock. Hannah was still asleep, she noted, as she rushed to the master bedroom to answer it.

It was Adam.

"Don't tell me you and Hannah are still in bed? How come she never sleeps late for me?"

He was joking. Menley knew it. The tone of his voice was amused and affectionate. Then why was she so quick to look for a double meaning in everything he said?

"You always bragged about the fresh ocean air," she said. "Looks as though Hannah has started to believe you." She thought about the dinner. "Adam, I had a lovely time last night."

"Oh, I'm glad. I was afraid to ask."

Just as I suspected, Menley thought.

"Anyone else there besides you and Elaine and John?"

"Scott Covey."

"That was nice. I told him in no uncertain terms that I needed to be able to reach him. Did he talk about the search?"

"Only that it was intrusive but not worrisome."

"Good. How are you doing, honey?"

I'm doing just fine, Menley thought. I imagined I heard a train roar through this house. I imagined I heard my dead child calling me. And I let Hannah scream for half an hour while I searched for him.

"Fine," she said.

"Why do I get the feeling that you're holding something back?"

"Because you're a good lawyer, trained to look for hidden meanings." She forced a laugh.

"No episodes?"

"I said I'm fine." She tried not to sound irritated or panicky. Adam could always see through her. She tried to change the subject. "Dinner really was pleasant, but Adam, whenever John utters the words, 'That reminds me of a story,' run for the hills. He does go on and on."

Adam chuckled. " 'Laine must be in love. Otherwise she wouldn't put up with it. The airport at five?"

"I'll be there."

. . .

After Hannah had been bathed and fed and was temporarily content in the keeping-room playpen, Menley called the psychiatrist in New York who was treating her for post-traumatic stress disorder. "I'm in a bit of trouble," she said, trying to sound matter-of-fact.

"Tell me about it."

Carefully choosing her words, she told Dr. Kaufman about waking up, imagining she was hearing the sound of the train, thinking she'd heard Bobby calling.

"And you decided not to pick up Hannah when she was crying?"

She's trying to find out if I was afraid I'd hurt the baby, Menley thought. "I was trembling so much I was afraid that if I picked her up, I'd drop her."

"Was she crying?"

"Screaming."

"Did that upset you very much, Menley?"

She hesitated, then whispered, "Yes, it did. I wanted her to stop."

"I see. I think we'd better increase your medication. I reduced it last week, and it may have been too soon. I'll have to Express Mail it to you. I can't prescribe out of state over the phone."

I could have her send it to Adam's office, Menley thought. He could bring it up. But I don't want Adam to know I spoke to the doctor. "I don't know if I gave you the address here," she said calmly.

When she hung up the phone, she went over to the table. Yesterday, after Jan Paley left, she'd glanced quickly through Phoebe Sprague's file of pictures, looking for one of Captain Andrew Freeman. Now she spent the next several hours going through all the files specifically looking for a picture. But she couldn't find one.

She compared her drawing with the one Jan had brought. Feature for feature, it was a perfect match. The only difference was that the sketch from the Brewster Library showed the captain at the wheel of his ship. How did I know what he looked like? she wondered again.

She reached for her sketchpad. A mental image of Mehitabel was filling her mind, demanding to be released. Wind-blown, shoulder-length brown hair; a delicate heart-shaped face; wide, dark eyes; small hands and feet; smiling lips; a blue linen gown with long sleeves, a high neck and a lace bib, the skirt billowing to the side.

She drew with swift, sure strokes, her trained fingers skillfully transferring the image to paper. When she was finished she held it against the sketch Jan had brought and realized what she had done.

In the Brewster Library sketch, a trace of Mehitabel's flowing skirt flared out behind the figure of the captain.

Menley grabbed her magnifying glass. The small marks on Andrew Freeman's sleeve as shown in the Brewster drawing were the tips of fingers—Mehitabel's fingers. Had she been standing behind her husband on his ship when the unknown artist sketched him nearly three hundred years ago? Did she look anything like the way I visualized her? Menley wondered.

Suddenly frightened, she buried the three sketches in the bottom of one of the files, picked up Hannah and walked outside into the sunlight.

Hannah cooed and pulled her mother's hair, and as Menley gently disentangled the small fingers, a thought came to her: last night when I woke up to the roaring of the train, Hannah was screaming.

"Did the train wake you up too?" she cried. "Was that why you were so frightened? Oh, Hannah, what is happening to us? What kind of craziness are you picking up from me?"

49

DISTRICT ATTORNEY ROBERT SHORE conducted the meeting in the conference room of his offices in the Barnstable County Courthouse. He sat at the head of the table, the medical examiner, detectives and expert witnesses along the sides. He had placed Nat Coogan at the opposite end, a tribute to the extensive work the detective had done on the case.

"What have we got?" Shore asked and nodded to Nat to begin laying out his facts.

Step by step, Nat presented the facts he had assembled.

The medical examiner was next. "The body was mutilated by marine scavengers. You are particularly interested in the condition of her hands. The fingertips of both hands were gone, which is to be expected. In a drowning it's one of the first places crabs will attack. The rest of the fingers of the left hand are intact. A narrow gold band, her wedding ring, was on the ring finger."

He held up a picture taken at the autopsy. "The right hand tells a different story. Besides the missing fingertips, the ring finger had been eaten to the bone between the knuckle and hand. That suggests it had suffered a previous trauma that caused the blood to rise to the surface and attract the scavengers."

"The husband claimed that the morning of the day she died, Vivian had been twisting and turning her emerald to get it off," Nat said. "Would that have caused the trauma?"

"Yes, but she must have been yanking at it mighty hard."

District Attorney Shore took the picture from the medical examiner. "The husband admits she was wearing the emerald on the boat but claims she must have switched it to the ring finger of her left hand. If it were loose, could it have slipped off in the water?"

"Certainly. But it never would have slipped off past the knuckle of the right hand. But here's something else." The medical examiner held up another autopsy photo. "There isn't much of her right ankle left, but there are some marks consistent with rope burn. It's possible she was tied up at some point and even dragged for a considerable distance."

Shore leaned forward. "Deliberately?"

"Impossible to tell."

"Let's talk about the alcohol content in her body."

"Between the vitreous humor, or in layman's words, eye fluid, and the blood, we've ascertained she'd consumed the equivalent of three glasses of wine. She'd have been listed as 'under the influence' if she'd been driving."

"In other words," Shore said, "she had no business scuba diving in that condition, but there's no law against it."

The two expert witnesses from the Coast Guard group in Woods Hole were next. One was carrying maritime charts, which he set up on a stand. With the aid of a pointer, he presented his findings. "If she disappeared here"—he indicated a spot a mile from Monomoy Island—"her body should have been washed toward the Vineyard and located somewhere around here." Again he pointed. "The other alternative is that, given the violent currents caused by the squall, she might have been washed into the Monomoy shore. One place she would not have been is where she was found, in Stage Harbor. Unless," he concluded, "unless she got caught in a fishing net and dragged there, which is also possible."

The expert on diving equipment spread out the gear Vivian Carpenter had been wearing the day of her death. "This stuff was pretty worn," he commented. "Wasn't she supposed to be rich?"

"I think I can speak to that," Nat said. "Vivian gave her husband new diving gear as a wedding present. His story is that she wanted to use his old rig to see if she liked diving. If she did, she'd buy a top-of-the-line set like his."

"Reasonable, I guess."

Tina's possible connection to Scott was discussed, with the district attorney playing devil's advocate. "Tina's engaged now?" he asked.

"Yes, to her old boyfriend," Nat said, then told them of his impression of Fred Hendin. Next he talked about the oil on the garage floor at Scott Covey's house.

"Pretty nebulous as evidence, I'd say," he admitted. "A good defense attorney—and Adam Nichols is tops—could blow that away."

The records taken from the Covey home were laid out. "Covey sure did his homework," Shore grunted. "There's nothing there. But what about Vivian? Where did she keep all her personal records?"

"In her safety deposit box," Nat said.

"And the husband wasn't a signatory on it?"

"No."

At the conclusion of the meeting, there was reluctant agreement that, based on the present facts, it would be almost impossible to get a grand jury to hand up an indictment of Scott Covey.

"I'm going to call Judge Marron in Orleans and ask him to schedule an inquest," Shore decided. "That way all the facts will be publicly aired. If he thinks we've got enough, he'll make a finding of evidence of criminal negligence or foul play and then we convene the grand jury."

He stretched. "Gentlemen, an informal poll. Forget what's admissible or not admissible for a jury. If you were voting innocent or guilty, how say you?"

He went around the table. One by one they quietly answered. "Guilty . . . Guilty . . . Guilty . . . Guilty . . . Guilty . . . Guilty . . . Guilty."

"Guilty," Shore agreed decisively. "It's unanimous. We may not be able to prove it yet, but we all believe Scott Covey is a murderer."

50

*A*DAM'S CLIENT, Susan Potter, wept quietly as she sat opposite him in his office at the Park Avenue law firm of Nichols, Strand and Miller. Twenty-eight years old, slightly plump, with dark red hair and blue-green eyes, she would have been very attractive if her features were not distorted by fear and stress.

Convicted of manslaughter in the death of her husband, she had been granted a new trial through Adam's appeal. It would begin in September.

"I just don't feel as though I can go through it again," she said. "I'm so grateful to be out of prison, but the thought that I might have to go back . . ."

"You won't," Adam told her. "But Susan, get this straight—have no contact with Kurt's family. Slam the phone down if his parents call you. Their goal is to get you to say something provocative, something that they can even loosely interpret as a threat."

"I know." She stood up to go. "You're on vacation and this is the second time you've come down because of my case. I hope you know how much I appreciate it."

"When we get you off for good is when I'll accept your words of appreciation." Adam walked around his desk and escorted her to the door.

As he opened it, she looked up at him. "I thank God every day of my life that you're handling my defense."

Adam saw the hero worship in her eyes. "Keep your chin up, Susan," he said matter-of-factly.

His fifty-year-old secretary, Rhoda, was in the outer office. She followed him back into his private room. "Honest to God, Adam, you do turn the ladies on. All your female clients end up falling in love with you."

"Come on, Rhoda. A lawyer is like a psychiatrist. Most patients fall in love with their shrink for a while. It's the arm-to-lean-on syndrome."

His words echoed in his ears as he thought about Menley. She had suffered another anxiety attack; he was sure of it. He could pick up the stress in her voice as clearly as someone with perfect musical pitch could detect an off-key note. It was part of his training, part of the reason he was a successful lawyer. But why wouldn't she talk about it? How bad had the attack—or attacks— been? he wondered.

The widow's walk. The only access to that precarious perch was a narrow ladder. Suppose she tried to carry Hannah up there and became dizzy. *Suppose she dropped the baby.*

Adam felt his throat close. The memory of Menley's face as she looked down at Bobby in the casket haunted him. Menley's sanity would never survive losing Hannah.

He knew what he had to do. Reluctantly he phoned his wife's psychiatrist. His heart sank when Dr. Kaufman said, "Oh, Adam, I was debating whether to call you. I didn't realize you were in town. When are you going back to the Cape?"

"This afternoon."

"Then I'll send Menley's new prescription over to you to take up to her."

"When were you talking to Menley?" he asked.

"Today." Dr. Kaufman's tone changed. "You didn't know that? Adam, why are you calling me?"

He told her that he was afraid Menley was having episodes of PTSD that she was not admitting to him. The doctor did not comment.

Then Adam told her how the baby-sitter had seen Menley on the widow's walk, and that Menley denied being there.

"Did she have Hannah with her?"

"No. The baby was with the sitter."

There was a pause. Then, speaking carefully, the doctor said, "Adam, I don't think Menley should be alone with Hannah, and I *do* think you should bring her back to New York. I want to admit her to the hospital for a little while. It's better to be safe. We don't need any more tragedies in your family."

51

*A*MY HAD SPENT the day at Nauset Beach with her friends. On the one hand it had been fun to be with them. On the other, however, she had been saving her baby-sitting money toward the purchase of a new car to use at college, and she was still short of having the amount she needed. Her father had promised that he would pay half, but she had to make up the difference.

"I know I could give it to you," her father often told her, "but remember what your mother used to say: 'You appreciate what you work for.' "

Amy did indeed remember. She remembered everything her mother said. Mom hadn't been at all like Elaine, Amy thought. She'd been what most people would call plain: no makeup, no high-fashion clothes, no airs. But she'd been real. Amy remembered how when Dad told those long-winded stories, she'd say, with affection, "John, dear, get to the point." She didn't laugh the way Elaine did, giggling uncontrollably, acting like he was Robin Williams or something.

Yesterday Amy had known that Mrs. Nichols was angry at her. She realized now she shouldn't have told her father about seeing Mrs. Nichols on the widow's walk, and about Mrs. Nichols denying she had been there. Of course, her father had told Elaine, who told Mr. Nichols; she had been in the room when Elaine phoned him.

But one thing had been bothering Amy. When she had been with her in the house yesterday, Mrs. Nichols had been wearing shorts and a white cotton shirt. But in that impression of her on the widow's walk, she'd been wearing some sort of long dress.

It had startled Amy and made her wonder suddenly if maybe Mrs. Nichols was a little crazy. She'd heard Elaine tell her father that Mrs. Nichols was probably in the midst of a nervous breakdown.

But what if Mrs. Nichols was right, that it was only an optical illusion because of the metal on the chimney? When she thought about it, Amy realized that only a few minutes after she thought she saw that figure, Mrs. Nichols came out of the house dressed in the shorts and tee shirt.

The whole thing was kind of scary and spooky, Amy thought. Or maybe I've just heard too many stories about Remember House, and just like Carrie Bell, I think I'm seeing things.

She wanted to try to explain to Mrs. Nichols. She looked at her watch. It was four o'clock. Yes, she'd phone.

Mrs. Nichols answered on the first ring. She sounded a little breathless. "Amy, I'm sorry, I can't talk right now. I'm on my way to the airport, and Hannah is in the car."

"It's just I'm so sorry if you thought I was talking about you," Amy stammered. "I didn't mean to do that. What I mean is, you see . . ." She tried to explain about the dress and that she was sure she'd been mistaken. "You came out of the house right afterward."

Then she waited. There was a pause before Mrs. Nichols said, "Amy, I'm glad you called. Thank you."

"I really miss working for you. I'm so sorry."

"It's all right, Amy. Are you free to baby-sit tomorrow? I really must study all the data I have from Mrs. Sprague, and I'll need you to watch Hannah."

52

*H*ENRY SPRAGUE took his wife for a walk along their favorite strip of beach, the one that eventually ran in front of Remember House. It was quarter past six when they saw Adam and Menley with their baby at the water's edge. They stopped to visit.

"I just got back from New York," Adam explained, "and I had to get some sand in my shoes right away. Come up and have a glass of wine with us."

It had been a bad day for Phoebe. After she and Henry and Jan Paley came back from Scott Covey's, she had been terribly agitated. She'd gone into the office and searched for her files, accusing Henry and Jan of stealing them. Henry reasoned it might be a good idea if she saw them where they were now while he explained again why Menley had them. And he wanted to tell Adam about talking to Scott.

He accepted the invitation, and they followed the Nicholses up from the beach to the house. As they crossed the lawn, he explained to Menley what he wanted to do.

Menley listened, her heart sinking, praying that Phoebe would not insist on taking her data back.

But in the keeping room, Phoebe Sprague only seemed pleased to see the neat stacks of files and papers and books. Lovingly she ran her fingers over them, and as her husband and Menley and Adam watched, her face cleared. The vague expression in her eyes receded. "I wanted to tell her story," she murmured as she opened the file of sketches.

Menley saw that Phoebe intended to look at all the pictures. When Phoebe came to the ones Menley had sketched, she held them up and cried, "Oh, you copied them from the painting I have of Mehitabel and Andrew together on the ship. I haven't been able to find that one. I thought I'd lost it."

Thank God, Menley thought. There *is* a picture I might have copied. With this damn medication, I know my head isn't on straight.

Phoebe stood for a moment, studying Mehitabel's face. She could feel herself stepping backward, being drawn into dark confusion, becoming lost again. She willed her mind to keep going. Her husband loved her, she thought, but he didn't believe her. That's why she died. I've got to warn Adam's wife. That's the plan for *her.*

Plan! Plan! She tried to hold onto the thought, but it had become meaningless.

Mehitabel. Andrew. Who else? Before her mind became cloudy and gray and empty again, she managed to whisper to Menley, "Mehitabel innocent. Tobias Knight. Answer in Mooncussers file."

53

GRAHAM AND ANNE CARPENTER received
the phone call from the district attorney late Wednesday afternoon.
They'd started to play golf but had quit after the ninth hole because
Anne wasn't feeling well.

Graham realized that it might have been a mistake to pressure
the authorities to openly accuse Scott Covey of being responsible for Vivian's death. The media was delighted to have a juicy
news story and had laid out every detail of Vivian's life they could
find.

Now the tabloids were referring to her as "the poor little rich
girl," "the outcast," "the pot-smoking rebel." Details of their private lives were being distorted and held up for public ridicule and
entertainment.

Anne was crushed and humiliated and bitter. "Maybe we should
have left it alone, Graham. We couldn't bring her back, and now
they're destroying her memory."

At least the inquest would clear the air, Graham thought as he
made their five o'clock martinis and carried the tray to the sunporch, where Anne was resting.

"A bit early isn't it?" she asked.

"A little," he agreed. "That was the district attorney on the
phone. The judge in Orleans is calling an inquest for Monday afternoon."

In response to her alarmed expression, he said, "At least the
circumstances will be aired. It's a public hearing, and after all the
facts are presented, we want the judge to decide one of three ways:

no evidence of foul play; no evidence of negligence; no evidence of criminal negligence."

"Suppose the judge decides there is no evidence of negligence or foul play?" Anne said. "We'll have gone through this disgusting publicity for nothing."

"Not for nothing, dear. You know that."

From inside they heard faint ringing. A moment later the housekeeper came to the door, carrying the cellular phone. "It's Mr. Stevens, sir. He said it's important."

"That's the investigator the insurance company put on Covey," Graham said. "I insisted on being informed immediately of anything he found."

Anne Carpenter watched as her husband listened intently and then asked rapid-fire questions. When he hung up, he looked exhilarated.

"Stevens is in Florida, at Boca Raton. That's where Scott spent last winter. Apparently he was visited a number of times by a flashy-looking brunette named Tina. Her last visit was a week before he came up here and married Vivian!"

54

As SOON AS she'd picked up Adam at the airport, Menley had a feeling that something had unsettled him. She understood what it was when they were preparing for bed and he gave her the package of medicine from Dr. Kaufman.

"Which one of you called the other?" she asked evenly.

"I called the doctor, who was trying to decide whether or not to call me."

"I think I'd rather talk about it in the morning."

"If that's what you want."

It was the way they had most often gone to bed in the year after Bobby's death and before she became pregnant with Hannah, Menley thought. An impersonal kiss; lying apart; disparate emotions separating them as effectively as a bundling board.

She turned on her side and pillowed her face in her hand. A bundling board. Odd that she'd made that comparison. She'd just come upon the definition of that fixture of colonial times. In the winter, when a young man and woman were courting, the house was frequently so cold that the couple would be allowed to lie together in the same bed, fully clothed, swathed in blankets and with a long wooden plank firmly in place between them.

How much did Dr. Kaufman tell Adam? Menley wondered. Did she feel it was her obligation to let him know about the flashback when I thought I heard the train and Bobby calling me?

Then Menley froze. Had the doctor told Adam that Hannah's crying had been profoundly disturbing, that I didn't trust myself to touch her? Did Adam tell the doctor about the widow's walk? I didn't bring that up to her.

Dr. Kaufman and Adam may be afraid I'll hurt Hannah, Menley thought. What did they decide to do? Would they insist on a full-time baby-sitter or nurse always being present when Adam wasn't there?

No, she thought, there was another, more terrible possibility. With a sinking heart, Menley was sure she had hit on the right answer. Adam will take me to New York, and Dr. Kaufman will sign me into a psychiatric hospital. I cannot let that happen. I cannot be away from Hannah. That would destroy me.

I am getting better, she told herself. I did manage to go over the railroad crossing when I drove Adam to the airport this week. Even the other night, when I thought I heard Bobby calling, I did come out of it by myself. I did go back to Hannah. I did not hurt her, and I did comfort her. And I want to stay here.

Being careful not to disturb Adam, Menley drew the blanket closer around her neck. In happier times if she woke up chilly she would simply slide into the warmth of Adam's arms. Not now. Not like this.

I simply can never allow Adam to see any sign of my anxiety, she told herself. I've got to beat him to the punch in the morning and say that I'd like to have Amy around all day to help with Hannah. In a day or two I'll have to tell him how much better I feel, that maybe the doctor was right, that the medication shouldn't have been reduced so quickly.

I don't like being dishonest with him, but he's not being honest with me, she thought. Elaine's call about dinner the other afternoon had been arranged ahead of time.

It will be so much easier to have a baby-sitter around all day in this house. I won't have the feeling of her being underfoot the way I do in the apartment. And Hannah is thriving here.

The new book is a fascinating project. Working always keeps me on an even keel. A David book with Andrew as the boy who grows up to become the captain of his own ship could be my best. I feel it.

I don't believe in ghosts, but Jan Paley's story about people who claim a presence in their old houses intrigues me and would intrigue readers. It would make a great historical article for *Travel Times*.

And I want to tell Mehitabel's story. Phoebe insists she is innocent and that the proof is in the Mooncusser file. That poor girl was condemned as an adulteress, publicly flogged, despised by her husband, and her baby was taken from her. Bad enough if she'd been guilty but unimaginable if she was innocent. I want to find the proof of her innocence, if it exists.

Do I feel a kinship with her because my husband may be conspiring with my psychiatrist to separate me from my baby and because

I'm innocent of what they believe about me, that I'm not capable of caring for her?

This must be the way it is for Scott Covey, she told herself. People watching, whispering, trying to find a way to lock you up. A smile tugged at her lips when she thought of Scott's raised eyebrow and hint of a wink as they listened to John labor through one of his interminable stories at dinner the night before.

Finally Menley felt herself relaxing and drifting off. She awakened with a start, not sure of how long she'd slept. She'd make sure Hannah was covered. As she slid out of bed, Adam jumped up and asked sharply, "Menley, where are you going?"

She bit back an angry retort and tried to sound offhand. "Oh, I woke up because I was chilly and thought I'd check the baby. Have you been awake, dear? Maybe you've looked in to see if she's covered."

"No, I've been asleep."

"I'll be right back."

There was a musty smell in the room. Hannah had turned over and was sleeping with her bottom raised, her legs tucked under her. Her blankets were scattered on the floor. The stuffed animals that had been on the dresser were arranged around her in the crib. The antique doll was propped in a sitting position in the cradle.

Frantically Menley tossed the toys back on the dresser, picked up the blankets, and shook them out.

"I didn't do that, Hannah," she whispered as she covered her daughter. "I didn't do that."

"What didn't you do, Menley?" Adam asked from the doorway.

55

*T*HURSDAY MORNING was cloudy, and a sharply cool breeze sent the residents of Chatham scurrying to their closets for long-sleeved shirts and jackets. It was the kind of day that Marge, Elaine's assistant, claimed "gave her pep."

The Atkins Real Estate Agency had a number of new listings, and Elaine had personally gone around to make flattering shots of the properties. She had developed and enlarged the photos, and the day before she had brought them into the office.

Feeling the coolness in the air when she awoke, Marge decided to go to the office early and take advantage of an uninterrupted hour to rearrange the display windows. She arrived there at seven-thirty and began removing the existing photos.

At ten of nine she was finished and standing out on the sidewalk, critically surveying her handiwork. Very nice, she thought, as she admired the effect.

The pictures were unusually good and showed the properties to excellent advantage. There was a lovely old Cape on Cockle Cove Ridge, a charming saltbox on Deep Water Lane, a contemporary on Sandy Shoes Lane and a dozen other lesser, but attractive, properties.

The most important listing was a waterfront estate on Wychmere Harbor. Elaine had hired the aerial photographer she always used to take a panoramic shot of that property. Marge had put it in the center of the window, in place of the framed Remember House aerial photo.

From behind her, Marge heard the sound of applause. She turned quickly.

"I'll buy all of them," Elaine said as she got out of her car.

"Sold!" Marge waited as Elaine walked up and stood beside her. "Honestly, what do you think?"

Elaine studied the exhibit. "I think they look great. I suppose it was time to take out my favorite, the Remember House shot."

"I honestly think so, especially since you're so sure the Nicholses are going to buy it."

Elaine preceded her into the agency. "I'm afraid that remains to be seen," she said soberly. "I'm getting the impression that Menley Nichols isn't a bit well."

"I never met her," Marge said, "but Adam Nichols is a lovely man. I remember how sad he looked when he came up here last year and you took him around. He rented the Spark cottage, near your house, didn't he?"

"That's right." Elaine spotted the photo of Remember House, propped against a chair. "I've got an idea," she said. "Let's send this over to Scott Covey. If everything gets straightened out for him, I wouldn't be surprised if he elected to stay on the Cape, and he and Vivian were crazy about that place. At least that way he'll keep the house in mind. Just in case the Nicholses don't take it."

"But suppose he isn't interested? If the property goes back on the market, you'll be sorry you gave it to him, Elaine."

"I've got the negative. I can make other copies."

She went into her own office. Marge began to transfer the pictures she'd taken from the window to the oversized album on the reception area table. The tinkling front door bell announced their first visitor.

It was the delivery boy from the florist. He was carrying a vase of long-stemmed roses.

"For Miss Atkins," he said.

"I never dreamed they were for me," Marge commented. "Take them in to her. You know the way."

After he left, Marge went in to admire the flowers. "Absolutely beautiful. This is getting to be a frequent occurrence. But what the heck is that?"

There was a streamer in the bouquet, with the number 106 pasted on it. "I know you're not that old, Elaine."

"John's just being sweet. That's how many days until we're married."

"He's a romantic, and God knows there are few of them left. Elaine, do you think the two of you will want to have a child?"

"He already has one, and I like to think that Amy and I are getting closer."

"But Amy's seventeen. She's going off to college. It would be different if she were a baby."

Elaine laughed. "If she were a baby, I wouldn't be marrying John. I'm just not that domestic."

The phone rang. "I'll get it." Elaine picked it up. "Atkins Real Estate, Elaine Atkins speaking." She listened. "Adam! . . . Is that bad? I mean an inquest sounds so intimidating. Of course I'll go over my testimony. Lunch with you would be fine. One o'clock? See you then."

When she hung up she told Marge, "It sounds like good news. They're convening an inquest on Vivian Covey's death, which means the media can be present. So this will be a chance for all of us to go to bat for Scott." She got up. "Where's the Remember House picture?"

"By my desk," Marge told her.

"Let's messenger it over to him with a note."

On her personal stationery, she quickly penned a few sentences in her clear, decisive handwriting.

Dear Scott,

I just heard about the inquest and welcome the chance to let the world know how happy you and Vivian were that beautiful afternoon when you were looking at Remember House. You enjoyed the view so much I wanted you to have this picture to remind you of it.

Yours,
Elaine.

56

*A*T TEN O'CLOCK on Thursday morning, as the breakfast service was winding down, Tina Aroldi used her fifteen-minute break to rush into the office of the Wayside Inn. The secretary was there alone.

"Jean, what was that detective doing looking under my car yesterday?" Tina demanded.

"I don't know what you mean," the secretary protested.

"You sure do know what I mean. Don't bother to lie. A couple of the busboys saw him through the window."

"There's nothing to lie about," Jean stammered. "The detective asked me to point out your car, then he came back and wanted to know if you ever answered the phone for reservations."

"I see."

Preoccupied, Tina went back to her station in the dining room. A few minutes after one, she was not pleased to see Scott's lawyer, Adam Nichols, come in with Elaine Atkins, the real estate broker, who often brought clients to the inn.

She saw Nichols gesturing toward her. Great. He wanted to be sure she was their waitress. The hostess seated them at one of her tables, and reluctantly, pad in hand, Tina went over to greet them.

She was surprised at the warm smile Nichols gave her. He sure is attractive, Tina thought, not drop-dead handsome, but there was something about him. You got a feeling he'd be a pretty exciting guy to be with. And you could tell he was smart.

Well, he might be smiling today, but the other morning when he came in with Scott, he sure hadn't been smiling, Tina reflected. He was probably one of those guys who was nice when he needed you.

She responded coolly to his greeting and asked, "Can I get you anything from the bar?"

They each ordered a glass of chardonnay. When she left them, Elaine said, "I wonder what's with Tina today?"

"I suspect she's nervous about being dragged in to testify at the inquest," Adam responded. "Well, she has to get over that. The district attorney is certainly going to subpoena her, and I want to make sure she creates a favorable impression."

They ordered hamburgers and shared a side order of onion rings. "It's a good thing I don't have lunch with you often," Elaine said. "I'd put on twenty pounds. I usually have a salad."

"This is like the good old days," Adam told her. "Remember how after our summer jobs we'd all load up on junk food, pile into that wreck of an outboard motorboat I had and call it our sunset sail?"

"I haven't forgotten."

"The other night, at your house with the old gang, I felt as though fifteen or twenty years had disappeared," Adam said. "The Cape does that to me. You do too, 'Laine. It's nice to feel like a kid sometimes."

"Well, you've had a lot to worry about. How is Menley doing?"

He hesitated. "She's doing okay."

"You don't look or sound as though you mean it. Hey, this is your old buddy you're talking to, Adam. Remember?"

He nodded. "I always could talk to you. The doctor thinks it would be wise to bring Menley back to New York and hospitalize her."

"You don't mean a psychiatric hospital, I hope."

"I'm afraid so."

"Adam, don't jump the gun. She seemed great at the party and at dinner the other night. Besides that, when I spoke to John, he said that Amy was going to be over at your place all day from now on."

"That's the only reason I'm able to be here. Menley told me this morning that she wants to work on her book, and she knows I'll be busy getting ready for the inquest, so she wanted to hire Amy for the entire day for a while."

"Then don't you think you should leave it at that? You're home in the evening."

"I guess so. I mean, this morning, Menley was herself. Relaxed, funny, enthusiastic about her book. You'd never think she's been experiencing post-traumatic stress—hallucinations, actually. Yesterday she told the doctor that she thought she heard Bobby calling her. She left Hannah screaming while she searched the house."

"Oh, Adam."

"So for her own good and for Hannah's safety, she has to be hospitalized. But as long as Amy can be there and I have to prepare for the inquest, I'll wait. After that, however, I'll take Menley back to New York."

"Will you stay there yourself?"

"I simply don't know. From what I understand, Doctor Kaufman wouldn't want me to visit Menley for a week or so. New York is damn hot, and our regular baby-sitter is away. If Amy helps out, minding Hannah during the day, I can certainly take care of her myself at night, so I may come back up here for at least that week."

He finished the last of the hamburger. "You know, if we really had wanted to make this like old times, we should have been drinking out of beer cans instead of wine glasses. No matter, I think I'll settle for coffee now."

He changed the subject. "Since the inquest is a public hearing, I can give a list of the people I want called to testify. That doesn't mean the district attorney won't frame his questions to try to put Scott in a bad light. Let's go over the sort of thing you might be asked."

They finished the coffee and had a second cup before Adam nodded in satisfaction. "You're a good witness, Elaine. When you're on the stand, emphasize how lonely Vivian seemed when she bought the house, how happy she was at her wedding reception; and talk about when she and Covey were house hunting, and all their plans for a baby. It's okay to let them know that Vivian had more than her share of New England thrift. That would help to explain why she didn't buy new diving gear right away."

When he was paying the check, he looked up at the waitress. "Tina, you finish work at two-thirty. I'd like to talk to you for about fifteen minutes after that."

"I have an appointment."

"Tina, you're going to receive a subpoena to appear in court next week. I suggest you discuss your testimony with me. I can assure you that if the judge rules unfavorably, it will be because he thinks you were the motive for Vivian's murder and maybe he'll even suspect you were involved. Being an accessory to murder is pretty serious."

Tina paled. "I'll meet you at the soda place next to the Yellow Umbrella Bookshop."

Adam nodded.

He walked down the block to the real estate agency with Elaine. "Hey," he said, looking in the display window, "where's the picture of my house?"

"Your house?"

"Well, maybe. Just keep in mind I have an option that I may decide to exercise."

"Sorry. I sent the picture over to Scott. I have to hedge my bets. If you don't buy it, there's a good chance he might. And Jan Paley could use the sale. She and Tom sank a lot of money in that renovation. I'll have another copy made up for you. I'll even throw in a really nice frame."

"I'll hold you to that."

Tina was clearly on the defensive when she spoke with Adam. "Listen, Mr. Nichols, I've got a nice boyfriend. Fred isn't going to like my having to testify in this thing."

"Fred has nothing to say about it. But he could help you."

"What do you mean?"

"He could verify that you two had dated for a while last summer, then broken up over Scott; that you got back together and now you're getting married."

"We didn't get back together right away. I dated other guys last winter."

"That's all right. The point is, I'd like to talk to Fred and decide whether he'd be a good witness."

"I don't know . . ."

"Tina, please get this straight. The faster Scott's name is cleared, the better it will be for you."

They were sitting at one of the small tables outside the soda shop. Tina toyed with the straw in her soda. "That detective is making me very nervous," she burst out. "Yesterday he was looking under my car."

"That's the sort of thing I need to know," Adam said quickly. "What was he looking for?"

Tina shrugged. "I don't know. I'm getting rid of it soon. Damn thing leaks like a sieve."

When they separated, Adam took Fred's phone number but promised he would wait to call until this evening, after Tina had a chance to explain what was going on.

He got in the station wagon and sat for a few minutes, thinking. Then he reached for the car phone and dialed Scott Covey's number.

When Covey answered, Adam said abruptly, "I'm on my way over."

57

PHOEBE HAD HAD a restless night. Several times a nightmare caused her to cry out in her sleep. One time she had screamed, "I don't want to go in there," another time she'd moaned, "Don't do that to me."

Finally, at dawn, Henry had managed to coax her into taking a strong sedative, and she had settled into drugged slumber.

Over his solitary breakfast, Henry tried to figure out what might have upset her. Yesterday, she had seemed relaxed when they walked on the beach. She appeared to enjoy the visit with Adam and Menley at Remember House. She'd been glad to see her files there, and had sounded absolutely lucid when she told Menley that the answer was in the Mooncusser file.

What answer? What did she mean? Clearly some aspect of her research had surfaced in her mind and she was trying to communicate it. But she'd also been clear when she talked about the sketch Menley had made of Captain Freeman and Mehitabel.

Henry brought his coffee into Phoebe's study. He'd received a letter from the director of the nursing home, suggesting that he select some mementos for Phoebe to have in her room when she went to live there. The director wrote that familiar objects, particularly those involving long-term memory, helped increase awareness in Alzheimer patients. I ought to start deciding what to pack for her, he thought. This is the place to look.

As always, sitting at Phoebe's desk brought back with knifelike sharpness the reality of how different things were for them now, as compared to a few years ago. After Phoebe retired from teaching, she'd spent every morning in here, happily absorbed in her research, working much as he imagined Menley Nichols worked.

Wait a minute, Henry thought. That picture of the captain and his wife Phoebe talked about yesterday was in the extra-large folder. That wasn't with the data I gave Menley. I didn't know another picture of them together existed. It seems to me that folder had a lot of other material on the Freemans and Remember House. Where would Phoebe have kept it? he wondered.

He looked around the room, taking in the floor-to-ceiling bookshelves, the end table by the sofa. Then he thought—of course, the corner cupboard.

He walked over to it. The open shelves of the fine antique held rare samples of early Sandwich glassware. He remembered how Phoebe had collected each of them lovingly, and he decided that a few of the pieces should be among the items she had with her in the nursing home.

The cabinet under the shelves was jampacked with books and papers and folders. I didn't realize she had all this stuff in here, Henry mused.

In the bewildering hodgepodge, he did manage to find the folder he was looking for, and in it the sketch of Captain Freeman and Mehitabel. The billowing of her skirt and the sails suggested a strong, cool wind. She was standing a little behind him rather than alongside, as though he were sheltering her. His face was strong and firm, hers soft and smiling; her hand was resting lightly on his arm. The unknown artist had caught the chemistry between them. You can tell they were lovers, Henry thought.

He glanced through the folder. Several times the word "mooncusser" caught his eye. This may be what Phoebe intended Menley to read, he decided.

"Oh, is that where I left the doll?"

Phoebe was in the doorway, her hair disheveled, her nightgown stained. Henry remembered that he had left the bottle of liquid sedative on the bedside table. "Phoebe, did you take more medicine?" he asked anxiously.

"Medicine?" She sounded surprised. "I don't think so."

She stumbled over to the cabinet and crouched beside him. "That's where I put the Remember House doll," she said, her tone excited and pleased.

She pulled papers from the deep bottom shelf, letting them scatter on the floor. Then she reached into the back of the cabinet, and pulled out an antique doll dressed in a long yellowing cotton gown. A lace-edged bonnet with satin streamers framed the delicately beautiful china face.

Phoebe stared at it, frowning. Then she handed it to Henry. "She belongs in Remember House," she said vaguely. "I meant to put her back, but I forgot."

58

*A*FTER LUNCH, Amy sat in front of the baby swing, playing with Hannah. "Clap hands, clap hands till Daddy comes home. Daddy has money and Mommy has none," she singsonged as she patted Hannah's hands together.

Hannah gurgled in delight, and Menley smiled. "That's a pretty sexist nursery rhyme," she said.

"I know," Amy agreed. "But it sticks in my head. My mother used to sing it to me when I was little."

Her mother's on her mind a lot, poor kid, Menley thought. Amy had arrived promptly at nine that morning, almost pathetically glad to be back. Menley knew her attitude reflected more than a desire to earn the baby-sitting money. She seemed genuinely happy to be there.

"My mother claims she tried to avoid singing to us," Menley

commented as she scrubbed the sink. "She's tone deaf and didn't want to pass it on to my brother and me. But she did." She swished water in the sink.

"Honestly, Hildy isn't very much use," she complained. "That cleaning woman who was just leaving when we arrived here left this place spotless. I wish she had come back."

"Elaine was mad at her."

Menley turned and looked at Amy. "Why was she mad at her?"

"Oh, I don't know," Amy said hurriedly.

"Amy, I think you *do* know," Menley said, sensing that this might be important.

"Well, it was just that Carrie Bell was scared that morning you arrived. She said she had heard footsteps upstairs, but there was no one there. Then, when she went into the nursery, the cradle was rocking by itself, or so she claimed. Elaine said that was ridiculous and she didn't want those kind of stories spread about the house, because it's for sale."

"I see." Menley tried not to sound excited. That's three of us she thought. Amy, Carrie Bell and me. "Do you know how I can reach Carrie?" she asked.

"Oh, sure. She's cleaned our house for years."

Menley reached for a piece of paper and jotted down the number Amy rattled off. "I'm going to see if she can come over again, and I'll ask Elaine to cancel Hildy."

Since it was still very cool, they agreed that Amy would bundle Hannah up and take her for a walk in the carriage. "Hannah likes to know what's going on," Amy said, smiling.

And don't we all, Menley thought as she settled down at the table and reached again for the Mooncusser file. For a moment she stared reflectively into space. This morning Adam had not bothered to mince words. "Menley," he had said, "I'm sure if you phone Dr. Kaufman you'll find she agrees with me. While you're having such shattering anxiety attacks and flashbacks I have to insist that Amy stay here with you and Hannah when I'm out."

Menley remembered the effort with which she had bitten back

an angry reply. Instead she had simply pointed out that it was her idea to have Amy with them, so he didn't need to be so overbearing. Even so, Adam had watched until Amy's car came into the driveway, then he had rushed out to have a word with her. After that he had closeted himself in the library, preparing for the inquest. He left the house at twelve-thirty, saying he'd be back late in the afternoon.

He talked privately to Amy because he doesn't even trust me to keep my word, Menley thought. Then she forced those thoughts from her mind and determinedly settled down to work.

Before lunch she'd been trying to make sense of the Mooncusser file, preparing her own notes, which she'd culled from the data Phoebe Sprague had put together.

She reread those notes:

The fifteen miles of treacherous currents and blind channels and shifting shoals that were the Chatham coastline were the undoing of countless vessels. They foundered and broke apart in blizzards and storms or sailed into sandbars, wrecking their hulls and sinking in the violent waters.

"Mooncussers" was the name given to the wreckers, who would rush to loot the cargos and snare the spoils. They would sail their small boats to the dying ship, carrying pinch bars, saws and axes, and would strip it clean of cargo and lumber and fixtures. Barrels and trunks and household goods were hoisted over the sides onto the waiting craft.

Even men of the cloth were wreckers. Menley had come across Phoebe's notes about the minister who in the middle of his sermon looked out the window, saw a ship in distress and immediately informed his congregation of the fortuitous happening. "Start fair," he'd yelped and rushed out of the meeting room, followed closely by his fellow scavengers.

Another story Phoebe had noted was of the minister who, when handed a note about a sinking ship, ordered his parishioners to bow their heads in silent prayer, while he himself slipped out in search of plunder. Returning five hours later, his booty tucked away, he found his obedient, stiff-necked and weary congregation still in place.

Wonderful stories, Menley thought, but what have they got to do with Tobias Knight? She continued to read; an hour later she finally came to a reference to him. He was listed as denouncing "the plundering gangs who stripped clean the cargo of flour and rum from the beached schooner *Red Jacket,* depriving the Crown of its salvedge."

Tobias was put in charge of that investigation. There was no mention of the success or failure of his mission.

But what is the connection to Mehitabel? Menley wondered. Certainly Captain Freeman wouldn't have been a wrecker.

And then she came upon another reference to Tobias Knight. In 1707 there was an election to replace him as selectman and assessor and to appoint Samuel Tucker to complete the building of the sheep pound that Knight had begun. The reason: "Tobias Knight no longer apeering in our midst to the greate disadvantage of the congregation."

Phoebe Sprague had noted: "Probably the 'greate disadvantage' was that they'd already paid him to build the pound. But what happened to him? No record of his death. Did he leave to avoid being pressed into service? 'Queen Anne's War,' the French and Indian war, was being fought. Or was his disappearance tied to the Crown investigation that began two years earlier?"

The Crown investigation! Menley thought. That's a new twist. Tobias Knight must have been quite a character. He threw Mehitabel to the winds. He led the search to recover the spoils from the *Red Jacket,* which meant he was investigating his own townspeople, and then he disappeared, leaving the sheep pound unfinished.

She got up and glanced at the clock. It was half past two. Amy had been out alone with the baby for nearly two hours. Concerned, she jumped up, went to the kitchen door and was relieved to see the carriage just turning onto the dirt road that marked the beginning of the property.

Will I ever get to the point where I'm not overly worried about Hannah? she wondered.

Stop thinking like that, she cautioned herself. You haven't even glanced at the ocean since you got out of bed, she thought. Take a look at it. It always does something for you.

She walked from the keeping room to the main parlor and opened the front windows, relishing the blast of salt-filled air. Tossed by the sharp breeze, the water was a mass of whitecaps. Cool as she knew it must be on the beach, she found herself yearning to walk there and feel the water on her ankles. How had Mehitabel felt about this house? She could visualize the way she would write the story.

They returned from the China trip and found the house completed. They examined it, room by room, remarking with joy on the posts and beams and paneling, the fine arrangement on the fireplaces of the bricks Andrew had commissioned from West Barnstable, the pilasters and carving that surrounded the great front door, with its crosslike panels.

They'd delighted in the fanlight they had admired in London, the way it cast lovely patterns over the entrance hall. Then they descended the steep slope to see their house as it would be observed from the beach.

"Tobias Knight be a fine builder," Andrew said as they stood looking up. The water was lapping at Mehitabel's skirt. She gathered it up and stepped onto dry sand, commenting, "I would love to feel the water on my ankles."

Andrew laughed. "A chill water it is, and you with child. I think it not advisable."

"Mrs. Nichols, are you all right?"

Menley spun around. Amy was in the doorway, Hannah in her arms. "Oh, of course, I'm fine. Amy, you're going to have to forgive me. When I write or sketch, I'm in a different world."

Amy smiled. "That's the way Professor Sprague used to describe writing when she visited my mother."

"Your mother and Professor Sprague were friends? I didn't know that."

"My mother and father belonged to a camera club. They were good amateur photographers. My father still is, of course. They met Professor Sprague through the club, and she and my mother got really friendly." Amy's tone changed. "That's where my father met Elaine. She's a member too."

Menley's throat went dry. Hannah was patting Amy's face. But she envisioned Amy looking different. Slimmer. Not as tall. Her blond hair darker, her face small and heart shaped. Her smile tender and sad as she kissed the top of the baby's head and rocked her in her arms. That was the way she would portray Mehitabel in the weeks between her baby's birth and the day she lost her.

Then Amy shivered. "It's really freezing cold in here, isn't it? Is it all right if I make a cup of tea?"

59

WHEN ADAM ARRIVED at Scott's house, he found him hosing down the garage. He frowned when he saw that Covey had been concentrating on an oil-stained area. "You're being very industrious," he observed.

"Not really. I've been meaning to do this for a while. Viv took a course on car maintenance a couple of years ago and fancied herself a mechanic for a while. She had an old Caddy, and she liked to pump her own gas and change the oil."

"Did the Caddy have an oil leak?" Adam asked quickly.

"I don't know whether it had a leak or if Viv was spilling half the oil. She always parked that car in this space. She bought the BMW after we were married."

"I see. Do you happen to know if the police took any pictures of the garage floor when they were here?"

Scott looked startled. "What's that supposed to mean?"

"Detective Coogan was looking under Tina's car yesterday. It has an oil leak."

Abruptly Scott turned off the hose and slammed it down. "Adam, can you understand what this is like for me? I'm going nuts. I have to tell you that as soon as the inquest is over, I'm getting out of here. Let them think what they want. They will anyhow."

Then he shook his head, as though clearing it. "Sorry. I shouldn't take it out on you. Come on inside. It's chilly out here. I thought August was supposed to be the best month of the year on the Cape."

"Other than being cool today, I haven't seen any weather to object to so far," Adam said mildly.

"Sorry again. Adam, I have to talk to you." He turned abruptly and led the way into the house.

Adam refused the offer of a beer, and while Scott went to get one for himself, used the time to study the living room carefully. It looked as though it needed a good straightening, but that could have been the result of the search. The police were not famous for restoring the premises they had searched to pristine order.

But there was something else Adam noted, an emptiness about the room. There was nothing personal anywhere, no photographs, no books, no magazines. The furniture wasn't shabby, but it was neither attractive nor coordinated. Adam remembered that Elaine had told him Vivian had bought the place furnished. It didn't look as though she had done anything to put her stamp on it, and if Scott Covey's personality was reflected in the room, Adam certainly couldn't spot it.

He thought of the keeping room of Remember House. In the two weeks they had been there, Menley had given it an inviting atmosphere, and she'd done it effortlessly. Geraniums lined the windowsills. The outsized wooden salad bowl was heaped with fruit. She had lugged a battered rocker from the small parlor and set it by the fireplace. A wicker basket that had probably been used for carrying logs was serving as a container for magazines and newspapers.

Menley was a natural homemaker. Adam thought uncomfortably of how he had dashed out this morning to warn Amy to stay with Menley until he got back. Menley wouldn't have sent Amy home, he told himself. She's just as concerned about those anxiety attacks as I am. She called Dr. Kaufman yesterday. She had even suggested having Amy in all day.

What was keeping Covey? How long did it take to pour a beer? And what in hell am I doing here? Adam asked himself. This is my vacation. My wife needs me and I let myself get talked into taking on this case.

He walked into the kitchen. "Any problem?"

Scott was sitting at the table, his arms folded, the beer untouched. "Adam," he said tonelessly. "I haven't been straight with you."

60

*N*AT COOGAN decided it would be a good idea to pay a second visit to Fred Hendin. Armed with the information that the insurance investigator had shared with him, he arrived at Hendin's home at four-thirty.

Hendin's car was in the driveway. Nat was not delighted to see that Tina's green Toyota was parked behind it. On the other hand, it might be interesting to observe them together, he thought.

He sauntered up the walk and rang the bell. When Hendin came to the door, he was visibly displeased. "Did I forget we had an appointment?" he asked.

"We don't," Nat said pleasantly. "Is it okay if I come in?"

Hendin stood aside. "It's not okay if you keep upsetting my girlfriend."

Tina was sitting on the couch, dabbing at her eyes with a handkerchief. "Why do you keep bothering me?" she demanded.

"I have no intention of bothering you, Tina," Nat said evenly. "We're conducting an investigation into a possible homicide. When we ask questions, it's to get answers, not to harass people."

"You're talking to people about me. You're looking at my car." Fresh tears gushed from her eyes.

You're a lousy actress, Nat thought. This is show-and-tell for Fred's benefit. He glanced at Hendin and saw irritation and sympathy on his face. And it's working, he thought.

Hendin sat down beside Tina, and his work-roughened hand closed over hers. "What's this about the car?"

"Haven't you noticed that Tina has a fairly serious oil leak?"

"I noticed it. I'm giving Tina a new car for her birthday. That's in three weeks. No point wasting money fixing up the other one."

"The floor of Scott Covey's garage has a pretty big oil stain," Nat said. "It didn't come from the new BMW."

"And it didn't come from my car," Tina snapped, her eyes suddenly dry.

Hendin stood up. "Mr. Coogan, Tina told me there'd be an inquest. Covey's lawyer is coming to talk to me, and I'm going to tell him exactly what I'm telling you now, so listen good. Tina and I broke up last summer because she was seeing Covey. She dated a lot of guys over the winter, and that's not my business. We've been back together since last April, and there hasn't been a night I haven't seen her, so don't try to make a big romance out of her bumping into Covey in that bar or stopping by his house to offer sympathy when his wife was missing."

He slung an arm around Tina's shoulders, and she smiled up at him. "It's a damn shame that you're spoiling all my surprises, but I have another one for this little lady. Besides the car, I bought her an engagement ring that I was going to give her on her birthday, but with the way things are, she's going to have it on her finger when we go into court next week. Now get out, Coogan. You and your questions make me sick."

61

So THIS IS WHERE the defense falls apart, Adam thought. In Vivian Carpenter's kitchen. "What do you mean you weren't being straight with me?" he snapped.

Scott Covey studied his untouched glass of beer. He did not look at Adam as he said, "I told you that I didn't see Tina from the time I married Vivian except that day in the pub and when she came here to offer condolences. That's true. What isn't true is the impression I gave you that she and I called it quits last summer."

"You saw her after you left the Cape last August?"

"She came down to Boca five or six times. I've been wanting to tell you; I'm sure your investigator will find out anyhow."

"The investigator I want is on vacation till next week. But you're right. He would have found out. And so will the district attorney's office, if they haven't already."

Scott pushed back his chair and got up. "Adam, I feel like a louse saying this, but it's true. I did break off with Tina last August. It wasn't just that I was seeing Viv. It was that Tina wanted to get serious and I didn't. Then when I got to Boca, I realized that I missed Viv a lot. Usually these summer romances fizzle. You know that. I phoned Viv and realized she felt the same way about me. She came down to Boca, we met in New York a few times and by spring we both were sure we wanted to get married."

"If you're telling the truth now, why didn't you tell it from the beginning?" Adam shot the question accusingly.

"Because Fred doesn't know that Tina was still seeing me over the winter. It didn't bother him that she dated other guys, but he really hates me because she dropped him for me last summer. That was the real reason she asked me to meet her. She wanted to see me face to face and hear me promise never to tell anyone that she'd been down to Florida."

"Did you see her after she walked out of the pub that day?"

Scott shrugged. "I called her and said that whatever she had to talk about, she'd have to say it on the phone. Then when I heard what it was, I laughed. I asked her who she thought I was going to tell about her coming to Boca. What kind of jerk did she think I was?"

"I think we're going to need a few witnesses at the inquest to testify that Tina was chasing you, and not the other way around. Is there anyone you can suggest?"

Scott brightened. "A couple of the other waitresses at the Daniel Webster Inn. Tina used to be friendly with them, but then they got mad at her. She told me they were sore because some of the regular customers who are big tippers requested to be seated at one of her tables."

"Tina seems to play all the angles," Adam said. "I hope her friend Fred doesn't mind having it publicly aired that she was lying to him." Why did I get myself into this? he wondered again. He still believed that Scott Covey's wife died in a tragic accident, but he also believed that Covey had been using Tina until Vivian decided to marry him. This guy may be innocent of murder, but it doesn't keep him from being a sleaze, he thought.

Suddenly this smallish kitchen seemed to close in on Adam. He wanted to get back to Menley and Hannah. They would have only a few days together before he had to take Menley to the hospital in New York. He would have to begin to prepare her for that. "Give me the names of those waitresses," he said abruptly.

"Liz Murphy and Alice Regan."

"Write them down. Let's hope they still work there." Adam turned and left the kitchen.

As he passed the dining room he glanced in. A large framed picture was on the table; it was the aerial view of Remember House Elaine had had in the window. He went over to examine it.

Beautiful photography, he thought. The house seemed majestically aloof. The colors were spectacular—the rich green-leaved branches of the trees surrounding the house, the purple-blue hydrangeas bordering the foundation, the blue-green ocean, tranquil with a lazy surf. You could even see strollers on the beach and a small boat anchored just below the horizon.

"I'd love to have this," he commented.

"It's a gift from Elaine," Scott said quickly. "Otherwise I'd give it to you. She seems to think that if you don't buy Remember House, I'd be interested."

"Would you be?"

"If Viv were alive, yes. As it stands, no." He hesitated. "What I mean is, in my present frame of mind, no. Maybe I'll feel differently if a judge clears me."

"Looking at this picture would certainly be an incentive to buy the place. It is for me," Adam said. Then he turned to leave. "I'm on my way. We'll talk later."

He was getting into his car when Henry Sprague waved him over. "I've found more material that I think Menley would be interested in," he explained. "Come in; let me give it to you."

The file was on the foyer table. "And Phoebe is very insistent that this doll belongs in Remember House. I don't know why she thinks that, but would you mind taking it with you?"

"Menley will probably be delighted to see it," Adam said. "It certainly is a genuine antique. Don't be surprised if it shows up sketched in her book. Thanks, Henry. How's Phoebe today?"

"Napping right now. She didn't have a good night. I don't know if I told you; I'm putting her in the nursing home as of the first of the month."

"You didn't tell me. I'm sorry."

As Adam tucked the file under his arm and picked up the doll, he was startled by a scream. "She's having another nightmare," Henry said, and rushed toward the bedroom, Adam behind him.

Phoebe was lying on the bed, her hands covering her face. Henry bent over and took her hands in his. "It's all right, dear," he said soothingly.

She opened her eyes, looked up at him, then turned her head and saw Adam holding the doll. "Oh, they did drown her," she sighed. "But I'm glad they decided to let the baby live."

62

*M*ENLEY PHONED Carrie Bell at four o'clock. Carrie's initial cautious response when Menley identified herself was replaced by genuine warmth when she realized the reason for the call.

"Oh, that's wonderful," she said. "I sure can use the money. I've lost a lot of work these two weeks."

"A lot of work?" Menley asked. "Why is that?"

"Oh, I shouldn't have said that. I'll be over tomorrow morning bright and early. Thank you, Mrs. Nichols."

Menley told Amy about the conversation. "Do you know what she could have meant about losing a lot of work?"

Amy looked uncomfortable. "It's just that Elaine recommends her to people who are selling or renting their houses. Carrie goes in for a couple of days and is really good at making a house look great. But Elaine says that, because she's a terrible gossip, she's not sending her out on new jobs. She even tried to get my father to fire her."

Over dinner, Menley told Adam about that conversation. "Don't you think that was mean?" she asked as she ladled a second helping of chili onto his plate. "From what Amy tells me, Carrie Bell is a hardworking single mother, supporting a three-year-old."

"This is your best chili ever," Adam commented. "To answer you, I know Carrie's good. She cleaned the cottage I took last year when I came up alone. But I also know that Elaine is a hard worker. It's no accident that she's as successful as she is, because she doesn't leave anything to chance. If she thinks Carrie Bell's gossip is hurting her chances of selling houses, Carrie's out of a job. Oh, did I mention that besides the food I like the ambience?"

Menley had turned off the overhead light and put the wall sconces on the dim setting. They were sitting opposite each other at the refectory table. All Phoebe Sprague's research data and books, as well as Menley's own notes and sketches, were now in the library.

"I decided that since we always eat in here, it's a shame to have it so cluttered," she explained.

That was only part of the truth, she acknowledged to herself. The rest was that when Adam had gotten home late in the afternoon and given her the heavy file he'd gotten from Henry Sprague, she had glanced through it and been shocked to see the sketch of Mehitabel and Andrew on the ship. It was exactly as she had visualized them. There has to be another picture of them in all this stuff, she thought, and I must have seen it. But it was one more example of forgetting something important.

That was when she decided to put the Remember House research aside for a few days and get the *Travel Times* article out of the way. She'd phoned Jan Paley, who agreed to line up some historical homes for her to visit.

"The stories you told me about the houses where people sense a presence would be perfect," she had told Jan. "I know the editor would love it." And I want to know what those people have to say, she'd thought.

"Did you do much writing today, or are you still digging through Phoebe's files?" Adam asked.

"Neither actually; I was working on something else." She told him about her call to Jan and what she planned to do.

Did I rush that explanation? Menley wondered. It sounded so rehearsed.

"Ghost stories?" Adam smiled. "You don't believe in that nonsense."

"I believe in legends." She noticed the chili had disappeared from his plate. "You were hungry. What did you have for lunch?"

"A hamburger, but that was a long time ago. 'Laine was with me. We went over her testimony for the inquest."

There was always something affectionate, even intimate, about the way Adam spoke when he referred to Elaine. She had to ask. "Adam, were you ever involved with Elaine, I mean more than as a big buddy?"

He looked uncomfortable. "Oh, we dated on and off as kids, and sometimes when I spent time at the Cape during law school, we got together."

"And never since then?"

"Oh, hell, Men, you don't expect me to kiss and tell. Before I met you, I used to bring the girl I was dating up here for a long weekend when my mother still had the big place. Other times I came alone. If neither one of us was busy, 'Laine and I would go out. But that was years ago. No big deal."

"I see." Get off it, Menley told herself. The last thing you need to start is a discussion on Elaine.

Adam was stretching his hand across the table. "I'm with the only girl I've ever really loved and wanted to be with," he said. He paused. "We've had more ups and downs in five years than most people experience in a lifetime. All I care about is getting through them and being on firm ground again."

Menley touched her fingertips to his. She pulled them back. "Adam, you're trying to tell me something, aren't you?"

With increasing horror, she listened as he told her his plan:

"Men, when I spoke to Dr. Kaufman, she said that she thought you would benefit from aggressive therapy. It's one thing to have a flashback to the accident. It's another to think you heard Bobby calling and run through the house looking for him. She wants you to be an inpatient for just a short time."

It was exactly what she had feared.

"I'm getting better, Adam."

"I know how hard you're trying. But after the inquest it would be better if we took her advice. You know you trust her."

In that moment she hated him and knew it showed in her face. She turned and saw that he had put the antique doll in Hannah's high chair. Now it stared at her with fixed china blue eyes, a parody of the miracle that was Hannah.

"We're not talking about trusting Dr. Kaufman, we're talking about trusting *me.*"

63

*J*AN PALEY had been surprised and pleased to receive the phone call from Menley Nichols that afternoon. Menley had asked about historical houses with legends attached to them.

"By historical, I mean good examples of early architecture, and by legends, I mean stories about an unexplainable presence, a ghost," Menley told her.

Jan had readily agreed to be her guide. She'd immediately sat down and made a list of the places she would take her.

The old Dillingham house in Brewster was one they would visit. It was the second oldest house on the Cape. Over the years some of the people who rented it claimed to have gotten the impression of a woman passing the door of one of the bedrooms.

The Dennis Inn was another place to take her. The proprietors even had a nickname for the playful spirit who constantly wrought havoc in the kitchen. They called her Lillian.

They could visit Sarah Nye, the friend she had mentioned to Menley when they spoke at Elaine's party. Sarah was sure she was sharing her house with the lady for whom it had been built in 1720.

And what about the saltbox in Harwich that now was an interior designer's shop on the entry level? The owners claimed they entertained a resident ghost and were convinced she was a sixteen-year-old who had died there in the nineteenth century.

Jan made some calls, set up appointments and phoned Menley back. "We're all set. I'll pick you up tomorrow morning at about ten o'clock."

"That's fine, and Jan, do you know anything about an antique doll that Phoebe Sprague was keeping? Henry told Adam that she insists it belongs in Remember House."

"Oh, did she find it?" Jan exclaimed. "I'm so glad. Tom discovered it under the eaves in the attic. God only knows how long it had been there. Phoebe wanted to show it to an antiques expert. Some research she had done suggested it actually might have belonged to Mehitabel. I didn't realize at that time that Phoebe's memory was beginning to slip. She put the doll somewhere and then couldn't find it."

"Why did she think it belonged to Mehitabel?" Menley asked Jan.

"Phoebe told me that a memoir she read mentioned that after her husband took her baby from her, Mehitabel could be observed standing on the widow's walk, holding a doll."

August 12th

64

SCOTT COVEY spent most of Friday on the boat. He packed a picnic lunch, brought along his fishing rods and passed the most peaceful day he had enjoyed in weeks. The golden warmth of August had returned in full measure, replacing the chill that had dominated yesterday. The ocean breeze was balmy again. His lobster pots were full.

After lunch he stretched out on the deck, clasped his hands under his head and rehearsed the testimony he would give at the inquest. He tried to remember all the negatives Adam Nichols had warned him about and how he could refute every single one.

His involvement with Tina last winter was going to be his biggest problem. Without seeming like a louse and a cad, how could he let the judge understand that she had been the one pursuing him?

And then something Vivian had told him came into his mind. In late June, when he had talked her through one of her periodic fits of tearful insecurity, she had sighed, "Scott, you're the kind of great-looking guy women naturally fall for. I try to understand that. I know other people instinctively understand it too. It's not your fault; you can't help it."

"Vivy," he said aloud, "I'm going to have you to thank for getting me through this inquest."

Looking up at the sky, he put his fingers to his lips and blew her a kiss.

65

ALL LITTLE DUCKS in a row, Nat Coogan thought as he went over the list of witnesses they had subpoenaed for the inquest. He was in the district attorney's office in Barnstable.

The DA, Robert Shore, was sitting behind his desk, going over his own notes. He had scheduled a conference at noon to coordinate final preparations for the inquest. "All right. We're going to get some bitching that we haven't given much notice to the people we've subpoenaed, but that's the way it goes. This is a high-profile case, and we can't let it drag on. Any problems?"

The meeting lasted an hour and a half. By then the two men were in agreement that they had a good case to present to the judge. But Nat felt he had to issue some words of warning: "Listen, I've seen this guy in action. He can cry on cue. He may not have made it as an actor on stage, but trust me—he might be able to earn his Tony in district court."

66

ON FRIDAY MORNING, Adam left Remember House as soon as Amy arrived. "I have to interview the waitresses who might balance any testimony about Tina visiting Scott in Florida," he explained to Menley.

"Jan is picking me up at ten," she said mechanically. "I should be back around two or two-thirty. Carrie Bell will be cleaning today, so she and Amy will both be in the house with Hannah. Is that satisfactory?"

"Menley!" He went to put his arms around her, but she turned and walked away from him.

"Do you want to tell me what's wrong?" Jan asked Menley as they drove over the bridge from Morris Island to the road that led to the lighthouse and Route 28.

"What's wrong is that my husband and my psychiatrist seem to agree that I belong in a padded cell."

"That's ridiculous."

"Yes, it is. And I'm not going to let it happen. Let's leave it at that. But, Jan, I have the feeling that Phoebe is trying to communicate something to me. The other day when she was at the house and saw her files, she looked at them, and I think she really understood what they were."

"It's possible," Jan agreed. "There are times when Phoebe does seem to have breakthroughs of memory."

"Her tone of voice was so urgent. She said that Mehitabel was innocent. Then she said something like, 'Tobias Knight. Answer in Mooncusser file.' Does that mean anything to you?"

"Not really. We know Tobias built Remember House, and that's about it. But when I was thinking of places to take you today I learned that he also built one of the oldest houses in Eastham. If you have time, we could swing by and take a look at it. It's run by the Eastham Historical Society, and they may have collected some information on him."

67

"*T*INA MET Scott Covey in here," Liz Murphy told Adam. "He came in for dinner with some of the people from the playhouse, and she played up to him like crazy. And nobody knows how to play up to a guy better than Tina."

Adam was interviewing the young waitress in the office of the Daniel Webster Inn in Sandwich. "That was in July of last year?"

"Early July. Tina was going around with Fred at the time. What a nice guy he is. But boy, she put the skids on him when Scott came into the picture."

"Did you think Scott was serious about Tina?"

"Heck no. We all agreed that Scott had big plans for himself. He wasn't going to ever settle down with someone who worked for a living. We told her she was crazy to dump Fred for him."

"As far as you know, did Tina see Scott over the winter?"

"She knew he was in Boca Raton, and she wanted to get a job there. But I guess he told her that if things worked out, he'd be back up on the Cape."

"And she knew he was going around with Vivian Carpenter?"

"She knew it and she didn't care."

Exactly what Scott told me, Adam thought. "Did Vivian know about Tina?"

"Unless Scott told her, I don't know how she would know."

"Do you know why Tina quit her job here?"

"She told me that Scott had gotten married and she was starting to see Fred again and wanted to be free evenings to be with him. She said that Fred gets up so early for work that he's in bed at ten o'clock at night. She wanted a job where she worked breakfast and lunch, but that wasn't available here."

"Liz, you're going to be subpoenaed as a witness at the inquest. Don't worry about it. The district attorney will ask you pretty much the same questions I've just asked."

The other waitress, Alice Regan, came on at eleven, so Adam waited to see her. Her story verified what Liz Murphy had told him. He knew the district attorney would hit Tina hard on choosing to work in Chatham, at a restaurant frequented by an ex-lover, but that would make Tina look bad, not Scott.

Adam drove down Route 6A and stopped at the Courthouse. In the district attorney's office, he submitted the names of Liz Murphy and Alice Regan to be added to the list of witnesses he wanted subpoenaed. "I may have one or two more," he told an assistant DA.

His next stop was in Orleans, to interview a fisherman whose boat had been swamped in the same squall that took Vivian Carpenter's life.

68

*C*ARRIE BELL bustled around the keeping room, dusting the inside of the cabinets as she chatted with Amy. "That is one adorable baby," she said. "And so good."

Amy was feeding Hannah her lunch.

As though she understood the compliment, Hannah turned a dazzling smile on Carrie and put her fist in the jar of peaches.

"Hannah!" Amy protested, laughing.

"And she's going to look a lot like her brother," Carrie announced.

"I think so too," Amy agreed. "That picture on Mrs. Nichols' dresser shows a real resemblance."

"It shows up even more in the video of Bobby that Mr. Nichols had up here last year." Carrie lowered her voice. "You know, I used to clean that little cottage he rented near Elaine's house. Well, one time I went in, and Mr. Nichols was watching a video of Bobby running to his mother. I swear, the look on his face almost broke my heart."

She picked up the antique doll. "You don't want to be taking this in and out of the high chair, Amy. Why don't I just put it in that old cradle in the baby's room? It kind of looks as though it belongs there."

69

*B*Y ONE O'CLOCK, a dozen pages of Menley's notebook were filled, and she had two hours of interviews on her tape recorder.

As Jan drove down Route 6 toward Eastham, Menley mused on the similarities in the experiences she had heard. "Everyone we talked to seems to feel that if there is something unexplainable in their house, it's a benevolent presence," she said. "But your friend in Brewster, Sarah, has never had any manifestation except that first one."

Jan looked at her. "Meaning?"

"Sarah told us that early one morning when she and her husband were asleep in bed, the sound of someone coming up the stairs awakened her. Then the door opened and she saw the imprint of footsteps on the carpet."

"That's right."

Menley flipped through her notebook. "Sarah said she felt a sense of comfort. Here's how she put it, 'It was like when you're a small child, and your mother comes into the room and covers you.' "

"Yes, that was the way she expressed it."

"And then she said she felt a pat on her shoulder, and it was as though someone were speaking, but she was hearing with her mind, not her ears. She knew it was Abigail Harding, the lady for whom the house had been built, and Abigail was telling her how happy she was that her home had been restored to its original beauty."

"That's always been the way Sarah described that experience."

"My point," Menley continued, "is that there was a reason for Abigail to contact Sarah. She had something to tell her. Sarah says she's never experienced anything specific again, and that when she has that feeling of a benevolent presence now, she may be simply sensing a tranquil atmosphere in the house. I think what I'm trying to say is that maybe some kind of unfinished business keeps a presence anchored to earth."

"It's possible," Jan agreed.

They stopped for a quick lunch at a small waterfront restaurant in Eastham, then went to see the house Tobias Knight had built in that town. It was on Route 6, surrounded by restaurants and shops.

"The location can't compare with Remember House," Menley remarked.

"Most of the captains' houses were set back from the water. The early settlers respected those nor'easters. But the house is similar to Remember House, if not quite as fancy. This one dates back to 1699. As you can see, there's no fanlight."

"The captain and Mehitabel brought the fanlight from England," Menley said.

"I didn't know that. You must have found that bit of information in Phoebe's material."

Menley did not answer. They went inside, stopped at the reception desk, picked up the literature on the house and then walked through the rooms. The beautifully restored mansion was similar in layout to Remember House. "The rooms are larger here," Jan observed, "but Remember House has finer detail."

Menley was silent on the drive back to Chatham. Something was bothering her, but she wasn't sure what it was. Now she was anxious to get home and have a chance to talk to Carrie Bell before she left.

70

*F*RED HENDIN worked on a carpentry crew with a small builder in Dennis who specialized in renovations. Fred liked the work, especially enjoying the feel of wood in his hands. Wood had a mind of its own as well as an inherent dignity. He viewed himself in much the same way.

Now that waterfront property was worth a fortune, it paid to renovate the budget homes that were situated on prime lots. The waterfront house they were working on was one of those. It was about forty years old, and they were practically rebuilding it. Part of the project was to gut the kitchen, replacing those pressboard cabinets that builders used in cheap housing with custom cherry-wood units.

Fred actually had his eye on a house opposite the one where he was working, a real handyman's special, with beach rights and a terrific view. He'd been watching the local real estate agents bring prospective buyers to see it, but none of them stayed long. They didn't look past the fact that the place was a mess. Fred knew that if he bought it and put in six months of hard work, he'd end up with one of the nicest homes anyone could want, plus he would have a good investment.

Only two weeks more till the end of August, he thought. Then the price would drop. Real estate activity pretty much died on the Cape during the winter.

Fred sat with the other guys in the crew, having lunch. They worked well together, and at breaks they shared a few laughs.

They began talking about the inquest into Vivian Carpenter Covey's death. Matt, the electrician, had done some work for Vivian in May, shortly after she was married. "Not an easy lady," he reported. "The day I was there her husband went to the store and stayed out a while. She sailed into him when he got back, said he wasn't going to make a fool of her. Told him to go pack his bags. Then she started crying and falling all over him when he reminded her she'd asked him to stop at the cleaners and that's what held him up. Believe me, that woman was a problem."

Sam, a recent addition to the crew asked, "Isn't there talk that Covey has a girlfriend, a waitress from around here who's a real hot number?"

"Forget it." Matt scowled as he glanced sideways at Fred.

Fred stuffed the napkin into his coffee container. "That's right. Forget it," he snapped, his previous good humor instantly gone. He pushed his chair back and left the table.

When he went back to work, it took him time to settle down. A lot of things were sticking in his craw. Last night after the detective left, Tina admitted that she'd been seeing Covey all last winter, making several trips down to Florida.

Does it matter? Fred asked himself as he hung the cabinets. As Tina had pointed out, she and Fred had not been dating then. But why did she have to lie about it? he asked himself. Then he wondered if she was also lying about seeing Covey after he was married. And what about in the past month since his wife died?

At the end of the day, when he arrived home to wait for Adam Nichols to keep their appointment, he was still wrestling with the question of whether or not he would ever be able to trust Tina again.

He wouldn't say anything to Covey's lawyer. For the present he would stick up for Tina and give her the engagement ring to wear at the inquest. From the way that detective talked, the police wouldn't mind involving Tina in a murder plot. She didn't seem to understand how serious all this had become.

No, he would stand by her for now, but if this bad feeling kept growing, he knew that as crazy as he was about Tina, he couldn't marry her. A man had to have his dignity.

Brooding, he thought about all the nice gifts he had given her this summer, like his mother's gold watch and pearls and pin. She kept them in that hollowed-out book that was really a jewelry box, on a shelf in her living room.

When the inquest was over, if he decided to call it quits with Tina, he would collect the engagement ring and them too.

71

*I*T WAS a busy afternoon at the agency. Elaine received two new listings from walk-ins and went out to inspect the properties. One of them she photographed immediately, a handsome replica of a square-rigger on Ryders Pond. "This should go fast," she assured the owner.

The other place had always been a rental and needed sprucing up. Tactfully she suggested that if the lawn were mowed and the shrubs trimmed, the overall effect could be enhanced. The house also needed a good cleaning. Reluctantly she offered to send Carrie Bell over—she had her drawbacks, but no one did a better job.

She called Marge on the car phone. "I'll go directly home. John and Amy are coming for dinner, and I want to develop the new pictures before I have to start cooking."

"You're getting very domestic," Marge kidded her.

"I might as well."

When she got home, Elaine made one more call, this time to Scott Covey. "Why not join us for dinner?"

"If you let me bring it. I just came in from the boat with a bucket of lobsters."

"I knew there was a reason I was calling you. Did you get the picture?"

"Yes, I did."

"You didn't even thank me," she teased. "But you know why I sent it."

"As a reminder, I know."

"See you later, Scott."

72

*C*ARRIE BELL was upstairs vacuuming when Jan dropped Menley off. Menley went up to her. "Amy has the baby out in the carriage, Mrs. Nichols," she explained. "Good as gold that baby is, let me tell you."

"She wasn't always that good." Menley smiled. She looked around. "Everything shines. Thanks, Carrie."

"Well, I like to leave things just right. I'm just about finished now. Do you want me to come next week?"

"I certainly do." Menley opened her pocketbook, took out her wallet and with a silent prayer began to steer the conversation where she wanted it to go. "Carrie, strictly between us, what frightened you the last time you were here?"

Carrie looked alarmed. "Mrs. Nichols, I know it's just my imagination, and like Miss Atkins says, I'm so heavy footed I probably stepped on a loose floorboard and that got the cradle rocking."

"Maybe. But you also thought you heard someone moving around upstairs. At least that's what Amy said."

Carrie leaned forward, and her voice lowered. "Mrs. Nichols, you promise you won't tell Miss Atkins a word about this?"

"I promise."

"Mrs. Nichols, I did hear something that day, and today I tried pounding my feet when I went into the nursery, and that cradle didn't budge."

"You didn't notice anything unusual today, then?"

"No. Nothing strange. But I'm a bit worried about Amy."

"Why? What happened?"

"Oh, nothing happened. I mean, just before Hannah woke up from her nap a little while ago, Amy was reading in the little parlor with the door closed. I thought I heard her crying. I didn't want to seem nosy so I didn't go in to her. I know she's worried about her father marrying Miss Atkins. Then later I asked her if anything was troubling her, and she denied it. You know how kids are. Sometimes they'll bare their souls. Other times they want you to MYOB."

"MYOB?"

"Mind your own business."

"Of course." Menley handed Carrie the folded bills. "Thanks very much."

"Thank you. You're a nice lady. And I tell you, I have a three-year-old, and I can understand how awful it must have been for you to lose that beautiful little boy. I got tears in my eyes when I saw that video of him last year."

"You saw a video of Bobby?"

"Mr. Nichols had it up here when he rented the cottage. Like I was telling Amy, he had the saddest expression watching it. It showed him in the pool with Bobby, and he lifted him out, and you called him, and he ran to you."

Menley swallowed over the lump in her throat. "That tape was made just two weeks before the accident," she said, trying to keep her voice steady. "I never could bear to watch it. It was such a happy day."

I want to see it now, she thought. I'm ready to see it.

Carrie put the money in her purse. "Miss Atkins was with Mr. Nichols that day, and he was telling her all about Bobby and how guilty he felt because he should have been with the two of you the day of the accident but played golf instead."

73

*I*T HAD BEEN a good day's work, Adam thought as he drove onto the private road that led to Remember House. Unfortunately it wasn't over. It was nearly three o'clock now and at five he'd leave to meet Fred Hendin.

But at least he'd be home for a couple of hours, and it was a perfect beach day. That is, if Menley was willing to go to the beach with him.

Amy's car was in the driveway. He had mixed feelings of relief and irritation. She was a nice, responsible kid, but it would be great to be alone with his family and not have someone always underfoot.

If I react this way, how does Menley feel, having someone around all the time? he wondered. Sick at heart, he realized that they were rapidly going back to the way it had been before the pregnancy with Hannah. Remote from each other. Both of them on edge.

There was no one in the house. Was Menley back yet, and if so, were they on the beach? He walked to the edge of the bluff and looked down.

Menley was sitting cross-legged on the blanket, Hannah propped against her. The perfect picture, Adam thought. Menley's hair was swirling behind her. Her slender body was tanned and lovely. She and Amy seemed to be deep in conversation.

Amy was lying on the sand facing Menley, leaning on her elbows, chin resting in her palms. It's got to be tough for her, he thought. Going away to college is always scary, and according to Elaine, she's still having a problem about her father remarrying. But Elaine had also said, "She doesn't know how lucky she is that John can afford to send her to Chapel Hill."

Elaine hadn't gone to college. At the end of the summer twenty-one years ago, when the rest of the crowd was heading for elite schools, her mother had just lost another job, so Elaine had gotten work as a typist in a real estate agency. Obviously she had done very well for herself, Adam reflected. Now she owned the agency.

At that moment Menley looked up. Adam scrambled down the steep path. When he reached them he had the feeling that he was an intruder. "Hi," he said, lamely.

Menley did not answer.

Amy sprang up. "Hi, Mr. Nichols. Are you home for good?"

"Yes, Adam, are you home for good?" Menley asked. "If you are, I know Amy would like to have a few hours to herself."

He decided to ignore her impersonal tone. "Go ahead, Amy. Thanks." He squatted down on the blanket and waited while Amy said good-bye to Hannah and Menley.

When she was out of earshot, he said, "I'll give her a chance to change, then I'll go up and get my bathing suit on."

"We'll come up with you. We've had enough of the beach."

"Damn it, Menley, knock it off."

"Knock what off?"

"Men, don't let this happen to us," he pleaded.

Hannah looked up at him uncertainly.

"It's all right, sweetheart," he said, "I'm just trying to make your mommy stop being mad at me."

"Adam, we can't reduce this to a tiff. I spoke to Dr. Kaufman. She's going to call us back at four-thirty. I am going to absolutely refuse to be hospitalized. I also have a call in to my mother in Ireland. I'm going to ask her to cut short her trip. If there is some way that you and Dr. Kaufman can sign me into a hospital against my will, then my mother, who is a registered nurse, will mind my baby, not your girlfriend 'Laine."

"What in the hell is that supposed to mean?"

"Adam, when you came up here last year, how much did you see of Elaine?"

"She's an old friend. Of course I saw her. And it meant nothing."

"As you said last night, you're not the kind to kiss and tell. But what was she doing watching vidoes of my little boy with you?"

"My God, Men, she happened to stop in when I was playing the tape. I wasn't just looking at Bobby in that video. I was looking at you."

"With your girlfriend."

"No, with an old buddy."

"Who has told her future stepdaughter that after you deposit me in a psychiatric hospital in New York, you'll be here with Hannah."

Adam stood up. "I'm going to change and go for a swim."

"Surely you're not planning to leave Hannah alone with me?"

He did not answer but turned and walked away.

Menley watched Adam climb the path. He was leaning forward, his hands in his pockets. She thought of what Carrie Bell had overheard him tell Elaine, that he felt guilty he hadn't been with her the day of the accident.

Adam had told her that right after Bobby died, and she had raged at him. "Don't try to make me feel better. You had a long-standing golf date. I didn't want you to change your plans for a last-minute invitation."

He'd never mentioned it to her again.

When Adam returned ten minutes later, she said, "Adam, I know myself. I am going to tell Dr. Kaufman that I am coming to grips with these anxiety attacks. I am also going to tell her that if you cannot and will not accept that fact, then our marriage is not going to last. The background of this house is of a husband who did not trust his wife. Don't perpetuate that mistake."

74

O<small>N THE DRIVE HOME,</small> Amy puzzled over whether or not to warn her father that Carrie Bell might tell him that she had been crying. Mrs. Nichols had asked her about it. "I wasn't crying," she'd protested. "Honestly. Carrie's hearing things."

She thought that Mrs. Nichols believed her, but her father would probably believe Carrie. Her father was always worried about her these days. If only he'd stop telling her how wonderful it was going to be to have a new mother.

I'll be eighteen next month, Amy thought. I wish Dad would stop trying to sell Elaine to me. I'm glad he is getting married again, but I wish it weren't to her.

Tonight she had wanted to go out with the crowd to Hyannis. But Elaine had decided she was going to fix a home-cooked meal, so her father had half ordered, half begged Amy to go with him.

"Don't hurt Elaine's feelings," he had urged.

I can't wait to get to college, Amy thought as she drove through the Main Street traffic into the rotary. Then she sighed. Oh, Mom, why did you have to go and die on us?

Maybe that was the reason she felt so close to Mrs. Nichols. Just the way she missed Mom, she knew Mrs. Nichols missed her little boy. But now Mrs. Nichols has Hannah.

And I have Elaine, she thought bitterly as she turned into her driveway.

But later she was glad her father had made her accompany him to Elaine's house. Scott Covey was there, and she helped him steam the lobsters he had brought. He was so nice, and even though he was having so many problems, he sure didn't take them out on anyone. He talked about Chapel Hill.

"One of the plays I toured in ran at the college for a couple of weeks," he told her. "Great town. You'll have a lot of fun."

During dinner, Amy noticed that they avoided any talk about the inquest. Elaine did ask if Carrie Bell had heard any more footsteps when she was cleaning today.

Amy seized the chance to get in something about the crying. "No, but in case she tells you she heard me crying, she was wrong."

"She heard crying?" Elaine asked. "Was it Menley?"

"Mrs. Nichols was out for a long time with Mrs. Paley, and when she came in she was fine." Amy did not want to talk about Mrs. Nichols with Elaine. She knew that Elaine thought Mrs. Nichols was on the verge of another breakdown. If I'd only brought my own car instead of going with Dad, she thought. I don't want to sit around here all night.

When Scott Covey started to talk about leaving, she saw her chance to get away. "Scott, would you mind dropping me off?" she asked, then tried to sound tired when she turned to her father. "Dad, I really have had a long day and I'd like to get home. Unless you want me to help with the dishes, Elaine."

"No, go right ahead. Taking care of a baby all day is work."

Now that she'd claimed to be tired, Amy realized there was nothing to do for the rest of the evening. She couldn't announce she was meeting her friends. There was nothing good on television, and she didn't want to ask Scott to drive her to rent a video. But wait a minute, she thought. Elaine has a terrific collection of old films. She lends them to Dad all the time.

"Elaine," she asked, "could I borrow one of your videos?"

"Any at all," Elaine said. "Take a couple of them. Just be sure to bring them back."

I know enough to return them, Amy thought resentfully. Her father was just starting to tell one of his long, pointless stories when she went into the family room.

The longest wall was covered with bookshelves. Fully half of them held videotapes, the titles facing out, in alphabetical order. Amy skimmed them and selected *The Country Girl* with Grace Kelly and *Horse Feathers,* the Marx brothers comedy.

She was about to leave when she remembered another oldie she'd always wanted to watch: *Birth of a Nation.* Was it here?

She read the *B* titles slowly and found it. As she took it from the shelf, several cassettes around it fell. Putting them back in place, she realized why they'd been sticking out. There was a cassette behind them, standing upright against the wall.

It was labeled BOBBY—EAST HAMPTON—LAST TAPE. Could this be the one of the Nicholses' little boy that Carrie Bell saw last year?

I'd love to see it, Amy thought. Elaine may not even realize it's here. It does belong to the Nicholses' and she might not want to lend it. I'll return it with the others and not say anything.

She dropped the cassettes in her shoulder bag and went back to the dining room.

Her father was just finishing his story.

Scott Covey was smiling politely. Elaine seemed convulsed with laughter. Amy wanted to strangle Elaine every time she heard that phony laugh. She thought, Mom would have said, "John, will you absolutely promise not to inflict that long-winded monologue on anyone again for at least a week?"

And then she would have laughed *with* Dad, not *at* him.

75

"*N*O, I have not increased the medication," Menley told Dr. Kaufman. "I haven't found it necessary."

She was on the phone in the library, Hannah in her lap. Adam was on the extension in the keeping room.

"Menley, I have a feeling you regard Adam and me as the enemy," Dr. Kaufman said.

"No, that isn't true. I did not tell you about the baby-sitter seeing me on the widow's walk for the simple reason that I thought she was mistaken. And now she has come to that conclusion too."

"Then whom did Amy see?"

"My guess is that she saw no one. There's a metal strip on that chimney. When the sun hits it, it gives an impression of someone moving."

"What about the flashback to hearing the train and Bobby calling you? You told me you were afraid to pick up Hannah."

"I didn't want her to cry anymore, but I was afraid to pick her up because I was trembling so much. I'm sorry I failed her at that moment. But even without a mother who's having an anxiety attack, babies are left to cry it out sometimes."

Hannah tugged her hair as she spoke. Menley bent her head. "Ouch."

"Menley!" Adam sounded startled.

"The baby is pulling my hair and I said 'ouch,' and Dr. Kaufman, please listen to what I'm trying to convey to you. Adam is ready to drop the phone and rush in here at the least hint of anything. I have to say I think you're treating the wrong patient."

She paused and bit her lip. "I'm going to get off now and let you two talk. Doctor, if you and Adam are able to sign me into a psychiatric facility against my will, you are going to wait until my mother is home from Ireland and can mind my baby. In the meantime, I will stay here in this lovely house and write my book. When I started having these anxiety attacks, you talked to both of us about the need for his support. Well, I don't feel that Adam has offered that to me, and I need it. The time will come, however, when I do not need it, and at that time I will neither need nor want him either."

She replaced the receiver quietly. "Well, Hannah," she said, "that's telling them."

It was exactly four-forty. At 4:43, Adam came to the door. "I always said I never wanted you to get mad at me." He hesitated. "I've got to see Fred Hendin now. I don't want to go. I'm sorry I got involved in this Covey case. But since we're being so stripped-down honest, I'd like to remind you that you were the one who urged me to help this guy out."

"Granted," Menley said.

"But when I get back, I'd like to take you out for dinner. You feed her nibs while I'm gone, and we'll bring her along. We used to do that with Bobby."

"Yes, we did."

"One more thing. You have a call in to your mother. When she phones, don't ask her to interrupt her vacation. Dr. Kaufman believes you're doing fine and I agree. Have a baby-sitter or not. That's up to you."

He was gone. Menley waited until she heard the sound of the keeping room door closing behind him before she said, "Hannah, sometimes you just have to stand up to people. We're going to be fine."

At six-thirty, just as she came out of the shower, her mother phoned from Wexford.

"Menley, they said it was urgent that I call you. What's wrong?"

Menley made a determined effort to sound cheery. "Nothing's wrong, Mom. I just wanted to see how you were. Hannah's telling herself jokes. She's lying on my bed, giggling . . . No, I didn't have a special reason for calling . . . Jack and Phyllis okay?"

She was still on the phone when Adam came into the bedroom. She waved him over. "Mom, let me brief Adam. He'll love it." Quickly she explained, "Phyl is now tracing my father's family. She's back five generations to 1860. She discovered Adrian Mc-

Carthy, a scholar from Trinity College. The McCarthys have gone up in her estimation. The hunt continues."

She handed him the phone. "Say a quick hello to your mother-in-law."

She studied Adam as he chatted with her mother, realizing how tired he looked. This has not been much of a vacation for him, she thought.

When he hung up, she said, "We don't have to eat out. The fish market isn't closed yet. Why don't you run down and get something."

"Actually, I would like that. Thanks, Men."

He returned with bay scallops, freshly picked ears of small-kernel corn, beef tomatoes and French bread.

Hannah watched the sunset with them. After they settled her in her crib, they prepared dinner together. By unspoken agreement, they did not discuss the conversation with Dr. Kaufman.

Instead, Adam told her about the meetings he had had that day. "Those waitresses will be good witnesses," he said, "and so will Tina's boyfriend. But Men, I have to tell you, Scott Covey is coming through more and more as an opportunist."

"But surely not a murderer."

"No, not that."

After dinner they both read for a while. They were still sensitive from the things that had been said earlier, so they talked very little.

They went to bed at ten-thirty, both sensing that they still needed space from each other. Menley felt uncommonly tired and fell asleep almost immediately.

"Mommy, Mommy." It was the afternoon at East Hampton two weeks before Bobby died. They were spending the weekend with Louis Miller, one of Adam's law partners. Lou was taking videos. Adam had Bobby in the pool. He'd put him on the deck. "Go to Mommy," he'd instructed.

Bobby ran to her, his arms outstretched, his smile joyous.
"Mommy, Mommy."

She swung him up and turned to the camera. "Tell us your
name," she instructed.

"Wobert Adam Nikko," he'd said proudly.

"And what do people call you?"

"Bobby."

"And do you go to school?"

"Nertry schoow."

"Nertry schoow," she'd repeated and the sound of laughter
closed the tape.

"Bobby. Bobby."

She was crying. Adam was leaning over her. "It's all right, Men."

She opened her eyes. "It was just a dream this time."

As Adam put his arms around her, they heard Hannah begin to
fuss. Menley pulled herself up.

"I'll go in to her," Adam said, quickly getting out of bed.

He brought her back to their room. "Here she is, Mama."

Menley closed her arms around the baby. A sense of peace and
healing came over her as Hannah snuggled close.

"Go to sleep, honey," Adam said quietly. "I'll put her nibs back
in a couple of minutes."

She drifted off, remembering Bobby's happy, sunny voice.
"Mommy, Mommy." By next summer Hannah would be able to
call to her too.

After a while she felt Hannah being taken from her arms. A few
minutes later Adam drew her to him and whispered, "Sweetheart,
the one thing you mustn't do is deny you're having flashbacks."

August 13th

76

LATE SATURDAY MORNING, Nat Coogan dutifully accompanied his wife into town. Their anniversary was coming up, and Debbie had seen a painting at one of the galleries that she thought would be perfect over their fireplace.

"It's a panoramic view of the ocean and shore," she told him. "I think if I were looking at it every day, I'd feel I was living on the water."

"If you like it, buy it, Babe."

"No, you have to see it first."

Nat was no judge of art, but when he saw the watercolor, he thought it was a pretty amateurish job, certainly not worth the two hundred dollar price tag.

"You don't like it. I can tell," Debbie said.

"It's okay."

The dealer intervened. "The artist is only twenty-one years old and has a lot of promise. This painting may be worth money someday."

I wouldn't hold my breath, Nat thought.

"We'll think about it," Debbie said. When they were outside, she sighed. "It didn't look that good today. Oh, well."

The art shop was on a path off Main Street. "Buy you lunch?" Nat asked when they reached the sidewalk.

"You probably want to get out on the boat."

"No, that's all right. We'll go to the Wayside. Tina's working today and I like her to see me hanging around. One of our few good chances to nail Covey is to get her rattled when she's testifying."

They passed the Atkins Real Estate Agency. Debbie stopped and looked in the window. "I always check to see what waterfront estate they're showing this week," she told Nat. "After all, we might win the lottery someday. I was so sorry when they took out that aerial photograph of Remember House. That was my favorite. I think it inspired me to get interested in the watercolor."

"Looks as though Marge is about to put the one of Remember House back," Nat observed.

Inside the office, Marge was opening the showcase window, and as they watched, she put the handsomely framed photograph in an empty space in the display area. Noticing them, Marge waved and came outside to speak to them. "Hello Detective Coogan," she said. "Anything I can help you with? We've got some very attractive listings."

"Unofficial business," Nat told her. "My wife is enamored of that picture." He pointed to the aerial photo of Remember House. "Unfortunately, that listing is a little out of our price range."

"That picture has brought in more traffic," Marge commented. "Actually this is a copy of the one you saw. Elaine made it for Adam Nichols and I'm just putting it in the window until he comes for it. She gave the original to Scott Covey."

"Scott Covey!" Nat exclaimed. "What would he want with it?"

"Elaine says he's expressed interest in Remember House."

"I'd have thought he couldn't wait to get away from the Cape," Nat said. "Provided he's free to go."

Marge was suddenly uncomfortably aware that she might be wandering into dangerous territory. She had heard that Nat Coogan was investigating Scott Covey. On the other hand, that was his job, and he and his wife were nice people and in the future could become clients. His wife was still admiring the picture of Remember House. Marge remembered that Elaine had said she had the negative and could always make copies.

"Would you want to have a print of this photograph?" she asked.

Debbie said, "I certainly would. I have just the spot for it."

"I know Elaine would make one up for you," Marge volunteered.

"Then that's settled," Nat decreed.

At the Wayside Inn, they found that Tina had phoned in sick. "I am getting her rattled," Nat said. "That's good."

It was when they were finishing their lobster rolls that Debbie suddenly observed, "That isn't the same picture, Nat."

"What do you mean?"

"There was something different about the picture of Remember House we saw this morning, and I just figured it out. The one that had been in the window earlier had a boat in it. The one Marge just showed us didn't. Isn't that odd?"

77

ON SATURDAY MORNING, Adam reminded Menley to tell Amy they wouldn't be needing her that day. He had a meeting with a marine expert the harbormaster at Chatham had recommended. "I want someone to balance the people from Woods Hole who are going to raise a question about where the body washed in, but it shouldn't take long. I'll be home by twelve or one."

Half a loaf, Menley thought. He may not have believed that I didn't have a flashback when I dreamed of Bobby, but at least he's willing to leave me alone with the baby.

"I want to work this morning," she said. "I'll have Amy baby-sit till lunchtime."

"Your decision, dear."

Amy arrived just as he was leaving. She was dismayed to hear Menley ask, "Adam, where is that tape of Bobby at East Hampton? I'm ready to see it now."

"It's in the apartment."

"The next time you go down will you bring it up?"

"Of course. We'll watch it together."

Should I tell them I have it? Amy wondered. They might not like the idea that I was looking at it. No, it would be better to return it to Elaine's house as fast as she could. Mr. Nichols might remember that he'd left it at the Cape and ask Elaine for it.

When Menley went into the library and closed the door, she realized instantly that something was different about the atmosphere. It was so chilly. That must be it. This room didn't get the morning sun. Even so, she decided not to move the data back into the keeping room. She was wasting too much time going through the stacks of files. She would spread them out on the floor, the way she worked in her office at home, and fasten on each one a sheet of paper on which she'd written the contents in large, bold print. That way she could find what she was looking for easily, and when she was finished, she could just close the door on the mess instead of straightening it out.

She spent the first hour spreading the data around to her satisfaction, then opened the new file from Phoebe Sprague and began to analyze the contents.

The sketches were on top. Again she studied the one of the Captain and Mehitabel on the ship, then taped it to the wall by her desk. Alongside it she hung her own sketches of them and the drawing Jan had brought from the Brewster Library. Almost interchangeable, she thought. I must have come across something like this in the files.

She had already planned the way she would work. She began by combing through the new material for any and every reference to Tobias Knight.

The first time she saw his name was in connection with the carrying out of Mehitabel's punishment. "At ye town meeting in Monomoit on the third Wednesday of August in ye year of our Lord one thousand seven hundred and five, Mehitabel, the wife of Captain Andrew Freeman was presented and the judgment of ye court carried out in the presence of her husband, her accusers, her penitent partner in adultery and ye town people who ventured forth from their homes and duties to witness and be warned of the punishment of unchastity."

The third Wednesday in August, Menley thought. That would be around this time. And Andrew watched her tortured. How could he?

There was a note that Phoebe had made: "Captain Freeman sailed that night, bringing with him the six-week-old infant and an Indian slave as nursemaid."

He left her in that condition and took her baby from her. Menley looked up at her sketch of Andrew Freeman. You didn't look strong and sure that day, I hope, she thought. She ripped the sketch from the wall, reached for a charcoal pencil, and with quick, sure strokes altered the confident expression.

She had intended to depict cruelty, but try as she would, when she was finished, the face of Andrew Freeman was that of a man ravaged by grief.

Maybe you had the grace to regret what you did to her, she thought.

Amy had brought Hannah in for a bottle of juice. Holding the baby, she stood uncertainly in the keeping room. From the front of the house she thought she could hear the sound of soft sobbing. That's what Carrie heard yesterday, she thought. Maybe Mrs. Nichols came back earlier than we realized.

Mrs. Nichols kept up such a good front when people were around, but she really was depressed, Amy thought, wondering briefly if it was her responsibility to talk to Mr. Nichols about it.

Then she listened again. No, that wasn't Mrs. Nichols crying. The breeze had started up the way it did yesterday and was making the sobbing sound that echoed in the chimney. Wrong again, Carrie, Amy thought.

August 14th

78

*O*N SUNDAY MORNING Adam insisted on going out for brunch after church. "We both ended up working last night, which wasn't the plan, and I have to spend at least an hour with Scott Covey this afternoon."

Menley could not refuse even though she wanted to stay at her desk. From town records in Phoebe Sprague's last file, she'd learned the circumstances of Mehitabel's death.

Captain Andrew Freeman had been gone for two years after he sailed, taking his infant daughter with him. Mehitabel had kept watch for him from the widow's walk of Nickquenum, as the house was known at that time.

When she spotted his sails, she had gone to the harbor to wait for him. "A piteous sight," according to a letter written by selectman Jonathan Weekes.

Clearly souferin, she homble knelt before him and begged for her babe. He told her his daughter-babe would never set eyes on an unchaste mother. He ordered Mehitabel begone from his home. But her sickliness and fatague was observed by all and she was caried there to be gathered that night to her heavenly account. It is said that Captain Freeman witnessed her death and that her last words were "Andrew, here I await my child and here cruelly wronged, I die sinless."

Menley discussed what she had learned with Adam as they had eggs Benedict at the Red Pheasant in Dennis.

"My father used to love this place," Adam said, looking around. "It's too bad he's not still here. He'd be a great help to you. He knew Cape history backward and forward."

"And God knows Phoebe Sprague knew it," Menley said. "Adam, do you think it would be all right to call the Spragues and see if Hannah and I could visit them while you're with Scott?"

Adam hesitated. "Phoebe says crazy things sometimes."

"Not always."

He made the call and came back to the table, smiling. "Phoebe's having a pretty good day. Henry said to come right over."

Eighteen days more, Henry thought as he watched Phoebe playing patty-cake with Hannah, who was sitting on Menley's lap. He dreaded the morning he would awaken without Phoebe beside him.

Today she was walking better. There was less of the uncertain shuffling that was her usual gait. He knew it wouldn't last. There were fewer and fewer moments of lucidity, but at least, thank heaven, there were no more nightmares. She'd slept fairly well the last couple of nights.

"My granddaughter loves patty-cake too," Phoebe told Hannah. "She's just about your age."

Laura was fifteen now. It was as the doctor said. Long-term

memory was the last to go. Henry was grateful for the look of understanding Adam's wife exchanged with him. What a pretty girl Menley is, he thought. In these couple of weeks her hair had become sunstreaked and her skin lightly tanned. The coloration brought out the deep blue of her eyes. She had a lovely smile, but today he noticed a difference in her, an indefinable air of sadness that hadn't been there before.

Then, when he heard her talking to Phoebe, he wondered if she was letting the research on Remember House get to her. It certainly was a tragic story.

"I came across the account of Mehitabel's death," she was telling Phoebe. "I guess when she knew Andrew wouldn't bring her the baby, she just gave up."

There was something Phoebe wanted to say. It had to do with Mehitabel and what was going to happen to Adam's wife. She would be dragged into that murky place where Andrew Freeman had left Tobias Knight to rot and then she would be drowned. If only Phoebe could explain that. If only the faces and voices of the people who were going to kill Adam's wife weren't hazy shadows. How could she warn her?

"Go away!" she cried, as she pushed at Menley and the baby. "Go away!"

"Vivian's mother and father are going to make strong, emotional witnesses," Adam warned Scott. "They're going to paint you as a fortune hunter who had a flashy girlfriend visiting him the week before the marriage, and who, after murdering their daughter, ripped a ring from her finger as a final act of greed."

Scott Covey was showing the strain of the impending inquest. They were sitting opposite each other at the dining room table, Adam's notes spread between them.

"I can only tell the truth," he said quietly.

"The *way* you tell it is what matters. You've got to convince that judge that you're as much a victim of that squall as Vivian was. I do have a good corroborating witness, a guy who almost lost his grandson when their boat was swamped. He would have lost him if he hadn't grabbed the kid by the foot as he was going over the rail."

"Would they have accused him of murdering the child if he hadn't been able to grab him?" Covey asked bitterly.

"That's exactly the thought we want to plant in the judge's mind."

When he left an hour later, Adam said, "No one can predict the outcome of these hearings. But we've got a good shot. Just remember, don't lose your temper, and don't criticize Vivian's parents. Get across that, yes, they're grieving parents and you are a grieving husband. Keep 'husband' in mind when they try to paint you as a murdering opportunist."

Adam was surprised to find Menley and Hannah waiting for him in the car. "I'm afraid I upset Phoebe," Menley told him. "I should never have mentioned Mehitabel to her. For some reason she got terribly agitated."

"There's no explaining what brings on those spells," Adam said.

"I don't know about that. Mine are triggered by stimulus, aren't they?"

"It's not the same." Adam put the key in the ignition.

Mommy, Mommy. Such a joyous sound. The night she thought she'd heard Bobby calling her. Had she been dreaming of the way he'd sounded that day in East Hampton? Had she attached a happy memory to a flashback? "When do you have to go to New York again?" she asked.

"We should hear the judge's decision either late tomorrow or Tuesday. I'll go down overnight Tuesday and stay until Thursday morning. But I swear that will be it on working this month, Men."

"I want you to bring up the tape of Bobby at East Hampton."

"I told you I would, honey." As Adam steered the car away from the curb, he wondered, what is that all about?

79

*F*RED HENDIN took Tina out for dinner on Sunday evening. She had said she had a headache when he called her in the morning, but agreed that fish and chips and a couple of drinks at Clancey's that evening would pick up her spirits.

They had a gin and tonic at the bar and Fred was surprised at how vivacious and animated Tina was. She knew the bartender and some of the patrons and kidded with them.

Fred thought she looked terrific in her red miniskirt and red-and-white top, and he could see that a number of other guys at the bar were giving her the eye. There was no doubt about it. Tina attracted men. She was the kind of woman a man could lose his head over.

Last year when they had been dating, she kept telling him that he was a real gentleman. Sometimes he wondered if that was a compliment. Then she dropped him like a hot potato when Covey came into the picture. Last winter when he tried to get back with her, she hadn't given him the time of day. Then suddenly in April she had called him. "Fred, why don't you drop around?" she had said as though nothing had happened.

Was she ready to settle for me only when she couldn't get Covey? he wondered, as Tina burst out laughing at a joke the bartender told.

He hadn't heard her laugh like that for a while. She seemed really happy tonight.

That's what it was, he realized suddenly. Even though she was nervous about testifying at the inquest, she seemed happy.

Over dinner, she asked him about the ring. "Fred, I would like to wear the engagement ring when I testify. Did you bring it?"

"Now you're trying to spoil what's left of the surprise. I'll give it to you when we get to your place."

Tina lived in a furnished apartment over a garage in Yarmouth. She wasn't much of a housekeeper and hadn't done much to personalize the place, but the minute they walked in, Fred noticed there was something different about the small sitting room. Some things were missing. She had a pretty good collection of rock music, but almost all the cassettes and CDs were gone. And so was the picture of her skiing with her brother's family in Colorado.

Was she planning a trip and not telling him about it? Fred wondered. And if so, was she going alone?

August 15th

80

MENLEY AWAKENED at dawn to the faint sound of sobbing. She pulled herself up on one elbow and strained to listen. No, it must be a seagull, she thought. The curtains were moving restlessly, and the good scent of the ocean was in the room.

She settled back on the pillow. Adam was in a deep sleep, snoring lightly. Menley remembered something her mother had said years ago. She'd been reading an advice column, probably Ann Landers or Dear Abby, and a woman had written in to complain that her husband's snoring kept her awake. The response was that to some women a husband's snoring would be the most welcome sound in the world. Ask any widow.

Her mother had commented, "Isn't that the truth?"

Mom raised us alone, Menley thought. I never experienced first-hand the interaction between happily married people. I never knew what it was like to see married people face problems and get through them.

Why think about that now? she wondered. Is it because I'm beginning to see a vulnerability in Adam that I didn't know existed? In a way I've always handled him with kid gloves. He's the attractive, successful, sought-after man who could have had anyone, but it was me he asked to marry him.

She realized there was no use trying to go back to sleep. She slipped out of bed, picked up her robe and slippers and tiptoed out of the room.

Hannah showed no signs of awakening, so Menley went down the stairs noiselessly and entered the library. With luck she might have two quiet hours before Adam and Hannah got up. She opened the new file.

Halfway through it, she found a group of papers clipped together that dealt with shipwrecks. Some of them she had already read about, such as the 1717 wreck of the pirate ship *Whidaw*. The mooncussers had picked its cargo clean.

And then she saw a reference to Tobias Knight: "The biggest house-to-house search for booty before the *Whidaw* was when the *Thankful* was lost in 1704 off Monomoy." Phoebe noted, "Tobias Knight was brought to Boston for questioning. He was developing an unsavory reputation and was suspected of being a mooncusser."

The next page was an account of the wreck of Captain Andrew Freeman's *Godspeed*. It was the copy of a letter to Governor Shute written by Jonathan Weekes, a selectman. The letter informed His Excellency that " 'on the thirty-first of August, in ye year of our Lord one thousand seven hundred and seven,' Captain Andrew Freeman set sail against all advice, 'there being a northeast breeze which was certain indication of an approaching storm.' The one survivor, Ezekiel Snow, a cabin boy, 'tells us the captain was distraught and much deranged, shouting he must return his daughter-babe to her mother's arms. All knew the baby's mother was dead and became much alarmed. The *Godspeed,* driven to the shoals, there broke up with a grievous loss of life.'

"Captain Freeman's body washed into Monomoit and he was buried alongside his wife, Mehitabel, since, in the testimony of the cabin boy, he went to his Maker crying out his love for her."

Something happened to make him change his mind, Menley thought. What was it? He was trying to bring the baby back to a mother already dead. He went to his Maker crying out his love for her.

81

EVEN THOUGH it was obviously going to be a hot day, Scott Covey chose to wear a navy summer-weight suit, long-sleeved white shirt and subdued navy-and-gray tie to the inquest. He had debated about wearing his green jacket, khakis and a sports shirt but realized they would not convey the impression he wanted to make on the judge.

He was uncertain about wearing his wedding ring. Would it look as though he were grandstanding? Probably not. He slipped it on.

When he was ready to go, he studied himself in the mirror. Vivian had told him that she was jealous of his ability to tan. "I burn and peel, burn and peel," she had sighed. "You just get this gorgeous tan, and your eyes look greener and your hair blonder and that many more girls turn their heads to look at you."

"And I'm looking at you," he had teased.

He surveyed his reflection from head to toe and frowned. He was wearing a new pair of Gucci loafers. Somehow they looked too picture perfect. He went to the closet and got out his old well-polished pair. Better, he thought, as he checked the mirror again.

His mouth suddenly dry, he said aloud, "This is it."

Jan Paley arrived to stay with Phoebe while Henry went to the inquest. "She was upset yesterday afternoon," Henry warned. "Something Menley said about Remember House disturbed her. I get the feeling she's trying to convey something to us and can't find the words."

"Maybe if I just talk about the house to her, it will come out," Jan suggested.

Amy arrived at Remember House at eight o'clock. It was the first time she had seen Mr. Nichols in a business suit, and she looked at him admiringly. He has a kind of elegance about him, she thought. He makes you feel that anything he does will be done well.

He seemed preoccupied, checking the papers in his briefcase, but he glanced up at her and smiled. "Hi, Amy. Menley's getting dressed and the baby is with her. Why don't you go upstairs and take over Hannah? We're starting to run late."

He was such a nice man, Amy thought. She hated to think that he was going to be wasting his time looking for the tape of little Bobby in New York when it was a few minutes away in Elaine's house. In a burst of confidence she said, "Mr. Nichols, can I tell you something, but don't let on you heard it from me?"

She thought he looked worried, but then he said, "Of course."

She explained about the tape, how she had noticed it, taken it home and put it back. "I didn't tell Elaine I had borrowed it, so she might get mad if she found out. It was just that I wanted to see what your little boy was like," she said almost apologetically.

"Amy, you've saved me a lot of trouble. We don't have any other copies, and my wife would have been really upset if that one disappeared. I left the Cape last year in a hurry, and Elaine had to ship a couple of things down to me. It will be easy to ask her to look for it without involving you."

He looked at his watch. "I've got to get moving. Oh, here they come."

Amy could hear footsteps on the staircase, then Mrs. Nichols came hurrying in, Hannah in her arms. "I'm all ready, Adam, or at least I think I am. This kid kept wiggling to the edge of the bed. She's all yours, Amy."

Amy reached for Hannah as Mrs. Nichols smilingly added, "Temporarily, of course."

82

*A*T 9:00 A.M. the courtroom in Orleans was filled to capacity. The media was out in full force. The extensive publicity around Vivian Carpenter Covey's death had attracted the sensation seekers who vied with friends and townspeople for the limited seating.

"It's like a tennis match," Nat heard one reporter whisper to another just before lunch.

It has to do with murder, not games, Nat thought, but we don't have enough to prove it today. The district attorney had presented the evidence well. Point by point he had built up his case: Covey's involvement with Tina until a week before he married Vivian; the bruised finger and missing ring; the failure to turn on the radio for the weather report; the fact that Vivian's body should not have washed in where it had been found.

The judge frequently had his own questions for the witnesses. With meticulous attention, he studied the charts and autopsy reports.

Tina made a discouragingly good witness for Covey. She readily admitted that he had warned her he was seeing Vivian, that she had gone to visit him in Boca Raton, hoping that he'd become interested in her again. "I was crazy about him," she said, "but I knew it was over when he married Vivian. He really was in love with her. I'm engaged to someone else now." From the witness chair, she smiled brilliantly at Fred.

During recess Nat saw the eyes of the spectators shift from Scott Covey, with his movie-star looks and poise, to Fred Hendin, squat and stolid with thinning hair and an air of profound embarrassment. You could read their minds. She had settled for Fred Hendin when she couldn't snare Covey from Vivian.

The testimony of Conner Marcus, the sixty-five-year-old resident of Eastham who had almost lost his grandson in the squall, might have clinched it even without Covey's testimony. "No one who wasn't out there can possibly understand how suddenly it came up," he said, his voice shaking with emotion. "One minute Terry, my little grandson, and I were fishing. Then the current got rough. Less than ten minutes later the waves were washing over the boat, and Terry was almost pulled into the water. I get down on my knees every night and thank God that I'm not in the boots of that young fellow." Tears in his eyes, he pointed at Covey.

With quiet authority, Elaine Atkins described the change in Vivian Carpenter when she met Scott Covey, and the marital happiness she witnessed. "The day they looked at Remember House, they talked about buying it. They wanted a large family. But Vivian said she would have to sell the other house first."

Nat had never heard that before. And it gave credence to Covey's story that he had been kept in the dark about the extent of Vivian's inheritance.

They recessed for lunch. In the afternoon, Vivian's lawyer from Hyannis was called and proved to be a dryly credible witness for

Covey. Henry Sprague came through solidly as a next-door neighbor who testified to the mutual devotion of the newlyweds. The
insurance investigator could only confirm what Tina had already
admitted: She had visited Covey in Boca Raton.

Both Carpenters testified. They admitted that their daughter had
always had emotional problems and had great difficulty in keeping
friends. They pointed out that at an imagined slight she would sever
a relationship, and they introduced the possibility that something
had happened to make Vivian turn on Scott and threaten to disin-
herit him.

Anne Carpenter talked about the emerald ring. "It never was too
tight," she said emphatically. "Besides, Vivy was superstitious
about it. She'd sworn to her grandmother that she'd never take it
off. She used to hold it to the light and admire it." Asked to describe
the ring, she said, "It was a beautiful, five-and-a-half carat Colombian stone with a large diamond on each side, and it was mounted
in platinum."

And then Covey got on the stand. He began his testimony in a
composed voice. He smiled when he talked about the early days of
dating Vivian. " 'Getting to Know You,' was our favorite song,"
he said.

He talked about the emerald ring: "It was bothering her. She
kept tugging at it that last morning. But I'm absolutely sure she was
wearing it on the boat. She must have switched it to her left hand."

And finally the description of losing her in the squall. Tears came
to his eyes, welled there, his voice broke, and when he shook his
head and said, "I can't stand thinking about how scared she must
have been," there were many moist eyes in the courtroom.

"I have nightmares where I'm searching through the water for
her and I can't find her," he said. "I wake up calling out to her."
Then he began to sob.

The judge's finding was that there was no evidence of negligence
and no evidence of foul play was almost anticlimatic.

The media asked Adam to make a statement.

"This has been a terrible ordeal for Scott Covey," he said. "Not only has he lost his young wife but he has been subjected to scandalous rumors and accusations. I hope this public airing has not only served to present the true circumstances surrounding this tragedy but will also allow this young man the peace and privacy he desperately needs."

Scott was asked his plans. "My father isn't well which is why he and my stepmother can't be here. I'm going to drive across the country to California to visit them. I'll stop in some of the cities where I've toured with shows and have friends, but mostly I just want time alone to decide what to do with the rest of my life."

"Will you stay on the Cape?" a reporter asked.

"I don't know," he said simply. "It holds a lot of heartache for me."

Menley was standing to the side, listening. You've done it again, Adam, she thought with pride. You're wonderful.

She felt a light touch on her arm. A woman in her late sixties said, "I wanted to introduce myself. I'm Norma Chambers. My grandchildren love your books and were so disappointed when you withdrew from renting my house for August."

"Renting your house? Oh, of course, you mean the first house Elaine arranged for us to take. But when there was a problem with the pipes, she switched us to Remember House," Menley said.

Chambers looked astonished. "'There was no problem. I had the house rented the day after you gave it up. Wherever did you get that idea?"

83

*A*FTER HE TESTIFIED, Henry Sprague phoned his house to see how Phoebe was doing. Jan urged him to stay until the end of the proceedings. "We're doing fine," she insisted.

It had not, however, been an easy day. Phoebe lost her balance going down the two steps to the backyard, and Jan barely managed to keep her from falling. At lunchtime, Phoebe picked up a knife and tried to eat the soup with it.

As Jan placed the spoon in her hand, she thought sadly of the many times she and Tom had dined here with the Spragues. In those days, Phoebe had been a gracious, witty hostess, presiding over a table bright with placemats and matching napkins and candles and a centerpiece she had created from flowers from her garden.

It was heartbreaking to realize that this woman who flashed her a look of pathetic gratitude for understanding that she hadn't known which utensil to use was the same person.

Phoebe napped after lunch, and when she awoke in mid-afternoon, she seemed more alert. Jan decided to try to find out what she might have been trying to convey about Remember House.

"The other day, Adam's wife and I went to talk to other people who have old houses," she began. "Adam's wife is writing an article about houses with legends attached to them. I think Remember House is the most interesting of all. Then we drove to Eastham and saw another house Tobias Knight had built. It's very much like Remember House but not as fancy, and the rooms are larger."

The rooms. Remember House. A musty smell came into Phoebe's nostrils. It smelled like a tomb. It was a tomb. She was at the top of a narrow ladder. There were piles of junk everywhere. She started to go through them, and her hands touched the skull. And the voices came from below, talking about Adam's wife.

"Inside the house," she managed to say.

"Is something inside Remember House, dear?"

"Tobias Knight," she mumbled.

84

SCOTT COVEY URGED Elaine and Adam and Menley and Henry to come back to his house for a glass of wine. "I won't keep you, but I do want to have a chance to thank you."

Adam glanced at Menley and she nodded. "A brief stop," he agreed.

Henry declined to stop at Covey's even for a few minutes. "Jan has been with Phoebe all day," he explained.

Menley was anxious to get back to Hannah but wanted a chance to ask Elaine about the reason she had switched them from renting Mrs. Chambers' house. Dropping by Scott Covey's place would give her the opportunity.

On the way there she and Adam discussed the inquest. "I wouldn't want to be Fred Hendin, with everyone listening to my fiancée talk about throwing herself at another man," she observed, "but he certainly stood up for her when he testified."

"If he's smart, he'll dump her," Adam said, "but I hope he doesn't. Scott's lucky that she backed up his story, but this inquest wouldn't preclude a grand jury being called if further evidence came out. Scott's got to be careful."

. . .

Scott opened a bottle of vintage bordeaux. "I hoped I'd be using it for this reason," he said. When it was poured he held up his glass. "This is not a celebration," he began. "It would only be that if Vivian were with us now. But I do want to toast you, my friends, for all that you've done to help me. Adam, you're the best. Menley, I know you urged Adam to help me. Elaine, what can I say except thank you."

He sipped and then said, "And now I want to share my future plans with you and only with you. I'm leaving here first thing in the morning, and I'm not coming back. I'm sure you can understand. I'll never walk down a street in this town without being pointed at and whispered about. I think that the Carpenters will be better able to get on with their lives if they don't run the risk of bumping into me. So Elaine, I'd like you to put this house on the market immediately."

"If that's what you want," Elaine murmured.

"I can't disagree with your thinking," Adam commented.

"Adam, I'll be on the road for a while. I'll phone your office next week, and if you have my bill ready I'll send you a check." He smiled. "Whatever it is, you were worth every penny."

A few moments later, Adam said, "Scott, if you're leaving early you'll want to pack."

Menley and Adam said their good-byes, but Elaine stayed behind to discuss details of leasing the house.

As they went down the walk to their car, Adam wondered why he didn't feel more triumphant. Why was his gut telling him he'd been had?

85

*A*FTER THE INQUEST, Nat Coogan did not have a celebratory glass of wine. Instead he sat in the family room, sipping a glass of cold beer, replaying the day in his mind. "This is what happens," he told Debbie. "Murderers get away with murder. I could spend the next two days citing cases where everybody knows the husband or the neighbor or the business partner committed the crime, but there just isn't enough proof to get a conviction."

"Will you keep working on the case?" Debbie asked.

Nat shrugged. "The trouble is, there's no smoking gun."

"In that case, let's plan our anniversary. Shall we have a party?"

Nat looked alarmed. "I thought I'd take you out for a fancy dinner alone and maybe we can check into a motel." He winked at her.

"The No-Tell Motel?" It was a long-standing joke between them.

Nat finished his beer. "Damn it, Deb," he said. "There *is* a smoking gun. And it's right under my nose. I know it is. But I can't find it!"

86

*A*S HE DROVE Tina home from the inquest, Fred Hendin had the sickening feeling that he might never be able to hold up his head again. He hadn't missed the fact that the spectators were comparing him with that gigolo, Scott Covey. Fred knew Covey was a smooth-talking phony, but that didn't make it easier that Tina freely admitted she had thrown herself at him all winter.

When Fred was on the stand he had done the best he could to back her up, and the judge's decision showed that he didn't feel that the affair between Tina and Covey had any connection with Vivian Carpenter's death.

Fred knew Tina better than she knew herself. A couple of times in the corridor during recess, she had glanced at Covey. There had been a look in her eye that said it all. A blind man could see she was still crazy about him.

"You're very quiet, Freddie," Tina said, slipping her arm around his.

"I guess I am."

"I'm so glad this is over."

"So am I."

"I'm going to see if I can take some time off and visit my brother. I'm sick of people whispering about me."

"I don't blame you, but Colorado is a long way to go just to get away."

"Not that far. About five hours from Logan Airport."

She leaned her head on his shoulder. "Freddie, I just want to go home now and collapse. Do you mind?"

"No."

"But tomorrow night, we'll have a nice dinner. I'll even cook."

Fred was painfully aware of how much he wanted to smooth the shiny dark hair that was tumbled on his sleeve. I'm nuts about you, Tina, he thought. That won't change. "Don't worry about cooking," he said, "but you can have a drink waiting for me. I'll be there by six."

87

"*WHAT MADE YOU QUESTION* 'Laine about the house in Eastham?" Adam asked as they drove home from the visit to Scott Covey.

"Because she lied about the reason for switching us to Remember House. There was nothing wrong with the pipes in the other place."

"From what she said, the Chambers woman who owns it would never admit the constant trouble she has with the pipes."

"In that case, why did Elaine rent it to someone else?"

Adam chuckled. "I think I see the picture. 'Laine probably realized that we might be good candidates to buy Remember House. I bet that's why she switched us. She always knew there were more ways than one to skin a cat."

"Including lying? Adam, you're a terrific lawyer, but sometimes I wonder about your blind spots."

"You're getting mean in your old age, Men."

"No, I'm getting honest."

They were driving onto Morris Island and down Quitnesset Lane. The late afternoon was turning cooler. The leaves on the locust trees were rustling, and a few had begun to fall. "It must be pretty here in other seasons," Menley observed.

"Well, in two weeks we have to decide whether we want to find that out for ourselves."

Amy had just finished feeding Hannah. The baby lifted her arms joyously when Menley bent over her.

"She's sticky," Amy warned as Menley lifted her from the high chair.

"That's fine with me. I've missed you," she told Hannah.

"I've missed her too," Adam said, "but your blouse is washable and this suit isn't. Hi, Toots." He blew a kiss at Hannah but kept out of her reach.

Menley said, "I'll take her upstairs. Thanks, Amy. Tomorrow afternoon about two all right with you? After I drop off the bread-winner at the airport, I do want to get in about four hours' work."

Amy nodded, and when Menley was out of earshot asked, "Did you speak to Elaine about the tape, Mr. Nichols?"

"Yes. She was sure she had returned it to me. You're positive you saw the right one?"

"You were all in it. You lifted Bobby out of the pool and told him to run to his mother. He called 'Mommy, Mommy' and then Mrs. Nichols asked him questions about his name and where he went to school."

"Nertry schoow," Adam said.

Amy saw the glint of tears in his eyes. "I'm so glad you have Hannah," she said quietly. "But that is the tape you're looking for, isn't it?"

"Yes, it is. Amy, Elaine doesn't like to admit to mistakes. Maybe you should just pick it up for me the next time you're at her house. It sounds like petty larceny, but it is ours, and I can't insist that she has it without perhaps causing trouble for you."

"I'd rather do it that way. Thanks, Mr. Nichols."

August 16th

88

*A*T SIX O'CLOCK on Tuesday morning, Scott Covey loaded the last of his bags into the BMW and made one more inspection of the house. Elaine was going to send someone in to give it a thorough cleaning, so that was not his concern. He looked again through the drawers in the bedroom and the closets for anything he might have missed.

Wait a minute, he thought. He had forgotten the eight or ten good bottles of wine that were still in cartons in the basement. No sense leaving them for the cleaning woman.

One thing nagged him, however—the pictures of Vivy. He wanted to put everything that had happened this summer behind him, but it might look callous to leave them here. He carried them to the car too.

He had put out the garbage and recycling bags. He wondered if he should rip the picture of Remember House out of the frame and completely tear it up. Then he shrugged. Forget it. Garbage pickup was in an hour.

Yesterday at the inquest, he had asked Vivian's lawyer, Leonard Wells, to handle her estate and probate her will. Now that the judge had cleared him, the family couldn't delay the transfer of assets. Wells told him he would have to sell a chunk of securities for taxes. The government certainly wanted plenty of other people's money.

I guess no matter how much you inherit, you feel that way, Scott thought.

He drove the car out of the garage and around the house. He paused for an instant; then he stepped on the accelerator.

"Good-bye, Vivy," he said aloud.

89

THEY SPENT Tuesday morning on the beach, just the three of them. They had brought the playpen down for Hannah and kept it under the shade of the umbrella. Adam lay in the sun and read the papers. Menley had magazines in her beach bag, but she had also brought a sheaf of papers from Phoebe's file.

The papers had a rubber band around them and didn't seem to be arranged in any particular order. Menley was getting the impression that, as the Alzheimer's disease started to make inroads, Phoebe's research became progressively more disorganized. It seemed as though she must have been gathering material and simply dumping it into the file. There were even recipes, clipped a few years ago from the *Cape Cod Times,* attached to stories of the early settlers.

"Tough sledding," she murmured.

Adam looked up. "What is?"

"Phoebe's most recent notes. They date back about four years, I think. It's obvious she was having real problems then. The pity is she must have realized she was losing her faculties. Many of the memos to herself are so terribly vague."

"Let's see." Adam glanced through the papers. "Now that's interesting."

"What is?"

"There's a reference to this place. 'Laine told me it got to be called Remember House because during a storm the house acts like a bellows. The way the wind whooshes against it sounds like someone calling 'Remmmmbaaaa.' "

"That's what Jan Paley told me."

"Then according to this, they're both wrong. Here's a copy of a town record from 1705. It records the birth of a child to Captain Andrew Freeman and his wife, Mehitabel, a daughter named Remember."

"The baby's name was Remember?"

"And look at this. It's a town record from 1712. 'Said property known as Nickquenum, a dwelling house and chattels and homestead bounded easterly by ye bank or clift to the salt water, southerly by the land of Ensign William Sears, southwesterly by ye land of Jonathan Crowell and northerly by ye land of Amos Nickerson by the will of Captain Andrew Freeman was passed to his wife and if she be deceased to his descendants. Mehitabel his wife having predeceased him, the sole heir is a daughter Remember listed on ye record of birth in the year of our Lord one thousand seven hundred and five. The whereabouts of said child being unknown, ye dwelling that has come to be known as Remember House is to be sold for taxes.' "

Menley shivered.

"Men, what is it?" Adam asked sharply.

"It's only that there's a story about one of the settlers in the late sixteen hundreds, a woman who knew she was going to die when her baby was born and directed that it be called Remember so it would always remember her. I wonder if Mehitabel knew of that. She may have suspected she was going to lose her child."

"Then if we do buy the house, maybe we'd better change its name back to the original. Have you any idea what Nickquenum means?"

"It's an Indian word that in essence means 'I am going home.' In the days of the early settlers, if a traveler was passing through hostile territory he only had to say that word and no one impeded him on his journey."

"You must have learned that from your research."

Did I? Menley wondered.

"I'm going for a quick swim," she said. "And I promise I won't go out too far."

"If you do, I'll rescue you."

"I hope so."

At one-thirty she dropped Adam at the Barnstable airport. "Here we go again," he said. "When I get back Thursday, we are starting a real vacation. No more work for me. And if I mind her nibs during the morning, will you be ready to be a beach bum or do some exploring in the afternoon?"

"You bet."

"We'll save Amy for a couple of dinners out."

"Alone, I hope."

On her way back from the airport, Menley decided to take a quick run to Eastham to see the Tobias Knight house again. "Now, Hannah," she instructed, "you must promise to behave. I need to get another look at this place. There's something that I don't understand."

There was a different volunteer, an older woman, Letitia Raleigh, at the old house's reception desk today. It had been a quiet afternoon, she told Menley, and she had time to chat.

Menley offered Hannah a cookie. "It's as hard as a dog biscuit," she said, "but it feels good to her because she's teething. I'll make sure she doesn't drop crumbs."

Content, Hannah settled down and Menley opened the subject of Tobias Knight. "I can't find very much about him," she explained.

"He was a bit of a mystery man," Raleigh confirmed. "Certainly a wonderful builder and ahead of his time. This house is nice, but I understand the one he built in Chatham was a showplace for that period."

"I rent it," Menley said. "It is beautiful, but the rooms are smaller than those in this house."

"I don't understand that. The dimensions are supposed to be the same." Raleigh rummaged through the desk. "There's a bio here we don't usually pass out. It's not too flattering of him. Here's his picture. Presentable if pompous, don't you think? And something of a dandy for those days."

The drawing was of an even-featured man of about thirty with a whisp of beard and longish hair. He was wearing breeches, a doublet, a cape and a high-collared ruffled shirt, and his shoes had silver buckles.

She lowered her voice. "According to this bio, Tobias left Eastham under a cloud. He got in trouble when he became involved with a couple of the goodwives, and a lot of people were sure he had a wrecker business going . . . that's a mooncusser, you know."

She skimmed the brochure and handed it to Menley. "Apparently in 1704, a few years after Tobias settled in Chatham, he was questioned by the Crown when all the cargo from the *Thankful* was missing. Everyone was sure he was guilty, but he must have found a way to hide his loot. He disappeared two years later. The theory is that it got too hot for him around Chatham and he took off to start fresh somewhere else."

"What was the cargo?" Menley asked.

"Clothing, blankets, household goods, coffee, rum—the reason it caused so much trouble is that it was all headed for the governor's mansion in Boston."

"Where did they usually hide all the cargo?"

"In sheds, buried on the shore, and some of them even had hidden rooms within their houses. These rooms were usually behind the fireplace."

90

ON TUESDAY MORNING, Nat Coogan left for work earlier than usual. As a matter of curiosity, he drove past Scott Covey's house to see if there was any sign of his getting ready to clear out. Nat had no doubt that now that the inquest was over and the decision favorable, Covey would shake the dust of the Cape from his shoes.

But early as he was, he could see that Covey was already gone. The shades were drawn and there were a couple of garbage bags on the side of the house for pickup. You don't need a search warrant to go through stuff that has been left for disposal, Nat thought as he parked his car.

One bag contained cans and bottles for recycling as well as sharp fragments of broken glass. The other had garbage and trash, including a frame with the rest of the broken glass stuck in it and a picture with long crisscross scratches. Oh my, my, Nat thought. There was the original aerial photo of Remember House, the one that had been in the real estate office window. Even in its mutilated condition it was clearer than the duplicate Marge had shown him in the office. But the section with the boat had been torn out. Why? Nat wondered. Why did he try to destroy it? Why not just leave it if he didn't want to be bothered carrying it? And why did he tear the boat out of the picture? And why was it missing from the copy print as well?

He put the mangled photo in the trunk of the car and drove to Main Street. Elaine Atkins was just opening up. She greeted him pleasantly. "I have that picture you want. I can get it framed if you like.'

"No, don't bother," Nat said quickly. "I'll take it now. Deb wants to take care of the framing herself." He reached for the print. He studied it. "Terrific! That's great photography!"

"I agree. A panoramic aerial photo can be a real selling tool, but just on its own, this one is wonderful."

"At the department we sometimes need aerial work done. Do you use someone around here?"

"Yes, Walter Orr from Orleans."

Nat continued to study the print. It was the same version that Marge had put in the window three days ago. Nat said, "Am I wrong, or when the picture was in the window did it have a boat in it?"

"The negative got damaged," Elaine said quickly. "I had to do some patching."

He noticed her heightened color. And why are you so nervous? he wondered.

"What do I owe you?" he asked.

"Nothing. I do my own developing."

"That's very nice of you, Miss Atkins."

91

TUESDAY WAS NOT an easy day for Fred Hendin. Knowing that he was about to give up Tina for good was an assault on his senses. He was thirty-eight now and had dated a number of girls over the years. At least half of them would probably have married him.

Fred knew that by some standards he was a good catch. He was a hard worker who made a comfortable living. He had been a devoted son and he would be a devoted husband and father. People would have been surprised to know exactly how robust his bank account was, although he had always had the feeling Tina could sense it.

Right now if he called up Jean or Lillian or Marcia, he knew he would have a dinner date tonight.

The trouble was that he had genuinely fallen in love with Tina. He had always known she could be moody and demanding, but when he went out with her on his arm, he felt like a king. And she could be lots of fun.

He had to get her out of his mind. All day he was distracted, thinking about her and about having to give her up. The boss had even called him on it a couple of times. "Hey, Fred, stop daydreaming. We've got a job to finish."

He looked again at the house across the road; somehow it didn't have the same appeal today. Oh, sure, he probably would buy it, but it wouldn't be the same. He had imagined Tina in it with him.

But a man had his dignity, his pride. He had to end it with Tina. The papers today were filled with the details of the inquest. Nothing had been left out: the condition of Vivian's right hand; the missing emerald ring; Tina's visits to Covey in Florida. Fred had winced to find his own name mentioned as Tina's on-again-off-again boyfriend, and now fiancé. The account made him look like a fool.

Yes, he had to end it. Tomorrow, when he drove her to the airport, he would tell her. But one thing concerned him. It would be just like Tina to refuse to give his mother's jewelry back to him.

At six o'clock when he got to Tina's and found that as usual she wasn't ready, he had turned on the television and then opened the jewelry box.

His mother's pearls and watch and pin were there, as well as the engagement ring he had just given Tina. It had served her purpose, and she probably couldn't wait to get it off her finger, he thought. He put the pieces in his pocket.

And then he stared. Buried underneath Tina's inexpensive chains and bracelets, he glimpsed a ring. It was a large green stone with a diamond on each side, mounted in platinum.

He picked it up and studied it. Even a fool would have recognized the clarity and depth of that emerald. Fred knew he was holding the family ring that had been ripped from Vivian Carpenter's finger.

When Menley arrived home from visiting the Tobias Knight house, Amy was sitting on the steps. "You must have thought I'd forgotten about you," Menley said apologetically.

"I knew you didn't." Amy unbuckled Hannah from the car seat.

"Amy, yesterday I overheard you talking to my husband about the tape of Bobby. Tell me about that."

Reluctantly Amy recounted how she happened to have it.

"Where is it now?"

"Home. I took it from Elaine's house last night when I borrowed more movie tapes. I was going to give it to Mr. Nichols when he gets back Thursday."

"Give it to me in the morning."

"Of course."

92

O*N THE DAY* after the inquest, Graham and Anne Carpenter decided to go on a cruise. "We need to get away," Graham decreed.

Anne, deeply depressed by recent events, agreed listlessly. Their other two daughters had come out for the hearing, and Emily, the older one, said bluntly, "Mother, you must stop blaming yourself. In her own way poor Vivy loved you and Dad very much, and I don't think she'd want to see you like this. Go on a trip. Get away from all this. Have a great time with Daddy, and you two take care of each other."

Tuesday evening, after Emily and Barbara and their husbands left, Anne and Graham sat out on the front porch, making plans for the trip. Anne's voice was brighter, and she laughed as they recalled some of the other cruises they had taken.

Graham had to put in words the way he felt: "It hasn't been pleasant for either of us to be depicted as horrible parents in the tabloids, and I'm sure they'll have a field day describing the inquest. But we did what we had to do, and I think that somewhere Vivian knows we tried to secure justice for her."

"And I pray she also knows we can do no more."

"Oh, look, there's Pres Crenshaw with Brutus."

They watched as their elderly neighbor walked slowly down the road past their gate, his German shepherd on a leash.

"Set your watch," Graham said. "Ten o'clock on the dot."

A moment later, a car drove past the gate. "Pres should be careful, that road is dark," Anne said.

They turned and went into the house.

93

*M*ENLEY INVITED Amy to stay for dinner. She sensed something forlorn about the young girl. "I'm just making a salad and linguine with clam sauce," she explained, "but you're welcome to share it."

"I'd love to."

She really is a nice kid, Menley thought, and actually she's not that much of a kid. She's almost eighteen and has a quiet poise that really is attractive. Plus she is more responsible than most adults. But she sure doesn't like the idea of her father marrying Elaine.

That was a subject Menley had no intention of bringing up, however. What she did introduce was Amy's preparations for college.

Discussing her plans, Amy became animated. "I've talked on the phone to my roommate. She sounds nice. We've decided on spreads and curtains. Her mother will help her buy them, and I'll pay my share."

"What have you done about clothes?"

"Elaine said she'll drive to Boston someday and we'll have a—wait, how does she put it—a 'fun girl day together.' Isn't that awful?"

"Amy, don't fight her," Menley said. "She's going to marry your father."

"Why? She certainly doesn't love him."

"Of course she does."

"Menley, I mean Mrs. Nichols, my father is a very boring man."

"Amy!" Menley protested.

"No, I mean it. He's nice and kind and good and successful but that's not what we're talking about. Elaine doesn't love him. He gives her corny gifts, at least he gives them in a corny way, and she puts on the big act. She's going to make him miserable and she knows that I know it and that's why she can't stand me."

"Amy, I hope Hannah doesn't talk about her father like that someday," Menley said, shaking her head even as she acknowledged that Amy was right on target.

"Are you kidding? Mr. Nichols is the kind of guy women want. And if you want to know something, the list starts with Elaine."

. . .

When Amy left, Menley walked through the house, locking up. She turned on the local weather channel and learned that a storm was brewing that would hit the Cape tomorrow in the late afternoon or early evening. I had better make sure we have a flashlight and candles just in case, she thought.

The phone rang as she was settling at her desk in the library. It was Jan Paley.

"I missed you yesterday when you were at Scott Covey's house," Jan said. "I wanted you to know that Phoebe was talking about Tobias Knight again. Menley, I think you're right. She is trying to tell us something about him."

"I stopped by his Eastham house today after I dropped Adam off," Menley said. "The receptionist showed me his picture. Jan, Tobias looked like a sneak and a dandy. I can't imagine why Mehitabel ever would have bothered with him. Another interesting point is that, according to the dates we have, she was already at least three months pregnant with Andrew Freeman's child when she was denounced."

She paused. "I guess I'm really thinking aloud. I've had two pregnancies, and the last thing in the world that would have intrigued me during the first three months of either one of them is to become involved in a love affair."

"Then what are you thinking?" Jan asked.

"Tobias Knight was a mooncusser. He was being questioned by the Crown about the cargo of the *Thankful* around the time he was seen visiting Mehitabel at unseemly hours. Suppose he wasn't visiting her? Suppose she never knew he was around? If he hadn't confessed to carrying on with Mehitabel, they'd have looked for another reason for him to be here. Suppose he hid some of the *Thankful* cargo on these grounds, or even in this house?"

"Oh, I don't think in the house," Jan protested.

"The dimensions of the first-floor rooms here are smaller than in the Eastham place. But from the outside the house is the same size. I'm going to poke around a bit."

"I don't think it will do you much good. If there ever was a storage area, it's probably been boarded up for the last two hundred years. But it is possible that one did exist at some time."

"Did anyone ever suggest that this house might have had a hidden room?"

"Not to me. And the last contractor did an awful lot of work. He's Nick Bean, from Orleans."

"Do you mind if I talk to him tomorrow?"

"Of course not. And feel free to poke around. Good night, Menley."

When she replaced the receiver, Menley leaned back in the chair and studied the drawings of Mehitabel and Andrew. On the ship they had looked so happy together.

Mehitabel had died swearing her innocence, and a week later Andrew had set sail into an oncoming storm, frantic to bring his baby back and crying out his love for his wife. Was it possible that he had been convinced of Mehitabel's innocence and been driven out of his mind with regret?

Every instinct told Menley that she was on the right track.

She settled back at the desk but now was not interested in going through the files. Something Amy had said at dinner had to be faced. Elaine might be engaged to another man, but she was in love with Adam. I sensed it that night at dinner, Menley thought. Elaine didn't forget she had that tape. She deliberately withheld it, knowing that it was irreplaceable to us. What use was it to her except to be able to look at Adam?

Or did she find another use for it?

At ten o'clock she went upstairs, changed into a nightgown and robe, and phoned Adam at the apartment in New York.

"I was just about to call you to say good night," he said. "How are my girls?"

"We're fine." Menley hesitated but knew she had to ask the question that was on her mind. "Amy stayed for dinner, and she made an interesting observation. She thinks Elaine is in love with you, and I have to say I agree with her."

"That's ridiculous."

"Is it? Adam, please understand that after Bobby died, I wasn't much of a wife to you for a year. Last summer I asked you for a separation, and we'd probably be divorced right now if I hadn't learned I was pregnant with Hannah. You got pretty close to Elaine in that time we were apart, didn't you?"

"It depends on what you call close. We've always been there for each other since we were kids."

"Adam, forget the buddy routine. Haven't you pulled that on her before? You said she was a rock when your father died. And over the years when you didn't have another serious girlfriend, you'd call her up. Wasn't that the pattern?"

"Menley, you can't think that I was involved with Elaine last year."

"Are you involved with her now?"

"My God, Menley, no!"

"I had to ask. Good night, Adam."

Adam heard the click in his ear. When he got to the apartment he had realized what had been bugging him. One day last winter when Menley was out, he had watched the tape of Bobby. It was where he had left it, in his desk drawer. He *had* brought it home last summer. Why did Elaine make a copy of it and not tell him about it?

94

O N WEDNESDAY MORNING, Nat brought his second cup of coffee into the family room and studied the two pictures of Remember House. He had painstakingly removed the mangled one from the frame, and now it was propped up on the mantel next to the copy Elaine had given him.

The destruction of the print he had taken from Scott Covey's garbage was even more apparent now that the picture was out of the frame. It looked as though the crisscross tears might have been made by a sharp knife or even a wedge of broken glass. There was a gaping hole where the boat had been.

The other print showed a faint smudge where the boat had been, as though Elaine had attempted to retouch the negative, but hadn't completed the job.

"Bye, Dad."

Nat's two sons, Kevin and Danny, sixteen and eighteen years old, stood in the doorway, grinning at him. "If you're trying to decide which one to buy, Dad, I'd vote for the one on the right," Kevin said.

"Someone sure didn't like the other one," Danny commented.

"I agree," Nat said. "The question is *why* didn't he like it? See you tonight, guys."

Debbie came in a few minutes later. "Still haven't figured it out?" she asked.

"Nothing makes sense. First of all, I can't believe that Elaine Atkins honestly thought that Scott Covey was in the market for that property. Then when he was clearing out, why didn't he just leave it in the house? Why go to all the trouble of smashing it and cutting out the boat? And why did Elaine blank out the boat in the copy? There has to be a reason."

Debbie picked up the torn photograph and turned it over. "Maybe you should talk to whoever took the picture. Look, his name is stamped on the back. Walter Orr. His phone number and address are here too."

"I know his name," Nat said. "Elaine gave it to me."

Debbie turned the pictures over again and smoothed the curling edges. "Look. The date and time this was taken is here on the bottom." She looked at the other picture. "It's not on the copy Elaine gave you."

Nat looked at the date. "July 15th at 3:30 P.M.!" he exclaimed.

"Is there anything significant about that date?"

"You bet there is," Nat said. "July 15th was the day Vivian Carpenter was drowned. Covey phoned the coastguard at 4:30 that afternoon." In two strides he was over to the phone.

A look of disappointment came over Nat's face as he listened to a recorded message. Then he gave his name and the phone number of the police station and finished by saying, "Mr. Orr, it is imperative I speak to you immediately."

When he hung up, he said, "Orr is on a job and will be back at four o'clock. So this will have to hold until then. But Deb, I just realized, when Marge offered us this copy, she said Elaine had the negative. And she's obviously already altered that. So if there is something to this, we may never find out what it is. Damn!"

95

THERE WAS a restless feeling in the air when Menley awakened at seven o'clock on Wednesday morning. The breeze was damp, and the room still shadowed. The light that penetrated around the shades was subdued, and no rays of sun danced on the windowsills.

She had slept well. Even though Hannah's room was close by and she had left both doors open, she had kept the baby monitor on the night table next to her. At two she had heard the baby stirring and checked her, but Hannah didn't wake up.

And no dreams, no flashbacks, thank God, Menley thought as she reached for a robe. She walked to the windows that overlooked the water and pulled up the shades. The ocean was gray, the waves still mild as they lapped at the shore. Thin sunlight peered around the heavy clouds that drifted over the water.

Ocean and sky and sand and space, she thought. This wonderful house, this special view. She was enjoying getting used to all this space. After her father died, her mother had given her brother the smaller bedroom to himself and moved Menley's twin bed into her room. When Jack went to college it was Menley's turn to get a room of her own, and thereafter when Jack was home, he slept on the pullout couch in the living room.

I remember how when I was little, I used to draw pictures of pretty houses with pretty rooms, Menley thought as she looked out over the ocean. But I never visualized a home like this, a location like this. Maybe that's why the house Adam and I had in Rye never got to me the way this one does.

Remember House would be a home of the heart, she thought. I can see coming up here for Thanksgiving and Christmas and the kind of summers Adam experienced growing up, and for long weekends in other seasons. That's a perfect balance to all the plusses of living in Manhattan, with Adam's office minutes away.

What had been Mehitabel's plans for her life? she wondered. Many wives of sea captains sailed with their husbands all over the world and brought their young children with them. Mehitabel had sailed with Andrew after they were married. Before everything went wrong, had she been looking forward to other trips?

It would make sense if Tobias Knight did build some sort of storage area on the grounds or in the house and that was why he had been seen around here. I'm going to write the story that way, she decided.

Why do I feel so strongly about her this morning? she wondered. And then she understood the reason. On the third Wednesday in August all those years ago, Mehitabel was condemned as an adulteress, flogged and returned here to find her husband had taken her baby away. Today was the third Wednesday in August.

A moment later Menley did not need the baby monitor to inform her that Hannah was awake and hungry. "I'm coming, Crabby," she called as she hurried into the nursery.

Amy arrived at nine o'clock. It was obvious that she was upset. It didn't take long to find out what was wrong. "Elaine was at our house when I got home last night," she said. "Mr. Nichols had asked her about the tape of Bobby, and I guess she must have figured out that I borrowed it. She asked me for it.

"I wouldn't give it to her. I said it belonged to you and I had promised to give it back to you. She said it was a backup copy she'd made because Mr. Nichols was so distraught last year she was afraid he'd lose it, and she knew you hadn't seen it." Tears glistened in Amy's eyes. "My dad sided with Elaine. He's mad at me too."

"Amy, I'm sorry you've had a problem about this. But I don't believe that Elaine made a copy of that tape with me in mind. And I'm glad you didn't give it to her. Where is it now?"

Amy reached in her bag. "Here it is."

Menley held the cassette in her hand for a moment, then laid it on the refectory table. "I'll watch it later. I think it would be a good idea if you put Hannah in the carriage and went for a walk. When that storm breaks, it's supposed to last until sometime tomorrow afternoon."

Adam phoned an hour later. "How's it going, love?"

"Fine," she told him, "but the weather's changing. There's a storm predicted."

"Did Amy bring the tape of Bobby?"

"Yes."

"Have you watched it yet?"

"No. Adam, trust me. I'm going to watch it this afternoon while Amy is with Hannah, but I know I can handle it."

When she hung up, she looked at the computer screen. The last sentence she had written before the phone had begun to ring was, "It would seem that Mehitabel implored her husband to trust her."

At eleven o'clock she reached the contractor Nick Bean, who had renovated the house. An affable man, Bean was both open and informative about Remember House. "Priceless workmanship," he said. "Not a nail anywhere in the original construction. All mortise-and-tenon joints."

She asked him what he knew about hidden rooms in the homes of early settlers.

"I've come across them in some of these old places," he explained. "People glamorize them. Originally they were called 'Indian rooms,' the idea being that they were where the family hid from the Indians when they were attacked."

Menley could hear the amusement in his voice as he continued: "Only one problem. The Indians on the Cape weren't hostile. Those rooms were where bootleg cargo was kept or where people who were going on a trip would hide their valuables. Their version of a safety deposit box, I guess you could call it."

"Do you think it's possible Remember House has a hidden storage area?" Menley asked.

"It's possible," Bean confirmed. "Seems to me my last workman on the job mentioned something about that. There's a fair amount of space between the rooms and the center of the house, where the chimneys were built. But that doesn't mean we'd ever find one if it exists. It may have been boarded over to the point where it would take a genius to locate it. One place to start looking is the minister's cabinet in the parlor. Sometimes a removable panel behind it led into a storage area."

A removable panel. As soon as Menley hung up, she hurried to check the minister's cabinet in the main parlor. It was to the left of the fireplace. She opened it, and a musty smell assailed her nostrils. I should leave the door open and let it air out, she thought. But the back of the built-in cabinet had no seams to indicate an entrance to a storage area.

Maybe when we own the house we can explore this further, she thought. You just can't go around smashing walls. She went back to the desk but realized she was becoming more and more distracted. She wanted to see the tape of Bobby.

She waited until after lunch, when Amy brought Hannah up for her afternoon nap. Then she picked up the cassette and brought it into the library. A lump was already forming in her throat when she put the tape in the VCR and pressed the start button.

They had visited one of Adam's partners in East Hampton that weekend. Lou Miller had a video camera and had brought it out on Sunday afternoon after brunch. Adam had Bobby in the pool. She had been sitting at the umbrella table talking with Lou's wife, Sherry.

Lou took shots of Adam teaching Bobby how to swim. Bobby looked so much like Adam, Menley thought. They were having such a good time together. Then Adam lifted Bobby onto the deck. She remembered Lou turning off the camera and saying, "Okay, enough of the aquacade. Let's get some shots of Bobby with Menley. Adam, put him on the deck. Menley, you call him."

She heard her own voice next. "Bobby, come on over here. I want you."

I want you, Bobby.

Menley dabbed at her eyes as she watched her two-year-old, arms outstretched, running toward her, heard him calling her, *"Mommy, Mommy."*

She gasped. It was the same joyous voice she had heard when she thought Bobby was calling her last week. He had sounded so vibrant, so alive. It was the way he had just started to say "Mommy" that struck her now. She and Adam had joked about it. Adam had said, "Sounds more like Mom-me, with the emphasis on *me.*"

That was exactly the way he had called to her the night that she'd searched the house for him. Had that been simply a vivid waking dream rather than a flashback? Dr. Kaufman had told her that happy memories would begin to replace the traumatic one. But the train whistle had certainly been a flashback.

The tape was rolling. Bobby flinging himself into her arms; turning him to the camera. "Tell us your name."

She began to sob as he said proudly, "Wobert Adam Nikko."

Tears choked her, and when the tape was finished, she sat for a few minutes, her face buried in her hands. And then a reassuring thought assuaged the pain: in another two years Hannah would be answering the same question. How would she pronounce Menley Hannah Nichols?

She heard Amy coming down the stairs and called to her. Amy came in, her expression concerned. "Are you okay, Mrs. Nichols?"

Menley realized that her eyes were still welling with tears. "I really am," she said, "but I'd like you to watch this with me."

Amy stood beside her as she rewound the videotape and played it again. When it was finished, Menley asked, "Amy, when Bobby was calling me, did you notice anything special about the way he sounded?"

Amy smiled. "You mean 'Mom-me'? It sounded as though he was saying, 'Hey, Mom, you come to me!' "

"That's what I thought. I just wanted to make sure I wasn't imagining that."

"Mrs. Nichols, do you ever get over losing someone you love?" Amy asked.

Menley knew Amy was thinking about her own mother. "No," she said, "but you learn to be grateful that you had the person at all, even though it wasn't long enough. And to quote my own mother, she always told my brother and me that she'd rather have had twelve years with my father than seventy years with anyone else."

She put an arm around Amy. "You'll always miss your mother the way I'll always miss Bobby, but we've both got to keep that thought in mind. I know I'm going to try."

Even as she was rewarded by Amy's grateful smile, Menley was struck by the thought that both times she had awakened to the sound of the train whistle, Hannah had heard it too.

The calling, the train. What if she hadn't imagined it?

96

*G*RAHAM AND ANNE CARPENTER spent most of Wednesday packing. At two o'clock, Graham saw the mail van go by and walked down to the mailbox.

When he took out the mail he glanced into the box and was surprised to see a small package in the far-back corner. It was wrapped in brown paper and tied with twine, so he knew it wasn't one of those soap samples that regularly made an appearance in the box.

The package was addressed to Anne, but there was no postage and no return address on it. Graham carried it up to the house and brought it to the kitchen, where Anne was talking to the house-keeper. When he told them about finding it, he saw a look of concern cross his wife's face.

"Do you want me to open it for you?" he asked.

Anne nodded.

He saw her expectant expression as he cut the twine. He won-dered if she was thinking the same thing he was. There was some-thing distinctly odd about the neatly lettered, tightly sealed package.

When he opened it, his eyes widened in shock. The fine deep green of the heirloom emerald ring gleamed through a plastic sand-wich bag.

The housekeeper gasped, "Isn't that . . . ?"

Anne grabbed the bag and pulled out the ring, folding it in her hand. Her voice was shrill, on the verge of hysteria as she cried, "Graham, where did this come from? Who brought it here? Re-member, I told you that emeralds always find their way home?"

97

NAT COOGAN was in his car on the way to Or-leans when he received a call at 3:15 from the district attorney's office. An assistant DA informed him that the emerald ring had been returned to the Carpenters' house last night and that at exactly 10:00 P.M. an elderly neighbor, Preston Crenshaw, had noticed a strange car slow up at the Carpenters' mailbox.

"We can't be sure that whoever was in the car left the ring, but it gives us something to go on," the assistant DA told him. "Mr. Crenshaw's description of the vehicle he saw is pretty good. A dark green or black Plymouth, Massachusetts plates with a 7 and a 3 or 8 in the numbers. We're running a check."

Plymouth, Nat thought. Dark green or black. Where had he seen one recently? Then he remembered. It had been in Fred Hendin's driveway, and then he had seen Fred and Tina in it after the inquest. "Tina Arcoli's boyfriend, Fred Hendin, drives a dark green Plymouth," he said. "Run a check on his plates."

He waited. The assistant DA came back on the phone, sounding triumphant. "Hendin's license plate number has both a 7 and a 3 in it. The boss says he wants you to go along when we pick him up for questioning."

"Then let's meet at Hendin's house at five o'clock. I'm on my way to something that may turn out to be another lead."

The aerial photographer, Walter Orr, had picked up his messages and returned Nat's call. Nat was to meet him in his office at four o'clock.

It's unraveling, Nat thought exultantly, snapping the phone back on the dashboard.

Ten minutes later he was turning off Route 6 onto the Orleans exit. Five minutes after that he was in Orr's office in the center of town.

Orr was about thirty, a brawny man who looked more like a dock-worker than a photographer. He was in the process of making coffee. "Long day," he told Nat. "I was doing a shoot in New London. Believe me, I was glad to get back here. That storm is going to hit us in a couple of hours, and I wouldn't want to be flying in it."

He held out a mug. "Coffee?"

Nat shook his head. "No thanks." He took out the mangled aerial photo. "You took this?"

Orr studied it briefly. "Yes, I did. Who slashed it?"

"That's part of what we're investigating. I understand Elaine Atkins hired you to take it and that she has the negative."

"That's right. She specifically wanted the negative and paid extra to get it."

"All right, take a look at this print." Nat unrolled the copy that Elaine had given him. "You see the difference?"

"Sure. The boat's been taken out. Who did that? Elaine?"

"That's what I'm told."

"Well, it's hers to mess around with, I guess."

"On the phone you told me that when you take aerial photos, the exact time and date is being registered on the film."

"That's right."

Nat pointed to the lower right-hand corner of the original photo. "This is marked Friday, 15 July, 3:30 P.M."

"And the year is above it."

"I see that. The point is that this is the absolutely accurate time the photo was made. Is that right?"

"Absolutely."

"I need to get a blowup of that missing boat. How many photos did you shoot, and is there another one that's similar?"

Orr hesitated. "Listen, is this important to you? You think the boat is carrying drugs or something?"

"It might be important to a lot of people," Nat said.

Orr pressed his lips together. "I know you're not here because you want to admire my photography. Just between us, I did sell Elaine the whole roll of film, but I made a duplicate negative of this shot for myself. I wouldn't have sold it to anyone else, but it's damn good photography. I wanted it as a sample of my work."

"That's very good news," Nat said. "Can you make another print, fast?"

"Sure. Exactly like this one?"

"Yes, exactly like the original, but it's really the boat I'm interested in."

"What do you want to know about it?"

"Everything that your skills can reveal to me." He scribbled the number of his cellular phone on the back of his card and handed it to Orr. "As soon as possible. I'll be waiting for your call."

98

*F*RED HENDIN was picked up shortly after five o'clock and brought to the district attorney's office in the courthouse. Quietly and courteously, he answered the questions that were flung at him. No, he had never met Vivian Carpenter. No, he had never met Scott Covey either, although he had seen him hanging around the Daniel Webster Inn last year. Yes, he was engaged to Tina Arcoli.

The ring? He had no idea what they were talking about. He hadn't been in Osterville last night. He had been out with Tina and then gone directly home to bed.

Yes, at the inquest he had heard a lot of talk about a missing ring. The *Cape Cod Times* yesterday gave a description of it. Nearly a quarter of a million dollars was a lot of ring. Whoever gave it back was certainly honest.

"I've got to get out of here," Fred told his interrogators. "I'm driving my fiancée to Logan Airport. She's got a flight to Denver at nine o'clock."

"I think Tina's going to miss her flight, Fred," Nat said. "We're going to bring her in now."

He watched as the telltale flush appeared on Fred's neck and worked its way up to his face. They were getting to him.

"Tina wants to visit her brother and his family," Fred said angrily. "All this business has upset her."

"It's upset a lot of people," Nat said mildly. "If you have sympathy for anyone, I suggest you start with the Carpenters. Don't waste it on Tina."

. . .

Nat drove with Bill Walsh, an investigator from the district attorney's office, to Tina's home. At first she refused to let them in, then finally opened the door.

They found her surrounded by luggage. The living room obviously had been stripped of personal belongings. She had no intention of coming back, Nat thought.

"I have no time for you," Tina snapped. "I have to make a plane. I'm waiting for Fred."

"Fred's at the district attorney's office, Tina," Nat told her. "We have to talk to him, and it's very important that we talk to you as well. If everything gets straightened out quickly, you can still make your plane."

Tina looked startled. "I have no idea why you want to talk to Fred or me. Let's get this over with fast."

99

*M*ENLEY WALKED Amy to the door. "Dad and I are going to Elaine's for dinner tonight," she said. "We're supposed to talk out my relationship with her."

"You mean to try to get it on a more even keel?" Menley asked.

"Last night she said something about not walking into such a hostile situation." Amy shrugged. "I'm going to tell her that I'll be in college in a couple of weeks and if there's a problem about my being around on school breaks, then I'll stay away. My grandmother still lives in Pennsylvania; she'll be glad to have me. At least then I won't have to watch Elaine make a jerk out of Dad."

"Sometimes it gets worse before it gets better," Menley said, opening the door. A gust of wind swept through the room. "I'm glad Adam isn't flying today," she commented.

After Amy left, Menley fed Hannah, bathed her, then watched the six o'clock news from Boston with the baby in her lap. At quarter past six a bulletin ran across the bottom of the screen. The storm would break at about seven, and a particular warning was issued to residents of the Cape and area islands.

"We'd better get the candles and flashlights out," Menley told Hannah. The sky was completely overcast. The water, dark gray and angry, was now crashing on the shore. The first drops of rain began to beat against the window. She went from room to room, turning on lights.

Hannah began to fuss, and Menley settled her in her crib, then came back downstairs. Outside the wind was increasing in velocity, and she heard the faint call that it made as it whooshed around the house: *Remmmmbaaaa . . .*

Adam phoned at quarter of seven.

"Men, the dinner I was staying for got canceled at the last minute. I grabbed a cab to the airport to make the direct flight. We were on the runway when they got word Barnstable Airport is closed. I'll take the shuttle to Boston and rent a car there. With luck I'll be home between nine-thirty and ten."

Adam was coming home tonight! "That's terrific," Menley said. "We'll weather the storm together."

"Always."

"You haven't had a chance to eat, have you?" she asked.

"No."

"I'll have dinner waiting. It probably will be by candlelight, and not just for effect."

"Men . . ." He hesitated.

"Don't be afraid to ask if I'm all right. Yes, I am."

"Did you watch the tape of Bobby?"

"Twice. Amy watched it with me the second time. Adam, remember how Bobby had just started to say 'Mom-me'?"

"Yes I do. Why, Men?"

"I'm not sure."

"Men, they're boarding. I'll have to go. See you in a little while."

Adam hung up and ran for the departure gate. He had watched the tape that he found in the library of the apartment. "Mom-*me.*" It almost sounded as though Bobby were calling Menley to him. Oh Christ, Adam thought, why didn't I get back to the Cape before the airport closed.

100

N*AT AND* Bill Walsh, the investigator, carried Tina's bags into one of the conference rooms. She sat down across from them at the table and pointedly looked at her watch. "If I'm not out of here in half an hour I'll miss my plane," she said. "Where's Fred?"

"He's down the hall," Nat said.

"What's he done?"

"Maybe nothing except be a delivery man. Tina, let's talk about Vivian Carpenter's missing emerald ring."

Her eyes narrowed. "What about it?"

"Then you know about it?"

"Anyone who reads the papers knows about it, to say nothing of all the talk at the inquest."

"Then you know it's not the kind of ring that would be mistaken for another one. Here, let me read the description of it from the insurance company." Nat picked up a sheet of paper. " 'Colombian emerald, five-and-a-half carats, fine deep green with no visible in-clusions, two fine emerald-cut diamonds, one-and-a-half carats each, on either side, mounted in platinum, value a quarter of a million dollars.' "

He laid down the paper and shook his head. "You can understand why the Carpenters wanted it back, can't you?"

"I don't know what you're talking about."

"A lot of people seem to think that ring was wrenched off Vivian's finger after she died, Tina. If true, that could get whoever has it now in big, big trouble. Why don't you think about that? Mr. Walsh will stay with you. I'm going in to talk to Fred."

He exchanged a glance with the investigator. Now Walsh could take the fatherly approach with Tina and, most important, he wouldn't leave her alone to go through her luggage. Nat had not missed the quick, nervous dart of Tina's eyes when he mentioned the ring. She thinks it's in her suitcase, he thought.

Fred Hendin looked up when Nat came into the room. "Is Tina here?" he asked quietly.

"Yes," Nat told him.

They had deliberately left Fred alone for nearly an hour. "Coffee?" Nat asked.

"Yes."

"Me too. It's been a long day."

The semblance of a smile passed over Fred Hendin's lips. "I guess you could say that."

Nat waited until the coffee was brought in, then leaned forward, man to man. "Fred, you're not the kind of guy who worries about fingerprints. My guess is that some of your prints are on that package that someone, and I emphasize *someone,* in a dark green Plymouth with the numbers 7 and 3 or 8 on his Massachusetts license plates, placed in the Carpenters' mailbox last night."

Hendin's expression did not change.

"The way I look at it," Nat said, "someone you know might have had that ring. And you remembered seeing her wear it, or maybe you saw it on her dresser or in her jewelry box, and after the inquest and reading all the papers, you got worried. Maybe you didn't want that person to be tied to what may have been a crime, so you helped her out *by getting the ring out of her possession.* Help me out, Fred. Isn't that the way it was?"

When Hendin remained silent, Nat said, "Fred, if Tina had the ring, she perjured herself at the inquest. That means she goes to prison unless she cuts a deal, which is what she should do. Unless she was in on a plot to kill Vivian Carpenter, she's small potatoes. If you want to help her, start to cooperate, because if you do, Tina will have to follow your very good example."

Fred Hendin's hands were folded. He seemed to be studying them. Nat knew what he must be thinking. Fred is an honest man. And proud. Every dollar he makes is earned honestly. Nat also reasoned that Fred knew enough about the law to be aware that, since Tina had said under oath she didn't know anything about an emerald ring, she could be in big trouble. That was why Nat was hinting that she could get out of trouble if she cooperated.

Nat also thought he had a pretty good idea of the way Tina thought. She would play every angle until she was backed into a corner. Hopefully they would accomplish that tonight. He knew that eventually they would track down Covey, but he didn't want to wait too long.

"I don't want Tina to get in trouble," Fred said, finally breaking the silence. "Falling for a snake like Covey shouldn't get anyone into trouble."

It sure as hell got Vivian Carpenter into trouble, Nat thought.

Then Fred Hendin said, "I took the emerald ring from Tina's jewelry box last night."

The investigator, Bill Walsh, kept a sympathetic expression as Tina snapped, "This is like living in Nazi Germany."

"Sometimes we have to ask innocent people to help in our investigations," Walsh said soothingly. "Tina, you keep looking at your luggage. Is there anything I can get for you?"

"No. Listen, if Fred can't drive me to Logan, I have to hire a cab, and that's going to cost me a fortune."

"With this lousy weather, I'll bet your flight is delayed. Want me to check?" Walsh picked up the phone. "What airline and what's your departure time?"

Tina listened while he confirmed her reservation. When he hung up, he was smiling broadly. "At least an hour delay, Tina. We've got plenty of time."

A few minutes later, Nat rejoined them. "Tina," he said, "I'm going to read you the Miranda warning."

Obviously stunned and confused, Tina listened in disbelief, read and signed the paper Nat gave her and waived her right to a lawyer. "I don't need one. I haven't done anything. I'll talk to you."

"Tina, do you know the penalty for being an accessory to murder in this state?"

"Why should I care?"

"At the very least you accepted a valuable ring that may have been torn from a victim's finger."

"That's a lie."

"You had the ring. Fred saw it and returned it to the Carpenters."

"He *what?*" She rushed to the pile of luggage in the corner and grabbed the carry-on bag. In one quick motion she unzipped it and pulled out a book.

One of those fake jewelry boxes, Nat thought, watching as Tina opened it to reveal the hollowed-out interior. He saw the color drain from her face. "The miserable sneak," she muttered.

"Who, Tina?"

"Fred knows where I keep my jewelry," she snapped. "He must have taken . . ." She stopped.

"Taken what, Tina?"

After a long moment, she said, "The pearls and pin and watch and engagement ring he gave me."

"Is that all? Tina, if you don't cooperate we have you cold on perjury."

She stared at Nat for a long moment. Then she sat down and buried her face in her hands.

The stenographer took down Tina's story. After the tragic death of his wife, Scott Covey had turned to her for comfort, and they had fallen in love again. He had found the emerald in his wife's jewelry box and given it to Tina as a token of their future life. But when those ugly rumors started, they had agreed that it would look very bad to admit he had the ring. They also agreed that she should keep seeing Fred until everything blew over.

"Do you have plans to join Scott?" Nat asked.

She nodded. "We're truly very much in love. And when he needed comfort . . ."

"I know," Nat said. "He turned to you." He paused. "Just as a matter of curiosity: You visited him at his house late at night sometimes and parked your car in his garage, didn't you?"

"Fred always left early in the evening. Sometimes I'd pay Scott a visit."

Tina was crying now. Nat wasn't sure if it was because she was beginning to see the serious implications of the questions or because she hadn't gotten away.

"Where is Scott now?"

"On his way to Colorado. He'll meet me there at my brother's house."

"Do you expect to hear from him before then?"

"No. He thought it was better to wait. He said that the Carpenters were powerful enough to have his car phone bugged."

Nat and the assistant district attorneys soberly discussed Tina's testimony. "Sure, we've got enough for a grand jury, but if she sticks to that story about how Covey gave her the ring after he found it—and she may well believe that it is true—we've got nothing concrete, nothing more damaging than his lying about the ring having been lost," one assistant said. "After his wife died, it was Covey's ring to give away."

The cellular phone in Nat's pocket began to ring. It was Walter Orr. "So how much do you want to know about that boat?" He sounded triumphant.

Don't play games, Nat thought. Trying to keep the irritation out of his voice, he asked, "What can you tell me?"

"It's an inboard/outboard motor, about twenty, twenty-three feet. There's a guy sunning on the deck."

"Alone?" Adam asked.

"Yes. Looks like the remains of lunch beside him."

"Is there a name on the boat?"

The response was just what Nat had been hoping to hear.

"Viv's Toy," Orr told him.

101

*T*HE PLANE CIRCLED Logan Airport for ten minutes before finally landing. Adam rushed out of the plane, then raced along the corridor to the terminal. A long line of people was waiting at the car-rental desk. It took another ten minutes before he had secured the necessary papers and flagged down a courtesy van to the pickup area. He called Menley again to say that he was on his way.

She was distracted. "I'm holding a flashlight and trying to light candles," she told him. "We just lost the lights. No, it's all right. They went on again."

Finally he was inching his way through the massive traffic that led into the Sumner Tunnel. It was quarter of nine before he was on Route 3, the road that led directly to the Cape.

Menley sounded perfectly calm, Adam thought, trying to reassure himself. But should I phone Elaine and ask her and John to go over and stay with her until I get home?

No. He knew Menley would never forgive him if he did that.

But why do I have this gut-level sense that there's a problem? he asked himself.

It was the same queasy feeling he had had the day of the accident. He had played golf that afternoon and reached home in time to pick up the phone when the policeman called.

He could still hear that restrained, sympathetic voice: "Mr. Nichols, I'm afraid I have bad news."

102

*A*FTER ADAM CALLED from the airport, Menley went upstairs and checked on Hannah. The baby was restless, though she did not awaken. Teething or just the noise of the wind? Menley wondered as she smoothed the blankets and tucked them around her daughter. She could hear the mournful shriek of the wind wrapping around the house, sounding more and more like a voice crying, *"Rememmmmmmberrrr . . ."*

Of course, it was her imagination, the powers of suggestion at work, she told herself firmly.

Downstairs, she could hear a shutter flapping. Giving the baby's back a final pat, Menley hurried down to try to secure the loose shutter. It was on one of the windows in the library. She opened the window, and gusts of rain drenched her as she reached out and pulled both the shutters over the glass and fastened them together.

The driving must be terrible, she thought. Adam, be careful. Had she said that to him? She realized suddenly she had been so busy resenting his concern for her that she had forgotten to show concern for him.

She tried to settle down, but was too restless to watch television. Adam wouldn't be home until at least nine-thirty, another hour and a half away. She decided to try to arrange the books on the library shelves in some sort of order.

Carrie Bell had obviously dusted them since Menley had looked through them a few weeks ago. But the pages of many of the oldest ones were swollen and torn. One of the past owners of the house had obviously been interested in acquiring secondhand books. The penciled prices on the inside cover of many of them were as low as ten cents.

She thumbed through some of the books as she organized them. The sporadic reading helped her to ignore the weather. Finally it was nine o'clock and time to start dinner. The book she was holding had been published in 1911 and was a dry history of sailing ships, illustrated with sketches. She knew she had glanced at it a few days after they had arrived in the house. And then, just as she was about to close it, she saw the familiar sketch of Andrew and Mehitabel on the ship. The caption read, "A ship captain and wife in the early seventeenth century, by an unknown artist."

Menley felt a great weight fall from her. I did see that picture and subconsciously copied it, she thought. She laid the book open on her desk under the pictures she had taped to the wall. The lights flickered again, dimming for a moment. In the deep shadows of the room, she had the unsettling feeling that the sketch she had made of Andrew with his ravaged, grief-filled expression in this light somehow resembled Adam.

As Adam is going to look very soon, flashed through her mind.

Ridiculous, Menley thought, and went into the kitchen where she took the precaution of lighting all the candles in case the electricity failed for good.

103

*A*DAM TURNED from Route 6 onto Route 137. Another seven miles, he told himself. Twenty minutes at the most. Provided you move it, he fumed at the driver several cars ahead who was traveling at a snail's pace. He didn't dare try to pass, though. There was moderate traffic coming in the other direction, and the roads were so wet he would probably cause a head-on collision.

Only another six miles, he said to himself a few minutes later, but his sense of urgency was steadily increasing. Now he was driving through whole sections that were in total darkness.

104

*M*ENLEY SWITCHED on the radio, twisted the dial and found the Chatham station that played forties music. She raised an eyebrow in surprise as the Benny Goodman orchestra went into the opening bars of "Remember." A particularly appropriate song, she thought. She picked up a serrated knife and began to slice tomatoes for a salad. "But you forgot to remember," the vocalist warbled.

The whooshing sound of the wind was growing stronger again. *"Reeememmmmmmberrrrr."*

Menley shivered as she reached for the celery. Adam will be here soon, she reminded herself.

There was a sudden noise. What was that? Had a door blown open? Or a window? Something was wrong.

She snapped off the radio. The baby! Was she crying? Was that a cry or a muffled, gagging sound? Menley hurried to the counter, grabbed the monitor and held it to her ear. She heard another throttled gasp and then nothing. The baby was choking!

She rushed from the kitchen into the hall and toward the staircase. Her feet barely touched the stairs as she raced to the second floor, and a moment later she was at the doorway of the nursery. There was no sound coming from the crib. "Hannah, Hannah," she cried.

Hannah was lying on her stomach, her arms outstretched, her body motionless. Frantically, Menley leaned down, turning the baby as she picked her up. Then her eyes widened in horror.

The china head of the antique doll rested against her hand. The painted face stared back at her.

Menley tried to scream, but no sound came from her lips. And then from behind her, a voice whispered, "I'm sorry, Menley. It's all over."

She spun around. Scott Covey was standing beside the cradle, a gun in his hand.

The cradle. Hannah was in it. Hannah, stirring, beginning to whimper. Relief flooded through Menley, followed by a surge of terror. She felt suddenly light-headed, besieged by a sense of unreality. Scott Covey? Why? "What are you doing here?" she managed to ask through lips so dry she almost could not form the words. "I don't understand. How did you get in?"

Covey's expression was the same as it always had been: courteous, attentive. He was wearing a sweat suit and sneakers. But they were dry. Why wasn't he drenched? Menley wondered.

"It doesn't matter how I got in, Menley," he said pleasantly. "The problem is that it took me longer to get here than I expected, but since Adam's in New York it doesn't matter."

Adam. Had he been talking to Adam?

It was as though he could read her thoughts. "Elaine told me, Menley."

"Elaine? I don't understand." Her mind was racing. What is going on? This can't be happening. This is a nightmare! Scott Covey? Why? She and Adam had befriended him. She had urged Adam to defend him. Adam had saved him from a murder charge. And Elaine? What did Scott have to do with Elaine? It all seemed so unreal.

But the gun in his hand was real.

Hannah whimpered louder, starting to wake up. Menley saw the annoyed look on Covey's face. He glanced down at the baby, and the hand with the gun moved.

"No!" she cried. Bending down, she grabbed Hannah from the cradle. Just as she pulled her close, the lights went out, and she ran from the room.

In the dark she rushed for the staircase. She had to focus. She knew every inch of the house. Scott didn't. If she could only get to the kitchen door before he found her. The ignition key was on the hook beside it. The station wagon was right outside. She only needed a minute. She ran down the sides of the steps, praying they wouldn't creak.

He wasn't behind her. He must have turned the other way; maybe he was looking for her in the other bedrooms. Please God, please God, just give me this one minute, she prayed.

A clap of thunder broke over the house, and Hannah began to scream.

The rush of the train, Bobby's cry, her own voice screaming.

Menley pushed the memory aside. She heard swift footsteps overhead. He was coming. Hugging Hannah tightly to her, she ran through the hall and into the kitchen. She raced across the room, wishing passionately she had not lit the candles. They were burning all too brightly now. Glancing over her shoulder, she saw Covey in the entrance from the hall. His expression was different now. His eyes were narrowed, his lips a knifelike slash.

Her fingers were closing over the car key when he caught her, pulling her roughly against him. "Menley, it's you, or it's you and the baby. Take your choice. Put her back in the cradle and come with me, because if you don't put her back, Adam will lose both of you."

His voice was quiet, level, almost matter-of-fact. It would have been easier if he had been nervous, if there had been some hesitancy. Then she might be able to reason with him. Why was he doing this? She kept trying to understand. Yet clearly he meant what he said. She had to get him away from Hannah.

"I'll put her back," she promised desperately. "I'll go with you."

He picked up one of the candles. She felt the gun pressed against her back as she led the way up to the nursery and laid the frightened, crying baby in the crib.

"The cradle," he said. "Put her in the cradle. And put the doll back in the crib."

"Why?" Delay, she thought, stall for time. Keep him talking. Adam can't be far away now. *Adam, hurry. Please hurry.*

"Because you're crazy, Menley, that's why. Crazy and hallucinating and depressed. Everyone, even Adam, is going to be so grateful that you didn't take the baby with you when you committed suicide."

"No. No. I won't."

"Either put the baby in the cradle or bring her with you. It's your choice, Menley. Either way, we are going now."

She had to get him away from Hannah. Alone, if he was taking her away in a car, she might be able to jump out, might be able to make a run for it. Somehow she might still save herself, but not here, not with Hannah in danger. She would have to leave Hannah here.

Menley laid the baby down, bringing fresh wails from the frightened infant. "Sshhh . . ." She pushed the cradle to start it rocking and looked up. "I'll go with you," she said, willing herself to be calm. Then suddenly she had to bite back a shriek.

A section of the wall behind Scott Covey was opening. A musty, stale odor was drifting in from the space behind it. Covey beckoned to her. "This way, Menley."

105

*A*S RAIN SLASHED against the windshield, Adam drove down the darkened main street of Chatham. He could not see more than a few feet ahead and forced himself not to speed. The road turned right. Now it ran along the ocean.

He passed the lighthouse. In five minutes he'd be home. Morris Island was just ahead. And then he came to the dip where Little Beach and Morris Island roads joined. It was flooded and the road was closed.

Without hesitating Adam drove through the barrier. As clearly as though she was in the car, he sensed that Menley was calling him.

106

*T*HE OPENING in the nursery wall wasn't more than a foot and a half wide, Menley realized, as Scott Covey nudged her through it.

"Go ahead, Menley," he said.

She heard a faint tap as the door closed behind her, and Hannah's cries became muffled. The candle's flickering light cast crazy shadows about the narrow space. Scott blew it out as he picked up a flashlight he had left lying on a pile of debris, its beam piercing the shadows of a small room piled with rotting clothes and broken furniture.

The musty odor was overpowering. It was the same smell she had noticed several times in Hannah's room and in the minister's cabinet downstairs. "You've been here before," she cried. "You've been in the baby's room other times."

"I've been here as little as possible, Menley," Covey told her. "There's a ladder in the corner. I'll follow you down it. Don't try anything."

"I won't," she said quickly, trying desperately to clear her head, to overcome this sense of unreality. He doesn't know Adam is coming, Menley thought. Maybe I can get him talking. Maybe distract him. Trip him. I'm stronger than he knows, she thought. I might be able to surprise him, get the gun away from him.

But could she use it? Yes. I don't want to die, she thought. I want to live and be with Adam and Hannah. I want the rest of my life. She felt anger surging through her.

She looked around her, taking in all that she could in the dim light. This place. It was what she had suspected. There *was* a hidden room in this house. More than just a room, in fact. Between the chimneys, the entire core of the house was storage space. Were these piles of rotting rags part of the cargo from the *Thankful?* she wondered.

Play for time, she told herself. Even though she knew Hannah must still be crying, she could not hear her. These walls were so thick that if she died in here, no one would ever find her.

If she died in here.

Was that Covey's plan? she asked herself.

"I'm not going to get out of here alive, am I?" she said.

"Aren't you?" He smiled. "What makes you think that?"

Menley felt a surge of pure hatred. Now he was toying with her.

But then he said, "Menley, I honestly am sorry about this. I'm doing what I have to do." His voice was completely sincere.

"Why? At least tell me *why.*"

"You can believe this or not," he said. "I didn't want to kill Vivian. She was crazy about me, always giving me presents when she came to Florida, but never a dime after we were married. No shared bank account, no assets in my name, no cash. Anything I wanted, she'd buy me, but would you believe, I had to ask her for every nickel I spent?" He shook his head in disbelief.

"And then she wanted me to sign something renouncing any interest in her estate if the marriage didn't last at least ten years. She said that would prove I loved her, that she'd heard people in the beauty parlor whispering that I'd married her for her money."

"And so you killed her?"

"Yes. Reluctantly. I mean, she wasn't a bad person, but she was making a fool of me."

"But what has that got to do with *me?* I helped you. I felt sorry for you. I urged Adam to defend you."

"You can blame Adam for being here now."

"Adam! Does Adam know you're here?" Even as she asked, she knew that wasn't possible.

"We've got to get moving. Menley, I'll make it simple. Elaine has always been crazy about Adam. A couple of times over the years she thought he was falling for her, but it never worked out. Last year when she thought you two were breaking up, she was sure he'd turn to her. Then he went rushing back to you, and she gave up. After that, she decided it was useless. But when Adam phoned about renting that place in Eastham, and she found out how emotionally unstable you were, she hit on this plan."

"Are you telling me you're doing this for Elaine? Why, Scott? I don't understand."

"No, I'm doing it for me. Elaine recognized my boat in that aerial photo of this place. She realized I was alone on the boat at 3:15, and that blew my story about what had happened to Vivian. She was ready to use that information. So we made a deal. She'd be my star character witness. And I'd help her try to drive you crazy. Adam had told her about your flashbacks and depression, and she figured that this old house with its legends and hidden rooms— which she had learned about from some workmen—would be the perfect place to push you over the edge. She planned it all; I just helped her carry it out.

"She brought me here to the house, showed me around, explained what she wanted done. That was the day that crazy woman wandered in and followed us up here. She's just lucky her husband came along when I took her for a walk in the ocean."

Menley shivered. He might have been talking about a walk along the shore. That's what Phoebe was trying to remember, to warn me, she thought.

Keep him talking. Keep him talking.

"The ring. What about the emerald? Where is that?"

He smiled. "Tina. She's quite a hot little number. And giving her the ring was a stroke of genius. In case they ever do try to indict me, she's an accessory. She'll have to keep her mouth shut. Elaine and I would have made a good team. We think the same way. She's been in and out of here at night. I guess she's pulled some stuff that's gotten under your skin, like dubbing your son's voice from the tape and playing it with the sound of the train for you at night. It certainly worked. The word around Chatham is that you're close to a total breakdown."

Where was Adam? Menley thought frantically. Would she hear him when he came? Not in here. She saw Covey glance over at the ladder. "Come on, Menley. You know it all now."

He waved the gun. Trying to follow the beam of the flashlight, she picked her way across the rough, uneven flooring. She tripped as she reached the gaping hole where she could see the top run of the ladder. Covey caught her before she fell.

"We don't want any marks on you," he said. "It was hard enough explaining the bruise on Vivian's finger."

The wood of the ladder was rough, and a splinter stabbed her palm. She felt with her feet for the rungs, descending carefully. Could she drop to the next level, somehow escape him? No. If she twisted an ankle, then she really would be helpless. Wait, she cautioned herself, wait.

She reached the area on the main floor. It was wider than that above; but there was debris scattered all about. Covey was right behind her. He stepped down from the final rung. "Take a look at this," he said, pointing the flashlight to what seemed to be a mound of rags. Then he kicked it with his foot. "There are bones under there. Elaine found them the day she showed me this place. Somebody's been buried in here for a long time. We talked about that being a good plan for you, Menley, to leave you here. But then if you just disappeared, Elaine was afraid Adam might spend the rest of his life hoping you'd come back."

She felt a moment of hope. He was not going to kill her in here. Outside, she might have a chance. As he shoved her ahead of him, she looked back at the bones. Phoebe had said Tobias Knight was in this house. Was that what she had meant?

"Over there." Holding the flashlight, Covey gestured toward an opening in the floor. She could smell dampness from a few feet below.

"Let yourself down slowly. There's no ladder." He waited until she had dropped through. Then he carefully let himself down beside her, closing the heavy trapdoor behind him, sealing the opening. "Stand over there."

Menley realized they were in a narrow storage area of the basement. Covey played the flashlight back and forth. A large yellow slicker was spread out on the ground where they had dropped through the hole, a pair of boots next to the slicker. That was why his clothing wasn't wet, she realized. He had come in this way.

With a swift movement, Covey picked up the slicker, and rolled the boots in it and threw the bundle under his arm.

Menley sensed a change in him. Now he wanted to get it over

with. He prodded her toward the wide basement door and pushed it up. "They'll think you went out this way," he said. "Makes you look a little crazier."

They'd think she left the baby alone and wandered out into a storm. Where was Covey's car? Maybe he was going to drive her somewhere. In the car she might have a chance to jump out or force him to crash. She turned toward the driveway, but he took her arm. "This way, Menley."

They were heading for the beach. He was going to drown her, she realized suddenly.

"Wait, Menley," he said. "Give me your sweater. In case your body never turns up, they'll at least know what happened."

The rain was pounding down, and the wind tore at her clothes. Her hair was drenched, falling forward in her face, covering her eyes. She tried to shake it back. Scott stopped, released her right hand. "Hold up your arm, Menley."

Numbly she obeyed. In a quick gesture, he ripped her sweater over her head and pulled it free, first of her left hand and then the right. Dropping the sweater on the ground, he grasped her arm and forced her down the path that led to the bluff and then to the sea. Tomorrow, with the torrents of rain, there wouldn't be a trace of his footsteps.

They'll find my sweater, Menley thought, and think I committed suicide. Would her body wash in? Vivian's had. Maybe they were counting on that. Adam. Adam, I need you.

The waves were slashing against the shore. The undertow would pull her down and out to sea, and she wouldn't have a chance. She stumbled as he hurried her down the steep path. Try as she might, she could not pull away from his viselike grip.

The full force of the storm struck them as they reached the place where only yesterday she had lounged on a blanket with Adam and Hannah. Now there was no beach, only the waves, breaking upon the land, eroding it, hungry to reclaim it.

"I'm really sorry, Menley," Scott Covey said. "But drowning

isn't that bad. It only took Vivy a minute or so. Just relax. It'll be over soon."

He pushed her into the water and, crouching, held her under the angry surf.

107

*A*DAM SAW the flickering candlelight in the kitchen as he rushed into the house. Finding no one there, he grabbed a flashlight and raced up the stairs.

"Menley," he shouted as he ran into the nursery. "Menley!"

He shone the light around the room.

"Oh God," Adam cried as the beam reflected on the china face of the antique doll.

And then a whimper came from behind him. He turned and played the light around the room until it found the gently rocking cradle. Hannah was there! Thank God! he thought. Hannah was all right!

But Menley—

Adam turned and ran to their bedroom. It was empty. He raced down the stairs and went from room to room.

Menley was gone!

It wasn't like Menley to leave Hannah alone. She would never do that. But she wasn't in the house!

What had happened? Had she heard Bobby's voice again? He knew he shouldn't have let her watch that tape. Shouldn't have left her alone.

Outside! She must have gone outside! Frantically, Adam rushed to the front door and opened it. The rain drenched him immediately as he stepped outside and began calling to her. "Menley!" he cried. "Menley, where are you?"

He raced across the front lawn, headed toward the path to the beach. Slipping in the heavy, wet grass, he fell. The flashlight flew out of his hand and disappeared over the edge.

The beach! She couldn't have gone down there, he thought frantically. Still he had to look. She had to be somewhere.

"Menley," he called out again. "Menley, where are you?"

He reached the path and clambered and slid down it. Below him the surf was roaring, while all about him was darkness. And then a bright flash of lightning illuminated the angry ocean.

Suddenly he saw her, her body surfacing on the crest of a huge wave.

108

*M*ENLEY HAD to will herself not to panic. She had held her breath until her lungs were bursting, forced her body to go limp when she was wild to struggle. She felt the water surging about them, Covey's strong hands holding her, pressing her down. And then he let her go. Quickly she turned her head, gulping air. Why had he released her? Did he think she was dead? Was he still there?

Then suddenly she understood. Adam! She heard Adam, calling out to her. Calling her name!

She started to swim just as a wave crashed over her. Momentarily stunned, she felt herself being pulled out by the powerful undertow.

Oh God, she thought, don't let me drown. Choking and gasping, she tried to tread water. The mountainous waves were everywhere, pulling her, sucking her down, tossing her forward. She forced herself to hold her breath when the water closed over her, to fight her way back up to the surface. Her only hope was to get into a cresting wave that would carry her back to land.

She swallowed more water, then flailed her arms and legs. Don't panic, she thought. Get into a wave.

She felt a surge building behind her, lifting her body up to the surface.

Now! she thought. Now! Swim! Fight! Don't let it pull you back.

Suddenly a bright flash of lightning illuminated everything around her—the sea, the bluff. Adam! There was Adam, sliding down the steep path toward her.

As the thunder crashed around her, she threw her body into the wave and rode it toward the shore, toward Adam.

He was only a few feet away from her as she felt the strong pull of the undertow drawing her back.

Then he was with her, his arm firmly around her, pulling her back to the shore.

109

*A*T *ELEVEN O'CLOCK* Amy and her father were saying good night to Elaine. The evening had been less than successful. Elaine had rehashed with Amy the importance of never taking anything without permission, and certainly never giving that object to another person. Her father had agreed, but she had gone on about it until even he had said, "I think we've milked this subject dry, Elaine."

They had been late eating dinner because the electricity failed for more than an hour, and the roast wasn't done. As they were finally finishing dessert, Elaine brought up Menley Nichols again.

"You must understand that Adam is very worried about Menley. She's in a state of serious depression, and seeing the tape of her little boy might upset her terribly, plus she's alone for two nights. That's a big worry for Adam."

"I don't think she's depressed," Amy said. "She was sad when she watched the tape, but we talked about it, and Mrs. Nichols said that you should be grateful when you've had the chance to love someone wonderful, even if you didn't have them very long. She told me that her mother always said she'd rather have been married to her father for twelve years than to someone else for seventy years."

Then Amy looked at her father and added, "I certainly agree with her." With some satisfaction she saw a flush come over his face. She was hurt and irritated at him for taking Elaine's part so vehemently about the tape. But then, I guess that's how it's going to be from now on, she thought.

Conversation throughout the entire meal had been strained. Plus Elaine seemed awfully nervous. Even Amy's father had noticed it. Finally he asked her if anything was wrong.

That was when Elaine dropped a bombshell. "John, I've been thinking," she said. "I believe we should delay the wedding for a while. I want it to be perfect for us, and that's just not going to be possible while Amy is clearly so unhappy."

You don't give a damn whether I'm happy or unhappy, Amy thought. I bet there's more to it than that. "Elaine, as you've said all summer, in another few weeks I'm going to be in college and starting my own adult life. You're marrying my father, not me. My only concern is my father's happiness, and that should be your concern as well."

Elaine's bombshell had come just as they were about to leave. Amy liked the dignified way her dad said, "I think this is something that you and I should talk about at another time, Elaine. I'll call you tomorrow."

When Elaine opened the front door, they saw a police car with its lights flashing pulling up in her driveway. "What can be wrong?" Elaine asked.

Amy sensed something odd about Elaine's voice. It sounded strained, as though she were frightened.

Nat Coogan got out of the squad car and paused for a moment, looking at Elaine Atkins as she stood in the doorway. He had just gotten home when the call came from the station. Scott Covey had gone to Morris Island and tried to murder Adam Nichols' wife. He had run away when Nichols showed up and had been caught at a roadblock on Route 6.

Now it was Nat Coogan's extreme pleasure to be the one to arrest Elaine Atkins. Ignoring the pelting rain, he went up the walk and stepped onto the porch. "Miss Atkins," he said. "I have a warrant for your arrest. I'll read you your rights, and then I'll have to ask you to please come along with me."

Amy and her father stared at Elaine as her face drained of all color. "That's ridiculous," she said, her voice shocked and angry.

Nat pointed to the driveway. "Scott Covey is in that car. We're just taking him in. He was so sure of himself, he told Menley Nichols the whole story of your interesting deal with him and all about how you wanted her out of the way so you could have Adam Nichols to yourself. You're just lucky that Covey didn't succeed in drowning her. This way you'll only have to face charges of attempted murder. But you will need a good lawyer, and I don't think you'd better count on Adam Nichols to defend you."

John Nelson gasped. "Elaine, what's going on? What's he talking about? Nat, surely you're—"

"Oh, shut up, John!" Elaine snapped. She looked at him with contempt.

There was a long silence while they stared at each other. Then Amy felt her father take her arm. "Come on, honey," he said, "we've been around here long enough. Let's go home."

110

WHEN MENLEY AWOKE on Thursday morning, sunbeams were bouncing off the windowsill, darting over the wide-planked floor. Her mind filled with memories of last night and quickly skipped to the moment when she knew she was safe, when they reached the house, and Adam had called the police while she ran to Hannah.

After the police finally left and they were alone, they took turns holding each other and holding Hannah. Then, both too weary to even think about eating, they brought the cradle into their room, unable to leave Hannah alone in the nursery until the storage area was cleaned out and permanently sealed.

Menley looked around. Adam and Hannah were still sleeping. Her eyes moved from one to the other, marveling at the miracle of being with them, of knowing that she was strong and whole.

I can go on with my life, she thought. Mehitabel and Andrew never had a second chance.

The police had looked into the storage area last night, saying they would be back to photograph it for evidence in the trials. They had examined the skeleton also. The silver buckles resting among the foot bones bore the initials T.K. Tobias Knight.

The side of the skull was caved in, as if by a heavy blow. My guess is that Captain Freeman had surprised Tobias here, Menley mused, and learning, or guessing, the true reason for his late-night visits to the house, struck him down for fostering the lie that had destroyed Mehitabel. Then he left the body here with the stolen cargo. He must have surmised the truth of his wife's innocence. We know he was out of his mind with grief when he sailed into the storm.

Phoebe and I were right. Mehitabel was innocent. She died protesting that fact and longing for her baby. When I write her story I'm going to put Phoebe's name on it too. It was the story she wanted so much to tell.

She felt Adam's arm go around her.

He turned her toward him. "Did I mention last night that you're a terrific swimmer?" he asked. Then the light tone disappeared from his voice. "Men, when I think that I was so obtuse about everything and that you almost died because of me, I could kill myself."

She put her finger on his lips. "Don't ever say that. When you told me there was no train whistle in the tape of Bobby, I began to suspect that something was going on. But you didn't know what I had been hearing, so I can't blame you for thinking I was crazy."

Hannah began to stir. Menley reached down and picked her up, bringing her into the bed with them. "Quite a night, wasn't it, Toots?" she asked.

Nat Coogan phoned as they were finishing breakfast. "I hate to bother you people, but we're having a struggle keeping the media away. Would you consider talking to them after our people finish the investigation?"

"We'd better," Adam replied. "Tell them we need a little more time to ourselves, then we'll see them at two o'clock."

Moments later, however, the phone rang again—a television station wanting to set up an interview. That call was followed by others, so many that they finally disconnected the phone, plugging it in only long enough for Menley to call Jan Paley, the Spragues and Amy.

When she hung up from her last call, she was smiling. "Amy sounds like a different person," she said. "Her dad keeps telling her that he wished he had half her common sense. I told her I feel the same way. She knew all along that Elaine was a phony."

"A very dangerous phony," Adam said quietly.

"Amy wants to baby-sit for us tomorrow night—for free! Her dad's paying for the whole car."

"We'll take her up on it. How is Phoebe doing?"

"Henry told her that we were safe and he was proud of her for trying to warn us. He's sure that she might have understood a little of what he was saying." Menley paused. "I'm so sorry for them."

"I know." Adam put his arm around her.

"And Joan's coming over. She said she would bring lunch makings and offered to pick up the mail, so I took her up on it."

When the police arrived to photograph the hidden room, Adam and Menley took chairs and Hannah's carriage out to the bluff. The water was calm now, and inviting, with gentle waves breaking on a shore that was in surprisingly good shape, considering the severity of the storm the night before. Menley knew that from now on, if she dreamed about that night, the dream would always end with Adam's hand closing over hers.

She looked back at the house and up at the widow's walk. The metal on the chimney was gleaming, the sunbeams bouncing off it through the shifting shadows cast by occasional clouds. Did that really cause an optical illusion that day Amy thought she saw me? she wondered.

"What are you thinking?" Adam asked.

"I'm thinking that when I write Mehitabel's story, I'm going to say that she was a presence in the house, awaiting her innocence to be proven and her baby's return."

"And if she were still a presence here, would you want to live in this house?" Adam said teasingly.

"I almost wish she were," Menley said. "We are going to buy it, aren't we? Hannah will love growing up summers on the Cape the way you did. And I love this house. It's the first place where I've ever really felt a deep sense of home."

"Of course we're buying it."

. . .

At noon, a few minutes after the police photographers left, Jan arrived. Her silent embrace spoke volumes. "The only mail for you was a letter from Ireland." Menley ripped it open immediately. "It's from Phyllis," she said. "Oh look at this, she really has done some heavy research on the McCarthys."

There was a sheaf of genealogical records, birth and death certificates, copies of newspaper items, a few faded photographs.

"You dropped her note," Adam said. He picked it up and handed it to her.

It read:

Dear Menley,

I'm so excited. I wanted you to see this right away. I've traced your family back to the first Menley, and it's a wonderful story. She was raised from infancy by her father's cousins, the Longfords, in Connemara. There's no record of where she was born, but the date was recorded as 1705. At seventeen she married Squire Adrian McCarthy of Galway, and they had four children. Part of the foundation of their mansion can still be seen. It overlooks the ocean.

She must have been quite a beauty (see enclosed snapshot of her portrait), and I see a distinct family resemblance between you and her.

But, Menley, this is the best part, and it's something Hannah might want to keep in mind if she decides that she likes your name better than hers but doesn't want to be known as "young Menley" or "little Menley."

The reason for your unusual name is that when she was little, your ancestor could not pronounce her real name and called herself Menley.

The name she was given at birth was Remember . . .

LET ME CALL YOU SWEETHEART

ACKNOWLEDGMENTS

No man is an island and no writer, at least not this one, writes alone. Special glowing thanks to my editors, Michael V. Korda and Chuck Adams, who are always the sine qua non of my books from conception to publication. Particularly and especially with this one and at this time, they've been wonderful.

A thousand thanks always to Eugene H. Winick, my literary agent, and Lisl Cade, my publicist. Their help is immeasurable.

A writer needs expert counsel. This book concerns plastic surgery. My thanks to Dr. Bennett C. Rothenberg of Saint Barnabas Hospital, Livingston, New Jersey, for his expert medical advice. Kudos to Kim White of the New Jersey Department of Corrections for her assistance. And once again, Ina Winick has vetted for me the psychological aspects of the story line. Thank you, Ina.

My offspring, all five of them, read the work in progress. From them I get much sound advice—legal: "Make sure you sequester the jury . . ."; or dialogue: "No one our age would say that. Put it this way . . ."—and always cheery encouragement. Thanks, kids.

Finally, my ten-year-old granddaughter, Liz, who in many ways was the role model for Robin. I would ask her, "Liz, what would you say if this were happening . . . ?" Her suggestions were "awesome."

I love you, one and all.

For my Villa Maria Academy classmates
in this special year,
with a particularly loving tip of the hat to
Joan LaMotte Nye
June Langren Crabtree
Marjorie Lashley Quinlan
Joan Molloy Hoffman

and in joyous memory of Dorothea Bible Davis

Heap not on this mound
  Roses that she loved so well;
Why bewilder her with roses,
  That she cannot see or smell?

Edna St. Vincent Millay,
"Epitaph"

As often as humanly possible he tried to put Suzanne out of his mind. Sometimes he achieved peace for a few hours or even managed to sleep through the night. It was the only way he could function, go about the daily business of living.

Did he still love her or only hate her? He could never be sure. She had been so beautiful, with those luminous mocking eyes, that cloud of dark hair, those lips that could smile so invitingly or pout so easily, like a child being refused a sweet.

In his mind she was always there, as she had looked in that last moment of her life, taunting him then turning her back on him.

And now, nearly eleven years later, Kerry McGrath would not let Suzanne rest. Questions and more questions! It could not be tolerated. She had to be stopped.

Let the dead bury the dead. That's the old saying, he thought, and it's still true. She would be stopped, no matter what.

1

Kerry smoothed down the skirt of her dark green suit, straightened the narrow gold chain on her neck and ran her fingers through her collar-length, dusky blond hair. Her entire afternoon had been a mad rush, leaving the courthouse at two-thirty, picking up Robin at school, driving from Hohokus through the heavy traffic of Routes 17 and 4, then over the George Washington Bridge to Manhattan, finally parking the car and arriving at the doctor's office just in time for Robin's four o'clock appointment.

Now, after all the rush, Kerry could only sit and wait to be summoned into the examining room, wishing that she'd been allowed to be with Robin while the stitches were removed. But the nurse had been adamant. "During a procedure, Dr. Smith will not permit anyone except the nurse in the room with a patient."

"But she's only ten!" Kerry had protested, then had closed her lips and reminded herself that she should be grateful that Dr. Smith was the one who had been called in after the accident. The nurses at St. Luke's-Roosevelt had assured her that he was a wonderful plastic surgeon. The emergency room doctor had even called him a miracle worker.

Reflecting back on that day, a week ago, Kerry realized she still hadn't recovered from the shock of that phone call. She'd been working late in her office at the courthouse in Hackensack, preparing for the murder case she would be prosecuting, taking advantage of the fact that Robin's father, her ex-husband, Bob Kinellen, had unexpectedly invited Robin to see New York City's Big Apple Circus, followed by dinner.

At six-thirty her phone had rung. It was Bob. There had been an accident. A van had rammed into his Jaguar while he was pulling out of the parking garage. Robin's face had been cut by flying glass. She'd been rushed to St. Luke's-Roosevelt, and a plastic surgeon had been called. Otherwise she seemed fine, although she was being examined for internal injuries.

Remembering that terrible evening, Kerry shook her head. She tried to push out of her mind the agony of the hurried drive into New York, dry sobs shaking her body, her lips forming only one word, "please," her mind racing with the rest of the prayer, *Please God, don't let her die, she's all I have. Please, she's just a baby. Don't take her from me . . .*

Robin was already in surgery when Kerry had arrived at the hospital, so she had sat in the waiting room, Bob next to her—with him but not with him. He had a wife and two other children now. Kerry could still feel the overwhelming sensation of relief she had experienced when Dr. Smith had finally appeared, and in a formal and oddly condescending manner had said, "Fortunately the lacerations did not deeply penetrate the dermis. Robin will not be scarred. I want to see her in my office in one week."

The cuts proved to be her only injuries, and Robin had bounced back from the accident, missing only two days of school. She had seemed to be somewhat proud of her bandages. It was only today, on their way into New York for the appointment, that she'd sounded frightened when she asked, "I will be okay, won't I, Mom? I mean my face won't be all messed up?"

With her wide blue eyes, oval face, high forehead and sculpted features, Robin was a beautiful child and the image of her father. Kerry had reassured her with a heartiness she hoped was truthful. Now, to distract herself, Kerry looked around the waiting room. It was tastefully furnished with several couches and chairs covered in a small floral print design. The lights were soft, the carpeting luxurious.

A woman who appeared to be in her early forties, wearing a bandage across her nose, was among those waiting to be called inside. Another, who looked somewhat anxious, was confiding to her attractive companion: "Now that I'm here, I'm glad you made me come. You look fabulous."

She does, Kerry thought as she self-consciously reached into her bag for her compact. Snapping it open, she examined herself in the mirror, deciding that today she looked every minute of her thirty-six years. She was aware that many people found her attractive, but still she remained self-conscious about her looks. She brushed the powder puff over the bridge of her nose, trying to cover the spray of detested freckles, studied her eyes and decided that whenever she was tired, as she was today, their hazel color changed from green to muddy brown. She tucked a stray strand of hair behind her ear, then with a sigh closed the compact and smoothed back the half bang that needed trimming.

Anxiously she fastened her gaze on the door that led to the examining rooms. Why was it taking so long to remove Robin's stitches? she wondered. Could there be complications?

A moment later the door opened. Kerry looked up expectantly. Instead of Robin, however, there emerged a young woman who seemed to be in her mid-twenties, a cloud of dark hair framing the petulant beauty of her face.

I wonder if she always looked like that, Kerry mused, as she studied the high cheekbones, straight nose, exquisitely shaped pouty lips, luminous eyes, arched brows.

Perhaps sensing her gaze, the young woman looked quizzically at Kerry as she passed her.

Kerry's throat tightened. I know you, she thought. But from where? She swallowed, her mouth suddenly dry. That face—I've seen her before.

Once the woman had left, Kerry went over to the receptionist and explained that she thought she might know the lady who just came out of the doctor's office. Who was she?

The name Barbara Tompkins, however, meant nothing to her. She must have been mistaken. Still, when she sat down again, an overwhelming sense of déjà vu filled her mind. The effect was so chilling, she actually shivered.

2

Kate Carpenter regarded the patients in the doctor's waiting room with something of a jaundiced eye. She had been with Dr. Charles Smith as a surgical nurse for four years, working with him on the operations he performed in the office. Quite simply, she considered him a genius.

She herself had never been tempted to have him work on her. Fiftyish, sturdily built with a pleasant face and graying hair, she described herself to her friends as a plastic surgery counterrevolutionary: "What you see is what you get."

Totally in sympathy with clients who had genuine problems,

she felt mild contempt for the men and women who came in for procedure after procedure in their relentless pursuit of physical perfection. "On the other hand," as she told her husband, "they're paying my salary."

Sometimes Kate Carpenter wondered why she stayed with Dr. Smith. He was so brusque with everyone, patients as well as staff, that he often seemed rude. He seldom praised but never missed an opportunity to sarcastically point out the smallest error. But then again, she decided, the pay and benefits were excellent, and it was a genuine thrill to watch Dr. Smith at work.

Except that lately she had noticed he was getting increasingly bad tempered. Potential new clients, directed to him because of his excellent reputation, were offended by his manner and more and more frequently were canceling scheduled procedures. The only ones he seemed to treat with flattering care were the recipients of the special "look," and that was another thing that bothered Carpenter.

And in addition to his being irascible, in these last months she had noticed that the doctor seemed to be detached, even remote. Sometimes, when she spoke to him, he looked at her blankly, as though his mind were far away.

She glanced at her watch. As she had expected, after Dr. Smith finished examining Barbara Tompkins, the latest recipient of the "look," he had gone into his private office and closed the door.

What did he do in there? she wondered. He had to realize that he was running late. That little girl, Robin, had been sitting alone in examining room 3 for half an hour, and there were other patients in the waiting room. But she had noticed that after the doctor saw one of the special patients, he always seemed to need time to himself.

"Mrs. Carpenter . . ."

Startled, the nurse looked up from her desk. Dr. Smith was staring down at her. "I think we've kept Robin Kinellen waiting

long enough," he said accusingly. Behind rimless glasses, his eyes
were frosty.

3

"I don't like Dr. Smith," Robin said matter-of-factly as Kerry
maneuvered the car out of the parking garage on Ninth
Street off Fifth Avenue.

Kerry looked at her quickly. "Why not?"

"He's scary. At home when I go to Dr. Wilson, he always
makes jokes. But Dr. Smith didn't even smile. He acted like he
was mad at me. He said something about how some people are
given beauty while others attain it, but in neither case must it
ever be wasted."

Robin had inherited her father's stunning good looks and was
indeed quite beautiful. It was true that this could someday be a
burden, but why would the doctor say such an odd thing to a
child? Kerry wondered.

"I'm sorry I told him I hadn't finished fastening my seat belt
when the van hit Daddy's car," Robin added. "That's when Dr.
Smith started lecturing me."

Kerry glanced at her daughter. Robin always fastened her seat
belt. That she hadn't this time meant that Bob had started the
car before she had had a chance. Kerry tried to keep anger out of

her voice as she said, "Daddy probably took off out of the garage in a hurry."

"He just didn't notice I hadn't had time to buckle it," Robin said defensively, picking up on the edge in her mother's voice.

Kerry felt heartsick for her daughter. Bob Kinellen had walked out on them both when Robin was a baby. Now he was married to his senior partner's daughter and was the father of a five-year-old girl and a three-year-old boy. Robin was crazy about her father, and when he was with her he made a big fuss over her. But he disappointed her so often, calling at the last minute to break a scheduled date. Because his second wife did not like to be reminded that he had another child, Robin was never invited to his home. As a result she hardly even knew her half brother and sister.

On the rare occasion when he does come through, and finally takes her out, look what happens, Kerry thought. She struggled to hide her anger, however, deciding not to pursue the subject. Instead she said, "Why don't you try to snooze till we get to Uncle Jonathan and Aunt Grace's?"

"Okay." Robin closed her eyes. "I bet they have a present for me."

4

While they waited for Kerry and Robin to arrive for dinner, Jonathan and Grace Hoover were sharing their customary late-afternoon martini in the living room of their home in Old Tappan overlooking Lake Tappan. The setting sun was sending long shadows across the tranquil water. The trees, carefully trimmed to avoid obstructing the lake view, were glowing with the brilliant leaves they would soon relinquish.

Jonathan had built the first fire of the season, and Grace had just commented that the first frost of the season was predicted for that evening.

A handsome couple in their early sixties, they had been married nearly forty years, tied by bonds and needs that went beyond affection and habit. Over that time, they seemed almost to have grown to resemble each other: both had patrician features, framed by luxuriant heads of hair, his pure white with natural waves, hers short and curly, still peppered with traces of brown.

There was, however, a distinctive difference in their bodies. Jonathan sat tall and erect in a high-backed wing chair, while Grace reclined on a sofa opposite him, an afghan over her useless legs, her bent fingers inert in her lap, a wheelchair nearby. For years a victim of rheumatoid arthritis, she had become increasingly more disabled.

Jonathan had remained devoted to her during the whole ordeal. The senior partner of a major New Jersey law firm specializing in high-profile civil suits, he had also held the position of state senator for some twenty years but had several times turned down the opportunity to run for governor. "I can do enough good or harm in the senate," was his often-quoted remark, "and anyhow, I don't think I'd win."

Anyone who knew him well didn't believe his protests. They knew Grace was the reason he had chosen to avoid the demands of gubernatorial life, and secretly they wondered if he didn't harbor some vague resentment that her condition had held him back. If he did, however, he certainly never showed it.

Now as Grace sipped her martini, she sighed. "I honestly believe this is my favorite time of year," she said, "it's so beautiful, isn't it? This kind of day makes me remember taking the train to Princeton from Bryn Mawr for the football games, watching them with you, going to the Nassau Inn for dinner . . ."

"And staying at your aunt's house and her waiting up to be sure you were safely in before she went to bed," Jonathan chuckled. "I used to pray that just once the old bat would fall asleep early, but she kept a perfect record."

Grace smiled. "The minute we would pull up in front of the house, the porch light started blinking." Then she glanced anxiously at the clock on the mantel. "Aren't they running late? I hate to think of Kerry and Robin in the thick of the commuter traffic. Especially after what happened last week."

"Kerry's a good driver," Jonathan reassured her. "Don't worry. They'll be here any minute."

"I know. It's just . . ." The sentence did not have to be completed; Jonathan understood fully. Ever since twenty-one-year-old Kerry, about to start law school, had answered their ad for a house-sitter, they'd come to think of her as a surrogate daughter. That had been fifteen years ago, and during that time Jonathan had been of frequent help to Kerry in guiding and shaping her career, most recently using his influence to have her name included on the governor's shortlist of candidates for a judgeship.

Ten minutes later the welcome sound of door chimes heralded Kerry and Robin's arrival. As Robin had predicted, there was a gift waiting for her, a book and a quiz game for her computer. After dinner she took the book into the library and curled up in a chair while the adults lingered over coffee.

With Robin out of earshot, Grace quietly asked, "Kerry, those marks on Robin's face *will* fade, won't they?"

"I asked Dr. Smith the same thing when I saw them. He not only practically guaranteed their disappearance, he made me feel as though I'd insulted him by expressing any concern about them. I have to tell you I have a hunch the good doctor has one big ego. Still, last week at the hospital, the emergency room doctor absolutely assured me that Smith is a fine plastic surgeon. In fact, he called him a miracle worker."

As she sipped the last of her coffee, Kerry thought about the woman she had seen earlier in Dr. Smith's office. She looked across the table at Jonathan and Grace. "An odd thing happened while I was waiting for Robin. There was someone in Dr. Smith's office who looked so familiar," she said. "I even asked the receptionist what her name was. I'm sure I don't know her, but I just couldn't shake the sensation that we had met before. She gave me a creepy feeling. Isn't that odd?"

"What did she look like?" Grace asked.

"A knockout in a kind of come-hither, sensually provocative way," Kerry reflected. "I think the lips gave her that look. They were kind of full and pouty. I know: Maybe she was one of Bob's old girlfriends, and I had just repressed that memory." She shrugged. "Oh well, it's going to bug me till I figure it out."

5

Y ou've changed my life, Dr. Smith . . . That was what Barbara Tompkins had said to him as she left his office
earlier today. And he knew it was true. He had changed
her and, in the process, her life. From a plain, almost mousy
woman who looked older than her twenty-six years, he'd transformed her into a young beauty. More than a beauty, actually.
Now she had spirit. She wasn't the same insecure woman who
had come to him a year ago.

At the time she had been working in a small public relations
firm in Albany. "I saw what you did for one of our clients," she
had said when she came into his office that first day. "I just
inherited some money from my aunt. Can you make me pretty?"

He had done more than that—he had transformed her. He had
made her beautiful. Now Barbara was working in Manhattan at
a large, prestigious P.R. firm. She had always had brains, but
combining those brains with that special kind of beauty had truly
changed her life.

Dr. Smith saw his last patient for the day at six-thirty. Then
he walked the three blocks down Fifth Avenue to his converted
carriage house in Washington Mews.

It was his habit each day to go home, relax over a bourbon
and soda while watching the evening news and then decide where
he wanted to dine. He lived alone and almost never ate in.

Tonight an unaccustomed restlessness overcame him. Of all the women, Barbara Tompkins was the one most like *her*. Just seeing her was an emotional, almost cathartic experience. He had overheard Barbara chatting with Mrs. Carpenter, telling her that she was taking a client to dinner that night in the Oak Room at the Plaza Hotel.

Almost reluctantly he got up. What would happen next was inevitable. He would go to the Oak Bar, look into the Oak Room restaurant, see if there was a small table from which he could observe Barbara while he dined. With any luck she wouldn't be aware of him. But even if she was, even if she saw him, he would merely wave. She had no reason to think that he was following her.

After they got home from dinner with Jonathan and Grace, and long after Robin was asleep, Kerry continued to work. Her office was in the study of the house she had moved to after Bob had left them and she sold the house they had bought together. She had been able to get the new place at a good price, when the real estate market was low, and she was grateful she had—she loved it. Fifty years old, it was a roomy Cape Cod with double dormers, set on a heavily treed two-acre lot. The only time she didn't love it was when the leaves began to fall, tons and tons of them. That would begin soon, she thought with a sigh.

Tomorrow she would be cross-examining the defendant in a murder case she was prosecuting. He was a good actor. On the stand, his version of the events that led up to the death of his supervisor had seemed entirely plausible. He claimed his superior had constantly belittled him, so much so that one day he had snapped and killed her. His attorney was going for a manslaughter verdict.

It was Kerry's job to take the defendant's story apart, to show that this was a carefully planned and executed vendetta against a boss who for good reasons had passed him over for promotion. It had cost her her life. Now he has to pay, Kerry thought.

It was one o'clock before she was satisfied that she had laid out all the questions she wanted to ask, all the points she wanted to make.

Wearily she climbed the stairs to the second floor. She glanced in on a peacefully sleeping Robin, pulled the covers tighter around her, then went across the hallway to her own room.

Five minutes later, her face washed, teeth brushed, clad in her favorite nightshirt, she snuggled down into the queen-sized brass bed that she had bought in a tag sale after Bob left. She had changed all the furniture in the master bedroom. It had been impossible to live with the old things, to look at his dresser, his night table, to see the empty pillow on his side of the bed.

The shade was only partially drawn, and by the faint light from the lamp on the post by the driveway, she could see that a steady rain had begun to fall.

Well, the great weather couldn't last forever, she thought, grateful that at least it was not as cold as predicted, that the rain would not change to sleet. She closed her eyes willing her mind to stop churning, wondering why she felt so uneasy.

She woke at five, then managed to doze off until six. It was in that hour the dream came to her for the first time.

She saw herself in the waiting room of a doctor's office. There was a woman lying on the floor, her large, unfocused eyes staring into nothingness. A cloud of dark hair framed the petulant beauty of her face. A knotted cord was twisted around her neck.

Then as Kerry watched, the woman got up, removed the cord from her neck and went over to the receptionist to make an appointment.

During the evening it crossed Robert Kinellen's mind to call and see how Robin had made out at the doctor's, but the thought had come and gone without being acted on. His father-in-law and the law firm's senior partner, Anthony Bartlett, had taken the unusual step of appearing at the Kinellens' house after dinner to discuss strategy in the upcoming income tax evasion trial of James Forrest Weeks, the firm's most important—and controversial—client.

Weeks, a multimillion-dollar real estate developer and entrepreneur, had become something of a public figure in New York and New Jersey during the past three decades. A heavy contributor to political campaigns, a prominent donor to numerous charities, he was also the subject of constant rumors about inside deals and influence peddling, and was rumored to have connections with known mobsters.

The U.S. attorney general's office had been trying to pin something on Weeks for years, and it had been the financially rewarding job of Bartlett and Kinellen to represent him during those past investigations. Until now, the Feds had always fallen short of enough evidence for a solid indictment.

"This time Jimmy is in serious trouble," Anthony Bartlett reminded his son-in-law as they sat across from each other in the study of the Kinellen home in Englewood Cliffs. He sipped a brandy. "Which of course means we're in serious trouble with him."

In the ten years since Bob had joined the firm, he had seen it become almost an extension of Weeks Enterprises, so closely were they entwined. In fact, without Jimmy's vast business empire, they would be left with only a handful of minor clients, and with billings inadequate to maintain the firm's operations. They both knew that if Jimmy were to be found guilty, Bartlett and Kinellen as a viable law firm would be finished.

"Barney's the one I worry about," Bob said quietly. Barney Haskell was Jimmy Weeks' chief accountant and codefendant in the current case. They both knew intense pressure was being put on him to turn government witness in exchange for a plea bargain.

Anthony Bartlett nodded. "Agreed."

"And for more than one reason," Bob continued. "I told you about the accident in New York? And that Robin was treated by a plastic surgeon?"

"Yes. How is she doing?"

"She'll be all right, thank goodness. But I didn't tell you the doctor's name. It's Charles Smith."

"Charles Smith." Anthony Bartlett frowned as he considered the name. Then his eyebrows rose and he sat bolt upright. "Not the one who . . . ?"

"Exactly," Bob told him. "And my ex-wife, the assistant prosecutor, is taking our daughter on regular visits to him. Knowing Kerry, it's only a matter of time before she makes the connection."

"Oh my God," Bartlett said miserably.

The Bergen County prosecutor's office was located on the second floor in the west wing of the courthouse. It housed thirty-five assistant prosecutors, seventy investigators and twenty-five secretaries, as well as Franklin Green, the prosecutor.

Despite the constantly heavy workload and the serious, often macabre, nature of the business, an air of camaraderie existed within the office. Kerry loved working there. She regularly received enticing offers from law firms, asking her to come work with them, but despite the financial temptations, she had elected to stay put and now had worked her way up to the position of trial chief. In the process she had earned herself a reputation as a smart, tough and scrupulous lawyer.

Two judges who had reached the mandatory retirement age of seventy had just vacated the bench, and now there were two openings. In his capacity as a state senator, Jonathan Hoover had submitted Kerry's name for one of the seats. She did not admit even to herself how much she wanted it. The big law firms offered much more money, but a judgeship represented the kind of achievement that no money could compete with.

Kerry thought of the possible appointment this morning as she punched in the code for the lock of the outside door and, at the click, shoved the door open. Waving to the switchboard operator, she walked at a quick pace to the office set aside for the trial chief.

By the standards of the windowless cubbyholes assigned to the new assistants, her office was reasonably sized. The surface of the worn wooden desk was so completely covered with stacks of files that its condition hardly mattered. The straight-backed chairs did not match, but were serviceable. The top drawer of the file had to be yanked vigorously to get it open, but that was only a minor irritation to Kerry.

The office had cross ventilation, windows that provided both light and air. She had personalized the space with thriving green plants that edged the windowsills, and with framed pictures that Robin had taken. The effect was that of functional comfort, and Kerry was perfectly content to have it as her office.

The morning had brought the first frost of the season, prompting Kerry to grab her Burberry as she left her house. Now she hung up the coat with care. She had bought it at a sale and intended it to have a long life.

She shook off the final vestiges of last night's troubling dream as she sat at her desk. The business at hand was the trial that would be resuming in an hour.

The murdered supervisor had two teenage sons whom she had been raising alone. Who was going to take care of them now? Suppose something happened to me, Kerry thought. Where would Robin go? Surely not to her father; she would not be happy, nor welcome, in his new household. But Kerry also couldn't picture her mother and her stepfather, both now over seventy and living in Colorado, raising a ten-year-old. Pray God I stay around at least till Robin is grown, she thought as she turned her attention to the file in front of her.

At ten of nine, her phone rang. It was Frank Green, the prosecutor. "Kerry, I know you're on your way to court, but stop by for just a minute."

"Of course." And it can only be a minute, she thought. Frank knows that Judge Kafka has a fit when he's kept waiting.

She found Prosecutor Frank Green seated behind his desk. Craggy-faced with shrewd eyes, at fifty-two he'd kept the hard physique that had made him a college football star. His smile was warm but seemed odd, she thought. Did he have his teeth bonded? she wondered. If so, he's smart. They do look good, and they'll photograph well when he's nominated in June.

There was no question that Green was already preparing for the gubernatorial campaign. The media coverage accorded his office was building, and the attention he was paying to his wardrobe was obvious to everyone. An editorial had said that since the present governor had served so well for two terms and Green was his handpicked successor, it seemed very likely that he would be chosen to lead the state.

After that editorial appeared, Green became known to his staff as "Our Leader."

Kerry admired his legal skills and efficiency. He ran a tight, solid ship. Her reservation about him was that several times in these ten years he had let an assistant who had made an honest mistake hang out to dry. Green's first loyalty was to himself.

She knew her possible nomination for a judgeship had increased her stature in his eyes. "Looks like the two of us will be going on to greater things," he had told her in a rare burst of exuberance and camaraderie.

Now he said, "Come in, Kerry. I just wanted to hear personally from you about how Robin is doing. When I learned that you had asked the judge to recess the trial yesterday, I was concerned."

She briefly told him about the checkup, reassuring him that all was under control.

"Robin was with her father at the time of the accident, wasn't she?" he asked.

"Yes. Bob was driving."

"Your ex may be running out of luck. I don't think he's going to get Weeks off this time. The word is they're going to nail him, and I hope they do. He's a crook and maybe worse." He made a gesture of dismissal. "I'm glad Robin's coming along okay, and I know you are on top of things. You're cross-examining the defendant today, aren't you?"

"Yes."

"Knowing you, I'm almost sorry for him. Good luck."

9

It was almost two weeks later, and Kerry was still basking in the satisfaction of the now concluded trial. She had gotten her murder conviction. At least the sons of the murdered woman would not have to grow up knowing that their mother's killer would be walking the streets in five or six years. That would have happened if the jury had fallen for the manslaughter defense. Murder carried a mandatory thirty-year sentence, without parole.

Now, once again seated in the reception area of Dr. Smith's office, she opened her ever-present briefcase and pulled out a newspaper. This was Robin's second checkup and should be fairly routine, so she could relax. Besides, she was anxious to read the latest about the Jimmy Weeks trial.

As Frank Green had predicted, the consensus was that it would not go well for the defendant. Previous investigations for bribery, inside trading and money laundering had been dropped for lack of sufficient evidence. But this time the prosecutor was said to have an airtight case. If it ever actually got started, that is. The jury selection had been going on for several weeks, and there seemed to be no end in sight. It no doubt makes Bartlett and Kinellen happy, she thought, to have all these billable hours piling up.

Bob had introduced Kerry to Jimmy Weeks once, when she had bumped into them in a restaurant. Now she studied his picture as he sat with her ex-husband at the defense table. Take away that custom-tailored suit and phony air of sophistication, and underneath you've got a thug, she thought.

In the picture, Bob's arm was draped protectively around the back of Weeks' chair. Their heads were close together. Kerry remembered how Bob used to practice that gesture.

She scanned the article, then dropped the newspaper back into her briefcase. Shaking her head, she remembered how appalled she had been when, shortly after Robin was born, Bob had told her he had accepted a job with Bartlett and Associates.

"All their clients have one foot in jail," she had protested. "And the other foot should be there."

"And they pay their bills on time," Bob had replied. "Kerry, you stay in the prosecutor's office if you want. I have other plans."

A year later he had announced that those plans included marrying Alice Bartlett.

Ancient history, Kerry told herself now as she looked around the waiting room. Today the other occupants were an athletic-looking teenage boy with a bandage across his nose and an older woman whose deeply wrinkled skin suggested the reason for her presence.

Kerry glanced at her watch. Robin had told her that last week she had waited in the examining room for half an hour. "I wish I'd brought a book with me," she had said. This time she'd made sure she had one.

I wish to God that Dr. Smith would set realistic appointment times, Kerry thought with irritation as she glanced in the direction of the examining rooms, the door to which was just opening.

Immediately, Kerry froze, and her glance became a stare. The young woman who emerged had a face framed by a cloud of dark hair, a straight nose, pouty lips, wide-set eyes, arched brows. Kerry felt her throat constrict. It wasn't the same woman she had seen last time—but it looked like her. Could the two be related? If they were patients, surely Dr. Smith couldn't be trying to make them look alike, she thought.

And why did that face remind her so much of someone else that it had brought on a nightmare? She shook her head, unable to come up with an answer.

She looked again at the others seated in the tiny waiting room. The boy had obviously had an accident and probably had broken his nose. But was the older woman here for something as routine as a face-lift, or was she hoping to have a totally different appearance?

What would it be like to look into the mirror and find a stranger's face staring back at you? Kerry wondered. Can you just pick a look that you want? Was it that simple?

"Ms. McGrath."

Kerry turned to see Mrs. Carpenter, the nurse, beckoning to her to come to the examining rooms.

Kerry hurried to follow her. Last visit she had asked the receptionist about the woman she had seen there and been told her name was Barbara Tompkins. Now she could ask the nurse about this other woman. "That young woman who just left, she looked familiar," Kerry said. "What is her name?"

"Pamela Worth," Mrs. Carpenter said shortly. "Here we are."

She found Robin seated across the desk from the doctor, her hands folded in her lap, her posture unusually straight. Kerry saw the look of relief on her daughter's face when she turned and their eyes met.

The doctor nodded to her and with a gesture indicated that she should take the chair next to Robin. "I have gone over with Robin the follow-up care I want her to take to insure that nothing impedes the healing process. She wants to continue to play soccer, but she must promise to wear a face mask for the rest of the season. We must not risk the slightest possibility of those lacerations being reopened. I expect that by the end of six months they'll no longer be visible."

His expression became intense. "I've already explained to Robin that many people come to me seeking the kind of beauty that was freely given to her. It is her duty to safeguard it. I see from the file that you are divorced. Robin told me her father was driving the car at the time of the accident. I urge you to warn him to take better care of his daughter. She is irreplaceable."

On the way home, at Robin's request, they stopped to have dinner at Valentino's in Park Ridge. "I like the shrimp there," Robin explained. But when they were settled at a table, she looked around and said, "Daddy brought me here once. He says it's the best." Her voice was wistful.

So that's why this is the restaurant of choice, Kerry thought. Since the accident, Bob had phoned Robin only once, and that had been during school hours. The message on the answering machine was that he guessed she was in school and that must mean she was doing great. There was no suggestion she return his call. Be fair, Kerry told herself. He did check with me at the office, and he knows that Dr. Smith said she is going to be okay. But that was two weeks ago. Since then, silence.

The waiter arrived to take their orders. When they were alone again, Robin said, "Mom, I don't want to go back to Dr. Smith anymore. He's creepy."

Kerry's heart sank. It was exactly what she had been thinking. And her next thought was that she only had his word that the angry red lines on Robin's face would disappear. I've got to have someone else check her out, she thought. Trying to sound matter-of-fact, she said, "Oh, I guess Dr. Smith is all right, even if he does have the personality of a wet noodle." She was rewarded by Robin's grin.

"Even so," she continued, "he doesn't want to see you for another month, and after that, maybe not at all, so don't worry about him. It's not his fault he was born without charm."

Robin laughed. "Forget the charm. He's a major creep."

When the food arrived, they sampled each other's choices and gossiped. Robin had a passion for photography and was taking a basic course in technique. Her present assignment was to capture the autumn leaves in transition. "I showed you the great shots I got of them just as they started to turn, Mom. I know the ones I took this week with the colors at peak are terrific."

"Sight unseen?" Kerry murmured.

"Uh-huh. Now I can't wait till they get dried up and then a good storm starts scattering everything. Won't that be great?"

"Nothing like a good storm scattering everything," Kerry agreed.

They decided to skip dessert. The waiter had just returned Kerry's credit card when she heard Robin gasp. "What is it, Rob?"

"Daddy's here. He sees us." Robin jumped up.

"Wait, Rob, let him come over to you," Kerry said quietly. She turned. Accompanied by another man, Bob was following the maître d'. Kerry's eyes widened. The other man was Jimmy Weeks.

As usual, Bob looked stunning. Even a long day in court did not leave a sign of fatigue on his handsome face. Never a wrinkle or a rumple about you, Kerry thought, aware that in Bob's presence she always had the impulse to check her makeup, smooth her hair, straighten her jacket.

On the other hand, Robin looked ecstatic. Happily she returned Bob's hug. "I'm sorry I missed your call, Daddy."

Oh, Robin, Kerry thought. Then she realized that Jimmy Weeks was looking down at her. "I met you here last year," he said. "You were having dinner with a couple of judges. Glad to see you again, Mrs. Kinellen."

"I dropped that name a long time ago. It's back to McGrath.

But you do have a good memory, Mr. Weeks." Kerry's tone was impersonal. She certainly wasn't going to say she was glad to see the man.

"You bet I have a good memory." Weeks' smile made the remark seem like a joke. "It helps when you're remembering a very attractive woman."

Spare me, Kerry thought, smiling tightly. She turned from him as Bob released Robin. Now he stretched out his hand to her.

"Kerry, what a nice surprise."

"It's usually a surprise when we see you, Bob."

"Mom," Robin implored.

Kerry bit her lip. She hated herself when she jabbed at Bob in front of their daughter. She forced a smile. "We're just leaving."

When they were settled at their table and their drink orders taken, Jimmy Weeks observed, "Your ex-wife sure doesn't like you much, Bobby."

Kinellen shrugged. "Kerry should lighten up. She takes everything too seriously. We married too young. We broke up. It happens every day. I wish she'd meet someone else."

"What happened to your kid's face?"

"Flying glass in a fender bender. She'll be fine."

"Did you make sure she had a good plastic surgeon?"

"Yes, he was highly recommended. What do you feel like eating, Jimmy?"

"What's the doctor's name? Maybe he's the same one my wife went to."

Bob Kinellen seethed inwardly. He cursed the lousy luck of meeting Kerry and Robin and having Jimmy ask about the accident. "It's Charles Smith," he said finally.

"Charles Smith?" Weeks' voice was startled. "You've got to be kidding."

"I wish I were."

"Well, I hear he's retiring soon. He's got big-time health problems."

Kinellen looked startled. "How do you know that?"

Jimmy W. looked at him coldly. "I keep tabs on him. You figure out why. It shouldn't take too long."

10

That night the dream returned. Again, Kerry was standing in a doctor's office. A young woman was lying on the floor, a cord knotted around her neck, her dark hair framing a face with wide unfocused eyes, a mouth open as though gasping for breath, the tip of a pink tongue protruding.

In her dream, Kerry tried to scream, but only a moaning protest came from her lips. A moment later Robin was shaking her awake. "Mom. Mom, wake up. What's wrong?"

Kerry opened her eyes, "What. Oh my God, Rob, what a rotten nightmare. Thanks."

But when Robin had returned to her room, Kerry lay awake, pondering the dream. What was triggering it? she wondered. Why was it different from the last time?

This time there had been flowers scattered over the woman's body. Roses. *Sweetheart roses.*

She sat up suddenly. That was it! *That* was what she had been trying to remember! In Dr. Smith's office, the woman today, and the woman a couple of weeks ago, the ones who had resembled each other so closely. She knew now why they seemed so familiar. She knew who they looked like.

Suzanne Reardon, the victim in the Sweetheart Murder Case. It had been nearly eleven years ago that she had been murdered by her husband. It had gotten a lot of press attention, crime of passion and roses scattered over the beautiful victim.

The day I started in the prosecutor's office was the day the jury found the husband guilty, Kerry thought. The papers had been plastered with pictures of Suzanne. I'm sure I'm right, she told herself. I sat in at the sentencing. It made such an impression on me. But why in the name of God would two of Dr. Smith's patients be look-alikes for a murder victim?

11

Pamela Worth had been a mistake. That thought kept Dr. Charles Smith sleepless virtually all Monday night. Even the beauty of her newly sculpted face could not compensate for her graceless posture, her harsh, loud voice.

I should have known right away, he thought. And, in fact, he had known. But he hadn't been able to help himself. Her bone structure made her a ridiculously easy candidate for such a transformation. And feeling that transformation take place under his fingers had made it possible for him to relive something of the excitement of the way it had been that first time.

What would he do when it wasn't possible to operate anymore? he wondered. That time was rapidly approaching. The
slight hand tremor that irritated now would become more pro-
nounced. Irritation would yield to incapacity.

He switched on the light, not the one beside his bed, but the
one that illuminated the picture on the wall opposite him. He
looked at it each night before he fell asleep. She was so beautiful.
But now, without his glasses, the woman in the picture became
twisted and distorted, as she had looked in death.

"Suzanne," he murmured. Then, as the pain of memory engulfed him, he threw an arm over his eyes, blocking out the
image. He could not bear to remember how she had looked then,
robbed of her beauty, her eyes bulging, the tip of her tongue
protruding over her slack lower lip and drooping jaw . . .

12

On Tuesday morning, the first thing Kerry did when she got to her office was to phone Jonathan Hoover.

As always, it was comforting to hear his voice. She got right to the point. "Jonathan, Robin had her checkup in New York yesterday, and everything seems to be fine, but I'd be a lot more comfortable with a second opinion, if another plastic surgeon concurred with Dr. Smith that there won't be any scarring. Do you know anyone who's good?"

Jonathan's voice had a smile. "Not by personal experience."

"You certainly never needed it."

"Thank you, Kerry. Let me make some inquiries. Grace and I both thought you should get a second opinion, but we didn't want to interfere. Did something happen yesterday that made you decide on this?"

"Yes and no. I have someone coming in right now. I'll tell you about it when I see you next."

"I'll get back to you with a name this afternoon."

"Thanks, Jonathan."

"You're welcome, Your Honor."

"Jonathan, don't say that. You'll jinx me."

As the phone clicked, she heard him chuckle.

Her first appointment that morning was with Corinne Banks, the assistant to whom, as trial chief, she had assigned a vehicular homicide case. It was on the court calendar for next Monday, and Corinne wanted to review some aspects of the prosecution she intended to present.

Corinne, a young black woman of twenty-seven, had the makings of a top-drawer trial lawyer, Kerry thought. A tap at the door, and Corinne came in, a large file under her arm. She was wreathed in smiles. "Guess what Joe dug up," she said happily.

Joe Palumbo was one of their best investigators.

Kerry grinned. "I can hardly wait."

"Our oh-so-innocent defendant who claimed he never was involved in another accident has a real problem. Under a phony driver's license, he has a string of serious traffic violations, including another death by auto fifteen years ago. I can't wait to nail that guy, and now I'm confident that we can." She laid down the file and opened it. "Anyhow, this is what I wanted to talk about . . ."

Twenty minutes later, after Corinne left, Kerry reached for the phone. Corinne's mention of the investigator had given her an idea.

When Joe Palumbo answered with his usual "Yup," Kerry asked, "Joe, have you got lunch plans?"

"Not a one, Kerry. Want to take me to Solari's for lunch?"

Kerry laughed. "I'd love to, but I have something else in mind. How long have you been here?"

"Twenty years."

"Were you involved with the Reardon homicide about ten years ago, the one the media called the Sweetheart Murder?"

"That was a biggie. No, I wasn't on it, but as I remember it was pretty open and shut. Our Leader made his name on that one."

Kerry knew that Palumbo was not enamored of Frank Green. "Weren't there several appeals?" she asked.

"Oh, yeah. They kept coming up with new theories. It seemed like it went on forever," Palumbo replied.

"I think the last appeal was turned down just a couple of years ago," Kerry said, "but something has come up that has me curious about that case. Anyhow, the point is, I want you to go to the files at *The Record* and dig out everything they printed on the case."

She could picture Joe good-naturedly rolling his eyes.

"For you, Kerry, sure. Anything. But why? That case is long gone."

"Ask me later."

Kerry's lunch was a sandwich and coffee at her desk. At one-thirty Palumbo came in, carrying a bulging envelope. "As requested."

Kerry looked at him affectionately. Short, graying, twenty pounds overweight and with a ready smile, Joe had a disarmingly benevolent appearance that did not reflect his ability to instinctively home in on seemingly unimportant details. She had worked with him on some of her most important cases. "I owe you one," she said.

"Forget it, but I do admit I'm curious. What's your interest in the Reardon case, Kerry?"

She hesitated. Somehow at this point it didn't seem right to talk about what Dr. Smith was doing.

Palumbo saw her reluctance to answer. "Never mind. You'll tell me when you can. See you later."

Kerry was planning to take the file home and begin to read it after dinner. But she could not resist pulling out the top clipping. I'm right, she thought. It was only a couple of years ago.

It was a small item from page 32 of *The Record,* noting that Skip Reardon's fifth appeal for a new trial had been turned down by the New Jersey Supreme Court, and that his attorney, Geoffrey Dorso, had vowed to find grounds for another appeal.

Dorso's quote was, "I'll keep trying until Skip Reardon walks out of that prison exonerated. He's an innocent man."

Of course, she thought, all lawyers say that.

13

For the second night in a row, Bob Kinellen dined with his client Jimmy Weeks. It had not been a good day in court.

Jury selection still dragged along. They had used eight of their peremptory challenges. But careful as they were being in choosing this jury, it was obvious that the federal prosecutor had a strong case. It was almost certain that Haskell was going to cop a plea.

Both men were somber over dinner.

"Even if Haskell does plead, I think I can destroy him on the stand," Kinellen assured Jimmy.

"You *think* you can destroy him. That's not good enough."

"We'll see how it goes."

Weeks smiled mirthlessly. "I'm beginning to worry about you, Bob. It's about time you got yourself a backup plan."

Bob Kinellen decided to let the remark pass. He opened the menu. "I'm meeting Alice at Arnott's later. Were you planning to go?"

"Hell, no. I don't need any more of his introductions. You should know that. They've done me enough harm already."

14

Kerry and Robin sat in companionable silence in the family room. Because of the chilly evening, they had decided to have the first fire of the season, which in their case meant turning on the gas jet and then pressing the button that sent flames shooting through the artificial logs.

As Kerry explained to visitors, "I'm allergic to smoke. This fire looks real and gives off heat. In fact, it looks so real that my cleaning woman vacuumed up the fake ashes, and I had to go out and buy more."

Robin laid out her change-of-season pictures on the coffee table. "What a terrific night," she said with satisfaction, "cold and windy. I should get the rest of the pictures soon. Bare trees, lots of leaves on the ground."

Kerry was seated in her favorite roomy armchair, her feet on a hassock. She looked up. "Don't remind me of the leaves. I get tired."

"Why don't you get a leaf blower?"

"I'll give you one for Christmas."

"Funny. What are you reading, Mom?"

"Come here, Rob." Kerry held up a newspaper clipping with a picture of Suzanne Reardon. "Do you recognize that lady?"

"She was in Dr. Smith's office yesterday."

"You've got a good eye, but it's not the same person." Kerry had just begun reading the account of Suzanne Reardon's murder. Her body had been discovered at midnight by her husband, Skip Reardon, a successful contractor and self-made millionaire. He had found her lying on the floor in the foyer of their luxurious home in Alpine. She had been strangled. Sweetheart roses were scattered over her body.

I must have read about that back then, Kerry thought. It certainly must have made an impression on me, to bring on those dreams.

It was twenty minutes later when she read the clipping that made her gasp. Skip Reardon had been charged with the murder after his father-in-law, *Dr. Charles Smith,* had told the police that his daughter lived in fear of her husband's insane attacks of jealousy.

Dr. Smith was Suzanne Reardon's father! My God, Kerry thought. Is that why he's giving her face to other women? How bizarre. How many of them has he done that to? Is that why he made that speech to me and Robin about preserving beauty?

"What's the matter, Mom? You look funny," Robin said.

"Nothing. Just interested in a case." Kerry looked at the clock on the mantel. "Nine o'clock, Rob. You'd better pack it in. I'll come up in a minute to say good night."

As Robin gathered her pictures, Kerry let the papers she was holding fall into her lap. She had heard of cases in which parents could not recover from the death of a child, where they had left the child's room unchanged, the clothes still in the closet, just as the child had left them. But to "re-create" her and do it over and over? That went beyond grief, surely.

Slowly she stood up and followed Robin upstairs. After she kissed her daughter good night, she went into her own room, changed into pajamas and a robe, then went back downstairs, made a cup of cocoa and continued to read.

The case against Skip Reardon did seem open and shut. He admitted that he and Suzanne had quarreled at breakfast the morning of her death. In fact, he admitted that in the preceding days they had fought almost continually. He admitted that he had come home at six o'clock that evening and found her arranging roses in a vase. When he asked her where they came from, she had told him it was none of his business who sent them. He said he had then told her that whoever sent them was welcome to her, that he was getting out. Then he claimed he had gone back to his office, had a couple of drinks, fallen asleep on the couch and returned home at midnight, to find her body.

There had been no one, however, to corroborate what he said. The file contained part of the trial transcript, including Skip's testimony. The prosecutor had hammered at him until he became confused and seemed to be contradicting himself. He had not made a very convincing witness, to say the least.

What a terrible job his lawyer had done in preparing him to testify, Kerry thought. She didn't doubt that, with the prosecutor's strong circumstantial case, it was imperative that Reardon take the stand to deny that he had killed Suzanne. But it was obvious that Frank Green's scathing cross-examination had completely unnerved him. There's no question, she thought, Reardon had helped to dig his own grave.

The sentencing had taken place six weeks after the trial ended. Kerry had actually gone in to witness it. Now she thought back to that day. She remembered Reardon as a big, handsome redhead who looked uncomfortable in his pin-striped suit. When the judge asked him if he wanted to say anything before sentence was passed, he had once again protested his innocence.

Geoff Dorso had been with Reardon that day, serving as assistant counsel to Reardon's defense lawyer. Kerry knew him slightly. In the ten years since then, Geoff had built a solid reputation as a criminal defense lawyer, although she didn't know him firsthand. She had never argued against him in court.

She came to the newspaper clipping about the sentencing. It included a direct quote from Skip Reardon: "I am innocent of the death of my wife. I never hurt her. I never threatened her. Her father, Dr. Charles Smith, is a liar. Before God and this court, I *swear* he is a liar."

Despite the warmth from the fire, she shivered.

15

Everyone knew, or thought they knew, that Jason Arnott had family money. He had lived in Alpine for fifteen years, ever since he had bought the old Halliday house, a twenty-room mansion on a crest of land that afforded a splendid view of Palisades Interstate Park.

Jason was in his early fifties, of average height, with scant brown hair, weathered eyes and a trim figure. He traveled extensively, talked vaguely of investments in the Orient and loved beautiful things. His home, with its exquisite Persian carpets, antique furniture, fine paintings and delicate objets d'art, was a feast for the eyes. A superb host, Jason entertained lavishly and was, in return, besieged with invitations from the great, the near great and the merely rich.

Erudite and witty, Jason claimed a vague relationship with the Astors of England, although most assumed this affectation was a figment of his imagination. They knew he was colorful and a little mysterious and totally engaging.

What they didn't know was that Jason was a thief. What no one ever seemed to piece together was that after a decent interval, virtually all of the homes he visited were burglarized by someone with a seemingly infallible method of bypassing security systems. Jason's only requirement was that he be able to carry away the spoils of his escapades. Art, sculpture, jewelry and tapestries were his favorites. Only a few times in his long career had he looted the entire contents of an estate. Those episodes had involved an elaborate system of disguises and importing renegade moving men to load the van that was now in the garage of his secret dwelling in a remote area in the Catskills.

There he had yet another identity, known to his widely scattered neighbors as a recluse who had no interest in socializing. No one other than the cleaning woman and an occasional repairman was ever invited inside the doors of his country retreat, and neither cleaning woman nor repairmen had an inkling of the value of the contents.

If his house in Alpine was exquisite, the one in the Catskills was breathtaking, for it was there that Jason kept the pieces from his looting escapades that he could not bear to part with. Each piece of furniture was a treasure. A Frederic Remington occupied the wall of the dining room, directly over the Sheraton buffet, on which a Peachblow vase glistened.

Everything in Alpine had been bought with money received for stolen property Jason had sold. There was nothing housed there that would ever catch the attention of someone with a photographic memory for a stolen possession. Jason was able to say with ease and confidence, "Yes, that's quite nice, isn't it? I got it at Sotheby's in an auction last year." Or, "I went to Bucks County when the Parker estate was on the block."

The only mistake Jason had ever made came ten years ago when his Friday cleaning woman in Alpine had spilled the contents of her pocketbook. When she retrieved them, she had missed her sheet of paper containing the security pass codes for four homes in Alpine. Jason had jotted them down, replaced the paper before the woman knew it was gone and then, tempted beyond control, had burglarized the four homes: the Ellots, the

Ashtons, the Donnatellis. And the Reardons. Jason still shuddered with the memory of his narrow escape that horrific night.

But that was years ago, and Skip Reardon was securely in prison, his avenues of appeal exhausted. Tonight the party was in full swing. Jason smilingly acknowledged the gushing compliments of Alice Bartlett Kinellen.

"I hope Bob will be able to make it," Jason told her.

"Oh, he'll be along. He knows better than to disappoint me."

Alice was a beautiful Grace Kelly–type blonde. Unfortunately, she had none of that late princess' charm or warmth. Alice Kinellen was cold as ice. Also boring and possessive, Jason thought. How does Kinellen stand her?

"He's having dinner with Jimmy Weeks," Alice confided as she sipped champagne. "He's up to here with that case." She made a slashing gesture across her throat.

"Well, I hope Jimmy comes too," Jason said sincerely. "I like him." But he knew Jimmy wouldn't come. Weeks hadn't been to one of his parties in years. In fact, he had kept a wide berth of Alpine after Suzanne Reardon's murder. Eleven years ago, Jimmy Weeks had met Suzanne at a party in Jason Arnott's house.

16

It was clear that Frank Green was irritated. The smile that he flashed so readily to show off his newly whitened teeth was nowhere in evidence as he looked across his desk at Kerry.

I suppose it's the reaction I expected, she thought. I should have known that, of all people, Frank wouldn't want to hear anyone questioning the case that made him, and especially not now, with talk of his candidacy for governor so prevalent.

After reading the newspaper file on the Sweetheart Murder Case, Kerry had gone to bed trying to decide what she should do regarding Dr. Smith. Should she confront him, ask him point-blank about his daughter, ask him why he was re-creating her in the faces of other women?

The odds were that he would throw her out of the office and deny everything. Skip Reardon had accused the doctor of lying when he gave testimony about his daughter. If he had lied, Smith certainly wouldn't admit it to Kerry now, all these years later. And even if he had lied, the biggest question of them all was, why?

By the time Kerry had finally fallen asleep, she had decided that the best place to start asking questions was with Frank Green, since he had tried the case. Now that she had filled Green in on the reason she was inquiring about the Reardon case, it was obvious that her question, "Do you think there is any possibility Dr. Smith was lying when he testified against Skip Reardon?" was not going to result in a helpful or even friendly response.

"Kerry," Green said, "Skip Reardon killed his wife. He knew she was playing around. The very day he killed her, he had called in his accountant to find out how much a divorce would cost him, and he went bananas when he was told that it would involve big bucks. He was a wealthy man, and Suzanne had given up a lucrative modeling career to become a full-time wife. He would have to pay through the nose. So questioning Dr. Smith's veracity at this point seems a waste of time and taxpayers' money."

"But there's something wrong with Dr. Smith," Kerry said slowly. "Frank, I'm not trying to make trouble, and no one more than I wants to see a murderer behind bars, but I swear to you that Smith is more than a grief-stricken father. He seems almost to be demented. You should have seen his expression when he lectured Robin and me about the necessity to preserve beauty, and how some people are given it freely and others have to attain it."

Green looked at his watch. "Kerry, you just finished a big case. You're about to take on another one. You've got a judgeship pending. It's too bad Robin was treated by Suzanne Reardon's father. If anything, he wasn't an ideal witness on the stand. There wasn't a drop of emotion in him when he talked about his daughter. In fact, he was so cold, so cut-and-dry that I was thankful that the jury even believed his testimony. Do yourself a favor and forget it."

It was clear the meeting was over. As Kerry stood up, she said, "What I am doing is having Dr. Smith's handiwork on Robin checked by another plastic surgeon, one that Jonathan found for me."

When she was back in her office, Kerry asked her secretary to hold the phone calls and sat for a long time gazing into space. She could understand Frank Green's alarm at the thought of her raising questions about his star witness in the Sweetheart Murder Case. Any suggestion that there might have been a miscarriage of justice certainly would result in negative publicity and no doubt would tarnish Frank's image as a potential governor.

Dr. Smith is probably an obsessively grieving father who is able to use his great skill to re-create his daughter, she told herself, and Skip Reardon is probably one of the countless murderers who say, "I didn't do it."

Even so, she knew that she couldn't let it rest at that. On Saturday, when she took Robin to visit the plastic surgeon Jonathan had recommended, she would ask him how many surgeons in his field would even consider giving a number of women the same face.

17

At six-thirty that evening, Geoff Dorso glanced reluctantly at the stack of messages that had come in while he was in court. Then he turned away from them. From his office windows in Newark, he had a magnificent view of the New York City skyline, a sight that after a long day on a trial was still soothing.

Geoff was a city kid. Born in Manhattan and raised there till the age of eleven, at which point the family moved to New Jersey, he felt that he had one foot on either side of the Hudson, and he liked it that way.

Thirty-eight years old, Geoff was tall and lean, with a physique that did not reflect the fact that he had a sweet tooth. His jet black hair and olive skin were evidence of his Italian ancestry. His intensely blue eyes came from his Irish-English grandmother.

Still a bachelor, Geoff looked the part. His selection of ties was hit-and-miss, and his clothes usually had a slightly rumpled look. But the stack of messages was an indication of his excellent reputation as an attorney specializing in criminal defense and of the respect he had earned in the legal community.

As he leafed through them, he pulled out the important ones and discarded the others. Suddenly he raised his eyebrows. There was a request to call Kerry McGrath. She had left two numbers, her office and her home. What's that about? he wondered. He didn't have any cases pending in Bergen County, her area of jurisdiction.

Over the years he had met Kerry at bar association dinners, and he knew she was up for a judgeship, but he didn't really know her. The call intrigued him. It was too late to get her at the office. He decided he would try her now, at home.

"I'll get it," Robin called, as the phone rang.

It's probably for you, anyhow, Kerry thought as she tested the spaghetti. I thought telephonitis didn't set in until the teen years, she mused. Then she heard Robin yelling for her to pick up.

She hurried across the kitchen to the wall phone. An unfamiliar voice said, "Kerry."

"Yes."

"Geoff Dorso here."

It had been an impulse to leave the message for him. Afterwards, Kerry was uneasy about having done it. If Frank Green heard that she was contacting Skip Reardon's attorney, she knew he would not be so gentle as he had been earlier. But the die was cast.

"Geoff, this is probably not relevant, but . . ." Her voice trailed off. Spit it out, she told herself. "Geoff, my daughter had an accident recently and was treated by Dr. Charles Smith—"

"Charles Smith," Dorso interrupted, "Suzanne Reardon's father!"

"Yes. That's the point. There is something bizarre going on with him." Now it was easier to open up. She told him about the two women who resembled Suzanne.

"You mean Smith is actually giving them his daughter's face?" Dorso exclaimed. "What the hell is that about?"

"That's what troubles me. I'm taking Robin to another plastic surgeon on Saturday. I intend to ask him about the surgical implications of reproducing a face. I'm also going to try to talk to Dr. Smith, but it occurred to me that if I could read the entire trial transcript beforehand, I'd have a better handle on him. I know I can get one through the office, it's in the warehouse somewhere, but that could take time and I don't want it getting around that I'm looking for it."

"I'll have a copy in your hands tomorrow," Dorso promised. "I'll send it to your office."

"No, better send it to me here. I'll give you the address."

"I'd like to bring it up myself and talk to you. Would tomorrow night about six or six-thirty be all right? I won't stay more than half an hour, I promise."

"I guess that would be okay."

"See you then. And thanks, Kerry." The phone clicked.

Kerry looked at the receiver. What have I gotten myself into? she wondered. She hadn't missed the excitement in Dorso's voice. I shouldn't have used the word "bizarre," she thought. I've started something I may not be able to finish.

A sound from the stove made her whirl around. Boiling water from the spaghetti pot had overflowed and was running down the sides onto the gas jets. Without looking, she knew that the al dente pasta had been transformed into a glutinous mess.

18

Dr. Charles Smith did not have office hours on Wednesday afternoon. It was a time usually reserved for surgical procedures or hospital follow-up visits. Today, however, Dr. Smith had cleared his calendar completely. As he drove down East Sixty-eighth Street, toward the brownstone where the public relations firm Barbara Tompkins worked for was located, his eyes widened at his good luck. There was a parking spot open across from the entrance of her building; he would be able to sit there and watch for her to leave.

When she finally did appear in the doorway, he smiled involuntarily. She looked lovely, he decided. As he had suggested, she wore her hair full and loose around her face; the best style, he had told her, to frame her new features. She was wearing a fitted red jacket, black calf-length skirt and granny shoes. From a distance she looked smart and successful. He knew every detail of how she looked up close.

As she hailed a cab, he turned on the ignition of his twelve-year-old black Mercedes and began to follow. Even though Park Avenue was bumper-to-bumper as was usual in the rush hour, keeping up with the taxi was not a problem.

They drove south, the cab finally stopping at The Four Seasons on East Fifty-second. Barbara must be meeting someone for a drink there, he thought. The bar would be crowded now. It wouldn't be difficult for him to slip in undetected.

Shaking his head, he decided to drive home instead. The glimpse of her had been enough. Almost too much, actually. For a moment he had really believed that she was Suzanne. Now he just wanted to be alone. A sob rose in his throat. As the traffic inched slowly downtown, he repeated over and over, "I'm sorry, Suzanne. I'm sorry, Suzanne."

19

If Jonathan Hoover happened to be in Hackensack, he usually tried to persuade Kerry to join him for a quick lunch. "How many bowls of cafeteria soup can any human being eat?" was his kidding question to her.

Today, over a hamburger at Solari's, the restaurant around the corner from the courthouse, Kerry filled him in on the Suzanne Reardon look-alikes and her conversation with Geoff Dorso. She also told him of her boss's less than favorable reaction to her suggestion that she might look into the old murder case.

Jonathan was deeply concerned. "Kerry, I don't remember much about that case except that I thought there wasn't any question of the husband's guilt. Whatever, I think you should stay out of it, especially considering Frank Green's involvement —very public as I remember—in securing the conviction. Look at the realities here. Governor Marshall is still a young man. He's served two terms and can't run for a consecutive third, but he loves his job. He wants Frank Green to take his place. Between us, they've got a deal. Green is to be governor for four years, then he gets to run for the senate with Marshall's support."

"And Marshall moves back into Drumthwacket."

"Exactly. He loves living in the governor's mansion. As of now it's a foregone conclusion that Green will get the nomination. He looks good, he sounds good. He's got a great track record, the Reardon case being an important part of it. And by a remarkable coincidence, he's actually smart. He intends to stick to the way Marshall's been running the state. But if anything upsets the apple cart, he's beatable in the primary. There are a couple of other would-be candidates panting for the nomination."

"Jonathan, I was talking about simply looking into things enough to see if the chief witness in a murder case had a serious problem that might have tainted his testimony. I mean, fathers grieve when their daughters die, but Dr. Smith has gone far beyond grief."

"Kerry, Frank Green made his name by prosecuting that case. It's what got him the media attention he needed. When Dukakis ran for president, a big factor in his defeat was the commercial that suggested he released a killer who then went on a crime spree. Do you know what the media would do if it were suggested that Green sent an innocent man to prison for the rest of his life?"

"Jonathan, you're getting way ahead of me. I'm not going in with that supposition. I just feel that Smith has a big problem, and it may have affected his testimony. He was the prosecution's main witness, and if he lied, it really casts doubt in my mind as to whether Reardon is guilty."

The waiter was standing over them, holding a coffeepot. "More coffee, Senator?" he asked.

Jonathan nodded. Kerry waved her hand over her cup. "I'm fine."

Jonathan suddenly smiled. "Kerry, do you remember when you were house-sitting for us and thought the landscaper hadn't put as many shrubs and bushes in as he had in the design?"

Kerry looked uncomfortable. "I remember."

"That last day you went around, counted all of them, thought you'd proven your point, dressed him down in front of his crew. Right?"

Kerry looked down at her coffee. "Uh-huh."

"You tell me what happened."

"He wasn't satisfied with the way some of the bushes looked, called you and Grace in Florida, then took them out, intending to replace them."

"What else?"

"He was Grace's cousin's husband."

"See what I mean?" His eyes had a twinkle. Then his expression became serious. "Kerry, if you embarrass Frank Green and put his nomination in jeopardy, chances are you can kiss your judgeship good-bye. Your name will be buried in a pile on Governor Marshall's desk, and I'll be quietly asked to submit another candidate for the vacancy." He paused, then took Kerry's hand. "Give this lots of thought before you do anything. I know you'll make the right decision."

20

Promptly at six-thirty that evening the chiming of the doorbell sent Robin racing to greet Geoff Dorso. Kerry had told her he was coming and that they would be going over a case for half an hour or so. Robin had decided to eat early and promised to finish her homework in her room while Kerry was busy. In exchange she was getting an unaccustomed weeknight hour of television.

She inspected Dorso with benevolence and ushered him into the family room. "My mother will be right down," she announced. "I'm Robin."

"I'm Geoff Dorso. How does the other guy look?" Geoff asked. With a smile he indicated the still-vivid marks on her face.

Robin grinned. "I flattened him. Actually it was a fender bender with some flying glass."

"It looks as though it's healing fine."

"Dr. Smith, the plastic surgeon, says it is. Mom says you know him. I think he's creepy."

"Robin!" Kerry had just come downstairs.

"From the mouths of babes," Dorso said, smiling. "Kerry, it's good to see you."

"It's good to see you, Geoff." I hope I mean it, Kerry thought as her gaze fell on the bulging briefcase under Dorso's arm. "Robin . . ."

"I know. Homework," Robin agreed cheerfully. "I'm not the neatest person in the world," she explained to Dorso. "My last report card had 'improvement needed' checked above 'home assignments.' "

"Also, 'uses time well' had a check above it," Kerry reminded her.

"That's because when I finish an assignment in school, I forget sometimes and start to talk to one of my friends. Okay." With a wave of her hand, Robin headed for the staircase.

Geoff Dorso smiled after her. "Nice kid, Kerry, and she's a knockout. In another five or six years you'll have to barricade the door."

"A scary prospect. Geoff, coffee, a drink, a glass of wine?"

"No, thanks. I promised not to take too much of your time." He laid his briefcase on the coffee table. "Do you want to go over this in here?"

"Sure." She sat next to him on the couch as he took out two

thick volumes of bound paper. "The trial transcript," he said, "one thousand pages of it. If you really want to understand what went on, I would suggest you read it carefully. Frankly, from start to finish, I'm ashamed of the defense we mounted. I know Skip had to take the stand, but he wasn't properly prepared. The state's witnesses weren't vigorously questioned. And we only called two character witnesses for Skip when we should have called twenty."

"Why was it handled that way?" Kerry asked.

"I was the most junior counsel, having just been hired by Farrell and Strauss. Farrell had been a good defense lawyer once upon a time, no doubt about that. But when Skip Reardon hired him, he was well past his prime and pretty much burned out. He just wasn't interested in another murder case. I really think Skip would have been better off with a much less experienced attorney who had some fire in his gut."

"Couldn't you have filled the gap?"

"No, not really. I was just out of law school and didn't have much to say about anything. I had very little participation in the trial at all. I was basically a gofer for Farrell. As inexperienced as I was, though, it was obvious to me that the trial was handled badly."

"And Frank Green tore him apart on cross-examination."

"As you read, he got Skip to admit that he and Suzanne had quarreled that morning, that he'd spoken to his accountant to find out what a divorce would cost, that he'd gone back to the house at six and again quarreled with Suzanne. The coroner estimated time of death to be between six and eight o'clock, so Skip could, by his own testimony, be placed at the scene of the crime at the possible time of the murder."

"From the account I read, Skip Reardon claimed he went back to his office, had a couple of drinks and fell asleep. That's pretty thin," Kerry commented.

"It's thin but it's true. Skip had established a very successful business, mostly building quality homes, although recently he had expanded into shopping malls. Most of his time was spent in the office, taking care of the business end, but he loved to put on work clothes and spend the day with a crew. That's what he'd done that day, before coming back to work at the office. The guy was tired."

He opened the first volume. "I've flagged Smith's testimony as well as Skip's. The crux of the matter is that we are certain that there was someone else involved, and we have reason to believe it was another man. In fact, Skip was convinced that Suzanne was involved with another man, perhaps even with more than one. What precipitated the second quarrel, the one that occurred when he went home at six o'clock, was that he found her arranging a bunch of red roses—sweetheart roses, I think the press called them—that he had not sent her. The prosecution maintained that he went into a rage, strangled her, then threw the roses over her body. He, of course, swears that he didn't, that when he left, Suzanne was still blithely puttering with the flowers."

"Did anyone check the local florists to see if an order for the roses had been placed with one of them? If Skip didn't carry them home, somebody delivered them."

"Farrell did at least do that. There wasn't a florist in Bergen County who wasn't checked. Nothing turned up."

"I see."

Geoff stood up. "Kerry, I know it's a lot to ask, but I want you to read this transcript carefully. I want you to pay particular attention to Dr. Smith's testimony. Then I'd like you to consider letting me be with you when you talk to Dr. Smith about his practice of giving other women his daughter's face."

She walked with Geoff to the door. "I'll call you in the next few days," she promised.

At the door, he paused, then turned back to Kerry. "There's one more thing I wish you'd do. Come down with me to Trenton State Prison. Talk to Skip yourself. On my grandmother's grave,

I swear you'll hear the ring of truth when that poor guy tells you his story."

21

In Trenton State Prison, Skip Reardon lay on the bunk of his cell, watching the six-thirty news. Dinnertime had come and gone with its dreary menu. As had become more and more the case, he was restless and irritable. After ten years in this place, he had managed for the most part to set himself on a middle course. In the beginning he had fluctuated between wild hope when an appeal was pending and crashing despair when it was rejected.

Now his usual state of mind was weary resignation. He knew that Geoff Dorso would never stop trying to find new grounds for an appeal, but the climate of the country was changing. On the news there were more and more reports criticizing the fact that repeated appeals from convicted criminals were tying up the courts, reports that inevitably concluded that there had to be a cutoff. If Geoff could not find grounds for an appeal, one that would actually win Skip his freedom, then that meant another twenty years in this place.

In his most despondent moments, Skip allowed himself to think back over the years before the murder, and to realize just how crazy he had been. He and Beth had practically been engaged. And then at Beth's urging he had gone alone to a party her sister and her surgeon husband were giving. At the last minute, Beth had come down with a bug, but she hadn't wanted him to miss out on the fun.

Yeah, *fun*, Skip thought ironically, remembering that night. Suzanne and her father had been there. Even now he could not forget how she looked the first time he saw her. He knew immediately she meant trouble, but like a fool he fell for her anyway.

Impatiently, Skip got up from the bunk, switched off the television and looked at the trial transcript on the shelf over the toilet. He felt as though he could recite it by heart. That's where it belongs, over the toilet, he thought bitterly. For all the good it's ever going to do me, I should tear it up and flush it.

He stretched. He used to keep his body in shape through a combination of hard work on the job site and a regular gym regimen. Now he rigidly performed a series of push-ups and sit-ups every night. The small plastic mirror attached to the wall showed his red hair streaked with gray, his face, once ruddy from outdoor work, now a pasty prison pallor.

The daydream he allowed himself was that by some miracle he was free to go back to building houses. The oppressive confinement and constant noise in this place had given him visions of middle-class homes that would be sufficiently insulated to insure privacy, that would be filled with windows to let in the outdoors. He had loose-leaf books filled with designs.

Whenever Beth came to see him, something he had tried to discourage of late, he would show the latest ones to her, and they would talk about them as though he really would one day be able to go back to the job he had loved, building homes.

Only now he had to wonder, what would the world be like, and what would people be living in when he finally got out of this terrible place?

22

Kerry could tell it was going to be another late night. She had started reading the transcript immediately after Geoff left and resumed after Robin went to bed.

At nine-thirty, Grace Hoover phoned. "Jonathan's out at a meeting. I'm propped up in bed and felt like chatting. Is this a good time for you?"

"It's always a good time when it's you, Grace." Kerry meant it. In the fifteen years she had known Grace and Jonathan, she had watched Grace's physical decline. She had gone from using a cane to crutches, finally to a wheelchair, and from being ardently involved in social activities to being almost totally housebound. She did keep up with friends and entertained with frequent ca-tered dinner parties, but as she told Kerry, "It's just gotten to be too much effort to go out."

Kerry had never heard Grace complain. "You do what you have to," she had said wryly when Kerry candidly told her how much she admired her courage.

But after a couple of minutes of familiar chatter, it became apparent that tonight there was a purpose to Grace's call. "Kerry, you had lunch with Jonathan today, and I'm going to be honest. He's worried."

Kerry listened as Grace reiterated Jonathan's concerns, con-cluding with, "Kerry, after twenty years in the state senate, Jonathan has a lot of power, but not enough to make the governor appoint you to a judgeship if you embarrass his chosen successor. Incidentally," she added, "Jonathan has no idea I'm calling you."

He must have really vented to Grace, Kerry thought. I wonder what she would think if she could see what I'm doing now. Feeling evasive the entire time, Kerry did her best to assure Grace that she had no intention or desire to ruffle feathers. "But Grace, if it developed that Dr. Smith's testimony was false, I think that Frank Green would be admired and respected if he recommended to the court that Reardon be given a new trial. I don't think that the public would hold it against him that he had in good faith relied on the doctor's testimony. He had no reason to doubt him.

"And don't forget," she added, "I'm far from being convinced that justice was denied in the Reardon case. It's just that by coincidence I've stumbled on this one thing, and I can't live with myself if I don't follow through on it."

When the conversation ended, Kerry returned to the transcript. By the time she finally laid it down, she had filled pages with notes and questions.

The sweetheart roses: Was Skip Reardon lying when he said he didn't bring or send them? If he was telling the truth, if he didn't send them, then who *did?*

Dolly Bowles, the baby-sitter who had been on duty in the house across the street from the Reardon home the night of the murder: She claimed she saw a car in front of the Reardons' house at nine o'clock that night. But neighbors were having a party at the time, and a number of their guests had parked in the street. Dolly had made a particularly poor witness in court. Frank Green had brought out the fact that she had reported "suspicious-looking" people in the neighborhood on six separate occasions that year. In each instance, the suspect turned out to be a legitimate deliveryman. The result was that Dolly came through as a totally unreliable witness. Kerry was sure the jury had disregarded her testimony.

Skip Reardon had never been in trouble with the law and was

considered a very solid citizen, yet only two character witnesses had been called: Why?

There had been a series of burglaries in Alpine around the time of Suzanne Reardon's death. Skip Reardon claimed that some of the jewelry he had seen Suzanne wearing was missing, that the master bedroom had been ransacked. But a tray full of valuable jewelry was found on the dresser, and the prosecution called in a part-time housekeeper the Reardons had employed who flatly testified that Suzanne always left the bedroom in a chaotic state. "She'd try on three or four outfits, then drop them on the floor if she decided against them. Powder spilled on the dressing table, wet towels on the floor. I often felt like quitting."

As she undressed for bed that night, Kerry mentally reviewed what she had read, and noted that there were two things she had to do: make an appointment to talk with Dr. Smith, and visit Skip Reardon at the State Prison in Trenton.

23

In the nine years since the divorce, Kerry had dated on and off, but there had never been anyone special. Her closest friend was Margaret Mann, her roommate at Boston College. Marg was blond and petite, and in college she and Kerry had been dubbed the long and the short of it. Now an investment banker with an apartment on West Eighty-sixth Street, Margaret was confidante, pal and buddy. On occasional Friday evenings, Kerry would have a sitter in for Robin and drive to Manhattan. She and Margaret would have dinner and catch a Broadway show or a movie or just linger over dessert for hours and talk.

The Friday night after Geoff Dorso left the transcript, Kerry arrived at Margaret's apartment and gratefully sank onto the couch in front of a platter of cheese and grapes.

Margaret handed her a glass of wine. "Bottoms up. You look great."

Kerry was wearing a new hunter green suit with a long jacket and calf-length skirt. She looked down at it and shrugged.

"Thanks. I finally got a chance to buy some new clothes and I've been sporting them all week."

Margaret laughed. "Remember how your mother used to put on her lipstick and say, 'You never know where romance may linger'? She was right, wasn't she?"

"I guess so. She and Sam have been married fifteen years now, and whenever they come East or Robin and I visit them in Colorado, they're holding hands."

Margaret grinned. "We should be so lucky." Then her expression became serious. "How's Robin? Her face is healing well, I hope."

"Seems to be fine. I'm taking her to see another plastic surgeon tomorrow. Just for a consultation."

Margaret hesitated, then said, "I was trying to find a way to suggest that. At the office I was talking about the accident and mentioned Dr. Smith's name. One of the traders, Stuart Grant, picked up on it right away. He said his wife consulted Smith. She wanted to do something about the bags under her eyes, but she never went back after the first visit. She thought there was something wrong with him."

Kerry straightened up. "What did she mean?"

"Her name is Susan, but the doctor kept slipping and calling her Suzanne. Then he told her he could do her eyes, but he'd rather do her whole face, that she had the makings of a great beauty and was wasting her life not taking advantage of it."

"How long ago was that?"

"Three or four years, I guess. Oh, and something else. Smith apparently also rambled on to Susan about how beauty brings responsibility, and that some people abuse it and invite jealousy and violence." She stopped, then asked, "Kerry, what's the matter? You have a funny look on your face."

"Marg, this is important. Are you sure that Smith talked about women inviting jealousy and violence?"

"I'm sure that's what Stuart told me."

"Do you have Stuart's phone number? I want to talk to his wife."

"In the office. They live in Greenwich, but I happen to know that the number's unlisted, so it will have to wait till Monday. What's this about, anyhow?"

"I'll tell you about it over dinner," she said distractedly. It seemed to Kerry that the trial transcript was on a Rolodex in her mind. Dr. Smith swore that his daughter was in fear for her life because of Skip Reardon's *unfounded* jealousy. Had he been lying? Had Suzanne given Skip reason to be jealous? And if so, of whom?

24

A t eight o'clock Saturday morning, Kerry received a phone call from Geoff Dorso. "I beeped in to the office and got your message," he told her. "I'm going to Trenton to see Skip this afternoon. Can you make it?" He explained that in order to register for the three o'clock visit, they would have to be at the prison by 1:45.

Almost as a reflex, Kerry heard herself say, "I'm sure I can make it. I'll have to make arrangements for Robin, but I'll meet you there."

Two hours later, Kerry and an impatient Robin were in Livingston, New Jersey, in the office of Dr. Ben Roth, a noted plastic surgeon.

"I'm going to miss the soccer game," Robin fretted.

"You'll be a little late, that's all," Kerry soothed. "Don't worry."

"Very late," Robin protested. "Why couldn't he see me this afternoon after the game?"

"Perhaps if you'd sent the doctor your schedule, he could have worked around it," Kerry teased.

"Oh, Mom."

"You can bring Robin in now, Ms. McGrath," the receptionist announced.

Dr. Roth, in his mid-thirties, warm and affable, was a welcome change from Dr. Smith. He examined Robin's face carefully. "The lacerations probably looked pretty bad right after the accident, but they were what we call superficial. They didn't deeply penetrate the dermis. You haven't got any problems."

Robin looked relieved. "Great. Thanks, Doctor. Let's go, Mom."

"Wait in the reception area, Robin. I'll be out in just a moment. I want to talk to the doctor." Kerry's voice carried what Robin called "the tone." It meant "and I don't want to hear any arguments."

"Okay," Robin said with an exaggerated sigh as she departed.

"I know you have patients waiting, so I won't be long, Doctor, but there is something I must ask you," Kerry said.

"I have time. What is it, Ms. McGrath?"

Kerry reduced to a few brief sentences a description of what she had seen in Dr. Smith's office. "So I guess I have two questions," she concluded. "Can you remake just any face to look like someone else, or does some fundamental factor, like a similar bone structure, have to be present? And knowing that it is possible to remake some faces so that they look alike, is this something that plastic surgeons do, I mean deliberately remake someone to look like someone else?"

It was twenty minutes later when Kerry rejoined Robin and they rushed to the soccer field. Unlike Kerry, Robin was not a natural athlete, and Kerry had spent long hours working with her, because her heart was set on being a good player. Now, as she watched Robin confidently kick the ball past the goalie, Kerry was still reflecting on Dr. Roth's flat statement: "It's a fact that some surgeons give everyone the same nose or chin or eyes, but I find it extremely unusual that any surgeon would in essence clone the faces of his patients."

At eleven-thirty she caught Robin's eye and waved good-bye. Robin would go home from the game with her best friend, Cassie, and would spend the afternoon at her house.

A few minutes later, Kerry was on the road to Trenton.

She had visited the state prison several times and always found the grim aspect of barbed wire and guard towers a sobering sight. This was not a place she looked forward to seeing again.

25

Kerry found Geoff waiting for her in the area where visitors were registered. "I'm really glad you made it," he said. They talked little while they waited for their scheduled meeting. Geoff seemed to understand that she did not want his input at this time.

Promptly at three o'clock a guard approached them and told them to follow him.

Kerry did not know what she expected Skip Reardon to look like now. It had been ten years since she had sat in at his sentencing. The impression she had retained of him was of a tall, good-looking, broad-shouldered young man with fiery red hair. But more than his appearance, it was his statement that had been burned into her mind: *Dr. Charles Smith is a liar. Before God and this court, I swear he is a liar!*

"What have you told Skip Reardon about me?" she asked Geoff as they waited for the prisoner to be escorted into the visiting area.

"Only that you've unofficially taken some interest in his case and wanted to meet him. I promise you, Kerry, I said 'unofficially.' "

"That's fine. I trust you."

"Here he is now."

Skip Reardon appeared, dressed in prison denims and an open-necked prison-issue shirt. There were streaks of gray through the red hair, but except for the lines around his eyes he still looked very much as Kerry recalled him. A smile brightened his face as Geoff introduced him.

A hopeful smile, Kerry realized, and with a sinking heart wondered if she shouldn't have been more cautious, perhaps waiting until she knew more about the case, instead of agreeing so readily to this visit.

Geoff got right to the point. "Skip, as I told you, Ms. McGrath wants to ask you some questions."

"I understand. And, listen, I'll answer them no matter what they are." He spoke earnestly, although with a hint of resignation. "You've heard that old saying, I have nothing to hide."

Kerry smiled, then went straight to the question that was to her the crux of this meeting. "In his testimony, Dr. Smith swore that his daughter, your wife, was afraid of you and that you had threatened her. You have maintained that he was lying, but what purpose would he have in lying about that?"

Reardon's hands were folded on the table in front of him. "Ms. McGrath, if I had any explanation for Dr. Smith's actions, maybe I wouldn't be here now. Suzanne and I were married four years, and during that time I never saw that much of Smith. She'd go into New York and have dinner with him occasionally, or he'd come out to the house, but usually when I was away on a business trip. At that time my construction business was booming. I was building all over the state and investing in land in

Pennsylvania for future development. I'd be gone a couple of days at a time on a fairly regular basis. Whenever I was with Dr. Smith, he seemed not to have much to say, but he never acted as though he didn't like me. And he certainly didn't act as though he thought his daughter's life was in danger."

"When you were with both him and Suzanne, what did you notice about his attitude toward her?"

Reardon looked at Dorso. "You're the guy with the fancy words, Geoff. What's a good way to put it? Wait a minute. I can tell you. When I was in parochial school, the nuns got mad at us for talking in church and told us we should have reverence for a holy place and holy objects. Well that's the way he treated her. Smith showed 'reverence' for Suzanne."

What an odd word to use about a father's attitude toward his daughter, Kerry thought.

"And he was also protective of her," Reardon added. "One night the three of us were driving somewhere for dinner and he noticed that Suzanne hadn't put on her seat belt. So he launched into a lecture about her responsibility to take care of herself. He actually got fairly agitated about it, maybe even a little angry."

It sounds like the same way he lectured Robin and me, Kerry thought. Almost reluctantly she admitted to herself that Skip Reardon certainly gave the appearance of being candid and honest.

"How did she act toward him?"

"Respectful, mostly. Although toward the end—before she was killed—the last few times I was with them, she seemed to be kind of irritated at him."

Kerry then ventured into other aspects of the case, asking him about his sworn testimony that just prior to the murder, he had noticed Suzanne wearing expensive pieces of jewelry that he had not given her.

"Ms. McGrath, I wish you'd talk to my mother. She could tell you. She has a picture of Suzanne that was run in one of the community papers, taken at a charity affair. It shows her with an old-fashioned diamond pin on the lapel of her suit. The picture was taken only a couple of weeks before she was murdered. I swear to you that that pin and a couple of other pieces of expensive jewelry, none of which I gave her, were in her jewelry box that morning. I remember it specifically because it was one of the things we argued about. Those pieces were there that morning and they weren't there the next day."

"You mean someone took them?"

Reardon seemed uncomfortable. "I don't know if someone took them or if she gave them back to someone, but I tell you there was jewelry missing the next morning. I tried to tell all this to the cops, to get them to look into it, but it was obvious from the beginning that they didn't believe me. They thought that I was trying to make it look like she had been robbed and killed by an intruder.

"Something else," he continued. "My dad was in World War II and was in Germany for two years after the war. He brought back a miniature picture frame that he gave to my mother when they became engaged. My mother gave that frame to Suzanne and me when we were married. Suzanne put my favorite picture of her in it and kept it on the night table in our room. When my mother and I sorted Suzanne's things out before I was arrested, Mom noticed it was missing. But I know it was there that last morning."

"Are you trying to say that the night Suzanne died, someone came in and stole some jewelry and a picture frame?" Kerry asked.

"I'm telling you what I know was missing. I don't know where it went, and of course I'm not sure it had anything to do with Suzanne's murder. I just know that suddenly those things weren't there and that the police wouldn't look into it."

Kerry looked up from her notes and peered directly into the eyes of the man facing her.

"Skip, what was your relationship with your wife?"

Reardon sighed. "When I met her, I fell like a ton of bricks. She was gorgeous. She was smart. She was funny. She was the kind of woman who makes a guy feel ten feet tall. After we were married . . ." He paused. "It was all heat and no warmth, Ms. McGrath. I was raised to think you're supposed to make a go of marriage, that divorce was a last resort. And, of course, there were some good times. But was I ever happy or content? No, I wasn't. But then I was so busy building up my company that I just spent more and more time at work and in that way was able to avoid dealing with it.

"As for Suzanne, she seemed to have everything she wanted. The money was rolling in. I built her the house she said she had dreamed of having. She was over at the club every day, playing golf or tennis. She spent two years with a decorator, furnishing the house the way she wanted it. There's a guy who lives in Alpine, Jason Arnott, who really knows antiques. He took Suzanne to auctions and told her what to buy. She developed a taste for designer clothes. She was like a kid who wanted every day to be Christmas. With the way I was working, she had plenty of free time to come and go as she pleased. She loved to be at affairs that got press coverage, so that her picture would be in the paper. For a long time I thought she was happy, but as I look back on it, I'm sure she stayed with me because she hadn't found any better setup."

"Until . . ." Geoff prompted.

"Until someone she met became important," Reardon continued. "That was when I noticed jewelry I hadn't seen before. Some pieces were antiques, others very modern. She claimed her father gave them to her, but I could tell she was lying. Her father has all her jewelry now, including everything I gave her."

When the guard indicated their time was up, Reardon stood and looked squarely at Kerry. "Ms. McGrath, I shouldn't be here. Somewhere out there the guy who killed Suzanne is walking around. And somewhere there has to be something that will prove it."

• • •

Geoff and Kerry walked to the parking lot together. "I bet you didn't have time for any lunch," he said. "Why don't we grab something fast?"

"I can't, I've got to get back. Geoff, I have to tell you that from what I heard today, I can't see a single reason for Dr. Smith to lie about Skip Reardon. Reardon says that they had what amounts to a reasonably cordial relationship. You heard him say that he didn't believe Suzanne when she told him that her father had given her some pieces of jewelry. If he started getting jealous about those pieces, well . . ." She did not finish the sentence.

26

On Sunday morning, Robin served at the ten o'clock mass. When Kerry watched the processional move down the aisle from the vestry, she always was reminded of how, as a child, she had wanted to be a server and was told it wasn't possible, that only boys were allowed.

Things change, she mused. I never thought I'd see my daughter on the altar, I never thought I'd be divorced, I never thought that someday I'd be a judge. *Might be* a judge, she corrected herself. She knew Jonathan was right. Embarrassing Frank Green right now was tantamount to embarrassing the governor. It could be a fatal blow to her appointment. Yesterday's visit to Skip Reardon might have been a serious mistake. Why mess up her life again? She had done it once.

She knew that she had worked her way through the emotional gamut with Bob Kinellen, first loving him, then being heartbroken when he left her, then angry at him and contemptuous of herself that she had not seen him for the opportunist he was. Now her chief reaction to him was indifference, except where

Robin was concerned. Even so, observing couples in church, whether her own age, younger, older—it didn't matter—seeing them always caused a pang of sadness. If only Bob had been the person I believed he was, she thought. If only he were the person *he* thinks he *is*. By now they would have been married eleven years. By now surely she would have had other children. She'd always wanted three.

As she watched Robin carry the ewer of water and the lavabo bowl to the altar in preparation for the consecration, her daughter looked up and met Kerry's gaze. Her brief smile caught at Kerry's heart. What am I complaining about? she asked herself. No matter what happens, I have her. And as unions go, it may have been far from perfect, but at least something good came of it. No one else except Bob Kinellen and I could have had exactly this wonderful child, she reasoned.

As she watched, her mind jumped back to another parent and child, to Dr. Smith and Suzanne. She had been the unique result of his and his former wife's genes. In his testimony, Dr. Smith had stated that after their divorce his wife moved to California and remarried, and he had permitted Suzanne to be adopted by the second husband, thinking that was in her best interests.

"But after her mother died, she came to me," he had said. "She needed me."

Skip Reardon had said that Dr. Smith's attitude toward his daughter bordered on reverence. When she heard that, a question that took Kerry's breath away had raced through her mind. Dr. Smith had transformed other women to look like his daughter. But no one had ever asked whether or not he had ever operated on Suzanne.

Kerry and Robin had just finished lunch when Bob called, suggesting he take Robin out to dinner that night. He explained that Alice had taken the children to Florida for a week, and he was driving to the Catskills to look at a ski lodge they might buy. Would Robin want to accompany him? he asked. "I still owe her dinner, and I promise I'll have her back by nine."

Robin's enthusiastically affirmative response resulted in Bob picking her up an hour later.

The unexpected free afternoon gave Kerry a chance to spend more time going over the Reardon trial transcript. Just reading the testimony gave her a certain amount of insight, but she knew that there was a big difference between reading a cold transcript and watching the witnesses as they testified. She hadn't seen their faces, heard their voices or watched their physical reactions to questions. She knew that the jury's evaluation of the demeanor of the witnesses had undoubtedly played a big part in reaching their verdict. That jury had watched and evaluated Dr. Smith. And it was obvious that they had believed him.

27

Geoff Dorso loved football and was an ardent Giants fan. It was not the reason he had bought a condominium in the Meadowlands, but as he admitted, it certainly was convenient. Nevertheless, on Sunday afternoon, sitting in Giant Stadium, his mind was less on today's very close game with the Dallas Cowboys than on yesterday's visit to Skip Reardon, and Kerry McGrath's reaction to both Skip and the trial transcript.

He had given the transcript to her on Thursday. Had she read it yet? he wondered. He had hoped that she would bring it up while they were waiting to see Skip, but she hadn't mentioned it. He tried to tell himself that it was her training to be skeptical, that her seemingly negative attitude after the visit to Skip didn't have to mean that she was washing her hands of the case.

When the Giants squeaked through with a last-second field goal as the fourth quarter of the game ended, Geoff shared in the lusty cheering but declined the suggestion of his friends that he join them for a couple of beers. Instead he went home and called Kerry.

He was elated when she admitted that she had read the transcript and that she had a number of questions. "I'd like to get together again," he said. Then a thought struck him. She can only say no, he reasoned, as he asked, "By any chance would you be free for dinner tonight?"

Dolly Bowles had been sixty when she moved in with her daughter in Alpine. That had been twelve years ago, when she was first widowed. She had not wanted to impose, but the truth was she had always been nervous about being alone and really didn't think she could go on living in the big house she and her husband had shared.

And, in fact, there was a basis, psychological at least, for her nervousness. Years ago, when she was still a child, she had opened the door for a deliveryman who turned out to be a burglar. She still had nightmares about the way he had tied up both her and her mother and had ransacked the house. As a result, she now tended to be suspicious of any and all strangers, and several times had irritated her son-in-law by pushing the panic button on the alarm system when she had been alone in the house and had heard strange noises or seen a man on the street she didn't recognize.

Her daughter Dorothy and her son-in-law Lou traveled frequently. Their children had still been at home when Dolly moved in with them, and she had been a help in taking care of them. But for the last several years they had been off on their own, and Dolly had had almost nothing to do. She had tried to pitch in around the house, but the live-in housekeeper wanted no part of her help.

Left with so much time on her hands, Dolly had become the neighborhood baby-sitter, a situation that worked out wonderfully. She genuinely enjoyed young children and would happily read to them or play games by the hour. She was beloved by just about everyone. The only time people got annoyed was when she made one of her all-too-frequent calls to the police to report suspicious-looking persons. And she hadn't done that in the last ten years, not since she was a witness at the Reardon murder trial. She shuddered every time she thought of that. The prosecutor had made such a fool of her. Dorothy and Lou had been mortified. "Mother, I begged you not to talk to the police," Dorothy had snapped at the time.

But Dolly had felt she had to. She had known Skip Reardon and liked him and just felt she had to try to help him. Besides, she really had seen that car, as had Michael, the five-year-old little boy with all the learning problems she had been minding that night. He had seen the car too, but Skip's lawyer had told her not to discuss it.

"That would only hurt our case," Mr. Farrell had said. "All we want you to do is to tell what you saw, that a dark sedan was parked in front of the Reardon house at nine and drove away a few minutes later."

She was sure she had made out one of the numbers and one of

the letters, a 3 and an L. But then the prosecutor had held up a
license plate at the back of the courtroom and she hadn't been
able to read it. And he had gotten her to admit that she was very
fond of Skip Reardon because he had dug out her car one night
when she got stuck in a snowdrift.

Dolly knew that just because Skip had been nice to her didn't
mean that he couldn't be a murderer, but in her heart she felt
that he was innocent, and she prayed for him every night. Sometimes, even now, when she was baby-sitting across the street
from the Reardon house, she would look out and think about
the night Suzanne was murdered. And she would think about
little Michael—his family had moved away several years ago—
who would be fifteen now, and how he had pointed to the
strange black car and said, "Poppa's car."

Dolly could not know that at the same time on that Sunday
evening that she sat looking out the window at what used to
be the Reardon house, some ten miles away, at Villa Cesare in
Hillsdale, Geoff Dorso and Kerry McGrath were talking about
her.

By tacit agreement, Kerry and Geoff refrained from any
discussion of the Reardon case until coffee was served.
During the earlier part of the meal, Geoff talked about
spending his youngest years in New York. "I thought of my New

Jersey cousins as living in the sticks," he said. "Then after we moved out ourselves and I grew up here, I decided to stay."

He told Kerry that he had four younger sisters.

"I envy you," she said. "I'm an only child, and I used to love to visit my friends' houses where there was a big family. I always thought it would be nice to have some siblings floating around. My father died when I was nineteen and my mother remarried when I was twenty-one and moved to Colorado. I see her twice a year."

Geoff's eyes softened. "That doesn't give you much family support," he said.

"No, I guess not, but Jonathan and Grace Hoover have helped to fill the gap. They've been wonderful to me, almost like parents."

They talked about law school, agreeing that the first year was a horror they would hate to have to endure again. "What made you decide to be a defense lawyer?" Kerry asked.

"I think it went back to when I was a kid. A woman in our apartment building, Anna Owens, was one of the nicest people I ever knew. I remember when I was about eight and ran through the lobby to catch the elevator, I slammed into her and knocked her over. Anyone else would have had a screaming fit, but she just picked herself up and said, 'Geoff, the elevator will come back, you know.' Then she laughed. She could tell how upset I was."

"That didn't make you become a defense lawyer." Kerry smiled.

"No. But three months later when her husband walked out on her, she followed him to his new girlfriend's apartment and shot him. I honestly believe it was temporary insanity, which was the defense her lawyer tried, but she went to prison for twenty years anyway. I guess the key phrase is 'mitigating circumstances.' When I believe those are present, or when I believe the defendant is innocent, as with Skip Reardon, I take the case." He paused. "And what made you become a prosecutor?"

"The victim and the family of the victim," she said simply. "Based on your theory I could have shot Bob Kinellen and pled mitigating circumstances."

Dorso's eyes flashed with mild irritation, then became amused. "Somehow I don't see you shooting anybody, Kerry."

"I don't either, unless . . ." Kerry hesitated, then continued, "Unless Robin were in danger. Then I'd do whatever it took to save her. I'm sure of that."

Over dinner, Kerry found herself talking about her father's death. "I was in my sophomore year at Boston College. He had been a Pan Am captain and later went into the corporate end and was made an executive vice president. From the time I was three years old, he took my mother and me all over. To me, he was the greatest man in the world." She gulped. "And then one weekend when I was home from college, he said he wasn't feeling right. But he didn't bother going to the doctor because he'd just had his annual physical. He said he'd be fine in the morning. But the next morning, he didn't wake up."

"And your mother remarried two years later?" Geoff asked softly.

"Yes, right before I graduated from college. Sam was a widower and a friend of Dad's. He'd been about to retire to Vail when Dad died. He has a lovely place there. It's been good for both of them."

"What would your father have thought of Bob Kinellen?"

Kerry laughed. "You're very perceptive, Geoff Dorso. I think he would have been underwhelmed."

Over coffee they finally discussed the Reardon case. Kerry began by saying frankly, "I sat in on the sentencing ten years ago, and the look on his face and what he said were imprinted in my memory. I've heard a lot of guilty people swear they were innocent—after all, what have they got to lose?—but there was something about his statement that got to me."

"Because he was telling the truth."

Kerry looked directly at him. "I warn you, Geoff, I intend to play devil's advocate, and while reading that transcript raises a lot of questions for me, it certainly doesn't convince me that Reardon is an innocent man. Neither did yesterday's visit. Either he's lying or Dr. Smith is lying. Skip Reardon has a very good reason to lie. Smith doesn't. I still think it's damaging that the very day Suzanne died, Reardon had discussed divorce and apparently flipped when he learned what it might cost him."

"Kerry, Skip Reardon was a self-made man. He pulled himself out of poverty and had become very successful. Suzanne had already cost him a fortune. You heard him. She was a big-time shopaholic, buying whatever struck her fancy." He paused. "No. Being angry and being vocal about it is one thing. But there's a hell of a difference between blowing off steam and murder. If anything, even though a divorce was going to be expensive, he was actually relieved that his sham marriage was going to be over, so he could get on with his life."

They talked about the sweetheart roses. "I absolutely believe Skip neither brought nor sent them," Geoff said as he sipped espresso. "So if we accept that, we then have the factor of another person."

As Geoff was paying the bill, they both agreed that Dr. Smith's testimony was the linchpin that had convicted Skip Reardon. "Ask yourself this," Geoff urged. "Dr. Smith claimed that Suzanne was afraid of Skip and his jealous rages. But if she were so afraid of him, how could she stand there and calmly arrange flowers another man had sent her, and not only arrange them, but flaunt them, at least according to Skip. Does that make sense?"

"*If* Skip was telling the truth, but we don't know that for an absolute fact, do we?" Kerry said.

"Well, I for one *do* believe him," Geoff said with passion. "Besides, no one testified in corroboration of Dr. Smith's testimony. The Reardons were a popular couple. Surely if he were abusive to her, someone would have come forward to say so."

"Perhaps so," Kerry conceded, "but then why were there no

defense fact witnesses to say that he wasn't insanely jealous? Why were there only two character witnesses called to help counter Dr. Smith's testimony? No, Geoff, I'm afraid that based on the information the jury was given, they had no reason not to trust Dr. Smith and believe him. Besides, aren't we in general conditioned to trust a physician?"

They were quiet on the drive home. As Geoff walked Kerry to her door, he reached for her key. "My mother said you should always open the door for the lady. I hope that's not too sexist."

"No, it isn't. Not for me at least. But maybe I'm just old-fashioned." The sky above them was blue-black and brilliant with stars. A sharp wind was blowing, and Kerry shivered from the chill.

Geoff noticed and quickly turned the key, then pushed open the door. "You're not dressed warmly enough for the night air. You'd better get inside."

As she moved through the entrance, he stayed on the porch, making no move to indicate that he expected her to invite him in. Instead he said, "Before I leave, I have to ask, where do we go from here?"

"I'm going in to see Dr. Smith as soon as he'll give me an appointment. But it's better that I go alone."

"Then we'll talk in the next few days," Geoff said. He smiled briefly and started down the porch steps. Kerry closed the door and walked into the living room but did not immediately turn on the light. She realized she was still savoring the moment when Geoff had taken the key from her hand and opened the door for her. Then she went to the window and watched as he backed his car out of the driveway and disappeared down the street.

Daddy is such fun, Robin thought as she contentedly sat next to him in the Jaguar. They had inspected the ski lodge Bob Kinellen was thinking about buying. She thought it was cool, but he said it was a disappointment. "I want one where we can ski to the door," he had said, and then he'd laughed. "We'll just keep looking."

Robin had brought her camera, and her father waited while she took two rolls of film. Even though there was only a little snow on the peaks, she thought the light on the mountains was fantastic. She caught the last rays of the setting sun, and then they started back. Her father said he knew a great place where they could get terrific shrimp.

Robin knew that Mom was mad at Daddy because he hadn't talked to her after the accident, but he *had* left a message. And it was true, she didn't get to see him much, but when they were together, he was great.

At six-thirty they stopped at the restaurant. Over shrimp and scallops, they talked. He promised that this year for sure they would go skiing, just the two of them. "Sometime when Mom's on a date." He winked.

"Oh, Mom doesn't date much," she told him. "I kind of liked someone who took her out a couple of times during the summer, but she said he was boring."

"What did he do?"

"He was an engineer, I think."

"Well, when Mommy's a judge, she'll probably end up dating another judge. She'll be surrounded by them."

"A lawyer came to the house the other night," Robin said. "He was nice. But I think it was just business."

Bob Kinellen had been only partially involved in the conversation. Now he became attentive. "What was his name?"

"Geoff Dorso. He brought over a big file for Mommy to read."

When her father suddenly became very quiet, Robin had the guilty feeling that maybe she had said too much, that maybe he was mad at her.

When they got back in the car, she slept the rest of the way, and when her father dropped her off at nine-thirty, she was glad to be home.

30

The senate and assembly of the State of New Jersey were having a busy fall. The twice-weekly sessions were almost one hundred percent attended, and for a good reason: The upcoming gubernatorial election, although still a year away, created a behind-the-scenes electricity that crackled through the atmosphere of both chambers.

The fact that Governor Marshall seemed intent on backing Prosecutor Frank Green as his successor did not sit well with a number of his party's other eager would-be candidates. Jonathan Hoover knew full well that any crack in Green's potential ability to be elected would be welcomed by other contenders. They would seize on it and create as much of a distraction as possible. If it got loud enough, it could easily shake loose Green's hold on the nomination. Right now it was far from a lock.

As president of the senate, Hoover had enormous power in party politics. One of the reasons he had been elected five times to four-year terms was his ability to take the long-range view when making decisions or when casting votes. His constituents appreciated that.

On days that the senate met, he sometimes stayed in Trenton and had dinner with friends. Tonight he would be dining with the governor.

Following the afternoon session, Jonathan returned to his private office, asked his secretary to take messages and closed the door. For the next hour he sat at his desk, his hands folded under his chin. It was the posture Grace called "Jonathan at prayer."

When he finally got up, he walked over to the window to stare at the darkening sky. He had made an important decision. Kerry McGrath's probing into the Reardon murder case had created a real problem. It was exactly the kind of thing the media would run with, trying to make it into something sensational. Even if in the end it came to nothing, which Jonathan fully expected, it would create a negative perception of Frank Green and would effectively derail his candidacy.

Of course, Kerry might just drop the whole thing before it got that far—he certainly hoped she would, for everyone's sake. Still, Jonathan knew it was his duty to warn the governor about her investigation so far and to suggest that, for the present, her name should not be submitted to the senate for approval of her judgeship. He knew it would be embarrassing to the governor to have one of his potential appointees effectively working against him.

31

On Monday morning Kerry found a package in her office, and inside was a Royal Doulton china figurine, the one called "Autumn Breezes." There was a note with it:

Dear Ms. McGrath,

Mom's house is sold and we've cleared out all our stuff. We're moving to Pennsylvania to live with our aunt and uncle.

Mom always kept this on her dresser. It had been her mother's. She said it made her happy to see it.

You've made us so happy by making sure that the guy who killed Mom pays for his crime that we want you to have it. It's our way of saying thanks.

The letter was signed by Chris and Ken, the teenage sons of the supervisor who had been murdered by her assistant.

Kerry blinked back tears as she held the lovely object. She called in her secretary and dictated a brief letter:

By law, I'm not allowed to accept any gifts, but, Chris and Ken, I promise you, if it were different, this would be one I'd cherish. Please keep it for me and for your mom.

As she signed the letter she thought about the obvious bond between these brothers, and between them and their mother. What would become of Robin if something happened to me? she wondered. Then she shook her head. There's nothing to be gained in being morbid, she thought. Besides, there was another, more pressing, parent/child situation to investigate.

It was time to pay a visit to Dr. Charles Smith. When she called his office, the answering service picked up. "They won't be in until eleven today. May I take a message?"

Shortly before noon, Kerry received a return call from Mrs. Carpenter.

"I'd like to have an appointment to speak with the doctor as soon as possible," Kerry said. "It's important."

"What is this in reference to, Ms. McGrath?"

Kerry decided to gamble. "Tell the doctor it's in reference to Suzanne."

She waited nearly five minutes, then heard Dr. Smith's cold, precise voice. "What do you want, Ms. McGrath?" he asked.

"I want to talk to you about your testimony at Skip Reardon's trial, Doctor, and I'd appreciate doing it as soon as possible."

By the time she hung up, he had agreed to meet with her in his office at seven-thirty the next morning. She mused that it meant she would have to leave home by six-thirty. And that meant she would have to arrange for a neighbor to phone Robin to make sure she didn't fall back asleep after Kerry had gone.

Otherwise, Robin would be fine. She always walked to school with two of her girlfriends, and Kerry was sure that she was old enough to get herself a bowl of cereal.

Next she phoned her friend Margaret at her office and got Stuart Grant's home phone number. "I talked to Stuart about you and your questions about that plastic surgeon, and he said his wife will be home all morning," Margaret told her.

Susan Grant answered on the first ring. She repeated exactly what Margaret had reported. "I swear, Kerry, it was frightening. I just wanted to have a tuck around the eyes. But Dr. Smith was so intense. He kept calling me Suzanne, and I know that if I had let him have his way, I wouldn't have looked like myself anymore."

Just before lunch, Kerry asked Joe Palumbo to stop by her office. "I have a little extracurricular situation I need your help with," she told him when he slumped in a chair in front of her desk. "The Reardon case."

Joe's quizzical expression demanded an answer. She told him about the Suzanne Reardon look-alikes and Dr. Charles Smith. Hesitantly she admitted that she had also visited Reardon in prison and that, while everything she was doing was strictly unofficial, she was beginning to have her doubts about the way the case was handled.

Palumbo whistled.

"And, Joe, I'd appreciate it if we could keep this just between us. Frank Green is not happy about my interest in the case."

"I wonder why," Palumbo murmured.

"The point is that Green himself told me the other day that Dr. Smith was an unemotional witness. Strange for a father of a murder victim, wouldn't you say? On the stand, Dr. Smith testified that he and his wife had separated when Suzanne was a baby and that a few years later he allowed her to be adopted by her stepfather, a man named Wayne Stevens, and that she grew up in Oakland, California. I'd like you to locate Stevens. I'd be very interested in learning from him what kind of girl Suzanne was growing up, and especially I want to see a picture of her taken when she was a teenager."

She had pulled out several pages of the Reardon trial transcript. Now she shoved them across the desk to Palumbo. "Here's the testimony of a baby-sitter who was across the street the night of the murder and who claims she saw a strange car in front of the Reardon house around nine o'clock that night. She lives—or lived—with her daughter and son-in-law in Alpine. Check her out for me, okay?"

Palumbo's eyes reflected keen interest. "It will be a pleasure,

Kerry. You're doing me a favor. I'd love to see Our Leader be the one on the hot seat for a change."

"Look, Joe, Frank Green's a good guy," Kerry protested. "I'm not interested in upsetting things for him. I just feel that there were some questions left open in the case, and frankly, meeting Dr. Smith and seeing his look-alike patients has spooked me. If there's a chance that the wrong man is in jail, I feel it's my duty to explore it. But I'll do it only if I am convinced."

"I fully understand," Palumbo said. "And don't get me wrong. In most ways I agree with you that Green is an okay guy. It's just that I prefer someone who doesn't run for cover every time someone in this office is taking heat."

32

When Dr. Charles Smith hung up the phone after talking to Kerry McGrath, he realized that the faint tremor that came and went in his right hand was beginning again. He closed his left hand over it, but even so, he could feel the vibrations in his fingertips.

He knew that Mrs. Carpenter had looked at him curiously when she told him about the McGrath woman's phone call. The mention of Suzanne had meant nothing to Carpenter, which no doubt had made her wonder what this mysterious call was all about.

Now he opened Robin Kinellen's file and studied it. He remembered that her parents were divorced, but he had not studied

the personal data Kerry McGrath had submitted along with
Robin's medical history. It said that she was an assistant prosecutor, Bergen County. He paused for a moment. He didn't remember ever having seen her at the trial . . .

There was a tap at the door. Mrs. Carpenter stuck her head in
the office to remind him that he had a patient waiting in exami-
nating room 1.

"I'm aware of that," he said brusquely, waving her away. He
turned back to Robin's file. She had come in for checkups on the
eleventh and the twenty-third. Barbara Tompkins had been in
for a checkup on the eleventh and Pamela Worth on the twenty-
third. Unfortunate timing, he thought. Kerry McGrath had probably seen both of them, and it had somehow triggered whatever
memory she had of Suzanne.

For long minutes he sat at the desk. What did her call really
mean? What interest had she in the case? Nothing could have
changed. The facts were still the same. Skip Reardon was still in
prison, and that's where he would remain. Smith knew that his
testimony had helped to put him there. And I won't change one
word of it, he thought bitterly. Not one word.

33

S andwiched between his two attorneys, Robert Kinellen and
Anthony Bartlett, Jimmy Weeks sat in federal district court
as the seemingly endless process of selecting a jury for his
income tax evasion trial dragged on.

After three weeks, only six jurors had been found acceptable to both prosecution and defense. The woman being questioned now was the kind he most dreaded. Prim and self-righteous, a pillar-of-the-community type. President of the Westdale Women's Club, she had stated; her husband the CEO of an engineering firm; two sons at Yale.

Jimmy studied her as the questioning went on and her attitude became more and more condescending. Sure she was satisfactory to the prosecution, no question about that. But he knew from the disdainful glance she swept in his direction that she considered him dirt.

When the judge was finished questioning the woman, Jimmy Weeks leaned over to Kinellen and said, "Accept her."

"Are you out of your mind?" Bob snapped incredulously.

"Bobby, trust me." Jimmy lowered his voice. "This will be a freebie." Then Jimmy glanced angrily down the defense table to where an impassive Barney Haskell sat watching the proceedings with his lawyer. If Haskell cut a deal with the prosecution and became their witness, Kinellen claimed he could destroy Barney on the stand.

Maybe. And maybe not. Jimmy Weeks wasn't so sure, and he was a man who always liked a sure thing. He had at least one juror in his pocket. Now he probably had two.

So far, there had only been the mention of Kinellen's ex-wife looking into the Reardon murder case, Weeks mused, but if anything actually went forward with it, he knew it could prove awkward for him. Especially if Haskell got wind of it. It might occur to him that he had another way to sweeten any deal he was trying to make with the prosecution.

34

Late that afternoon, Geoff Dorso's secretary buzzed him on the intercom. "Miss Taylor is here," she said. "I told her I was sure you couldn't see her without an appointment. She said it will only take a few minutes and that it's important."

For Beth Taylor to just show up without calling first, it had to be important. "It's okay," Geoff said. "Send her in."

His pulse quickened as he waited. He prayed that she wasn't there to tell him that something had happened to Skip Reardon's mother. Mrs. Reardon had had a heart attack shortly after Skip's conviction and another one five years ago. She had managed to bounce back from both, declaring that there was no way on earth that she was going to die while her son was still in prison for a crime he didn't commit.

She wrote Skip every day—cheery, happy letters, full of plans for his future. On a recent visit to the prison, Geoff had listened as Skip read him an excerpt from one he had received that day: "At mass this morning, I reminded God that while all things come to him who waits, we've waited long enough. And you know, Skip, the most wonderful feeling came over me. It was almost as though I was hearing in my mind a voice saying, 'not much longer.' "

Skip had laughed wryly. "You know, Geoff, when I read this, I almost believed it."

When his secretary escorted Beth into his office, Geoff came around his desk and kissed her affectionately. Whenever he saw her, the same thought always flashed immediately into his mind: What a different life Skip would have had if he had married Beth Taylor and never met Suzanne.

Beth was Skip's age, almost forty now, about five feet six, a comfortable size 12, with short, wavy brown hair, lively brown eyes and a face that radiated intelligence and warmth. She had been a teacher when she and Skip were dating fifteen years ago. Since then she had earned her master's degree and now worked as a guidance counselor in a nearby school.

By her expression today it was obvious she was deeply troubled. Indicating a comfortable seating area at the end of the room, Geoff said, "I know they made a fresh pot of coffee half an hour ago. How about it?"

Her smile came and went. "I'd like that."

He studied her expression as they made casual chatter and he poured them both some coffee. She looked worried rather than grief-stricken. He was now sure nothing had happened to Mrs. Reardon. Then another possibility occurred to him. Good God, has Beth met someone she's interested in and doesn't know how to tell Skip? He knew that such a thing might happen—perhaps even *should* happen—but he knew that it would be rough on Skip.

As soon as they were settled, Beth came directly to the point. "Geoff, I talked to Skip on the phone last night. He sounds so terribly depressed. I'm really worried. You know how much talk there is about cutting off repeated appeals from convicted murderers. Skip has practically been kept alive on the hope that someday one of the appeals will be upheld. If he ever gives up that hope completely—I know him, he'll want to die. He told me about that assistant prosecutor visiting him. He's sure she doesn't believe him."

"Do you think he's becoming suicidal?" Geoff asked quickly. "If so, we have to do something about it. As a model prisoner, he's getting more privileges. I should warn the warden."

"No, no! Don't even think about reporting that!" Beth cried. "I don't mean he'd do anything to himself now. He knows he'd be killing his mother too. I just . . ." She threw out her hands in a helpless gesture. "Geoff," she burst out, "is there any hope I can give him? Or maybe I'm asking if you realistically believe you'll find grounds to file a new appeal."

If this were a week ago, Geoff thought, I'd have had to tell her that I've gone over every inch of this case and I can't find even a suggestion of new grounds. Kerry McGrath's call, however, had made the difference.

Careful not to sound overly encouraging, he told Beth about the two women Kerry McGrath had seen in Dr. Smith's office and of Kerry's growing interest in the case. As he watched the radiant hope grow on Beth's face, he prayed that he was not leading her and Skip down a path that would ultimately prove to be another dead end.

Beth's eyes were filling with tears. "Then Kerry McGrath still is looking into the case?"

"Very definitely. She's quite something, Beth." As Geoff heard himself saying those words, he was visualizing Kerry; the way she tucked a lock of blond hair behind her ear as she was concentrating, the wistful look in her eyes when she talked about her father, her trim, slender body, her rueful, self-deprecating smile when Bob Kinellen's name came up, the joyful pride that emanated from her when she talked about her daughter.

He was hearing her slightly husky voice and seeing the almost shy smile she gave him when he had taken the key and opened the door for her. It was obvious to him that after her father's death, no one had ever taken care of Kerry.

"Geoff, if there are grounds for an appeal, do you think we made a mistake last time by not telling about me?"

Beth's question yanked him back to the present. She was referring to one aspect of the case that had never come out in court. Just prior to Suzanne Reardon's death, Skip and Beth had started to see each other again. A few weeks earlier, they had bumped into each other, and Skip had insisted on taking her to lunch. They had ended up talking for hours, and he had confessed to her how unhappy he was and how much he regretted their breakup. "I made a stupid mistake," he had told her, "but for what it's worth, it's not going to last much longer. I've been married to Suzanne for four years, and for at least three of them I've been wondering how I ever let you go."

On the night Suzanne died, Beth and Skip were scheduled to have dinner together. She had had to cancel at the last minute, however, and it was then that Skip had gone home to find Suzanne arranging the roses.

At the time of the trial, Geoff had agreed with Skip's chief counsel, Tim Farrell, that to put Beth on the stand was a double-edged sword. The prosecution no doubt would try to make it seem that in addition to avoiding the expense of a divorce, Skip Reardon had another compelling reason for killing his wife.

On the other hand, Beth's testimony might have been effective in dispelling Dr. Smith's contention that Skip was insanely jealous of Suzanne.

Until Kerry had told him about Dr. Smith, and about the look-alikes, Geoff had been sure that they had made the right decision. Now he was less sure. He looked squarely at Beth. "I didn't tell Kerry about you yet. But now I want her to meet you, and to hear your story. If we have any chance at all for a new and successful appeal, all the cards have to be on the table."

35

When she was ready to leave the house for her early morning appointment with Dr. Smith, Kerry shook awake a protesting Robin. "Come on, Rob," she urged. "You're always telling me I treat you like a baby."

"You do," Robin mumbled.

"All right. I'm giving you a chance to prove your independence. I want you to get up now and get dressed. Otherwise you'll fall asleep again. Mrs. Weiser will phone at seven to be sure you didn't let yourself fall back asleep. I left cereal and juice out. Make certain the door is locked when you leave for school."

Robin yawned and closed her eyes.

"Rob, please."

"Okay." With a sigh Robin swung her legs over the side of the bed. Her hair fell forward over her face as she rubbed her eyes.

Kerry smoothed it back. "Can I trust you?"

Robin looked up with a slow, sleepy smile. "Uh-huh."

"Okay." Kerry kissed the top of her head. "Now remember, same rules as any other time. Don't open the door for anyone.

I'll set the alarm. You deactivate it only when you're ready to leave, then reset it. Don't take a ride from anyone unless you're with Cassie and Courtney and it's one of their parents."

"I know. I know." Robin sighed dramatically.

Kerry grinned. "I know I've given you the same spiel a thousand times. See you tonight. Alison will be here at three."

Alison was the high school student who stayed with Robin after school until Kerry came home. Kerry had thought about having her come over this morning to see Robin off but had acceded to her daughter's vigorous protest that she wasn't a baby and could get herself off to school.

"See you, Mom."

Robin listened to Kerry's steps going down the stairs, then went over to the window to watch the car pull out of the driveway.

The room was chilly. By seven o'clock, when she usually got up, the house was toasty warm. Just for a minute, Robin thought as she slipped back into bed. I'll just lie here for a minute more.

At seven o'clock, after the phone had rung six times, she sat up and answered it. "Oh, thanks, Mrs. Weiser. Yes, I'm sure I'm up."

I am now, she thought as she hurried out of bed.

36

Despite the early hour, the traffic into Manhattan was heavy. But at least it was moving at a reasonable clip, Kerry thought. Nevertheless it took her a full hour to drive from New Jersey, down what was left of the West Side Highway and across town to Dr. Smith's Fifth Avenue office. She was three minutes late.

The doctor let her in himself. Even the minimal courtesy he had shown on Robin's two visits was lacking this morning. He did not greet her except to say, "I can give you twenty minutes, Ms. McGrath, and not a second more." He led her to his private office.

If that's the way we're going to play it, Kerry thought, then fine. When she was seated across his desk from him, she said, "Dr. Smith, after seeing two women emerge from this office who startlingly resembled your murdered daughter, Suzanne, I became curious enough about the circumstances of her death to take time this last week to read the transcript of Skip Reardon's trial."

She did not miss the look of hatred that came over Dr. Smith's face when she mentioned Reardon's name. His eyes narrowed, his mouth tightened, deep furrows appeared on his forehead and in vertical slashes down his cheeks.

She looked directly at him. "Dr. Smith, I want you to know

how terribly sorry I am that you lost your daughter. You were a divorced parent. I'm a divorced parent. Like you, I have an only child, a daughter. Knowing the agony I was in when I received the call that Robin had been in an accident, I can only imagine how you felt when you were told about Suzanne."

Smith looked at her steadily, his fingers locked together. Kerry had the feeling that there was an impenetrable barrier between them. If so, the rest of their conversation was entirely predictable. He would hear her out, make some sort of statement about love and loss, and then usher her to the door. How could she break through that barrier?

She leaned forward. "Dr. Smith, your testimony is the reason Skip Reardon is in prison. You said he was insanely jealous, that your daughter was afraid of him. He swears that he never threatened Suzanne."

"He's lying." The voice was flat, unemotional. "He truly was insanely jealous of her. As you said, she was my only child. I doted on her. I had become successful enough to give her the kinds of things I could never give her as a child. It was my pleasure from time to time to buy her a piece of fine jewelry. Yet, even when I spoke to Reardon, he refused to believe that they had been gifts from me. He kept accusing her of seeing other men."

Is it possible? Kerry wondered. "But if Suzanne was in fear for her life, why did she stay with Skip Reardon?" she asked.

The morning sun was flooding the room in such a way that it shone on Smith's rimless glasses, making it so that Kerry could no longer see his eyes. Could they possibly be as flat as his expressionless voice? she thought to herself. "Because unlike her mother, my former wife, Suzanne had a sense of deep commitment to her marriage," he responded after a pause. "The grave mistake of her life was to fall in love with Reardon. An even graver mistake was not to take his threats seriously."

Kerry realized she was getting nowhere. It was time to ask the question that had occurred to her earlier, but that possibly held implications she wasn't sure she was prepared to face. "Dr. Smith, did you ever perform any surgical procedures of any kind on your daughter?"

It was immediately clear that her question outraged him. "Ms. McGrath, I happen to belong to the school of physicians who would never, except in dire emergency, treat a family member. Beyond that, the question is insulting. Suzanne was a natural beauty."

"You've made at least two women resemble her to a startling degree. Why?"

Dr. Smith looked at his watch. "I'll answer this final question, and then you will have to excuse me, Ms. McGrath. I don't know how much you know about plastic surgery. Fifty years ago, by today's standards, it was quite primitive. After people had nose jobs, they had to live with flaring nostrils. Reconstructive work on victims born with deformities such as a harelip was often a crude procedure. It is now very sophisticated, and the results are most satisfying. We've learned a great deal. Plastic surgery is no longer for only the rich and famous. It is for anyone, whether he or she needs it, or simply wants it."

He took off his glasses and rubbed his forehead as though he had a headache. "Parents bring in teenagers, boys as well as girls, who are so conscious of a perceived defect that they simply can't function. Yesterday I operated on a fifteen-year-old boy whose ears stuck out so much that they were the only thing one saw when looking at him. When the bandages come off, all his other quite pleasing features, which had been obscured by this of-fending problem, will be what people see when they look at him.

"I operate on women who look in the mirror and see sag-ging skin or baggy eyes, women who had been beautiful girls in their youth. I raise and clamp the forehead under the hairline, I tighten the skin and pull it up behind the ears. I take twenty years off their appearance, but more than that, I transform their self-deprecation into self-worth."

His voice rose. "I could show you before-and-after pictures of accident victims whom I have helped. You ask me why several of my patients resemble my daughter. I'll tell you why. Because in these ten years, a few plain and unhappy young women came into this office and I was able to give them her kind of beauty."

Kerry knew he was about to tell her to leave. Hurriedly, she asked, "Then why several years ago did you tell a potential patient, Susan Grant, that beauty sometimes is abused, and the result is jealousy and violence? Weren't you talking about Suzanne? Isn't it a fact that Skip Reardon may have had a reason to be jealous? Perhaps you did buy her all the jewelry Skip couldn't account for, but he swears he did not send Suzanne those roses she received on the day of her death."

Dr. Smith stood up. "Ms. McGrath, I should think in your business you ought to know that murderers almost inevitably plead innocence. And now, this discussion is over."

There was nothing Kerry could do except follow him from the room. As she walked behind him, she noticed that he was holding his right hand rigidly against his side. Was that a tremor in his hand? Yes, it was.

At the door he said, "Ms. McGrath, you must understand that the sound of Skip Reardon's name sickens me. Please call Mrs. Carpenter and give her the name of another physician to whom she can forward Robin's file. I do not want to hear from you or see you or your daughter again."

He was so close to her that Kerry stepped back involuntarily. There was something genuinely frightening about the man. His eyes, filled with anger and hatred, seemed to be burning through her. If he had a gun in his hand right now, I swear he'd use it, she thought to herself.

37

After she locked the door and started down the steps, Robin noticed the small dark car parked across the street. Strange cars weren't common on this street, especially at this hour, but she didn't know why this one gave her an especially funny feeling.

It was cold. She shifted her books to her left arm and zipped her jacket the rest of the way to her neck, then quickened her steps. She was meeting Cassie and Courtney at the corner a block away and knew they probably were already waiting. She was a couple of minutes late.

The street was quiet. Now that the leaves were almost gone, the trees had a bare, unfriendly look. Robin wished she had remembered to wear gloves.

When she reached the sidewalk, she glanced across the street. The driver's window in the strange car was opening slowly, stopping after it had been lowered only a few inches. She stared at it as hard as she could, hoping to see a familiar face inside, but the bright morning sun reflected in such a way that she could see nothing. Then she saw a hand reach out, pointing something at her. Suddenly panicked, Robin began to run. With a roar, the car came rushing across the road, seemingly aimed right toward her. Just as she thought it was going to come up the curb and hit her, it swerved into a U-turn and then raced down the block.

Sobbing, Robin ran across the lawn of their neighbor's house and frantically rang the doorbell.

When Joe Palumbo finished his investigation of a break-in in Cresskill, he realized that it was only nine-thirty. Since he was a scant few minutes away from Alpine, it seemed like a perfect opportunity to look up Dolly Bowles, the baby-sitter who had testified at the Reardon murder trial. Fortunately, he also happened to have her phone number with him.

Dolly initially sounded a little guarded when Palumbo explained that he was an investigator with the Bergen County prosecutor's office. But after he told her that one of the assistant prosecutors, Kerry McGrath, very much wanted to hear about the car Dolly had seen in front of the Reardon house the night of the murder, she announced that she had been following the trial Kerry McGrath recently had prosecuted and was so glad that the man who shot his supervisor had been convicted. She told Palumbo about the time she and her mother had been tied up in their home by an intruder.

"So," she finished, "if you and Kerry McGrath want to talk to me, that's fine."

"Well, actually," Joe told her somewhat lamely, "I'd like to come over and talk to you right now. Maybe Kerry will talk to you later."

There was a pause. Palumbo could not know that, in her mind, Dolly was seeing again the derisive expression on the face of Prosecutor Green when he cross-examined her at the trial.

Finally she spoke. "I think," she said, with dignity, "that I would be more comfortable discussing that night with Kerry McGrath. I think it's best we wait until she is available."

39

It was 9:45 before Kerry got to the courthouse, much later than she normally arrived. Anticipating the possibility of receiving a bit of flack about it, she had phoned to say she had an errand and was going to be late. Frank Green was always at his desk promptly at seven o'clock. It was something they joked about, but it was obvious he believed that his entire staff should be on board with him. Kerry knew he would have a fit if he learned that her errand was to see Dr. Charles Smith.

When she punched in the code that admitted her to the prosecutor's office, the switchboard operator looked up and said, "Kerry, go right into Mr. Green's office. He's expecting you."

Oh boy, Kerry thought.

As soon as she walked into Green's office, she could see he was not angry. She knew him well enough to be able to read his mood. As usual he came directly to the point. "Kerry, Robin is fine. She's with your neighbor, Mrs. Weiser. Emphatically, she is all right."

Kerry felt her throat tighten. "Then what's wrong?"

"We're not sure and maybe nothing. According to Robin, you left the house at six-thirty." There was a glint of curiosity in Green's eyes.

"Yes, I did."

"When Robin was leaving the house later, she said she noticed a strange car parked across the street. When she reached the sidewalk, the window on the driver's door opened slightly, and she was able to see a hand holding some kind of object. She couldn't tell what it was, and she wasn't able to see the driver's face. Then the car started up and veered across the street so suddenly she thought it would come up on the sidewalk and hit her, but it quickly went into a U-turn and took off. Robin ran to your neighbor's house."

Kerry sank into a chair. "She's there now?"

"Yes. You can call her, or go home if that would reassure you. My concern is, does Robin have an overactive imagination, or is it possible someone was trying to frighten her and ultimately frighten you?"

"Why would anyone want to frighten Robin or me?"

"It's happened before in this office after a high-profile case. You've just completed a case that got a lot of media attention. The guy you convicted of murder was clearly an out-and-out sleaze and still has relatives and friends."

"Yes, but all of them I met seemed to be pretty decent people," Kerry said. "And to answer your first question, Robin is a level-headed kid. She wouldn't imagine something like this." She hesitated. "It's the first time I let her get herself out in the morning, and I was bombarding her with warnings about what to do and not do."

"Call her from here," Green directed.

Robin answered Mrs. Weiser's telephone on the first ring. "I knew you'd call, Mom. I'm okay now. I want to go to school. Mrs. Weiser said she'd drive me. And Mom, I've still got to go out this afternoon. It's Halloween."

Kerry thought quickly. Robin was better off in school than sitting at home all day, thinking about the incident. "All right, but I'll be there at school to pick you up at quarter of three. I don't want you walking home." And I'll be right with you when you trick-or-treat, she thought. "Now let me talk to Mrs. Weiser, Rob," she said.

When she hung up, she said, "Frank, is it all right if I leave early today?"

His smile was genuine. "Of course it is. Kerry, I don't have to tell you to question Robin carefully. We have to know if there's any chance someone really was watching for her."

As Kerry was leaving, he added, "But isn't Robin a bit young to see herself off to school?"

Kerry knew he was fishing to find out what had been so important that she had left Robin alone at home at six-thirty.

"Yes, she is," she agreed. "It won't happen again."

Later that morning, Joe Palumbo stopped by Kerry's office and told her about his call to Dolly Bowles. "She doesn't want to talk to me, Kerry, but I'd still like to go with you when you see her."

"Let me phone her now."

Her six-word greeting, "Hello, Mrs. Bowles, I'm Kerry McGrath," led to being on the receiving end of a ten-minute monologue.

Palumbo crossed his legs and leaned back in the chair as with some amusement he watched Kerry try to interject a word or question. Then he was irritated when, after Kerry finally got an opportunity to say that she would like to bring her investigator, Mr. Palumbo, with her, it was obvious the answer was no.

Finally she hung up. "Dolly Bowles is not a happy camper about the way she was treated by this office ten years ago. That was the gist of the conversation. The rest is that her daughter and son-in-law don't want her talking about the murder or what she saw anymore, and they're coming back from a trip tomorrow. If I want to see her, it's got to be about five o'clock today. That's going to take some juggling. I told her I'd let her know."

"Can you get out of here in time?" Joe asked.

"I have a few appointments I'm canceling anyhow." She told Palumbo about Robin and the incident this morning.

The investigator rose to his feet and tried to close the jacket that always strained over his generous middle. "I'll meet you at your place at five," he suggested. "While you're with Mrs. Bowles, let me take Robin for a hamburger. I'd like to talk to her about this morning." He saw the look of disapproval on Kerry's face and hastened to speak before she could protest. "Kerry, you're smart, but you're not going to be objective about this. Don't do my job for me."

Kerry studied Joe thoughtfully. His appearance was always a little disheveled, and his paperwork was usually somewhat disorganized, but he was just about the best there was at his job. Kerry had seen him question young children so skillfully that they didn't realize every word they said was being analyzed. It would be very helpful to have Joe's spin on this. "Okay," she agreed.

40

On Tuesday afternoon, Jason Arnott drove from Alpine to the remote area near Ellenville in the Catskills where his sprawling country home, hidden by the surrounding mountain range, concealed his priceless stolen treasures.

He knew the house was an addiction, an extension of the sometimes uncontrollable drive that made him steal the beautiful things he saw in the homes of his acquaintances. For it was beauty, after all, that made him do those things. He loved beauty, loved the look of it, the feel. Sometimes the urge to hold something, to caress it, was so strong it was almost overwhelming. It was a gift, and as such, both a blessing and a curse. Someday it would get him in trouble. As it almost had already. It made him impatient when visitors admired carpets or furniture or paintings or objets d'art in his Alpine home. Often he amused himself by contemplating how shocked they would be if he were to blurt out, "This place is ordinary by my standards."

But, of course, he never would say that, for he had no desire to share his private collection with anyone. That was his alone. And must be kept that way.

Today is Halloween, he thought dismissively as he drove swiftly up Route 17. He was glad to get away. He had no desire to be victimized by children endlessly ringing his doorbell. He was tired.

Over the weekend he had stayed at a hotel in Bethesda, Maryland, and used the time to burglarize a Chevy Chase home at which he had attended a party a few months earlier. At that gathering, the hostess, Myra Hamilton, had rattled on about her son's upcoming wedding, which would take place on October 28th in Chicago, effectively announcing to one and all that the house would be empty on that date.

The Hamilton house was not large, but it was exquisite, filled with precious items the Hamiltons had collected over the years. Jason had salivated over a Fabergé desk seal in sapphire blue with a gold egg-shaped handle. That and a delicate three-by-five-foot Aubusson with a central rosace that they used as a wall hanging were the two things he most wanted to wrest from them.

Now both objects were in the trunk of his car, on their way to his retreat. Unconsciously, Jason frowned. He was not experiencing his usual sensation of triumph at having achieved his goal. A vague, indefinable worry was nagging at him. Mentally he reviewed the modus operandi of entering the Hamilton home, going over it step by step.

The alarm had been on but easy to disengage. Clearly the house was empty, as he had anticipated. For a moment, he had been tempted to go through the place quickly, looking for anything of great value he might have missed noticing at the party. Instead he stuck to his original plan, taking only those things he had scoped out earlier.

He had barely inched his way into the traffic on Route 240 when two police cars, sirens screaming and lights flashing, raced past him and turned left onto the street he had just exited. It was obvious to him that they were on their way to the Hamilton home. Which, of course, meant that he had somehow triggered a silent alarm that operated independently of the master system.

What other kind of security did the Hamiltons have? he wondered. It was so easy to conceal cameras now. He had been wearing the stocking mask he always put on when entering one of the houses he had chosen to honor with his attention, but at one point this night he had pulled it up to examine a bronze figurine, a foolish thing to do—it had proved to be of no real value.

One chance in a million that a camera caught my face, Jason reassured himself. He would dismiss his misgivings and go on with his life, albeit a bit more cautiously for a while.

The afternoon sun was almost lost behind the mountains when he pulled into his driveway. At last he felt a measure of buoyancy. The nearest neighbor was several miles away. Maddie, the weekly cleaning woman—large, stolid, unimaginative and unquestioning woman that she was—would have been in yesterday. Everything would be shining.

He knew she didn't recognize the difference between an Aubusson and a ten-dollar-a-yard carpet remnant, but she was one of those rare creatures who took pride in her work and was satisfied only with perfection. In ten years, she had never so much as chipped a cup.

Jason smiled to himself, thinking of Maddie's reaction when she found the Aubusson hanging in the foyer and the Fabergé desk seal in the master bedroom. *Hasn't he got enough stuff to dust?* she would wonder and go on with her chores.

He parked the car at the side door and, with the rush of anticipation that always surged over him when he came here, entered the house and reached for the light switch. Once again, the sight of so many beautiful things made his lips and hands moist with pleasure. A few minutes later, after his overnight case, a small bag of groceries and his new treasures were safely inside, he locked the door and drew the bolt. His evening had begun.

His first task was to carry the Fabergé seal upstairs and place it on the antique dressing table. Once it was in place, he stood back to admire it, then leaned over to compare it with the miniature frame that had been on his night table for the past ten years.

The frame represented one of the few times he had been fooled.

It was a decent Fabergé copy, but certainly not the real thing. That fact seemed so obvious now. The blue enamel looked muddy when compared to the deep color of the desk seal. The gold border encrusted with pearls was nothing like authentic Fabergé workmanship. But from inside that frame, Suzanne's face smiled back at him.

He didn't like to think about that night, almost eleven years ago. He had gone in through the open window of the sitting room of the master bedroom suite. He knew the house was supposed to be empty. That very day, Suzanne had told him about her dinner engagement for the evening, and the fact that Skip would not be home. He had the security code, but when he got there, he saw that the window was wide open. When he entered the upstairs floor, it was dark. In the bedroom he spotted the miniature frame he had seen earlier; it was on top of the night table. From across the room it looked authentic. He was just examining it closely when he heard a raised voice. Suzanne! Panicking, he had dropped the frame in his pocket and hidden in a closet.

Jason looked down at the frame now. Over the years he had sometimes wondered what perverse reason kept him from removing Suzanne's picture from it, or from throwing the whole thing away. The frame was, after all, only a copy.

But as he stared at it this night, he understood for the first time why he had left the picture and frame intact. It was because it made it easier for him to blot out the memory of how gruesome and distorted Suzanne's features had been when he made his escape.

41

"Well, we've got our jury impaneled and it's a good one," Bob Kinellen told his client with a heartiness he did not feel.

Jimmy Weeks looked at him sourly. "Bobby, with a few exceptions, I think that jury stinks."

"Trust me."

Anthony Bartlett backed up his son-in-law. "Bob's right, Jimmy. Trust him." Then Bartlett's eyes strayed to the opposite end of the defense table where Barney Haskell was sitting, his expression morose, his hands supporting his head. He saw that Bob was looking at Haskell too, and he knew what Bob was thinking.

Haskell's a diabetic. He won't want to risk years in prison. He's got dates and facts and figures that we'll have a hell of a time contradicting . . . He knew all about Suzanne.

The opening arguments would begin the next morning. When he left the courthouse, Jimmy Weeks went directly to his car. As the chauffeur held the door open, he slid into the backseat without his usual grunted good-bye.

Kinellen and Bartlett watched the car pull away. "I'm going back to the office," Kinellen told his father-in-law. "I've got work to do."

Bartlett nodded. "I would say so." There was an impersonal tone to his voice. "See you in the morning, Bob."

Sure you will, Kinellen thought as he walked to the parking garage. You're distancing yourself from me so that if my hands get dirty, you're not part of it.

He knew that Bartlett had millions salted away. Even if Weeks was convicted and the law firm went under, he would be all right. Maybe he would get to spend more time in Palm Beach with his wife, Alice Senior.

I'm taking all the risks, Bob Kinellen thought as he handed his ticket to the cashier. I'm the one who risks going down. There had to be a reason Jimmy insisted on leaving the Wagner woman on the jury. What was it?

42

Geoff Dorso phoned Kerry just as she was about to leave the office. "I saw Dr. Smith this morning," she told him hurriedly, "and I'm seeing Dolly Bowles around five. I can't talk now. I've got to meet Robin at school."

"Kerry, I'm anxious to know what happened with Dr. Smith, and what you learn from Dolly Bowles. Can we have dinner?"

"I don't want to go out tonight, but if you don't mind a salad and pasta . . ."

"I'm Italian, remember?"

"About seven-thirty?"

"I'll be there."

When she picked up Robin at school, it was clear to Kerry that her daughter's mind was much more on Halloween trick-or-treating than on the early-morning incident. In fact, Robin seemed to be embarrassed about it. Taking her cue from her daughter, Kerry dropped the subject, for now at least.

When they reached home, she gave Robin's teenage sitter the afternoon off. This is the way other mothers live, she thought as, with several of them, she trailed a cluster of trick-or-treating children. She and Robin arrived back at their place just in time to let Joe Palumbo in.

He was carrying a bulging briefcase, which he tapped with a satisfied smile. "The records of the office investigation of the Reardon case," he told her. "It'll have Dolly Bowles' original statement. Let's see how it compares with what she has to say to you now."

He looked at Robin, who was wearing a witch's costume. "That's some outfit, Rob."

"It was between this and being a corpse," Robin told him.

Kerry did not realize she had winced until she caught the look of understanding in Palumbo's eyes.

"I'd better be on my way," she said hurriedly.

During the twenty-minute drive to Alpine, Kerry realized her nerves were on edge. She had finally gotten Robin to talk briefly about the incident that morning. By then, Robin was trying to play the whole thing down. Kerry wanted to believe that Robin had exaggerated what had happened. She wanted to conclude that someone had stopped to check an address and then realized he was on the wrong block. But Kerry knew her daughter would not have exaggerated or imagined the incident.

. . .

It was obvious to Kerry that Dolly Bowles had been watching for her. As soon as she was parked in the driveway of the massive Tudor house, the door was yanked open.

Dolly was a small woman with thinning gray hair and a narrow, inquisitive face. She was already talking when Kerry reached her, ". . . just like your picture in *The Record*. I was so sorry I was busy baby-sitting and couldn't make it to the trial of that awful man who killed his supervisor."

She led Kerry into a cavernous foyer and indicated a small sitting room to the left. "Let's go in here. That living room is too big for my taste. I tell my daughter my voice echoes in it, but she loves it 'cause it's great for parties. Dorothy loves to throw parties. When they're home, that is. Now that Lou is retired, they never settle down; they're here and there, hither and yon. Why they need to pay a full-time housekeeper is beyond me. I say, why not have someone come in once a week? Save the money. Of course, I don't really like to be alone overnight, and I suppose that has something to do with it. On the other hand . . ."

Oh my God, Kerry thought, she's a sweet woman, but I'm just not in the mood for this. She chose a straight-backed chair, while Mrs. Bowles settled on the chintz-covered couch. "Mrs. Bowles, I don't want to take too much of your time and I have someone minding my daughter, so I can't stay too long . . ."

"You have a daughter. How nice. How old is she?"

"Ten. Mrs. Bowles, what I'd like to know—"

"You don't look old enough to have a ten-year-old daughter."

"Thank you. I can assure you I feel old enough." Kerry felt as though she had driven into a ditch and might never get out. "Mrs. Bowles, let's talk about the night Suzanne Reardon died."

Fifteen minutes later, after she had heard all about Dolly baby-sitting across the street from the Reardons, and how Michael, the little boy she was minding that night, had serious developmental problems, she managed to isolate one nugget of information.

"You say that you are positive that the car you saw parked in front of the Reardons did not belong to one of the guests at the neighbors' party. Why are you so sure of that?"

"Because I talked to those people myself. They were entertaining three other couples. They told me who the guests were. They're all from Alpine, and after Mr. Green made me feel like such a fool on the stand, I called each of them myself. And you know what? None of those guests was driving Poppa's car."

"*Poppa's car!*" Kerry exclaimed incredulously.

"That's what Michael called it. You see, he had a real problem with colors. You'd point to a car and ask him what color it was, and he wouldn't know. But no matter how many cars were around, he could pick out one that was familiar, or one that looked just like a familiar car. When he said 'Poppa's car' that night, he had to have been pointing at the black Mercedes four-door sedan. You see, he called his grandfather Poppa and loved to ride with him in his car—his black Mercedes four-door sedan. It was dark, but the torch light at the end of the Reardons' driveway was on so he could see it clearly."

"Mrs. Bowles, you testified that you had seen the car."

"Yes, although it wasn't there at seven-thirty when I got to Michael's house, and when he pointed it out it was pulling away, so I didn't get a good look at it. Still, I had an impression of a 3 and an L on the license plate." Dolly Bowles leaned forward intensely, and behind the round glasses her eyes widened. "Ms. McGrath, I tried to tell Skip Reardon's defense attorney about this. His name was Farrer—no, Farrell. He told me that hearsay evidence usually isn't admissible and, even if it were, hearsay evidence from a developmentally disabled child would only dilute my testimony that I'd seen the car. But he was wrong. I don't see why I couldn't have told the jury that Michael became all excited when he thought he had seen his grandfather's car. I think that would have helped."

Her voice lost its faint quaver. "Ms. McGrath, at a couple of minutes past nine o'clock that night, a black Mercedes four-door sedan drove away from the Reardon home. I know that for a fact. Absolutely."

43

Jonathan Hoover was not enjoying his predinner martini this evening. Usually he savored this time of day, sipping the smooth gin diluted with precisely three drops of vermouth and enhanced with two olives, sitting in his wing chair by the fire, conversing with Grace about the day.

Tonight, added to his own concerns, it was obvious that something was troubling Grace. If the pain was worse than usual he knew she would never admit it. They never discussed her health. Long ago he had learned not to ask more than a perfunctory, "How do you feel, dear?"

The answer was inevitably, "Not bad at all."

The increasing rheumatic assault on her body did not prevent Grace from dressing with her innate elegance. Nowadays she always wore long loose sleeves to cover her swollen wrists and in the evening, even when they were alone, chose flowing hostess gowns that concealed the steadily progressing deformity of her legs and feet.

Propped up as she was, in a half-lying position on the couch, the curvature in her spine was not apparent, and her luminous gray eyes were beautiful against the alabaster white of her complexion. Only her hands, the fingers gnarled and twisted, were visible indicators of her devastating illness.

Because Grace always stayed in bed till midmorning, and Jonathan was an early riser, the evening was their time to visit and gossip. Now Grace gave him a wry smile. "I feel as though I'm looking in a mirror, Jon. You're upset about something too, and I bet it's the same thing that was bothering you earlier, so let me go first. I spoke to Kerry."

Jonathan raised his eyebrows. "And?"

"I'm afraid she has no intention of letting go of the Reardon case."

"What did she tell you?"

"It's what she *didn't* tell me. She was evasive. She listened to me, then said that she had reason to believe that Dr. Smith's testimony was false. She did acknowledge that she had no concrete reason to believe that Reardon wasn't the murderer, but she felt it was her obligation to explore the possibility that there might have been a miscarriage of justice."

Jonathan's face flushed to a deep, angry red. "Grace, there's a point where Kerry's sense of justice approaches the ludicrous. Last night I was able to persuade the governor to delay submitting to the senate the names of candidates for appointment to the bench. He agreed."

"Jonathan!"

"It was the only thing I could do short of asking him to withhold Kerry's appointment for the present. I had no choice. Grace, Prescott Marshall has been an outstanding governor. You know that. Working with him, I've been able to lead the senate in getting necessary reforms into law, in revising the tax structure, in attracting business to the state, in welfare reform that doesn't mean depriving the poor while searching out the welfare cheats. I want Marshall back in four years. I'm no great fan of Frank Green, but as governor he'll be a good benchwarmer and won't undo what Marshall and I have accomplished. On the other hand, if Green fails, and if the other party gets in, then everything we've accomplished will be taken apart."

Suddenly the intensity the anger had inspired drained from his face and he looked to Grace only very tired and every minute of his sixty-two years.

"I'll invite Kerry and Robin to dinner Sunday," Grace said. "That will give you another chance to talk sense to her. I don't think anyone's future should be sacrificed for that Reardon man."

"I'm going to call her tonight," Jonathan told her.

Geoff Dorso rang the doorbell at exactly seven-thirty and once again was greeted by Robin. She was still wearing her witch's costume and makeup. Her eyebrows were thick with charcoal. Pasty white powder covered her skin except where the lacerations streaked her chin and cheek. A wig of tangled black hair flapped around her shoulders.

Geoff jumped back. "You scared me."

"Great," Robin said enthusiastically. "Thanks for being on time. I'm due at a party. It's starting right now, and there's a prize for the scariest costume. I need to be going."

"You'll win in a landslide," Geoff told her as he stepped into the foyer. Then he sniffed. "Something smells good."

"Mom's making garlic bread," Robin explained, then called, "Mom, Mr. Dorso's here."

The kitchen was at the back of the house. Geoff smiled as the door swung open and Kerry emerged, drying her hands on a towel. She was dressed in green slacks and a green cowl-neck sweater. Geoff couldn't help but notice how the overhead light accentuated the gold streaks in her hair and the spray of freckles across her nose.

She looks about twenty-three, he thought, then realized that her warm smile did not disguise the concern in her eyes.

"Geoff, good to see you. Go inside and be comfortable. I have to walk Robin down the block to a party."

"Why not let me do that?" Geoff suggested. "I've still got my coat on."

"I guess that would be okay," Kerry said slowly, assessing the situation, "but be sure to see her inside the door, won't you? I mean, don't just leave her at the driveway."

"Mom," Robin protested, "I'm not scared anymore. Honest."

"Well, I am."

What's that about? Geoff wondered. He said, "Kerry, all of my sisters are younger than I am. Until they went to college, I was forever dropping them off and picking them up, and God help me if I didn't see them safely inside wherever they were going. Get your broom, Robin. I assume you have one."

As they walked along the quiet street, Robin told him about the car that had frightened her. "Mom acts cool about everything, but I can tell she's freaking out," she confided. "She worries about me too much. I'm sort of sorry I told her about it."

Geoff stopped short and looked down at her. "Robin, listen to me. It's a lot worse *not* to tell your mother when something like that happens. Promise me you won't make that mistake."

"I won't. I already promised Mom." The exaggerated painted lips separated in a mischievous smile. "I'm real good at keeping promises except when it comes to getting up on time. I hate getting up."

"So do I," Geoff agreed fervently.

Five minutes later, when he was sitting on a counter stool in the kitchen watching Kerry make a salad, Geoff decided to try a direct approach. "Robin told me about this morning," he said. "Is there a reason to worry?"

Kerry was tearing freshly washed lettuce into the salad bowl. "One of our investigators, Joe Palumbo, talked to Robin this afternoon. He's concerned. He thinks that a car doing a reckless U-turn a few feet from where you're walking could make anybody jumpy, but Robin was so specific about the window opening and then a hand appearing with something pointing at her . . . Joe suggested that somebody might have taken her picture."

Geoff heard the tremor in Kerry's voice.

"But why?"

"I don't know. Frank Green feels that it might be connected to that case I just prosecuted. I don't agree. I could have nightmares wondering if some nut may have seen Robin and developed a fixation. That's another possibility." She began to tear the lettuce with savage force. "The point is, what can I do about it? How do I protect her?"

"It's pretty tough to carry that worry alone," Geoff said quietly.

"You mean because I'm divorced? Because there was no man here to take care of her? You've seen her face. That happened when she was with her father. Her seat belt wasn't fastened, and he's the kind of driver who floors the accelerator and then makes sudden stops. I don't care whether it's macho stuff or just the fact that Bob Kinellen is a risk taker, in his case, Robin and I are better off alone."

She ripped the final piece of lettuce, then said apologetically,

"I'm sorry. I guess you picked the wrong night for pasta in this house, Geoff. I'm not much company. But then that doesn't matter. What is important are my meetings with Dr. Smith and Dolly Bowles."

Over salad and garlic bread she told him about her encounter with Dr. Smith. "He hates Skip Reardon," she said. "It's a different kind of hatred."

Noting the look of confusion on Geoff's face, she added, "What I mean is that typically when I deal with relatives of victims, most of them despise the murderer and want him to be punished. What they're expressing is anger so entwined with grief that both emotions are flying out of them. Parents will frequently show you baby pictures and graduation pictures of the murdered daughter, then tell you the kind of girl she was and if she won a spelling bee in the eighth grade. Then they break down and cry, their grief is so overwhelming, and one of them, usually the father, will tell you he wants five minutes alone with the killer, or he'll say that he'd like to pull the switch himself. But I didn't get any of that from Smith. From him I got only hatred."

"What does that say to you?" Geoff asked.

"It says that either Skip Reardon is a lying murderer or we need to find out whether Smith's intense animosity to Skip Reardon preceded Suzanne's death. As part of the latter consideration, we also need to know exactly what Smith's relationship with Suzanne was. Don't forget, by his own testimony, he didn't lay eyes on her from the time she was an infant till she was nearly twenty. Then one day she just appeared in his office and introduced herself. From her pictures you can see she was a remarkably attractive woman."

She stood up. "Think about that while I put together the pasta. Then I want to tell you about Dolly Bowles and 'Poppa's car.'"

Geoff was almost unaware of how delicious the linguine with clam sauce tasted as he listened to Kerry's report of her visit to Dolly Bowles. "The thing is," she concluded, "from what Dolly

tells me, both our office and your people brushed aside even the possibility that little Michael might have been a very reliable witness."

"Tim Farrell interviewed Dolly Bowles himself," Geoff recalled. "I kind of remember a reference to a learning-disabled five-year-old seeing a car, but I passed over it."

"It's a long shot," Kerry said, "but Joe Palumbo, the investigator I told you about who spoke to Robin, brought the Reardon file with him this afternoon. I want to go through it to see what names might have come up—of men Suzanne was possibly getting cozy with. It shouldn't be too hard to check with the Motor Vehicle Division to see if any of those named owned a black Mercedes sedan eleven years ago. Of course, it's possible the car was registered in someone else's name, or even rented, in which case we won't get anywhere."

She looked at the clock over the kitchen stove. "Plenty of time," she said.

Geoff knew she was talking about getting Robin. "What time is the party over?"

"Nine. There usually aren't weeknight parties, but Halloween really is the kids' special night, isn't it? Now how about espresso or regular coffee? I keep meaning to buy a cappuccino machine but never seem to find the time."

"Espresso is fine. And while we're having it, I'm going to tell you about Skip Reardon and Beth Taylor."

When he finished giving her the background of Beth's relationship with Skip, Kerry said slowly, "I can see why Tim Farrell was afraid to use Taylor as a witness, but if Skip Reardon was in love with her at the time of the murder, it tends to take some of the credibility away from Dr. Smith's testimony."

"Exactly. Skip's whole attitude about seeing Suzanne arranging flowers given to her by another man can be summed up in two words: 'Good riddance.' "

The wall phone rang and Geoff looked at his watch. "You said

nine o'clock for Robin, didn't you? I'll get her while you're on the phone."

"Thanks." Kerry reached for the receiver. "Hello."

She listened, then said warmly, "Oh, Jonathan, I was going to call you."

Geoff got up, and with a "see you" motion of his hand, went into the foyer and reached in the closet for his coat.

As they walked back home, Robin said she had had a good time at the party even though she had not won first prize for her costume. "Cassie's cousin was there," she explained. "She had on a dorky skeleton outfit, but her mother had sewed soup bones all over it. I guess that made it special. Anyhow, thanks for walking me, Mr. Dorso."

"You win some, you lose some, Robin. And why don't you call me Geoff?"

The moment Kerry opened the door for them, Geoff could see that something was terribly wrong. It was an obvious effort for her to keep an attentive smile on her face as she listened to Robin's enthusiastic description of the party.

Finally Kerry said, "Okay, Robin, it's after nine and you promised . . ."

"I know. Off to bed and no dragging my heels." Robin kissed Kerry quickly. "Love you, Mom. Good night, Geoff." She bounced up the stairs.

Geoff watched as Kerry's mouth began to quiver. He took her arm, led her into the kitchen and closed the door. "What's the matter?"

She tried to keep her voice steady. "The governor was supposed to be submitting three names to the senate tomorrow for approval of judicial appointments. Mine was to be one of them. Jonathan has asked the governor to postpone the action for now, because of me."

"Senator Hoover did that to you!" Geoff exclaimed. "I thought he was your big buddy." Then he stared at her. "Wait a minute. Does this have something to do with the Reardon case and Frank Green?"

He didn't need her nod to know he was right. "Kerry, that's lousy. I'm so sorry. But you said 'postponed,' not 'withdrawn.' "

"Jonathan would never withdraw my nomination. I know that." Now Kerry's voice was becoming steadier. "But I also know that I can't expect him to go out on a limb for me. I told Jonathan about seeing Dr. Smith and Dolly Bowles today."

"What was his reaction?

"He wasn't impressed. He feels that by reopening this case I am needlessly bringing into question both the capability and the credibility of Frank Green, and that I'm leaving myself open to criticism for wasting taxpayers' money on a case that was decided ten years ago. He pointed out that five appeals courts have confirmed Reardon's guilt."

She shook her head, as though trying to clear her mind. Then she turned away from Geoff. "I'm sorry to have wasted your time this way, Geoff, but I guess I've decided that Jonathan is right. A murderer is in prison, put there by a jury of his peers, and the courts have been consistent in upholding his conviction. Why do I think I know something they don't?"

Kerry turned back and looked at him. "The killer is in prison, and I'm just going to have to let this drop," she said with as much conviction as she could muster.

Geoff's face tightened in suppressed anger and frustration. "Very well, then. Good-bye, Your Honor," he said. "Thanks for the pasta."

45

I n the laboratory of FBI headquarters in Quantico, four agents watched the computer screen freeze on the profile of the thief who had broken into the Hamilton home in Chevy Chase over the weekend.

He had pulled the stocking mask up so that he could have a better look at a figurine. At first, the image taken by the hidden camera had seemed impossibly blurry, but after some electronic enhancement, a few details of the face were visible. Probably not enough to make a real difference, thought Si Morgan, the senior agent. It's still pretty difficult to see much more than his nose and the outline of his mouth. Nonetheless, it was all they had, and it might just jog someone's memory.

"Get a couple of hundred of these run off and see that they're circulated to the families in every break-in that matches the profile of the Hamilton case. It's not much, but at least we now have a chance of getting that bastard."

Morgan's face turned grim. "And I only hope that when we get him we can match his thumbprint to the one we found the night Congressman Peale's mother lost her life because she'd canceled her plans to go away for the weekend."

46

It was still early morning as Wayne Stevens sat reading the newspaper in the family room of his comfortable Spanish-style house in Oakland, California. Retired two years from his modestly successful insurance business, he looked the part of a contented man. Even in repose, his face maintained a genial expression. Regular exercise kept his body trim. His two married daughters and their families both lived less than half an hour away. He had been married to his third wife, Catherine, for eight years now, and in that time had come to realize that his first two marriages had left much to be desired.

That was why when the phone rang he had no premonition that the caller was about to evoke unpleasant memories.

The voice had a distinct East Coast accent. "Mr. Stevens, I'm Joe Palumbo, an investigator for the Bergen County, New Jersey, prosecutor's office. Your stepdaughter was Suzanne Reardon, was she not?"

"Suzanne Reardon? I don't know anyone by that name. Wait a minute," he said. "You're not talking about Susie, are you?"

"Is that what you called Suzanne?"

"I had a stepdaughter we called Susie, but her name was Sue

Ellen, not Suzanne." Then he realized the inspector had used the past tense: "was." "Has something happened to her?"

Three thousand miles away, Joe Palumbo gripped the phone. "You don't know that Suzanne, or Susie as you call her, was murdered ten years ago?" He pushed the button that would record the conversation.

"Dear God." Wayne Stevens' voice fell to a whisper. "No, of course I didn't know it. I send a note to her every Christmas in care of her father, Dr. Charles Smith, but I've heard nothing from her in years."

"When did you last see her?"

"Eighteen years ago, shortly after my second wife, Jean, her mother, died. Susie was always a troubled, unhappy and, frankly, *difficult* girl. I was a widower when her mother and I married. I had two young daughters and I adopted Susie. Jean and I raised the three together. Then, after Jean died, Susie received the proceeds of an insurance policy and announced that she was moving to New York. She was nineteen then. A few months later I received a rather vicious note from her saying she'd always been unhappy living here and wanted nothing to do with any of us. She said that she was going to live with her real father. Well, I phoned Dr. Smith immediately, but he was extremely rude. He told me that it had been a grave mistake to allow me to adopt his daughter."

"So Suzanne, I mean Susie, never spoke to you herself?" Joe asked quickly.

"Never. There seemed to be nothing to do but let it go. I hoped in time she'd come around. What happened to her?"

"Ten years ago her husband was convicted of killing her in a jealous rage."

Images ran through Wayne Stevens' head. Susie as a whiny toddler, a plump, scowling teenager who turned to golf and tennis for recreation but seemed to take no pleasure in her own prowess in either sport. Susie listening to the jangle announcing phone calls that were never for her, glowering at her stepsisters when their dates came to pick them up, slamming doors as she stomped upstairs. "Jealous because she was involved with another man?" he asked slowly.

"Yes." Joe Palumbo heard the bewilderment in the other man's voice and knew that Kerry's instinct was right when she had asked him to delve into Suzanne's background. "Mr. Stevens, would you please describe your stepdaughter's physical appearance?"

"Sue was . . ." Stevens hesitated. "She was not a pretty girl," he said quietly.

"Do you have pictures of her you could send me?" Palumbo asked. "I mean, those that were taken closest to the time she left to come East."

"Of course. But if this happened over ten years ago, why are you bringing it up now?"

"Because one of our assistant prosecutors thinks there's more to the case than came out at the trial."

And boy, was Kerry's hunch right! Joe thought as he hung up the phone after having secured Wayne Stevens' promise to send the pictures of Susie by overnight mail.

47

K erry was barely settled in her office Wednesday morning
when her secretary told her that Frank Green wanted to
see her.

He did not waste words. "What happened, Kerry? I understand that the governor has postponed presenting the nomina-
tions for judgeship. The indication was that he was having a
problem with your inclusion. Is something wrong? Is there anything I can do?"

Well, yes, as a matter of fact there is, Frank, Kerry thought.
You can tell the governor that you welcome any inquiry that
might reveal a gross miscarriage of justice, even if you're left with
egg on your face. You could be a stand-up guy, Frank.

Instead she said, "Oh, I'm sure it will all go through soon."

"You're not on the outs with Senator Hoover, are you?"

"He's one of my closest friends."

As she turned to go, the prosecutor said, "Kerry, it stinks to
be twisting in the wind, waiting for these appointments. Hey,
I've got my own nomination coming up. Right? I get nightmares
hoping it doesn't get screwed up somewhere."

She nodded and left him.

Back in her office, she tried desperately to keep her mind on
the trial schedule. The grand jury had just indicted a suspect in a
bungled gas station holdup. The charge was attempted murder

and armed robbery. The attendant had been shot and was still in intensive care. If he didn't make it, the charge would be upgraded to murder.

Yesterday the appeals court had overturned the guilty verdict of a woman convicted of manslaughter. That had been another high-profile case, but the appeals court decision that the defense had been incompetent at least did not reflect badly on the prosecutor.

They had planned that Robin would hold the Bible when she was sworn in. Jonathan and Grace had insisted that they would buy her judicial robes, a couple of everyday ones and a special one for ceremonial occasions. Margaret kept reminding her that, as her best friend, she would be allowed to hold the robe Kerry would wear that day and assist her in putting it on. "I, Kerry McGrath, do solemnly swear that I will . . ."

Tears stung her eyes as she heard Jonathan's impatient voice again. *Kerry, five appeals courts have found Reardon guilty. What's the matter with you?* Well, he was right. Later this morning, she would call him and tell him that she had dropped the whole matter.

She became aware that someone had knocked on her door several times. Impatiently she brushed the backs of her hands across her eyes and called, "Come in."

It was Joe Palumbo. "You're one smart lady, Kerry."

"I'm not so sure. What's up?"

"You said it occurred to you to wonder if Dr. Smith ever did any work on his daughter."

"He all but denied it, Joe. I told you that."

"I know you did, and you also had me check on Suzanne's background. Well, listen to this."

With a flourish, Joe laid a tape recorder on the desk. "This is most of my call to Mr. Wayne Stevens, Suzanne Reardon's stepfather." He pressed the button.

As Kerry listened, she felt a new wave of confusion and conflicting emotions sweep over her. *Smith's a liar,* she thought as she remembered his outrage at even the suggestion that he had performed any surgical procedure on his daughter. He's a liar and he's a good actor.

When the recorded conversation was finished, Palumbo smiled in anticipation. "What next, Kerry?"

"I don't know," she said slowly.

"You don't know? Smith's lying."

"We don't know that yet. Let's wait for those pictures from Stevens before we get too excited. Lots of teenagers suddenly blossom after they get a good haircut and a makeover at a salon."

Palumbo looked at her in disbelief. "Sure they do. And pigs have wings."

Deidre Reardon had heard the discouragement in her son's voice when she spoke to him on Sunday and Tuesday, which was why she decided on Wednesday to make the long trip by bus and train and another bus to the Trenton prison to see him.

A small woman who had passed on to her son her fiery red hair, warm blue eyes and Celtic complexion, Deidre Reardon now looked every day of her age, which would soon be seventy. Her compact body hinted of frailness, and her step had lost much of its bounce. Her health had forced her to give up her job as a saleswoman at A&S, and now she supplemented her social security check by doing some clerical work at the parish office.

The money she had saved during the years when Skip was doing so well and was so generous to her was gone now, most of it spent on the court costs of the unsuccessful appeals.

She arrived at the prison in midafternoon. Because it was a weekday, they could only communicate by telephone, with a window between them. From the minute Skip was brought in and she saw the look on his face, Deidre knew that the one thing she feared had happened. Skip had given up hope.

Usually when he was very discouraged, she tried to get his mind off himself with gossip about the neighborhood and the parish, the kind of gossip that someone would enjoy who was away but expected to come home soon and wanted to be kept up on events.

Today she knew such small talk was useless. "Skip, what's the matter?" she asked.

"Mom, Geoff called last night. That prosecutor who came down to see me. She's not going to follow up. She's pretty much washed her hands of me. I made Geoff be honest and not snow me."

"What was her name, Skip?" Deidre asked, trying to keep her voice matter-of-fact. She knew her son well enough to avoid offering platitudes now.

"McGrath. Kerry McGrath. Apparently, she's going to be made a judge soon. With my luck they'll put her on the appeals court so if ever Geoff does find another reason to file an appeal, she'll be there to kick it out."

"Doesn't it take a long time for judges to be put on the appeals court?" Deidre asked.

"What does it matter? We don't have anything *but* time, do we, Mom?" Then Skip told her that he had refused Beth's call today. "Mom, Beth has to get on with her life. She never will if all her life is tied up with worrying about me."

"Skip, Beth loves you."

"Let her love someone else. I did, didn't I?"

"Oh, Skip." Deidre Reardon felt the shortness of breath that always preceded the numbness in her arm and the stabbing pain in her chest. The doctor had warned that she was going to need another bypass operation if the angioplasty next week didn't work. She hadn't told Skip about that yet. She wouldn't now either.

Deidre bit back tears as she saw the hurt in her son's eyes. He had always been such a good kid. She had never had a hint of trouble with him when he was growing up. Even as a baby, when he was tired, he hadn't gotten crabby. One of her favorite stories about him was of the day he had toddled from the living room of the apartment into the bedroom and pulled his security blanket through the bars of the crib, wrapped himself up in it and gone to sleep on the floor under the crib.

She had left him alone in the living room while she started supper, and when she couldn't find him, she had gone racing through the tiny apartment, shouting his name, terrified that somehow he had gotten out, maybe was lost. Deidre had that same feeling now. In a different way, Skip was getting lost.

Involuntarily she reached out her hand and touched the glass. She wanted to put her arms around him, that fine, good man who was her son. She wanted to tell him not to worry, that it would be all right, just as she had years ago when something had hurt him. Now she knew what she had to say.

"Skip, I don't want to hear you talk like this. You can't decide that Beth isn't going to love you anymore, because she is. And I'm going to see that Kerry McGrath woman. There has to be a reason why she came to see you in the first place. Prosecutors don't just drop in on convicted people. I'm going to find out why she took an interest in you, and why she's turning her back on you now. But you've got to cooperate; don't you dare let me down by talking like this."

Their visiting time was up much too quickly. Deidre managed

not to cry until after the guard had led Skip away. Then she dabbed her eyes fiercely. Her mouth set in a determined line, she stood up, waited for the stab of chest pain to pass and walked briskly out.

It feels like November, Barbara Tompkins thought as she walked the ten blocks from her office on Sixty-eighth Street and Madison Avenue to her apartment on Sixty-first and Third Avenue. She should have worn a heavier coat. But what did a few blocks of discomfort matter when she felt so good?

There wasn't a day that she didn't rejoice in the miracle that Dr. Smith had performed for her. It seemed impossible that less than two years ago, she had been stuck in a drudge P.R. job in Albany, assigned to getting mentions in magazines for small cosmetics clients.

Nancy Pierce had been one of the few clients she had enjoyed. Nancy always joked about being the Plain Jane with a total inferiority complex because she worked with gorgeous models. Then Nancy took an extended vacation and came back looking like a million dollars. Openly, even proudly, she told the world she had had aesthetic surgery.

"Listen," she had said. "My sister has the face of Miss America, but she's always fighting her weight. She says inside her there's a thin gal trying to fight her way out. I always said to myself that inside me there was a very pretty gal trying to fight her way out. My sister went to the Golden Door. I went to Dr. Smith."

Looking at her, at her new ease and confidence, Barbara had promised herself, "If I ever get money, I'll go to that doctor too." And then, dear old Great Aunt Betty had been gathered to her reward at age eighty-seven and left $35,000 to Barbara, with the instruction that she kick up her heels and have fun with it.

Barbara remembered that first visit to Dr. Smith. He had come into the room where she was sitting on the edge of the examining table. His manner was cold, almost frightening. "What do you want?" he had barked.

"I want to know if you can make me pretty," Barbara had told him, somewhat tentatively. Then, gathering courage, she'd corrected herself. "Very pretty."

Wordlessly, he had stood in front of her, turned a spotlight on her, held her chin in his hand, run his fingers over the contours of her face, probed her cheekbones and her forehead and studied her for several long minutes.

Then he had stepped back. "Why?"

She told him about the pretty woman struggling to get out of the shell. She told him about how she knew that she shouldn't care so much, and then burst out, "But I *do* care."

Unexpectedly he had smiled, a narrow, mirthless, but nevertheless genuine smile. "If you didn't care, I wouldn't be bothered," he had told her.

The procedure he prescribed had been incredibly involved. The operations gave her a chin and reduced her ears, and took the dark circles from under her eyes and the heavy lids from over them, so that they became wide and luminous. The surgery made her lips full and provocative and removed the acne scars from her cheeks and narrowed her nose and raised her eyebrows. There had even been a process to sculpt her body.

Then the doctor sent her to a salon to have her hair changed from mousy tan to charcoal brown, a color that enhanced the creamy complexion he had achieved through acid peeling. Another expert at the salon taught her about the subtleties of applying makeup.

Finally, the doctor told her to invest the last of her windfall in clothes and sent her with a personal shopper to the Seventh Avenue designer workrooms. Under the shopper's guidance, she accumulated the first sophisticated wardrobe she had ever owned.

Dr. Smith urged her to relocate to New York City, told her where to look for an apartment and even took personal interest by inspecting the apartment she had found. Then he insisted that she come in every three months for checkups.

It had been a dizzying year since she had moved to Manhattan and started the job at Price and Vellone. Dizzying but exciting. Barbara was having a wonderful time.

But as she walked the last block to her apartment, she glanced nervously over her shoulder. Last night, she had had dinner with some clients in The Mark Hotel. When they were leaving, she had noticed Dr. Smith seated alone at a small table off to the side.

Last week she had caught a glimpse of him in the Oak Room at the Plaza.

She had dismissed it at the time, but the night last month when she met clients at The Four Seasons, she had had the impression that someone was watching her from a car across the street when she hailed a taxi.

Barbara felt a surge of relief as the doorman greeted her and opened the door. Then once again she looked over her shoulder.

A black Mercedes was stopped in traffic directly in front of the apartment building. There was no mistaking the driver, even though his face was turned partly away as though he were looking across the street.

Dr. Smith.

"You okay, Miss Tompkins?" the doorman asked. "You look like you don't feel so great."

"No. Thank you. I'm fine." Barbara walked quickly into the foyer. As she waited for the elevator, she thought, he *is* following me. But what can I do about it?

50

Although Kerry had fixed Robin one of their favorite meals—baked chicken breasts, baked potatoes, green beans, green salad and biscuits—they ate in near silence.

From the moment Kerry arrived home and Alison, the high school baby-sitter, had whispered, "I think Robin's upset," Kerry had bided her time.

As she prepared dinner, Robin sat at the counter doing her homework. Kerry had waited for a time to talk to her, for some sign, but Robin seemed extraordinarily busy with her assignments.

Kerry even made certain to ask, "Are you sure you're finished, Rob?" before she put their dinner on the table.

After she began to eat, Robin visibly relaxed. "Did you finish your lunch today?" Kerry asked, finally breaking the silence, trying to sound casual. "You seem hungry."

"Sure, Mom. Most of it."

"I see."

Kerry thought, she is so like me. If she's hurt, she handles it herself. Such a private person.

Then Robin said, "I like Geoff. He's neat."

Geoff. Kerry dropped her eyes and concentrated on cutting chicken. She didn't want to think about his derisive, dismissive comment when he left the other night. *Good-bye, Your Honor.*

"Uh-huh," she responded, hoping that she was conveying the fact that Geoff was unimportant in their lives.

"When is he coming back?" Robin asked.

Now it was Kerry's turn to be evasive. "Oh, I don't know. He really just came because of a case he's been working on."

Robin looked troubled. "I guess I shouldn't have told Daddy about that."

"What do you mean?"

"Well, he was saying that when you're a judge, you'll probably meet a lot of judges and end up marrying one of them. I didn't mean to talk about you to him, but I said a lawyer I liked had come to the house on business the other night, and Daddy asked who it was."

"And you told him it was Geoff Dorso. There's nothing wrong with that."

"I don't know. Daddy seemed to get upset with me. We'd been having fun, then he got quiet and told me to finish my shrimp. That it was time to get home."

"Rob, Daddy doesn't care who I go out with, and certainly Geoff Dorso has no connection to him or any of his clients. Daddy is involved in a very tough case right now. Maybe you had kept his mind off it for a while, and then when dinner was almost over, he started thinking about it again."

"Do you really think so?" Robin asked hopefully as her eyes brightened.

"I really think so," Kerry said firmly. "You've seen me when I'm in a fog because I'm on a trial."

Robin began to laugh. "Oh boy, have I!"

· · ·

At nine o'clock, Kerry looked in on Robin, who was propped up in bed reading. "Lights out," she said firmly as she went over to tuck her in.

"Okay," she said reluctantly. As Robin snuggled down under the covers, she said, "Mom, I was thinking. Just because Geoff came here on business doesn't mean we can't ask him back, does it? He likes you. I can tell."

"Oh, Rob, he's just one of those guys who likes people, but certainly he's not interested in me especially."

"Cassie and Courtney saw him when he picked me up. They think he's cute."

I think he is too, Kerry thought as she turned out the light.

She went downstairs, planning to tackle the chore of balancing her checkbook. But when she got to her desk, she gazed for a long minute at the Reardon file Joe Palumbo had given her yesterday. Then she shook her head. Forget it, she told herself. Stay out of it.

But it wouldn't hurt just to take a look at it, she reasoned. She picked it up, carried it to her favorite chair, laid the file on the hassock at her feet, opened it and reached for the first batch of papers.

The record showed that the call had come in at 12:20 A.M. Skip Reardon had dialed the operator and shouted at her to connect him to the Alpine police. "My wife is dead, my wife is dead," he had repeated over and over. The police reported they had found him kneeling beside her, crying. He told the police that as soon as he came into the house he had known she was dead and had not touched her. The vase that the sweetheart roses had been in was overturned. The roses were scattered over the body.

The next morning, when his mother was with him, Skip Reardon had claimed he was sure a diamond pin was missing. He said he remembered it in particular because it was one of the pieces he had not given her, that he was certain another man must have given her. He also swore that a miniature frame with Suzanne's picture that had been in the bedroom that morning was gone.

At eleven o'clock, Kerry got to Dolly Bowles' statement. It was essentially the same story she had narrated when Kerry visited her.

Kerry's eyes narrowed when she saw that a Jason Arnott had been questioned in the course of the investigation. Skip Reardon had mentioned him to her. In his statement, Arnott described himself as an antiques expert who for a commission would accompany women to auctions at places like Sotheby's and Christie's and advise them in their efforts in bidding on certain objects.

He said that he enjoyed entertaining and that Suzanne often came to his cocktail parties and dinners, sometimes accompanied by Skip, but usually alone.

The investigator's note showed that he had checked with mutual friends of both Suzanne and Arnott, and that there was no suggestion of any romantic interest between them. In fact one friend commented that Suzanne was a natural flirt and joked about Arnott, calling him "Jason the neuter."

Nothing new here, Kerry decided when she had completed half the file. The investigation was thorough. Through the open window, the Public Service meter reader had heard Skip shouting at Suzanne at breakfast. "Boy, was that guy steaming," was his comment.

Sorry, Geoff, Kerry thought as she went to close the file. Her eyes were burning. She would skim through the rest of it tomorrow and return it. Then she glanced at the next report. It was the interview with a caddie at the Palisades Country Club, where Suzanne and Skip were members. A name caught her eye, and she picked up the next batch of papers, all thought of sleep suddenly gone.

The caddie's name was Michael Vitti, and he was a fountain of information about Suzanne Reardon. "Everybody loved to caddie for her. She was nice. She'd kid around with the caddies and gave big tips. She played with lots of the men. She was good, and I mean *good*. A lot of the wives got sore at her because the men all liked her."

Vitti had been asked if he thought Suzanne was involved with any of the men. "Oh, I don't know about that," he said. "I never saw her really alone with anyone. The foursomes always went back to the grill together, you know what I mean?"

But when pressed he said that just maybe there was something going on between Suzanne and Jimmy Weeks.

It was Jimmy Weeks' name that had jumped out at Kerry. According to the investigator's notes, Vitti's remark wasn't taken seriously because, although Weeks was known to be a ladies' man, on being questioned about Suzanne, he absolutely denied that he had ever seen her outside the club and said that he had been having a serious relationship with another woman at that time, and besides, he had an ironclad alibi for the entire night of the murder.

Then Kerry read the last of the caddie's interview. He admitted that Mr. Weeks treated all the women pretty much alike and called most of them things like Honey, Darlin' and Lovey.

The caddie was asked if Weeks had a special name for Suzanne.

The answer: "Well, a couple of times I heard him call her 'Sweetheart.' "

Kerry let the papers drop in her lap. Jimmy Weeks. Bob's client. Was that why his attitude changed so suddenly when Robin told him that Geoff Dorso had come to see her on business?

It was fairly widely known that Geoff Dorso represented Skip Reardon and had been trying doggedly, but unsuccessfully, for ten years to get a new trial for him.

Was Bob, as Jimmy Weeks' counsel, afraid of what a new trial might entail for his client?

A couple of times I heard him call her Sweetheart. The words haunted Kerry.

Deeply troubled, she closed the file and went up to bed. The caddie had not been called as a witness at the trial. Neither had Jimmy Weeks. Did the defense team ever interview the caddie? If not, they should have, she thought. Did they talk to Jason Arnott about any other men Suzanne might have seemed interested in at his parties?

I'll wait for the pictures to come in from Suzanne's stepfather, Kerry told herself. It's probably nothing, or at least nothing more than what I told Joe today. Maybe Suzanne just had a good makeover done when she came to New York. She did have money from her mother's insurance policy. And Dr. Smith did, in effect, deny that he ever did any procedure whatsoever on Suzanne.

Wait and see, she told herself. Good advice, since it was all she could do for the present anyway.

51

On Thursday morning, Kate Carpenter arrived at the office at quarter of nine. There were no procedures scheduled, and the first patient wasn't arriving until ten o'clock, so Dr. Smith had not come in yet.

The receptionist was at her desk, a worried look on her face. "Kate, Barbara Tompkins wants you to phone her, and she specifically asked that Dr. Smith not be told about her call. She says it's very important."

"She's not having any problems because of the surgery?" Kate asked, alarmed. "It's been over a year."

"She didn't say anything about that. I told her you'd be along very soon. She's waiting at home to hear from you."

Without stopping to take off her coat, Kate went into the closet-sized private office the accountant used, closed the door and dialed Tompkins' number.

With increasing dismay she listened as Barbara related her absolute conviction that Dr. Smith was obsessively following her. "I don't know what to do," she said. "I'm so grateful to him.

You know that, Mrs. Carpenter. But I'm beginning to be frightened."

"He's never approached you?"

"No."

"Then let me think about it and talk to a few people. I beg you not to discuss this with anyone else. Dr. Smith has a wonderful reputation. It would be terrible to have it destroyed."

"I'll never be able to repay Dr. Smith for what he did for me," Barbara Tompkins said quietly. "But please get back to me quickly."

52

At eleven o'clock, Grace Hoover phoned Kerry and invited her and Robin for Sunday dinner. "We haven't seen nearly enough of you two lately," Grace told her. "I do hope you can come. Celia will outdo herself, I promise."

Celia was the weekend housekeeper and a better cook than the Monday-to-Friday live-in. When she knew Robin was going to be coming, Celia made brownies and chocolate chip cookies to send home with her.

"Of course we'll come," Kerry said warmly. Sunday is such a family day, she thought as she hung up the phone. Most Sunday afternoons she tried to do something special with Robin, like going to a museum or a movie or occasionally to a Broadway show.

If only Dad had lived, she thought. He and Mother would be living nearby at least part of the time. And if only Bob Kinellen had been the man I thought he was.

Mentally she shook herself to shrug off that line of reflection. Robin and I are darn lucky to have Jonathan and Grace, she reminded herself. They'll always be there for us.

Janet, her secretary, came in and closed the door. "Kerry, did you make an appointment with a Mrs. Deidre Reardon and forget to tell me?"

"Deidre Reardon? No, I did not."

"She's in the waiting room and she says she's going to sit there until you see her. Shall I call security?"

My God, Kerry thought. Skip Reardon's mother! What does she want? "No. Tell her to come in, Janet."

Deidre Reardon got directly to the point. "I don't usually force my way into people's offices, Ms. McGrath, but this is too important. You went to the prison to see my son. You had to have had a reason for that. Something made you wonder if there had been a miscarriage of justice. I know there was. I know my son, and I know that he is innocent. But why after seeing Skip did you not want to help him? Especially in light of what's been uncovered about Dr. Smith."

"It's not that I didn't want to help him, Mrs. Reardon. It's that I *can't* help him. There's no new evidence. It's peculiar that Dr. Smith has given other women his daughter's face, but it's not illegal, and it might be simply his way of coping with bereavement."

Deidre Reardon's expression changed from anxiety to anger. "Ms. McGrath, Dr. Smith doesn't know the meaning of the word 'bereavement.' I didn't see much of him in the four years Suzanne and Skip were married. I didn't want to. There was something absolutely unhealthy about his attitude toward her. I remember one day, for example, there was a smudge on Suzanne's cheek. Dr. Smith went over to her and wiped it off. You'd have thought he was dusting a statue the way he studied her face to make sure he'd gotten it all. He was proud of her. I'll grant you that. But affection? *No*."

Geoff had talked about how unemotional Smith was on the stand, Kerry thought. But that doesn't prove anything.

"Mrs. Reardon, I do understand how you must be feeling—" she began.

"No, I'm sorry, you don't," Deidre Reardon interrupted. "My son is incapable of violence. He would no more have deliberately taken that cord from Suzanne's waist and pulled it around her neck and strangled her than you or I would have done such a thing. Think about the kind of person who could commit a crime like that. What kind of monster is he? Because that monster who could so viciously kill another human being was in Skip's house that night. Now think about Skip."

Tears welled in Deidre Reardon's eyes as she burst out, "Didn't some of his essence, his goodness, come through to you? Are you blind and deaf, Ms. McGrath? Does my son look or sound like a murderer to you?"

"Mrs. Reardon, I looked into this case only because of my concern over Dr. Smith's obsession with his daughter's face, not because I thought your son was innocent. That was for the courts to decide, and they have. He has had a number of appeals. There is nothing I can do."

"Ms. McGrath, I think you have a daughter, don't you?"

"Yes, I do."

"Then try to visualize her caged for ten years, facing twenty years more in that cage for a crime she didn't commit. Do you think your daughter would be capable of murder someday?"

"No, I do not."

"Neither is my son. Please, Ms. McGrath, you are in a position to help Skip. Don't abandon him. I don't know why Dr. Smith lied about Skip, but I think I've come to understand. He was jealous of him because Skip was married to Suzanne, with all that implies. Think about that."

"Mrs. Reardon, as a mother I understand how heartbroken

you are," Kerry said gently as she looked into the worn and anxious face.

Deidre Reardon got up. "I can see that you're dismissing everything I'm telling you, Ms. McGrath. Geoff said that you're going to become a judge. God help the people who stand before you pleading for justice."

Then as Kerry watched, the woman's complexion became ghastly gray.

"Mrs. Reardon, what is it?" she cried.

With shaking hands, the woman opened her purse, took out a small vial and shook a pill into her palm. She slipped it under her tongue, turned and silently left the office.

For long minutes Kerry sat staring at the closed door. Then she reached for a sheet of paper. On it, she wrote:

1. Did Doctor Smith lie about operating on Suzanne?
2. Did little Michael see a black, four-door Mercedes sedan in front of the Reardons' house when Dolly Bowles was baby-sitting him that night? What about the partial license-plate numbers Dolly claims she saw?
3. Was Jimmy Weeks involved with Suzanne, and, if so, does Bob know anything about it, and is he afraid of having it come out?

She studied the list as Deidre Reardon's honest, distressed face loomed accusingly in her mind.

53

Geoff Dorso had been trying a case in the courthouse in Newark. At the last minute he had gotten a plea bargain for his client, an eighteen-year-old kid who had been joyriding with friends in his father's car when he had crashed into a pickup truck whose driver had sustained a broken arm and leg.

But there had been no alcohol involved, and the boy was a good kid and genuinely contrite. Under the plea bargain he got a two-year suspension of his driver's license and was ordered to do one hundred hours of community service. Geoff was pleased— sending him to jail instead of college would have been a serious mistake.

Now, on Thursday afternoon, Geoff had the unusual luxury of unscheduled time, and he decided to drop in on the Jimmy Weeks trial. He wanted to hear the opening arguments. Also, he admitted to himself, he was anxious to see Bob Kinellen in action.

He took a seat in the back of the courtroom. There were plenty of media representatives present, he noticed. Jimmy Weeks had managed to avoid indictment so many times that they had taken to calling him "Teflon Jimmy," a takeoff on the Mafia mobster who had been known as "The Teflon Don," now in prison for life.

Kinellen was just starting his opening statement. He's smooth, Geoff thought. He knows how to play to the jury, knows when to sound indignant, then outraged, knows how to ridicule the charges. He is also picture-perfect in appearance and presentation, Geoff thought, trying to imagine Kerry married to this guy. Somehow he couldn't see it. Or maybe he didn't want to see it, he admitted to himself. At least, he thought, taking some comfort, she certainly didn't seem to be hung up on Kinellen.

But then, why should that matter? he asked himself, as the judge declared a recess.

In the corridor he was approached by Nick Klein, a reporter for the *Star-Ledger*. They exchanged greetings, then Geoff commented, "A lot of you guys around, aren't there?"

"Fireworks expected," Nick told him. "I have a source in the attorney general's office. Barney Haskell is trying to make a deal. What they're offering him isn't good enough. Now he's hinting he can tie Jimmy to a murder that someone else is serving time for."

"I sure wish I had a witness like that for one of my clients," Geoff commented.

54

At four o'clock, Joe Palumbo received delivery of an Express Mail package with the return address of Wayne Stevens in Oakland, California. He immediately slit it open and eagerly reached inside for the two stacks of snapshots held together with rubber bands. A note was clipped to one of them.

It read:

Dear Mr. Palumbo,

The full impact of Susie's death hit me only after I began putting these photos together for you. I am so sorry. Susie was not an easy child to raise. I think these pictures tell the story. My daughters were very attractive from the time they were infants. Susie was not. As the girls grew up, that led to intense jealousy and unhappiness on Susie's part.

Susie's mother, my wife, had great difficulty watching her stepdaughters enjoy their teen years while her own child was so desperately insecure and basically friendless. I'm afraid the situation caused a great deal of friction in our home. I think I always entertained the hope that a mature and well-adjusted Susie would show up at the door one day and have a wonderful reunion with us. She had many gifts that she did not appreciate.

But for now, I hope these pictures will help.

> Sincerely,
> Wayne Stevens

Twenty minutes later, Joe went into Kerry's office. He dropped the snapshots on her desk. "Just in case you think Susie—sorry, I mean Suzanne—became a beauty because of a new hairdo," he commented.

At five o'clock, Kerry phoned Dr. Smith's office. He had already left for the day. Anticipating that, she next asked, "Is Mrs. Carpenter available?"

When Kate Carpenter came to the phone, Kerry said, "Mrs. Carpenter, how long have you been with Dr. Smith?"

"Four years, Ms. McGrath. Why are you asking?"

"Well, from something you said, I had an idea that you had been with him longer than that."

"No."

"Because I wanted to know if you were there when Dr. Smith either operated on his daughter, Suzanne, or had a colleague operate on her. I can tell you what she looked like. In your office I saw two patients and asked their names. Barbara Tompkins and Pamela Worth are both dead ringers for Dr. Smith's daughter, at least as she looked after extensive plastic surgery, not as she was born."

She heard the woman gasp. "I didn't know Dr. Smith had a daughter," Mrs. Carpenter said.

"She died nearly eleven years ago, murdered, as the jury decided, by her husband. He is still in prison and continues to protest his innocence. Dr. Smith was the principal witness against him."

"Ms. McGrath," Mrs. Carpenter said, "I feel terribly disloyal to the doctor, but I think it's very important that you speak to Barbara Tompkins immediately. Let me give you her number." Then the nurse explained about the frightened woman's call.

"Dr. Smith is stalking Barbara Tompkins!" Kerry said, as her mind raced with the possibilities of what such an action might mean.

"Well, following her, anyhow," Mrs. Carpenter said defensively. "I have both her numbers, home and office."

Kerry took them. "Mrs. Carpenter, I must talk to Dr. Smith and I doubt very much that he will agree to see me. Is he going to be in tomorrow?"

"Yes, but he has a very full schedule. He won't be done until sometime after four o'clock."

"I'll be there then, but don't tell him I'm coming." A question occurred to Kerry. "Does Dr. Smith own a car?"

"Oh, yes. His home is in Washington Mews. He lives in a converted carriage house and it has a garage, so it's easy for him to keep one."

"What kind of car does he drive?"

"The same one he's always driven. A four-door Mercedes sedan."

Kerry gripped the phone. "What color is it?"

"Black."

"You say 'always driven.' You mean he *always* selects a black Mercedes sedan?"

"I mean he drives the same one he's driven for at least twelve years. I know, because I've heard him talking about it to one of his patients who happens to be a Mercedes executive."

"Thank you, Mrs. Carpenter." As Kerry returned the receiver to its cradle, Joe Palumbo reappeared. "Hey, Kerry, was Skip Reardon's mother in here to see you?"

"Yes."

"Our Leader saw and recognized her. He was rushing out to a meeting with the governor. He wants to know what the hell she was doing in here asking for you."

55

When Geoff Dorso got home on Thursday night, he stood at the window of his condominium and stared at the New York skyline. All day the memory of how he had sarcastically called Kerry "Your Honor" had been plaguing him, but he resolutely had pushed it out of his mind. Alone now, and at the end of his day, he had to face it.

What a hell of a nerve I had, he thought. Kerry was decent

enough to call me and ask to read the transcript. She was decent enough to talk to Dr. Smith and Dolly Bowles. She made the trek to Trenton to meet Skip. Why shouldn't she worry about losing her judgeship, especially if she honestly doesn't believe that Skip is innocent?

I had no right to speak to her that way, and I owe her an apology, he thought, although I wouldn't blame her if she hung up on me. Face it, he told himself. You were convinced that the more she looked into the Sweetheart Murder Case, the more she would believe that Skip was innocent. But why should he be so sure? She certainly has the right to agree with the jury and with the appeals court, and it was a cheap shot to insinuate that she was being self-serving.

He shoved his hands in his pockets. It was November 2. In three weeks it would be Thanksgiving. Another Thanksgiving in prison for Skip. And in that time Mrs. Reardon would be going in for another angioplasty. Ten years of waiting for a miracle had taken its toll on her.

One thing, however, had come out of all this, he reminded himself. Kerry might not believe in Skip's innocence, but she had opened two lines of inquiry that Geoff would follow up on. Dolly Bowles' story of "Poppa's car," a black four-door Mercedes, was one, and the other was Dr. Smith's bizarre need to duplicate Suzanne's face in other women. At least they both were new angles on what had become a very familiar story.

The ringing of the phone interrupted his thoughts. He was tempted not to answer it, but years of listening to his mother jokingly say, "How can you not answer the phone, Geoff? For all you know it's news about a pot of gold," made him reach for it.

It was Deidre Reardon calling to tell him about her visit with Skip, and then with Kerry McGrath.

"Deidre, you didn't say that to Kerry?" Geoff asked. He made no effort to conceal how upset he was with what she had done.

"Yes, I did. And I'm not sorry," Mrs. Reardon told him.

"Geoff, the only thing that's keeping Skip going is hope. That woman singlehandedly put out that hope."

"Deidre, thanks to Kerry I have some new angles that I'm going to pursue. They could be very important."

"She went down to see my son, looked into his face, questioned him and decided he was a killer," Mrs. Reardon said. "I'm sorry, Geoff. I guess I'm getting old and tired and bitter. I don't regret a word of what I said to Kerry McGrath." She hung up without saying good-bye.

Geoff took a deep breath and dialed Kerry's number.

When Kerry got home and the sitter had left, Robin looked at her critically. "You look bushed, Mom."

"I am bushed, kiddo."

"Tough day?"

"You could call it that."

"Mr. Green on your back?"

"He will be. But let's not talk about it. I think I'd rather forget it for the moment. How was your day?"

"Fine. I think Andrew likes me."

"Really!" Kerry knew that Andrew was considered the coolest boy in the fifth grade. "How do you know that?"

"He told Tommy that even with my face banged up, I'm better looking than most of the dorks in our class."

Kerry grinned. "Now that's what I call a compliment."

"That's what I thought. What are we having for dinner?"

"I stopped at the supermarket. How does a cheeseburger sound?"

"Perfect."

"No, it's not, but I try. Oh well, I guess you'll never have much reason to brag about your mother's home cooking, Rob."

The phone rang and Robin grabbed it. It was for her. She tossed the receiver to Kerry. "Hang up in a minute, okay? I'll take it upstairs. It's Cassie."

When she heard Robin's exuberant "I'm on," Kerry replaced the receiver, carried the mail into the kitchen, laid it on the counter and began to sort through it. A plain white envelope with her name and address in block printing caught her eye. She slit it open, pulled out a snapshot, looked at it and went cold.

It was a color Polaroid of Robin coming down the walk outside their house. Her arms were full of books. She was dressed in the dark blue slacks she had worn on Tuesday, the day she had been frightened by the car that she thought was going to hit her.

Kerry's lips felt rubbery. She bent over slightly as though reeling from a kick in the stomach. Her breath came in short, fast gasps. Who did this? Who would take Robin's picture, drive a car at her, then mail the picture to me, she wondered, her thoughts dazed and confused.

She heard Robin clattering down the stairs. Quickly she shoved the picture in her pocket. "Mom, Cassie reminded me that I'm supposed to be watching the Discovery Channel now. The program is about what we're studying in science. That doesn't count as entertainment, does it?"

"No, of course not. Go ahead."

The phone rang again as Kerry sank into a chair. It was Geoff Dorso. She cut off his apologies. "Geoff, I just opened the mail." She told him about the picture. "Robin was right," she half whispered. "There *was* someone watching her from that car. My God, suppose he had pulled her into it. She'd have disappeared, just like those kids in upstate New York a couple of years ago. Oh my God."

Geoff heard the fear and despair in her voice. "Kerry, don't say anything else. Don't let Robin see that picture or realize that you're upset. I'm on my way. I'll be there in half an hour."

56

D r. Smith had sensed something amiss in Kate Carpenter's attitude toward him all day. Several times he had caught her staring at him with a questioning look. Why? he wondered.

As he sat in his library that evening, in his usual chair, sipping his usual after-office cocktail, he pondered the possible reasons for her odd behavior. He was sure Carpenter had detected the slight tremor in his hand when he performed the rhinoplasty the other day, but that wouldn't explain the looks she had given him. Whatever was on her mind now was something more troubling, of that he was certain.

It had been a terrible mistake to follow Barbara Tompkins last night. When his car was caught in traffic in front of her apartment building, he had turned away as much as possible, but even so, he thought she might have seen him.

On the other hand, midtown Manhattan was a place where people did frequently catch a glimpse of people they knew. So his being there really wasn't so unusual.

But a quick, casual glimpse wasn't enough. He wanted to see Barbara again. Really see her. Talk to her. She wasn't due for a checkup for another two months. He had to see her before then. He couldn't wait that long to watch the way her eyes, now so luminous without the heavy lids that had concealed their beauty, smiled at him across the table.

She wasn't Suzanne. No one could be. But like Suzanne, the more Barbara became accustomed to her beauty, the more her personality enhanced it. He recalled the sullen, plain creature who had first appeared in his office; within a year of the operation Suzanne had capped the transformation with her total change of personality.

Smith smiled faintly, remembering Suzanne's provocative body language, the subtle moves that made every man turn to look at her. Then she had begun to tilt her head just a little, so that she gave whomever she was talking with the sense of being the only person in the universe.

She had even lowered the tone of her voice until it had a husky, intimate quality. Teasingly she would run a fingertip over the hand of the man—and it was always a man—who was chatting with her.

When he had commented on the personality transformation she had undergone, she had said, "I had two good teachers, my stepsisters. We reversed the fairy tale. They were the beauties and I was ugly Cinderella. Only instead of a fairy godmother, I have you."

Toward the end, however, his Pygmalion fantasy had begun to turn into a nightmare. The respect and the affection she had seemed to have for him had begun to fade. She seemed no longer willing to listen to his counsel. Toward the end she had gone beyond simple flirting. How many times had he warned her that she was playing with fire, that Skip Reardon would be capable of murder if he found out the way she was carrying on?

Any husband of a woman that desirable would be capable of murder, Dr. Smith thought.

With a jolt he looked down angrily at his empty glass. Now there wouldn't be another chance to reach the perfection he had achieved in Suzanne. He would have to give up surgery before a

disaster occurred. It was too late. He knew he was in the beginning stages of Parkinson's.

If Barbara wasn't Suzanne, she was of all his living patients the
most striking example of his genius. He reached for the phone.

Surely that wasn't stress in her voice, he thought, when she
picked up the receiver and said hello.

"Barbara, my dear, is anything wrong? This is Dr. Smith."

Her gasp was audible, but then she said quickly, "Oh, no, of
course not. How are you, Doctor?"

"I'm fine but I think you might be able to do me a favor. I'm
stopping in at Lenox Hill Hospital for a moment to see an old
friend who is terminal, and I know I'll be feeling a bit down.
Would you have mercy on me and join me for dinner? I could
stop by for you at about seven-thirty."

"I, I don't know . . ."

"Please, Barbara." He tried to sound playful. "You did say
that you owed me your new life. Why not spare me two hours of
it?"

"Of course."

"Wonderful. Seven-thirty then."

"All right, Doctor."

When Smith hung up, he raised his eyebrows. Was that a
note of resignation in Barbara's voice? he wondered. She almost
sounded as though he had *forced* her into meeting him.

If so, it was one more way in which she was beginning to
resemble Suzanne.

57

Jason Arnott could not shake the feeling that something was wrong. He had spent the day in New York with fifty-two-year-old Vera Shelby Todd, trailing after her as she took him on her endless hunt for Persian carpets.

Vera had phoned him that morning and asked if he could be available for the day. A Rhode Island Shelby, she lived in one of the handsome manor houses in Tuxedo Park and was used to getting her way. After her first husband died, she had married Stuart Todd but decided to keep the Tuxedo Park place. Now, using Todd's seemingly unlimited checkbook, Vera frequently availed herself of Jason's infallible eye for rare finds and bargains.

Jason had first met Vera not in New Jersey, but at a gala the Shelbys gave in Newport. Her cousins had introduced them, and when Vera realized how relatively close he lived to her Tuxedo Park home, she had begun inviting him to her parties and eagerly accepting invitations to his gatherings as well.

It always amused Jason that Vera had told him every detail of the police investigation into the Newport robbery he had committed years ago.

"My cousin Judith was so upset," she had confided. "She couldn't understand why someone would take the Picasso and the Gainsborough and pass up the Van Eyck. So she brought in some art expert, and he said that she had a discriminating crimi-nal: The Van Eyck is a fake. Judith was furious, but for the rest of us who had had to listen to her bragging about her peerless knowledge of the great masters, it's become a family joke."

Today, after having exhaustively examined ludicrously expen-sive rugs ranging from Turkomans to Safavids, with Vera finding none of them to be exactly what she had in mind, Jason was wild to get home and away from her.

But first, at her insistence they had a late lunch at The Four Seasons, and that pleasant interlude perked Jason up consider-ably. At least until, as she finished her espresso, Vera had said, "Oh, did I forget to tell you? You remember how five years ago my cousin Judith's place in Rhode Island was burglarized?"

Jason had pursed his lips. "Yes, of course I do. Terrible experi-ence."

Vera nodded. "I should say. But yesterday Judith got a photo-graph from the FBI. There was a recent burglary in Chevy Chase, and a hidden camera caught the robber. The FBI thinks it may be the same person who broke into Judith's house and dozens of others."

Jason had felt every nerve in his body tingle. He had only met Judith Shelby a few times and hadn't seen her at all in almost five years. Obviously she hadn't recognized him. Yet.

"Was it a clear picture?" he asked casually.

Vera laughed. "No, not at all. I mean from what Judith says, it's in profile and the lighting is bad and a stocking mask was pushed up on the guy's forehead but was still covering his head. She said she could just about make out something of the nose and mouth. She threw it out."

Jason stifled a spontaneous sigh of relief, although he knew he had nothing to celebrate. If the photo went out to the Shelbys, it probably also went out to dozens of others whose homes he had broken into.

"But I think Judith is finally over her Van Eyck incident," Vera continued. "According to the information with the photograph, that man is considered dangerous. He's wanted for questioning in the murder of Congressman Peale's mother. She apparently stumbled in on him during a robbery at her house. Judith almost went home early the night her place was burglarized. Just think what might have happened if she'd found him there."

Nervously, Jason pursed his lips. They had tied him to the Peale death!

When they left The Four Seasons, they shared a taxi to the garage on West Fifty-seventh Street where both had parked. After an effusive good-bye and Vera's strident promise, "We'll just keep looking. The perfect rug for me is out there somewhere," Jason was at last on his way home to Alpine.

How indistinct was the picture the hidden camera had taken of him? he wondered as he drove in the steadily moving afternoon traffic up the Henry Hudson Parkway. Would someone look at it and find that it reminded him, or her, of Jason Arnott?

Should he cut and run? he asked himself as he crossed the George Washington Bridge and turned onto the Palisades Parkway. No one knew about the place in the Catskills. He owned it under an assumed name. Under other alternate identities, he had plenty of money in negotiable securities. He even had a fake passport. Maybe he should leave the country immediately.

On the other hand, if the picture was as indistinguishable as Judith Shelby found it, even if some people saw a resemblance to him, they would find it patently absurd to tie him to a theft.

By the time Jason exited onto the road into Alpine, he had made up his mind. With the exception of this photograph, he was almost sure he had left no tracks, no fingerprints. He had been extremely careful, and his caution had paid off. He simply couldn't give up his wonderful lifestyle just because of what might happen. He had never been a fearful man. If he had been, he certainly wouldn't have lived this life for so many years.

No, he would not panic. He would just sit tight. But no more jobs for a long time, he promised himself. He didn't need the money, and this was a warning.

He got home at quarter of four and went through the mail. One envelope caught his eye and he slit it open, pulled out the contents—a single sheet of paper—studied it, and burst out laughing.

Surely no one would link him to that vaguely comical figure with the stocking mask pushed up and the grainy caricature of a profile literally inches away from the copy of the Rodin figurine.

"Vive le junk," Jason exclaimed. He settled in the den for a nap. Vera's constant stream of talk had exhausted him. When he awoke, it was just time for the six o'clock news. He reached for the remote control and turned on the set.

The lead story was that Jimmy Weeks' codefendant, Barney Haskell, was rumored to be cutting a deal with the attorney general.

Nothing like the deal I could cut, Jason thought. It was a comforting reminder. But of course it would never happen.

Robin turned off the science program just as the doorbell rang. She was delighted to hear Geoff Dorso's voice in the foyer and came running out to greet him. She could see that both his face and her mother's were serious. Maybe they had a fight, she thought, and want to make up.

Throughout the meal, Robin noticed that her mother was unusually quiet, while Geoff was funny, telling stories about his
sisters.

Geoff is so nice, Robin thought. He reminded her of Jimmy
Stewart in that movie she watched with her mother every Christmas, *It's a Wonderful Life*. He had the same sort of shy, warm
smile and hesitant voice, and the kind of hair that looked as
though it wouldn't ever really stay in place.

But Robin noticed that her mother seemed to be only half
listening to Geoff's stories. It was obvious something was up
between them and that they needed to talk—without her in the
room. So she decided to make the big sacrifice and work on her
science project upstairs in her room.

After she had helped clear the table, she announced her plans
and caught the look of relief in her mother's eyes. She does want
to talk to Geoff alone, Robin thought happily. Maybe this is a
good sign.

Geoff listened at the bottom of the stairs. When he heard the
click of Robin's bedroom door closing, he went back into the
kitchen. "Let's see the picture."

Kerry reached into her pocket, drew it out and handed it to
him.

Geoff studied it carefully. "It looks to me as though Robin had
it straight when she told what had happened," he said. "That car
must have been parked directly across the street. Someone caught
her coming head-on from the house."

"Then she was right about the car racing toward her," Kerry
said. "Suppose it hadn't swerved into a U-turn? But Geoff,
why?"

"I don't know, Kerry. But I do know that this has to be treated
seriously. What are you thinking of doing about it?"

"Showing this to Frank Green in the morning. Getting a check
to see if any sex offenders have moved into the area. Driving Robin to school on my way to work. Not letting her walk
home with the other kids but having the sitter pick her up.

Notifying the school so that they're aware that someone may be after her."

"What about telling Robin?"

"I'm not sure. Not yet anyhow."

"Did you let Bob Kinellen know yet?"

"Good Lord, it never occurred to me. Of course Bob has to know about this."

"I'd want to know if it were my child," Geoff agreed. "Look, why don't you give him a call and let me pour us another coffee."

Bob was not at home. Alice was coldly civil to Kerry. "He's still at the office," she said. "He practically lives there these days. Is there a message I can give him?"

Only that his oldest child is in danger, Kerry thought, and she doesn't have the advantage of a live-in couple to be there to protect her when her mother is working. "I'll call Bob at the office. Good-bye, Alice."

Bob Kinellen picked up the phone on the first ring. He paled as he listened to Kerry's recounting of what had happened to Robin. He had no doubt who had taken the picture. It had Jimmy Weeks' signature all over it. That was the way he worked. Start a war of nerves, then step it up. Next week there would be another picture, taken from long range. Never a threat. No notes. Just a picture. A get-the-message-or-else situation.

It wasn't an effort for Kinellen to sound concerned and to agree with Kerry that it would be better if Robin were driven to and from school for a while.

When he hung up, he slammed his fist on the desk. Jimmy was spinning out of control. They both knew that it was all over if Haskell completed his deal with the U.S. attorney.

Weeks figured that Kerry would probably call me about the picture, Bob thought. It's his way of telling me to warn her away from the Reardon case. And it's his way of telling me I'd better find a way to get him off on this tax evasion charge or else. But what Weeks doesn't know, he told himself, is that Kerry doesn't get scared off. In fact, if she perceived that picture as a warning to her, it would be like waving a red flag in front of a bull.

But Kerry doesn't understand that when Jimmy Weeks turns on someone, it's all over for that person, he thought.

Bob's mind jumped back to the day nearly eleven years ago when Kerry, three months pregnant, had looked at him with eyes that were both astonished and furious. "You're quitting the prosecutor's office to go with that law firm? Are you crazy? All their clients have one foot in jail. And the other foot should be there," she'd said.

They had had a heated argument that ended with Kerry's contemptuous warning, "Just remember this, Bob. There's an old saying: Lie down with dogs and you'll get up with fleas."

D r. Smith took Barbara Tompkins to Le Cirque, a very chic, very expensive restaurant in midtown Manhattan. "Some women enjoy quiet little out-of-the-way places, but I suspect you enjoy the high-profile spots where one can see and be seen," he said to the beautiful young woman.

He had picked her up at her apartment and did not miss the fact that she had been ready to leave immediately. Her coat was on a chair in the small foyer, her purse on the table beside it. She did not offer him an aperitif.

She doesn't want to be alone with me, he had thought.

But at the restaurant, with so many people around them and the attentive maître d' hovering nearby, Barbara visibly relaxed. "It's a lot different from Albany," she said. "I'm still like a kid having a daily birthday."

He was stunned for a moment by her words. So similar to Suzanne, who had compared herself to a kid with an ever-present Christmas tree and gifts always waiting to be opened. But from being an enchanted child, Suzanne had changed into an ungrateful adult. I asked so little of her, he thought. Shouldn't an artist be allowed to take pleasure in his creation? Why should the creation be wasted among leering dregs of humanity while the artist suffers for a glimpse of it?

Warmth filled him as he noticed that in this room filled with attractive, elegant women, sidelong glances rested on Barbara. He pointed that out to her.

She shook her head slightly as though dismissing the suggestion.

"It's true," Smith persisted. His eyes became cold. "Don't take it for granted, Suzanne. That would be insulting to me."

It was only later, after the quiet meal was over and he had seen her back to her apartment, that he asked himself if he had called her Suzanne. And if so, how many times had he slipped?

He sighed and leaned back, closing his eyes. As the cab jostled downtown, Charles Smith reflected how easy it had been to drive past Suzanne's house when he was starved for a glimpse of her. When she wasn't out playing golf, she invariably sat in front of the television and never bothered to draw the drapes over the large picture window in her recreation room.

He would see her curled up in her favorite chair, or sometimes he would be forced to witness her sitting side by side on the couch with Skip Reardon, shoulders touching, legs stretched out on the cocktail table, in the casual intimacy he could not share.

Barbara wasn't married. From what he could tell there wasn't anyone special in her life. Tonight he had asked her to call him

Charles. He thought about the bracelet Suzanne had been wearing when she died. Should he give it to Barbara? Would it endear him to her?

He had given Suzanne several pieces of jewelry. Fine jewelry. But then she had started accepting other pieces from other men, and demanding that he lie for her.

Smith felt the glow from being with Barbara ooze away. A moment later he realized that for the second time the cabbie's impatient voice was saying, "Hey, mister, you asleep? You're home."

60

Geoff did not stay long after Kerry had called Kinellen. "Bob agrees with me," she told him as she sipped the coffee.

"No other suggestions?"

"No, of course not. Sort of his usual, 'You handle it, Kerry. Anything you decide is fine.' "

She put down the cup. "I'm not being fair. Bob honestly did seem concerned, and I don't know what else he could suggest."

They were sitting in the kitchen. She had turned off the overhead light, thinking they would carry their coffee into the living room. Now the only illumination in the room came from the dim light in a wall fixture.

Geoff studied the grave face across the table from him, aware of the hint of sadness in Kerry's hazel eyes, the determination in the set of her generous mouth and finely sculpted chin, the vulnerability, in her overall posture. He wanted to put his arms around her, to tell her to lean on him.

But he knew she didn't want that. Kerry McGrath did not expect or want to lean on anyone. He tried again to apologize for his dismissive remark to her the other night, suggesting that she was being self-serving, and for Deidre Reardon's intrusive visit to her office. "I had a hell of a nerve," he said. "I know that if you believed in your heart that Skip Reardon was innocent, you of all people would not hesitate in trying to help him. You're a stand-up guy, McGrath."

Am I? Kerry wondered. It was not the moment to share with Geoff the information she had found in the prosecutor's file about Jimmy Weeks. She would tell him, but first she wanted to see Dr. Smith again. He had angrily denied that he had touched Suzanne surgically, but he had never said that he hadn't sent her to someone else. That meant that technically he wasn't a liar.

As Geoff left a few minutes later, they stood for a moment in the foyer. "I like being with you," he told her, "and that has nothing to do with the Reardon case. How about our going out to dinner on Saturday night and bringing Robin with us?"

"She'd like that."

As Geoff opened the door he leaned down and brushed her cheek with his lips. "I know it's unnecessary to tell you to double lock the door and to turn on the alarm, but I will suggest you don't do any heavy thinking about that picture after you go to bed."

When he was gone, Kerry went upstairs to check on Robin. She was working on her science report and did not hear her mother come in. From the doorway Kerry studied her child. Robin's back was to her, her long dark brown hair spilling over her shoulders, her head bent in concentration, her legs wrapped around the rungs of the chair.

She is the innocent victim of whoever took that picture, Kerry thought. Robin is like me. Independent. She's going to hate having to be driven to and picked up from school, hate not being able to walk over to Cassie's by herself.

And then in her mind she heard again Deidre Reardon's pleading voice begging her to ask herself how she would like to see her child caged for ten years for a crime she didn't commit.

61

The plea bargaining was not going well for Barney Haskell. At 7:00 A.M. on Friday morning he met attorney Mark Young in his handsome law office in Summit, half an hour and a world away from the federal courthouse in downtown Newark.

Young, head of Barney's defense team, was about the same age he was, fifty-five, but there the resemblance ended, Barney thought sourly. Young was smoothly elegant even at this early hour, dressed in his lawyer's pin-striped suit that seemed to fit like a second skin. But Barney knew that when the jacket came off, those impressive shoulders disappeared. Recently the *Star-Ledger* had done a write-up on the high-profile lawyer, including the fact that he wore one-thousand-dollar suits.

Barney bought his suits off the rack. Jimmy Weeks had never paid him enough to allow him to do otherwise. Now he was facing years in prison if he stuck with Jimmy. So far the Feds were hanging tough. They would only talk reduced sentence, not a free ride, if he handed Jimmy over to them. They thought they could convict Weeks without Barney.

Maybe. But maybe not, Barney thought. He figured they were bluffing. He had seen Jimmy's lawyers get him off before. Kinellen and Bartlett were good, and they had always managed to get him through those past investigations without any real damage.

This time, though, judging from the U.S. attorney's opening statement, the Feds had plenty of hard evidence. Still, they had to be scared that Jimmy would pull another rabbit out of his hat.

Barney rubbed his hand over his fleshy cheek. He knew he had the innocent look of a dumb bank clerk, an aspect that had always been helpful. People tended not to notice or remember him. Even the guys closest to Weeks never paid much attention to him. They thought of him as a gofer. None of them had realized he was the one who converted the under-the-table cash into investments and took care of bank accounts all over the world.

"We can get you into the witness protection program," Young was saying. "But only after you've served a minimum of five years."

"Too much," Barney grunted.

"Look, you've been hinting you can tie Jimmy to a murder," Young said as he examined a ragged edge on his thumbnail. "Barney, I've milked that as far as I can. You've got to either put up or shut up. They'd love to hang a murder on Weeks. That way they'll never have to deal with him again. If he's in for life, his organization probably would collapse. That's what they're gunning for."

"I can tie him to one. Then they'll have to prove he did it. Isn't there talk that the U.S. attorney on this case is thinking about running for governor against Frank Green?"

"If each gets his party's nomination," Young commented as he reached in his desk drawer for a nail file. "Barney, I'm afraid you'll have to stop talking in circles. You'd better trust me with whatever it is you're hinting about. Otherwise I won't be able to help you make an intelligent choice."

A frown momentarily crossed Barney's cherubic face. Then his forehead cleared and he said, "All right. I'll tell you. Remember the Sweetheart Murder Case, the one involving that sexy young wife who was found dead with roses scattered all over her? It was ten years ago, but it was the case that Frank Green made his name on."

Young nodded. "I remember. He got a conviction on the husband. Actually it wasn't that hard, but the case got a lot of publicity and sold a lot of newspapers." His eyes narrowed. "What about it? You're not saying Weeks was connected to that case, are you?"

"You remember how the husband claimed he didn't give his wife those roses, that they must have been sent by some man she was involved with?" At Young's nod, Haskell continued, "Jimmy Weeks sent those roses to Suzanne Reardon. I should know. I delivered them to her house at twenty of six the night she died. There was a card with them that he wrote himself. I'll show you what was on it. Give me a piece of paper."

Young shoved the telephone message pad at him. Barney reached for his pen. A moment later he handed back the pad. "Jimmy called Suzanne 'Sweetheart,' " he explained. "He had made a date with her for that night. He filled out the card like this."

Young examined the paper Barney pushed back to him. It held six notes of music in the key of C, with five words written underneath: "I'm in love with you." It was signed "J."

Young hummed the notes, then looked at Jimmy. "The opening phrase of the song 'Let Me Call You Sweetheart,' " he said.

"Uh-huh. Followed by the rest of the first line of the song, 'I'm in love with you.' "

"Where is this card?"

"That's the point. Nobody mentioned it being in the house

when the body was found. And the roses were scattered over her body. I only delivered them, then I kept going. I was on my way to Pennsylvania for Jimmy. But afterwards I heard the others talking. Jimmy was crazy about that woman, and it drove him nuts that she was always playing up to other guys. When he sent her those flowers he had already given her an ultimatum that she had to get a divorce—and stay away from other men."

"What was her reaction?"

"Oh, she liked to make him jealous. It seemed to make her feel good. I know one of our guys tried to warn her that Jimmy could be dangerous, but she just laughed. My guess is that that night she went too far. Throwing those roses over her body is just the kind of thing Jimmy would do."

"And the card was missing?"

Barney shrugged. "You didn't hear nothing about it at the trial. I was ordered to keep my mouth shut about her. I do know that she kept Jimmy waiting or stood him up that night. A couple of the guys told me he exploded and said he'd kill her. You know Jimmy's temper. And there was one other thing. Jimmy had bought her some expensive jewelry. I know, because I paid for it and kept a copy of the receipts. There was a lot of talk about jewelry at the trial, stuff the husband claimed he hadn't given her, but anything they found, the father swore he gave her."

Young tore the sheet of paper Barney had used off the pad, folded it and put it in his breast pocket. "Barney, I think you're going to be able to enjoy a wonderful new life in Ohio. You realize that you've not only delivered the U.S. attorney a chance to nail Jimmy for murder but also to annihilate Frank Green for prosecuting an innocent man."

They smiled across the desk at each other. "Tell them I don't want to live in Ohio," Barney joked.

They left the office together and walked down the corridor to the bank of elevators. When one arrived and the doors started to part, Barney sensed immediately that something was wrong.

There was no light on inside it. Gut instinct made him turn to run.

He was too late. He died immediately, moments before Mark Young felt the first bullet shred the lapel of his thousand-dollar suit.

62

Kerry heard about the double homicide on WCBS Radio as she was driving to work. The bodies were discovered by Mark Young's private secretary. The report stated that Young and his client Barney Haskell had been scheduled to meet in the parking lot at 7:00 A.M., and it was surmised that Young had disengaged the alarm system when he opened the downstairs door of the small building. The security guard did not come on duty until eight o'clock.

The outside door was unlocked when the secretary arrived at 7:45, but she thought Young had simply forgotten to relock it, as she reported he often had in the past. Then she had taken the elevator upstairs and made the discovery.

The report concluded with a statement from Mike Murkowski, the prosecutor of Essex County. He said it appeared both men had been robbed. They might have been followed into the building by potential muggers and then lost their lives when they tried to resist. Barney Haskell had been shot in the back of his head and neck.

The CBS reporter asked if the fact that Barney Haskell reportedly had been in the process of plea bargaining in the Jimmy Weeks case, and was rumored to be about to connect Weeks to a murder, was being considered as a possible motive for the double slaying. The prosecutor's sharp answer was, "No comment."

It sounds like a mob hit, Kerry thought as she snapped off the radio. And Bob represents Jimmy Weeks. Wow, what a mess!

As she had expected, there was a message from Frank Green waiting on her desk. It was very short. "See me." She tossed off her coat and went across the main hall to his private office.

He did not waste words. "What was Reardon's mother doing coming in here and demanding to see you?"

Kerry chose her words carefully. "She came because I went down to the prison to see Skip Reardon and he received from me the correct impression that I didn't see anything new that would be grounds for an appeal."

She could see the lines around Green's mouth relax, but it was clear he was angry. "I could have told you that. Kerry, ten years ago if I had thought there was one *shred* of evidence to suggest Skip Reardon's innocence, I'd have run it into the ground. There wasn't. Do you know what kind of hay the media would make of this if they thought my office was investigating that case now? They'd love to portray Skip Reardon as a victim. It sells papers —and it's the kind of negative publicity they love to print about political candidates."

His eyes narrowed, and he thudded his fingers on the desk for emphasis. "I'm damn sorry you weren't in the office when we were investigating that murder. I'm damn sorry you didn't see that beautiful woman strangled so viciously that her eyes had almost popped out. Skip Reardon had shouted at her so loudly in the morning that the meter reader who overheard them wasn't sure whether he should call the cops before something happened. That was his statement under oath on the stand. I happen to think you'll make a good judge, Kerry, if you get the chance, but a good judge exercises judgment. And right now I think yours is lousy."

If you get the chance.

Was that a warning? she wondered. "Frank, I'm sorry if I've upset you. If you don't mind, let's move on to something else." She took Robin's picture from the pocket of her jacket and handed it to him. "This came in a plain white envelope in yesterday's mail. Robin is wearing the outfit she had on Tuesday morning when she said she saw that unfamiliar car parked across the street and thought someone might be after her. She was right."

The anger vanished from Green's face. "Let's talk about protecting her."

He agreed with Kerry's plan to notify the school, and to drop Robin off and have her picked up. "I'll find out if we have any convicted sex offenders recently released or moved into the area. I still think that sleaze you convicted last week may have friends who want to get back at you. We'll request that the Hohokus police keep an eye on your house. Do you have a fire extinguisher?"

"A sprinkler system."

"Get a couple of extinguishers just in case."

"You mean in case of a firebomb?"

"It's been known to happen. I don't want to frighten you, but precautions have to be taken."

It was only as she turned to leave that he mentioned the murder in Summit.

"Jimmy Weeks worked fast, but your ex is still going to have a hell of a time getting him off, even *without* Haskell's plea bargain."

"Frank, you talk as though it's a foregone conclusion that this was a hit!"

"Everybody knows it was, Kerry. The wonder is that Jimmy waited this long to get Haskell. Be glad you got rid of Weeks' mouthpiece when you did."

63

Bob Kinellen did not hear the news about Barney Haskell and Mark Young until he entered the courthouse at ten of nine and the media pounced on him. As soon as he heard what had happened, he realized that he had been expecting it.

How could Haskell have been so stupid as to think Jimmy would let him live to testify against him?

He managed to appear appropriately shocked, and to sound convincing when, in answer to a question, he said that Haskell's death would in no way change Mr. Weeks' defense strategy. "James Forrest Weeks is innocent of all charges," he said. "Whatever deal Mr. Haskell was trying to make with the U.S. attorney would have been exposed in court as self-serving and dishonest. I deeply regret the death of Mr. Haskell and my fellow attorney and friend Mark Young."

He managed to escape into an elevator and brush past other media representatives on the second floor. Jimmy was already in the courtroom. "Heard about Haskell?"

"Yes, I did, Jimmy."

"Nobody's safe. These muggers are everywhere."

"I guess they are, Jimmy."

"It does kind of level the playing field though, doesn't it, Bobby?"

"Yes, I would say so."

"But I don't like a level playing field."

"I know that, Jimmy."

"Just so you know."

Bob spoke carefully. "Jimmy, someone sent my ex-wife a picture of our little girl, Robin. It was taken as she was leaving for school on Tuesday by the same person who was in a car that made a last-minute U-turn right in front of her. Robin thought he was going to come up on the sidewalk and run her over."

"They always joke about New Jersey drivers, Bobby."

"Jimmy, nothing had better happen to my daughter."

"Bobby, I don't know what you're talking about. When are they going to make your ex-wife a judge and get her out of the prosecutor's office? She shouldn't be poking around in other people's business."

Bob knew that his question had been asked and answered. One of Jimmy's people had taken the picture of Robin. He, Bob, would have to get Kerry to back off investigating the Reardon case. And he had better see to it that Jimmy was acquitted in this one.

"Good morning, Jimmy. Morning, Bob."

Bob looked up to see his father-in-law, Anthony Bartlett, slip into the chair next to Jimmy.

"Very sad about Haskell and Young," Bartlett murmured.

"Tragic," Jimmy said.

At that moment the sheriff's officer motioned to the prosecutor and Bob and Bartlett to step inside the judge's chambers. A somber Judge Benton looked up from his desk. "I assume you have all been made aware of the tragedy involving Mr. Haskell and Mr. Young." The attorneys nodded quietly.

"As difficult as it will be, I believe that, given the two months already invested in this trial, it should continue. Fortunately, the jury is sequestered and won't be exposed to this news, including the speculation that Mr. Weeks may be involved. I will simply tell them that the absence of Mr. Haskell and Mr. Young means that Mr. Haskell's case is no longer before them.

"I will instruct them not to speculate on what happened and not to let it affect their consideration of Mr. Weeks' case in any way.

"Okay—let's continue."

The jury filed in and settled in their seats. Bob could see the quizzical looks on their faces as they looked over to Haskell's and Young's empty chairs. As the judge instructed them not to speculate on what had happened, Bob knew damn well that that was exactly what they were doing. They think he pled guilty, Bob thought. That's not going to help us.

As Bob pondered how badly this would hurt Weeks, his eyes rested on juror number 10, Lillian Wagner. He knew that Wagner, prominent in the community, so proud of her Ivy League husband and sons, so aware of her position and social status, was a problem. There had to be a reason Jimmy demanded he accept her.

What Bob did not know was that an "associate" of Jimmy Weeks had quietly approached Alfred Wight, juror number 2, just before the jury had been sequestered. Weeks had learned that Wight had a terminally ill wife and was nearly bankrupt from the medical expenses. The desperate Mr. Wight had agreed to accept $100,000 in exchange for a guarantee that his vote would be Not Guilty.

64

K erry looked with dismay at the stack of files on the worktable beside her desk. She knew she had to get to them soon; it was time to assign new cases. In addition, there were some plea bargains she had to discuss with Frank or Carmen, the first assistant. There was so much to be done there, and she should be focusing her attention.

Instead she asked her secretary to try to reach Dr. Craig Riker, the psychiatrist she sometimes used as a prosecution witness in murder trials. Riker was an experienced, no-nonsense doctor whose philosophy she shared. He believed that, while life does deal some pretty tough blows, a person just has to lick his wounds and then get on with it. Most important, he had a way of defusing the obfuscating psychiatric jargon spouted by the shrinks the defense attorneys lined up.

She especially loved him when, asked if he considered a defendant insane, he answered, "I think he's nuts, but not insane. He knew exactly what he was doing when he went into his aunt's home and killed her. He'd read the will."

"Dr. Riker is with a patient," Kerry's secretary reported. "He'll call you back at ten of eleven."

And true to his word, at exactly ten of eleven Janet called in that Dr. Riker was on the phone. "What's up, Kerry?"

She told him about Dr. Smith giving other women his daughter's face. "He denied in so many words that he did any work on Suzanne," she explained, "which could be true. He may have referred her to a colleague. But is making other women look like Suzanne a form of grieving?"

"It's a pretty sick form of grieving," Riker told her. "You say he hadn't seen her from the time she was a baby?"

"That's right."

"And then she appeared in his office?"

"Yes."

"What kind of guy is this Smith?"

"Rather formidable."

"A loner?"

"I wouldn't be surprised."

"Kerry, I need to know more and I'd certainly like to know whether or not he operated on his daughter, asked a colleague to do the job, or if she had the surgery before she went to him."

"I hadn't thought about the last possibility."

"But if, and I stress the word, *if,* he met Suzanne after all those years, saw a plain or even a palpably homely young woman, operated on her, created a beauty and then was enchanted by what he'd done, I think we've got to look for erotomania."

"What is that?" Kerry asked.

"It covers a lot of territory. But if a doctor who is a loner meets his daughter after all those years, transforms her into a beauty and then has the sense of having done something magnificent, we could argue that it falls into that category. He's possessive of her, even in love with her. It's a delusional disorder that often applies to stalkers, for example."

Kerry thought of Deidre Reardon telling her how Dr. Smith treated Suzanne as an object. She told Dr. Riker about Smith patting away a smudge on Suzanne's cheek and then lecturing her on preserving beauty. She also told him of Kate Carpenter's conversation with Barbara Tompkins, and of the latter's fear that Smith was stalking her.

There was a pause. "Kerry, I've got my next patient coming in. Keep me posted, won't you? This is a case I'd love to follow."

65

Kerry had intended to leave the office early so she could be at Dr. Smith's office just after his last appointment. She had changed her mind, however, realizing that it would be better to wait until she had a better perspective on Dr. Smith's relationship with his daughter. She also wanted to be home with Robin.

Mrs. Reardon believed that Smith's attitude toward Suzanne was "unhealthy," she thought.

And Frank Green had remarked on how Smith had been totally unemotional on the stand.

Skip Reardon had said his father-in-law wasn't around their house much, that when Suzanne saw him, they usually met alone.

I need to talk to someone who knew these people and who has no axe to grind, Kerry thought. I'd also like to talk to Mrs. Reardon again, more calmly. But what can I say to her? That a mobster who happens to be on trial right now was known to call Suzanne Sweetheart when he played golf with her? That a golf caddie sensed that there might be something going on between them?

Those disclosures might only nail Skip Reardon's coffin a little more tightly shut, she reasoned. As a prosecutor I could argue that even if Skip wanted a divorce so he could get back together with Beth, it would have infuriated him if he had learned that Suzanne was running around with a multimillionaire while charging three-thousand-dollar Saint Laurent suits to him.

She was just leaving the office at five o'clock when Bob phoned. She caught the tension in his voice. "Kerry, I need to stop by for a few minutes. Will you be home in an hour or so?"

"Yes."

"I'll see you then," he said, and hung up.

What was bringing Bob to the house? she wondered. Concern about the picture of Robin she'd received? Or had he had an unexpectedly tough day in court? That was certainly possible, she told herself, remembering how Frank Green had commented that even without Haskell's testimony the government would be able to convict Jimmy Weeks. She reached for her coat and slung her shoulder bag over her arm, remembering wryly how for the year and a half of her marriage, she had joyfully rushed home from work to spend the evening with Bob Kinellen.

When she arrived home, Robin looked at her accusingly. "Mom, why did Alison pick me up at school and drive me home? She wouldn't give me a reason, and I felt like a jerk."

Kerry looked at the sitter. "I won't hold you up, Alison. Thanks."

When they were alone, she looked into Robin's indignant face. "That car that frightened you the other day . . . ," she began.

When she was finished, Robin sat very still. "It's kind of scary, isn't it, Mom?"

"Yes, it is."

"That's why when you came home last night you looked all tired and beat up?"

"I hadn't realized I looked quite that bad, but yes, I was pretty heartsick."

"And that's why Geoff came running up?"

"Yes, it is."

"I wish you'd told me last night."

"I didn't know how to tell you, Rob. I was too uptight myself."

"So what do we do now?"

"Take a lot of precautions that may be a nuisance until we find out who was across the street last Tuesday and why he was there."

"Do you think if he comes back, he'll run me over next time?"

Kerry wanted to shout, "No, I don't." Instead she moved over to the couch where Robin was sitting and put an arm around her.

Robin dropped her head on her mother's shoulder. "In other words, if the car comes at me again, duck."

"That's why the car isn't going to get the chance, Rob."

"Does Daddy know about this?"

"I called him last night. He's coming up in a little while."

Robin sat upright. "Because he's worried about me?"

She's pleased, Kerry thought, as though Bob has done her a favor. "Of course, he's worried about you."

"Cool. Mom, can I tell Cassie about this?"

"No, not now. You've got to promise, Robin. Until we know who's pulling this—"

"And have cuffed him," Robin interjected.

"Exactly. Once that's done, then you can talk about it."

"Okay. What are we going to do tonight?"

"Just crash. We'll send out for pizza. I stopped on the way home and rented a couple of movies."

The mischievous look Kerry loved came into Robin's face. "R-rated, I hope."

She's trying to make me feel better, Kerry thought. She's not going to let me know how scared she is.

At ten of six, Bob arrived. Kerry watched as, with a whoop of joy, Robin ran into his arms. "What do you think about me being in danger?" she asked.

"I'm going to let you two visit while I get changed," Kerry announced.

Bob released Robin. "Don't be long, Kerry," he said hurriedly. "I can only stay a few minutes."

Kerry saw the instant pain on Robin's face and wanted to throttle Kinellen. Toss her a little TLC for a change, she thought angrily. Struggling to keep her tone of voice even, she responded, "Down in a minute."

She changed quickly into slacks and a sweater, but deliberately waited upstairs for ten minutes. Then, as she was about to come down, there was a knock at her door and Robin called, "Mom."

"Come in." Kerry started to say, "I'm ready," when she saw the look on Robin's face. "What's wrong?"

"Nothing. Dad asked me to wait up here while he talks to you."

"I see."

Bob was standing in the middle of the study, obviously uncomfortable, obviously anxious to be gone.

He hasn't bothered to take off his coat, Kerry thought. And what did he do to upset Robin? Probably spent the whole time telling her how rushed he was.

He turned when he heard her footsteps. "Kerry, I've got to get back to the office. There's a lot of work I have to do for tomorrow's session. But there's something very important I have to tell you."

He pulled a small sheet of paper out of his pocket. "You heard what happened to Barney Haskell and Mark Young?"

"Obviously."

"Kerry, Jimmy Weeks has a way of getting information. I'm not sure how, but he does. For example, he knows that you went to see Reardon in prison Saturday."

"Does he?" Kerry stared at her ex-husband. "What difference would that make to him?"

"Kerry, don't play games. I'm worried. Jimmy is desperate. I just told you that he has a way of finding out things. Look at this."

Kinellen handed her what seemed to be a copy of a note written on a six-by-nine-inch sheet torn from a pad. On it were six musical notes in the key of C, and underneath were the words, "I'm in love with you." It was signed "J."

"What's this supposed to be?" Kerry asked, even as she mentally hummed the notes she was reading. Then, before Bob had a chance to answer, she understood, and her blood ran cold. They were the opening notes to the song "Let Me Call You Sweetheart."

"Where did you get this and what does it mean?" she snapped.

"They found the original in Mark Young's breast pocket when they went through his clothes at the morgue. It was Haskell's writing, and on a sheet of paper torn from the pad next to Young's phone. The secretary remembers putting a fresh pad there last night, so Haskell had to have jotted it down sometime between seven and seven-thirty this morning."

"A few minutes before he died?"

"Exactly. Kerry, I'm certain it's connected to the plea bargain Haskell was trying to make."

"The plea bargain? You mean the homicide he was hinting he could connect to Jimmy Weeks was the Sweetheart Murder Case?" Kerry could not believe what she was hearing. "Jimmy *was* involved with Suzanne Reardon, wasn't he? Bob, are you telling me that whoever took Robin's picture and came within an inch of running her over works for Jimmy Weeks, and this is his way of scaring me off?"

"Kerry, I'm not saying anything except leave it alone. For Robin's sake, *leave it alone.*"

"Does Weeks know you're here?"

"He knows that, for Robin's sake, I'd warn you."

"Wait a minute." Kerry looked at her former husband with disbelief. "Let me get this straight. You're here to warn me off because your client, the thug and murderer you represent, has given you a threat, veiled or otherwise, to convey to me. My God, Bob, how low you have gone."

"Kerry, I'm trying to save my child's life."

"Your child? All of a sudden she's so important to you? Do you know how many times you've devastated her when you didn't show up to see her? It's insulting. Now get out."

As he turned, she snatched the paper from his hand. "But I'll take this."

"Give that to me." Kinellen grabbed her hand, forcing her fingers open and pulling the paper from her.

"Dad, let go of Mom!"

They both whirled to see Robin standing in the doorway, the fading scars bright once more against the ashen pallor of her face.

66

D
r. Smith had left the office at 4:20, only a minute or so after his last patient—a post–tummy-tuck checkup—had departed.

Kate Carpenter was glad to see him go. She found it disturbing just to be around him lately. She had noticed the tremor in his hand again today when he removed the skull stitches from Mrs. Pryce, who had had an eyebrow lift procedure. The nurse's concern went beyond the physical, however; she was sure that mentally there was something radically wrong with the doctor as well.

The most frustrating thing for Kate, though, was that she didn't know where to turn. Charles Smith was—or at least had been—a brilliant surgeon. She didn't want to see him discredited, or drummed out of the profession. If circumstances were different, she would have talked to his wife or best friend. But in Dr. Smith's case, she couldn't do that—his wife was long gone, and he seemed to have no friends at all.

Kate's sister Jean was a social worker. Jean probably would understand the problem and be able to advise her on where to turn to get Dr. Smith the help he obviously needed. But Jean was on vacation in Arizona, and Kate didn't know how to reach her even if she wanted to.

At four-thirty Barbara Tompkins phoned. "Mrs. Carpenter, I've had it. Last night, Dr. Smith called and practically demanded that I have dinner with him. But then he kept calling me Suzanne. And he wants me to call him Charles. He asked if I had a serious boyfriend. I'm sorry, I know I owe him a lot, but I think he is really creepy, and this is getting to me. I find that even at work I'm looking over my shoulder, expecting to see him lurking somewhere. I can't stand it. This can't go on."

Kate Carpenter knew she couldn't stall any longer. The one possible person who came to her mind in whom she might confide was Robin Kinellen's mother, Kerry McGrath.

Kate knew she was a lawyer, an assistant prosecutor in New Jersey, but she was also a mother who was very grateful that Dr. Smith had treated her daughter in an emergency. She also realized that Kerry McGrath knew more about Dr. Smith's personal background than did she or anyone else on his staff. She wasn't sure why Kerry had been checking on the doctor, but Kate didn't feel that it was for any harmful purpose. Kerry had shared with her the information that Smith had been not only divorced but also was the father of a woman who was murdered.

Feeling like Judas Iscariot, Mrs. Kate Carpenter gave Barbara

Tompkins the home phone number of Bergen County Assistant Prosecutor Kerry McGrath.

For a long time after Bob Kinellen left, Kerry and Robin sat on the sofa, not talking, shoulders touching, legs up on the coffee table.

Then, choosing her words carefully, Kerry said, "Whatever I said, or whatever the scene you just witnessed might have implied, Dad loves you very much, Robin. His worry is for you. I don't admire the fixes he gets himself into, but I respect his feeling for you even when I get so angry I throw him out."

"You got mad at him when he said he was worried about me."

"Oh, come on, those were just words. He makes me so angry sometimes. Anyhow, I know that you're not going to grow up to be the kind of person who lets herself drift into problems that are obvious to everyone else, then pleads situational ethics— meaning 'this may be wrong but it's necessary.' "

"That's what Dad's doing?"

"*I* think so."

"Does he know who took my picture?"

"He *suspects* he knows. It has to do with a case Geoff Dorso has been working on and that he's tried to get me to help him with. He's trying to get a man out of prison that he's convinced is innocent."

"Are you helping him with it?"

"Actually, I'd pretty well decided that by getting involved I was stirring up a hornet's nest for no reason. Now I'm beginning to think I may have been wrong, that there are a couple of very good reasons to think that Geoff's client indeed may have been unfairly convicted. But on the other hand, I'm certainly not going to put you in any danger to prove it. I promise you that."

Robin stared ahead for a moment and then turned to her mother. "Mom, that doesn't make sense. That's totally unfair. You're putting Dad down for something, and then you're doing the same thing. Isn't *not* helping Geoff if you think his client shouldn't be in prison 'situational ethics'?"

"Robin!"

"I mean it. Think about it. Now can we order the pizza? I'm hungry."

Shocked, Kerry watched as her daughter stood up and reached for the bag with the video movies they were planning to watch. Robin examined the titles, chose one and put it in the VCR. Just before she turned it on, she said, "Mom, I really think that guy in the car the other day was just trying to scare me. I don't think he really would have run me over. I don't mind if you drop me off at school and Alison picks me up. What's the dif?"

Kerry stared at her daughter for a moment, then shook her head. "The dif is that I'm proud of you and ashamed of myself." She hugged Robin quickly, then released her and went into the kitchen.

A few minutes later, as she was getting out plates for the pizza, the phone rang and a hesitant voice said, "Ms. McGrath, I'm Barbara Tompkins. I apologize for bothering you, but Mrs. Carpenter, in Dr. Charles Smith's office, suggested that I call you."

As she listened, Kerry grabbed a pen and began jotting notes on the message pad. *Dr. Smith was consulted by Barbara . . . He showed her a picture . . . Asked her if she wanted to look like*

this woman . . . Operated on her . . . Began counseling her . . .
Helped her select an apartment . . . Sent her to a personal shop-
per . . . Now is calling her "Suzanne" and stalking her . . .

Finally Tompkins said, "Ms. McGrath, I'm so grateful to Dr.
Smith. He's turned my life around. I don't want to report him to
the police and ask for a restraining order. I don't want to hurt
him in any way. But I can't let this go on."

"Have you ever felt you were in physical danger from him?"
Kerry asked.

There was a brief hesitation before Tompkins answered
slowly, "No, not really. I mean he's never tried to force himself
on me physically. He's actually been quite solicitous, treating me
as though I were fragile somehow—like a china doll. But I also
get a sense occasionally of terrible, restrained anger in him, and
that it could easily be unleashed, maybe on me. For example,
when he showed up to take me out to dinner last night, I could
tell he wasn't happy that I was ready to immediately get out of
my apartment. And for a moment I thought he might lash out.
It's just that I didn't want to be alone with him. And now I feel
as if I outright *refused* to see him, he could get very, very angry.
But as I told you, he's been so good to me. And I know a restraining order could seriously damage his reputation."

"Barbara, I'm going in to see Dr. Smith on Monday. He
doesn't know it, but I am. I think from what you tell me, and
particularly from the fact that he calls you Suzanne, that he's
suffering from some sort of breakdown. I hope he might be per-
suaded to seek help. But I can't advise you not to speak to the
New York police if you're frightened. In fact, I think you
should."

"Not yet. There's a business trip I was going to make next
month, but I can rearrange my schedule and take it next week.
I'd like to talk to you again when I come back; then I'll decide
what I should do."

•   •   •

When she hung up, Kerry sank into a kitchen chair, the notes of the conversation in front of her. The situation was getting much more complicated. Dr. Smith had been stalking Barbara Tompkins. Had he also been stalking his own daughter? If so, it was very likely that it was *his* Mercedes Dolly Bowles and little Michael had seen parked in front of the Reardon house the night of the murder.

She remembered the partial license numbers Bowles claimed to have seen. Had Joe Palumbo had a chance to check them against Smith's car?

But if Dr. Smith had turned on Suzanne the way Barbara Tompkins feared he might turn on her, if he was the one responsible for her death, then why was Jimmy Weeks so afraid of being connected to Suzanne Reardon's murder?

I need to know more about Smith's relationship with Suzanne before I see him, before I know which questions to ask him, Kerry thought. That antique dealer, Jason Arnott—he might be the one to speak to. According to the notes she had found in the file, he had been just a friend but went into New York frequently with Suzanne to auctions and whatever. Perhaps Dr. Smith met them sometimes.

She placed a call to Arnott, leaving a message requesting him to call her back. Kerry then debated about making one more call.

It would be to Geoff, asking him to set up a second meeting at the prison with Skip Reardon.

Only this time she would want to have both his mother and his girlfriend, Beth Taylor, there as well.

Jason Arnott had planned to stay quietly at home on Friday night and prepare a simple dinner for himself. With that in mind he had sent his twice-weekly cleaning woman shopping, and she had returned with the filet of sole, watercress, pea pods and crisp French bread he had requested. But when Amanda Coble phoned at five o'clock to invite him to dinner at the Ridgewood Country Club with Richard and her, he had accepted gladly.

The Cobles were his kind of people—superrich but marvelously unpretentious; amusing; very, very smart. Richard was an international banker and Amanda an interior designer. Jason successfully handled his own portfolio and keenly enjoyed talking with Richard about futures and foreign markets. He knew that Richard respected his judgment and Amanda appreciated his expertise in antiques.

He decided they would be a welcome diversion after the disquieting time he had spent in New York yesterday with Vera Todd. And in addition, he had met a number of interesting people through the Cobles. In fact, their introduction had led to a most successful forage in Palm Springs three years ago.

He drove up to the front door of the club just as the Cobles surrendered their car to the parking valet. He was a moment behind them going through the front entrance, then waited as they greeted a distinguished-looking couple who were just leaving. He recognized the man immediately. Senator Jonathan Hoover. He'd been at a couple of political dinners where Hoover put in an appearance but they'd never met face to face.

The woman was in a wheelchair but still managed to look regal in a deep blue dinner suit with a skirt that came to the tips of high-laced shoes. He had heard that Mrs. Hoover was disabled, but had never seen her before. With an eye that instantly absorbed the smallest detail, he noted the position of her hands, clasped together, partially concealing the swollen joints of her fingers.

She must have been a knockout when she was young, and before all this happened, he thought as he studied the still-stunning features dominated by sapphire blue eyes.

Amanda Coble glanced up and saw him. "Jason, you're here." She waved him over and made the introductions. "We're talking about those terrible murders in Summit this morning. Both Senator Hoover and Richard knew the lawyer, Mark Young."

"It's pretty clear that it was a mob hit," Richard Coble said angrily.

"I agree," Jonathan Hoover said. "And so does the governor. We all know how he's cracked down on crime these eight years, and now we need Frank Green to keep up the good work. I can tell you this: If Weeks were being tried in a state court, you can bet the attorney general would have completed the plea bargain and gotten Haskell's testimony, and these murders never would have happened. And now Royce, the man who bungled this whole operation, wants to be governor. Well, not if I can help it!"

"Jonathan," Grace Hoover murmured reprovingly. "You can tell it's an election year, can't you, Amanda?" As they all smiled, she added, "Now we mustn't keep you any longer."

"My wife has been keeping me in line since we met as college freshmen," Jonathan Hoover explained to Jason. "Good seeing you again, Mr. Arnott."

"Mr. Arnott, haven't we met before as well?" Grace Hoover asked suddenly.

Jason felt his internal alarm system kick in. It was sending out a strong warning. "I don't think so," he answered slowly. I'm sure I'd have remembered, he thought. *So what makes her think we've met?*

"I don't know why, but I feel as though I know you. Well, I'm sure I'm wrong. Good-bye."

Even though the Cobles were their usual interesting selves and the dinner was delicious, Jason spent the evening heartily wishing he had stayed home alone and cooked the filet of sole.

When he got back to his house at ten-thirty, his day was further ruined by listening to the one message on his answering machine. It was from Kerry McGrath, who introduced herself as a Bergen County assistant prosecutor, gave her phone number, asked him to call her at home till eleven tonight or first thing in the morning. She explained that she wanted to talk to him unofficially about his late neighbor and friend, the murder victim, Suzanne Reardon.

On Friday evening, Geoff Dorso went to dinner at his parents' home in Essex Fells. It was a command performance. Unexpectedly, his sister Marian, her husband, Don, and their two-year-old twins had come in from

Boston for the weekend. His mother immediately tried to gather together her four other children, their spouses and offspring, to welcome the visitors. Friday was the only night all the others could make it at once, so Friday it would have to be.

"So you will postpone any other plans, won't you, Geoff?" his mother had half pleaded, half ordered when she had called him that afternoon.

Geoff had no plans, but in the hopes of building up credit against another demand invitation, he hedged: "I'm not sure, Mom. I'll have to rearrange something, but . . ."

Immediately he was sorry for having chosen that tack. His mother's voice changed to a tone of lively interest as she interrupted, "Oh, you've got a date, Geoff! Have you met someone nice? Don't cancel it. Bring her along. I'd love to meet her!"

Geoff groaned inwardly. "Actually, Mom, I was just kidding. I don't have a date. I'll see you around six."

"All right, dear." It was clear his mother's pleasure in his acceptance was tempered by the fact that she wasn't about to be introduced to a potential daughter-in-law.

As he got off the phone, Geoff admitted to himself that if this were tomorrow night, he would be tempted to suggest to Kerry that she and Robin might enjoy dinner at his parents' home. She'd probably run for the hills, he thought.

He found it suddenly disquieting to realize that several times during the day the thought had run through his mind that his mother would like Kerry very, very much.

At six o'clock he drove up to the handsome, rambling Tudor house that his parents had bought twenty-seven years ago for one-tenth of its present value. It was an ideal family home when we were growing up, he thought, and it's an ideal family home now with all the grandchildren. He parked in front of the old carriage house that now was the residence of his youngest and still-single sister. They'd all had their turn at using the carriage house apartment after college or graduate school. He'd stayed there when he was at Columbia Law School, then for two years after that.

We've had it great, he acknowledged as he breathed in the cold November air and anticipated the warmth of the inviting, brightly lighted house. His thoughts turned toward Kerry. I'm glad I'm not an only child, he said to himself. I'm grateful Dad didn't die when I was in college and Mother didn't remarry and settle a couple of thousand miles away. It couldn't have been easy for Kerry.

I should have called her today, he thought. Why didn't I? I know she doesn't want anyone hovering over her, but, on the other hand, she doesn't really have anyone to share her worries with. She can't protect Robin the way this family could protect one of our kids if there were a threat.

He went up the walk and let himself into the noisy warmth, so typical when three generations of the Dorso clan gathered.

After effusive greetings to the Boston branch and a casual hello to the siblings whom he saw regularly, Geoff managed to escape into the study with his father.

Lined with law books and signed first editions, it was the one room off limits to exploring youngsters. Edward Dorso poured a scotch for his son and himself. Seventy years old, he was a retired attorney who had specialized in business and corporate law and once numbered among his clients several Fortune 500 companies.

Edward had known and liked Mark Young and was anxious to hear any behind-the-scenes information about his murder that Geoff might have picked up in court.

"I can't tell you much, Dad," Geoff said. "It's hard to believe the coincidence that a mugger or muggers just happened to botch a robbery and kill Young, just when his fellow victim, Haskell, was about to plea bargain in return for testifying against Jimmy Weeks."

"I agree. Speaking of which, I had lunch in Trenton today with Sumner French. Something that would interest you came up. There is a planning board official in Philadelphia they're positive gave Weeks inside information ten years ago, about a new highway being built between Philly and Lancaster. Weeks picked up some valuable property and made a huge profit selling it to developers when the plans for the highway were made public."

"Nothing new about inside tips," Geoff observed. "It's a fact of life and almost impossible to police. And frequently difficult to prove, I might add."

"I brought this case up for a reason. I gather that Weeks bought some of these properties for next to nothing because the guy who had the options on them was desperate for cash."

"Anyone I know?"

"Your favorite client, Skip Reardon."

Geoff shrugged. "We travel in close circles, Dad, you know that. It's just one more way Skip Reardon was pushed down the tube. I remember Tim Farrell talking at the time about how Skip was liquidating everything for his defense. On paper, Skip's financial picture looked great, but he had a lot of optioned land, a heavy construction mortgage on an extravagant house and a wife who seemed to think she was married to King Midas. If Skip hadn't gone to prison, he'd be a rich man today, because he was a good businessman. But my recollection is that he sold off all the options for fair market value."

"Not fair market if the purchaser has privileged information," his father said tartly. "One of the rumors I heard is that Haskell, who was Weeks' accountant even then, was aware of that transaction too. Anyhow it's one of those pieces of information that may be useful some way, some day."

Before Geoff could comment, a chorus of voices from outside the study shouted, "Grandpa, Uncle Geoff, dinner's ready."

"And it has come, the summons, kind . . . ," Edward Dorso quoted as he stood and stretched.

"Go ahead, Dad, I'll be right behind you. I want to check my messages." When he heard Kerry's husky, low voice on the answering machine tape, he pressed the receiver to his ear.

Was Kerry actually saying that she wanted to go to the prison and see Skip again? That she wanted to have his mother and Beth Taylor there? "Hallelujah!" he said aloud.

Grabbing Justin, his nephew who had been sent to get him, Geoff scrambled to the dining room, where he knew his mother was impatiently waiting for everyone to sit down so that grace could be offered.

When his father had concluded the blessing, his mother added, "And we're so grateful to have Marian and Don and the twins with us."

"Mother, it's not as though we live at the North Pole," Marian protested, winking at Geoff. "Boston is about three and a half hours away."

"If your mother had her way, there'd be a family compound," his father commented with an amused smile. "And you'd all be right here, under her watchful eye."

"You can all laugh at me," his mother said, "but I love seeing my whole family together. It's wonderful to have three of you girls settled, and Vickey with a steady boyfriend as nice as Kevin."

Geoff watched as she beamed at that couple.

"Now if I could just get our only son to find the right girl . . ." Her voice trailed off as everyone turned to smile indulgently at Geoff.

Geoff grimaced, then smiled back, reminding himself that when his mother wasn't riding this horse, she was a very interesting woman who had taught medieval literature at Drew University for twenty years. In fact, he had been named Geoffrey because of her great admiration for Chaucer.

Between courses, Geoff slipped back into the den and phoned Kerry. He was thrilled to realize that she sounded glad to hear from him.

"Kerry, can you go down and see Skip tomorrow? I know his mother and Beth will drop everything to be there when you come."

"I want to, Geoff, but I don't know if I can. I'd be a wreck leaving Robin, even at Cassie's house. The kids are always outside, and it's right on an exposed corner."

Geoff didn't know he had the solution until he heard himself say, "Then I've got a better idea. I'll pick you both up, and we can leave Robin here with my folks while we're away. My sister and her husband and their kids are here. And because of them, the other grandchildren will be dropping by. Robin will have plenty of company, and if that isn't enough, my brother-in-law is a captain in the Massachusetts State Police. Believe me, she'll be safe."

70

Jason Arnott lay sleepless most of the night, wrestling with trying to decide how to treat the call from Assistant Prosecutor Kerry McGrath, even, as she so delicately put it, in an "unofficial" capacity.

By 7:00 A.M. he'd made up his mind. He would return her call and, in a courteous, civil, but distant tone, inform her that he would be delighted to meet with her, provided it would not take too long. His excuse would be that he was about to leave on a business trip.

To the Catskills, Jason promised himself. I'll hide out at the house. Nobody will find me there. In the meantime, this will all blow over. But I can't look as though I have anything to be concerned about.

The decision made, he finally fell into a sound sleep, the kind of sleep he enjoyed after he had successfully completed a mission and knew he was home free.

He called Kerry McGrath first thing when he woke up at nine-thirty. She picked up on the first ring. He was relieved to hear what seemed to be genuine gratitude in her tone.

"Mr. Arnott, I really appreciate your calling, and I assure you this is unofficial," she said. "Your name came up as having been a friend and antiques expert for Suzanne Reardon, years ago. Something has developed about that case, and I'd very much appreciate an opportunity to talk to you about the relationship you saw between Suzanne and her father, Dr. Charles Smith. I promise, I'll only take a few minutes of your time."

She meant it. Jason could spot a phony, had made a career of it, and she wasn't a phony. It wouldn't be hard to talk about Suzanne, he told himself. He frequently had shopped with her the way he shopped with Vera Shelby Todd yesterday. She had been at many of his parties, but so had dozens of other people. No one could make anything of that.

Jason was totally amenable to Kerry's explanation that she had a firm commitment to be picked up at one and would so much appreciate visiting him within the hour.

71

Kerry decided to bring Robin with her when she drove to Jason Arnott's house. She knew that it had upset Robin to see her struggling with Bob the night before over the copy of the Haskell note, and she reasoned that the drive to

Alpine would give them a half hour each way to chat. She blamed herself for the scene with Bob. She should have realized that there was no way he would let her have the note. Anyhow, she knew what it said. She had jotted it down just as she had seen it so she could show it to Geoff later.

It was a sunny, crisp day, the kind, she thought, that renews the spirit. Now that she knew she had to look seriously into the Reardon case and really see it through, she was determined to do it quickly.

Robin willingly had agreed to come along for the ride, although she pointed out that she wanted to be back by noon. She wanted to invite Cassie over for lunch.

Kerry then told her about the plan for her to visit Geoff's family while she went to Trenton on business.

"Because you're worried about me," Robin said matter-of-factly.

"Yes," Kerry admitted. "I want you where I know you'll be okay, and I know you'll be fine with the Dorsos. Monday, after I drop you off at school, I'll have a talk with Frank Green about all this. Now, Rob, when we get to Mr. Arnott's house, you come in with me, but you do know I have to talk privately to him. You brought a book?"

"Uh-huh. I wonder how many of Geoff's nieces and nephews will be there today. Let's see, he has four sisters. The youngest isn't married. The one next to Geoff has three kids, a boy who's nine—he's the one closest to my age—and a girl who's seven and a boy who's four. Geoff's second sister has four kids, but they're kind of little—I think the oldest is six. Then there's the one with the two-year-old twins."

"Rob, for heaven sake, when did you learn all this?" Kerry asked.

"The other night at dinner. Geoff was talking about them. You were kind of out of it, I guess. I mean, I could tell you weren't listening. Anyhow I think it will be cool to go down there. He says his mother's a good cook."

As they were leaving Closter and entering Alpine, Kerry glanced down at her directions. "It's not far now."

Five minutes later they drove up a winding road to Jason Arnott's European-style mansion. The bright sun played on the structure, a breathtaking combination of stone, stucco, brick and wood, with towering leaded-pane windows.

"Wow!" Robin said.

"Sort of makes you realize how modestly *we* live," Kerry agreed, as she parked in the semicircular driveway.

Jason Arnott opened the door for them before they could find the buzzer. His greeting was cordial. "Ms. McGrath, and is this your assistant?"

"I said it would be an unofficial visit, Mr. Arnott," Kerry said, as she introduced Robin. "Perhaps she could wait here while we talk." She indicated a chair near a life-size bronze sculpture of two knights in combat.

"Oh, no. She'll be much more comfortable in the little study." Arnott indicated a room to the left of the entrance hall. "You and I can go into the library. It's just past the study."

This place is like a museum, Kerry thought as she followed Arnott. She would have loved to have had the chance to stop and study the exquisite wall coverings, the fine furniture, the paintings, the total harmony of the interior. Keep your mind on what you're doing, she warned herself. You promised him you'd only be half an hour.

When she and Arnott were seated opposite each other on handsome morocco armchairs, she said, "Mr. Arnott, Robin suffered some facial injuries in a car accident several weeks ago and was treated by Dr. Charles Smith."

Arnott raised his eyebrows. "The Dr. Charles Smith who was Suzanne Reardon's father?"

"Exactly. On each of two follow-up visits, I saw a patient in his office who bore a startling resemblance to Suzanne Reardon."

Arnott stared at her. "By coincidence, I hope. Surely you're not saying that he is deliberately re-creating Suzanne?"

"An interesting choice of words, Mr. Arnott. I'm here because, as I told you on the phone, I need to know Suzanne better. I need to know what her relationship with her father really was, and so far as you knew it, with her husband."

Arnott leaned back, looked up at the ceiling and clasped his hands under his chin.

That's so posed, Kerry thought. He's doing it to impress me. Why?

"Let me start with meeting Suzanne. It would be about twelve years ago now. One day she simply rang the bell. I must tell you she was an extraordinarily beautiful girl. She introduced herself and explained that she and her husband were in the process of building a house in the neighborhood, that she wanted to furnish it with antiques and that she'd heard that I went with good friends to assist them in their bidding at auctions.

"I told her that that was true, but I did not consider myself an interior designer, nor did I intend to be considered a full-time advisor."

"Do you charge for your services?"

"In the beginning I did not. But then, as I realized I was having a very good time accompanying pleasant people on these jaunts, warning them off bad bargains, helping them to get fine objects at excellent prices, I set a fair commission rate. At first I was not interested in becoming involved with Suzanne. She was rather smothering, you see."

"But you did become involved?"

Arnott shrugged. "Ms. McGrath, when Suzanne wanted something, she got it. Actually, when she realized that flirting outrageously with me was only annoying me, she turned on the charm in a different way. She could be most amusing. Eventually we became very good friends; in fact, I still miss her very much. She added a great deal to my parties."

"Did Skip come with her?"

"Seldom. He was bored, and frankly my guests did not find him simpatico. Now don't misunderstand me. He was a well-mannered and intelligent young man, but he was different from most of the people I know. He was the kind of man who got up early, worked hard and had no interest in idle chatter—as he publicly told Suzanne one night when he left her here and went home."

"Did she have her own car that evening?"

Arnott smiled. "Suzanne never had a problem getting a ride."

"How would you judge the relationship between Suzanne and Skip?"

"Unraveling. I knew them for the last two years of their marriage. At first they seemed to be very fond of each other, but eventually it became clear that she was bored with him. Toward the end they did very little together."

"Dr. Smith said that Skip was wildly jealous of Suzanne and that he threatened her."

"If he did, Suzanne did not confide that to me."

"How well did you know Dr. Smith?"

"As well as any of her friends did, I suppose. If I went into New York with Suzanne on days when his office was closed, he often managed to show up and join us. Finally, though, his attention seemed to annoy her. She'd say things like, 'Serves me right for telling him that we were coming here today.' "

"Did she show him she was annoyed?"

"Just as she was quite public in displaying her indifference to Skip, she made no effort to hide her impatience with Dr. Smith."

"You knew that she had been raised by her mother and a stepfather?"

"Yes. She told me her growing-up years were miserable. Her stepsisters were jealous of her looks. She once said, 'Talk about Cinderella—in some ways I lived her life.' "

That answers my next question, Kerry thought. Obviously Suzanne had not confided to Arnott that she had grown up as the plain sister named Susie.

A sudden question occurred to her. "What did she call Dr. Smith?"

Arnott paused. "Either Doctor or Charles," he said after a moment.

"Not Dad."

"Never. At least not that I recall." Arnott looked pointedly at his watch.

"I know I promised not to take up too much of your time, but there's one more thing I need to know. Was Suzanne involved with another man? Specifically, was she seeing Jimmy Weeks?"

Arnott seemed to consider before answering. "I introduced her to Jimmy Weeks in this very room. It was the one and only time he was ever here. They were quite taken with each other. As you may know, there has always been a formidable feeling of power about Weeks, and that instantly attracted Suzanne. And, of course, Jimmy always had an eye for a beautiful woman. Suzanne bragged that after they met, he started appearing frequently at the Palisades Country Club, where she spent a lot of her time. And I think Jimmy was already a member there as well."

Kerry thought about the caddie's statement as she asked, "Was she happy about that?"

"Oh, very. Although I don't think she let Jimmy know it. She was aware that he had a number of girlfriends, and she enjoyed making him jealous. Do you remember one of the early scenes in *Gone With the Wind,* the one where Scarlett collects everyone else's beaux?"

"Yes, I do."

"That was our Suzanne. One would think she'd have out-grown that. After all, it's quite an adolescent trick, isn't it? But there wasn't a man Suzanne didn't try to dazzle. It didn't make her very popular with women."

"And Dr. Smith's reaction to her flirting?"

"Outraged, I would say. I think that if it had been possible, Smith would have built a guardrail around her to keep others away from her, pretty much the way museums put guardrails around their most precious objects."

You don't know how close you are to the mark, Kerry

thought. She recalled what Deidre Reardon had said about Dr. Smith's relationship to Suzanne, that he treated her as an object. "If your theory is correct, Mr. Arnott, wouldn't that be a reason for Dr. Smith to resent Skip Reardon?"

"Resent him? I think it went deeper than that. I think he hated him."

"Mr. Arnott, did you have any reason to think that Suzanne was given jewelry by any man other than her husband and father?"

"If she was, I wasn't privy to it. Suzanne had some very fine pieces, that I *do* know. Skip bought her a number of things every year for her birthday, and again for Christmas, always after she pointed out exactly what she wanted. She also had several one-of-a-kind older Cartier pieces that I believe her father gave her."

Or so he said, Kerry thought. She got up. "Mr. Arnott, do you think Skip Reardon killed Suzanne?"

He rose to his feet. "Ms. McGrath, I consider myself very knowledgeable about antique art and furnishings. I'm less good at judging people. But isn't it true that love and money are the two greatest reasons to kill? I'm sorry to say that in this case both of these reasons seem to apply to Skip. Don't you agree?"

From a window, Jason watched Kerry's car disappear down the driveway. Thinking over their brief exchange, he felt he had been sufficiently detailed to seem helpful, sufficiently vague so that she, like both the prosecution and defense ten years ago, would decide there was no purpose in questioning him further.

Do I think Skip Reardon killed Suzanne? No, I don't, Ms. McGrath, he thought. I think that, like far too many men, Skip might have been *capable* of murdering his wife. Only that night someone else beat him to it.

72

Skip Reardon had endured what was arguably one of the worst weeks of his life. Seeing the skepticism in Assistant Prosecutor Kerry McGrath's eyes when she had come to visit him had completed the job that the news about possibly no more appeals had begun.

It was as though a Greek chorus were chanting the words endlessly inside his head: *"Twenty more years before even the possibility of parole."* Over and over again. All week, instead of reading or watching television at night, Skip had stared at the framed pictures on the walls of his cell.

Beth and his mother were in most of them. Some of the pictures went back to seventeen years ago, when he was twenty-three years old and had just begun dating Beth. She had just started her first teaching job, and he had just launched Reardon Construction Company.

In these ten years he had been incarcerated, Skip had spent many hours looking at those pictures and wondering how everything had gone so wrong. If he hadn't met Suzanne that night, by now he and Beth would have been married fourteen or fifteen years. They probably would have two or three kids. What would it be like to have a son or a daughter? he wondered.

He would have built Beth a home they would have planned together—not that crazy, modern, vast figment of an architect's imagination that Suzanne had demanded and that he had come to detest.

All these years in prison he had been sustained by the knowledge of his innocence, his trust in the American justice system and the belief that someday the nightmare would go away. In his fantasies, the appeals court would agree that Dr. Smith was a liar, and Geoff would come down to the prison and say, "Let's go, Skip. You're a free man."

By prison rules, Skip was allowed two collect phone calls a day. Usually he called both his mother and Beth twice a week. At least one of them came down to see him on Saturday or Sunday.

This week Skip had not phoned either one of them. He had made up his mind. He would not let Beth visit him anymore. She had to get on with her life. She'd be forty her next birthday, he reasoned. She should meet someone else, get married, have kids. She loved children. That was why she had chosen teaching and then counseling as a career.

And there was something else that Skip decided: He wasn't going to waste any more time designing rooms and houses with the dream that someday he would get to build them. By the time he got out of prison—if he ever did get out—he would be in his sixties. It would be too late to get started again. Besides, there would be no one left to care.

That was why on Saturday morning, when Skip was told his lawyer was phoning him, he took the call with the firm intention of telling Geoff to forget about him as well. He too should get on to other things. The news that Kerry McGrath was coming down to see him as well as his mother and Beth angered him.

"What does McGrath want to do, Geoff?" he asked "Show Mom and Beth exactly *why* they're wasting their time trying to get me out of here? Show them how every argument *for* me is an argument *against* me? Tell McGrath I don't need to listen to that again. The court's done a great job of convincing me."

"Shut up, Skip," Geoff's firm voice snapped. "Kerry's interest in you and this murder case is causing her a hell of a lot of trouble, including a threat that something could happen to her ten-year-old daughter if she doesn't pull out."

"A threat? Who?" Skip looked at the receiver he was holding as though it had suddenly become an alien object. It was impossible to comprehend that Kerry McGrath's daughter had been threatened because of him.

"Not only *who?* but *why?* We're sure Jimmy Weeks is the 'who.' The 'why' is that for some reason he's afraid to have the investigation reopened. Now listen, Kerry wants to go over every inch of this case with you, and with your mother and Beth. She has a bunch of questions for all of you. She also has a lot to tell you about Dr. Smith. I don't have to remind you what his testimony did to you. We'll be there for the last visiting period, so plan to be cooperative. This is the best chance we have had of getting you out. It may also be the last."

Skip heard the click in his ear. A guard took him back to his cell. He sat down on the bunk and buried his face in his hands. He didn't want to let it happen, but in spite of himself, the flicker of hope that he thought he had successfully extinguished had jumped back to life and now was flaming throughout his being.

73

eoff picked up Kerry and Robin at one o'clock. When they reached Essex Fells, Geoff brought Kerry and Robin into the house and introduced them around. At the end of the family dinner the night before, he had briefly explained to the adults the circumstances of his bringing Robin for a visit.

Immediately his mother's instincts had zeroed in on the fact that this woman Geoff insisted on calling "Robin's mother" might have special significance for her son.

"Of course, bring Robin over for the afternoon," she had said. "Poor child, that anyone could even think of harming her. And Geoff, after you and her mother—Kerry, did you say her name was?—come back from Trenton, you must stay and have dinner with us."

Geoff knew his vague "We'll see" cut no ice. Chances are, unless something untoward happens, we will eat at my mother's table tonight, he said to himself.

Instantly he detected the approval in his mother's eyes as she took in Kerry's appearance. Kerry was wearing a belted camel's hair coat over matching slacks. A hunter green turtleneck sweater accentuated the green tones in her hazel eyes. Her hair was brushed loosely over her collar. Her only makeup other than lip blush seemed to be a touch of eye shadow.

Next he could see that his mother was pleased by Kerry's sincere, but not effusive, gratitude for letting Robin visit. Mom had always stressed that voices should be well modulated, he thought.

Robin was delighted to hear that all nine grandchildren were somewhere in the house. "Don is taking you and the two oldest to Sports World," Mrs. Dorso told her.

Kerry shook her head and murmured, "I don't know . . ."

"Don is the brother-in-law who's the captain in the Massachusetts State Police," Geoff told her quietly. "He'll stick by the kids like glue."

It was clear that Robin expected to have a good time. She watched as the two-year-old twins, chased by their four-year-old cousin, pell-melled past them. "Sort of like baby rush hour around here," she observed happily. "See you later, Mom."

In the car, Kerry leaned back against the seat and sighed deeply.

"You're not worried, are you?" Geoff asked quickly.

"No, not at all. That was an expression of relief. And now let me fill you in on what I didn't tell you before."

"Like what?"

"Like Suzanne's years growing up, and what she saw when she looked in the mirror in those days. Like what Dr. Smith is up to with one of the patients whom he has given Suzanne's face. And like what I learned from Jason Arnott this morning."

Deidre Reardon and Beth Taylor were already in the visitors' reception room in the prison. After Geoff and Kerry registered with the clerk, they joined them, and Geoff introduced Kerry to Beth.

While they waited to be called, Kerry deliberately kept the conversation impersonal. She knew what she wanted to talk about when they were with Skip, but she wanted to save it until then. She did not want to lose the spontaneity of having the three of them trigger each other's memories as she raised the different points. Understanding Mrs. Reardon's restrained greeting, she concentrated on chatting with Beth Taylor, whom she liked immediately.

Promptly at three o'clock they were led to the area where family members and friends were allowed contact visits with the prisoners. It was more crowded today than it had been when Kerry visited last week. Dismayed, Kerry realized that it might have been better to have officially asked for one of the private conference rooms that were available when both prosecutor and defense attorney requested a joint visit. But that would have meant going on record as a Bergen County assistant prosecutor paying a visit to a convicted murderer, something she still was not quite ready to do.

They did manage to get a corner table, whose location filtered out some of the background noise. When Skip was escorted in, Deidre Reardon and Beth both jumped up. After the guard removed Skip's handcuffs, Beth held back while Deidre hugged her son.

Then Kerry watched as Beth and Skip looked at each other. The expressions on their faces and the very restraint of their kiss told more of what was between them than would have the most ardent, demonstrative embraces. In that moment Kerry vividly relived the memory of that day in court when she had seen the agony on Skip Reardon's face as he was sentenced to a minimum of thirty years' imprisonment, and had listened to his heartrending protest that Dr. Smith was a liar. Thinking back on it, she realized that, knowing very little about the case at the time, she still had felt she heard the ring of truth in Skip Reardon's voice that day.

She had brought a yellow pad on which she had written a series of questions, leaving room under each to make notes of their answers. Briefly she told them everything that had impelled her to make this second visit: Dolly Bowles' story about the presence of the Mercedes the night Suzanne died; the fact that Suzanne had been extremely plain growing up; Dr. Smith's bizarre re-creation of her face when operating on current patients; Smith's attraction to Barbara Tompkins; the fact that Jimmy Weeks' name had come up in the investigation; and, finally, the threat to Robin.

Kerry felt that it was a credit to the three of them that after their initial shock over hearing the disclosures, they did not waste time reacting among themselves. Beth Taylor reached for Skip's hand as she asked, "What can we do now?"

"First, let's clear the air by saying I now have grave doubts whether Skip is guilty, and if we uncover the kinds of things I expect to find, I'll do my best to help Geoff get the verdict reversed. This is how I see it," Kerry told them. "A week ago, Skip, you surmised after we talked, that I didn't believe you. That really isn't accurate. What I felt, and what I thought, was that there was nothing I had heard that couldn't be interpreted in two ways—for you or against you. Certainly there was nothing I heard that would provide grounds for a new appeal. Isn't that right, Geoff?"

Geoff nodded.

"Dr. Smith's testimony is the main reason that you were convicted, Skip. The one great hope is to discredit that testimony. And the only way I can see to do that is to back him into a corner by exposing some of his lies and confronting him with them."

She did not wait for any of them to speak. "I already have the answer to the first question I intended to ask—Suzanne never told you that she'd had plastic surgery. And incidentally, let's cut the formalities. My name is Kerry."

For the remaining hour and fifteen minutes of the visit she fired questions at them. "First of all, Skip, did Suzanne ever mention Jimmy Weeks?"

"Only casually," he said. "I knew he was a member of the club and that she sometimes played in a foursome with him. She used to brag about her golf scores all the time. But when she knew I was getting suspicious that she was involved with someone, she began to mention only the names of the women she played with."

"Isn't Weeks the man on trial for income tax evasion?" Deidre Reardon asked.

Kerry nodded.

"That's incredible. I thought it was terrible that the government is harassing him. Last year I was a volunteer on the cancer drive, and he let us hold it on the grounds of his estate in Peapack. He underwrote the whole thing and then made a huge donation. And you are saying that he was involved with Suzanne and that he's threatening your little girl!"

"Jimmy Weeks has made sure his public image as basic good guy has been carefully nurtured," Kerry told her. "You're not the only one who thinks he's a victim of government harassment. But trust me—nothing could be further from the truth." She turned to Skip. "I want you to describe the jewelry that you believe Suzanne had received from another man."

"One piece was a gold bracelet with zodiac figures engraved in silver, except for the Capricorn symbol. That was the centerpiece, and all encrusted with diamonds. Suzanne was a Capricorn. It was obviously a very expensive piece. When I asked about it, she told me her father had given it to her. The next time I saw him, I thanked him for his generosity to her, and, just as I expected, he didn't know what I was talking about."

"That's the kind of item we might be able to trace. We can put out a flyer to jewelers in New Jersey and Manhattan for openers," Kerry said. "It's surprising how many of them can either identify a piece they've sold years before, or recognize someone's style when it's a one-of-a-kind design."

Skip told her about an emerald-and-diamond ring that looked like a wedding band. The diamonds alternated with the emeralds and were set in a delicate pink-gold band.

"Another one she claimed her father gave her?"

"Yes. Her story was that he was making up for the years he hadn't given her anything. She said that some of the pieces were family jewelry from his mother. That was easier to believe. She also had a flower-shaped pin that was obviously very old."

"I remember that one," Deidre Reardon said. "It had a smaller bud-shaped pin attached to it by a silver chain. I still have a picture I cut out of one of the local papers showing Suzanne wearing it at some sort of fund-raiser. Another heirloom-type piece was the diamond bracelet Suzanne was wearing when she died, Skip."

"Where was Suzanne's jewelry that night?" Kerry asked.

"Except for what she was wearing, in her jewelry case on top of her dressing table," Skip said. "She was supposed to put it in the lockbox in her dressing room, but she usually didn't bother."

"Skip, according to your testimony at the trial several items were missing from your bedroom that night."

"There were two things missing that I'm positive of. One was the flower pin. The problem is that I can't swear it was in the jewelry box that day. But I can swear that a miniature frame that was on the night table was gone."

"Describe it to me," Kerry said.

"Let me, Skip," Deidre Reardon interrupted. "You see, Kerry, that little frame was exquisite. It was reputed to have been made by an assistant to the jeweler Fabergé. My husband was in the army of occupation after the war and bought it in Germany. It was a blue enamel oval with a gold border that was encrusted with pearls. It was my wedding present to Skip and Suzanne."

"Suzanne put a picture of herself in it," Skip explained.

Kerry saw the guard at the door look at the wall clock. "We've only got a few minutes," she said hurriedly. "When did you last see that frame, Skip?"

"It was there that last morning when I got dressed. I remember particularly, because I looked at it when I was changing the stuff in my pockets to the suit I'd just put on. That night, when the detectives told me they were taking me in for questioning, one of them came up to the bedroom with me while I got a sweater. The frame was gone."

"If Suzanne was involved with someone else, is it possible she gave that picture of herself to someone that day?"

"No. It was one of her best pictures, and she liked looking at it. And I don't think even she would have had the guts to give my mother's wedding present away."

"And it never showed up?" Kerry asked.

"Never. But when I tried to say it might have been stolen, the prosecutor argued that if a thief had been there, all that jewelry would have been gone."

The bell signaled the end of visiting hours. This time when Skip got up, he put one arm around his mother, the other around Beth, and drew them to him. Over their heads, he looked at Kerry and Geoff. His smile made him seem ten years younger. "Kerry, you find a way to get me out of this place and I'll build a house for you that you'll never want to leave for the rest of your life." Then he suddenly laughed. "My God," he said, "In this place, I can't believe I said that."

Across the room, convict Will Toth was sitting with his girl-friend, but he gave most of his attention to the group with Skip Reardon. He had seen Skip's mother, the lawyer and the girl-friend here any number of times. Then last week he had recognized Kerry McGrath when she visited Skip. He would know her anywhere—McGrath was the reason he would spend the next fifteen years in this hellhole. She had been the prosecutor at his trial. It was clear that today she was being very cozy with Reardon; he had noticed that she spent the whole time writing down what he was telling her.

Will and his girlfriend stood up when the signal came that visiting hours were over. As he kissed her good-bye, he whispered, "Call your brother as soon as you get home and tell him to pass the word that McGrath was down here again today and taking lots and lots of notes."

74

S i Morgan, senior FBI agent in charge of investigating the Hamilton theft, was in his office at Quantico on Saturday afternoon, going over computer printouts concerning that case and the others believed to be related.

They had asked the Hamiltons, along with burglary victims in similar cases, to furnish names of all guests who attended any gathering or party at their homes during the several months before they were victimized. The computer had created a master file and then a separate list of the names that appeared frequently.

The trouble, Si thought, is that so many of these people travel in the same circles that it's not uncommon to see certain people included regularly, especially at the big functions.

Nevertheless there were about a dozen names that turned up consistently. Si studied that alphabetized list.

The first one was Arnott, Jason.

Nothing there, Si thought. Arnott had been quietly investigated a couple of years ago and passed as clean. He had a healthy stock portfolio, and his personal accounts didn't show the sudden infusions of cash associated with burglary. His interest income was also consistent with his lifestyle. His income tax statement accurately reflected his stock market transactions. He was well respected as an art and antiques expert. He entertained frequently and was well liked.

If there was a red flag in his profile, it was that Arnott was perhaps a little too perfect. That and the fact that his in-depth knowledge of antiques and fine art was consistent with the selective first-rate-only approach the thief took to the victims' possessions. Maybe it wouldn't hurt to run a check on him again if nothing else shows up, Si thought. But he was much more interested in another name on the frequent list, Sheldon Landi, a man who had his own public relations firm.

Landi certainly seems to rub shoulders with the beautiful people, Si mused. He doesn't make much money, yet he lives high. Landi also fit the general profile of the man the computer told them to look for: middle-aged; unmarried; college educated; self-employed.

They had sent out six hundred flyers with the security-camera photo to the names culled from the guest lists. So far they had received thirty tips. One of them came from a woman who had phoned to say she thought the culprit might be her ex-husband. "He robbed me blind the whole time we were married and lied his way into a big settlement when we were divorced, and he has that kind of pointy chin I see in the picture," she'd explained eagerly. "I'd check on him if I were you."

Now, as he leaned back in his desk chair, Si thought about that call and smiled. The ex-husband the woman was talking about was a United States senator.

75

Jonathan and Grace Hoover were expecting Kerry and Robin around one o'clock. They both believed that a leisurely Sunday afternoon meal was a civilized and restful custom.

Unfortunately, the brightness of Saturday had not lasted. Sunday had dawned gray and chilly, but by noon the house was pleasantly filled with the succulent aroma of roasting lamb. The fire was blazing in their favorite room, the library, and they were contentedly settled there as they awaited their guests.

Grace was absorbed in the *Times* crossword puzzle, and Jonathan was deep in the paper's "Arts and Leisure" section. He looked up when he heard Grace murmur in annoyance and saw that the pen had slipped from her fingers onto the carpet. He watched her laboriously begin the process of bending over to retrieve it.

"Grace," he said reprovingly, as he sprang up to get it for her.

She sighed as she accepted the pen from him. "Honestly, Jonathan, what would I ever do without you?"

"You'll never have to try, dear. And may I say that the sentiment is mutual."

For a moment she held his hand to her face. "I know it is,
dear. And believe me, it is one of the things that gives me the
strength to carry on."

On the way over to the Hoovers', Kerry and Robin talked about
the previous evening. "It was much more fun staying at the
Dorsos' house for dinner than going to a restaurant," Robin
exulted. "Mom, I like them."

"I do too," Kerry admitted without reluctance.

"Mrs. Dorso told me that it isn't that hard to be a good cook."

"I agree. I'm afraid I let you down."

"Oh, Mom." Robin's tone was reproachful. She folded her
arms and stared straight ahead at the narrowing road that indicated they were approaching Riverdale. "You make good pasta,"
she said defensively.

"I do, but that's about it."

Robin changed the subject. "Mom, Geoff's mother thinks he
likes you. So do I. We talked about it."

"You what?"

"Mrs. Dorso said that Geoff never, ever brings a date home.
She told me you're the first since his prom days. She said that it
was because his little sisters used to play tricks on his dates and
that now he's gun shy."

"Probably," Kerry said offhandedly. She turned her mind from
the realization that coming back from the prison, she had been
so weary that she had closed her eyes for just a minute and
awakened later, resting against Geoff's shoulder. And that it had
felt so natural, so right.

The visit with Grace and Jonathan Hoover was, as expected,
thoroughly agreeable. Kerry did know that at some point they

would get around to discussing the Reardon case, but it wouldn't be before coffee was served. That was when Robin was free to leave the table to read or try one of the new computer games Jonathan always had waiting for her.

As they ate, Jonathan entertained them with talk about the legislative sessions and the budget the governor was trying to get through. "You see, Robin," he explained, "politics is like a football game. The governor is the coach who sends in the plays, and the leaders of his party in the senate and the assembly are the quarterbacks."

"That's you, isn't it?" Robin interrupted.

"In the senate, yes, I guess you could call me that," Jonathan agreed. "The rest of our team protects whoever is carrying the ball."

"And the others?"

"Those from the other team do their damnedest to break up the game."

"Jonathan," Grace said quietly.

"Sorry, my dear. But there have been more attempts at pork-barreling this week than I've seen in many years."

"What's that?" Robin asked.

"Pork-barreling is an ancient but not necessarily honorable custom wherein legislators add unnecessary expenses to the budget in order to win favor with the voters in their district. Some people carry it to a fine art."

Kerry smiled. "Robin, I hope you realize how lucky you are to be learning the workings of government from someone like Uncle Jonathan."

"All very selfish," Jonathan assured them. "By the time Kerry is sworn in for the Supreme Court in Washington, we'll be getting Robin elected to the legislature and have her on her way too."

Here it comes, Kerry thought. "Rob, if you're finished, you can see what's up with the computer."

"There's something there you'll like, Robin," Jonathan told her. "I guarantee it."

The housekeeper was going around with the coffeepot. Kerry was sure she would need the second cup. From here on it's all going downhill, she thought.

She did not wait for Jonathan to ask about the Reardon case. Instead she presented everything to him and Grace exactly as she knew it, and concluded by saying, "It's clear Dr. Smith was lying. The question is how much was he lying? It's also clear that Jimmy Weeks has some very important reason not to want that case reopened. Otherwise why would he or his people be involving Robin?"

"Kinellen actually threatened that something could happen to Robin?" Grace's tone was icy with contempt.

"Warned is the better word, I think." Kerry turned, appealing to Jonathan. "Look, you must understand that I don't want to upset anything for Frank Green. He would make a good governor, and I know you were talking to me as well as explaining to Robin what goes on in the legislature. He would carry out Governor Marshall's policies. And Jonathan, dammit, I want to be a judge. I know I can be a good one. I know I can be fair without being a pushover or a bleeding heart. But what kind of judge would I make if, as a prosecutor, I turned my back on something that more and more appears to be a flagrant miscarriage of justice?"

She realized her voice had gone up slightly. "Sorry," she said. "I'm getting carried away."

"I suppose we do what we must," Grace said quietly.

"My thought is that I'm not trying to ride a horse down Main Street and wave to the crowd. If something is wrong I'd like to find out what it is and then let Geoff Dorso carry the ball. I'm going to see Dr. Smith tomorrow afternoon. The key is to discredit his testimony. I frankly think he's on the verge of a breakdown. Stalking someone is a crime. If I can push him enough to get him to break down and admit that he lied on the stand, that he didn't give Suzanne that jewelry, that someone else may well have been involved, then we've got a new ball game. Geoff Dorso could take over and file a motion for a new trial. It will take a few months for it to be properly filed and heard. By then Frank could be governor."

"But you, my dear, may not be a member of the judiciary." Jonathan shook his head. "You're very persuasive, Kerry, and I admire you even while I worry about what this may cost you. First and foremost, though, is Robin. The threat may be just that, a threat, but you must take it seriously."

"I do take it seriously, Jonathan. Except when she was with Geoff Dorso's family, she hasn't been out of my sight all weekend. She won't be left alone for a minute."

"Kerry, anytime you feel your house isn't safe, leave her here," Grace urged. "Our security is excellent, and we'll keep the outside gate closed. It's alarmed, so we'll know if anyone tries to come in. We'll find a retired cop to drive her back and forth from school."

Kerry put her hand over Grace's fingers and gave them a hint of a squeeze. "I love you two," she said simply. "Jonathan, please don't be disappointed that I have to do this."

"I'm proud of you, I guess," Jonathan said. "I'll do my best to keep your name in for the appointment but . . ."

"But don't count on it. I know," Kerry said slowly. "Goodness, choices can be pretty tough, can't they?"

"I think we'd better change the subject," Jonathan said briskly. "But keep me posted, Kerry."

"Of course."

"On a happier note, Grace felt well enough to go out to dinner the other night," he said.

"Oh, Grace, I'm so glad," Kerry said sincerely.

"We met someone there who's been on my mind ever since, purely because I can't remember where I've met him before," Grace said. "A Jason Arnott."

Kerry had not thought it necessary to talk about Jason Arnott.

For the moment she decided to say nothing except, "Why do you think you know him?"

"I don't know," Grace said. "But I'm sure that either I've met him before, or I've seen his picture in the paper." She shrugged. "It will come to me eventually. It always does."

76

The sequestered jury in the Jimmy Weeks trial did not know about the assassination of Barney Haskell and Mark Young, but the media were making sure that everyone else did. Over the weekend many newspaper columns had been dedicated to the investigation, and every television news program featured seemingly endless scene-of-the-crime coverage.

A frightened witness, whose identity was not revealed, had finally phoned the police. He had been on his way to withdraw cash from an ATM and had seen a dark blue Toyota pull into the parking lot of the small building that housed Mark Young's law office. That was at ten after seven. The front right tire of the witness's car had felt wobbly, and he had pulled over to the curb to examine it. He was crouched beside it when he saw the door of the office building open again and a man in his thirties run back to the Toyota. His face was obscured, but he was carrying what appeared to be an oversized gun.

The witness got part of the Toyota's out-of-state license number. Good police work tracked the car down and identified it as one that had been stolen Thursday night in Philadelphia. Late Friday, its burned-out frame was found in Newark.

Even the slight possibility that Haskell and Young had been the victims of a random mugging disappeared in light of that evidence. It was obviously a mob hit, and there was no doubt it had been ordered by Jimmy Weeks. But the police were unsure as to how to prove it. The witness would not be able to identify the gunman. The car was gone. The bullets that had killed the victims were undoubtedly from an unlicensed gun that was now at the bottom of a river, or would be exchanged for a toy at Christmas with no questions asked.

On Monday, Geoff Dorso once again spent a few hours at the Jimmy Weeks trial. The government was building its case brick by brick, with solid, seemingly irrefutable evidence. Royce, the U.S. attorney who seemed intent on being the candidate for governor opposite Frank Green, was resisting the impulse to grandstand. A scholarly-looking man with thinning hair and steel-framed glasses, his strategy was to be utterly plausible, to close off any alternate explanations for the outrageously complicated business affairs and money transfers of Weeks Enterprises.

He had charts that he referred to with the help of a long pointer, the kind Geoff remembered the nuns using when he was in grammar school. Geoff decided that Royce was a master at making Weeks' affairs easy for the jurors to grasp. One did not have to be a mathematical whiz or a CPA to follow his explanations.

Royce got the pilot of Jimmy Weeks' private plane on the stand and hammered at him. "How often did you fill out the appropriate paperwork for the corporate jet? . . . How often did Mr. Weeks use it solely for his private parties? . . . How often did he lend it to friends for their private entertainment? . . . Wasn't it billed to the company every single time the engines were turned on in that jet? . . . All those tax deductions he took for so-called business expenses were really for his personal joyrides, weren't they?"

When it was Bob Kinellen's turn to cross-examine, Geoff saw that he turned on all his charm, trying to make the pilot trip himself up, trying to confuse him on dates, on the purpose of the trips. Once again, Geoff thought that Kinellen was good, but probably not good enough. He knew that there was no way of being sure what was going on in the jurors' minds, but Geoff didn't think they were buying it.

He studied the impassive face of Jimmy Weeks. He always came to the courtroom dressed in a conservative business suit, white shirt and tie. He looked the part he was trying to play—a fifty-year-old businessman-entrepreneur with a variety of enterprises, who was the victim of a tax-collecting witch-hunt.

Today Geoff was observing him from the viewpoint of the connection he had had with Suzanne Reardon. What was it? he wondered. How serious had it been? Was Weeks the one who had given her the jewelry? He had heard about the paper found on Haskell's lawyer that might have been the wording on the note that accompanied the roses given to Suzanne Reardon the day she died, but with Haskell dead and the actual note still missing, it would be impossible to prove any connection to Weeks.

The jewelry might provide an interesting angle, though, Geoff realized, and one worth investigating. I wonder if he goes to any one place to buy baubles for his girlfriends? he asked himself. Who did I date a couple of years ago who told me she'd been out with Weeks? he wondered. The name wouldn't come, but he would go through his daily reminders of two and three years ago. He was sure he had marked it down somewhere.

When the judge called a recess, Geoff slipped quickly out of the courtroom. He was halfway down the corridor when from behind him he heard someone call his name. It was Bob Kinellen. He waited for him to catch up. "Aren't you taking a lot of interest in my client?" Kinellen asked quietly.

"General interest at this point," Geoff replied.

"Is that why you're seeing Kerry?"

"Bob, I don't think you have even the faintest right to ask that question. Nevertheless I'll answer it. I was glad to be there for her after you dropped the bombshell that your illustrious client is threatening her child. Has anyone nominated you for Father of the Year yet? If not, don't waste your time waiting for the phone to ring. Somehow I don't think you'll make it."

77

On Monday morning, Grace Hoover stayed in bed longer than usual. Even though the house was comfortably warm, the winter cold seemed to somehow find its way into her bones and joints. Her hands and fingers and legs and knees and ankles ached fiercely. After the legislature completed the present session, she and Jonathan would go to their home in New Mexico. She reminded herself that it would be better there, that the hot, dry climate always helped her condition.

Years ago, at the onset of her illness, Grace had decided that she would never succumb to self-pity. To her, that was the dreariest of all emotions. Even so, on her darkest days she admitted to herself that besides the constantly increasing pain, it had been devastating to have to constantly lessen her activities.

She had been one of the few wives who actually enjoyed going to the many affairs that a politician such as Jonathan had to attend. God knows it wasn't that she wanted to spend hours at them, but she relished the adulation Jonathan received. She was so proud of him. He should have been governor. She knew that.

Then, after Jonathan made the obligatory appearances at these functions, they would enjoy a quiet late dinner, or on the spur of the moment decide to escape somewhere for the weekend. Grace smiled to herself, remembering how twenty years after they were married, someone they chatted with at an Arizona resort remarked that they had the look of honeymooners.

Now the nuisance of the wheelchair, and the necessity of bringing along a nurse's aide to help her bathe and dress, made a hotel stay a nightmare for Grace. She would not let Jonathan give her that kind of assistance and was better off at home, where a practical nurse came in daily.

She had enjoyed going to the club for dinner the other night. It was the first time in many weeks that she had been out. But that Jason Arnott—isn't it funny that I can't get him out of my mind? she thought as she restlessly tried to flex her fingers. She had asked Jonathan about him again, but he could reason only that possibly she had been with him at some fund-raiser Arnott may have attended.

It had been a dozen years since Grace went to any of those big events. By then she had been on two canes, and disliked jostling crowds. No, she knew it was something else that triggered her memory of him. Oh well, she said to herself, it will come in time.

The housekeeper, Carrie, came into the bedroom with a tray. "I thought you'd be ready for a second cup of tea around now," she said cheerfully.

"I am, Carrie. Thanks."

Carrie laid down the tray and propped up the pillows. "There. That's better." She reached in her pocket and pulled out a folded sheet of paper. "Oh, Mrs. Hoover, this was in the wastebasket in the senator's study. I know the senator was throwing it away, but I still want to ask if it's all right if I take it. All my grandson

Billy talks about is being an FBI agent someday. He'd get such kick out of seeing a genuine flyer they sent out." She unfolded it and handed it to Grace.

Grace glanced at it and started to hand it back, then stopped. Jonathan had shown this to her on Friday afternoon, joking, "Anyone you know?" The covering letter explained that the flyer was being sent to anyone who had been a guest at gatherings in homes that were burglarized shortly afterwards.

The grainy, almost indistinguishable picture was of a felon in the process of committing a robbery. He was believed to be responsible for many similar break-ins, almost all of them following a party or social function of some kind. One theory was that he might have been a guest.

The covering letter concluded with the promise that any information would be kept confidential.

"I know the Peales' Washington home was broken into a few years ago," Jonathan had said. "Terrible business. I had been there to Jock's victory party. Two weeks later his mother came home early from a family vacation and must have walked in on the thief. She was found at the bottom of the staircase with a broken neck, and the John White Alexander painting was missing."

Maybe it was because I know the Peales that I paid so much attention to this picture, Grace thought as she gripped the flyer. The camera must have been below him, the way his face is angled.

She studied the blurry image, the narrow neck, sharp-tipped nose, pursed lips. It wasn't what you'd notice when you look directly at someone's face, she thought. But when you're looking up at him from a wheelchair, you see him from this angle.

I would swear this looks like that man I met at the club the other night, Jason Arnott, Grace thought. Was it possible?

"Carrie, hand me the phone, please." A moment later Grace was speaking to Amanda Coble, who had introduced her to Jason Arnott at the club. After the usual greetings, she brought the conversation around to him. She confessed that she was still plagued by the impression that she had met him before. Where did he live? she asked. What did he do?

When she hung up, Grace sipped the now cooling tea and studied the picture again. According to Amanda, Arnott was an art and antiques expert, and he traveled in the best social circles from Washington to Newport.

Grace called Jonathan in his Trenton office. He was out at the time, but when he got back to her at three-thirty that afternoon, she told him what she believed she had figured out, that Jason Arnott was the burglar the FBI was looking for.

"That's quite an accusation, dear," Jonathan said cautiously.

"I've got good eyes, Jonathan. You know that."

"Yes, I do," he agreed quietly. "And frankly, if it were anyone other than you, I would hesitate to pass the name along to the FBI. I don't want to put anything in writing, but give me the confidential number on that flyer. I'll make a phone call."

"No," Grace said. "As long as you agree that it's all right to speak to the FBI, I'll make the call. If I'm dead wrong, you're not connected to it. If I'm right, I at least get to feel that at last I've done something useful again. I very much liked Jock Peale's mother when I met her years ago. I'd love to be the one who found her killer. No one should be allowed to get away with murder."

78

Dr. Charles Smith was in a very bad mood. He had spent a solitary weekend made more frustratingly lonely by the fact that he could not reach Barbara Tompkins. Saturday had been such a beautiful day, he thought she might enjoy a drive up through Westchester, with a stop for an early lunch at one of the little inns along the Hudson.

He got her answering machine, however, and if she was home, she did not return his call.

Sunday was no better. Usually on Sunday Smith forced himself to look in the "Arts and Leisure" section of the *Times* to find an off-Broadway play or a recital or a Lincoln Center event to attend. But he had no heart for any of it that day. Most of Sunday was passed lying on top of his bed, fully dressed, studying the picture of Suzanne on the wall.

What I achieved was so incredible, he said to himself. *That painfully plain, bad-tempered offspring of two handsome parents had been given back her birthright—and so much more. He had given her beauty so natural, so breathtaking, that it inspired awe in those who encountered it.*

On Monday morning he tried Barbara at the office and was told that she was on a business trip to California, that she would not be back for two weeks. Now he really was upset. He knew that was a lie. In the course of conversation at dinner on Thursday night, Barbara had mentioned something about looking forward to a business lunch at La Grenouille this Wednesday. He remembered because she said she had never been to that restaurant and was especially looking forward to it.

For the rest of Monday, Smith found it difficult to concentrate on his patients. Not that his schedule was very busy. He seemed to have fewer and fewer patients, and those who came in for initial consultation seldom came back. Not that he really cared —so few of them had the potential for genuine beauty.

And once again he felt Carpenter's eyes following him. She was very efficient, but he had decided it might be time to let her go. He had noticed that the other day, during the rhinoplasty, she had watched him like an anxious mother, hoping her child will perform his part in the school play without stumbling.

When his three-thirty appointment canceled, Smith decided to go home early. He would get the car and drive up to Barbara's office and park across the street. She usually left a few minutes after five, but he wanted to be there early just in case. The thought that she might be deliberately evading him was intolerable. If he learned that was true . . .

He was just stepping from the building lobby onto Fifth Avenue when he saw Kerry McGrath approaching. He looked around quickly for some way to avoid her, but it was impossible. She was blocking his path.

"Dr. Smith, I'm glad I caught you," Kerry said. "It's very important that I speak to you."

"Ms. McGrath, Mrs. Carpenter and the receptionist are still in the office. Any assistance you require can be handled by them." He turned and tried to walk past her.

She fell into step beside him. "Dr. Smith, Mrs. Carpenter and the receptionist can't discuss your daughter with me, and neither one of them is responsible for putting an innocent man in prison."

Charles Smith reacted as though she had thrown hot tar on him. "How dare you?" He stopped and grabbed her arm.

Kerry realized suddenly that he was about to strike her. His face was contorted with fury, his mouth twisted in a narrow snarl. She felt the trembling of his hand as his fingers pinched her wrist.

A man passing by looked at them curiously and stopped. "Are you all right, miss?" he asked.

"Am I all right, Doctor?" Kerry asked, her voice calm.

Smith released her arm. "Of course. Of course." He started to walk quickly down Fifth Avenue.

Kerry kept stride with him. "Dr. Smith, you know you will have to talk to me eventually. And I think it would be a much better idea to hear me out before things get out of hand and some very unpleasant situation occurs."

He did not respond.

She stayed next to him. She realized his breathing was rapid. "Dr. Smith, I don't care how fast you walk. I can outrun you. Shall we go back to your office, or is there some place around here where we could get a cup of coffee? We have got to talk. Otherwise I'm afraid you're going to be arrested and charged with being a stalker."

"Charged . . . with . . . what?" Again Smith whirled to face her.

"You have frightened Barbara Tompkins with your attention. Did you frighten Suzanne as well, Doctor? You were there the night she died, weren't you? Two people, a woman and a little boy, saw a black Mercedes in front of the house. The woman remembered part of the license plate, a 3 and an L. Today I learned that your license plate has an 8 and an L. Close enough to make it possible, I would say. Now, where shall we talk?"

He continued to stare at her for several moments, anger still flaring in his eyes. She watched as resignation gradually took its place, as his whole body seemed to go slack.

"I live down this street," he said, no longer looking at her. They were near the corner, and he pointed to the left.

Kerry took the words as an invitation. Am I making a mistake going inside with him? she wondered. He seems to be at the breaking point. Is there a housekeeper there?

But she decided whether she was alone with Smith or not, she might not get this chance again. The shock value of what she had said to him might have cracked something in his psyche. Dr. Smith, she was sure, did not mind seeing another man in prison but would not relish the prospect of facing the court in any way as a defendant.

They were at number 28 Washington Mews. Smith reached for his key and with a precise gesture inserted it in the lock, turned it and pushed the door open. "Come in if you insist, Ms. McGrath," he said.

The tips continued to filter in to the FBI from people who had been guests at one or more of the various burglarized homes. They now had twelve potential leads, but Si Morgan thought he had struck gold when on Monday afternoon his chief suspect, Sheldon Landi, admitted that his public relations firm was a coverup for his real activity.

Landi had been invited in for questioning, and for a brief moment Si thought he was about to hear a confession. Then Landi, perspiration on his brow, his hands twisting together whispered, "Have you ever read *Tell All*?"

"That's a supermarket tabloid, isn't it?" Si asked.

"Yes. One of the biggest. Four million circulation a week." For an instant there was a bragging note in Landi's tone. Then his voice dropped almost to the point of being inaudible as he said, "This must not go beyond this room, but I'm *Tell All*'s chief writer. If it ever gets out, I'll be dropped by all my friends."

So much for that, Si thought, after Landi left. That little sneak is just a gossipmonger; he wouldn't have the guts to pull off any of those jobs.

At quarter of four, one of his investigators came in. "Si, there's someone on the Hamilton case confidential line I think you should talk to. Her name is Grace Hoover. Her husband is New Jersey State Senator Hoover, and she thinks she saw the guy we're looking for the other night. It's one of the birds whose name has come up before, Jason Arnott."

"Arnott!" Si grabbed the phone. "Mrs. Hoover, I'm Si Morgan. Thank you for calling."

As he listened, he decided that Grace Hoover was the kind of witness lawmen pray to find. She was logical in her reasoning, clear in her presentation and articulate in explaining how, looking up from her wheelchair, her eyes were probably at the same angle as the lens of the surveillance camera in the Hamilton house.

"Looking straight at Mr. Arnott you would think his face was fuller than it appears when you're looking up at him," she explained. "Also when I asked him if we knew each other, his lips pursed together very tightly. I think it may be a habit he has when he's concentrating. Notice how they're scrunched in your picture. My feeling is that when the camera caught him, he was concentrating very much on that statuette. I would guess he was deciding whether or not it was genuine. My friend tells me he's quite an expert on antiques."

"Yes, he is." Si Morgan was excited. At last he had struck gold! "Mrs. Hoover, I can't tell you how much I appreciate this call. You do know that if this leads to a conviction, there's a substantial reward, over one hundred thousand dollars."

"Oh, I don't care about that," Grace Hoover said. "I'll simply send it on to a charity."

When Si hung up he thought of the tuition bills that were sitting on his desk at home for the spring semester at his sons' colleges. Shaking his head he turned on the intercom and sent for the three investigators who were working on the Hamilton case.

He told them that he wanted Arnott followed round the clock. Judging from the investigation they had made of him two years ago, if he was the thief, he had done an excellent job of concealing his tracks. It would be better to trail him for a while. He might just lead them to where he was keeping stolen property.

"If this isn't another red herring, and we can get proof he's committed the burglaries," Si said, "our next job will be to nail the Peale murder on him. The boss wants that one solved big time. The president's mother used to play bridge with Mrs. Peale."

D r. Smith's study was clean, but Kerry noticed that it had the shabby look of a room that had endured years of neglect. The ivory silk lamp shades, the kind she remembered from her grandmother's house, were darkened with age. One of them had at some point been scorched, and the silk around the burn mark was split. The overstuffed velour chairs were too low and felt scratchy.

It was a high-ceilinged room that could have been beautiful, but to Kerry it seemed frozen in time, as though it were the setting for a scene in a black-and-white movie made in the forties.

She had slipped off her raincoat, but Dr. Smith did not attempt to take it from her. The lack of even the gesture of courtesy seemed to suggest that she would not be staying long enough for him to bother. She folded the coat and draped it on the arm of the chair in which she was sitting.

Smith sat rigidly erect in a high-backed chair that she was sure he never would have chosen if he were alone.

"What do you want, Ms. McGrath?" The rimless glasses enlarged eyes that chilled with their hostile probing.

"I want the truth," Kerry said evenly. "I want to know why you claimed that it was you who gave Suzanne jewelry, when, in fact, it was given to her by another man. I want to know why you lied about Skip Reardon. He never threatened Suzanne. He may have lost patience with her; he may have gotten angry at her. But he never threatened her, did he? What possible reason would you have for swearing that he did?"

"Skip Reardon killed my daughter. He strangled her. He strangled her so viciously that her eyes hemorrhaged, so violently that blood vessels in her neck broke, her tongue hung out of her mouth like a dumb animal's . . ." His voice trailed off. What had started as an angry outburst ended almost as a sob.

"I realize how painful it must have been for you to examine those pictures, Dr. Smith." Kerry spoke softly. Her eyes narrowed as she saw that Smith was looking past her. "But why have you always blamed Skip for the tragedy?"

"He was her husband. He was jealous, insanely jealous. That was a fact. It was clear to everyone." He paused. "Now, Ms. McGrath, I don't want to discuss this any further. I demand to know what you mean by accusing me of stalking Barbara Tompkins."

"Wait. Let's talk about Reardon first, Doctor. You are wrong.

Skip was not insanely jealous of Suzanne. He did know she was seeing someone else." Kerry waited. "But so was he."

Smith's head jerked as though she had slapped him. "That's impossible. He was married to an exquisite woman and he worshiped her."

"*You* worshiped her, Doctor." Kerry hadn't expected to say that, but when she did, she knew it was true. "You put yourself in his position, didn't you? If you had been Suzanne's husband and had found out she was involved with another man, you'd have been capable of murder, wouldn't you?" She stared at him.

He did not blink. "How dare you! Suzanne was my daughter!" he said coldly. "Now get out of here." He stood and moved toward Kerry as though he might grab her to throw her out.

Kerry jumped up, clutching her coat, and stepped back from him. With a glance she checked to see that, if necessary, she could get around him to the front door. "No, Doctor," she said, "*Susie Stevens* was your daughter. *Suzanne* was your creation. And you felt you owned her, just as you believe you own Barbara Tompkins. Doctor, you were in Alpine the night Suzanne died. Did you kill her?"

"Kill Suzanne? Are you crazy?"

"But you were there."

"I was not!"

"Oh yes you were, and we're going to prove it. I promise you that. We're going to reopen the case and get the innocent man you condemned out of prison. You were jealous of him, Dr. Smith. You punished him because he had constant access to Suzanne and you didn't. But how you tried! In fact, you tried so hard that she became sick of your demands for her attention."

"That's not true." The words escaped through his clenched teeth.

Kerry saw that Smith's hand was trembling violently. She lowered her voice, took a more conciliatory tone. "Dr. Smith, if you didn't kill your daughter, someone else surely did. But it wasn't

Skip Reardon. I believe that you loved Suzanne in your own way. I believe that you wanted her murderer to be punished. But do you know what you've done? You've given Suzanne's killer a free ride. He's out there laughing at you, singing your praises for covering up for him. If we had the jewelry Skip is sure you didn't give Suzanne, we could try to trace it. We might be able to find out who did give it to her. Skip is certain that at least one piece is missing and may have been taken that night."

"He's lying."

"No, he isn't. It's what he's been saying from the beginning. And something else was stolen that night—a picture of Suzanne in a miniature frame. It had been on her night table. Did you take it?"

"I was not in that house the night Suzanne died!"

"Then who borrowed your Mercedes that night?"

Smith's "Get out!" was a guttural howl.

Kerry knew she had better not stay any longer. She circled around him but at the door turned to him again. "Dr. Smith, Barbara Tompkins spoke to me. She is alarmed. She moved up a business trip solely to get away from you. When she returns in ten days, I'm going to personally escort her to the New York police to lodge a complaint against you."

She opened the door to the old carriage house, and a blast of cold air swept into the foyer. "Unless," she added, "you come to terms with the fact that you need both physical and psychological help. And unless you satisfy me that you have told the full truth about what happened the night Suzanne died. And unless you give me the jewelry you suspect may have been given to her by a man other than you or her husband."

When Kerry bundled up her collar and thrust her hands in her pockets for the three-block walk to her car, she was aware neither of Smith's probing eyes studying her from behind the grille in the study window, nor of the stranger parked on Fifth Avenue who picked up his cellular phone and called in a report of her visit in Washington Mews.

81

The U.S. attorney, in cooperation with the Middlesex and Ocean County prosecutor's offices, obtained a search warrant for both the permanent residence and the summer home of the late Barney Haskell. Living apart from his wife most of the time, Barney resided in a pleasant split-level house on a quiet street in Edison, an attractive middle-income town. His neighbors there told the media that Barney had never bothered with any of them but was always polite if they met face to face.

His other home, a modern two-story structure overlooking the ocean on Long Beach Island, was where his wife resided year round. Neighbors there told the investigators that during the summer Barney was around a lot, had always spent a good amount of time fishing on his twenty-three-foot Chris-Craft, and that his other hobby was carpentry. His workshop was in his garage.

A couple of neighbors said his wife had invited them in to show off the massive white-oak hutch Barney had made to house their entertainment center last year. It seemed to be his pride and joy.

The investigators knew that Barney had to have had solid

evidence against Jimmy Weeks to back up his attempted plea bargain. They also knew that if they didn't find it quickly, Jimmy Weeks' people would ferret it out and destroy it.

Despite the screeching protests of his widow, who cried that Barney was a victim, and that this was her home even if poor Barney's name was on it, and that they had no right to destroy it, they took apart everything, including the oak hutch that was nailed to the wall of the television room.

When they had ripped the wood from the plaster, they found themselves looking at a safe large enough to house the records of a small office.

As the media gathered outside, television cameras recorded the arrival on the scene of a retired safecracker now on the payroll of the United States government. Fifteen minutes later the safe was opened, and shortly afterwards, at 4:15 P.M. that afternoon, U.S. Attorney Royce received a phone call from Les Howard.

A second set of books for Weeks Enterprises had been found, as well as day-at-a-glance date books going back fifteen years, in which Barney had chronicled Jimmy's appointments along with his own notations about the purpose of the meetings and what was discussed.

A delighted Royce was told that there were also shoe boxes with copies of receipts for high-tag items, including furs and jewelry and cars for Jimmy's various girlfriends, which Barney had flagged "No sales tax paid."

"It's a bonanza, a treasure trove," Howard assured Royce. "Barney sure must have heard that old adage, 'Treat your friend as though he may become your enemy.' He has to have been preparing since day one to barter his way out of prison by throwing Jimmy to us if they ever got indicted."

The judge had adjourned the trial until the next morning rather than start with a new witness at four o'clock. Another break, Royce thought. After he hung up the phone, a smile continued to linger on his lips as he savored the splendid news. He said aloud, "Thanks, Barney, I always knew you'd come through." Then he sat in silence while he considered his next move.

Martha Luce, Jimmy's personal bookkeeper, was scheduled to be a defense witness. They already had her sworn statement that the records she had kept were totally accurate and the only set that existed. Given the choice of turning government witness in exchange for immunity from a long prison sentence, Royce decided that it shouldn't be too hard to convince Ms. Luce where her best interests lay.

82

Jason Arnott had awakened late on Sunday morning with flulike symptoms and decided not to go to the Catskill house as planned. Instead he spent the day in bed, getting up only long enough to prepare some light food for himself. It was at times such as this that he regretted not having a live-in housekeeper.

On the other hand, he thoroughly enjoyed the privacy of having the house to himself without someone underfoot. He brought books and newspapers to his room and spent the day reading, in between sipping orange juice and dozing.

Every few hours, however, he compulsively pulled out the FBI flyer to reassure himself that no one could possibly tie him to that grainy caricature of a picture.

By Monday evening he was feeling much better and had completely convinced himself that the flyer was not a threat. He reminded himself that even if an FBI agent showed up at the door to subject him to routine questioning because he had been one of the guests at a Hamilton party, they would never be able to connect him to the theft.

Not with that picture. Not with his phone records. Not with a single antique or painting in this house. Not with the most scrupulous financial check. Not even with the reservation at the hotel in Washington the weekend of the robbery at the Hamilton home, since he had used one of his fake identities when he checked in.

There was no question. He was safe. He promised himself that tomorrow, or certainly by Wednesday, he would drive up to the Catskills and spend a few days enjoying his treasures.

Jason could not know that the FBI agents had already obtained a court order allowing them to tap his phone and were now quietly surveying his house. He could not know that from now on he wouldn't make a single move without being observed and without being followed.

83

Driving north out of Manhattan's Greenwich Village, Kerry was caught in the first surge of rush hour traffic. It was twenty of five when she pulled her car out of the garage on Twelfth Street. It was five past six when she turned into her driveway and saw Geoff's Volvo parked in front of the other door of the two-car garage.

She had called home from the car phone as she was leaving the garage, and had been only partially reassured to talk to both Robin and Alison, the sitter. She had warned them both not to go out under any circumstances and not to open the door for anyone until she got home.

Seeing Geoff's car made her realize that Alison's car was gone. Had Geoff come because of a problem? Kerry turned off the engine and lights, scrambled from her car, slammed the door behind her and ran toward the house.

Robin had obviously been watching for her. The front door opened as she raced up the steps.

"Rob, is anything wrong?"

"No, Mom, we're fine. When Geoff got here he told Alison it was all right to go ahead home, that he'd wait for you." Robin's face became worried. "That was okay, wasn't it? I mean letting Geoff in."

"Of course." Kerry hugged Robin. "Where is he?"

"In here," Geoff said as he appeared at the door of the kitchen. "I thought that having had one Dorso home-cooked meal on Saturday night, you might be game for another tonight. Very simple menu. Lamb chops, a green salad and baked potato."

Kerry realized she was both tense and hungry. "Sounds wonderful," she sighed as she unbuttoned her coat.

Geoff quickly moved to take it from her. It seemed natural that as he put it over one arm, he slid the other arm around her and kissed her cheek. "Hard day at the factory?"

For a brief moment she let her face rest in the warm spot beneath his neck. "There have been easier ones."

Robin said, "Mom, I'm going upstairs to finish my homework, but I do think since I'm the one in danger, I should know exactly what's going on. What did Dr. Smith say when you saw him?"

"Finish your homework and let me unwind for a few minutes. I promise a full report later."

"Okay."

Geoff had turned on the gas fire in the family room. He had brought in sherry and had glasses ready alongside the bottle on the coffee table there. "I hope I'm not making myself too much at home," he apologized.

Kerry sank onto the couch and kicked off her shoes. She shook her head and smiled. "No, you're not."

"I've got news for you, but you go first. Tell me about Smith."

"I'd better tell you about Frank Green first. I told him I was leaving the office early this afternoon, and I told him why."

"What did he say?"

"It's what he *didn't* say that hung in the air. But in fairness to him, even though I think he was choking on the words, he told me that he hoped I didn't think he would rather see an innocent man in prison than be politically embarrassed himself." She shrugged. "The problem is, I wish I could believe him."

"Maybe you can. How about Smith?"

"I got to him, Geoff. I know I did. The guy is cracking up. If he doesn't start telling the truth, my next move is to get Barbara Tompkins to file a stalking complaint against him. The prospect of that shocked him right down to his toes, I could tell. But I think rather than risk having it happen, he'll come through and we'll get some answers."

She stared into the fire, watching the flames lick at the artificial logs. Then she added slowly, "Geoff, I told Smith that we had two witnesses who saw his car that night. I threw at him that maybe the reason he was so anxious to see Skip convicted was because he was the one who killed Suzanne. Geoff, I think he was in love with her, not as a daughter, maybe not even just as a woman, but as his *creation.*"

She turned to him. "Think about this scenario. Suzanne is sick of having her father around her so much, of having him show up wherever she goes. Jason Arnott told me that much, and I believe him. So on the evening of the murder, Dr. Smith drives out to see her. Skip has come and gone, just as he claimed. Suzanne is in the foyer, arranging flowers from another man. Don't forget, the card was never found. Smith is angry, hurt and jealous. It isn't just Skip he has to contend with; now it's Jimmy Weeks as well. In a fit of rage he strangles Suzanne, and because he's always hated Skip, he takes the card, makes up the story of Suzanne being afraid of Skip and becomes the prosecution's principal witness.

"This way Skip, his rival for Suzanne's attention, is not only punished by spending at least thirty years in prison, but the police don't look elsewhere for a suspect."

"It makes sense," Geoff said slowly. "But then why would Jimmy Weeks be so worried about your reopening the case?"

"I've thought about that too. And, in fact, you could make an equally good argument that he was involved with Suzanne. That they quarreled that night, and he murdered her. Another scenario is that Suzanne told him about the land in Pennsylvania that Skip had optioned. Could Jimmy have inadvertently told her about the highway going through and then have killed her to keep her from telling Skip? He picked up those options for next to nothing, I gather."

"You've done a lot of thinking today, lady," Geoff said. "And you've made a damn good case for either scenario. Did you happen to listen to the news on the way home?"

"My brain needed a rest. I listened to the station with the golden oldies. Otherwise I'd have gone mad in that traffic."

"You made a better choice. But if you had listened to a news station, you'd know that the stuff Barney Haskell was planning to swap for a plea bargain is now in the U.S. attorney's hands. Apparently Barney kept records like nobody else ever kept records. Tomorrow, if Frank Green is smart, instead of resisting your investigation he'll request access to any records they can find of jewelry Weeks bought in the months before Suzanne's murder. If we can tie him to stuff like the zodiac bracelet, we've got proof Smith was a liar." He stood up. "I would say, Kerry McGrath, that you have sung for your supper. Wait here. I'll let you know when it's ready."

Kerry curled up on the couch and sipped the sherry, but even with the fire the room felt somehow less than comfortable. A moment later she got up and walked into the kitchen. "Okay if I watch you play chef? It's warmer in here."

Geoff left at nine o'clock. When the door closed behind him, Robin said, "Mom, I've got to ask you. This guy Dad is defending? From what you tell me, Dad's not going to win the case. Is that right?"

"Not if all the evidence we believe has been found is what it's cracked up to be."

"Will that be bad for him?"

"No one likes to lose a case, but no, Robin, I think the best thing that could ever happen to your father is to see Jimmy Weeks convicted."

"You're sure Weeks is the one who's trying to scare me?"

"Yes, I'm about as sure as I can get. That's why the sooner we can find out his connection to Suzanne Reardon, the sooner he won't have any reasons to try to scare us off."

"Geoff's a defense attorney, isn't he?"

"Yes, he is."

"Would Geoff ever defend a guy like Jimmy Weeks?"

"No, Robin. I'm pretty sure he wouldn't."

"I don't think he would either."

At nine-thirty, Kerry remembered that she'd promised to report to Jonathan and Grace about her meeting with Dr. Smith. "You think he may break down and admit he lied?" Jonathan asked when she reached him.

"I think so."

Grace was on the other extension. "Let's tell Kerry my news,

Jonathan. Kerry, today I've either been a good detective or made an awful fool of myself."

Kerry had not thought it important to bring up Arnott's name on Sunday when she told Jonathan and Grace about Dr. Smith and Jimmy Weeks. When she heard what Grace had to say about him, she was glad that neither one of them could see the expression on her face.

Jason Arnott. The friend who was constantly with Suzanne Reardon. Who, despite his seeming frankness, had struck Kerry as being too posed to be true. If he was a thief, if, according to the FBI flyer Grace described, he was also a murder suspect, where did he fit in the conundrum surrounding the Sweetheart Murder Case?

Dr. Charles Smith sat for long hours after he forced Kerry to leave. "Stalker!" "Murderer!" "Liar!" The accusations she had thrown at him made him shudder with revulsion. It was the same revulsion he felt when he looked at a maimed or scarred or ugly face. He could feel his very being tremble with the need to change it, to redeem it, to make things right. To find for it the beauty that his skilled hands could wrest from bone and muscle and flesh.

In those instances the wrath he felt had been directed against the fire or the accident or the unfair blending of genes that had caused the aberration. Now his wrath was directed at the young woman who had sat here in judgment of him.

"Stalker!" To call him a stalker because a brief glimpse of the near perfection he had created gave him pleasure! He wished he could have looked into the future and known that this was the way Barbara Tompkins would express her thanks. He would have given her a face all right—a face with skin that collapsed into wrinkles, eyes that drooped, nostrils that flared.

Suppose McGrath took Tompkins to the police to file that complaint. She had said she would, and Smith knew she meant it.

She had called him a murderer. *Murderer!* Did she really think that he could have done that to Suzanne? Burning misery raced through him as he lived again the moment when he had rung the bell, over and over, then turned the handle and found the door unlocked.

And Suzanne there, in the foyer, almost at his feet. Suzanne— but not Suzanne. That distorted creature with bulging, hemor-rhaged eyes, and gaping mouth and protruding tongue—that was not the exquisite creature he had created.

Even her body appeared awkward and unlovely, crumpled as it was, the left leg twisted under the right one, the heel of her left shoe jabbing her right calf, those fresh red roses scattered over her, a mocking tribute to death.

Smith remembered how he had stood over her, his only thought an incongruous one—that this is how Michelangelo would have felt had he seen his *Pietà* broken and defaced as it had been by the lunatic who attacked it years ago in St. Peter's.

He remembered how he had cursed Suzanne, cursed her be-cause she had not heeded his warnings. She had married Reardon against his wishes. "Wait," he had urged her. "He's not good enough for you."

"In your eyes, no one will ever be good enough for me," she had shouted back.

He had endured the way they looked at each other, the way their hands clasped across the table, the way they sat together, side by side on the couch, or with Suzanne on Reardon's lap in the big, deep chair, as he had seen them when he had looked through the window at night.

To have to endure all that had been bad enough, but it was too much when Suzanne became restless and began seeing other men, none of them worthy of her, and then came to him, asking for favors, saying "Charles, you must let Skip think you bought me this . . . and this . . . and this . . ."

Or she would say, "Doctor, why are you so upset? You told me I should have all the good times I've missed. Well, I'm having them. Skip works too hard. He isn't fun. You take risks when you operate. I'm just like you. I take risks too. Now remember, Doctor Charles, you're a generous daddy." Her impudent kiss, flirting with him, sure of her power, of his tolerance.

Murderer? No, Skip was the murderer. As he stood over Suzanne's body, Smith had known exactly what had happened. Her loutish husband had come home to find Suzanne with flowers from another man, and he had exploded. Just as *I* would, Smith had thought when his eye fell on the card half hidden by Suzanne's body.

And then, standing there over her, a whole scenario had played itself out in his mind. Skip, the jealous husband—a jury might be lenient with a man who killed his wife in a moment of passion. He might get off with a light sentence. Or maybe even no sentence at all.

I won't let that happen, he had vowed. Smith remembered how he had closed his eyes, blotting out the ugly, distorted face in front of him and, instead, seeing Suzanne in all her beauty. *Suzanne, I promise you that!*

It had not been hard to keep the promise. All he had to do was take the card that had come with the flowers, then go home and wait for the inevitable call that would tell him that Suzanne, his daughter, was dead.

When the police had questioned him, he had told them that Skip was insanely jealous, that Suzanne feared for her life, and, obeying the last request she made of him, he claimed he had given her all the pieces of jewelry that Skip had questioned.

No, let Ms. McGrath say all she might want. The murderer was in jail. And he would stay there.

It was almost ten o'clock when Charles Smith got up. It was all over. He couldn't operate anymore. He no longer wanted to see Barbara Tompkins. She disgusted him. He went into the bedroom, opened the small safe in the closet and took out a gun.

It would be so easy. Where would he go? he wondered. He did believe that the spirit moves on. Reincarnation? Maybe. Maybe this time he would be born Suzanne's peer. Maybe they would fall in love. A smile played on his lips.

But then, as he was about to close the safe, he looked at Suzanne's jewelry case.

Suppose McGrath was right. Suppose it hadn't been Skip but another person who had taken Suzanne's life. McGrath had said that person was laughing now, mockingly grateful for the testimony that had condemned Skip.

There was a way to rectify that. If Reardon was not the killer, then McGrath would have all that she needed to find the man who had murdered Suzanne.

Smith reached for the jewelry case, laid the gun on top of it and carried both to his desk in the study. Then with precise movements he took out a sheet of stationery and unscrewed the top from his pen.

When he was finished writing, he wrapped the jewelry case and the note together and managed to force them into one of the several Federal Express mailers that he kept at home for convenience. He addressed the package to Assistant Prosecutor Kerry McGrath at the Bergen County Prosecutor's Office, Hackensack, New Jersey. It was an address he remembered well.

He put on his coat and muffler and walked eight blocks to the Federal Express drop that he had used on occasion.

It was just eleven o'clock when he returned home. He took off his coat, picked up the gun, went back into the bedroom and stretched out on the bed, still fully dressed. He turned off all the lights except the one that illuminated Suzanne's picture.

He would end this day with her and begin the new life at the stroke of midnight. The decision made, he felt calm, even happy.

At eleven-thirty the doorbell began to ring. Who? he wondered. Angrily he tried to ignore it, but a persistent finger was pressed against it. He was sure he knew what it was. Once there had been an accident on the corner, and a neighbor had run to him for help. After all, he was a doctor. If there had been an accident, just this one more time his skill might be put to use.

Dr. Charles Smith unlocked and opened his door, then slumped against it as a bullet found its mark between his eyes.

85

On Tuesday morning, Deidre Reardon and Beth Taylor were already in the reception room of Geoff Dorso's law office when he arrived at nine o'clock.

Beth apologized for both of them. "Geoff, I'm so sorry to come without calling first," she said, "but Deidre has to go into the hospital for the angioplasty tomorrow morning. I know it will rest her mind if she has a chance to talk to you for a few minutes and give you that picture of Suzanne we talked about the other day."

Deidre Reardon was looking at him anxiously. "Oh, come on, Deidre," Geoff said heartily, "you know you don't have to make excuses for seeing me. Aren't you the mother of my star client?"

"Sure. It's all those billing hours you're logging," Deidre Reardon murmured with a relieved smile, as Geoff took her hands in his. "It's just that I'm so embarrassed at the way I barged into that lovely Kerry McGrath's office last week and treated her like dirt. And then to realize her own child has been threatened because Kerry's trying to help my son."

"Kerry absolutely understood how you felt that day. Come back to my office. I'm sure the coffeepot's on."

"We will only stay five minutes," Beth promised as Geoff placed a coffee mug in front of her. "And we won't waste your time saying it's been a glimpse of heaven to think that finally there's real, genuine hope for Skip. You know how we feel, and you know how grateful we are for everything you are doing."

"Kerry saw Dr. Smith late yesterday afternoon," Geoff said. "She thinks she got to him. But there are other developments as well." He told them about Barney Haskell's records. "We may at last have a chance to track the source of the jewelry we think Weeks gave Suzanne."

"That's one of the reasons we're here," Deidre Reardon told him. "Remember I said I had a picture that showed Suzanne wearing the missing set of antique diamond pins? As soon as I got home from the prison Saturday night I went to get it out of the file and couldn't find it. I spent all Sunday and yesterday ransacking the apartment, looking for it. Of course it wasn't there. Stupidly, I had forgotten that at some point I'd covered it with one of those plastic protectors and put it with my own personal papers. Anyway, I finally found it. With all the talk about the jewelry the other day, I felt it important for you to have it."

She handed him a legal-size manila envelope. From it, he extracted a folded page from *Palisades Community Life,* a tabloid-sized weekly paper. As he opened it Geoff noticed the date, April 24th, nearly eleven years ago and barely a month before Suzanne Reardon died.

The group picture from the Palisades Country Club took up the space of four columns of print. Geoff recognized Suzanne Reardon immediately. Her outstanding beauty leaped from the page. She was standing at a slight angle, and the camera had clearly caught the sparkling diamonds on the lapel of her jacket.

"This is the double pin that disappeared," Deidre explained, pointing to it. "But Skip doesn't know when he last saw it on Suzanne."

"I'm glad to have this," Geoff said. "When we can get a copy of some of those records Haskell kept, we may be able to trace the pin."

It almost hurt to see the eager hope on both their faces. Don't let me fail them, he prayed as he walked them back to the reception room. At the door he hugged Deidre. "Now remember, you get this angioplasty over and start feeling better. We can't have you sick when they unlock the door for Skip."

"Geoff, I haven't walked barefoot through hell this long to check out now."

After having taken care of a number of client calls and queries, Geoff decided to call Kerry. Maybe she would want to have a fax of the picture Deidre had brought in. Or maybe I just want to talk to her, he admitted to himself.

When her secretary put her through, Kerry's frightened voice sent chills through Geoff. "I just opened a Federal Express package that Dr. Smith sent me. Inside was a note and Suzanne's jewelry case and the card that must have come with the sweetheart roses. Geoff, he admits he lied about Skip and the jewelry. He told me that by the time I read this he'll have committed suicide."

"My God, Kerry, did—"

"No, it's not that. You see, he *didn't*. Geoff, Mrs. Carpenter from his office just called me. When Dr. Smith didn't come in for an early appointment, and didn't answer the phone, she went to his house. His door was open a crack and she went in. She found his body lying in the foyer. He'd been shot, and the house ransacked. Geoff, was it because someone didn't want Dr. Smith to change his testimony and was looking for the jewelry? Geoff, who is doing this? Will Robin be next?"

86

At nine-thirty that morning, Jason Arnott looked out the window, saw the cloudy, overcast sky and felt vaguely depressed. Other than some residual achiness in his legs and back, he was over the bug or virus that had laid him low over the weekend. But he could not overcome the uneasy sense that something was wrong.

It was that damn FBI flyer, of course. But he had felt the same way after that night in Congressman Peale's house. A few of the downstairs lamps that were on an automatic switch had been on when he got there, but the upstairs rooms were all dark. He had been coming down the hallway, carrying the painting and the lockbox that he had pried from the wall, when he heard footsteps coming up the stairs. He had barely had time to hold the painting in front of his face when light flooded the hallway.

Then he had heard the quavering gasp, "Oh, dear God," and knew it was the congressman's mother. He hadn't intended to hurt her. Instinctively he had rushed toward her, holding the painting as a shield, intending only to knock her down and grab her glasses so he could make his getaway. He had spent a long time talking with her at Peale's inaugural party, and he knew she was blind as a bat without them.

But the heavy portrait frame had caught the side of her head harder than he intended, and she had toppled backwards down the stairs. He knew from that final gurgle that she made before she went still that she was dead. For months afterward he had looked over his shoulder, expecting to see someone coming toward him with handcuffs.

Now, no matter how hard he tried to convince himself otherwise, the FBI flyer was giving him that same case of the jitters.

After the Peale case, his only solace had been to feast his eyes on the John White Alexander masterpiece *At Rest,* which he had taken that night. He kept it in the master bedroom of the Catskill house just as Peale had kept it in his master bedroom. It was so amusing to know that thousands of people trooped through the Metropolitan Museum of Art to gaze on its companion piece, *Repose.* Of the two, he preferred *At Rest.* The reclining figure of a beautiful woman had the same long sinuous lines as *Repose,* but the closed eyes, the look on the sensual face reminded him now of Suzanne.

The miniature frame with her portrait was on his night table, and it amused him to have both in his room, even though the imitation Fabergé frame was unworthy of the glorious company it kept. The night table was gilt and marble, an exquisite example of Gothic Revival, and had been obtained in the grand haul when he had hired a van and practically emptied the Merriman house.

He would call ahead. He enjoyed arriving there to find the heat on and the refrigerator stocked. Instead of using his home phone, however, he would call his housekeeper on a cellular phone that was registered to one of his aliases.

Inside what seemed to be a repair van of Public Service Gas and Electric the signal came that Arnott was making a call. As the agents listened, they smiled triumphantly at each other. "I think we are about to trace the foxy Mr. Arnott to his lair," the senior agent on the job observed. They listened as Jason concluded the conversation by saying, "Thank you, Maddie. I'll leave here in an hour and should be there by one."

Maddie's heavy monotone reply was, "I'll have everything ready for you. You can count on me."

87

Frank Green was trying a case, and it was noon before Kerry was able to inform him of Smith's murder and the Federal Express packet she had received from him late that morning. She was fully composed now and wondered why she had allowed herself to lose control when Geoff had phoned. But her emotions were something that she would explore later. For now, the knowledge that Joe Palumbo was parked outside Robin's school, waiting to escort her home and then stand watch at the house until Kerry got home, was enough to help relieve her immediate fears.

Green went carefully through the contents of the jewelry box, comparing each piece with those Smith had mentioned in the letter he had included in the package to Kerry. "Zodiac brace-let," he read. "That's right here. Watch with gold numerals, ivory face, diamond and gold band. Okay. Here it is. Emerald and diamond ring set in pink gold. That's right here. Antique diamond bracelet. Three bands of diamonds attached by dia-mond clasps." He held it up. "That's a beauty."

"Yes. You may remember Suzanne was wearing that bracelet when she was murdered. There was one more piece, an antique diamond pin or double pin, that Skip Reardon had described.

Dr. Smith doesn't mention it, and apparently he didn't have it, but Geoff just faxed me a picture from a local newspaper showing Suzanne wearing that pin only a few weeks before she died. It never showed up in the items found at the house. You can see that it's very much like the bracelet and obviously an antique. The other pieces are beautiful, but very modern in design."

Kerry looked closely at the blurred reproduction and understood why Deidre Reardon had described it as evoking a mother-and-child image. As she'd explained, the pin appeared to be in two parts, the larger being a flower, the smaller a bud. They were attached by a chain. She studied it for a moment, perplexed because it looked oddly familiar.

"We'll watch out for this pin to see if it is mentioned in Haskell's receipts," Green promised. "Now let's get this straight. As far as you know, everything the doctor mentioned, excluding this particular pin, is the total of the jewelry Suzanne asked the doctor to tell Skip he gave her?"

"According to what Smith wrote in his letter, and it does coincide with what Skip Reardon told me Saturday."

Green put down Smith's letter. "Kerry, do you think you might have been followed when you went to see Smith yesterday?"

"I think now I probably was. That's why I'm so concerned about Robin's safety."

"We'll keep a squad car outside your house tonight, but I wouldn't be unhappy to have you and Robin out of there and in some more secure place with all this coming to a head. Jimmy Weeks is a cornered animal. Royce may be able to tie him to tax fraud, but with what you've uncovered, we may be able to tie him to a murder."

"You mean because of the card Jimmy sent with the sweetheart roses?" The card was already being analyzed by handwriting experts, and Kerry had reminded Green of the paper found in Haskell's lawyer's pocket after both men had been murdered.

"Exactly. No clerk in a flower shop drew those musical notes. Imagine describing an inscription like that over the phone. From what I understand, Weeks is a pretty good amateur musician. The life of the party when he sits down at the piano. That kind. With that card—and if the jewelry ties in to those receipts—the Reardon case is a whole new ball game.

"And if Skip is granted a new trial, he'll be entitled to release on bail pending that trial—or dismissal of the charges," Kerry said evenly.

"If the scenario plays out, I'll recommend that," Green agreed.

"Frank, there's one other point I have to raise," Kerry said. "We know that Jimmy Weeks is trying to scare us off this investigation. But it may be for some reason other than we think. I have learned that Weeks picked up Skip Reardon's options on valuable Pennsylvania property when Skip had to liquidate. He apparently had inside information, so there's a good chance the whole transaction was illegal. It's certainly not as major a crime as murder—and we still don't know, of course; he *may* have been Suzanne's killer—but if the IRS had that information, along with the tax evasion charges and what-have-you, Weeks could be put away for a long time as it is."

"And you think he's worried that your probing into the Reardon murder case might expose those earlier deals?" Green asked.

"Yes, it's very possible."

"But do you really think that is sufficient to make him threaten you through Robin? That seems a little extreme to me." Green shook his head.

"Frank, from what I have learned from my ex-husband, Weeks is ruthless enough and arrogant enough to go to almost any lengths to protect himself, and it would make no difference what the charge—it could be murder or it could be stealing a newspaper. But all this aside, there's still another reason why the murder scenario may not play out, even if we can tie Jimmy Weeks to Suzanne," Kerry said. Then she began to fill him in on Jason Arnott's connection to Suzanne and Grace Hoover's theory that he was a professional thief.

"Even if he is, are you tying him to Suzanne Reardon's murder?" Green asked.

"I'm not sure," Kerry said slowly. "It depends on whether or not he is involved in those thefts."

"Sit tight. We can get that flyer faxed in from the FBI right away," Green decreed as he pressed the intercom. "We'll find out who's running the investigation."

Less than five minutes later his secretary brought in the flyer. Green pointed out the confidential number. "Tell them to put me through to the top guy on this."

Sixty seconds later, Green was on the phone with Si Morgan. He turned on the phone's speaker so that Kerry could listen too.

"It's breaking now," Morgan told him. "Arnott has another place, in the Catskills. We've decided to ring the doorbell and see if the housekeeper will talk to us. We'll keep you posted."

Kerry gripped the arms of her chair and turned her head toward the detached voice coming out of the speaker phone. "Mr. Morgan, this is terribly important. If you can still contact your agent, ask him to inquire about a miniature oval picture frame. It's blue enamel with seed pearls surrounding the glass. It may or may not hold a picture of a beautiful dark-haired woman. If it's there, we'll be able to connect Jason Arnott to a murder case."

"I can still reach him. I'll have him ask about it, and I'll get back to you," he promised.

"What was that about?" Green asked as he snapped off the speaker.

"Skip Reardon has always sworn that a miniature frame that was a Fabergé copy disappeared from the master bedroom the day Suzanne died. That and the antique pin are the two things we can't account for as of now."

Kerry leaned over and picked up the diamond bracelet. "Look at this. It's from a different world from the other jewelry." She held up the picture of Suzanne wearing the antique pin. "Isn't it funny? I feel as though I've seen a pin like that before, I mean the little one joined to the big one. It may just be because it came up repeatedly in statements from Skip and his mother at the time of the investigation. I've read that file until I'm dizzy."

She laid the bracelet back in the case. "Jason Arnott spent a great deal of time with Suzanne. Maybe he wasn't the neuter he tried to make himself out to be. Think of it this way, Frank. Let's say he fell for Suzanne too. He gave her the antique pin and the bracelet. It's exactly the kind of jewelry he would select. Then he realized that she was fooling around with Jimmy Weeks. Maybe he came in that night and saw the sweetheart roses and the card we believe Jimmy sent."

"You mean he killed her and took back the pin?"

"And her picture. From what Mrs. Reardon tells me, it's a beautiful frame."

"Why not the bracelet?"

"While I was waiting for you this morning, I looked at the pictures taken of the body before it was moved. Suzanne had a gold link bracelet on her left hand. You can see it in the picture. The diamond bracelet, which was on the other arm, doesn't show. I checked the records. It was pushed up on her arm under the sleeve of her blouse so that it wasn't visible. According to the medical examiner's report it had a new and very tight security clasp. She may have shoved the bracelet out of sight because she had changed her mind about wearing it and was having trouble getting it off, or she may have been aware that her attacker had come to retrieve it, probably because it was a gift from him, and she may have been hiding it. Whatever the reason, it worked, because he didn't find it."

While they waited for Morgan to call back, Green and Kerry worked together to prepare a flyer, with pictures of the jewelry in question, that would be distributed to New Jersey jewelers.

At one point Frank observed, "Kerry, you do realize that if Mrs. Hoover's hunch works out, it means that a tip from our state senator's wife will have caught the murderer of Congressman Peale's mother. Then if Arnott is tied to the Reardon case . . ."

Frank Green, gubernatorial candidate, Kerry thought. He's already figuring how to sugarcoat having convicted an innocent man! Well, that's politics, I guess, she told herself.

88

Maddie Platt was not aware of the car that followed her when she stopped at the market and did the shopping, carefully gathering all the items she had been instructed to get. Nor did she notice it continued to follow her when she drove farther out of Ellenville, down narrow, winding roads to the rambling country house owned by the man she knew as Nigel Grey.

She let herself in and ten minutes later was startled when the doorbell rang. Nobody ever dropped in at this house. Furthermore, Mr. Grey had given her strict orders never to admit anyone. She was not about to open the door without knowing who it was.

When she peeked out the side window she saw the neatly dressed man standing on the top step. He saw her and held up a badge identifying him as an FBI agent. "FBI, ma'am. Would you please open the door so I can talk to you?"

Nervously, Maddie opened the door. Now she stood inches

from the badge showing the unmistakable FBI seal and identifying picture of the agent.

"Good afternoon, ma'am. I'm FBI agent Milton Rose. I don't
mean to startle or upset you, but it's very important that I speak
with you about Mr. Jason Arnott. You are his housekeeper,
aren't you?"

"Sir, I don't know any Mr. Arnott. This house is owned by
Mr. Nigel Grey, and I've worked for him for many years. He's
due here this afternoon, in fact he should be here shortly. And I
can tell you right now—I am under strict orders not to ever let
anyone in this house without his permission."

"Ma'am, I'm not asking to come in. I don't have a search
warrant. But I still need to talk to you. Your Mr. Grey is really
Jason Arnott, whom we suspect has been responsible for dozens
of burglaries involving fine art and other valuable items. He
might even be responsible for the murder of a congressman's
elderly mother, who may have surprised him during the burglary
of her home."

"Oh my God," Maddie gasped. Certainly Mr. Grey had always been completely a loner here, but she had just assumed that
this Catskill home was where he escaped to for privacy and
relaxation. She now realized that he might well have been "escap-
ing" here for very different reasons.

Agent Rose went on to describe to her many of the stolen
pieces of art and other items that had disappeared from homes
where Arnott had previously attended social functions. Sadly,
she confirmed that virtually all of these items were in this house.
And, yes, the miniature oval blue frame encrusted with seed
pearls, with a woman's picture in it, was on his night table.

"Ma'am, we know that he will be here soon. I must ask you
to come with us. I'm sure you didn't know what was happening,
and you're not in any trouble. But we are going to make a telephone application for a search warrant so that we can search
Mr. Arnott's home and arrest him."

Gently, Agent Rose led the bewildered Maddie to the waiting car. "I can't believe this," she cried. "I just didn't know."

At twelve-thirty, a frightened Martha Luce, who for twenty years had been bookkeeper to James Forrest Weeks, sat twisting a damp handkerchief as she cowered in the office of U.S. Attorney Brandon Royce.

The sworn statement she had given to Royce months ago had just been read back to her.

"Do you stand by what you told us that day?" Royce asked as he tapped the papers in his hand.

"I told the truth as far as I knew it to be the truth," Martha told him, her voice barely above a whisper. She cast a nervous sidelong glance at the stenotypist and then at her nephew, a young attorney, whom she had called in a panic when she learned of the successful search of Barney Haskell's home.

Royce leaned forward. "Miss Luce, I cannot emphasize strongly enough how very serious your position is. If you continue to lie under oath, you do so at your own peril. We have enough to bury Jimmy Weeks. I'll lay out my cards. Since Barney Haskell has unfortunately been so abruptly taken from us, it will be helpful to have you as a living witness"—he emphasized the word "living"—"to corroborate the accuracy of his records. If you do not, we will still convict Jimmy Weeks, but then, Miss Luce, we will turn our full attention to you. Perjury is a very serious offense. Obstructing justice is a very serious offense. Aiding and abetting income tax evasion is a very serious offense."

Martha Luce's always timid face crumbled. She began to sob. Tears that immediately reddened her pale blue eyes welled and flowed. "Mr. Weeks paid every single bill when Mama was sick for such a long time."

"That's nice," Royce said. "But he did it with taxpayers' money."

"My client has a right to remain silent," the nephew/attorney piped up.

Royce gave him a withering glance. "We've already established that, counselor. You might also advise your client that we're not crazy about putting middle-aged women with misguided loyalties in prison. We're prepared, this one—and only this one—time, to offer total immunity to your client in exchange for full cooperation. After that, she's on her own. But you remind your client" —here Royce's voice was heavy with sarcasm—"that Barney Haskell waited so long to accept a plea bargain offer that he never got to take it."

"Total immunity?" the nephew/lawyer asked.

"Total, and we'll immediately put Ms. Luce in protective custody. We don't want anything to happen to her."

"Aunt Martha . . . ," the young man began, his voice cracking.

She stopped sniffling. "I know, dear. Mr. Royce, perhaps I always suspected that Mr. Weeks . . ."

90

The news that a cache had been found in a hidden safe in Barney Haskell's summer home was, to Bob Kinellen, the death knell of any hope of getting Jimmy Weeks an acquittal. Even Kinellen's father-in-law, the usually unruffleable Anthony Bartlett, was clearly beginning to concede the inevitable.

On this Tuesday morning, U.S. Attorney Royce had requested and been granted that the lunch recess be extended an hour. Bob suspected what that maneuver meant. Martha Luce, a defense witness, and one of their most believable because of her timid, earnest demeanor, was being leaned on.

If Haskell had made a copy of the books he had kept, Luce's testimony swearing to the accuracy of Jimmy's records was probably being held as a weapon over her head.

If Martha Luce turned prosecution witness in exchange for immunity, it was all over.

Bob Kinellen sat silently looking at every possible thing in the room other than his client. He felt a terrible weariness, like a weight crushing him, and he wondered at what moment it had invaded him. Thinking back over the recent days, he suddenly knew. It was when I delivered a threat concerning my own child, he said to himself. For eleven years he had been able to keep to the letter of the law. Jimmy Weeks had the right to a defense, and his job was to keep Jimmy from getting indicted. He did it by legal means. If other means were also being used, he did not know nor did he want to know about them.

But in this trial he had become part of the process of circumventing the law. Weeks had just told him the reason he'd insisted on having Mrs. Wagner on the jury: She had a father in prison in California. Thirty years ago he had murdered an entire family of campers in Yosemite National Park. He knew he intended to hold back the information that juror Wagner had a father in prison and make that part of Weeks' appeal. He knew, too, that was unethical. Skating on thin ice was over. He had gone beyond that. The burning shame he had felt when he heard Robin's stricken cry as he struggled with Kerry still seared him. How had Kerry explained that to Robin? *Your father was passing along a threat his client made about you? Your father's client was the man who ordered some bum to terrify you last week?*

Jimmy Weeks was terrified of prison. The prospect of being locked up was unbearable to him. He would do anything to avoid it.

It was obvious that Jimmy was wildly upset. They had lunch in a private room of a restaurant a few miles from the courtroom. After the orders were taken, Jimmy said abruptly, "I don't want any talk about plea bargaining from you two. Understand?"

Bartlett and Kinellen waited without responding.

"In the jury room, I don't think we can count on the wimp with the sick wife not to buckle."

I could have told you that, Bob thought. He didn't want to discuss any of this. If his client had tampered with that juror, it was without his knowledge, he reassured himself. *And Haskell was the victim of a mugging,* an interior voice mocked.

"Bobby, my sources tell me the sheriff's officer in charge of the jury owes you a favor," Weeks said.

"What are you talking about, Jimmy?" Bob Kinellen toyed with his salad fork.

"You know what I'm talking about. You got his kid out of trouble, big trouble. He's grateful."

"And?"

"Bobby, I think the sheriff's officer has to let that prune-face, uptight Wagner dame know that her daddy, the murderer, is going to make big headlines unless she comes up with some reasonable doubt when this case goes to the jury."

Lie down with dogs and you'll get up with fleas. Kerry had told him that before Robin was born.

"Jimmy, we already have grounds for a new trial because she didn't reveal that fact. That's our ace in the hole. We don't need to take it any further." Bob shot a glance at his father-in-law. "Anthony and I are sticking our necks out by not reporting that to the court as it is. We can get away with claiming that it only came to our attention after the trial was over. Even if you're convicted you'll be out on bail, and then we delay and delay and delay."

"Not good enough, Bobby. This time you've got to put yourself on the line. Have a friendly chat with the sheriff's officer. He'll listen. He'll talk to the lady who already is in trouble for lying on her questionnaire. Then we have a hung jury, if not an acquittal. And then we delay and delay and delay while you two figure out a way to make sure we get an acquittal next time."

The waiter returned with their appetizers. Bob Kinellen had ordered the escargots, a specialty here that he thoroughly enjoyed. It was only when he finished and the waiter was removing the plate that he realized he hadn't tasted a thing. Jimmy isn't the only one who's being backed into a corner, he thought.

I'm right there with him.

91

Kerry went back to her office after the call from Si Morgan came through. She was now convinced that Arnott was irrevocably tied in some way to Suzanne Reardon's death. Just how, though, would have to wait until he was in FBI custody and she and Frank Green had had a chance to interrogate him.

There was a pile of messages on her desk, one of which, from Jonathan, was marked "Urgent." He had left his private number at his local office. She called him immediately.

"Thanks for calling back, Kerry. I have to come over to Hackensack and I want to talk to you. Buy you lunch?"

A few weeks ago, he had started the conversation with "Buy you lunch, Judge?"

Kerry knew the omission today was not accidental. Jonathan played it straight. If the political fallout from her investigation cost Frank Green the nomination, she would have to forget about a judgeship, no matter how justified she had been. That was politics, and besides, there were plenty of other highly qualified people panting for the job.

"Of course, Jonathan."

"Solari's at one-thirty."

She was sure she knew why he was calling. He had heard about Dr. Smith and was worried about her and Robin.

She dialed Geoff's office. He was having a sandwich at his desk.

"I'm glad I'm sitting down," he told her when she filled him in about Arnott.

"The FBI will be photographing and cataloguing everything they find in the Catskill house. Morgan said the decision hasn't been made whether to move everything into a warehouse or to just invite the people who've been robbed to come and identify their stuff right at that site. However they do it, when Green and I go up to talk to Arnott we want Mrs. Reardon along to positively identify the picture frame."

"I'll ask her to postpone going in for the angioplasty for a few days. Kerry, one of our associates was in federal court this morning. He tells me that Royce requested an extra hour for the lunch break. The word is that he may be offering immunity to Jimmy Weeks' bookkeeper. He's not going to take a chance on losing another prize witness by playing hardball."

"It's coming to a head, then?"

"Exactly."

"Have you called Skip about Smith's letter?"

"Right after I talked to you."

"What was his reaction?"

"He started to cry." Geoff's voice became husky. "I did too. He's going to get out, Kerry, and you're the reason."

"No, you're wrong. You and Robin are. I was ready to turn my back on him."

"We'll argue about that another time. Kerry, Deidre Reardon's on the other phone. I've been trying to reach her. I'll talk to you later. I don't want you and Robin alone in your place tonight."

Before Kerry left to meet Jonathan, she dialed Joe Palumbo's cellular phone. He answered on the first ring. "Palumbo."

"It's Kerry, Joe."

"Recess is over. Robin is back inside. I'm parked in front of the main entrance, which is the only unlocked door. I'll drive her home and stay with her and the sitter." He paused. "Don't worry, Momma. I'll take good care of your baby."

"I know you will. Thanks, Joe."

It was time to meet Jonathan. As she hurried out to the corridor and rushed through the just-closing elevator door, Kerry kept thinking about the missing pin. Something about it seemed so familiar. The two parts. The flower and the bud, like a mother and child. A momma and a baby . . . why did that seem to ring a bell? she wondered.

Jonathan was already seated at the table, sipping a club soda. He got up when he saw her coming. His brief, familiar hug was reassuring. "You look very tired, young lady," he said. "Or is it very stressed?"

Whenever he talked to her like that, Kerry felt the remembered warmth of the days when her father was alive and felt a rush of gratitude that Jonathan in so many ways had been a surrogate father to her.

"It's been quite a day so far," she said as she sat down. "Did you hear about Dr. Smith?"

"Grace called me. She heard the news when she was having breakfast at ten o'clock. Sounds like more of Weeks' handiwork. We're both heartsick with worry about Robin."

"So am I. But Joe Palumbo, one of our investigators, is outside her school. He'll stay with her till I get home."

The waiter was at the table. "Let's order," Kerry suggested, "and then I'll fill you in."

They both decided on onion soup, which arrived almost immediately. While they were eating, she told him about the Federal Express package with all the jewelry and the letter from Dr. Smith.

"You make me ashamed that I tried to dissuade you from your investigation, Kerry," Jonathan said quietly. "I'll do my best, but if the governor decides Green's nomination is in jeopardy, it would be like him to take it out on you."

"Well, at least there's hope," Kerry said. "And we can thank

Grace for the tip she gave the FBI." She told him what she had learned about Jason Arnott. "I can see where Frank Green is already planning to defuse negative publicity about Skip Reardon being unfairly prosecuted. He's dying to announce that the cat burglar who murdered Congressman Peale's mother was captured because of a tip from the wife of Senator Hoover. You're going to come out of this as his best friend, and who can blame him? God knows you're probably the most respected politician in New Jersey."

Jonathan smiled. "We can always stretch the truth and say that Grace consulted Green first and he urged her to make the call." Then the smile vanished. "Kerry, how does Arnott's possible guilt in the Reardon case affect Robin? Is there a possibility that Arnott is the one who took that picture of her and sent it to you?"

"No way. Robin's own father passed along the warning and in essence admitted that Jimmy Weeks had that picture taken."

"What's the next step?"

"Probably that Frank Green and I will bring Deidre Reardon up to the Catskills first thing tomorrow morning to positively identify that miniature frame. Arnott should be being cuffed right about now. They'll keep him in the local jail, at least for the present. Then, once they start connecting the stolen goods to specific burglaries, they'll begin arraigning him in different locations. My guess is they're itching to try him first for the murder of Congressman Peale's mother. And, of course, if he was responsible for Suzanne Reardon's death, we'll want to try him here."

"Suppose he won't talk?"

"We're sending flyers to all the jewelers in New Jersey, naturally concentrating on Bergen County since both Weeks and Arnott live here. My guess is that one of those jewelers will recognize the more contemporary jewelry and tie it to Weeks, and that the antique bracelet will turn out to be from Arnott. When it was found on Suzanne's arm it obviously had a new clasp, and the bracelet is so unusual some jeweler might remember it. The more we can find to use in confronting Arnott, the easier it should be to make him try to strike a deal."

"Then you expect to leave early in the morning for the Cats-kills?"

"Yes. I'm certainly not going to leave Robin alone in the house in the morning again, but if it turns out that Frank wants to be on the road very early, I'll see if the sitter will stay over."

"I have a better idea. Let Robin stay with us tonight. I'll drop her off at school in the morning, or, if you want, you can have that Palumbo man pick her up. Our house has state-of-the-art security. You know that. I'll be there, of course, and I don't know whether you realize that even Grace has a gun in her night table drawer. I taught her to use it years ago. Besides, I really think it would be good for Grace to have Robin visit. She's been rather down lately, and Robin is such fun to have around."

Kerry smiled. "Yes, she is." She thought for a moment. "Jona-than, that really could work. I really should get some work in on another case I'll be trying, and then I want to go through the Reardon file with a fine-toothed comb to see if there's anything more I can pick up to use when we question Arnott. I'll call Robin when I know she's home from school and tell her the plan. She'll be delighted. She's crazy about you and Grace, and she loves the pink guest room."

"It used to be yours, remember?"

"Sure. How could I forget? That's back when I was telling Grace's cousin, the landscaper, that he was a crook."

92

The extended recess over, U.S. Attorney Royce returned to court for the afternoon trial session of the United States versus James Forrest Weeks. He went secure in the knowledge that behind her timid, unassuming facade, Martha Luce had the memory of a personal computer. The damning evidence that would finally nail Jimmy Weeks was spilling from her as she responded to the gentle prodding of two of Royce's assistants.

Luce's nephew/attorney, Royce admitted to himself, had possibilities. He insisted that before Martha began singing, the bargain she was striking had to be signed and witnessed. In exchange for her honest and forthright cooperation, which she would not later rescind, any possible federal or other criminal or civil charges would not be pressed against her either now or in the future.

Martha Luce's evidence would come later, however. The prosecution case was unfolding in a straightforward way. Today's witness was a restaurateur who in exchange for having his lease renewed admitted to paying a five-thousand-dollar-a-month cash bonus to Jimmy's collector.

When it was the defense's turn to cross-examine, Royce was kept busy jumping to his feet with objections as Bob Kinellen jabbed at the witness, catching him in small errors, forcing him to admit that he had never actually seen Weeks touch the money, that he really couldn't be sure that the collector hadn't been working on his own. Kinellen is good, Royce thought, too bad he's wasting his talent on this scum.

Royce could not know that Robert Kinellen was sharing that same thought even as he grandstanded to a receptive jury.

93

Jason Arnott knew there was something terribly wrong the minute he walked in the door of his Catskill home and realized that Maddie was not there.

If Maddie's not here and she didn't leave a note, then something is happening. It's all over, he thought. How long before they would close in on him? Soon, he was sure.

Suddenly he was hungry. He rushed to the refrigerator and pulled out the smoked salmon he had asked Maddie to pick up. Then he reached for the capers and cream cheese and the package of toast points. A bottle of Pouilly-Fuissé was chilling.

He prepared a plate of salmon and poured a glass of wine. Carrying them with him, he began to walk through the house. A kind of final tour, he thought, as he assessed the riches around him. The tapestry in the dining room—exquisite. The Aubusson in the living room—a privilege to walk on such beauty. The Chaim Gross bronze sculpture of a slender figure holding a small child in the palm of her hand. Gross had loved the mother-and-child theme. Arnott remembered that Gross's mother and sister had died in the Holocaust.

He would need a lawyer, of course. A good lawyer. But who? A smile made his lips twitch. He knew just the one: Geoffrey Dorso, who for ten years had so relentlessly worked for Skip Reardon. Dorso had quite a reputation and might be willing to take on a new client, especially one who could give him evidence that would help him spring poor Reardon.

The front doorbell rang. He ignored it. It rang again, then continued persistently. Arnott chewed the last toast point, relishing the delicate flavor of the salmon, the pungent bite of the capers.

The back doorbell was chiming now. Surrounded, he thought. Ah, well. He had known it would happen someday. If he had only obeyed his instincts last week and left the country. Jason sipped the last of the wine, decided another glass would be welcome and went back to the kitchen. There were faces at all the windows now, faces with the aggressive, self-satisfied look of men who have the right to exercise might.

Arnott nodded to them and held up the glass in a mocking toast. As he sipped, he walked to the back door, opened it, then stood aside as they rushed in. "FBI, Mr. Arnott," they shouted. "We have a warrant to search your home."

"Gentlemen, gentlemen," he murmured, "I beg you to be careful. There are many beautiful, even priceless objects here. You may not be used to them, but please respect them. Are your feet muddy?"

94

K erry called Robin at three-thirty. She and Alison were at the computer, Robin told her, playing one of the games Uncle Jonathan and Aunt Grace had given her. Kerry told her the plan: "I have to work late tonight and be on the way by seven tomorrow. Jonathan and Grace really would like to have you stay with them, and I'd feel good knowing you're there."

"Why was Mr. Palumbo parked outside our school and why did he drive me home and why is he parked outside now? Is it because I'm in really big danger?"

Kerry tried to sound matter-of-fact. "Hate to disappoint you, but it's just a precaution, Rob. The case is really coming to a head."

"Cool. I like Mr. Palumbo, and, okay, I'll stay with Aunt Grace and Uncle Jonathan. I like them too. But what about you? Will Mr. Palumbo stay in front of the house for you?"

"I won't be home till late, and when I get there, the local cops will drive by every fifteen minutes or so. That's all I need."

"Be careful, Mom." For a moment, Robin's bravado vanished, and she sounded like a frightened little girl.

"You be careful, sweetheart. Do your homework."

"I will. And I'm going to ask Aunt Grace if I can pull out her old photo albums again. I love looking at the old clothes and hairstyles, and if I remember it right, they are arranged in the order they were taken. I thought I might get some ideas, since our next assignment in camera class is to create a family album so that it really tells a story."

"Yeah, there are some great pictures there. I used to love to go through those albums when I was house-sitting," Kerry reminisced. "I used to count to see how many different servants Aunt Grace and Uncle Jonathan grew up with. I still think about them sometimes when I'm pushing the vacuum or folding the wash."

Robin giggled. "Well, hang in there. You may win the lottery someday. Love you, Mom."

At five-thirty, Geoff phoned from his car. "You'll never guess where I am." He didn't wait for an answer. "I was in court this afternoon. Jason Arnott had been trying to reach me. He left a message."

"Jason Arnott!" Kerry exclaimed.

"Yes. When I got back to him a few minutes ago, he said he has to talk to me immediately. He wants me to take his case."

"Would you represent him?"

"I couldn't because he's connected to the Reardon case, and I wouldn't if I could. I told him that, but he still insists on seeing me."

"Geoff! Don't let him tell you anything that would have lawyer-client privilege."

Geoff chuckled. "Thank you, Kerry. I never would have thought of that."

Kerry laughed with him, then explained the arrangement she had made for Robin for the night. "I'm working late right here. When I start home I'll let the Hohokus cops know I'm on the way. It's all set."

"Now be sure you do." His voice became firm. "The more I've thought about you going into Smith's house alone last night, the more I realize what a lousy idea it was. You could have been there when he was shot, just the way Mark Young was gunned down with Haskell."

Geoff signed off after promising to call and report to Kerry after he had seen Arnott.

It was eight o'clock before Kerry had finished the work she needed to do in preparing for an upcoming case. Then once again she reached for the voluminous Reardon file.

She looked closely at the pictures of the death scene. In his letter, Dr. Smith had described entering the house that night and finding Suzanne's body. Kerry closed her eyes at the awful prospect of ever finding Robin like that. Smith said he had deliberately removed the "Let Me Call You Sweetheart" card because he was so sure Skip had murdered Suzanne in a fit of jealous rage, and he didn't want him to escape maximum punishment, to get off with a reduced sentence.

She believed what Smith had written—most people don't lie when they plan to kill themselves, she reasoned. And what Dr. Smith had written also supports Skip Reardon's story. So now, Kerry thought, the murderer is the man who visited that house between the time Skip left at around six-thirty, and when the doctor arrived at around nine o'clock.

Jason Arnott? Jimmy Weeks? Which one had killed Suzanne? she wondered.

At nine-thirty Kerry closed the file. She hadn't come up with any new angles in her plan to question Arnott tomorrow. If I were in his boots, she thought, I'd claim that Suzanne gave me the picture frame that last day because she was afraid a couple of pearls were getting loose and wanted me to have it fixed. Then, when she was found dead, I didn't want to become involved in a murder investigation, so I kept the frame.

A story like that could easily hold up in court because it was entirely plausible. The jewelry, however, was a different story. It all came back to the jewelry. It she could prove that Arnott gave Suzanne those valuable antique pieces, there was no way he could get away with saying it was a gift of pure friendship.

At ten o'clock she left the now-quiet office and went into the parking lot. Realizing suddenly that she was starving, she drove to the Arena diner around the corner and had a hamburger, french fries and coffee.

Substitute a cola for the coffee, and you have Robin's favorite meal, she thought, sighing inwardly. I have to say I miss my baby.

The momma and the baby . . .

The momma and the baby . . .

Why did that singsong phrase keep echoing in her head? she wondered again. Something about it seemed wrong, so terribly wrong. But what was it?

She should have called and said good night to Robin before she left her office, she realized suddenly. Why hadn't she? Kerry ate quickly and got back in the car. It was twenty of eleven, much too late to call. She was just pulling out of the lot when the car phone rang. It was Jonathan.

"Kerry," he said, his voice low and taut, "Robin is in with Grace. She doesn't know I'm calling. She didn't want me to worry you. But after she fell asleep she had a terrible nightmare. I really think you should come over. So much has been going on. She needs you."

"I'll be right there." Kerry switched the turn signal from the right to the left one, pressed her foot on the accelerator and rushed to get to her child.

95

It was a long and miserable ride from New Jersey up the thruway to the Catskills. An icy rain began falling around Middletown, and traffic slowed to a crawl. An overturned tractor trailer that blocked all lanes caused an extra hour to be added to the already torturous trip.

It was a quarter of ten before a tired and hungry Geoff Dorso arrived at the Ellenville police headquarters, where Jason Arnott was being held. A team of FBI agents was waiting to question Arnott as soon as he had had the chance to speak to Geoff.

"You're wasting your time waiting for me," Geoff had told them. "I *can't be his lawyer*. Didn't he tell you that?"

A handcuffed Arnott was escorted into the conference room. Geoff had not seen the man in the nearly eleven years since Suzanne's death. At that time, he had been considered to have a relationship with Suzanne Reardon that combined friendship and business. No one, including Skip, ever suspected that he had any other interest in her.

Now Geoff studied the man closely. Arnott was somewhat more full-faced than Geoff remembered, but he still had that same urbane, world-weary expression. The lines around his eyes suggested deep fatigue, but the turtleneck cashmere shirt still looked fresh under his tweed jacket. Country gentleman, cultivated connoisseur, Geoff thought. Even in these circumstances, he certainly looks the part.

"It's good of you to come, Geoff," Arnott said amiably.

"I really don't know why I'm here," Geoff replied. "As I warned you on the phone, you are now connected to the Reardon case. My client is Skip Reardon. I can tell you that nothing you may say to me is a privileged communication. You've had your Miranda warning. I am not your lawyer. I will repeat anything you say to the prosecutor, because I intend to try to place you in the Reardon house the night of Suzanne's death."

"Oh, I was there. That's why I sent for you. Don't worry. That isn't privileged information. I intend to admit it. I asked you here because I can be a witness for Skip. But in exchange, once he is cleared, I want you to represent me. There won't be any conflict of interest then."

"Look, I'm not going to represent you," Geoff said flatly. "I've spent ten years of my life representing an innocent man who got sent to prison. If you either killed Suzanne, or know who did, and you let Skip rot in that cell all this time, I'd burn in hell before I would raise a finger to help you."

"You see, now that's the kind of determination I want to hire." Arnott sighed. "Very well. Let's try it this way. You're a criminal defense attorney. You know who the good ones are whether they're from New Jersey or elsewhere. You promise to find me the best attorney money can buy, and I'll tell you what I know of Suzanne Reardon's death—which, incidentally, I am not responsible for."

Geoff stared at the man for a moment, considering his offer. "Okay, but before we say another word, I want to have a signed and witnessed statement that any information you give me will not be privileged, and that I can use it in whatever way I see fit to assist Skip Reardon."

"Of course."

The FBI agents had a stenotypist with them. She took down

Arnott's brief statement. When he and a couple of witnesses had signed it, he said, "It is late and it has been a long day. Have you been thinking about what lawyer I should have?"

"Yes," Geoff said. "George Symonds, from Trenton. He's an excellent trial lawyer and a superb negotiator."

"They're going to try to convict me of deliberate murder in the death of Mrs. Peale. I swear it was an accident."

"If there's a way to get it down to felony murder, he'll find it. At least you wouldn't face the death penalty."

"Call him now."

Geoff knew that Symonds lived in Princeton, having once been invited to dinner at his home. He also remembered that the Symonds phone was listed in his wife's name. Using his cellular phone, he made the call in Arnott's presence. It was ten-thirty.

Ten minutes later, Geoff put the phone back. "All right, you've got a top-drawer lawyer. Now talk."

"I had the misfortune to be in the Reardon house at the time Suzanne died," Arnott said, his manner suddenly grave. "Suzanne was so wildly careless of her jewelry, some of which was quite beautiful, that the temptation proved too great. I knew Skip was supposed to be in Pennsylvania on business, and Suzanne had told me she had a date with Jimmy Weeks that evening. You know, odd as it may seem, she really had quite a crush on him."

"Was he in the house while you were there?"

Arnott shook his head. "No, the way they had arranged it, she was to drive to the shopping mall in Pearl River, leave her car there and join him in his limo. As I understood it, she was meeting Jimmy early that night. Obviously I was wrong. There were a few lights on downstairs when I got to Suzanne's house, but that was normal. They came on automatically. From the back I could see that the windows of the master bedroom were wide open. It was child's play to climb up, since the second-story roof of that very modern house slopes almost to the ground."

"What time was that?"

"Precisely eight o'clock. I was on my way to a dinner party in

Cresskill; one of the reasons for my long and successful career is that almost invariably I could furnish an impeccable set of witnesses as to my whereabouts on particular nights."

"You went into the house . . . ," Geoff encouraged.

"Yes. There wasn't a sound, so I assumed everyone was away as planned. I had no idea that Suzanne was still downstairs. I went through the sitting room of the suite, then into the bedroom and over to the night table. I'd only seen the picture frame in passing and had never been sure if it was a genuine Fabergé; obviously I had never wanted to seem too interested in it. I picked it up and was studying it when I heard Suzanne's voice. She was shouting at someone. It was quite disconcerting."

"What was she saying?"

"Something to the effect of 'You gave them to me and they're mine. Now get out. You bore me.' "

You gave them to me and they're mine. The jewelry, Geoff thought. "So that must mean that Jimmy Weeks had changed plans and arranged to pick Suzanne up that night," he reasoned.

"Oh, no. I heard a man shout, 'I have to have them back,' but it was much too refined a voice to have been Jimmy Weeks, and it certainly wasn't poor Skip." Arnott sighed. "At that point, I dropped the frame in my pocket, almost unconsciously. A dreadful copy as it turns out, but Suzanne's picture has been a pleasure, so I have enjoyed having it. She was so entertaining. I do miss her."

"You dropped the frame in your pocket," Geoff prodded.

"And realized suddenly that someone was coming upstairs. I was in the bedroom, you remember, so I jumped into Suzanne's closet and tried to hide behind her long gowns. I hadn't closed the door completely."

"Did you see who came?"

"No, not the face."

"What did that person do?"

"Made straight for the jewelry case, picked among Suzanne's baubles and took out something. Then, apparently not finding everything he wanted, he began going through all the drawers. He seemed rather frantic. After only a few minutes he either found what he was looking for or gave up. Fortunately he didn't go through the closet. I waited as long as I could, and then, knowing that something was terribly wrong, I slipped downstairs. That's when I saw her."

"There was a lot of jewelry in that case. What did Suzanne's killer take?"

"Given what I learned during the trial, I'm sure it must have been the flower and the bud . . . the antique diamond pin, you know. It really was a beautiful piece: one of a kind."

"Did whoever it was that gave Suzanne that pin also give her the antique bracelet?"

"Oh, yes. In fact, I think he was probably trying to find the bracelet as well."

"Do you know who gave Suzanne the bracelet and the pin?"

"Of course I know. Suzanne kept few secrets from me. Now mind you, I can't swear he was the one in the house that night, but it does make sense, doesn't it? So see what I mean? My testimony will help to deliver the real murderer. That's why I should have some consideration, don't you agree?"

"Mr. Arnott, who gave Suzanne the bracelet and pin?"

Arnott's smile was amused. "You won't believe me when I tell you."

96

It took Kerry twenty-five minutes to drive to Old Tappan. Every turn of the wheel seemed interminable. Robin, brave little Robin, who always tried to hide how disappointed she was when Bob sloughed her off, who today had so successfully hidden how scared she was—it had finally become too much for her. I never should have left her with anyone else, Kerry thought. Even Jonathan and Grace.

Even Jonathan and Grace.

Jonathan had sounded so odd on the phone, Kerry thought.

From now on, *I'll* take care of my baby, Kerry vowed.

The momma and the baby—there it was again, that phrase stuck in her mind.

She was entering Old Tappan. Only a few minutes more now.

Robin had seemed so pleased at the prospect of being with Grace and Jonathan and of going through the photo albums.

The photo albums.

Kerry was driving past the last house before reaching Jonathan's. She was turning into the driveway. Almost unconsciously she realized that the sensor lights did not go on.

The photo albums.

The flower-and-bud pin.

She had seen it before.

On Grace.

Years ago, when Kerry first started to work for Jonathan.

Grace used to wear her jewelry then. Many pictures in the album showed her wearing it. Grace had joked when Kerry admired that pin. She'd called it "the momma and the baby."

Suzanne Reardon was wearing Grace's pin in that newspaper picture! That must mean . . . Jonathan? Could he have given it to her?

She remembered now that Grace had told her that she had asked Jonathan to put all her jewelry in the safe-deposit box. "I can't put it on without help, and I can't get it off without help, and I would only worry about it if it were still in the house."

I told Jonathan I was going in to see Dr. Smith, Kerry realized. Last night, after I came home, I told Jonathan I thought Smith would crack, she said to herself. Oh my God! He must have shot Smith.

Kerry stopped the car. She was in front of the handsome limestone residence. She pushed the driver's-side door open and rushed up the steps.

Robin was with a murderer.

Kerry did not hear the faint pealing of the car telephone as she pressed her finger on the doorbell.

97

Geoff tried to phone Kerry at home. When there was no answer, he tried her car phone. Where was she? he wondered frantically. He was dialing Frank Green's office when the guard led Arnott away.

"The prosecutor's office is closed. If this is an emergency, dial . . ."

Geoff swore as he dialed the emergency number. Robin was staying with the Hoovers. Where was Kerry? Finally someone answered the emergency line.

"This is Geoff Dorso. I absolutely must reach Frank Green. It concerns a breaking murder case. Give me his home number."

"I can tell you he's not there. He was called out because of a murder in Oradell, sir."

"Can you get through to him?"

"Yes. Hold on."

It was a full three minutes before Green got on the line. "Geoff, I'm in the middle of something. This had better be important."

"It is. Very important. It has to do with the Reardon case. Frank, Robin Kinellen is staying at Jonathan Hoover's home tonight."

"Kerry told me that."

"Frank, I've just learned that Jonathan Hoover gave that antique jewelry to Suzanne Reardon. He'd been having an affair with her. I think he's our killer, and Robin is with him."

There was a long pause. Then in an unemotional voice Frank Green said, "I'm in the home of an old man who specialized in repairing antique jewelry. He was murdered early this evening. There's no evidence of a robbery, but his son tells me his Rolodex with the names of his customers is missing. I'll get the local cops over to Hoover's place fast."

98

Jonathan opened the door for Kerry. The house was dimly lit and very quiet. "She's settled down," he said. "It's all right."

Kerry's fists were hidden in the pockets of her coat, clenched in fear and anger. Still she managed to smile. "Oh, Jonathan, this is such an imposition for you and Grace. I should have known Robin would be frightened. Where is she?"

"Back in her room now. Fast asleep."

Am I crazy? Kerry wondered as she followed Jonathan upstairs. Did my imagination go hog wild? He seems so normal.

They came to the door of the guest bedroom, the pink room as Robin called it, because of the soft pink walls and draperies and quilt.

Kerry pushed the door open. In the glow provided by a small night-light, she could see Robin on her side in her usual fetal position, her long brown hair scattered on the pillow. In two strides Kerry was beside the bed.

Robin's cheek was cupped in her palm. She was breathing evenly.

Kerry looked up at Jonathan. He was at the foot of the bed, staring at her. "She was so upset. After you got here, you decided to take her home," he said. "See, her bag with her school clothes and books is packed and ready. I'll carry it for you."

"Jonathan, there was no nightmare. She didn't wake up, did she?" Kerry said, her voice even.

"No," he said indifferently. "And it would be easier for her if she didn't wake up now."

In the dim glow of the night-light, Kerry saw that he was holding a gun.

"Jonathan, what are you doing? Where's Grace?"

"Grace is fast asleep, Kerry. I felt it was better that way. Sometimes I can tell that one of her more powerful sedatives is necessary to help ease the pain. I dissolve it in the hot cocoa I bring her in bed every night."

"Jonathan, what do you want?"

"I want to keep on living just as we're living now. I want to be president of the senate and friend of the governor. I want to spend my remaining years with my wife, whom I really do love, still. Sometimes men stray, Kerry. They do very foolish things. They let young, beautiful women flatter them. Perhaps I was susceptible because of Grace's problem. I knew it was foolish of me; I knew it was a mistake. Then all I wanted to do was to take back the jewelry I had so stupidly given that vulgar Reardon girl, but she wouldn't part with it."

He waved the revolver. "Either wake up Robin or pick her up. There isn't any more time."

"Jonathan, what are you going to do?"

"Only what I have to do, and then only with great regret. Kerry, Kerry, why did you feel you had to tilt at windmills? What did it matter that Reardon was in prison? What did it matter that Suzanne's father claimed as his gift the bracelet that could have so desperately harmed me? Those things were meant to be. I was supposed to continue to serve the state I love, and to live with the wife I love. It was sufficient penance to know that Grace had so easily spotted my betrayal."

Jonathan smiled. "She is quite marvelous. She showed me that picture and said, 'Doesn't that remind you of my flower-and-bud pin? It makes me want to wear it again. Please get it out of the safe-deposit box, dear.' She knew, and I knew that she knew, Kerry. And suddenly from being a middle-aged romantic fool . . . I felt soiled."

"And you killed Suzanne."

"But only because she not only refused to return my wife's gems but had the gall to tell me she had an interesting new boyfriend, Jimmy Weeks. My God, the man's a thug. A mobster. Kerry, either wake up Robin or carry her as she sleeps."

"Mom," Robin was stirring. Her eyes opened. She sat up. "Mom." She smiled. "Why are you here?"

"Get out of bed, Rob. We're leaving now." He's going to kill us, Kerry thought. He's going to say that Robin had a nightmare and I came to get her and drove off with her.

She put her arm around Robin. Sensing something was wrong, Robin shrank against her. "Mom?"

"It's all right."

"Uncle Jonathan?" Robin had seen the gun.

"Don't say anything else, Robin," Kerry said quietly. What can I do? she thought. He's crazy. He's out of control. If only Geoff hadn't gone to see Jason Arnott. Geoff would have helped. Somehow, Geoff would have helped.

As they were going down the stairs, Jonathan said quietly, "Give me your car keys, Kerry. I'll follow you out, and then you and Robin will get in the trunk."

Oh God, Kerry thought. He'll kill us and drive us somewhere and leave the car and it will look like a mob killing. It will be blamed on Weeks.

Jonathan spoke again as they crossed the foyer: "I am truly sorry, Robin. Now open the door slowly, Kerry."

Kerry bent down to kiss Robin. "Rob, when I spin around, you run," she whispered. "Run next door and keep screaming."

"The door, Kerry," he prodded.

Slowly she opened it. He had turned off the porch lights so that the only illumination was the faint glow thrown off by the torchère at the end of the driveway. "My key is in my pocket," she said. She turned slowly, then screamed, "Run, Robin!"

At the same moment she threw herself across the foyer at Jonathan. She heard the gun go off as she hurtled toward him, then felt a burning pain in the side of her head, followed immediately by waves of dizziness. The marble floor of the foyer rushed up to greet her. Around her she was aware of a cacophony of sound: Another gunshot. Robin screaming for help, her voice fading into the distance. Sirens approaching.

Then suddenly only the sirens, and Grace's broken cry, "I'm sorry, Jonathan. I'm sorry. I couldn't let you do this," she said. "Not this. Not to Kerry and Robin."

Kerry managed to pull herself up and press her hand against the side of her head. Blood was trickling down her face, but the dizziness was receding. As she looked up, she saw Grace slide from her wheelchair onto the floor, drop the pistol from her swollen fingers and gather her husband's body in her arms.

99

The courtroom was packed for the swearing-in ceremony of Assistant Prosecutor Kerry McGrath to the judiciary. The festive hum of voices subsided into silence when the door from the chambers opened and a stately procession of black-robed judges marched in to welcome a new colleague to their midst.

Kerry quietly walked from the side of the chamber and took her place to the right of the bench as the judges went to the chairs reserved for them in front of the guests.

She looked out at the assembly. Her mother and Sam had flown in for the ceremony. They were sitting with Robin, who was ramrod straight on the edge of her seat, her eyes wide with excitement. There was barely a trace of the lacerations that had brought them to that fateful meeting with Dr. Smith.

Geoff was in the next row with his mother and father. Kerry thought of how he had rushed down in the FBI helicopter to come to her in the hospital, how he had been the one to comfort a hysterical Robin and then bring her home to his family when the doctor insisted Kerry stay overnight. Now she blinked back tears at what she saw in his face as he smiled at her.

Margaret, old friend, best friend, was there, fulfilling her vow to be part of this day. Kerry thought of Jonathan and Grace. They had planned to be present too.

Grace had sent a note.

I am going home to South Carolina and will live with my sister. I blame myself for everything that happened. I knew Jonathan was involved with that woman. I also knew it wouldn't last. If only I had ignored that picture in which she was wearing my pin, none of this would have happened. I didn't care about the jewelry. That was my way of warning Jonathan to give her up. I didn't want his career ruined by scandal. Please forgive me and forgive Jonathan if you can.

Can I? Kerry wondered. Grace saved my life, but Jonathan would have killed Robin and me to save himself. Grace knew Jonathan had been involved with Suzanne and might even have been her murderer, yet she let Skip Reardon rot in prison all those years.

Skip, his mother and Beth were somewhere in the crowd. Skip and Beth were getting married next week; Geoff would be best man.

It was customary for a few close friends or associates to make brief remarks before the swearing-in. Frank Green went first. "Searching my memory, I cannot imagine any person—man or woman—who is more suited to assume this high position than Kerry McGrath. Her sense of justice led her to request me to reopen a murder case. Together we faced the appalling fact that a vengeful father had condemned his daughter's husband to prison, while the real killer was enjoying freedom. We . . ."

That's my boy, Kerry thought. Lemonade from lemons. But in the end, Frank had stood by her. He had personally met with the governor and urged that her name be placed before the senate for confirmation.

Frank had been the one to clear up the Jimmy Weeks connection to Suzanne Reardon. One of his sources, a small-time hood who had been a gofer for Jimmy, supplied the answer. Suzanne indeed had been involved with Jimmy, and he had given her jewelry. He had also sent the roses to her that night and was supposed to meet her for dinner. When she didn't show up, he had become furious and in drunken anger had even said he would kill her. Since Weeks was not generally given to idle threats, a couple of his people thought he really had been the murderer. He was always afraid that if his connection to her came out, her death would be pinned on him.

Now the assignment judge, Robert McDonough, was speaking, talking about how when Kerry came into the courtroom for the first time eleven years ago as a brand-new assistant prosecutor, she had looked so young that he thought she was a college kid on a summer job.

I was a brand-new bride too, Kerry thought wryly. Bob was an assistant prosecutor then. I only hope he has the brains to stay away from Jimmy Weeks and his ilk from now on, she mused. Weeks had been convicted on all counts. Now he was facing another trial for tampering with a juror. He had tried to blame that on Bob but hadn't been able to make it stick. But Bob had narrowly missed being indicted himself. And Weeks wouldn't get anywhere if he complained about the juror whose father had been incarcerated. He knew that during the trial and could have asked then that she be replaced by an alternate. Maybe all this would scare Bob before it was too late. She hoped so.

Judge McDonough was smiling at her. "Well, Kerry, I think it's time," he said.

Robin came forward, carrying the heavy Bible. Margaret rose and walked behind her, the black robe over her arm, waiting to present it to Kerry after the oath. Kerry raised her right hand, placed her left hand on the Bible and began to repeat after Judge McDonough: "I, Kerry McGrath, do solemnly swear . . ."

Other Bestselling Authors with Omnibus Editions
from Random House Value Publishing:

MARY HIGGINS CLARK
Volume 1: *Weep No More, My Lady*
Stillwatch
A Cry In The Night

Volume 2: *Where Are The Children?*
A Stranger Is Watching
The Cradle Will Fall

Volume 3: *While My Pretty One Sleeps*
Loves Music, Loves To Dance
All Around The Town

SUE GRAFTON
Volume 1: *A Is For Alibi*
B Is For Burglar
C Is For Corpse

Volume 2: *D Is For Deadbeat*
E Is For Evidence
F Is For Fugitive

CLIVE CUSSLER

DEAN KOONTZ

MICHAEL CRICHTON

MAEVE BINCHY

COLLEEN McCULLOUGH